# Fox Creek

# M. E. TORREY

# Fox Creek

BOOK 1 OF THE FOX CREEK PLANTATION TRILOGY

SLY FOX
PUBLISHING

Published by Sly Fox Publishing, LLC., POB 45, Fox Island, WA 98333

SLY FOX 1ST EDITION, SEPTEMBER 2025.



*Publisher's Note:* This is a work of fiction. Names, characters, places, and incidents either are the product of the author's imagination or are used fictitiously, and any resemblance to actual persons, living or dead, business establishments, events, or locales is entirely coincidental.

First paperback edition, September 2025
First hardcover edition, September 2025
First electronic edition, September 2025

Trade Paperback ISBN: 979-8-9914555-0-3
Hardcover ISBN: 979-8-9914555-2-7
Electronic ISBN: 979-8-9914555-1-0

Library of Congress Control Number: 2024918756

www.metorrey.com

Printed in the United States of America; set in Garamond Pro.

*To Carl Lee Gann*

# Book One

*"Those are the same stars, and that is the same moon,*
*that look down upon your brothers and sisters,*
*and which they see as they look up to them,*
*though they are ever so far away from us, and each other."*

Sojourner Truth

# *Chapter 1*

## *March 1843*

THE MORNING THE WAGON came to take Monette away, the air was biting crisp, and a sheen of frost covered the cane fields.

Awakened before dawn, Monette rubbed her eyes, yawned, and stretched, asking her nurse, Heloise, what was the matter. Instead of the usual kiss and the mug of *chocolat chaud*, Heloise threw back the covers and said, "Hurry, *ma petite.* Get dressed while I start a fire in the grate. There is only cold water for washing this morning."

Normally, in the brightness of the day, the child's bedroom was filled with color—the lemon yellow of the walls, the lavish *courtepointe* on the tester bed, its indigo cloth embroidered with metallic gold thread, the dollhouse in the corner, orange, pink, and cream, painted with both precision and whimsy. But in the vague light of predawn, all was gray and ugly and cold, as if the colors lay exhausted.

Heloise knelt beneath the marble mantel, lantern beside her on the floorboards. At the first hiss of flame, the plantation bell pealed through the semi-darkness. On any other morning, hearing the bell, Monette would roll over, burrow deep under her covers, and close her eyes, letting the resonance of the bell wrap around her in low, undulating waves. But on this morning, Monette was confused.

Why had Heloise awakened her so early? Before a fire roared in the grate, warming her room and her wash water? Tired, shivering, fumbling with countless ties, buttons, and hooks, and frightened by Heloise's silence, Monette began to cry. A soft, delicate whimpering.

The nurse sighed and stood to help. "Do not cry, *ma petite.* Hush now."

The nurse's voice, quiet though it was, filled the bedchamber.

Monette allowed the words to soothe her, to scatter the confusion, the fear, like a fire dispelling shadow. They were words of comfort, as caressing as if Papa Léon held Monette in his arms once again and pressed his lips into her hair. Monette closed her eyes while Heloise fussed with the back of her dress, pretending Papa Léon was still here and that she could sit on his lap anytime she wanted. Wrap her arms around him. Feel his warmth, the tickle of his whiskers, the smell of tobacco as he laughed.

She had stared at her father that day. *That day.* She had crept around the casket, slowly, making no sound. Surrounded by dozens of flickering candles, she stared at his pale, thin body, at the glittering gold coins on his closed eyes, the red rosary in his hand. She wondered why Papa Léon did not sit up and take her on his horse to the cane fields. Wondered why he did not want to have supper with her, with guest after shimmering guest, while Monette sat beside him, a tiny sapphire among diamonds.

There in the parlor, she had pressed her cheek against his hand, quickly pulling back, startled at the coldness, the hardness, the rosary clattering to the floor. Her nostrils suddenly filled with the fragrance of greenhouse roses. She fled the room—fled from the horrible gold coins, from the sickening smell, from his cold, hard hand.

Since his death, Monette had been frightened. So many whispers. So many people looking at her, then quickly away, as if she were now a ghost.

"Heloise—"

"Hush, *ma petite.*"

"Heloise, do I look like a ghost?"

"*Mon Dieu!* What kind of question is that? You invite the evil spirits with such talk. Even your *gris-gris* cannot protect you. Now, if you hush and be good, I shall give you a gift."

"What is it?" asked Monette. But she saw her nurse's eyes close in secrecy beneath her colorful *tignon* and knew it was useless to ask again. She could only stand patiently while Heloise smoothed and whispered, clucked and buttoned until all was done, and nothing remained but to sit.

It seemed hours later when Monette heard the rumble of wagon wheels. She set aside her new rag doll and crept to the dormered window, careful not to awaken Heloise, who dozed an old woman's slumber in her chair before the fire. Monette drew aside the velvet curtain.

At the far end of the *allée*, draped under the canopy of live oaks, a wagon approached, pulled by two mules. Even from a distance, Monette heard the clank and groan, the din growing louder and louder until she was amazed Heloise could sleep at all. Finally, the wagon stopped in front of the *grande maison*. The driver, a stranger to Monette, handed the reins to Uncle Lazare, climbed stiffly out of the wagon, glanced around once, then ascended the steps and disappeared under the eave of the *galérie*.

Pierre Auguste Dominique drummed his fingers on the arm of his chair, listening to nothing but the click of his manicured fingernails, the snap of the fire, and the tick of the mantel clock.

The parlor was vast, heavily furnished, the ceiling soaring fifteen feet above his head, designed for coolness, as was typical. The home was old, built even before the colonies rose in arms to wrest their independence from England, a struggle that concerned not at all those in French Louisiana—those who owed their allegiance to France and none other. (Though rumor had it that their new monarch, Louis XVI, was as ineffective as he was unremarkable.)

It was early still, the corners of the room yet dusted with shadow. Sunlight filtered through the pulled-back drapes. It was a weak sun, a winter's sun, despite the fact that it was mid-March, a time of year when Louisiana should burst with warmth and wisteria.

Up until his father's death three weeks ago, Pierre had been a banker, not a planter. As the only son, he'd always known that someday, *someday*, he would inherit this home of his childhood. For all of Pierre's twenty-eight years, the plantation had been an exemplar of elite society. It was known throughout the region—and even as far distant as Paris—for the fine *fêtes*, the banquets, the extravagant balls, the *soirées* on the bayou, all delicately spiced with gentle laughter and delicious conversation.

There were days at the bank—stuporous, drugged days that made Pierre almost long for the clamoring, desperate days of recession—when he'd consoled himself with dreams of Papa's plantation. For weeks on end, each time he closed his eyes, he saw fields ripened with cane, blackened with laborers, the landing piled high with hogsheads of sugar and molasses. What red-blooded man wouldn't dream such a dream? An entire plantation devoted to one's livelihood, one's comfort. It was only natural for Pierre to long for the day when he could trade in his ledger and ink stains for a wineglass and a riding crop.

Now Pierre tightened his jaw and stared at the fire, thinking, *but nothing has been the way I imagined. Never, never in my darkest dreams could I have pictured this. Oh, Papa, I always knew you were a foolish man, but until now, I did not realize the extent of your folly. How could you do this to me? To me—your son. Flesh of your flesh.*

Yes, he'd known of his father's debt. After all, hadn't Papa Léon come into the Bank of Louisiana every year, always needing more money? Pierre smiled wryly. Rare was the planter who *didn't* borrow money. It was common practice. Borrow money to build a sugarhouse, harvest the crop, purchase more land and slaves, borrow money for a new steam mill. Expand, expand, expand.

And hadn't these last few years been hard on everyone, forcing all to run to the banks for help? The financial panic of '37, the yellow fever outbreak in '39, worms in the cotton the following year coinciding with a ruinous flood—and now, in 1843, the winter's unusual severity.

Instead of the fantasy of wealth and ease he'd once envisioned, his father's death marked the beginning of a nightmare from which Pierre had yet to awaken.

Two weeks ago, cloaked in the stillness of Papa Léon's dusty, shuttered office, Pierre had unlocked the drawer and opened the ledger. He studied the figures, nodding, understanding. But Pierre's empathy soon melted into horror as he turned page after page. *No, no, it cannot be!* After spending all night poring over the account books—loosening his *cravate,* mopping the sweat from his brow despite the chill—there came a knock upon the door. A representative from Citizens Bank handed Pierre a claim against the estate for forty thousand dollars, payable in thirty days. Forty thousand dollars! A fortune! How would he ever get enough money? But it was only the beginning. An avalanche of creditors soon arrived from every banking institution in New Orleans. While Pierre had known Papa was in debt, he'd never imagined the extent. A nightmare . . .

Pierre's fingers tightened around the arms of the chair—squeezing, strangling—his knuckles turning white. It was time to put things back to their natural order before he lost everything. All unnecessary expenses must be trimmed away. Now. Today.

Another hour passed before he heard the distant rattle of a wagon approaching. He waited, unmoving, until he heard the man's tread upon the *galérie,* heavy and cloddish. Pierre stood to greet his visitor, smiling through his impatience, trying not to scowl when the man crushed his hand in the vulgar way of all Americans. *"Bonjour,* Monsieur Finney. You had no difficulties finding the plantation, no?"

"Was right where you told me."

"Wine?" offered Pierre, extricating his hand.

"Well, if you got whiskey, I'd be much obliged to you."

Pierre gave orders in French to a servant. To Finney he said, "You wish to sit?" motioning to a set of chairs. Pierre sat opposite Finney and smiled, thinking, An odious man. A true American. "I understand from your advertisement you pay cash."

"Yes, sir. You understand correctly." Finney smiled, and Pierre resisted the urge to stare at the man's huge, tobacco-stained teeth. They reminded him of a braying jackass.

Being forced to sit opposite a speculator with jackass teeth tested even Pierre's cultivated manners. Having to sell *nègres* was a situation every planter—every respectable planter, that is—dreaded and avoided. It was mortifying. Pierre would have preferred dealing with a Creole, someone who understood discretion, but that was impossible. Such an occupation was too base. A Creole would never stoop so low.

"Top dollar for prime negroes," Finney was saying. "Less for older or younger ones, you understand, of course. And I don't take no sick ones. Bad for business."

Two whiskey tumblers later, Pierre led the way to the barn, unaware of a succession of black faces at each window, peering from behind every building, a gaggle of children, pointing, whispering, flitting from one magnolia to the next like phantom butterflies. Pierre closed the barn door behind him, shutting out the sharp chill, closing in the smells of cypress, hay, and axle grease.

Thirty *nègres,* men and women, stood in a line—scrubbed and shining, fingernails cleaned, woolly hair combed through—all wearing their Sunday best.

Pierre heard Finney say, "Strip," and watched the American shove a plug of tobacco between his lower teeth and lip. *Abruti.* He sensed the hesitation of the *nègres*, saw the threatening scowl of the overseer, the tightening of his hand on the butt of his whip.

The examinations took twenty minutes, no more. A contemptible process that made Pierre sigh with relief when it was finally over, and he and Finney stepped out of the barn into the cold sunshine. The distance to the *grande maison* was a half mile, and along the way they talked.

"Now Monsieur Dominique, no offense now, but some of them is older than thirty. You know I didn't advertise for no negroes older than thirty or younger than ten."

Pierre frowned. In fact, by all accounts, the oldest servant was only twenty-nine. All were of good stock—gardeners, laundresses, seamstresses, coachmen—spoiled as they were. "Monsieur Finney, I had my first gray hair at age sixteen, yes? Gray hair does not necessarily mean old age."

"That sure is true enough. Yep, true enough. You don't have to tell me you've got yourself a fine crop of young negroes, gray hair or no. But it ain't me we're talking about here, it's the buyer. And sometimes the buyer's eyes ain't so good as mine, 'cause, you see, I got years of experience. Now if I can't get top dollar at the market 'cause the buyers don't know no better, well then, I can't give you top dollar, now can I?"

"What kind of offer are you willing to make?"

"Well now, let's see here." Finney took off his hat, ran a hand through his greasy, limp hair, and spat a stream of tobacco juice. "Considering them gray hairs and all, I just don't think I could pay you more than eighteen thousand dollars for the lot and still sleep at night."

Pierre did not have to pretend surprise. "Why, Monsieur Finney, if I did not know you better, I would think you were insulting me, no? That is a trifling $600 per negro. You and I both know they sell for much more in New Orleans, especially with such skills."

"Last year, maybe that was true. But this year's winter hit hard. Not just you, but everybody's got darkies to sell. Too many sellers and not enough buyers. Now you're a smart enough man, Monsieur Dominique, to understand that when you got too many sellers and not enough buyers, prices drop. It may not be purty, but it's the godawful truth. Simple economics is what it is."

Pierre walked on. Unfortunately, the trader was right. Half of Papa's livestock had died of cold this winter, and Pierre knew the same was true elsewhere. Once again, planters were in desperate trouble. And *nègres* brought quick money. "Twenty-seven thousand," said Pierre, thinking he must sell some land as well.

"Nineteen."

"Twenty-six." Although loathe to converse more than necessary with the slave trader, Pierre haggled some more, listing reason upon reason why these *nègres* were worth more than Finney was willing to pay. Such bargaining was, after all, custom, and an insult to both parties to do anything less.

"Twenty-three thousand," Pierre finally said, "and if you refuse, I shall be forced to contact another speculator. You understand, yes? How did you say—simple economics?"

"Well then, when you put it like that, I guess you got yourself a deal."

But when Finney thrust out his hand to conclude the deal, Pierre shook his head. *"S'il vous plaît,"* he said with a bow. "I must beg your indulgence. I have one more negro to sell. Come. She is in the great house."

As Theophilus Finney followed the Frenchman into the *grande maison*, he could scarcely contain his excitement over his good fortune. Such a deal! Twenty-three thousand dollars for thirty of the healthiest, finest-looking negroes he'd ever seen. Not a scratch, limp, bad eye, or snaggle-tooth among them. Buyers would scramble over themselves in New Orleans to scoop them up. Even at scrape bottom prices, he figured to make three to four thousand, minimum. Considering their skills, possibly as much as ten thousand dollars!

Finney accepted another glass of whiskey, furrowing his brow, anxious to be on his way, wondering whom Monsieur Dominique was going to try and pawn off on him.

A hundred-year-old washer woman? A blind seamstress? A cook with no arms and one leg out sideways? Damned Frenchmen. For men of such honor, they sure were a crafty bunch. No telling who or what they'd sell.

Monsieur Dominique gave an order to one of the servants. Finney heard footsteps ascend a staircase. A door opening. Overhead, an old woman's soft, muffled cry.

Finney shifted uncomfortably, watching Monsieur Dominique lean against the marble mantel, his wineglass in his hand, firelight leaping upon his legs. The tick of the mantel clock sounded especially loud. He heard nothing more until, of a sudden, a small child was standing in the doorway, shyly glancing back and forth at the two of them.

Monsieur Dominique motioned her to go stand before Finney. With only a slight hesitation, she obeyed, stopping just out of Finney's reach, her little boots making no sound on the floral rug beneath.

She was about six years old, by his guess, a mulatto, her skin the color of coffee with cream. Finney recognized in her delicate frame the slender features of Monsieur Dominique, the rosy, sensitive lips—so effeminate on a man yet becoming on such a small female child—the tender, dainty fingers, the slender nose, so unlike the splayed-out noses of full-blooded negro wenches. She was dressed in the clothing of a planter's daughter, all flounces, frills, and ruffles. The child watched him with large, amber eyes, an unusual eye color even for a mulatto.

Finney cleared his throat. "Now Monsieur Dominique, you know well as I do that it's against the law in Louisiana to sell a child under ten years of age without its mama." Finney licked his lips. If the mother was as pretty as the daughter . . .

"The mother is dead. I believe she died in childbirth, or shortly thereafter. A Congo slave."

Finney was surprised. He did not pretend to know much about Creoles and their arrogant, foppish ways, but this much he knew: Creole men did not mix with full-blooded African slaves. It was a social disgrace. A violation of caste. No wonder the Frenchman wanted to be rid of the child. "I'm supposing you have written proof of the mother's death?"

"*Oui*. You shall have it before you leave."

"Your child?" Finney didn't usually ask such personal questions—didn't care, really. After all, it was bad for business. But he was curious. The Frenchman was a peculiar sort.

Monsieur Dominique pierced him with a haughty look. "Of course not. She is an unwanted expense—and I am tired of unwanted expenses." The Frenchman hesitated before adding, "Besides, the child should follow the status of her mother. It is in her blood; it cannot be helped."

Finney looked back at the girl. A child like this would not be difficult to sell. She'd make someone a fine pet. White women were fond of that sort of thing, and sometimes spent extravagant amounts of money. "Most I can offer is a hundred dollars. She's too young and has weak blood. Won't be able to work none—carry a glass of water, maybe."

"Three hundred dollars," the Frenchman replied, a snap in his voice, disdain flashing in his eyes. Without waiting for confirmation, he said, "So the total is twenty-three thousand three hundred dollars, no?"

Finney pretended not to see the disdain and answered in the affirmative. He rose from his seat and shook hands with Monsieur Dominique.

Damned foppy Frenchman. Shakes hands like a fish.

—ell—

Huddled in the back of the wagon, Monette hugged her doll to her chest, wrapping it beneath her woolen cape to keep it warm. "Hush, *ma petite*," she whispered, glancing up at her bedroom window. She could see nothing beyond the velvet drapes. Where was Heloise? Never before had she traveled without her nurse. She hugged her doll tighter. "Do not worry, little baby. Heloise will come. She is only fetching her walking stick."

Monette watched as the man with big teeth fastened a line of men and women to the back of the wagon. Chained together two by two, they stared at her, and she looked away. So many of them—only a few she vaguely recognized. She shrank against the side of the wagon, the rough planks hard and unforgiving, all the while searching the windows and doors of the *grande maison*. Heloise! *Tout de suite!* I am alone!

The wagon lurched forward, and Monette cried aloud. The groan of the wheels. The heavy clank of chains as the men and women trotted after. The thumping of her heart. Heloise! Where are you?

The bouncing jarred her teeth. She slammed against the side of the wagon, bruising her shoulder. Tears stung her eyes. One of the black men spoke to her, but she pretended not to hear, turning away and sobbing harder. Oh, Heloise, what is happening?

Then, from far away, she heard a rumbling. At first, she thought it was a distant thunder—the beginnings of a storm, a deluge—but soon realized the sound came from the cane fields. For a moment, she stopped crying and listened as the rumbling grew into a full-throated roar. Then she saw them: a seething mass of black poured like heavy smoke toward the wagon. Closer, closer . . . men, women, children, casting aside farm implements as they ran, stumbling over furrows, weeping, shrieking, arms outstretched. My wife! My son! *Maman!* The men and women chained to the wagon cried out. The mules moved faster, forcing them to trot.

Then the roaring crowd enveloped Monette like fire. Black fire. Fire that screamed crimson screams. *No! No!* Fire that clung to the men and women, refusing to let go, pulling against the chains, begging, wrenching—until skin ripped and blood flowed. *No! No!* A whip cracked the air. A gun fired, belching black smoke. She heard the smack of leather on flesh and shrieked, throwing herself to the floor of the wagon. She plugged her ears with her fingers. She rocked back and forth. *Papa Léon, oh, Papa Léon.* She began to sing a nursery rhyme—one he had sung to her many times—as if he held her in his arms once more, as if he buried his lips in her hair and whispered, My daughter, *ma chérie.*

# Chapter 2

FOR DAYS NOW THE rain had pummeled Cyrus, pounding him into the muck. It was a freezing rain, intermittent yet vicious, and the boy's jaw ached from clenching his teeth. At first, the mud provided a sense of warmth—a blanket of stinking ooze that sucked at his feet with every step, protecting him from the driving, chilling rain. But after four days of travel, his feet now scratched and bleeding, he could only remember warmth as a sensation from long ago—a memory to be cherished like a piece of molasses candy, savored one lick at a time.

"Dress him up fine," Missus had told his mother, her pale, bony finger wagging through the doorway. "I'm taking him to town."

Mama had beamed and fussed, so proud her son would accompany Missus to town, slicked and shining like a new copper penny. With a bucket of water from the bayou and a bar of lye soap, Mama scrubbed Cyrus' skin till it smarted. He pulled back and frowned, saying, "Mama, it hurts," but she shook her head and tsked and said a big boy like him shouldn't be scared of a little soap and water. Besides, it was an honor being asked to go to town with Missus. And Missus wouldn't want no dirty boy next to her, now would she?

After the scrubbing, Cyrus dressed in his best clothes—clothes he hadn't worn for several months. He followed Mama's gaze as she studied his wrists poking out from the sleeves, his pants, ending just below mid-shin. Mama grunted and put her hands on her hips, saying, "Maybe Missus gonna take you to town to buy you some new clothes. Lord knows you needs them bad. I wish she take your sister too, but she ain't growing like you is."

Cyrus squeezed his feet into last year's shoes. They pinched his toes and heels. "They's too tight, Mama," he complained. But she shushed him and said Missus was ready and calling for him, and to be good and don't be sassing none, you hear?

Even when they neared town and Cyrus saw the double line of men chained to the hitching post like mules, even then he did not know. Even when he followed Missus into the store, bells jangling, the strong, sweet smell of tobacco thick and cloying, glancing around him for a new set of clothes, he was unaware of the sudden interest of the white men gathered at the far corner. Cyrus followed Missus. Greetings exchanged. Cyrus stared at the floorboards, his face blank, his feet pinched and throbbing. Where my new clothes?

"How old are you, boy?"

"T-t-t-ten," stuttered Cyrus, still gazing at the floor.

There was a giggle from somewhere.

"You always talk like that, boy?"

"N-n-no."

Missus sighed. "I know, he talks bad. And he's a little dull, but that don't hurt none in a negro. He's a good worker, does what he's asked. You can see for yourselves he's strong and healthy. Cyrus, open your mouth and show them your teeth."

The men peered into Cyrus' mouth. They felt his muscles and watched him with folded arms as he jumped, squatted, and walked lively. Cyrus was glad to do all those things—just so long as he didn't have to talk. When he was done, he stood panting, staring at the floor again, thinking, They figuring to fit me for my new clothes. And I needs shoes bad. Real bad.

"Five dollars a pound," said one of the men.

Beside him, Missus shook her head. "Nine dollars a pound, no less. Look at him, gentlemen. He's strong as an ox. In a year or so he'll make a good plow boy. Just 'cause I'm a widow woman ain't no reason to be taking advantage of this here situation. I know what this boy's worth."

They haggled while Cyrus blinked once, twice. He wasn't listening to them anymore. Instead, a terrible understanding bubbled within his head—expanding, seeping like poison, cold, viscous—through his brain, his ears, his nostrils, his mouth.

*She gonna sell me.*

"I said, sit on the scale, boy," one of the men repeated.

When Cyrus did not move, hands grabbed him and shoved him onto a scale where he was weighed like a bag of wheat or a hog.

*Mama . . .*

Outside, they led him to the lone man standing at the end of the line and handcuffed their wrists together. They fastened an iron collar around Cyrus' neck, passing the long central chain through the hasp of the padlock. Cyrus heard Missus get into her buggy—heard the snap of reins, the creak of leather harness, the rumble of wheels as she drove away.

*Mama . . .*

Even before the coffle left town—three men on horseback driving, one in front, one in the middle, and one bringing up the rear—the clouds opened, and a cold, drowning rain began. Within an hour, Cyrus lost both his shoes, sucked off his feet by the deepening muck.

*Mama . . .*

Four days of rain. Four days of exhaustion—his limbs shaking, his jaw clenched to keep his teeth from chattering. Four days of cold, lumpy food—food that stuck in his throat even while he wolfed it down. Four days of whispers under the hanging moss. Where you from, what your name, you gonna eat that? Nights of pretending. Pretending to sleep in a tent that did not leak, that did not reek of mud and piss. Pretending not to awaken more tired than when he lay down.

At the edge of a large bayou, the chain of men halted. During the dry season, the bayou was twenty, maybe thirty feet across at most. But now, the opposite bank could scarcely be discerned through the veil of rain. On both banks, tree trunks, branches, all manner of brush lay half-submerged.

The lead white man walked his horse through the brush and into the bayou.

At first, the coffle did not move. Cyrus stared, like everyone, at the swollen waters, knowing he could not swim, wondering if the log he saw was an alligator or the swirling branch a snake. Then the white man in the middle of the line rode to the front and brandished his whip.

"Move!"

After a moment's hesitation, the two lead black men plunged into the bayou.

"Move!"

Halfway across, with the chain of men stretched out, the two lead men vanished, swallowed without a sound into a hole in the muck.

Immediately, the two men just behind were yanked beneath the waters, and the chain tightened as the line of men pulled back to keep themselves from going under. Then the two lead men surfaced—covered with mud, gasping—lunging like harnessed animals toward the opposite bank.

"Move!"

Unable to stop the forward momentum, unwilling to feel the lick of the lash, each pair disappeared in turn with a choked cry beneath the surface, yanked off their feet by the collar around their necks.

"Goddammit, move!"

Cyrus dug in his feet, pulling against the chain. No! No! But his feet slipped, and the water wrapped itself about his waist—deeper, deeper. Then the men in front of him fell beneath the water, the chain snapped taut, his head whipped back, and he was pulled under.

*Mama!*

He landed at the bottom of the bayou, face down, dragged. Mud in his nostrils, his ears, his mouth—tasting of death and decay. Already his lungs burned. He tried to crawl, to claw his way through the ooze, out of the hole, but he couldn't move his handcuffed arm. As if the man he was handcuffed to had suddenly turned to stone. He pulled against the weight, lungs screaming. Cyrus knew he was dying. He could feel it—in the pound of his head, in the blackness that pulsed through his thoughts, in the pain and heaviness of his arm that refused to let him move. He struggled for the surface one last time, surprised to feel the kick of what felt to be a hoof, dimly aware that someone had him by the iron collar, and that he was being lifted up and out, his arm on fire.

The camp was centrally located at the juncture of several footpaths and cart trails. A bayou (easily crossed should such an occasion be necessary) slept nearby—a winding serpent, waking only with the passing of a breeze or an alligator across its spine. The grass of the camp rarely suffered to grow upright—in places long-dead, where thousands of feet had walked, run, and shuffled through the years. Gullies of mud—tracks from countless wagon wheels—crisscrossed the struggling grass. Hitched to the low branches of a tree, horses snoozed, waking only to eat and tramp the ground into a soupy, manure mush.

Monette awakened, knowing by the damp, chilled, stiffened feeling between her legs that she had wet herself. The first time she had done so, Finney had cursed, unlocking one of the women from the chain and ordering the woman to change Monette and wash her clothes in the bayou. The woman had looked at him, uncomprehending, fear in her face, until Finney, frustrated, had turned to Monette to translate.

So, in the cold of the afternoon, Monette had been stripped naked—stripped of her woolen cape, her dress, her lace pantalettes, her woolen stockings, her doll, and her red flannel *gris-gris* bag (filled with salt and pepper, red agate, sweetgrass, bone, stick, and a plait of black hair—all necessary, Heloise had warned her again and again, for protection against evil spirits). Monette had cried and shivered, ignoring the woman's brief attempts to comfort her as the woman bathed her with cold water from the bayou—water Monette shied away from because it was cloudy and dirty and smelly.

Monette hadn't seen her clothes or her *gris-gris* again. Instead, she was clad in coarse homespun—ugly, ill-fitting clothing that caused her to scratch until her skin turned an angry red. She cried for her clothes, her *gris-gris*. She cried for her doll, unceasing and shrill, until Finney gave it back, saying, "Jesus Christ, shut up, will you?" Monette wiped her tears, cradled her doll, and stuck her thumb in her mouth. *Ma petite.*

Now she had wet herself again. Cold, she lay huddled beneath her blanket in the corner of the wagon behind the driver's seat, the tarp frozen about her waist, her doll clamped to her chest. She gazed at the ragged canopy of cypress overhead, at the weak morning light struggling to penetrate the chilling mist that snaked around the trunks of trees and through the curling of moss. The camp was stirring. She heard the snap of new fire, the occasional hurried whisper. When the aroma of bacon caused her stomach to growl, she sat up.

"Do not worry, *ma petite.* You shall have your breakfast soon. I shall feed you until you are plump and happy." She pressed her lips into her doll's yarn hair. "You shall have butter cakes with raspberry jam and custard tarts for dessert. And if you are very, very good, I shall give you a cup of *chocolat chaud.*"

Monette ate her breakfast of boiled bacon and cornmeal sweetened with molasses, feeding bits to her doll. By now, the light was stronger, yet it was still dim, choked, and the air colder, damp, and penetrating.

After licking her fingers, she carefully gathered all the crumbs and was tossing them away when she saw them. Three white men on horseback approached through the woods. Behind them, emerging from the mist in a ghostly swirl, trailed a coffle of black men. Monette saw the shifting whites of their eyes. All was silent except for the clank of chains and the soft shuffle of feet.

When they drew near, Finney called a greeting. "Morning, Wirt! Thought maybe y'all drowned or something. Been waiting here a spell."

Wirt dismounted and stretched. "Yeah, I know. Woulda been here sooner but got hung up."

"That so?"

"Got everything under control now. Just had to bust a few hides, is all. By golly, that coffee sure smells good . . ."

Soon, Wirt and Finney hunkered down around the fire, drinking their coffee. While they talked, one of the other white men rode over to the wagon where Monette sat. She watched as he dismounted, lifting a black boy off the saddle with him.

"Go on, get in," he said, pointing to the wagon.

The boy blinked at the white man before slowly crawling over the tarp and into the wagon. The white man led his horse away.

Monette didn't want anyone in the wagon with her. She shrank into her corner, pulling her blanket tightly around her, keeping her doll hidden so the black boy couldn't steal it. He settled on the opposite side from her and tugged the tarp over him as far as it would go, the canvas stiff and crackling, his back against a barrel of supplies. Monette tried not to look, tried to ignore him, to pretend it really didn't matter that she now had to share her wagon with someone else, but she couldn't help herself. She peered out of the corner of her eye.

He was a big boy, so much bigger than she, older too, and as black as coffee beans. Dried mud caked his arms, his neck and face, even his nose—a nose wide and strong like the men who worked in Papa Léon's fields. His full lips quivered. Monette's eyes widened in amazement as the trembling of his lips grew worse. His breathing grew ragged, and he shut his eyes. Soon a tear streaked a lone trail down his cheek.

He is sad, she thought with surprise. Monette sat still, keenly aware of her cold, stiffened clothes, of her unpleasant smell, of the doll pressed against her chest, of her blanket wrapped about her and the meager warmth it offered. Perhaps, she thought, I should share my blanket. Perhaps he is sad because he is cold. Even as she thought it, she was also aware of her fear—almost paralyzing, choking. But what if he took away her doll forever and ever? What if he stole her blanket and then she was cold every night? Or what if he was like that mean boy who sometimes waited for her behind the *grande maison* so he could yank her hair and call her nasty names? Besides, he was so dirty—*sale de façon répugnante.*

Then she noticed the boy cradling his muddied arm and saw it was swollen and discolored. He is hurt, she thought. Sad and hurt. *Pauvre garçon.* Monette hesitated before slowly inching away from her position in the corner. Together with her doll and her blanket, she crept over the roughened planks that separated them, stopping an arm's length away. The boy's eyes remained closed. She reached out a cautious hand, lifted the canvas, and placed the doll in the boy's lap. He opened his eyes and blinked in surprise, as if seeing her for the first time, another tear dropping from his eyelash.

She remained alert, ready to flee. But when he did not tug her hair, did not call her nasty names, she spread her blanket over the two of them, tucking it in at the edges so no draft of cold air could seep through. Already, she could feel his warmth. She lay against him then, thumb in her mouth, holding the hand of her doll in his lap as the first flakes of snow fell out of the sky and filtered through the trees—lazy snowflakes, wet, covering them in a blanket of white.

# Chapter 3

ONE HUNDRED MILES UPRIVER from New Orleans and east of
the Mississippi, the Fox Creek Plantation bell awakened young
Katherine Emma Jensey. An unearthly ringing, strange and muffled,
caused her to open her eyes in the predawn. She stared at the bed canopy
for a moment—a bewildered moment, in which her dreams yet lingered.
Dreams that tasted of sugar, sounded of soft voices, and echoed with
Tiptop's hoofbeats as Kate rode her pony through the pine forest of West
Feliciana Parish—a landscape as familiar to her as her lavender-scented
sheets, or perhaps even the whisper of her breath.

Proudly dubbed "English Louisiana" by its Anglo-Saxon inhabitants,
the twin parishes of East and West Feliciana were as British as New
Orleans was French. Many of its settlers had been Loyalists, fleeing the
Eastern Seaboard during and after the Revolutionary War—uprooting
households, toting along servants, children, seeds, and blooded hounds,
seeking nothing but land where they could continue living in the grand
manner to which they were accustomed. They were delighted with what
they found. Named "Feliciana," meaning "Happy Land," by the original
Spanish settlers, West Feliciana was a vista of rolling hills, streams, foxes,
and colorful birds, with a climate friendly to cotton, perique tobacco, rice,
and just about anything else that sprouted from a seed or hatched from an
egg.

Now, decades after her grandfather had settled the land, seven-year-old
Kate pushed aside the mountain of quilts, piled one atop the other to
protect her from the unusual cold—the culmination of a winter her
grandmother, Mehitable, had declared was the worst in all her recollection.
Putting on her slippers, ignoring the gooseflesh that danced across her fair

skin like wind across a lake, Kate crossed the room, drew back the curtain, and gasped.

A fairytale land of white stretched as far as she could see, hushed under the muted light. It hung heavy on the branches of the live oaks and magnolias, carpeted the stretches of lawn like a vast coat of ermine, and was sprinkled like sugar on the pine wood far across the creek. "Snow," she whispered, her child's breath steaming the glass pane. And in that whispering, the word at once became sacred and indelibly delicious.

Scarcely able to contain her excitement, she hurried through the back loggia to her older brother's room, relieved Mammy Hester was nowhere in sight to reprimand her, to declare, "Lord a'mercy, Missie Kate, what you doing running around half-naked in nothing but your nightgown? Sure as angels do fly, you's gonna catch your death."

Kate shook Breck's shoulder, telling him to hurry and wake up, still shaking him even after he roused and sat up, his brown, wavy hair tousled and sticking out in all directions. Disregarding his complaints of sleepiness and cold, she dragged him from his bed and smiled smugly when she whipped back the drapes and saw his mouth drop in surprise.

"It's called snow!" she declared. "Real snow, like what they have up North. I've heard tell you can throw it at one another, and it sticks to your eyelashes."

Breck leaned his forehead against the glass, staring at the wonderland below. His breath fogged the window. "Did you ever see anything so pretty?"

Kate thought hard. She'd seen marvelous, colorful, even scary costumes at Mardi Gras; she'd studied a butterfly with velvet wings of yellow and black while her mother caressed her hair and whispered, "Enjoy it, dear Katherine, God means for us to enjoy it." And once, when Mrs. Smith came to visit, she'd swept into the parlor like a queen—all sparkles and jewels and silks and manners and a mouth pursed like a cherry. "Well," said Kate, finally deciding, "that time when we saw fireworks bursting in the sky? Remember that? Mama declared it was pretty as a picture, and I thought so too."

Breck smiled down at her. At eight years old, he was a healthy, handsome child, square-jawed and strong-boned. His smile touched his soft, brown eyes, even crinkling the pink, puckered scar at the side of his right eye where Kate had struck him with a stick just a few months earlier. She'd cried for hours, it seemed. Then she felt his thin arms wrap around her, and heard him whisper, "Stop crying, Kate. I know you didn't mean it." She stopped crying then, even though in the back of her mind she knew she had, in fact, meant to whack him with the stick. Good and hard. She'd been angry, mad as the buzz of wasps, but was relieved to stop crying—it was beginning to hurt her head—and besides, Grandma Mehitable said it wasn't seemly for young ladies to carry on so.

"Come on. Let's go play before it disappears!" said Kate.

When Breck nodded enthusiastically, they quickly pulled on some of Breck's clothing over their nightclothes, then ran down the stairs, out the rear loggia, and into the crisp morning air.

First, they stomped a path, marveling at their footprints, shocked at the coldness already seeping through their boots—like half-melted ice from the icehouse. Then they raced to the pond, shouting, Do you think the fish are still alive?

They cracked the ice and peered beneath, praying to see a flash of orange, a flash of white, meaning the carp had lived through this terrible, mighty, godawful storm. But they saw only murky darkness. They ignored Mammy Hester calling for them from behind the big house, and instead scrambled up the live oak, a tree whose limbs stretched out over the pond as though to dominate both land and sea. Perched high on a branch, Breck and Kate began throwing snowballs at a boy, choosing him as their target simply because he was the only one around—and because Footy happened to be Breck's best friend.

By the time his britches had soaked through and a shy sun peeped over the treetops, Breck heard a muffled gallop, the sound of hooves drumming the snow. Beneath the vast canopy of trees and running parallel to the creek, a man rode. Even from a distance, Breck could tell he was tall. He sat high in the saddle, his back straight and his body relaxed, a born horseman. Six hounds loped before him.

"It's Papa!" shrieked Kate, already scrambling down the tree trunk.

"Yes," whispered Breck, "Papa's home."

———ele———

It had been an exhilarating hunt—a fire hunt, William's favorite. Not all gentlemen appreciated a fire hunt. They didn't think it gave the animals a sporting chance, what with the flame of the torches both startling and stunning prey in the dead of night, their eyes glowing like embers, creating perfect targets. But William Thomas Jensey was never one to turn down a good hunt, and he found urging his horse through the piney woods and swamps at night—torches ablaze, rifle at the ready—about as exhilarating as life could get. It was then he felt most *primal.* As if in the raw interplay of prey and predator he glimpsed the undercurrent, the primordial secret of life itself—a secret normally coifed, hushed, and regulated under layers of polite society.

The hounds had found the deer at midnight. It staggered to its feet, a six-point stag, eyes wide with stupor. A bullet between the eyes brought him down. "That was a fine shot," said William's brother-in-law, John. "A fine shot."

William was especially impressed with his newest hound, Rascal—a purebred black-and-white spotted pup, only ten months old. He'd been a gift from William's factor in New Orleans in thanks for his patronage. No sooner were they on their way again than Rascal roused two more—a doe and her fawn.

"That's a fine hound," said John. "A fine hound."

Yes, it had been a good hunt, and William felt refreshed.

At first light, when the first flakes of snow began to fall, William shrugged it off, thinking it would not stick. But as the landscape around him gradually turned a ghostly white under the glow of the torches, he bade farewell to John. He gave orders to Sam and Primus to bring half the venison home by noon, no later. With his hounds before him and his horse beneath him, he headed home to Fox Creek Plantation, pleasantly exhausted.

Decades ago—some sixteen years after the end of the American Revolution—William's father, Octavian, had heard of Louisiana. He'd heard of the fine land that didn't have to lie fallow, producing abundant crops year after year, perhaps generation after generation. Octavian, the eighth of twelve children, heeded the call to the West at the age of twenty, seeking to make a name for himself away from the shadows of his squabbling siblings. His mother begged him not to go, but despite her effusion of tears and, subsequently, letters, go he did. He left the tobacco lands of South Carolina, plucking himself like a ripe plum from a family tree that prided itself on having remained rooted in the same spot for more than 150 years.

With three house servants, three books (*Twelfth Night,* the *Iliad,* and the *Aeneid*), his favorite sporting rifle, his hound, and his horse, Octavian arrived in the Felicianas. He liked what he saw—the woody hills, rich not only in pine but also in blue poplar, oak, and cypress, and dotted with streams that flowed into the mighty Mississippi. He chose his land, then paid some Kentuckians to take him down the great river to the city of New Orleans. There he received a grant of one thousand acres from the Spanish government and purchased nine brute negroes. Then he headed back upriver, determined to build a house every bit as grand as the one he'd left.

Beautifully situated on a slight swell of ground, the Fox Creek Plantation big house was a large, comfortable frontier home of twelve rooms, six above and six below (plus three rooms in the attic, but no one counted the attic). The house was framed with cypress beams and blue poplar cut from Jensey land, with hand-fashioned bricks finishing the exterior walls. Six heavy Doric columns of rounded brick rose from the first-floor gallery, with six colonnettes of cypress supporting the roof on the upper gallery. Altogether—with its hand-carved wooden balustrades and its large central doorway with arched transom—the home, while maybe not as grand as the family estate in South Carolina, nevertheless had a pleasing, domestic effect. Though not yet able to build every structure he envisioned, Octavian further mapped out the entire plantation complex, every inch designed with an eye to symmetry, function, and, of course, the future.

Satisfied, Octavian settled into a life that suited him (despite whispers that he'd chosen poorly in marriage). For the next few decades, he sired children, built barns and stables and cabins and whatnot, harvested crops, hunted the woods with abandon, dabbled in politics, and did his civic duty as was expected of every planter and gentleman.

Upon Octavian's death in 1831, William, his only son, then just eighteen, assumed the mantle of plantation lord and master. He'd been studying for the bar at Harvard, bored, distracted, wishing he were a little more concerned about his studies so he could become, in his father's words, "An ornament to the nation." William wasn't supposed to feel relief at the news of his father's death—but relieved he was.

The letter came on a frigid day in mid-January, when the fire from the pot-bellied stove did little to dispel the chill of the dormitory. William opened the envelope with shivering hands, expecting the usual letter from his father chronicling the demands of plantation management. Instead, he was surprised to see the scrawled penmanship of his mother. She wrote that his father, Octavian, had died suddenly of a bilious fever of undetermined nature. William felt an immediate rush of relief—no more school, no bar exam—followed swiftly by a wave of guilt for not thinking of his father first. Before the day was out, William boarded a vessel bound south, and upon arriving at West Feliciana, took charge of Fox Creek, the plantation his father had wrested out of the raw land, a cotton plantation then spanning 2200 acres, with eighty-one negro hands.

Three years after his father's death, William married Sarah Margaret Breck, a belle from the adjoining plantation, Woodleigh. Eighteen years of age, Sarah was, in the opinion of the community at large, as refined, genteel, and beautiful as God had ordained women to be. Most approved of the match—even envied it. Most were quick to forget William's crooked teeth, his unruly, acorn-brown hair, and his somewhat heavy, uneven brow—instead feeling drawn to his considerable height and force of personality.

Yes, it was well known that William Jensey was a force to be reckoned with, a man who knew what it meant to be both a gentleman and a master, a delicate balance of character that some men never achieved. Indeed, in the nine and a half years since his marriage, William had fathered two children, purchased 600 more acres of forested land, built twelve more slave cabins, added sixty-five slaves through both purchase and natural increase, and bred the finest racehorses and blooded hounds West Feliciana Parish had ever seen.

That was in addition to the 613 bales of cotton ginned this year alone, the last of which was shipped only last week. Even the prolonged, harsh winter, the loss of some livestock, and the knowledge that he would have to replant his corn hadn't dampened William's spirits. It had been a good year.

A good year and a good hunt. . . .

The first indication that all was well was the scent of the kitchen fires. The second indication was the sound of the axe in the forest. By the time he reined to a halt before his children, William was pleased. The snowfall appeared to have had no effect on the normal operations of his plantation. From where he sat in his saddle, he could see the carpenters busy building the new hospital, the stockman rounding up the milk cows, and, in the distance, the stableboys leading blanketed horses for brisk walks.

"Papa!" shrieked Kate. Frozen-faced, freckled, with auburn hair hanging past her waist in limp, soggy strings, she bounded toward him, jumping up and down.

William bent over and scooped her up with one arm, setting her before him on the saddle, telling her to look in his pocket if she wanted a surprise. After a bit of digging, she pulled out an object and gasped with delight.

"A whistle!" she cried.

She blew into the whistle, which produced a reedy, mellow sound.

William smiled and looked at Breck, who stood holding the horse's halter, waiting expectantly. William withdrew another whistle from his other pocket and handed it to his son.

"Did you carve it?"

"Last night. Found a good willow tree and thought you might like it."

"I do like it." Breck gave the whistle a toot before slipping it into his pocket. The dogs surrounded Breck, panting, tongues lolling from the long run. "Did you kill any deer, Papa?"

"Three. That new pup there, Rascal. He found two of them."

Breck knelt beside the spotted pup and scratched behind his ears. "Good boy."

"Most of the other dogs were dead tired, but not Rascal. He'd like to have found another four or five deer if I'd let him."

Breck smiled up at him—an intelligent, appreciative smile filled with admiration—and William warmed toward his son. He was a good boy, a fine son, and someday William would be proud to leave Breck these lands, this home. "Son," he said, making a sudden decision, "I'd like to give you Rascal."

Breck's smile changed to a look of astonishment. "What?"

"You heard me. He's yours."

"Hear that, boy? You're mine!" Breck threw his arms around the dog's neck. The hound whined and wagged his tail.

"Take good care of him, and someday I'll take you on your first fire hunt."

Breck stood, eyes widening. "A fire hunt," he breathed, as if he couldn't believe what he'd heard.

William had thought Kate was not listening, for since he had given her the whistle, she had only stopped blowing it long enough to draw another breath. Now she turned around in the saddle. "I want to go on a fire hunt too!" she declared, her green eyes flashing with that rambunctiousness that William often found vexing—so unlike the gentle, green eyes of his wife.

"You," said William, "are too young." Suddenly, William felt anxious to be home—anxious to hold his wife, to warm his feet by the fire, to cradle a hot cup of tea in his hands. He reached down and, as he had Kate, scooped Breck up and placed him behind him on the horse. He felt his son's thin arms wrap around his waist. William frowned. Breck's hands were as frozen as Kate's.

"Footy!"

"Yes, Mars?" The boy Footy stood about twenty feet away, his skinny body motionless.

"Take the dogs to the kennels. Give them their breakfast. Give an extra ration of meat to Rascal."

"Yes, Mars."

William wheeled his horse and headed toward the big house.

Kate's room was delicate, decorated with just enough pink to be pretty. A ruffled canopy draped atop a four-poster bed, matching the bed ruffle, the curtains, and a comfortable armchair. The walls and woodwork were painted a cool, summery white, and the dark cypress floor gleamed with polish and smelled of lemon. In the corner stood a mirrored armoire, into which Kate occasionally practiced her smile, coupled with a smart toss of her pigtails. Above the brick fireplace, a mantel and mirror stretched almost to the ceiling, and today, atop the thick Aubusson carpet, a copper tub gleamed before the roaring fire.

"Mind them foots, Missie Kate," said Mammy Hester, as she poured another kettle of steaming water into the tub.

Kate drew in her feet, watching as more bubbles formed, careful to hold her willow whistle out of the water so it wouldn't get wet. Such a grand time! She wished it could snow every day, although she did have to admit it was rather cold. By the time Papa had set her on the ground behind the big house, handing her over to Mammy Hester with a sharp reprimand for Mammy to take better care, Kate's teeth chattered, and she could no longer feel her hands or feet.

"Up to your room," ordered Mammy Hester. "Into the tub. What you doing running 'round, screaming like an Injun? Mercy sakes, Missie Kate, ain't I learnt you better than that?"

Mammy Hester already had the water boiling, so it wasn't long before steaming water filled the tub and Kate began to thaw. Along with the thaw came the pain. Yet it was a delicious pain, sweet as a child's first snowfall. But now, flushed, Kate declared she was too hot.

Clucking her tongue, Mammy Hester knelt beside Kate and began scrubbing her with a soapy washrag. "It's no wonder you's hot, chile. I 'bout boils you to death trying to warm you up."

"See my whistle? Papa carved it from a willow tree last night." Kate blew hard. She pretended it was a trumpet and that she was about to go on a fox hunt.

"That's mighty fine."

"When I go to New Orleans next week, I'm taking it with me."

"Why, honey chile, your Mama might have something to say about that. She gonna take you to the theater, and for certain she don't want no whistle blowing while all them white folks be singing."

"Then I'll bring it to the horse races."

"Chile, you knows good and well that the last thing your Papa needs is you under his foots while he's at the races, especially if you's blowing a whistle." Mammy Hester sighed and wrung out the washrag. "'Sides, that racing and gambling stuff ain't no place for a young lady like yourself."

"Breck gets to go."

"Breck is a man, or leastways, he will be someday."

Disappointed, since the answers were always the same, Kate sighed, wiping the beads of sweat from her forehead. "After my bath, can I go back outside and play in the snow? I promise to stay dry and not to scream."

Mammy Hester shook her head, firelight painting her cocoa-colored skin with a golden hue. To Kate, Mammy Hester seemed old—older than the bony nag Papa kept because it was his first horse ever, older than Miss Partridge, who, according to Papa, had both feet in the grave and was sinking fast. But the soft folds of Mammy's face and the skin sagging beneath her eyes, Kate knew, could be deceiving, for Mammy was strong as a whalebone corset—strong enough to carry a demijohn of molasses or to brush Kate bald-headed while trying to rid her mane of tangles.

"I plans to go see my Demps this afternoon." Mammy Hester peered at Kate from beneath her white turban. "There won't be no one to draw your bath when you comes back half froze to death. 'Sides, I think you done seen enough trouble for one day, Missie Kate."

Kate sighed again. She hated it when Mammy Hester left. Every two weeks or thereabouts, Mammy visited her husband and children and grandchildren where they lived at Woodleigh Plantation, where Kate's mother had grown up. Mammy Hester usually stayed the night and didn't return until late the next day, sometimes after Kate was in bed and asleep. "It's not fair. Nothing's fair."

"Honey chile, has I ever told you life is fair?"

Knowing it was useless to argue, thinking that this magical day was turning out to be just another day in which the adults spoiled everything, Kate sighed for a third time while Mammy bade her lift her feet so she could scrub them toes. But as Mammy scrubbed, there came an odd sound from outside. At first, Kate couldn't place it. Then she knew. She sat up, water swirling around the tub with a rush. "Bells!"

Mammy Hester rose, grunting, knees popping, and moved to the window, her starched white apron and calico skirt swishing. Although she was almost sixty years old, her hearing was as sharp as ever. She drew aside the curtain and peered out.

A carriage glided down the front lane, different from anything Mammy had ever seen. It had no wheels—instead, it just whisked along, slick as you please, pulled by two white, prancing horses. Her heart sank when she saw who it was. Behind the coachman, bundled under a heap of furs, sat one of Mars William's sisters, Miss Virginia—a woman, in Mammy Hester's opinion, more loud-mouthed and demanding than any woman had a right to be. And squeezed next to Miss Virginia like possums in a pouch were all those children of hers. Mammy Hester closed her eyes, wishing it weren't so. Company always meant extra work, and no one could be spared. No one.

"What is it?" asked Kate.

"It am your Aunt Virginia and all them chilluns."

Kate didn't notice that Mammy Hester's voice had gone flat. Instead, she sprang out of the tub and onto the carpet in a shower of droplets and bubbles, shouting *hooray* and declaring that this was the best day of her life! Standing before the fire as Mammy Hester rubbed her body with a towel, Kate shivered with excitement. Cousin Cordelia! The last time Cousin Cordelia came to visit, Kate had stayed up until well past midnight playing Old Maid and Chase-the-Ace with molasses-sticky fingers, and then they'd whispered in bed for what seemed hours and hours—at least until Cordelia fell asleep and Kate could no longer shake her awake.

She could scarcely hold still while Mammy Hester clad her in her plaid woolen dress and heated the irons to curl her hair. She could hear them below: cousins Juliana, Joseph, and Cordelia. She could even hear the hungry wail of baby Betsy, still not quite loud enough to drown out Mammy's constant reproofs.

"Stop your wiggling, chile, you's gonna burn yourself."

"For heaven's sake, stop all that fool jumping. You's gonna make my teeth fall out."

One by one, sausage curls bounced hot against her neck and tiny ringlets danced across her forehead, coaxed and patted with rose-scented pomade. Then finally, with a kiss from Mammy Hester—a kiss as dry as autumn leaves, she was released.

Sarah Margaret Breck Jensey, mistress of Fox Creek Plantation, considered herself fortunate. Fortunate not so much in terms of the quantifiable—such as how many silken gowns or fancy headdresses she owned, or the fact that a new *barouche* carriage with velvet seats was delivered just last week from Boston (to the envy of all)—but more in terms of the immeasurable: family, security, warmth, and love. The type of fortune more frequently enjoyed by those who valued matters of the heart more than the estimation of others.

Not that others did not highly esteem Sarah Jensey, for they did. Voted Belle of the State at just eighteen years of age, these nine years later, Sarah was still renowned for her beauty and sense of style, and as such continued to be a favored subject of conversation in fashionable circles. "Did you see the white taffeta Miss Sarah wore last night?" "You don't suppose she dyes her hair with henna, do you?" (this, said in a conspiratorial whisper) "Surely that auburn can't be natural—" "Orange? Why, I never allow the color near me. Miss Sarah says it's most unbecoming on a lady." "I couldn't agree more. I think it's perfectly vulgar."

Miss Sarah was also a useful exemplar in preparing young girls for the rigors of the ladies' toilette and in the management of skin, hair, teeth, and general health. Mammies all over the parish scrubbed little white faces, saying, "Now hush that whining. It's for certain Miss Sarah Jensey never squallered such, and look at her skin now. Peaches and cream." Mammies brushed copious manes of hair and ordered children to chew charcoal twice a week to sweeten the breath and prevent tooth decay, while mothers everywhere demanded daughters rise early and retire to rest in good season—a necessary discipline, according to Miss Sarah, to maintain grace and good humors.

But Miss Sarah was admired for more than just her skin-deep attributes or as an exemplar of health, more than even for her gift in coaxing the spindliest of plants to grow into a blossoming marvel; she was admired most because when folks entered her home—perhaps warming their hands by the fire, or parched with thirst should the weather be intolerably warm—they felt enveloped in the warmth of her hospitality. As if she were genuinely delighted to see them upon her doorstep, young and old, announced and unannounced alike.

On the snowy day Sarah's sister-in-law, Virginia, and her nieces and nephew arrived, Sarah had been planning to do a thorough inventory of the medicines, and then roll more pills and prepare more tinctures, as they were running dangerously low in this season of aches and coughs. After which, if there was time, she'd planned to write another page or so in her book on etiquette and health for young ladies—a project which she'd, as yet, told no one about, unsure of both her authority and aptitude as a writer, keeping the manuscript pages locked in the drawer of her desk until such secret was forthcoming. She received the news of the guests' arrival with an inward groan and a weariness that settled in her bones like winter cold.

"Have the servants stoke the fires in every room," she told Uncle Henry, the manservant, hoping her disappointment did not show. "Prepare the guest rooms and inform the cook that there will be four more for each meal until further notice. Tell Aunt Delia there's a nice ham in the smokehouse that would do well for tonight's supper."

A few minutes later, Sarah stood in the parlor of the Fox Creek big house, kissing the frosty-red cheeks of her relatives and asking after their journey. Telling them how good it was to see them. How kind of them to drop by. That Aunt Delia's potato and corn chowder was already bubbling in the kitchen, and in the meantime, please warm themselves before the fire and rest a spell. For surely, they must be weary . . .

# Chapter 4

Tʜᴇ ᴡɪɴᴛᴇʀ's sɴᴏᴡ ᴡᴀs two days past when William leaned over the split-rail fence, watching as the three-year-old colt completed his third mile. Chestnut coat rippling, black mane and tail streaming, beautifully proportioned and fully sixteen hands, Chancet appeared to move effortlessly, gliding over the dirt track with a determination and a power that made William shake his head in wonder. Bottomless, absolutely bottomless.

As the colt flew past, the third-mile pacer horse fell off, and the fourth-mile pacer horse began her run. William's horse trainer, gray-headed Uncle Abram, consulted his timer and whistled softly. "One minute and fifty-four seconds for the third mile."

Not bad. Not great, but not bad. Other horses had done it faster—he'd seen them. But rarely had William seen a horse with more pluck, more courage, or more of a desire to run. And the stamina, God! the stamina. It was unbelievable. It was everything William had hoped for—everything he'd paid for. The blood of two of the greatest American thoroughbreds coursed through Chancet's veins: Diomed and Sir Archy. Thoroughbreds from a time when stamina outweighed sprinting ability. When stamina was king, and four-mile heats were mere afternoon strolls.

William propped one booted leg on the lowest railing of the fence as Chancet rounded the curve of the oval and began the backstretch. Visible over the cotton plants, the horse's head and neck bobbed. Cato, the jockey, clung to Chancet's back, seeming to float along the tops of the cotton. The fourth-mile pacer horse, Yellow Bird, ran on the outside at Chancet's flank. The air was bitter cold, and clouds of white billowed out of the horses' nostrils.

"That Chancet sure do like to run. He 'most flying. Seem to me like he going even faster."

Silent, William watched the horse and rider a while before saying, "By God, Uncle Abram, I believe you're right."

Little by little, Chancet pulled away from Yellow Bird, a filly that had kept up with Chancet during the second mile. Chancet was three lengths ahead when he approached the final stretch, clods of dirt flying behind him, the drum of hooves louder and louder until the horse sailed past with a great heave of breath, fully five lengths ahead of Yellow Bird.

"By God," William said again, struck with admiration.

"Seven minutes and thirty-four seconds!"

"Unbelievable."

"That last lap was one minute and forty-eight seconds!"

It was one of the fastest one-mile segments William had ever heard of. And for it to come at the end of four miles, when most horses were played out . . .

Uncle Abram whooped and did a little dance. "Mars William, that colt gonna win you a heap of money!"

"That's what I'm counting on, Uncle Abram. That's what I'm counting on," William said, feeling like doing a little whoop and dance himself.

"Think he can beat Black Harry?"

Black Harry was the terror of the New Orleans racetracks and had been for three years running. His owner, Marshall McCain, was a planter just outside of Baton Rouge and a personal friend of William's. A friend William would love to beat. For the past year, just the sight of Chancet in the paddock or on the track made William dream of beating Black Harry—beating Marshall. If any horse could beat Black Harry, it was Chancet—a colt that had hit the straw running on the night he was foaled and hadn't stopped yet. Even before Chancet was weaned, William had seen evidence of a champion: his stride, his spirit, his speed, and, oh God! his strength. Until now, he'd kept Chancet a carefully guarded secret. But come Saturday at the Metairie track, all of New Orleans would know Chancet.

"I think," said William slowly, watching as Cato took Chancet through his cool-down, "that Marshall's in for a big surprise."

Uncle Abram grinned, his white teeth shining in his coal-black face. "That sure is fine by me, Mars William. I's getting awful tired of that Black

Harry winning all the time. Black Harry this, and Black Harry that. Don't seem right. Ain't natural." The old trainer turned back toward Chancet, his eyes dancing with an excitement William recognized, for he felt it within himself. It was love. The pure love of horseflesh. The joy of seeing a horse run. Of seeing a horse race—and win. William knew he was lucky, for Uncle Abram was a fine trainer—the best. He knew his business. Through the years, William had received numerous offers for Uncle Abram, some of them quite high. But always, William refused. He would sooner part with his right arm than with Uncle Abram. And now, with this new colt that flew like the devil, bestowed with greatness from generations past—well, Uncle Abram was a part of that, and William knew it.

After instructing Uncle Abram and Cato regarding the upcoming race, William spent the rest of the afternoon with Quincy, his negro driver. Together they sorted through next week's rations while, one by one, William went over his list of items that needed to be accomplished before his return.

By the time William headed back to the big house, the sun was setting, splashing the fields and forests with a crisp, winter lavender. William was ready. Ready as he'd ever be. Tomorrow, with his family, he'd embark for New Orleans. He bounded up the stairs, pleased to find Sarah resting in their room, her auburn braid flung across the pillow. The room smelled of lilac. The scent of his wife. He heard the rustle of linens as she rolled over and sat up, sleep yet stamped upon her face in the waning light, the imprint of a crease on her cheek.

"William? Is everything all right?"

He took off his hat, sat on the edge of the bed, and caressed her cheek with his fingertips, realizing too late that his hand was icy. Instead of protesting, she reached up and grasped his hand, then, one by one, slowly kissed the tips of his fingers.

A warmth spread through him, spark to tinder. In that moment, heart beating faster, he felt an immense satisfaction with life. He knew were he to die now, draw his last breath and collapse into her arms, he could truthfully say he'd lived a life worth living.

He drew her to him and kissed her deeply before pushing her back onto the pillows.

*Sarah . . .*

It was a bold streak of light: a heavenly brushstroke painted upon a canvas of stars. Despite the comet's boldness, Breck had difficulty seeing the road and wished he'd brought a lantern. It was a considerable distance from the big house to the cypress quarter, an eight- to ten-minute walk at least, and in the darkness, it took even longer. But the risk of lighting a lantern was too great; Breck knew he wasn't supposed to be out past dark. Everyone thought him to be in bed. He headed toward the yellow glow of the negro quarters, weak light seeping from between the planked walls of the cabins where the chinks had not been stuffed with rags and mud.

A double row of cabins, eight on each side, faced one another across a dirt lane, each cabin housing one family. Footy lived in the third cabin on the left. Across the way, past the grist mill and the smithy and cooper shops, sat another sixteen cabins—the pine quarter—but Breck rarely visited there.

As he approached the cabins, he heard the deep contraalto of a woman's song—her voice rich and thick as the maple syrup he poured on his hotcakes. So different from the songs of the fields, with their rhythmic cadence. So different from the hand-clapping, foot-stomping, calico-swirling, toe-tapping tunes of Saturday nights when Grandma Mehitable would exclaim, "My, but aren't they a happy bunch of darkies!" Different, too, from Cousin Juliana, standing in the parlor with her hands clasped before her, singing with her trained child's voice.

When he stepped onto the small gallery and knocked on Footy's door, the singing stopped. Then the door creaked open, a sliver of light shone in his face, and Footy's father said, "Now Mars Breck, don't be standing there shivering—come on in and warm yourself. We been expecting you."

Breck stepped into the cabin, thankful to leave the chill air behind. It was one room, rectangular, with a brick fireplace and chimney on one side, and a shuttered window opposite. Tonight, the embers glowed, and besides the ever-present reek of smoke, he smelled remnants of a pork and cornmeal supper.

Footy's mother sat cradling an infant before the fire. "Evening, Mars Breck," she said, looking up briefly while the infant suckled noisily, and a spat of embers burst up the chimney. Footy's four sisters chimed in, a staircase of voices from three to thirteen years old, saying, "Hello," and "How do, Mars Breck?"

"Evening," he replied, thankful when everyone returned to what they were doing. Footy's pallet lay against the back wall, a pallet he normally shared with three of his sisters. Footy lay on it alone now, a blanket in disarray around his legs and hips. Breck sat next to him and touched his hand. It was dry and feverish.

Footy's eyes opened, startled, unfocused. Then awareness settled, and he said simply, "You came."

A washrag lay across Footy's forehead. Breck took it and dipped it in a bowl of water beside the pallet, like he'd seen Mammy Hester do when Kate was sick. He wrung it out and placed it back on Footy's forehead, anxious for his friend, hoping it would make him well. "Mama said you were sick."

"I's ailing something terrible." Footy's voice was so soft, Breck had to lean forward to hear. "My chest burns like it on fire."

Breck didn't know what to say. It was the first time he'd known Footy to be sick. Sitting here beside him, wondering what to say certainly wasn't like climbing a tree, or fishing, or hunting for birds' eggs. During those times, they alternately yelled, whooped, and in the quieter hours, perhaps under the stillness of shade, told each other their dreams and secrets. "I hope you get better," he said now, aware of his awkwardness and how loud his voice sounded in the enclosed space.

But Footy didn't seem to notice Breck's awkwardness. He shifted in his bed, wincing as if in pain. He was a thin child to begin with—downright skinny. Together with his hair shaved close to his head and his large teeth, which Breck always teased him about, his illness made him look skeletal. Watching him, Breck became frightened, wondering if his friend—his best friend since as far back as he could remember—was going to die. He glanced at Footy's mother and saw her glance down quickly at the baby, as if she had been observing him but didn't want him to know. She began to hum, a soft crooning meant to put the baby to sleep. *Does she know?* Breck wondered. *Is Footy going to die?*

Breck licked his lips, turning back to Footy. "I brought you something." He pulled his gift out of his pocket, hoping it would cure Footy even if the washrag didn't.

"Your whistle."

"I want you to have it."

Footy hesitated, drawing his brows together, turning the whistle over in his hands. "But Mars William done made it hisself."

Without looking, Breck knew Footy's mother was watching again. Listening. "That's why I want you to have it. It's special, you see. You can signal me with it."

Footy wrinkled his brow, seeming to mull over the implication. "Does you mean if I needs you to come quick like, I can blow the whistle?"

"If I hear it, I'll come running. I promise."

The child brought the whistle to his lips, took a breath, and blew. But instead of the reedy, mellow sound Breck was expecting, Footy exploded into a fit of coughing, his chest rattling like bullets in a box. He gasped for breath, eyes glazed with pain. Breck stood, unsure of what to do, until Footy's father stood beside him, and Breck knew it was time to go.

"I'm leaving for New Orleans tomorrow with my family," Breck said between Footy's bursts of coughing. "Except Grandma Mehitable's not coming. She's going to stay with my Aunt Virginia for a few weeks—says the city gives her a headache. Um, anyway, I won't be home for a while."

"He knows, Mars Breck," Footy's father answered.

"Well, I'll be seeing you," Breck said, knowing it was inadequate, feeling a pain in his throat, his heart.

But Footy had already closed his eyes.

Breck slipped out the door, shutting it behind him. Again, the chill of darkness encompassed him, and he felt his way down the steps, deciding to wait on the bottom step until his eyes adjusted. From inside, he heard the creak of a chair, the sound of someone walking across the room. Then they were talking, and he realized they were talking about him.

Their voices came distinctly through the door—through the walls really—and he knew they believed he had left. He knew he should leave, walk down the road immediately, darkness or not, but he felt rooted to the step.

"He gots a good heart." It was Footy's father, Obediah.

"Maybe he do, maybe he don't. Who can say for true? All's I know is sooner or later all white boys grows into their fathers. I seen it happen before. Plenty a times. White boys can't help who they is any more than a calf can help being a cow."

"It ain't his fault, Retta. He just a boy."

"Sure, it ain't his fault. I ain't never said it was. All's I's saying is white is white. Ain't nothing never gonna change that."

Breck heard Obediah sigh. "So, what you expect me to do 'bout it?"

"I expects you to throw that blamed whistle into the fire, that's what I expects."

"Now Retta, that whistle was a gift from Mars Breck, you know that well as I does."

"That's what I's saying, if you had ears to listen. Soon's we starts accepting gifts and such like, what you think Mars William gonna say 'bout that? He gonna be wondering where we got such fancy things, and we's gonna be in a lick of trouble trying to explain ourselves."

Obediah said, "Now you know Mars Breck ain't gonna let that happen."

"Is you thick in the head, or does I need to come over there and whack some sense into you? I already done told you that sooner or later they grows into their fathers. Mind my words, Obediah, the day's coming when Mars Breck gonna just stand aside and not say nothing, no matter who be trying to explain theirselves. And you know I's right. Now toss that whistle into the fire 'fore Footy wakes up and throws a fuss."

Breck blinked in the darkness. Overhead, there was a rustle of wind through the trees, and in the cabin, a sigh like the hiss of flame, then silence. He sat, unsure of what he'd heard. He sat, unable to move, so confused, his heart heavy like a chunk of wood, not understanding.

*White is white . . . all white boys grows into their fathers. . . .*

Then the plantation bell rang ten o'clock, and the dogs began to howl.

# Chapter 5

A S FAR AS STEAMERS went, the *Glory Belle* was a small one, a packet built to navigate the larger bayous and even the smaller ones if the waters ran high. And, as far as steamers went, she was ugly, squat, with none of the fancy trim, elegant parlors, or tasteful music of the larger steamers. But her route was regular, something passengers appreciated. She stopped at numerous landings along the bayous, picking up passengers, letting others disembark, before pointing her bow toward the Mississippi for the short jaunt to the city. On this day, the clouds hung full and heavy, and the air smelled of rain and soot as her decks teemed with Creole, American, Irish, Cajun, and German, a gumbo of languages.

No one gave the coffle a second glance. It was, after all, a common sight, as common as red beans and rice. A coffle of slaves. Slaves aboard a steamer, bound for the countless slave pens on Gravier, Baronne, and Moreau Streets. Slaves primed for auction under the vast rotundas of the St. Charles and St. Louis hotels, destined to fall under the hammer at Congo Square or at the Maspero's Exchange Coffee House at 440 Chartres Street, where the auctioneer's voice boomed as loud as a boiler explosion, where his jokes were laughed at and repeated in every coffee house and tavern in the *Vieux Carré*. Male slaves in the prime of their lives, chains clinking with every movement. Adult females too, filthy but comely, sure to clean up smart with a little soap and water (as any savvy buyer would recognize). A handful of children, well-fed, bound to be favorites with the crowds.

Ever since the day in the wagon when Monette had covered him with her blanket, Cyrus had kept her close. She seemed content to stay. It had taken him a while before he'd plucked up the courage to ask her her name. Upon her whispered reply, he said, "I's Cyrus," and pulled her close, holding her as tight as the doll she snuggled. Not caring that she was just a little girl, younger even than his sister. She was someone. Someone who knew his name.

So that first night in the snow-covered wagon, they'd slept in one another's arms, the warmest Cyrus had been since leaving home. Even so, for Cyrus, it was a fitful sleep, peppered with remembered voices.

*How old are you, boy?*

*You always talk like that, boy?*

*Five dollars a pound.*

*I said, sit on the scale, boy.*

Waking with a start, with a cry cut short, he'd found Monette watching him, her amber eyes so large under the pale, moonlit sky, that Cyrus felt if he could but wrap himself in their depths, the pain in his heart would cease.

She touched his trembling lip with her finger.

"Do not cry, *mon ami.*"

Two days after that, the *Glory Belle* had chugged up the bayou, black smoke billowing from her twin stacks, blasting her whistle, a low, throaty bellow that nonetheless pierced his ears. Cyrus stared hard, blinking with wonder, saying to Monette, "I ain't never seen nothing like that." Then she surprised him. Said she'd ridden one before. All the way to a big city where buildings were taller than trees, and where ladies in silk and feathers pinched her cheeks before going on stage and singing beautiful songs. He'd looked at her then, this little girl he kept so close, saying, "You sure is a puzzlement to me."

Then, hand-in-hand, they'd followed the coffle aboard. Finney, Wirt, and the other traders seemed content to leave the children alone, letting them settle in a tight spot beside the railing, safe beneath their blanket, where they could watch the water as it swirled by. One by one, the bayous slipped away—until the morning when the land split wide open, and they churned out upon a great river to join a fleet of other boats.

Floating craft of every description jammed the Mississippi. Shanty boats hugged the water's edge, slapped together with lumber scrounged from the river. The boatmen searched for the next tributary, the next settlement, where they could peddle their pots and pans. On the decks, women sewed. With rows of hides tacked behind them on the cabin wall, with squealing pigs and children running around and lines of freshly laundered clothes waving above their heads, the women rocked with the motion of the boat, needles flashing in and out, while the men poled the river. They steered away from the soot-belching steamers, from the roiling wake that made their pots sway and clank, from the steamboat crews who screamed for them to get the hell out of the way.

Blacksmiths plied the river on floating smithies, asking, "Mister, need them horses shod today?" while dentists shouted, "Get your extractions here! Guaranteed painless!" Flatboats slipped downriver, laden with lumber, flour, furs, whiskey, hemp, and tobacco, while barges from Pittsburgh headed for the New Orleans market, loaded with coal and the latest gossip from the North, all in feverish demand this frigid winter.

Cyrus' arm still hurt, and today it pounded with each beat of his heart. Monette seemed to know when his arm hurt, for she reached over and gently pulled it to her chest, cradling it along with her doll.

"It hurts. It hurts real bad."

Monette furrowed her brow. "If my nurse Heloise were here, she would wrap it in clay mud and give you a cup of hot chocolate to drink."

Cyrus had never had a cup of hot chocolate before, and he told her so.

"*Que c'est délicieux!* I'm sure you would like it."

Cyrus nodded. "I'd like to try some, that's for true." He wondered what it would taste like, whether it would taste like molasses, or coffee, and again he marveled at Monette—the girl who talked so strangely, who sipped hot chocolate and went to the big city to watch ladies sing. "I ain't never been to the big city before neither. Fact of the matter is, I ain't never been nowhere 'cept home, 'less you count the store."

"Where is your home?"

"Somewheres back there, I guess," Cyrus said, pointing back to where they'd come from. "Same as you." He peered behind the packet, past the flotilla of ramshackle boats and elegant steamers, remembering the mud, the labyrinth of bayous, the washed-out trails. It was too far. Too confusing.

"I miss Heloise," said Monette, her voice so soft he could barely hear her.

"I miss my mama," he whispered.

Monette looked at him with her big amber eyes, her brow furrowed once again, her lips trembling. Then she slipped her thumb into her mouth and laid her head on his chest.

For a long time, Cyrus stroked her hair, thinking. Through nights of watching the falling star, through mornings and afternoons of tramping through the mud, of sitting in the wagon with Monette, he'd wrestled with his thoughts, thinking and thinking until his head ached, pounding with the same force as his arm. *Why Missus done sell me? What I do bad?*

Maybe it was when he tripped, spilling a bucket of fresh milk over the kitchen floor, sprawling on his belly, watching as it seeped into the floorboards. Missus had looked shocked, blinked, then said simply, "Clean it up." But he was tired that day—too tired to give it anything but a token swipe. Maybe after the floor began to stink, reeking for weeks—a sour, rotten smell—maybe that was when she decided to sell him. Or maybe it was the time his sister jumped from the hayloft into a pile of straw. "Whooee!" she said, bits of straw poking from her braids, "That was heaps of fun! C'mon Cyrus!" He joined her. Jumping the afternoon away instead of slopping out the muck like Missus had told him. Maybe that was why. Cyrus didn't know the answer. He was beginning to realize he'd probably never know why—why Missus done sold him.

With this realization, a new understanding grew within him. He knew now he would never see his mother or his sister again. And with this knowledge, this final understanding, his chest stabbed with raw pain, as if he'd leapt out of the hayloft, not knowing that a pitchfork lay hidden beneath the straw.

It came as a relief when, minutes later, Cyrus noticed that the steamer was slowing. Its two paddle wheels were churning to a stop, the stacks no longer billowing copious amounts of soot. Cyrus lifted his head from the railing. Monette must have sensed it too, for she lifted her head from his chest, pulled her thumb from her mouth, and glanced around quickly. "Look!" she said, pointing.

Cyrus twisted around and stared, his mouth dropping open in surprise.

"It's the big city, *oui?*" she said, her voice tinged with pride. "The one I was telling you about."

Huge cotton warehouses, sugar magazines, wholesale stores, steam presses, and brick hotels lined the waterfront in both directions for a league or more. Church spires and steeples towered, and in the distance, a great white dome gleamed. Between the buildings and the river stretched an esplanade, broad and long, bustling with workers and passengers, the very air howling with racket—whistles, shouts, the rumble of wagon wheels—a babel of confusion and noise. Roustabouts loaded and unloaded cargo. Mules hauled drays filled with newly arrived merchandise, while here and there flatboat crews relaxed on barrels—smoking, drinking, tossing dice, and playing cards. Enormous steamships were moored at the wharf alongside three-masters, schooners, brigantines, barges, and scows, all crammed together, three deep, six deep, so tall, so wide—a maze of gangplanks leading from one boat to the next.

The *Glory Belle* blew her whistle and docked fore and aft between two steamers while her crew clambered aboard the adjacent ship with lines to secure her. Under a cloud of soot, the passengers prepared to disembark, gathering up belongings, calling children to their sides.

Finney stood. He removed his hat, swiped his hand through his long, greasy hair, spat a stream of tobacco juice over the rail, and said loud enough for Cyrus to hear, "Now listen up. We're heading into the city, and you're all gonna come real peaceful like. I don't want no trouble. You there." He pointed to the lead pair. "Follow me. Wirt, take up the rear. Like I said. I don't want no trouble."

Cyrus grasped Monette's hand in his, pulled her close, and whispered, "Don't be scared none, I's right here," although his own heart skittered with dread.

"But where are they taking us?"

"Someplace nice, Monette. Someplace real nice."

With a command from Finney, the coffle left the *Glory Belle.* Two by two. Chains clanking. Over the adjacent boats. Across each gangplank. Through the bustle and stink of the waterfront. Over the levee. Down the narrow streets. A coffle of slaves.

Monette awakened in the darkness, dreaming of Papa Léon. His long, white hair tied behind his neck, the wrinkles framing his eyes of ocean-blue, the tenderness of his mouth. For a sweet moment that lingered like a bedtime kiss, she believed he was with her. They strolled through the orchard, plucking peaches that took two hands to hold.

*You must be gentle,* ma chérie. Douce. *Otherwise, they will bruise.*

Then she heard the snores, the weepings, the whispers of the people around her—many people, crammed side by side, feet to heads. She smelled the stink of exhalations, straw jabbing her cheek like a stale reminder of what used to be. Remembering, she began to cry softly. Memory scraped her heart raw, snatched her breath away. She did not understand, only knowing that Papa Léon was gone, and that she, too, was also gone—somehow stolen from a life that had been theirs. So, she pushed the dream away, telling it to come no more, for the pain of waking was greater than the joy of dreaming.

Monette nestled into the crook of Cyrus' shoulder, closing her eyes when he wrapped his good arm around her. *"Mon frère,"* she whispered into the night.

*My brother . . .*

When morning came, she followed Cyrus into the yard and, like the others, obeyed the shouted directions of the white men and scrubbed her face and ears in the trough of cold water, pretending she could not remember Heloise bathing and dressing her, pretending it had always been this way—people jostling for position like dogs, shoulders rubbing, water spilling from between cupped hands, while the dirt underfoot turned damp.

After breakfast, she stood, bracing herself against one of the ivy-covered walls that surrounded the courtyard, while Cyrus combed her hair using his good arm, his other arm splinted. Within the yard were three outbuildings, plus two privies and a cistern. A jumble of haphazard rooflines peeped over the brick enclosure like curious neighbors. Monette's head jerked as the comb snagged on the tangles.

"Sorry," Cyrus said with each tug. "Sorry."

She blinked back tears, not wanting him to know how much it hurt, instead drawing air through her nostrils. Air laden with a jumble of everything—cold bacon fat, the wail of a baby, a mother's hush, the stink of the nearby privy. Three crows perched on the privy roof exchanged caws like squabbling siblings, all the while a beehive of people shat, scrubbed, and shaved, voices brittle as the morning chill.

She saw Finney step out of the passageway and scan the crowded yard. Upon spying her, he started in her direction, weaving between people, cheek distended with tobacco, carrying a parcel under his arm. She dropped her gaze, her breath catching.

Then he was standing before her, boots still spattered with the mud of the journey. A spurt of tobacco juice landed on a weed a few feet away. "Put this on." He handed her the parcel. It was pillow-sized, wrapped in burlap, and tied with string.

She took it, saying nothing, wondering what was inside. *"Merci."*

"Here. Put these in your hair." He dropped a handful of ribbons on top of the package—the palest of greens, lavenders, blues, yellows. Soft and new. Monette blinked and glanced up at him.

"Make sure she puts them in her hair," Finney said to Cyrus. "And make sure she has that doll with her each time she goes outside. That'll look real purty."

"Open your present, Monette," Cyrus urged, once Finney left. "Then I can tie them ribbons in your hair."

She set the package on the ground, untied the string, and pulled back the folds of burlap. It was her dress. Green, the color of Papa Léon's absinthe *frappé.* Rows of ruffles, ribbons of velvet. Heloise's favorite. It smelled and felt freshly laundered. "My dress," she said, astonished. She'd never thought to see it again. In fact, she'd tried to forget about her dress. To forget that her new clothes scratched and made her itch, that they were ill-fitting and ugly, and made her feel filthy.

Cyrus fingered the fabric, looking at her sideways. "This yours?"

*"Oui, mon frère.* And my cape and my pantalettes. Oh, and my stockings and boots too! Now my feet shall be warm. And look, here is my *gris-gris."* She slipped the amulet over her head and under her clothing, smiling when she felt the familiar small bag nestle against her chest.

"Is you a princess?" Cyrus asked, his voice quiet.

Monette laughed and shook her head, anxious to feel the ribbons in her hair. *"Non.* At least, I don't think so."

"A queen?"

Again, she giggled, realizing it had been many days, weeks even, since she'd laughed, surprised at how good it felt. *"Non, mon ami!"*

Cyrus smiled then, a gleaming grin of straight, white teeth that lit up his face. The sadness vanished from his eyes as he began to laugh too, finally catching his breath long enough to say, "I ain't never knowed someone like you before. Never."

Together, they gathered her belongings and entered the outbuilding. While Cyrus fumbled with her buttons and hooks and tied her hair with ribbons, she told him about her life with Papa Léon, a subject she hadn't wanted to talk about until now. About feeding the swans in the pond, riding her pony through the orange groves and fields of cane, playing hide-and-seek behind statues and fountains.

"Then why Papa Léon done sell you?" Cyrus asked simply.

Her laughter, her joy at getting her dress back, dissolved like salt in water. She could say nothing while Cyrus tied the last ribbon, a pale-yellow ribbon that hovered beside her ear like a whisper: *Why Papa Léon done sell you . . . sell you . . .*

She had no answer. Even the question caused her mind to swirl until she felt sick to her stomach. And through the mist of confusion, the tangle of unuttered questions, she remembered that man—that man who looked like her father, and yet who stared at her with a hardness in his eyes.

Just then, a commotion came from outside.

"I think they call for us," she said, fleeing the outbuilding into the crispness of the morning sunshine.

Cyrus' hand slipped over hers.

"Don't you fret none," he whispered. "From now on, I's gonna take care of you."

She heard Finney rather than saw him, for the crowd pressed in close. She saw nothing but shirts tucked into pants, shifting feet, a babe held on a woman's hip, an arm around a waist.

"Here's your new clothes: a fine calico dress, apron, and turban for each woman, and a suit and hat for each man. And everyone gets a pair of new shoes. Now, ain't that nice?"

Monette heard Finney expel juice from his mouth.

"Don't want no one saying we don't treat you right. Now, when I give the word, I want everyone to line up real orderly-like, and fetch your clothes. We open for business at ten o'clock sharp, and I want all you darkies looking smart and lively."

From somewhere, a fiddle began to play—a jaunty, skirt-swishing melody made for dancing. The crowd surged forward. Cyrus squeezed her hand.

"Did you hear that, Monette? I's gonna get me some new clothes too, and some new shoes. Lordy, this am a good day."

When Cyrus reached the front of the line, the white men looked him over and then handed him his clothes, hat, and shoes. Cyrus tucked the bundle under his arm and raced toward the outbuilding, hollering, "C'mon, Monette! It my turn now."

Soon he stood before her, grinning, standing proud in his stiff black pants and jacket, his white shirt buttoned to the throat, a top hat perched on his head. "And look!" he pointed to the ground. "New shoes! I gots new shoes!"

Monette had forgotten how big he was, and now, with his hat towering above her, and his clothes only a few shades darker than his skin, he seemed a stranger—a man, almost. She said nothing, peeping at him shyly, wondering if he was still her friend, her brother.

To the sound of the fiddle, Monette fetched her doll and, together with Cyrus, joined the others in the yard.

Upon the instructions of the white men, and while she yet wondered what was happening and where they were going and why, everyone filed out of the yard, feet shuffling through the passageway and into the showroom, where the paneled doors were thrown back, opening the showroom completely to the street. Then, like water released from a bottleneck, they streamed out the doors and onto the *banquette*.

# *Chapter 6*

UPON OPENING ITS DOORS in 1837, the St. Charles Hotel of New Orleans was the largest and grandest hotel in the nation. Built by the renowned architects Dakin and Gallier the elder, its four-story-high Corinthian portico dominated the skyline, its white dome soaring to one hundred eighty-five feet above St. Charles Street.

While the Creoles scoffed, saying no hotel was finer than the St. Louis in the *Vieux Carré,* the Americans knew differently. From around the nation, the American elite—politicians, planters, bankers, everyone who was anyone—gathered upon the marble steps of the St. Charles. Under its Ionic columns, under its vast, echoing dome reaching up and up like St. Peter's Basilica in Rome, stretching like the finger of Adam toward God, gentlemen congregated, discussing crops, livestock, the weather, the latest prices of slaves, the next day's horse races, the troubles brewing in Mexico, and next year's presidential election. They reclined in clusters of comfortable chairs scattered throughout the rotunda as cigar smoke swirled in a slow-moving blue haze.

"Damn near lost half my hogs this winter. Sorriest weather since I can remember."

"Snowed in Natchez. Eight inches. Says so right here in the paper."

"Maybe on account of the comet. Maybe our weather's changed for good. Maybe it'll never be warm again."

"Poppycock. Nothing but hysteria if you ask me," said an arthritic old colonel with a face like a bloodhound. With great effort, he dug himself out of the deeply cushioned chair and leaned forward on his cane.

"Losing hogs isn't hysteria," the first man replied.

"Don't get me wrong. I'm not saying it isn't cold. Sure, it's cold. I'm just saying it's poppycock to blame it on a comet."

"The Millerites say it's the end of the world."

"Miller's been preaching that rot for almost twenty years," said another, shaking the snuff from his handkerchief, "and it hasn't happened yet. What kind of fool would believe such rubbish?"

Another gentleman cleared his throat, adjusted his gold-rimmed spectacles, and held his newspaper at arm's length to read. "Says right here that a colored Millerite in Brooklyn was buried in his cellar during a snowstorm. Some passers-by heard him crying for help and dug him out. The colored man says, 'Is de end come?'"

"What'd they tell him?"

"Of course, they told him it wasn't the end of anything, much less the world. So, he says, 'Well, by gosh! I tought it had, and dey plum forgot dis saint altogedder!'"

The gentlemen chuckled.

"Well, what do you expect of Northerners?" The old colonel tapped his cane on the floor as the laughter died down. "They haven't the sense God gave a mule. Always sticking their noses into other people's business where they don't belong. Take those abolitionists, for example. They seem to know how to live our lives better than we know ourselves."

Several murmured assent, William Jensey among them. He enjoyed the company of men like himself—planters who understood his hardships, who understood what it meant to replant fields of corn, to lose a negro to fever, to be forced to whip an entire hoe gang who, for three days running, had done but a half day's work, to be forever in debt, borrowing even more money from the banks to snap up the adjacent land before someone else did, hoping the worm would not destroy their cotton crop before they could repay the loan.

Today William was content to say nothing, half-listening to the conversation, half-watching the scores of people who swarmed in, around, and through the rotunda of the St. Charles in its service as the hotel lobby. Rising from the center of the rotunda, spiraling upward in a graceful curve, a staircase led to the upper stories, terminating in a circular room under the dome where the entire city could be viewed. Up those stairs, burly porters marched, laden with trunks and parcels, cautioned by ladies who rustled of silk to take care and not drop anything. Men arrived, removed their top hats, and gazed up at the dome before striding to the front desk and signing their names with a flourish. Black mammies, their aprons stiff and snowy, held the hands of their young charges. The children stared wide-eyed at the hundreds of silver bells dinging through the bustling air; five in succession, three at a time—room 117, room 382, room 136—summoning a legion of white-coated attendants.

William reclined in his chair, absently smoking his cigar, unaware of the many who glanced at him, seeing a towering man. He was lean, weathered, with acorn-brown hair in need of a trim, looking the epitome of the rugged pioneer, yet at the same time appearing the perfect gentleman in his new frock coat and polished half-boots, and in the respectful tipping of his top hat should a well-dressed couple pass nearby with their entourage of servants and children. Nothing in his demeanor betrayed the fact that he would have preferred an all-night dancing frolic to a formal ball, a fish fry to a chandeliered black-tie banquet, or a round of ribald jokes with his friends rather than engaging in political debate. (With the exception of a few worthy issues that caused his blood to boil, he found politics rather dull, reminding him of the years spent at Harvard, where boyish pranks were vastly more satisfying to his soul than becoming, in his father's words, an ornament to the nation.)

"I'd like to see those abolitionists pick five hundred acres of cotton by themselves with just their own white hands," one gentleman was saying.

"Oh, they'd die of heat long before they'd finish even one row. Whites can't tolerate the heat like the negroes. It's a well-documented fact."

"More than likely, it would rain on the field and ruin the cotton because it took them too long."

"Cotton-picking idiots, is what they are."

"Or they'd die of fever afterward."

"Yet," said the colonel, "like everyone else, Northerners wear clothing made of cotton and then turn around and demand more. They sprinkle sugar in their tea, sugar grown right here in Louisiana using the very slave labor they abhor. Now where's the logic in that, I ask you? Abolitionists are stupider than the Millerites and far more fanatical."

"Fanatics are trouble."

"Fanatics start wars," he replied. "If they keep it up, there's going to be one. You mark my words. I'm not giving over one hundred thousand dollars' worth of personal property just because someone says it's the right thing to do. Poppycock! Where's my financial compensation? Where's the labor force to replace it?" He thumped his cane for emphasis. "They're fanatical idiots, those abolitionists. Haven't a clue what they're talking about."

"Hear, hear."

The gentleman with gold spectacles said, "Says right here in the paper that a Dr. Hagan of Vicksburg gave permission for his servant Richard to visit Virginia. Says Richard not only had a pass from his master, but one hundred dollars in gold in his purse and a good supply of silver coin for ready use."

"And?" The colonel leaned forward.

"Says that on his way back from Virginia, Richard stopped in Cincinnati to wait for a boat to take him to Vicksburg. The abolitionists pestered him so much that he was forced to take the mail boat to Louisville to get away from them. He told the abolitionists that he knew his own business best, and that he should return to his master, who treated him well and allowed him as many privileges as he wanted. He reached home, and now here it is in the paper. Says so right here."

The cane tapped the floor. "There you have it. Proof is in the pudding, as they say."

Such talk made William feel suddenly hot, and now he loosened his cravat. He agreed with the gentlemen, believing the abolitionists stirred a pot that was no concern of theirs, a pot that would soon come to a boil. Like other planters, William had legally bought and paid for his labor force. No one—especially sanctimonious, holier-than-thou scoundrels like the abolitionists—was going to tell him what to do. His negroes were rightfully his by law. He agreed that if the abolitionists were not stopped, it could indeed, someday, come to bloodshed. Bloodshed was something William would do everything in his power to avoid, but even so, for himself, he knew that if the abolitionists tried to take even one of his negroes, they'd be staring up the barrel of his rifle for their last look at life.

His father, Octavian, had taught him long ago that slavery was a necessary component of a well-ordered society, economic considerations aside. It was necessary that there be a class of people designated to perform the menial tasks of life, necessary so that those who were better appointed, both intellectually and morally, could aspire to greatness, to fulfill their destiny to which they were born. Besides, as his father was fond of saying, and as every gentleman at the St. Charles Hotel could affirm, slavery had a long history of proven success. Would ancient Greece have risen to such intellectual heights had Aristotle or Plato spent their days plowing the fields, driving the team of oxen, or—God forbid—emptying the chamber pots? Could the Roman Empire have spread its *Pax Romana* throughout Europe, Asia, and Northern Africa had the emperors or the senate been required to clean the stables, or prepare their own meals, or milk the cows morning and night? Slavery was a simple fact of life in any well-ordered society. William firmly believed that the North's modern emphasis on the rights of every man to pursue industry and wealth, regardless of social station, was an invitation to anarchy.

"Look at the French Revolution," William had told his son Breck only a week ago in just such a conversation. "The social classes were demolished. Now, the most anyone can aspire to is simple survival. In a hundred years, what will her culture be but a reminiscence of past glory? If such a thing happens in America, Son, before you know it, you will have negroes as your neighbors, calling the land theirs, demanding the same rights and privileges. Not only negroes, but poor whites too. God forbid they should mix with impunity—black and white—for then you will witness the destruction of the fabric of society, and our infant nation, so recently weaned and destined for greatness, will perish under the demands of the masses."

While William rarely allowed himself such political discourse—political extravagance, really (he had far too many other things to worry about besides abstract ponderings)—on such occasions he found it liberating, as if it were a sore that needed lancing. Liberating especially with an audience as attentive and intelligent as his son. Such a discourse was certainly necessary to maintain his bearings in a nation increasingly bending its ear to the ravings of lunatics.

It took William a while to realize they were talking to him, that they'd asked him the same question twice, maybe three times. "Don't you have a horse entered in tomorrow's four-mile races, Mr. Jensey?"

Before he could answer, the spectacled man nodded, saying, "Here it is. Right on the first page. Name's Chancet. An untried three-year-old."

"He any good?" the old colonel inquired, peering at William.

"The best," he replied, satisfied when all the gentlemen nodded, and a round of snuffing and smoking ensued. William's stables were renowned throughout Louisiana, his horses fast, well-trained, bred in the healthy air of West Feliciana's lush, rolling hills. Just last year, his stables had been featured in New York's *Spirit of the Times,* the ultimate sporting magazine for gentlemen. So, when William Jensey said a horse was the best, men believed him.

All except one.

"That so?" a voice boomed from behind him, practically in his ear. "Think he can beat Black Harry?"

William smiled. There was no mistaking that voice—blunt, jaunty, and sharp-edged all at once. He rose from his chair, turned, and grasped the man's hand. "Hey there, Marshall. Thought you'd never get here."

Marshall McCain was a few years younger than William, and short, the top of his head scarcely reaching William's chest. But his diminutive size was deceiving, for he was strong and wiry as twisted rope. William himself had seen Marshall hoist a man twice his size over his head and heave him like cordwood through a split-rail fence. Cigar clenched between his teeth, smoke billowing from him like a coal-fed locomotive, Marshall pumped William's hand in both of his.

"Champagne for everyone!" he ordered from a passing waiter. "And bring the best caviar you've got!" He swaggered to an empty chair, exchanging greetings as he went, his step as jaunty and commanding as his voice, his legs bowed from life in the saddle.

"Well?" Marshall said once everyone was seated, fixing William with a challenging stare. His eyes were small, intelligent, framed by a face that might have been deemed handsome were it not for the pockmarks and crooked nose.

William leaned forward, aware all the men watched and listened. "I think," he said slowly, "your Black Harry is about to gallop right off his pedestal."

Marshall looked around in mock surprise. "Why bless my ears. Hear that, gentlemen? William Jensey thinks his little colt can beat my Black Harry."

Some of the men smiled, but most didn't.

Taking a long drag on his cigar, Marshall turned back to William. "Seeing as Black Harry holds the record at the Metairie track—and all of Louisiana, for that matter—that's quite a statement, don't you agree, gentlemen?"

William knew Marshall was attempting to intimidate him, and a lesser man would have retreated. But William Jensey was not a man to be intimidated, which was one of the reasons why his friendship with Marshall was strong, why they respected one another, recognizing the same strengths in each other that they saw within themselves. Instead of answering, William said nothing, content to let the men around them shift uncomfortably in their seats.

"Tell you what," said Marshall after a while, chewing on his cigar. "I've got five hundred dollars that says Black Harry whips your horse's sorry ass."

William sensed the intake of breath. Sensed the listening attention from more than those just gathered in this intimate circle. Even the waiter, his tray loaded with caviar, empty glasses, and two bottles of champagne, stood frozen at Marshall's elbow, staring at William.

William inhaled deeply. "No," he finally said.

There was a collective sigh of Biblical proportions, an audible exhale of breath. The waiter's tray dropped a few inches as if it had suddenly become too heavy. Disappointment flashed across Marshall's face. A few listeners outside the circle began to move away.

William allowed himself a moment's satisfaction, savoring the sweetness of competition, the joys of horseflesh, wondering if it ever got any better than this, before he said loud enough for everyone to hear, "One thousand."

Marshall's eyes widened, and a slow grin spread across the small man's features. "Hear that, gentlemen?" he reached for a bottle of champagne and, after a brief struggle, popped the cork. He raised the foaming bottle above his head and said, "We've got ourselves a horse race!"

Sitting and listening once again—to the conversation, the tinkle of bells, a distant rumble of thunder—William drained two glasses of champagne. Betting a thousand dollars was reckless. Foolish, even. Yes, he was here to race his horse, but more importantly, he'd come to New Orleans to purchase some much-needed field hands and to give his family a respite from what he knew could be a very isolated existence. He'd never before wagered such a large sum, and knew its loss would be something he could ill afford. But somehow, when Marshall was around, he did things he wouldn't normally do. It was part of their friendship. Marshall brought out the best in him. Or was it his worst? William shook his head, smiling, unsure of the answer.

"My, but he is tall," the store owner remarked for at least the third time. "Are you quite certain he's only eight years old?"

"Quite certain," Sarah replied, her voice just as calm as the first time he'd asked. "I can't keep up with him. I expect he's going to be tall, just like his father."

"Ain't that the gospel truth!" exclaimed Mammy Hester, who hovered behind Sarah like a mother hen.

Already, Breck had been measured, pinned, pulled, tucked, buttoned, and told to stand straight and not move an inch. A most exquisite torture. It seemed forever before they finally released him—the reluctant owner of two new pairs of pants, three white linen shirts, a pair of durable patent leather brogans, two hats, six embroidered handkerchiefs, and a coat of the finest merino. But instead of leaving the clothing establishment, followed by servants laden with the purchases, Breck was told to sit and be a good boy, for now it was his sister's turn.

With a sigh of boredom, Breck pulled on a thread dangling from a button on the back of the settee. He picked and yanked until, to his mortification, the button popped off. He glanced up, wondering if anyone had seen him, relieved to find that they were not paying him the slightest attention, gathered instead around Kate as she squealed with delight at the hats, gloves, and dress material.

"A dress suitable for the theater," Sarah was saying. "And, of course, she must have new petticoats."

"Certainly, Madame."

"Lord a'mercy, Missie Kate," said Mammy Hester, clapping her thin hands together, "you's sure gonna look fine."

Breck sighed again and tried to push the button back into the socket, blinking in frustration when it kept falling out. Ever since his visit to Footy's cabin a few days ago, ever since he'd sat atop the step in the darkness and overheard Footy's parents, Breck had felt this sense of frustration, this vague feeling of incomprehension, as if there was some fundamental truth he could not understand, a truth as elusive as fog in the wind. He'd spoken of it to no one, not even aboard the steamer the next day when his father asked him if something ailed him. He'd shaken his head, mumbled no, feeling relieved when his father said nothing more, taking him instead to check on his prize racehorse and to see the boilers.

Now Breck held the button in the socket, wondering if Footy was dead. "Breck?"

"Yes, Mama?" He looked up, careful not to release the button.

"Would you like to go shopping with Mammy Hester? She's going to the market to purchase some herbs." His mother gave him a tender look, as if she sensed his restlessness.

Breck shook his head *no*. Shopping for herbs didn't sound much more exciting than shopping for clothes. Besides, if he got up right now, he'd have to let go of the button, and then everyone would know he'd been naughty. "No, thank you, Mama. I'll stay right here."

He was immediately sorry for his decision, for upon Mammy Hester's departure, Sarah turned to the proprietor. "Now I'd like to see some materials for myself. I'm partial to organdies, marceline, and *chiné* silks, preferably in violets and greens. Oh, and I adore bustles."

Breck sank back into the settee with a groan. More buttoning, tucking, pinning, and such. He would be stuck here at least until suppertime, and already his stomach growled. Breck made a sudden decision. He placed the button on the settee, strode to the door, and left. Herb shopping was definitely better than clothes shopping.

He glanced up and down the street, unsure of which way Mammy Hester had gone. Just as he was about to give up and return to the store, he spied Mammy Hester just across the boulevard, recognizing her thin form, her blue turban, her fichu of white lawn, her swaying gingham skirts. It was the widest street he'd ever seen, with a triple row of sycamores running down the center. He hesitated briefly before bounding across the street, careful to dodge the carriages. "Mammy Hester, wait for me! I've changed my mind!"

It didn't matter that she couldn't possibly hear him through the clatter of hooves, the jingle of harness, and the cries of street vendors selling their wares, for he prided himself on being a fast runner and knew he would soon catch up, despite the fact that she walked at a furious pace, faster than he'd ever seen her move before.

He reached the other side, hurrying across the planks that spanned the brimming gutter, searching the crowd, frowning because he'd lost her. No matter. He was certain he'd seen her turn down the side street just up ahead. He raced along the *banquette*. Although the wind blew a nasty chill, the cold air revived his body from the stupor of boredom, and running kept him warm.

"Mammy Hester, wait for me!"

A block or two ahead, he saw a flash of blue. He bounded down another street. Around the corner. Again, he lost her. Again, the flash of blue.

When he finally caught up to her, grabbing her hand and wondering why she kept walking at her frantic pace when surely she'd heard him calling for her, he stepped back in surprise as a stranger's face peered at him from beneath a blue turban. When the woman said, *"Oui? Puis-je vous aider en quoi que ce soit, petit gars?"* he backed away, embarrassed, not understanding.

Impatience flashed across the woman's face, while Breck stammered an apology in English, feeling his face flush. Then, after an awkward silence, the stranger shrugged and resumed her furious pace, leaving him standing alone on the *banquette.*

Where was Mammy Hester? He looked up and down the street, knowing even so that he'd followed the wrong person. Mammy Hester could be anywhere. Much as he hated the thought, he knew he must retrace his steps to the clothing store. He turned and headed back in the direction he had come.

Several blocks later, he knew he was lost.

Breck stood beside the gutter, thinking. While following the woman, he'd paid little heed to the streets and landmarks, having focused on the blue turban as his objective and little else. He knew it was useless to try to remember which way he'd come, for now that he was lost, he remembered very little. He wished he could ask someone for help—someone who spoke English—but everyone bustled about, fortified against the cold, their turned-up collars and pulled-down hats a seeming barrier against unsolicited communication. Breck shivered and wrapped his thin arms around himself. He set out in what he believed was the proper direction, skirting a rat that poked through the refuse in the gutter.

At first, he did not notice the strangeness of the city, but as he ventured through the streets, it seeped into him—a ghostly seeping, like whispered lies. This was not the New Orleans he knew. This was not the brilliantly lit rotunda of the St. Charles, nor the vast avenues of commerce where magnificent Greek edifices soared, where everyone spoke English and was understood. Here, the streets were narrow, bordered with water-filled gutters that reeked of excrement, of rotted food, dead things, manure, and mold—each city block an island. Buildings crowded shoulder to shoulder. Balconies of lacework iron jutted over the *banquettes.* From behind slivers of curtain, Breck glimpsed a face every now and then—faces that seemed to watch him. A white child. Alone. Breck hurried, wishing he'd thought to bring his new coat.

A man stepped off the *banquette.* His skin was mink-brown, and he was dressed in an elegant frock coat, a richly embroidered vest, and a *cravate* tied in a bow and pinned with a diamond. The man raised his beaver top hat as Breck passed, saying, *"Bonjour, Monsieur. Excusez-moi si je vous pose une question, mais puis-je vous être utile? Vous vous êtes peut-être perdu? Non?"*

Breck stared. Should such a man, dressed to the nines with diamonds and cravats, ever set foot on Fox Creek, Breck knew his father would waste no time caning him as an impudent upstart. Feeling his face flush with the sudden, unwelcome image of his father caning this man, Breck tore his gaze away and hurried down the street.

He smelled the riverfront before he saw it, knowing he'd gone the wrong way even as he heard the blast of the steamers and the shouts of the roustabouts. Here it was colder still. The wind swept through the vast square before him and tore through his thin clothing. He sat on the front step of a church and wrapped his arms about his shivering legs, resting his forehead on his knees as tears welled and threatened to fall.

The familiar frustration swelled in his chest, pulsing alongside his heart, mocking him, as if nothing he could ever say or do would rid him of it. He was too young. He could not understand. The world was too complex.

*The day's coming when Mars Breck gonna just stand aside and not say nothing...*

*All white boys grows into their fathers.*

*Look at the French Revolution.*

*Our nation ... will perish ...*

Breck pushed the tears down, refusing to cry. But even as he forced the tears away, the frustration remained—rising, swelling like an injury.

It was then he realized he was not alone. Two steps above and some three feet away sat an old man, his black face grizzled with whiskers. Breck was suddenly self-conscious, wondering how long the man had been sitting there. A milky film covered one of his eyes, the lid half-closed, but with his other eye, he watched Breck. His clothing was filthy, torn, his hands knotted and scarred, one finger missing. He cradled a bowl filled with what appeared to be stew. Surrounded now by the pungent, steaming aroma, Breck remembered his hunger. He put a hand to his stomach as it growled.

Without a word, the man held out the bowl to Breck. Uncertain if it was polite—if it was safe—Breck nonetheless took the bowl, welcoming the heat against his icy fingers. He shoveled in a spoonful of the stew, startled by the spices that immediately set his tongue aflame. Laden with fish, shrimp, and crab, it was the most delectable food he'd ever eaten. The man grinned, seeming amused at Breck's watery eyes and the effects of the spices, surely burning like fire on his face. Embarrassed again, Breck turned away from the old man and his staring eye, gulping down spoonful after spoonful. He didn't mean to finish it all, but before he knew it, the spicy stew was gone, the bowl scraped clean, and he was licking his lips—and a spot on his thumb where the stew had dripped. He felt ashamed then, afraid even, knowing he'd devoured the man's meal—perhaps his only meal. But when he turned back to thank the man, to apologize for his appetite and to return the bowl, Breck was shocked to see the steps as wind-swept and bare as when he'd first arrived.

He sat holding the bowl while it grew cold in his hands, finally leaving it on the step where the man had been sitting. Then, rubbing his hands together, feeling even colder despite the influx of warmth into his stomach, Breck descended the stairs and started across the square, not knowing where else to go. As he broke into a run, feeling the wind against the wetness of his eyes, he wondered if anyone was looking for him yet. Whether he would ever see home again. Wishing he'd never pulled the button out of the settee.

# Chapter 7

T HE AFTERNOON WAS COLD, and a wet wind sliced through the narrow street in short but savage gusts. Passersby blinked against the wind, cloaks flapping, their steps clipped and brisk, occasionally glancing up at the negroes lined across the front of the building. Some stopped. Examined the merchandise. Haggled and moved on. A few stepped inside the showroom to examine the stock at greater length—perhaps to conclude the deal.

Cyrus felt as if he'd stood there forever, grinning, teeth frozen to the wind, his arm aching.

A few days ago, after the disbursement of new clothing and to the merry strains of the fiddle, they'd filed out of the showroom and onto the *banquette.* With the white men directing, they arranged themselves across the front of the building—men on one side of the bay window, women on the other, and children at the far end—sixty-two in all: a line of new suits and top hats, bright calicos, freshly starched aprons, scrubbed faces, and colorful *tignons.* Cyrus stood with the children, next to Monette—next to her petite, laced and ruffled figure. He stood tall, proud in his new-smelling clothes, in his stiff new shoes that creaked when he walked and didn't pinch his toes. "Don't you fret none," he told her again and again, squeezing her hand. "I's gonna take care of you."

So, on that first day, when a white woman knelt in front of Monette, saying what a pretty thing she was and asking her name, Cyrus had answered: "H-h-her name Monette," he said. "W-w-we's brother and s-s-sister. We g-g-g-gots to be buyed t-t-together."

He recalled the revulsion—the pulling away of the white woman, the grunt of disgust. She left in a swirl of skirts, followed by her two servants, ignoring Finney's pleas to come back, come back—that they had plenty more merchandise, both fresh and cheap—that the boy was a liar, that they weren't brother and sister.

The next thing Cyrus knew, two traders grabbed his arms, one on each side. They yanked him through the showroom, down the passageway, and back into the yard where the morning had begun.

It was the first time he'd ever been beaten.

*Truly* beaten.

Now, he stood not with the children, but with the men—grinning, always grinning—fiercely determined to do nothing wrong, thinking, Ain't no one never gonna beat me again. I's gonna be good. Real good.

"How old are you, boy?" A man stopped in front of him.

Cyrus stared at the man's boots, muddy from last night's rain—at the mud-tipped walking cane as it tapped the *banquette.* The man had the voice of someone older, one even older than the greasy-haired slave trader called Finney.

"Th-th-thirteen," Cyrus said from behind his teeth, blinking away the lie.

The man didn't seem to notice, for he reached out and began probing Cyrus' shoulders and arms. The splint was gone—removed whenever Cyrus stepped onto the *banquette* so as not to, according to Finney, dishearten any customers. Cyrus stiffened, knowing what was coming. When the man reached his injury, pain erupted through Cyrus—a visceral explosion of bone and sinew—and he clenched his teeth to keep from crying aloud, widening his grin even as tears scalded the backs of his eyes.

Again, the man didn't seem to notice anything unusual, for he said, "Turn around, boy."

Heart and knees rubbery from the shock, Cyrus turned as Finney strolled up the *banquette* and stopped beside the customer.

"He's a fine, strong buck," Finney said. "Takes orders real good. Been vaccinated against smallpox. If you like, we can take him inside for a more thorough going-over."

"What kind of work does he do?"

"Well now, what kind of work did you have in mind?"

"I own a shipping business." The man continued to prod Cyrus—poking his back, his buttocks, his thighs. "I need workers to load and unload cargo. They've got to be strong. And young. I want them young. What's your name, boy?"

Cyrus turned back around, eyes lowered. "Cy-Cy-Cyrus."

"Good God. Does he always talk like that?"

"'Course not," said Finney.

"Ever been whipped, boy?"

"'Course he hasn't. See how happy he is?"

"I asked the boy. Ever been whipped, boy?"

Cyrus glanced up at Finney's narrowed eyes, remembering.

That first day they'd dragged him into the yard, ordering him to strip naked. They placed a pole horizontally behind both his knees, told him to squat over it, to loop his arms beneath the pole. There he'd squatted, unable to move, penis dangling between his legs, exposed while they beat him with a large wooden paddle bored with holes. It left no marks, they said. A few blisters is all. For a while, he'd screamed for his mama, but it was only when he fell silent, when he ceased to flinch with every whack, that the beating ceased.

Do like we tell you, boy, they said, and you won't get beat no more. You want to get sold to a good man, don't you? they said, prodding him with the paddle.

Cyrus nodded, scarcely conscious, struggling for breath, lying in the yard, dirt in his nostrils. They said, No respectable gentleman wants to buy a stupid darky who lies and talks bad. Only bad men buy those kind of darkies 'cause they know they can whip 'em up right. So do what we say, and we'll see you go to a decent man. Understand, boy? Understand? From now on, you're thirteen years old. You're a man. Old enough to do a man's work. Understand, boy? You hear what we're saying? You're a man now.

They left him there, that first day. Left him in the yard. He'd lain in agony for what? An hour? Two? While his back and buttocks rippled with spasms. He'd lain there unable to move, certain he was going to die, when he felt hands on his shoulders. He knew it was her.

"Cyrus," she said, her voice quivering. "Cyrus, *mon ami, mon frère. Ça va?* Are you hurt?"

He let her help him up, biting his lip, determined not to cry, to be good, real good, so they would never beat him again. He followed her, staggering to the blanket that they shared, his weight on her frail shoulders.

He allowed her to cover his nakedness, to wipe the dirt from his face, to lean in close and kiss his quivering lips.

Now Cyrus swallowed hard, tasting fear, smiling at the man's muddy boots. "N-n-no."

"Let me see your back. Lift up your shirt."

Cyrus did as he was asked, the wind slapping his bare flesh. He felt the tip of the walking cane as it was thrust under his shirt like a tent pole, lifting his clothing higher. No one spoke as the man examined him. Finally, the man grunted, the walking cane was removed, and Cyrus lowered his shirt.

"Like I was saying, he's a good boy. Won't give you a lick of trouble. Does everything you tell him. You'll get fifty, sixty years of hard work out of him. I'm giving you a deal when I say I'll let you have him for a thousand dollars."

The customer burst out laughing, spat, and walked away. Cyrus stared at the bricks in the *banquette,* at their pattern, at the mud settling in the cracks, the tiny bubbles in the man's spittle.

"Wait!" Finney called after him. "Nine hundred dollars! Eight fifty! Last chance, 'cause I'm sending a pile of them to auction next week!" When the man didn't answer, Finney yelled, "I've got others! Some of them talk fine enough to be lawyers. Hell, preachers even."

As the tap of the man's cane faded away, Finney turned to Cyrus, his voice hard. "You just shut your trap from now on, you hear? Stupid black bastard."

Nodding, grinning, not understanding what he'd done wrong, his forearm still throbbing, Cyrus felt weak with relief when Finney left and took up his post again just outside the entrance.

Cyrus glanced down the line, past the men, the women, spotted the green of Monette's dress and thought, Ain't no one buyed her yet.

The afternoon wore on. Servants hurried by on some errand, baskets hooked over their arms. Carriages slopped and swayed through the mud and the occasional half-sunken cobblestone, candle lamps aflame in the deepening gloom. The blasts of steamships bellowed through the streets on gusts of wind that grew increasingly bitter, stinking of brine and soot.

Cyrus clamped a frozen hand to his hat. His cheeks hurt from smiling. It was then that he saw him: across the street, huddled in the darkened recess of a doorway, a white boy stared at him.

Cyrus blinked, startled, wondering briefly if he was seeing things. But no—there *was* a boy, thin, so obviously cold. From across the distance, they watched one another. It was a strange watching—as if the boy knew Cyrus was not really a man, but a boy, big for his age. As if the white boy saw beneath Cyrus' grin—saw instead the broken arm, the beating, the hole in the bayou, the forever loss of his mother and sister.

From overhead came a rumble of thunder, loud and threatening, followed by a flurry of wind. Just as quickly, a curtain of rain fell between the two boys—heavy, gray—as if the show was over, the stage lights extinguished.

"Move inside!" cried Finney. "Double quick!"

Cyrus hurried toward the entrance, curious about the boy, yet anxious—like the others—to move inside the showroom, out of the rain and where a fire blazed. When he glanced back through the veil of rain, to his surprise, he saw the boy dash toward him into the street—directly into the path of a carriage. He heard the curse of the driver, the scream of the horses as the reins were hauled taut, and the horses reared back. Around him people gasped. A woman shrieked. Then there was a moment—a moment only—when Cyrus glimpsed the expression on the boy's face. It was a look of shock, of terror, before the boy disappeared beneath the flailing hooves.

It was the kind of afternoon that every mother dreads, the kind that causes her to wake in the belly of the night, quivering and praying that such a trial will never come to pass. That maybe—dear God, maybe—she can arrive at the end of her days surrounded by every child she'd ever pushed from her womb, replete with satisfaction at life's abundance, contented, arms outstretched to embrace the joys yet to come. . . .

While Sarah stood arrayed in sparkling emerald silk, the clothier circling her with a mouthful of pins, Kate remarked offhand, "Mama, where's Breck?"

After a quick search of the establishment, Sarah assured Kate, saying that perhaps he'd gone with Mammy Hester after all. But even as she said it, even before Mammy Hester returned alone, with a basket of herbs hanging over her thin arm, Sarah knew.

The next couple of hours went by in a blur. She bundled up Kate and hurried to the waiting hack, fumbling with her green *barège* veil just as a blinding, vicious rain burst from the sky. Behind her, the proprietor was inquiring as to what he should do with her purchases—Should he wait to hear from her? Would she be returning momentarily?—while Mammy Hester was praying loudly, "Sweet Jesus! Oh, sweet Jesus! My poor little baby boy! Protect him, sweet Jesus! Send your mighty armies of angels! Oh, sweet Jesus!"

"To the St. Charles Hotel!" Sarah cried to the driver, ordering Kate and Mammy Hester up to their rooms and out of the way the moment they arrived.

Immediately, the gentlemen in the rotunda galvanized into action. Cigars were extinguished. Overcoats secured. Gentlemen divided into groups. William directed, hat on his head, voice thundering. Off they went, on horses, in covered carriages, out into the crackling lightning storm, into the driving rain that fell so fast and hard that they vanished from sight in a heartbeat.

Sarah sat in the area normally occupied by gentlemen guests, saying nothing, surrounded by ladies who patted her hand, who whispered among themselves and dabbed their eyes with handkerchiefs as the rotunda flashed with lightning. Every story she'd ever heard of a lost child meeting a terrible end returned to her in lurid detail. The little Irish boy, newly arrived from his native island, separated from his family in the bustle of the wharf, his body found the next day downriver, floating in the reeds. . . . The ten-year-old girl from a prominent New Orleans family, said to be bright and cheerful and already a beauty, stolen away—her body found weeks later in a cemetery, mutilated, violated. . . .

Then, like a breeze filtering down the dome, faintly heard at first, word spread that Breck had been found. At first Sarah didn't believe it, sitting straight and saying nothing, twisting her handkerchief into knots. Then she saw William's unmistakable figure enter the rotunda, a muddied child limp in his arms, overcoat tinged with blood. She stood and felt the life drain from her, thinking, *Dear Jesus, he's dead.*

William approached, leaving a trail of water behind him, the brim of his hat dripping with every movement of his head. "Have someone fetch the doctor," he said to her. "I'm taking him to his room." To a nearby servant, he said, "Room 201. We need a strong fire, hot water, and towels. And a tray of food, including broth and bread." But when the servant did not move, instead staring open-mouthed at the seemingly lifeless boy, William barked, "Now!"

By the time the doctor arrived, Breck lay in bed, changed and dry, and the fire roared in the grate. Sarah turned away when the doctor stitched the head wound, and then bled the child, pressing her face against William's sodden shirtfront, filling her ear with her husband's heartbeat.

*It was my fault—all my fault.*

"He'll recover," the doctor said in a huddled conference by the door, "so long as he doesn't take ill from his experience. Other than that nasty cut on his head, just bruises and scrapes. Nothing broken, thank heaven. Keep him warm, make certain he gets plenty of rest, and if he takes a turn for the worse, you must fetch me without delay."

Once the doctor was gone, Sarah put her face in her hands and wept. William's arms wrapped about her, and she let him pull her close. "Hush, wife, hush. Breck will be all right."

"It was my fault."

"It was an accident. A mistake. Hush, Sarah."

"How could I have been so—so careless?"

"That's enough now."

Then she felt his kisses atop her head, the coolness of his hands in her hair, loosening the pins. In a cascade of auburn curls, her hair tumbled out of its restraint, down her shoulders and back.

"Sarah," he whispered, his lips brushing her forehead, her dampened cheeks. "Sarah, my love." He kissed her then—a long kiss that quickened her breath and made her heart beat faster, a kiss lingering and soft, creating a heat within her.

She closed her eyes, leaning her head back as he kissed her neck, as he pressed her against his body. His body—so lean, so hard—she knew she should not be thinking such thoughts, but could not help herself. She loved him. All of him.

But when he undid the top hook of her bodice, she pushed him away. "Not here. Not with Breck in the room. Not now. How can you even think it?" She sat in a chair beside Breck's bed, smoothing her hair, her dress, her breath still trembling. From behind her, William said nothing, but she sensed his passion, palpable.

He moved her hair aside and fastened her bodice before leaning down and pressing his lips against the top of her head. "I love you, my wife," he whispered.

She heard him walk to the hallway door, felt the breeze of its opening, and then he was gone, shutting it softly behind him.

As the day turned to evening, she alternately read from her prayer book or set it aside when she wearied of praying, once glancing up briefly as a servant entered to stoke the fire. Occasionally, she brushed Breck's hand with her fingers, wondering when he would awaken, whether he could feel her touch. His breathing was soft and even.

It was only after she'd read the prayer for the sick two dozen times over that Breck finally awakened, his brown eyes gazing about the room with the unfocused look of someone recently ill.

"Mama?"

In a rustle of skirts, she sat next to him on the bed. The flicker of candlelight and the glow of embers illuminated his features—his square jawline that held the promise of strength, strength like his father's; the puckered scar at the side of his eye that would never, Sarah knew, disappear entirely. She placed her palm flat on his bandaged forehead, knowing even so that it was too soon for a fever. "How do you feel? How's your head?"

"I'm hungry."

During her years of nursing the sick at the plantation, she'd learned hunger was a good sign—a body mending. "I have a tray of food right here. And I've kept the broth warm beside the fire."

After drinking half the broth and eating a few bites of bread, he fell back against the pillows, clearly exhausted, soon asleep. Sarah hoped he would sleep the night through.

She was again reading the prayer for the sick when William returned.

"I've hired a tutor for Breck." He yanked his cravat from his neck and tossed it on the floor, as if glad to be rid of it.

"A tutor?"

"He's from Philadelphia. Comes highly recommended."

"But why? I mean, why now? Today? And what about Mrs. Rivers?" Mrs. Rivers was an elderly widow from St. Marysville who traveled to the various plantations, teaching the younger children reading, writing, and arithmetic. Sarah had always thought her to be a pleasant woman, though prone to forgetfulness—such as where she'd laid her spectacles (usually atop her head), or whether she was supposed to come to the Jensey plantation on Wednesday or Thursday afternoons.

William stood at the window, parted a curtain, and gazed into the darkness beyond. Though the thunder and lightning had moved away, the wind still rattled the window, rain pounding the glass. When he let the curtain drop and turned back to her, Sarah recognized that look he always had when his mind was already made up. It was a hard look, resolute, reminding her so much of his mother (a comparison that had infuriated him the one time she'd said as much). "Listen, Sarah, what happened today would not have happened if Breck had been better able to communicate. Don't look at me like that. You know I've been meaning to get rid of Mrs. Rivers for a long time now. She's an old biddy who can barely remember to put in her teeth, much less recall two times two. To expect her to teach languages, not to mention chemistry and economics—well, you might as well expect her to jump on Chancet tomorrow and beat Black Harry around the track. It's laughable."

Sarah said nothing.

Then, as so often happened, William's face softened, the hard lines suddenly erased. He crossed the room and knelt beside her, smelling of dampness and cigars, his eyes filled with concern. "Mrs. Rivers was adequate for a while, Sarah, but Breck needs more. He needs to know how to speak French fluently, among other things. He needs to know higher math and Latin and, well—everything. And I intend to get him what he needs."

She turned from her husband and gazed at Breck, at his still form. Of course, William was right. He was always right. He was a good father, and a faithful and attentive husband. William himself hadn't been able to complete his education, forced as he was to take over the management of a plantation at an age younger than most, and so it moved Sarah to see such thoughtfulness for the educational well-being of their son. "And Katherine?"

William blinked as if he'd forgotten he had another child. "She'll receive her education alongside Breck. Who knows? If the teacher's worth his salt, maybe she'll finally settle down and stop getting into so much confounded mischief."

"But where will this man sleep? I mean, where will we put him? And how much are we paying him?"

William smiled and covered her lips with his finger. "Shh. No more questions, my love. Not now. Now we have better things to do."

She did not resist when he took her hand and led her from Breck's room into theirs, a room bright with fire and thick with warmth. The coverlet was already turned down, and on her pillow lay a single purple flower. Even as he kissed her, she wondered how he'd gotten an iris in the midst of such coldness, and how lovely it was—the first flower of spring. But as he slipped her clothing away, layer after layer, she forgot even that. . . .

## Chapter 8

ON THE FOLLOWING MONDAY, thousands of readers around New Orleans, William Jensey among them, picked up their edition of *The Weekly Picayune,* anxious to read the recap of Saturday's horse race for themselves. Already, Chancet was the talk of the town (even though, on race day, the weather had been thin and disagreeable, and the road to the Metairie Course was so muddy from the previous day's thunderstorm that most sensible people stayed home).

As was expected, Black Harry, known to be a good mudder, was the hands-down favorite against the other three horses, Chancet being the distant long shot, as no one expected an untried three-year-old to be able to withstand the grueling effects of a four-mile heat (much less two or three additional heats should more be required). Really, most expected Chancet to be distanced in the first heat, finished for the day, and the talk in the grandstand, the infield, surrounding the outer rail, and even in the judges' stand was to that effect. But Chancet surprised everyone except William when he nosed by the distance marker at the last possible second, despite a nasty stumble during the third mile that nearly unseated Cato.

The odds didn't improve for Chancet during the forty-five minutes between heats, though he held his head high, with eyes alert, and showed no obvious signs of distress—a fact observed by all who crowded around the judges' stand while the horses were washed and rubbed, and the jockeys weighed.

But following the second four-mile heat—a heat in which those who had been sitting at their leisure in the grandstand were sitting no longer—the betting went crazy, as if a plug had suddenly been removed from an anthill. General Bonaparte was distanced. The filly, Sue Ann, lost a bit of her sprightly step. But neither General Bonaparte nor Sue Ann was the reason the betting went crazy; it was because, as Chancet rounded that last bend of the last mile, everyone knew they were watching a fighter—a horse who would later be described as "whipcord every inch of him," by *The Weekly Picayune.* For, as the crowd stood to their feet, as the thin air mingled with shouts and the smash of hooves, Chancet caught up to Black Harry, and they crossed the finish line together.

Half said Chancet had won, and half said Black Harry had won, and the judges declared it a dead heat. Black Harry would need to run again if he wanted the best two of three—something Black Harry hadn't had to do for his last fifteen races. By now, William was forced to contain his smile, which, he knew, should he allow it full rein, would add more fuel to the betting fire, as his reactions were being observed by any and all. As it was, he maintained a blank expression, appearing almost bored to an outside observer—an expression that betrayed nothing of the raw joy that quaked his insides, a raw joy only tempered by the fact that his son wasn't there to share it with him.

Odds were nearly even by the start of the third heat, when, to the tap of the drum, both Chancet and Black Harry sprang away as if the distance were a mere race around the block, leaving Sue Ann in a splatter of mud within the first quarter mile. The crowd cried out when Chancet slipped again, allowing Black Harry to pull ahead by four lengths. But dismay soon turned to dumbfounded admiration when, during the last mile, Chancet gained steadily. Even those whose money was on Black Harry couldn't help but shake their heads, knowing this was a race that would be talked about for months—for years possibly—that Chancet was a piece of horseflesh worth reckoning. In the final stretch, while Black Harry's rider was laying on the lash and the spurs, Chancet coolly edged past Black Harry to take it by a neck, distancing Sue Ann.

Chancet, now the heavy favorite, won the fourth heat handily, distancing Black Harry, who was neither in the mood nor the condition for another heat.

No longer needing to harness his joy, William grinned as the crowd parted for Marshall. The smaller man walked up to William, his swagger no less cocky, the ubiquitous cigar clenched in his teeth. They clasped hands.

"Well," drawled Marshall, "it sticks in my craw like a rotten possum to have to say it, but I'll say it anyway. Congratulations, big boy. You got me."

William shook his head, still grinning, hardly able to believe his good fortune. "Had me worried there for a while."

The mayor of New Orleans, who was listening, as were dozens of other men crowded elbow-to-elbow, said, "Got yourself a little firecracker there, Mr. Jensey. Fine piece of horseflesh. Wouldn't want to sell him now, would you?"

"Sorry, I—"

"I've got three thousand dollars I'll give you today."

"Well, that's mighty generous, but I—"

"Four thousand," said a man from behind Marshall.

"Forty-five hundred," said the mayor, without missing a step.

"How about your trainer?" said another man. "Who's your trainer?"

"My own Uncle Abram. He's been with me ever since—"

"I'll give you fifteen hundred for him!"

"Sixteen hundred!"

"Two thousand for the jockey!"

"Why, I'll give you six thousand for the lot—horse, trainer, and jockey!"

"Sixty-five hundred!"

"Seven thousand!"

"Gentlemen, gentlemen, please!" William held up his hands against the flattering onslaught. "I'm afraid that no one—neither horseflesh nor otherwise—is for sale at this time. I mean to enjoy all of them for just a few more races, at least, if you'll allow. After all, I'm sure you'll agree there's no point in racing horses if a man can't enjoy a few wins every now and again, is there?" There was a brief moment of silence, during which William heard only the soft patter of rain on his hat, the whinny of a horse in the distance. Then the men began to chuckle, and the air of competition was replaced by a friendly air of amusement and banter, all accompanied by resounding claps on William's back.

"By god," said Marshall, "coming from you, that was an outright verbosity."

"Keep me in mind for when you *do* want to sell, Mr. Jensey."

"Enjoy your wins, Mr. Jensey."

"Maybe your trainer could give my trainer a few pointers—"

"I must say," said Marshall, as the crowd finally dispersed, leaving the two men alone, "I'm cheered by the thought that our newly formed rivalry is not so quickly ended."

"I'm certain we would have found something else to contend about."

"Goes without saying, big boy."

William wrapped an arm around Marshall's shoulder and began strolling nowhere in particular, saying, "Now, about that bet of ours . . ."

So, on the following Monday, the winner of not only the thousand-dollar bet from Marshall, but the $750 Jockey Club purse, William—after folding up his newspaper, finishing his tea, and extinguishing his cigar—left the barroom at the St. Charles and began attending to business. He met with his factor, who pumped his hand vigorously in both of his, congratulating him for his win at the track (and also asking after Breck's welfare), then offered William a chair. Together, they discussed the status of William's crops and livestock. Needed supplies. The ramifications of the weather. The need for credit. Overall, William was content with his affairs. He left his factor's office in a state of optimism bordering on euphoria, believing this would be the year to shatter the harvest records of all his previous years. Come the end of the week, all that remained was for William to purchase some field hands.

Now he bounded up the hotel's spiral staircase and entered Breck's room, pleased to see his son sitting up, head swathed in a clean bandage. The room was stuffy, its air belying the crisp freshness of the out-of-doors that still clung to William's coat like dew. Mammy Hester had been sitting next to the window sewing, but upon William's entrance, she set aside her sewing, curtsied, and left.

William had wanted to wait until his son was well enough before telling him about the horse race (as it was known that too much excitement could be injurious to the health), but Breck was perceptive. Perhaps overly so. A trait that had caught William off guard more than once. "Chancet won, didn't he?"

"I thought you were supposed to be resting."

"I am."

"Feeling better?"

"Yes."

"How's the head?"

"Fine."

Tossing his hat, newspaper, and gloves onto the bedside table, William asked, "Where's your mother?"

"Resting."

"Ah, at least someone knows how it's done."

"He won, didn't he?"

"Yes, Son, he won." William sat on the bed beside Breck and regaled him with the details of the race, unable to stop the fervor from overtaking his voice or the grin that spread across his face like silliness on a jester. He was pleased with Breck's answering smile, even though he knew that, were Sarah to discover them talking horses and wagers and upsets of the century, she'd doubtless summon the doctor to lecture them both on the dangers of overstimulation and the powers of rest. As it was, William couldn't help but believe that the tale of such a victory held a curious curative power of its own—unchronicled in the annals of medical history but intrinsically understood in the minds and hearts of every lover of the races.

"Wish I could have been there," said Breck.

"Next time."

"When can I get out of bed?"

"When the doctor says you can, and from what I've heard, that won't be for another few days, maybe not until next week."

Sighing, Breck sank back into his pillow, suddenly looking tired. For the first time, William noticed the bruise-like shadows beneath the boy's eyes. Perhaps Sarah was right. It was too much excitement, too soon. He rang the bell for the servant and rose to go, just as Mammy Hester entered the room, toting a tray of food that smelled of gruel and the peculiar odor of arrowroot.

"Papa?"

William paused at the door, hat, newspaper, and gloves in hand. "Yes?"

"Don't worry," his son said with a wink. "I won't tell Mama you told me."

Kate sat atop the grand spiral staircase of the St. Charles Hotel, her chin on her knees, picking at a loose thread dangling from her frock.

Ever since her brother Breck had gotten lost, the trip to New Orleans had been perfectly spoiled. Up until then, it had been a parade of new bonnets, fashionable short cloaks, and jointed dolls, topped by an evening at the theater (even though she'd fallen asleep before it was over).

Now, for the last week, it was as if Kate didn't exist. Unless, of course, she existed only to be told to be quiet or to go play with her doll and be a good girl. She was tired of her doll. She was tired of being a good girl. It seemed everyone was having fun except her. Breck got to stay in bed, while Mama covered him with damp washrags and Mammy Hester fed him one spoonful at a time, saying, Poor baby, poor baby. But when Kate tried to take a nibble, or opened her mouth to be fed, she was told to stop being so naughty and to go to her room and keep herself occupied.

It simply wasn't fair.

Tears welled in Kate's eyes, and her vision shimmered. She snapped the thread and tossed it over the edge of the staircase, watching as it spiraled down. When it disappeared from sight, she knew just what to do. She would get lost. Just like Breck.

Fortified by her decision, anxious to lie in bed and have everyone hover over her and feed her whatever she wanted and say poor baby, poor baby, she hurried down the steps, around and around.

Soon she was running. Through the crowded portico and down the marble steps to the street, where gawkers strained their eyes upward for a glimpse of the great white dome. Several people gave her a sidelong glance, and she realized her cheeks were damp with tears. She ignored them, and crossed the street, dodging a mule-drawn omnibus whose driver blew his trumpet at her. She ran down the *banquette,* not wanting to be lost so close to the hotel.

After a while, she glanced back, out of breath, slowing to a walk when she could barely see the hotel. Now that she had run away, now that she was lost, really lost, she felt a prickle of uncertainty. How long would she have to stay lost before she was found? Even though it was a pleasant April day and the sun warmed her face, if she stayed lost too long, she knew she would have to turn around and go back. She didn't want to be out after dark.

Soon the buildings parted, and a vast expanse of green spread beside her. Under the coolness of the shade trees, white-turbaned mammies chatted as they minded their strollers. Older children hooted and ran on the lawn, playing games of tag amid low-flying birds. Kate recognized the park. She'd visited it many times before with Breck and Mammy Hester. Stepping into the park through the iron gate, she sat on one of the sun-warmed benches, wondering who would be the first to find her and how long she would have to wait.

The afternoon trickled on, and she grew restless. Nighttime was still a very long way away. Finally, she could stand it no more, and asked a group of boys if she could play.

"Only if you're it," said one boy, a stout child with freckles sprinkled across his cheeks like cinnamon.

Soon, she dashed about, shrieking with delight, breathless with laughter, racing to touch the fastest boy. "You're a nanny goat!" she cried when she finally tagged him. She sprinted to hide behind the trunk of a shade tree, screaming, "Can't catch me! Can't catch me!" half-dreading, half-hoping he would. Then out onto the grass she raced, dashing to within inches of the nanny goat's fingertips and back again.

Being lost was such fun!

The sun dipped low, and a cool breeze lifted the damp hair from her forehead when she heard a voice behind her. "Why, Miss Katherine Jensey, is that you?"

Panting, Kate turned to see Mrs. Fusser, accompanied by her servant. Kate knew Mrs. Fusser because she sometimes ate breakfast with Mama in the ladies' parlor. Mrs. Fusser ate precisely one hard-boiled egg every morning—salt, no pepper—and had eyes that bulged so much Kate thought they might someday pop from her head. Now those hard-boiled, buggy eyes stared at Kate. "What on earth are you doing out here, running about and screaming like a savage? Where is your Mammy?"

Kate swallowed hard. This was not at all what she had envisioned when imagining her rescue. Mrs. Fusser, of all people. All bother and buggy eyes. "I'm lost," whispered Kate, a tiny tear welling in one eye but stubbornly refusing to fall.

"Lost? With the hotel just a few blocks away? I've never heard such nonsense! Your mother will have a thing or two to say about that! Not to mention your father! Now come along with me, young lady." With the servant in tow, Mrs. Fusser marched Kate straight out of the park and back down St. Charles Avenue.

It was a dejected Kate who trailed behind Mrs. Fusser, walking no faster when the woman turned and said, "Don't be a laggard!"

A sense of foreboding filled Kate, much like the time she'd burned her finger by poking it into a forbidden peach pie.

*Mama will know*, she thought. *Mama will know.*

The door to Breck's room opened in response to Mrs. Fusser's sharp rap. Dim light spilled into the hall as Mama appeared in the doorway. "Why, Mrs. Fusser! Katherine!" Kate saw the questions in her mother's eyes. "But what—"

"That daughter of yours was by herself at Lafayette Square, playing with some boys," said Mrs. Fusser. "If I hadn't walked past and seen her, there's no telling what would have become of her. As it was, she was screaming and tumbling about like a savage. I mean, look at her! Grass stains all over her frock and petticoats—they used to be white, I presume—her hair a regular rat's nest, and heaven only knows what kind of abominable language she picked up—"

"Thank you, Mrs. Fusser," interrupted Mama with a smile. "I'll handle it from here." Sarah pulled Kate inside the room and gently closed the door.

Kate scarcely noticed Breck sitting up in bed, alert and watching, scarcely heard Mammy Hester's exclamation, "Lord a'mercy! What you gone and done now, honey chile?" as Sarah ushered her to a chair, ordering her to sit and explain herself.

Now the tears flowed. Real tears. Tears of the past week's anguish. The past week's nonexistence. Kate laid her face in her hands and sobbed. "I was lost, Mama."

"But Katherine, you know the way to and from Lafayette Square. It's only a short walk from the hotel. You've been there dozens of times."

"That's the gospel truth," said Mammy Hester. "I know that's the truth, 'cause I takes you there myself."

"I was lost, Mama, really I was." Tears spilled through her fingers. She was sorry for her ruined frock, sorry for her messy hair, wishing she'd never had such a stupid idea as getting lost.

Then, suddenly, like waking from a bad dream, Sarah was beside her, wrapping her arms around her, enfolding Kate in billows of lilac and lace. "Oh, Katherine, my little darling. I'm so sorry. It's been a hard week for you, I know."

Kate said nothing, so relieved, content to stay wrapped in her mother's arms. Sarah stroked Kate's hair, seemingly oblivious to the tangles, as Kate closed her eyes, still hiccuping with tiny sobs, thinking, *I've been found.*

After a while, Sarah drew back and brushed the hair from Kate's eyes. "What if," she said with a half-smile, "you and I go out tonight?"

Kate gasped, scarcely believing her ears. "Really?"

"Well, I don't see why not. The doctor says your brother is fully recovered and can leave his bed tomorrow. Isn't that right, Breck?" Without waiting for an answer, Mama continued, "And your father is with the gentlemen tonight, so it makes perfect sense for you and me to go to the theater and enjoy a night out. William's boy, Henry, can accompany us."

"The theater? Do you mean it?"

She nodded. "I hear *The Wood Demon* and *The Fairy of the Whitesheaf* are playing tonight at the American Theatre. If we hurry, we can catch the opening."

It was one of the happiest nights of young Kate's life. Leaning over the balustrade of their box, holding her mother's gloved hand in her own, she watched, enraptured, as Miss Ince danced the *Cracovienne,* and Miss MayBelle sang, her clear, sweet voice vibrating up to the highest gallery. It was a night of diamonds, of violins, of bravos.

"Mama," she whispered between shows, almost afraid to speak, as if it would break a spell. "I'm so happy." Her mother smiled at her then, and Kate thought she was the most beautiful mother in the whole wide world. Then the brilliant gaslights dimmed again, the audience hushed, the curtain rose, and *The Fairy of the Whitesheaf* began. But long before it ended, Kate fell asleep, dreaming of nymphs and fairies and owning a name as grand as Miss Ince or Miss MayBelle.

Sarah sat holding her daughter's hand, watching Kate as she slept. The evening seemed to have worked a kind of magic on the child. A spark had danced in Kate's eyes from the moment Sarah had suggested a night out together. It was all the child had needed—her mother, all to herself. Sarah chided herself for not recognizing how much Kate craved affection. It seemed so obvious now, but when her thoughts had been occupied solely with Breck's care, she hadn't noticed—no more than she'd noticed what time it was, or when she'd taken her last meal.

An immense love for her daughter swept over her. There was no doubt Kate was a difficult child—headstrong, boisterous, selfish on occasion—but sometimes those very traits made Sarah love her all the more. How different she was from Sarah herself. Kate struggled to do the simplest things—sewing, sitting still, listening—yet became fiercely determined when faced with a tree to climb, a game to win, or her mother's waning attention. Kate did everything with her whole heart, or not at all. She was a child of passion. So like William.

A memory surfaced, one forgotten until now. The day after Breck had been found, Sarah had sat in her chair beside him, believing she was alone, her face buried in her hands, weeping. Then, suddenly, when she lifted her head, there was little Kate, watching her with a most sorrowful expression. With unexpected tenderness, Kate had placed both hands on Sarah's cheeks and said with a quivering voice, "It will be all right, Mama. Please don't cry."

Now Sarah sighed, grateful for these fleeting glimpses into Kate's softer side, thinking of the years ahead when that tender side would need to be cultivated and nurtured. Sarah knew that someday her daughter would become a lady—the wife of a planter, the *chatelaine* of a plantation—a woman of grace and social refinement rather than a child of impetuous temperament. Such molding of character would not be easy; it would test both of them to their limits. For now, Sarah was content simply to love her.

Sarah placed a hand on her belly, sensing the child within. She was only a few weeks along at most—a Christmas baby. Even with Breck and Kate, she'd known this early. A growing awareness, as well as a changing body. It made for a long pregnancy. Even so, she warmed at the thought of another child in her arms. William's child.

God has blessed me, she thought. Indeed, He has blessed me with great abundance. But even as her heart warmed, a familiar fear, long submerged, began to worm its way into her awareness, boring holes through her contentment. No, she thought. It is enough to be happy.

A child is a blessed event.

I am, among women, blessed.

# *Chapter 9*

HER BREAKFAST CAME UP quickly. A queasy tightness. Monette said nothing, merely bending at the waist, observing with detachment as bile, bacon, and cornbread splattered onto the marble floor.

"Look out!"

It would have been funny. The way the white men jumped. Leaping as if dancing. But she didn't care, even though tiny flecks of vomit had spattered her dress, even when one of the men stuck his face in front of her and yelled, "What the hell's the matter with you?"

The dullness had started last night, when Finney gathered everyone into the yard and told them their time in the pen was finished, and that those not sold would go to auction tomorrow because he was leaving for St. Louis on Sunday. That's when it started. The nothingness.

*Auction . . .*

She'd slept fitfully all night, waking with a gasp whenever she did manage to drift off.

Cyrus tried to comfort her, but she said nothing. Could say nothing. "Don't you fret none, Monette," he whispered in the darkness. "I won't let nothing happen to you. I's gonna keep us together. We's brother and sister, remember?"

*Auction . . .*

She didn't know what "auction" meant. Didn't ask. Staring at the emptiness of the rafters above her, her ears filled with the sounds of weeping, she remembered seeing a black man swinging from the branch of a tree, a rope around his neck, his blood-red eyes bulging from their sockets. She wondered if that was "auction."

Upon rising in the morning, she'd gone through the usual motions. Get dressed. Wash in the trough. Stand while Cyrus untangled her hair and tied it with ribbons. Eat breakfast. Hold her doll. Listen to instructions. All the while thinking nothing. Feeling nothing. Then, instead of lining up on the street like usual, they'd followed Finney down the *banquette* in rows of two—some of them chained—into a giant white building that towered up and up and echoed with bells and voices and the fall of a hammer.

Now a woman scraped vomit off the marble floor. Monette watched, dully aware that it was her own, and that it stank.

"You sick, Monette?" Cyrus felt her forehead. "You ain't hot. Leastways, I don't think you is. You's cold. Real cold. I felt a piece of ice once, and that was cold. You's cold like that. Once I was so hot my mama said you could fry a egg on my head. My sister, she was gonna try too. She gots a egg from the henhouse, but Mama knowed and made her go put the egg back 'fore Missus found out."

He held her hand and chattered more. A nervous chatter. But she didn't listen, seeing instead a man swinging slowly, a rope around his neck.

*Auction . . .*

Somewhere, right now, people were being auctioned. She heard voices rise, a scream every now and then, a baby crying, and the pound of a hammer. It was the sound of *auction.* A dense prickle started at the base of her spine, and with each cry, each slam of the hammer, it crept upward like tentacles.

Then Cyrus was grabbing her, sticking his face in front of her own like the white man had done. His face was strangely contorted, and she thought she could feel his heartbeat through the touch of his hands. "Monette! It almost your turn. Oh, Monette! Speak to me!" He tugged on the sleeve of one of the white men. "M-m-mister Wirt, p-p-please s-sell us t-t-together! I p-promises to w-w-work hard. I w-w-won't n-n-never make you s-s-sorry."

But the man grabbed Cyrus and yanked him away from Monette. "I'm already sorry, you dumb ass. Now get away from her before I have to beat you again. And she ain't your sister." Cyrus was pulled out of her line of vision.

Someone was pushing her up a set of stairs. "No crying now, you hear?" Finney's voice. "Look happy."

Monette stepped onto a platform, wooden planks beneath her boots, suddenly aware of a sea of faces stretched out before her. Tens, hundreds of people. Men, women, children, white and black. All staring at her. Gasping.

"Oh, isn't she sweet!" someone said.

"Just like a porcelain doll!"

"Papa, I want her!"

In an instant, Monette's nothingness vanished.

Instead, a terrible trembling seized her, and she was suddenly, viciously, alive.

High overhead, under the great expanse of the dome, two birds wheeled and dove. Occasionally they alighted on some projection or staircase, but never for long. Off they flittered again, silent above Breck's head, swooping and diving. He wondered how long they had been there, flying in circles. What happened to birds caught inside the dome? Did they never find their way out, instead circling and circling until they dropped, exhausted, to the floor? Did they live there for years, descending to eat a few crumbs before ascending again for their daily routine of circling? Or did they observe the people flooding in and out of the hotel entrance and, one day, decide to follow them? Breck pondered these questions, feeling the familiar frustration rising despite his attempts to keep it suppressed.

It was the first day following Breck's confinement. While his limbs quaked with weakness and dizziness threatened, he refused to return to his bed. He was tired of lying in bed. Tired of being coddled. Instead, he sat in one of the comfortable chairs in the rotunda, ten feet from the front of the platform, with his family around him. The crowd milled about, some lounging in the chairs, all chatting and laughing, waiting for the next negro to be put on the block.

Already Papa had purchased two negroes. Both male. Good specimens, by the look of them, although Breck was the first to admit he really didn't know much about purchasing negroes. Papa tried to help him, though.

"Look for a liveliness in the eyes," he said. "But beware of defiance. A defiant negro will make you sorry you were ever born. And stay away from the sulky ones. Sometimes, no matter what you do, they never amount to anything."

But regardless of how hard Breck tried, he couldn't detect liveliness, or defiance, or sulkiness. Instead, when he looked into their eyes, he saw Footy's eyes—fever-filled and wracked with pain. He saw the eyes of the elegant black man who dressed like white, with diamonds and top hat. And the milky eye of the old man who had given Breck his bowl of gumbo. Rather than let the familiar frustration creep back into his heart, he watched the birds circling overhead, finding it much less complicated than gazing into the eyes of men about to be sold.

"I need a new laundress," Sarah was saying to William. "Ever since Diana died, the white clothes have had a gray cast, and some of them have come back considerably smaller, with scorch marks from the irons. Oh, how I miss her. No one knows how to wash clothes like Diana. Anyway, I've instructed the new girl again and again, but she's too young, and I suspect she doesn't know her business. Try to find someone older, so she's had some experience."

"How old?" asked William.

"At least, I'd say, twenty-two or thereabouts. Oh, and make sure she comes guaranteed."

William nodded.

Suddenly, from all around Breck, the ladies gasped—a feminine chorus, an intake of perfumed breath, gloved hands covering lips.

"Oh, isn't she sweet!"

"Just like a porcelain doll!"

Kate pulled William's sleeve, pointed, and said, "Papa, I want her!"

Atop the block stood a girl. They were right, Breck thought. She was like a porcelain doll—but like none he'd ever seen before. Delicate. Princess-like. Her skin, *café au lait,* smooth and unblemished. Dressed in pantalettes and a velvet dress adorned with ribbons and ruffles, she squeezed a rag doll against her chest, staring at everyone with wide, amber-colored eyes.

Breck knew immediately what she was feeling. It was not liveliness, or defiance, or sulkiness. It was fear—stark, cold, primal fear.

"I want her, Papa! Please, Papa!" Kate jumped up and down, her auburn pigtails bouncing.

William frowned. "I didn't come here to buy negroes who can't work. And I certainly don't want a mulatto. Nothing but trouble. They get airs and think they're better than the other negroes, and before you know it, you've got a situation."

"Name's Monette!" bellowed the auctioneer, his voice echoing throughout the rotunda. "Fluent in both English and French! Obedient personality. Vaccinated against smallpox. A fine pet for your wife or playmate for your daughter! Comes with the clothes and doll you see here. I'll start the bidding at two hundred dollars!"

"Two hundred!" yelled someone from behind Breck.

"I have two hundred. Do I hear two-fifty?"

"Two-fifty!"

Kate began to cry. "Papa, please!"

"Three hundred!"

"Papa, please!"

At first Breck thought Kate's desire to own Monette was purely whimsical, like getting a puppy or a new jointed doll. But now he detected a desperation to her voice, hysteria almost.

His mother spoke close to William's ear, but even so, Breck heard what she said. "At least think about it. Katherine's acted so strange of late. Perhaps this is just what she needs—someone her own age to occupy her time and play games with her. Settle her down. You know the plantation can get positively lonely, especially for a young girl. Please, William."

Still, he said nothing.

"Three-fifty!"

"The bid is three-fifty! Three-fifty!" The auctioneer's voice rolled like thunder—constant, deep, booming. "Do I hear four hundred? Four hundred!"

"Four hundred!"

"I have a bid of four hundred from the fine lady in the back."

"Besides," Mama was saying, "you said yourself you want Breck to learn French. What better way than to have a playmate who speaks fluent French?"

Breck watched the slave girl, saw her trembling body, the rainbow of ribbons in her hair quivering like butterflies. Her chest moved in and out with shallow, quickened breaths as she placed one foot behind the other until she stood at the back of the block, her gaze darting from person to person as if at any moment they might eat her alive. Breck was reminded of the time the hounds at Fox Creek had cornered an injured wildcat. The last thing he'd seen before the wildcat disappeared beneath a snarl of teeth and claws was its desire to live—a wide-eyed plea of such raw intensity that Breck was taken aback, haunted for weeks afterward.

*Plea denied.*

He realized his own muscles were tense and trembling. Sweat broke out on his forehead and his upper lip, and he wondered vaguely if he was sick again.

"The bid is four hundred. Do I hear four-fifty?" The auctioneer paused. "Four-fifty? Now, come on, folks, someone so smart she can speak two languages ought to be worth at least four-fifty!"

A few people chuckled.

Breck tugged the leg of his father's pantaloons.

William looked down. "What is it?"

"Buy her," whispered Breck. "Please."

His father rubbed his forehead as if stricken with a sudden headache. "I give up." Then, rising to his full height, William raised his hand and hollered, "Four-fifty!"

"Ah, we have a new bidder right here in the front. Four-fifty to Mr. Jensey. Do I hear five? Five hundred? Last chance now, folks. Dig out your gold and give me a bid of five hundred. Take this child home to your daughter. Looks like she's made of honey. A child as sweet as this ought to get you a nice thank-you kiss from your wife! Five hundred. I said five hundred. How about four seventy-five? Four seventy-five going once, going twice—*sold* to Mr. Jensey for four-fifty."

Kate shrieked and clapped. "Thank you, Papa, oh thank you!" She flung her arms around his waist. William reached down and picked her up, then smiled when her arms encircled his neck and she planted a kiss on his cheek.

"Now that's one happy little customer," said the auctioneer, smiling.

The people around them chuckled, and a few clapped.

After the mulatto was led away, Breck sank into his chair, drawing his long legs beneath him, his heart banging fast as a rabbit's. Perhaps he should go to bed. Perhaps being pampered by Mammy Hester—having food shoved down his throat like a baby bird until he felt close to retching—perhaps that was better than sitting here watching an auction. He'd been to auctions before, but he'd never felt so involved. So helpless. He hated the feeling and ground his teeth together, staring at the birds circling overhead.

He ignored the next four negroes up for sale, barely looking when Mama purchased the laundress she wanted—a negress named Minty. Twenty-four years old, healthy, fully guaranteed, especially skilled with flat irons and fancy wash.

"Pay attention now, Breck," said his father. "This is how you learn."

"Are you feeling all right, dear?" his mother said, placing her palm on his forehead. "Do you want to go back to your room?"

Breck was about to say yes when something arrested his attention: stepping onto the block was a boy he recognized.

"Breck, darling, are you all right?" Sarah repeated.

Breck nodded, brushing her arm away. He stared at the boy, remembering. It was on the day he'd been hit by the carriage. He'd taken shelter in a doorway. Across the street from him stretched a long line of negroes for sale: men, women, children—everyone sharply dressed. Breck hunkered down in the doorway, sitting on the step, wrapping his thin arms around himself, observing while a customer examined the boy, lifting his shirt up with his cane. He heard snatches of questions—except when a carriage rattled its way between, or the wind howled. Then the customer was laughing and walking away. Breck stared at the boy, mesmerized by his grin. Breck had watched him for a long time before the boy noticed him.

When their gazes finally locked, Breck knew the grin was a lie.

He still didn't know what had come over him, what could possibly have made him dash out into the street without looking. Perhaps it was the slow fire burning in the showroom, an invitation to warmth. Perhaps it was because the only person who knew he was out there—knew he was alone, lost—was leaving. All Breck remembered was that one moment he was sitting in a doorway, and the next he was dashing across the street, through the puddles, through the driving rain, and that's where his memory ended.

Now Breck looked into the boy's eyes and saw the shock of recognition course through the boy as he saw Breck. Again, the boy grinned. A huge, white-toothed grin.

"Name's Cyrus," boomed the auctioneer. "Thirteen years old and vaccinated against smallpox. Folks, we've got ourselves a fine, strapping young man. He'll make a good plow hand or a terrific cane cutter. Whatever you want him to do, he'll do. Take off your shirt, boy, and let them see those muscles. Turn all the way around. That's it. Now, folks, imagine how big he'll be in just a few years. Gentlemen, I'll start the bidding at five hundred dollars, but you know he's worth a lot more."

"Five hundred!"

"Five-fifty!"

"Six hundred!"

"The bid is six hundred. Do I hear six-fifty? Six-fifty—"

Then Cyrus did a strange thing. Staring at Breck, his silly grin still plastered on his face, the boy began to dance. Up there on the platform, naked from the waist up, his shirt hanging from his pants, he shuffled his feet, his arms swaying, hips gyrating. Embarrassed laughter tittered through the crowd.

"Why, look at that!" exclaimed the auctioneer. "We got ourselves a performer! Someone guaranteed to make you laugh."

It was a silly-looking dance, as silly as his grin, but Breck was not laughing. When the boy stared at him again, swinging his hips, shuffling his feet, Breck knew: *he wants me to buy him.*

"Now, gentlemen, you saw what he can do. He's willing and obedient. Do I hear six-fifty?"

"Six-fifty!"

"Seven hundred!"

"The bid is seven hundred. Give me seven-fifty. I said seven hundred and fifty dollars. Seven hundred's a good bid, gentlemen, but not good enough. You'll get forty, fifty years of hard work out of him. Think of all the fat, strapping pickaninnies you'll have running around. Now, what do you say? Give me seven-fifty."

Breck stood, aware of his weakness, his trembling, and of his father standing beside him.

"Seven-fifty!" cried Breck.

He sensed the intake of breath. He saw the surprise mirrored on everyone's faces—Cyrus, the auctioneer, the slave trader who hovered in the background. Breck glanced up quickly and saw the same surprise on William's face, but his father nodded his head. "If that's what you think, Son."

The auctioneer said nothing until he saw William's nod. Then he boomed, "Did you hear that? This young fellow here has more gumption than any of you! Seven-fifty is what he bid! Now, are you going to let him have this darky for such a measly price, or are you going to give me eight hundred? I said eight hundred."

"Eight hundred!"

"Eight-fifty!" hollered Breck, fighting the darkness that wavered at the edges of his vision.

"The bid is eight-fifty. Do I hear nine? Nine hundred. Nine hundred dollars, gentlemen. Not too much to ask. Nine hundred dollars going once, going twice—*sold* to young Jensey for eight-fifty!"

# Book Two

*"I played among the wildflowers and wandered, in high glee, over hill and hollow, enchanted with the beauty of nature, and knew not that I was a slave, and son of a slave."*

B. J. Vance Lewis

# Chapter 1

### *June 1843*

ALREADY, FOX CREEK PLANTATION felt like home to Monette. Though she'd scarcely lived there for a handful of weeks, it was hard for her to remember that it had not always been this way. Papa Léon, Heloise, rides on horseback through the cane fields—these distant memories evoked such searing pain that Monette refused to think of them. Instead, like closing a book, she shut the memories from her mind and pretended her life had always been at Fox Creek. And so, the chapters of her former life faded until they seemed no more than a game she used to play.

From that first day following the auction, Monette had felt loved and wanted. Reeking of vomit, having wet herself again, she was whisked to Mammy Hester's room on the upper floor of the St. Charles, where she was undressed and made to stand in a basin of water. As Mammy ran the cool washrag over Monette's body, soaking the rag doll which Monette refused to surrender, the old woman whispered again and again, "Poor little chile. What they gone and done to you?"

Finally arriving at Fox Creek, Monette climbed into a trundle bed beside Kate's four-poster as if she'd always lived there, slept there, and known nothing else for all her life. She'd fallen asleep holding Kate's hand as Kate whispered a story about a princess, a story that quickly merged with dreams the way twilight blends with night.

Since then, her days were filled with companionship. For the first time in her life, she played with children her own age. Kate taught her to skip rope. Breck showed her how to play marbles. She climbed trees, swung on swings, and shared the saddle with Kate as they rode Kate's pony through the forest and fields. She played battle with Kate, Breck, Footy, and Cyrus. They called her Private Monette. Breck promised her a promotion if she followed orders. Monette didn't know what a promotion was, but she was eager to find out, and so did everything they told her—marching, scouting, guarding, and standing at attention.

In May, William completed a playhouse for Kate. It measured just eight feet by six, with a ceiling so low that anyone taller than Breck had to stoop. Not that it mattered, for Kate allowed no one but Monette and herself to enter. Inside, they swept, washed dishes, dusted, and chatted over pretend tea and biscuits. When the air grew too stifling, they sat out on the miniature gallery in pint-sized rocking chairs, sipping lemonade and gossiping about news of the neighborhood.

"I've been told Miss Botswa colors her hair," Kate would say.

"Do tell."

"They say she's actually very old, and if she didn't color her hair, she would die."

"*Bonté divine!* Is this true?"

"Miss Botswa's maid told the coachman who told Mammy Hester's husband who told Mammy Hester. And everyone knows Mammy Hester doesn't lie, so it must be true."

"Do tell."

"I would rather drop dead than color my hair. It just isn't right. Proper ladies don't dye their hair."

"*Non.* Most certainly not. Proper ladies are *comme il faut,*" Monette said, translating when Kate didn't understand.

On Monette's first full day at Fox Creek, Miss Sarah had taken Monette aside, saying, "You are to be Breck and Kate's little French teacher. While they will receive formal instruction from Mr. Gilbert, you will talk with them in French and help them to understand—especially Kate, for she has difficulty in that regard. If she says something wrong or poorly, please correct her." Then, to Monette's delight, Miss Sarah had spoken a few words of French to her, and though her French really wasn't very good, it warmed Monette to know she had tried.

"I will," Monette had promised her. *"Je serai leur petit professeur de français."*

Often, during the morning hours while Kate was closeted in the schoolroom receiving formal instruction from Mr. Gilbert, Monette left the big house and meandered down to Fox Creek to play. It was only a few minutes' stroll under the vast canopy of trees, and the way was pleasant. Magnolias, ponderosa pine, and sprawling live oaks shaded the azalea shrubs, whose brown, wilted blossoms crunched under her feet as she skipped across the lawn.

On this day in early June, the creek was low, but even so, it measured forty feet at its widest and six to seven feet deep. The sides of the creek sloped gently upward, covered with buff-colored loess and crowned with a ridge of trees and brambles. Once, when Monette came to the creek, it was still muddy after a recent rainfall, and Mammy Hester scolded her, saying, "Gators eat chilluns what have muddy shoes."

Now, she surveyed the water and surrounding vegetation for alligators before taking off her slippers, pulling up her pantalettes, and sinking her feet into the loess at the water's edge. It had the texture and softness of sand, and its coolness felt refreshing, for the day was hot. After wading a while, water tickling her lower legs, she arranged some leaves on the bank and sat on top. Scooping the loess with her hands, she patted it into shapes, humming, wondering what Kate was doing now. Whether she was learning her letters, listening to a lecture about decorum (sitting straight and paying attention), or whether she was pretending to listen and instead inventing a story to tell Monette later. Monette hoped the latter, for Kate's stories were a treasure trove of heroes and villains, princesses and faraway kingdoms.

So engrossed was Monette in her play that she did not realize anyone was behind her until he spoke.

"What's that you's building?"

Monette looked behind her in surprise. It was Cyrus, with Footy beside him. Both of them held fishing poles.

"What's that you's building?" Cyrus asked again.

Monette looked to where Cyrus pointed. Beside her was a mound of damp loess, crudely formed into a building. Crude as it was, she recognized the steeply pitched roof, the dormer where her bedroom window looked out across the vast *allée,* the *galérie* where Papa Léon rocked her to sleep in his arms. Monette hesitated before reaching out and pressing the building flat. *"Rien,"* she said. "It was nothing." She washed her hands in the creek and stood, looking at the two boys.

They were an odd pair. Cyrus—thickly built, almost man-like—towered over Footy, who was a couple of years younger and skinny as a bedpost. Both Cyrus and Footy were clad in coarse linen shirts that hung to mid-thigh. Neither of them wore pants, and Monette knew from unintentional exposure that, like the other black children on the plantation, they were naked beneath their single garment. Mosquito bites, scabs, and scars dotted their bare legs and feet. Atop their heads perched freshly woven hats made from palmetto fronds.

"Can you make me a hat like yours, *mon ami?*" she asked.

Cyrus grinned, his brown eyes flashing. "Sure enough, little Sister." He set down his fishing stick and began digging in a dirt-filled gourd. "I can make you a dozen hats while I waits for the fish to bite."

Footy said, "That's 'cause he can't catch no fish. He gots all the time in the world to make you hats."

Monette giggled.

"Don't you listen to him none, little Sister," Cyrus said, crouching as he pulled a wiggling worm from the gourd. "Yesterday I done cotched me two fish. One for me and one for Footy."

"I done told you and told you," said Footy, with a tone of exasperation. "She ain't your sister."

"Is so."

"Breck says she ain't. Besides, any fool with eyes and ears can tell she ain't your sister nohow. Ain't that right, Monette? Tell him it ain't so. Tell him in that fine Frenchy language of yours and make him answer. If he really your brother, then he can talk Frenchy too."

"Don't matter none what you say," said Cyrus. He peered up at Footy while shielding his eyes from the sun. "Don't matter none, 'cause Monette and I, we's together here on this creek, 'stead of on opposite sides of the world." Cyrus turned back to the task at hand and threaded the worm on his hook. "That's all that matters," he concluded.

Footy shook his head. "Is you stupid or something? I's standing right here by this creek with Monette too, and that sure don't make her my sister."

"By the time you's done yakking," said Cyrus, casting his line into the water, "I's gonna have me a dozen hats and a heap of fish besides. Here, Monette, hold this here stick while I goes and fetches you some weaving stuff. If a fish bites, yank him out of the water real quick-like." Handing the stick to Monette, he trotted off into the brush and disappeared.

Footy stared after him, saying, "That's the fastest I ever seen him move. You must of cast a spell on him or something. He ain't naturally so affected in the head."

Monette sat down again, content to hold the fishing stick, wishing she could catch a fish for Cyrus. She knew that would make him happy. "We're just friends," she said to Footy. "Good friends."

"Yup, I knows how that goes. Me and Breck, we's good friends too. We's like this." He crossed his fingers to show her how close they were.

Cyrus was gone a long time. When he returned, Footy remarked that he must have gathered enough palmetto fronds to build a house. But Cyrus ignored Footy and dropped his bundle of fronds, revealing a bouquet of wildflowers clutched in his hand. "These flowers is for you," he said to Monette.

She exchanged the fishing stick for the bouquet. *"Oh, mon frère, elles sont très belles! Merci bien!"*

Cyrus didn't understand what she said, but from the look on her face and the fact that she sniffed each flower, he knew she was pleased. Suddenly self-conscious, he lowered his eyes and scuffed the ground with his big toe, giddy with happiness. He enjoyed doing things for her. He loved being with her, giving her gifts, and seeing her light up with pleasure.

On the day of the auction, he thought he'd never see Monette again. With so many people crowded into the rotunda, all bidding and shouting rapidly, like whenever Missus would rattle off a list of chores, Cyrus had despaired, knowing it was impossible that he and Monette would be purchased by the same person.

But then came the miracle: the boy from the doorway. Mars Breck, they called him. Cyrus had recognized him, danced for him, and, amazingly, everything had turned out just as Cyrus had promised Monette it would. It seemed silly now that he'd ever been worried, that his heart had nearly torn in two with grief. They were together just like before, and they were safe.

Cyrus propped his fishing stick between his knees and began to weave a hat. I's gonna make it beautiful, he thought, just like she is. While Footy fished and chatted and Monette hummed, Cyrus carefully wove the fronds over and under, back and forth, occasionally setting it on Monette's head to see if the fit was right. His right wrist and hand were a little stiff, but Miss Sarah said the break had healed well, and the stiffness would soon go away.

He well remembered the reaction of Mars William when he discovered Cyrus had a broken arm. Standing beside his son, the man had frowned and, like everyone else, asked Cyrus what had happened. Upon Cyrus' slow, stuttered reply, the man's eyes narrowed. He turned to Breck and said, "No way you could've known, Son. Better luck next time."

Cyrus had swallowed his fear, afraid they were going to sell him back to Finney. He tugged on the tall man's sleeve. "I-I's g-g-gonna be g-g-good," he said, grinning his widest grin. "I-I's g-g-g-gonna d-d-do every-th-thing you s-s-says." Without replying, the man shrugged him off and walked away, leaving Cyrus with his new master, Breck. Cyrus remembered the shame he felt, wishing for the thousandth time he could speak properly in front of white folks.

But none of that mattered now, because they hadn't sold him back. They'd put both him and Monette on another steamship, much bigger and fancier than the *Glory Belle,* and only a short while later, they'd arrived here at the plantation. It didn't matter that Monette got to live in the big house while he shared a cabin with four other men and boys in the cypress quarter. At least he and Monette were together during the days. At least they were safe.

Just then, the fishing stick between Cyrus' knees jerked. Cyrus threw the half-completed hat aside and grabbed the stick. "I gots a bite!" With a quick tug, he yanked the fish from the water. A flash of silver flew over his head in a rainbow of droplets and landed behind him on the hat. Together with Footy and Monette, he stared at the flopping fish. "It am a beauty," he breathed.

"*Oui. Très jolie.*"

"That fish ain't so big," said Footy, returning to his fishing spot.

"That fish is bigger than any fish you got," said Cyrus.

"That's 'cause I's waiting for the big one. It just ain't come along yet."

Cyrus removed the hook from the fish's mouth and set the fish aside. "Then you's gonna be waiting a long time, 'cause I just cotched the biggest fish. He sure do like my worm best."

"Ain't got nothing to do with whether he like your worm or my worm or some such foolishness." Footy scowled. "Worms is worms. My daddy say it all in the technique. And I gots technique." He waggled his fishing stick up and down in the water a few times, then sat back.

Cyrus dug in his gourd of dirt again and baited his hook. "Seems to me," he said quietly, "like my fish ain't heard of no technique. He just hungry."

"You just keep on mumbling," said Footy, checking his line. "I gots to be ready to yank me up a whale."

After casting his line and securing the stick between his knees, Cyrus inspected the hat. "It ain't hurt none," he reassured Monette. "Just a little wet and fishy, is all." He scooted closer to her and began weaving the hat once again. It pleased him that she watched him work. "It gonna look real purty. 'Specially on you."

By the time he finished the hat, the sun was straight overhead, and Cyrus' stomach growled. He set aside his fishing stick and placed the hat on Monette's head. "There," he said proudly.

"*Merci, mon frère.*" Smiling, she stood, turned around once, and then looked at him from beneath the brim. "How do I look? Kate says green is a good color for me. How does she say? . . . 'Brings out my eyes.'"

But before Cyrus could tell her how pretty she was, that green was dandy and so were her eyes, there were shouts from the brush, and then both Kate and Breck appeared on the bank, followed by Breck's dog, Rascal.

"Oh, there you are," said Kate to Monette, approaching. "I've been looking for you. I brought a surprise. C'mon, let's go to—" and she leaned over and whispered in Monette's ear.

Monette's face brightened, and she clapped her hands. "*Oui!*"

Together, the two girls disappeared up and over the bank, into the brush and under the trees.

"*Au revoir, Cyrus! Au revoir, Footy! Merci!*" called Monette as she left, waving her bouquet of flowers in the air.

Cyrus watched them go, a heaviness in his chest. He swiped his forehead with his arm, suddenly hot.

"Who wants to go rafting?" asked Breck.

But Cyrus never answered, for no sooner had Breck asked his question than Cyrus' fishing stick jerked and, quick as a snake, flew through the air and disappeared under the water. Cyrus had forgotten about it. "My stick! My hook!"

As he scrambled after it, he tripped over his feet and tumbled face-first into the water, while both Footy and Breck collapsed into gales of laughter.

Save for the stray branches that protruded like arms akimbo, the clearing
was about seventy feet across. In the center grew the most magnificent
magnolia, which, had the family at Fox Creek or the community at large
been aware of the tree, would have been declared the finest around,
a stellar example of God's handiwork. Whispering, creeping, the girls
settled beneath the spreading branches. It was here, sheltered within its
bosom, that the girls felt protected against the sun and the world. That,
should there come a deluge of proportions akin to Noah's flood, the
girls would remain untouched. That, should there come wildfire, locusts,
disease—cataclysms of any and all description—again, they would remain
as unscathed as the angels in heaven. After all, it was a secret place, magical
almost, accessible only through a tunnel of dense shrubbery and curtains
of Spanish moss, a hideaway that selectively opened its bowers, drawing
young girls into its pink-blossomed embrace, respiring air that, despite the
oppressive heat, smelled as sweet and enchanting as a fairy tale.

"Now for the surprise," said Kate, opening up her basket. "I asked Mama
first, and then Aunt Delia, and they both said yes." From her basket, she
withdrew two napkins, two thick slices of bread and butter, a slab of jujube
paste, lemon tarts, and a bottle of tamarind juice.

Monette clapped her hands. "Hooray! A picnic! It is the same word in
French, *oui?* We say, *pique-nique.* That, at least, should be very easy for you
to remember."

For a while, they ate in companionable silence. Kate was famished.
Spending all morning forming her letters until her hand cramped, and
then having to sit straight and tall while Mr. Gilbert taught French, was
more than she could tolerate. She longed to learn French, to speak it like
Monette, but learning was *such* a tiresome process. Kate licked her fingers
clean of butter and jujube, asking, "What's that on your head?"

Monette touched her hat. "Do you like it?"

Kate bit into a tart and studied the hat. It was lizard-green and crudely
made. The ends of the fronds were not tied off and instead stuck out
in all directions. Worst of all, it didn't match Monette's pink and yellow
plaid dress, one of Kate's favorite hand-me-downs. "No," she said with her
mouth full, "it's ugly."

"Cyrus made it for me," said Monette. "I watched him. It took him all morning."

"Where's your bonnet? The pretty one with velvet ribbons?"

"I lost it." Monette removed her hat. "Do you really think it's ugly?"

Kate shrugged. "Mama would never let me wear something like that. It's not ladylike enough."

"Oh." Monette set her hat on the ground.

"Where did you lose your bonnet?"

"Down by the creek, last week. I left it by mistake, and the next day it was gone."

"Probably floated away," said Kate.

"*Oui*, probably."

Kate finished her tart and poured herself more tamarind juice. "More juice?"

"*Oui, s'il vous plaît.*"

"Are you going to eat the rest of your tart?" Kate asked, smothering her disappointment when Monette replied, *"Oui, que c'est délicieux."*

Monette was such a slow eater, taking dainty bites, wiping the sides of her mouth with her napkin. Kate wished she could take dainty bites like Monette, but whenever Kate was hungry, all thoughts of daintiness vanished from her head. Mama was always saying, Slow down, Katherine dear. Don't gulp. Don't slurp. Sit up straight. Don't talk with your mouth full. Use your napkin. Say please. Say thank you. Say excuse me.

Kate sighed and lay back on the grass. Clouds of magnolia blossoms floated above her, and the air chorused with cicadas, the chirrup of birds, and the croak of frogs. Bees droned from one blossom to the next. Butterflies danced—flashes of color, flitting here, then there, seemingly without purpose—unlike the hummingbirds, which hovered industriously, wings a-blur, beaks thrust into blossoms like tiny swords. They're happy to be alive, thought Kate. With that thought, she realized that she, too, was happy to be alive. Making a sudden decision, Kate sat up and removed her own bonnet, placing it on Monette's head. "Here. You can have my bonnet. I have three others." She tied the ribbon, then sat back with a smile of accomplishment and generosity.

"Now I shall give you something in return. A *lagniappe*. When I used to go to the city, the shopkeepers would give me *lagniappe*. It is, how do you say—a token of appreciation. My favorite was at Ma'amzelle Rosalie's. She used to give me praline candies. I love pralines—" Monette chatted as she sorted through her bouquet, separating out some flowers. Then she began weaving them together: trumpet-shaped golden flowers as big as her fist, clusters of tiny lavender blooms, crimson blossoms the size of teacups.

"What are you doing?" asked Kate.

"Why, I am making you a crown."

Kate observed, fascinated by the deft way Monette's fingers formed the chain. The air smelled of nectar, of lemons, of lavender—a *potpourri* of fragrance so thick that when Kate breathed through her mouth, she could taste the heady sweetness. "Where did you learn to do that?"

Monette shrugged. "I can't remember."

"Who taught you?"

"No one taught me. At least, not that I remember."

"Will you teach me?"

Pleased with Kate's interest and delighted with her new bonnet, Monette looked at Kate—at her green eyes, her auburn hair dappled with sunshine—and smiled. "Certainly, *mon amie. Bien sûr.* But first, we must pick some flowers for you." Together, they gathered an abundant bouquet from the glade, then sat cross-legged, their pantaletted knees touching, heads bent together like members of a ladies' sewing club. As they wove, Monette listened while Kate told her a story about a poor little orphan girl who had only rags to wear, just one shoe, and was very hungry besides.

"She wandered from place to place, begging, but no one would help her. 'No!' the mean people cried, swatting her with a switch. 'You are too dirty, and you stink! Go away! We don't want your kind around here!'"

"I would cry if someone did that to me," said Monette. "That is very mean."

"She did cry. Great bucketfuls."

"*Pauvrette.* Poor little orphan girl."

"Yes, poor, poor little orphan girl." Kate shook her head sadly. "When people threw their scraps to the dogs, she had to fight the dogs for the scraps so she could eat: bones with rotting meat, bread crusts with green mold—"

"Fruit with bugs in it," added Monette, brushing away a bee that had come to investigate the blossomed crown.

"Yes, fruit with bugs in it. And worms. Anyway, one day she was walking along when she came across a—a girl crying. This girl was dressed very nicely, in jewels and silks. In fact, this girl was a princess. But she was a very sad princess."

"Why was she sad? Was she wearing an ugly hat?"

"Well, she was sad because, well—" One of the blossoms tore apart in Kate's hands. She tossed it away and grabbed another. "She was sad because she had no one to play with; that's why, and so she was very lonely."

"I would be very sad, too, I think."

"Well, of course, the orphan girl said *she* would be her friend, and so, from that day on, they became the best of friends. Everything they did, they did together. Like us."

"And they lived happily ever after?"

"Not yet," said Kate, flashing Monette a green-eyed glance before turning to a cluster of honeysuckle. "Because, you see, the orphan girl had to live secretly in the castle cellar because the princess knew that no one would allow her to play with a stinky little orphan. Such a thing was forbidden."

Monette shuddered, imagining what it must have been like to live in the cellar: dark, cold, and filthy, with rats scurrying about, rubbing their fur and tails against her one bare foot. "How horrible!"

"Yes, horrible it was. But the years went by, and one day the princess became the queen and let the orphan out of the cellar. When you're the queen, mind you, you can do things like that. She dressed the little orphan in silken gowns and jewels and made her a princess."

"The orphan became a princess?" Monette said with a gasp, thinking how wonderful it all was.

"Yes, and they were both very beautiful, too. But first, the orphan had to take a bath, of course, and comb the rats' nests out of her hair."

"This is a good story, *mon amie*."

"They were both so beautiful, the most beautiful in all the land. They lived happily ever after, playing together forever and ever and ever. The end."

Monette clapped. *"Bon travail!"*

"You liked my story?"

In answer, Monette leaned forward and placed her finished crown on Kate's head, her fingers sticky with flower juice. "It is my favorite, *princesse.*"

Kate reached up, touching the blossoms as if the silky petals were made of gold, rubies, diamonds, and emeralds. "I am a princess."

Monette touched her own new bonnet, imagining it as a crown, thinking it far better than her other hat. Besides being soft and comfortable, it didn't tickle her head or crackle in her ears or stink like a fish.

Kate held up her finished flower chain. "How does it look?"

"*Magnifique*," said Monette, although the chain looked somewhat battered, with stems and stray leaves poking out every which way.

"It's a necklace for you, *princesse*." Kate smiled and draped it over Monette's head. Then, just as the blossoms tickled Monette's cheeks, Kate gasped, "Oh dear!" and at the same time jumped up and began tossing things into the basket as if a whirlwind were on its way.

"What is the matter?"

"Mama said to not be gone too long. Monsieur Déclouet comes this afternoon to teach music and dance. C'mon. We have to hurry!"

"*Oui!*" Monette stood and helped Kate gather their things. The last time Monsieur Déclouet came, Monette had danced the afternoon away. Now she was as excited as Kate. What a wonderful day this was turning out to be! "*Tout de suite!*" she cried, clapping. "We shall dance like little princesses!"

They left the clearing. But before Monette ducked down to crawl through the tunnel of bushes, she glanced back. There, under the tree, lay the hat of palmetto fronds. I have forgotten it, she thought. But then she remembered that they were in a hurry. There was no time. Besides, she thought, I have a new bonnet, a *couronne* for a *princesse*. With this happy thought, she parted the curtain of Spanish moss and crawled through the tunnel after Kate.

## Chapter 2

"Now curtsy! Extend the right foot, draw up the left! *Non! Non!* Not like cows! Like fairies! Like little princes and princesses! Like this!" Standing in the center of the parlor, Monsieur Déclouet lifted the corners of his long-tailed coat with thumbs and forefingers and curtsied. The coat came to his knees and gathered tightly about the waist like a dress.

A homely man, thought Mehitable, as she watched the lessons through a sliver in her bedroom doorway. His methods are deplorable. And I swear he binds himself with corsets.

"You see? Now try yourselves! Step with the right foot, draw up the left! Better! Improvement. I see improvement! Now Monsieur Breck, *s'il vous plaît*, take your partner's hand and twirl her!"

Kate's dress swirled in a perfect circle, and both she and the little mulatto laughed. Monette clapped her hands, a habit which Mehitable thought to be particularly annoying. A habit which had already awakened her from countless naps. Naps which, at her age and in her condition, were tantamount to medicine.

Prancing to the piano, Déclouet tossed the skirts of his coat behind him, seated himself, and pounded the keyboard. "Dance!" he cried. "Twirl!" he thundered.

Ridiculous.

The man's face was long and slender, and his mouth, filled with crooked teeth, opened to cavernous effect when he sang, which he now did. The song filled the room, punctuated occasionally with "Change partners!" "Twirl!" "Faster!" Finally, with one massive, merciful chord, the song ended. Déclouet clapped and stood. "Well done! Bravo! And now, lessons in deportment! Come! Everybody sit! *Non! Non!* Not like kangaroos sit. Bouncing is torture for the spine, Mademoiselle Katherine. You must sit like little kings and queens. Elegance! We must have *élégance! Oui,* little Monette. *Très bien!"*

Mehitable did not wait to see more. She closed the door and smoothed her hair in her mirror. At no time in her life had her hair ever been considered luxurious, and now it was downright thin, her scalp visible through iron-gray hair. No matter. Old ladies were allowed to have thin hair. She affixed her sun bonnet, fetched her cane, and left her bedroom through the office. The office was shuttered, vacant. At this time of day, her son, William, was rarely in his office. Anyway, it did not matter, for it was not William whom she determined to see. It was her daughter-in-law, Sarah. Sarah was the wife, the mistress. Sarah was responsible for the machinations of the Jensey household. It was Sarah's responsibility, her *duty* as mistress, to set things to right. Mehitable passed through the office, stepped through the rear loggia, and into the bright afternoon sunshine.

That she should have to be outside at this time of day irritated Mehitable. By all rights, she should be enjoying her afternoon nap. After all, it was a necessity. The heat of the afternoons frequently overwhelmed her, and she suffered from the most excruciating headaches. Lying down with a cool washrag on her forehead prevented the headaches, and the afternoons, as a consequence, became endurable. Until Monsieur Déclouet came, that is. Plus, that stupid clapping mulatto. Mehitable shook her head and clucked her tongue in vexation as she marched toward the gardens. Already, she could feel a headache gathering behind her eyes.

By the time she found Sarah in the potting shed, Mehitable was damp with perspiration, and her temples throbbed. She stood in the doorway and leaned on her cane, catching her breath, mopping her face with her handkerchief, before Sarah turned and saw her.

"Mother!" Sarah exclaimed, pulling off her gloves and wiping her hands on a rag. "What on earth are you doing outside? You know your headaches!"

Still struggling for breath, Mehitable could say nothing. Blasted heat!

"Here, Mother, sit."

Grateful for Sarah's assistance, Mehitable allowed herself to be led into the potting shed, to a wooden chair in the corner. The chair was too small, really—made for someone more Sarah's size, but Mehitable was too exhausted to argue. It squawked as Mehitable settled herself. She fanned her face and loosened the ties of her bonnet. Flies droned around her head—a buzz of wings, heat, humidity, and headache.

Sarah said to the houseboy, Nat, "Run and fetch Miss Mehitable a cool glass of water from the well. And have Aunt Delia wrap a chunk of ice in a cloth. Tell her I said so. Hurry now."

"Yes, Miss Sarah."

It seemed forever before Nat finally returned with ice and a glass of water. Not for the first time, Mehitable was grateful for Jensey water. It was the coolest, most refreshing water in the parish. Perhaps in all of Louisiana, for that matter. Mehitable took the glass and guzzled the contents, unable to suppress the usual belch that followed.

"Here, Mother," said Sarah, taking the glass from her. She removed Mehitable's bonnet and pressed the linen-wrapped ice to her forehead. "Rest for a bit."

The ice felt good. Drops of water slid down her face and trickled under the folds of her chin. "Land sakes," Mehitable managed to say. Little by little, her headache receded. Such a relief, and yet such a bother, she thought. This was entirely unnecessary. I should not even be out here on such a day, suffering as I am. "All because of that man."

"What man?"

Mehitable sighed, impatient. For as much as she liked her daughter-in-law, loved her even, at times she found her obtuse. Especially about certain matters. A selective obtuseness that bordered on stubbornness. How much of it was pure stupidity and how much of it was calculated stubbornness, Mehitable didn't know. Well, Mehitable thought, I may not be as stupid, but I am equally as stubborn. "That fool of a dancing man, of course. Who else would I be talking about?"

"His name is Monsieur Hypolyte Déclouet, Mother, and you know he is no fool. He's an excellent instructor of both dancing and singing. He comes highly recommended. He just has peculiar ways, is all."

The ice had melted. It never lasted long in such weather. "Oh, mercy," moaned Mehitable. "Be a good girl, dear Sarah, and massage my temples." She closed her eyes while her daughter-in-law moved behind her chair. Sarah's touch was cool in the hot, moist air. "More vigorous, dear, harder. Nat, boy, come here and fan the flies from me." Soon she felt a breeze on her face. That, combined with Sarah's touch, almost made the heat bearable. It was terrible to be so old and infirm. "As I was saying, highly recommended or not, his methods are uncommon. It will be a wonder if the children don't turn into dancing kangaroos or flying fairies."

"But your own daughter thinks highly of Monsieur Déclouet. After all, her Juliana's accomplished so much under his tutelage in just a few months."

"Any idiot with ears can hear that Juliana has natural talent. All he did was tell her to open her mouth and let it out. Anyone could have done that. Oh, my head! Harder, dear!"

"Mother, why don't you let me take you back to your bedroom where you can rest?"

Mehitable swatted Sarah's hands away, turned, and glared at her. Sometimes her daughter-in-law amazed her. It *was* stupidity. Definitely stupidity. "Just how do you suggest I do that with all that blasted racket? That's what I'm trying to tell you." In a fit of impatience, she snatched her bonnet from her lap, put it on, stood to her feet, and faced the younger woman. "I've not the energy to say this more than once. You must get rid of that terrible man, that Monsieur what's-his-name."

"Mother, please. You're unwell."

"Of course, I'm unwell. Everyone knows I'm unwell. I've been ill for years, and I'm not getting any better. Surely someday I shall sicken and die."

"At least sit back down."

Mehitable was, in fact, feeling rather unsteady, so she did what Sarah asked and sat in the chair, closing her eyes. The heat, land sakes, the heat! And where on earth is my breeze? Opening her eyes, she saw that the boy had stopped his fanning, and his chin drooped to his chest. She had no patience for such laziness. Leaning forward, she poked a rigid finger into his chest and barked, "Wake up!" satisfied when his eyes snapped open, his head jerked up, and the fanning resumed.

Sarah knelt beside her and grasped her hands. "Perhaps we should talk about this later when you're feeling better."

"Nonsense," said Mehitable. Then her tone softened, for Sarah's expression was one of love and concern. Mehitable patted her hand. She really was a good woman, stupid or not. "Sarah dear, the house is simply too small for all this educating. What with Mr. Gilbert roaming around upstairs spouting mathematics and what not, and that fool dancing away downstairs, it's simply more than a woman my age can tolerate."

"But the children must have their education. Besides, Monsieur Déclouet only comes twice a week. Surely you can make allowances for just two afternoons a week."

"What's-his-name's methods are deplorable, and he's an idiot besides."

"I'm terribly sorry, Mother, but I'm pleased with the children's progress under Monsieur Déclouet."

"Pleased! That ruckus pleases you?" Mehitable said, frowning. It was then that she recognized the all-too-familiar look on her daughter-in-law's face. The steady gaze, no longer so loving and concerned. The firm set to the jaw. Yes, it *was* stubbornness. Definitely stubbornness. Suddenly, Mehitable didn't feel well. No, not well at all. "You see, my dear, I'm afraid with all the ruckus I might have an attack and die." Saying this, Mehitable pressed her handkerchief to her forehead and bit her lip. There, her headache was returning.

Standing, Sarah sighed and resumed her work at the potting table, pulling on her India rubber gloves. Her mother-in-law indeed suffered from headaches, and her afternoon naps certainly appeared to revive her. Such resting in the afternoon during the hottest part of the day was quite common. Sarah herself often rested, unable to keep going in such heat and dampness. But the woman's constant references to her ailments, to her supposed impending death, wearied Sarah. She had work to do. Before Mehitable came to the shed, Sarah had been potting her peach cuttings, which had sat in water for two weeks. It was time to plant them. The day was fast waning, and she had yet to start her blackberry preserves, to mix the medicines for the next morning's litany of complaints, to fetch the provisions from the storehouse for the cook, or to supervise the cutting of a new shipment of calico—the list of things to accomplish was endless. It always was. No sooner did Sarah complete a task than it needed doing again—a day, a week, or a month later.

"Already I've heard improvements in Katherine's singing," she said, hoping she did not sound as tired as she felt, wishing this conversation were ended. "She has much promise, even more so than Juliana. She has perfect pitch and a beautiful tone. A joy to listen to."

"Again, natural talent, I say."

For a while, they said nothing. Sarah knew that her own presence was difficult for Mehitable. After all, when Sarah had assumed the mantle of mistress ten years ago, Mehitable had already been mistress of Fox Creek for twenty-five years. The once-popular daughter of a prominent judge from Baton Rouge, Mehitable had, in her quarter century as mistress, gained in both strength of will and girth, becoming a large, proud woman who guarded her master keys with the fierceness of a jailor.

Now those keys hung on a *chatelaine* at Sarah's waist, a testament to her station as mistress of Fox Creek. For Mehitable to relinquish such a station was difficult; such responsibility and command did not go away lightly. Every day, it seemed, there was something about which they butted heads. (At one time, Sarah had fostered the hope that Mehitable would move to South Carolina as she'd been threatening, to live with her youngest daughter, Phereba, who had moved there after her wedding three years ago. But, despite Mehitable's threats and intimations, the much-promised migration was not forthcoming.)

Now Sarah hoped Mehitable would either fall asleep or return to her room. Her presence was just too tiring. Today, especially, Sarah didn't feel well; nausea and fatigue circled around her like the flies. It was only a matter of time before her pregnancy became noticeable. As yet, she had told no one. Each day her corsets pinched her all the more, and at times it seemed she could scarcely breathe.

"At least get rid of that stupid mulatto girl."

Sarah frowned. A new conversation. "Monette?"

"She's a bad influence on Kate. It's a known fact that too much intimacy with a darky can corrupt a white child. After all, the negro is so recently from the jungle."

"I really don't want to talk about this right now, Mother." Sarah planted one of the cuttings in the soil and patted down the dirt. The cuttings had sprouted well in the water.

"If you were to remove our civilizing influence, the negro race would revert to their natural, savage state."

"Mother—"

"The girls share the same bed; they wear each other's clothes and hair ribbons, and I've seen them drink from the same cup. Today, when Kate returned from her picnic, that little darky was wearing Kate's bonnet. Now

Kate is covered with freckles. Her skin is ruined. I'm telling you, it's not good. It's that darky's influence."

"I'll remind Katherine to wear her bonnet."

"Really, Sarah, you must be more firm. You can't allow William's daughter to turn into a savage. There are enough of them as it is. Now, as I was saying, you simply must get rid of that mulatto."

"Monette's a bright, tractable negress. Someday she will make a fine little maid. Besides, I think Monette's been good for Katherine." A sudden wave of nausea coursed through Sarah, and, just as quickly, passed. Already she had vomited today, alone, behind the rose bushes.

"*Good?* For heaven's sake. You and I both know Kate's a corruptible child. Easily influenced. To allow that little mulatto such unsupervised freedom with her is inviting trouble, you mark my words. No telling where she's come from. Nothing but trouble will come of this."

Perhaps, thought Sarah, I should finish my plantings tomorrow. It's time to start the preserves, and Mehitable hates the kitchen. Sarah pulled off her gloves. "Nat, water the ones I've potted, set them outside, and then I want you to sweep out the shed and close it up. I'll be in the kitchen putting away preserves. Come see me when you're finished."

"Yes, Miss Sarah."

"What does my William think about all this?" said Mehitable, standing to her feet with a grunt.

"About what?"

"That mulatto."

Sarah brushed the hair from her forehead, knowing she left a dirty smudge. "William," she said wearily, looking her mother-in-law in the eye, "has given me complete control in the matter."

Mehitable narrowed her eyes and snapped, "Fiddle-faddle. A husband and wife are one person, and that person is the husband."

"Perhaps. But that is between me and my husband. Now come with me, Mother. I'm going back to the house." Sarah handed Mehitable her cane and, without waiting for an answer, put her hand under Mehitable's arm and steered the woman toward the doorway.

# Chapter 3

A SCREAM AWAKENED HER. Sarah sat bolt upright in bed, knowing. It is Tamar. Her time has come.

Without waking William, she dressed quickly. Even so, with a minimum of petticoats and undergarments, it was a while before she stepped outside onto the back porch. They were waiting for her with lanterns, as she'd known they would be.

"Tamar's time done come, Miss Sarah, please hurry."

Sarah recognized Tabb, Tamar's husband. Had it already been nine months since Tamar and Tabb were married? Somehow, the time had slipped by.

The hospital had been completed only two weeks prior, in early June, and already Sarah marveled that she could ever have gotten along without it. Before, the very ill or women in labor made do in their own cabins, creating unnecessary fuss and inconvenience for all (especially for Sarah, as forays into the quarters in the dead of night exhausted her).

Now there was a place for the sick close by, in the yard that spread in a square behind the big house kitchen, the kitchen being a separate building located a safe distance from the back of the big house itself. The yard's split-rail fence enclosed a variety of other buildings: laundry house, dairy and well house, storehouse, loom house, nursery for the little ones, cabins for the domestics—fourteen buildings in all, counting the new hospital that still had that sweet, raw-lumber smell.

One story high, the hospital was three rooms long. One room was for the men, one for the women, and one set aside for women lying-in. It was into that last room that Sarah now stepped. She did not have to tell the men to stay outside. They knew better than to enter and had already settled themselves on the front gallery for what might be a long night's vigil, especially for a first confinement.

The room stank of steam and sweat. It was a plain room, unadorned, with planked walls and flooring, and three beds side-by-side. Against the far wall stood a table and a chair. Light emanated from a solitary candle atop the table and from a low fire in the fireplace. An iron pot filled with bubbling water and linens hung over the fire. Sarah was pleased. Her hospital attendant, Aunt Page, had obviously done her job well. The room was tidy, ready for the first birth within its walls.

On the far bed next to the table, Tamar lay under the thin gauze of the mosquito net. Aunt Page hovered beside her, reaching under the gauze and wiping Tamar's forehead with a wet rag. The room was stiflingly hot.

Yesterday, Sarah had suspected that Tamar was in labor. The baby had turned a few weeks prior, and Tamar's lower back had hurt. "It won't be long," Sarah had told her. "Tonight, perhaps. Or tomorrow." She'd given Tamar a dose of castor oil, then given precise instructions to Aunt Page, ordering her to spread a fresh linen. After observing Tamar for a while, Sarah had returned to the big house for supper.

Now, seized by a contraction, Tamar screamed again.

She was a young woman, just sixteen, born at Fox Creek before Sarah had married William. Sarah gently hushed her and then lifted the bed sheet and examined her. Half an hour, an hour at most. Again, Sarah was pleased. Tamar was healthy. Strong. One of the fastest cotton pickers they had.

"Everything's fine," Sarah assured her, lowering the bed sheet.

"Oh, Miss Sarah," whispered Tamar, her eyes wide with fear. "I's so scared. And it hurts so bad. I never thought anything could hurt so bad."

"There's nothing to worry about, Tamar. It won't be long. Just try to relax and don't push yet."

Sarah held the woman's hand, murmuring soft words each time a contraction hit. Tamar's eyes rolled up in her head, and she shrieked. Sweat glistened on her face, and she began to pant. This will be me, Sarah realized. Come December. With that thought, nausea rolled through her, mingled with a growing, stabbing fear. She closed her eyes and swallowed hard. Not here. Not now.

The births of both Breck and Kate had been difficult. Over thirty hours' labor for each of them, hours mingled with screams, with hushed whispers, ending with a final, releasing rush of blood and flesh. Both had been big babies.

"The biggest babies I've ever seen," her brother John had said. He was seven and a half years her senior and a respected doctor.

Over time, she'd forgotten her pain. Until now. Now, bile rising in her throat, Sarah thought, *I must endure it again. While my body rips asunder.*

She leaned over a ceramic basin and vomited, thinking, *I must tell William. Tonight.*

Finished, she wiped her mouth, sensing the shock from both Aunt Page and Tamar, imagining their unuttered questions, knowing that rumors would fly throughout the quarters come tomorrow. "Something I ate," was all she said.

An hour later, the child was born—a plump, healthy boy. While Aunt Page changed the linens, Sarah rubbed the squalling newborn with lard and, using a soft flannel, washed him in blood-warm water and soap. "He's beautiful," she said, smiling as she handed the child to Tamar, once the umbilical cord was dressed and the baby swaddled in a soft cloth. "What's his name?"

Tamar cradled the infant. "His name's Basil. That's his granddaddy's name. That's what me and Tabb decides." Then she glanced up. "That's all right with you, ain't it, Miss Sarah?"

"It's a nice name."

With the birth over, and Sarah satisfied that Tamar's womb had contracted sufficiently, her own weariness returned. After giving further instructions to Aunt Page and showing Tamar how to breastfeed, Sarah left the hospital. She answered the father's questions briefly before returning to the big house and climbing the steps to her own room, still shuttered in darkness. In half an hour, the plantation bell would ring. In an hour, it would be dawn.

William awoke when his wife entered, hearing the rustling of her skirts and petticoats, her soft, weary sigh, and the creak of the floorboards. When she finally climbed under the mosquito net and into bed, he reached for her, pulling her close. "Sarah," he whispered, covering her lips with his own, pressing himself against her. Such softness.

But to his surprise, she pushed him away. "Not now, William. I'm too tired."

He frowned and lay back on his pillow. Closing his eyes, he thought, this is a hell of a way to start the day. Then, just as he began to drift back into sleep, he felt her against him. Once again, he stirred.

She laid her head in the crook of his arm. "I have something to tell you."

He said nothing as she ran her fingers through the hair on his chest. He wrapped his arm around her and pulled her close, breathing in her scent.

"William, we are going to have another baby."

At first, he was uncomprehending, as if she'd told him they needed a new milk cow, or that her mother was coming to visit. Then the words sank in. Welcome words.

A baby.

A son.

William propped himself up on an elbow, scarcely believing, hesitating to say anything, as if to speak would break the spell of the incredible, the impossible. They'd tried for so long . . . Breck's recent carriage accident had brought to the surface an old fear, one that William had suppressed out of helplessness: should anything, God forbid, happen to Breck, he had no other heirs. Who would take over the plantation? Who would care for his mother, for Sarah, and for Kate? William placed his hand on Sarah's cheek. "A baby?" He could feel her nodding in the darkness. In a fit of joy, he embraced her—this woman of his heart, his wife. "I've waited a long time."

"I know."

"I'd about given up—"

"I know. Me, too."

"When is the baby due?"

"Christmas."

"So, you've known?"

"For two months."

"Why didn't you tell me?"

"I didn't want you to worry."

"My God, Sarah, do you know how much I love you?"

"Yes—yes, I do."

"Who else knows about the baby?"

"No one."

"My God, Sarah." And while the room gradually changed from darkness to dawn (forget the damn bell, forget the damn chores, the damnable list of to-dos) William was content to simply hold his wife, their hearts beating in a joyful duet, her breath warm against his skin, lengthening as she slipped back into sleep.

Word spread quickly that Miss Sarah had vomited on the night Basil was born. So, when William announced that they would soon have a new master, everyone acted surprised, although everyone already knew. They accepted the jugs of whiskey as a token of good fortune and drank to the unborn master.

There were one hundred and fifty-three hands at Fox Creek, including baby Basil. Come Sunday mornings, William called all hands to the yard and distributed their weekly rations. Clean, combed, and wearing their Sunday best, they stood in three lines before him, while, beginning with the household servants, he called each family forward for inspection and distribution. Four and a half pounds of pork, plus enough corn to grind a peck of meal per adult, less for children. Molasses, tobacco, and one pound of coffee. Plus, depending upon the season, sweet potatoes, green peas, or snap beans. Children four years old and under received two quarts of milk per week, and new mothers one pint per day for two months following the birth of a child (not to mention a month of rest and a new dress, compliments of Miss Sarah). All agreed they were generous rations.

It was on one of those Sundays in June, a heavy, oppressive day of heat and insects, that William took a second look at the boy called Cyrus. The child stood before him, woolly head bowed, bare feet shifting in the steaming mud as he swatted at the occasional mosquito. Following his initial fury on the day of the auction, William was actually quite impressed. While the boy was not thirteen years old as advertised (his teeth indicating he was closer to ten or eleven), the boy, indeed, was strong. Now that his arm had healed, Cyrus was capable of tasks normally set aside for three-quarter hands. And the boy was willing. That, thought William, was perhaps the most important quality in a good negro: willingness. Speech be damned. Intelligence be damned. What did it matter how someone talked or thought, so long as they plowed the field or hoed the cotton? So long as they followed instructions, went to bed on time, and arose each morning at the sound of the bell?

Already, it seemed, the boy had grown since April. If he kept growing at this rate, someday he would be a gigantic bull of a man. William nodded, approving. Come cotton-picking season, he decided, he would move the boy to the fields.

On the same Sunday that William made his decision regarding Cyrus, he oversaw his son, Breck, as he called each family forward and inspected them before turning them over to William for the distribution of their rations. Previously, Breck had always observed the inspections; this was the first time William asked him to perform them.

"Look for dirty faces," he instructed Breck. "Look for dirty eyes, dirty hands, uncombed hair, and dirty clothes. Everyone must be clean. Cleanliness does not come naturally to them; it is only under our influence that they are clean."

Pleased with Breck's thorough manner, and agreeing with him that the negroes indeed looked clean and presentable, that nothing and no one required further attention at present, William dismissed the hands, bade them rest and relax for the remainder of the day, and then headed inside the house, his arm about his son's shoulders. "Well done," he said, smiling, feeling a warm satisfaction.

To William, Breck seemed older and wiser than his nine years and one month. Perhaps it was his height that gave such an impression, or the way he devoured his studies. More and more, William felt compelled to begin Breck's education in the ways of a planter: the seasons of the crops, the financial aspects, the management of the negroes, the delicate balance of rewards and punishments, and each Sunday's inspection and distribution of rations. So much to learn. Initially, the learning would be that much more difficult because, like his father before him, William refused to employ an overseer. He never had and never would. Again and again, he heard horror stories from his neighbors about this overseer or that one. A sudden passel of little mulattos running around. The cotton destroyed because the overseer had been blind to worms until it was too late. A mutinous gang of negroes, who, one night, hacked the overseer to death with their cane machetes—afterward the whole lot of them executed according to the law. A severe financial loss, and all because of an incompetent overseer. No, none of that for William.

Instead, William used three negro drivers, with Quincy as the head driver. These three men were respected among his negro force—intelligent, responsible for the crops and the workers, and answerable only to William. It was the way Octavian had taught him, and William saw no reason to change. Of course, it took much supervision on William's part, for everyone knew that negroes, by nature, were incapable of self-government: want of discretion, judgment, et cetera. Most every day—except when he was hunting, fishing, or at the races—found William in the fields, observing from atop his horse, discoursing with the driver about the day's expectations and yesterday's accomplishments, and speaking with the blacksmith, the tanner, the cobbler, the cooper, and the carpenter. . . . It was this that Breck would have to learn—a massive undertaking that would require knowledge, strength of character, and a backbone of iron.

# Chapter 4

As June seeped into July, besides remaining miserably hot, torrents of rain swelled Fox Creek to its banks, while the swamps crept to the edges of the fields like living, breathing creatures. William told his brother-in-law, John, he'd never seen so many alligators in his life, and shot seven of them when he discovered two of his prize hounds were missing.

On these rainy days, days when the rain fell straight down with the sound of rushing water, the field women were sent to the loom house, where they carded wool or spun cotton under the supervision of the seamstress, while the men cleaned the ginhouse, hauled rails, split wood, cleared new land, or repaired roads. Between downpours, men plowed, while women hoed the fields free of grass, a never-ending, cyclical task that had to be started again immediately after the last field was hoed.

While Breck and Kate were closeted in the schoolroom with Mr. Gilbert, an army of children—Cyrus, Footy, Nat, and others—often followed Sarah into her ornamental gardens, where she directed them at the various tasks. Waving away mosquitoes, the little army swept the brick walkways, raked and carted off leaves and debris, weeded, trimmed, and dug. Then, when the clouds overhead darkened and thunder rolled across the land, Sarah hurriedly dismissed the troops and returned indoors to rest.

Despite the heavy rains, which should have proved devastating, William was pleased with his cotton crop. His neighbors all agreed that he had the best crop in the parish. Unlike theirs—yellow and sickly—by the ninth day of July, the cotton crop at Fox Creek was head-high and bolling fast.

In a generous mood, William halted production for a day and gave the one hundred and fifty-three hands a dinner and dance. Behind the big house, next to the kitchen, seven tables groaned under the weight of so much food: turkey, beef, chicken, and pig—baked, broiled, roasted, and fried—along with rice, green beans, peas, sweet potatoes, stewed collards, stewed apples, pickles, jellied tarts, peach pies, frosted cakes, milk, juice, and, of course, whiskey.

Both Miss Sarah and William watched as the negroes ate, drank, and danced, William thinking, I must build them a dance hall. A fine dance hall. One far away from here where they can dance on Saturday nights and not disturb the household. Taking the head carpenter aside, William gave orders for its construction, pleased with Obediah's answering smile.

Then, beginning the next day, the delicate balance of the plantation toppled.

When one-fourth of the negroes didn't show for work, complaining of aching stomachs and spinning heads, it was attributed to drunkenness. But when, late that night, the first negro died, a child, William sent for John for a diagnosis: worms, fevers, measles, soupy bowels, and runny eyes—it seemed everyone had something wrong with them.

The sicknesses weren't just confined to Fox Creek. From all around the parish, there came word of this neighbor sick, or that negro dead. If that weren't enough, whispers of yellow fever blew upriver from the great Mississippi port, whispers that filled West Feliciana Parish with alarm. Immediately, all business transactions with New Orleans were delayed until, with the advent of cooler weather, the epidemic would undoubtedly pass, as it always did.

Meanwhile, no ships from New Orleans were allowed into the port town of Bayou Clare, and at Holy Trinity Episcopal Church in St. Marysville, they held a special candlelight vigil for the safety of their parish. Yellow fever—a particularly dreaded scourge because it killed with such spectacular violence. Lord, keep this plague from us, they prayed. And almost as an afterthought, Lord, protect those in New Orleans.

While the wealthy of New Orleans fled to the healthy air surrounding Lake Pontchartrain, and while those left behind tried to escape the poisonous night air by sealing themselves behind closed doors and windows, life pulsed on for those in the country. There were fields to be hoed. Gardens to be tended. Children to be born. Wood to be chopped. Soon, the cotton-picking season would begin. And in that pulse of country life, William himself became ill, not with yellow fever, but with the recurring swamp fever.

Breck enjoyed his lessons with Mr. Gilbert, a serious, bespectacled man who made Breck feel as if learning was the most important occupation a man could have.

While Kate struggled to form her letters—laborious, scrawling blotches of ink—Breck was rapidly advancing in both reading and writing, and, encouraged by Mr. Gilbert, one morning copied a chapter from Shakespeare without a mistake and with only a few misplaced splotches of ink.

Soon, Breck was immersed in maps, copying the names of countries and their capital cities, and repeating them aloud until he had them memorized.

Then, one day, just as Mr. Gilbert drilled Breck on his multiplication tables and Kate on her sums, the tutor shivered violently, rubbed his temples, and surprised Breck by standing and saying, "I think that's enough for one day."

It was only eight o'clock in the morning.

While Kate exclaimed, "Hooray!" and vanished from the schoolroom, Breck remained, twirling the globe on its axis and poring over the first chapter of *Kenilworth* until his mother came and told him there would be no more lessons for a while.

"But why?"

"I'm afraid Mr. Gilbert is confined to his room in the attic. He's taken ill with swamp fever, just like your father."

"Will he die?"

"I don't know. He might. You see, being from Philadelphia, he's not acclimated like we are, and so he's taking it pretty hard. They always do."

Breck pondered this information, then asked, "But how will I learn my lessons?"

"I don't know. Pray he gets better, I suppose. I'm sorry, Breck, really I am. I know how much you've enjoyed your schooling."

For the next few days, Breck rattled around, aimless. The house was so stifling. So closed and sickly. Even Monsieur Déclouet had ceased riding his horse from plantation to plantation, so now there were no lessons of any kind. In the mornings, Mammy Hester told Breck to find something to do and stay out of the way. Even his mother had no time for him, carrying supplies from the storehouse to the hospital to the big house and back again, pausing only long enough to check him for fever and slip half an onion into his pocket for protection against poisonous vapors.

One day, weary of the drabness of indoors, he tucked a few books under his arm (hoping Mr. Gilbert wouldn't mind), and headed outside to read.

Upon Mammy Hester's insistence, he took a torch with him to purify the miasma. "You stay away from those swamps and that creek, you hear?" she added as he walked away. "Them gators is powerful hungry."

So, with his dog Rascal, Breck selected a secluded spot in a strip of pine forest that ran between two cotton fields. Here, the forest was somewhat dry, the land set on a knoll. On that first day, he set his torch into the ground, sat on a log, and opened a book, reading while Rascal slept beside him. On his second day there, Cyrus and Footy found him.

For the last few weeks, Breck had found less and less time to spend with them. During his dinner break, he usually tried to find them. Then the three of them went fishing, hunted for Indian treasures, or poled Fox Creek on their makeshift raft. But lately, it seemed that Cyrus and Footy were kept busy helping Mama in the garden, fetching wood for the kitchen fires, or some such. With Breck in school five days a week, and Cyrus and Footy now performing small tasks, their time together was limited to stolen minutes and an occasional lazy Sunday afternoon, when all the hands had the day off. Much as Breck loved his school lessons, he realized he missed Cyrus and Footy, most especially Footy. He missed the times when they'd had nothing to do together but play.

"What you doing?" Footy asked, telling Rascal to hush and go back to sleep when he gave a groggy, obligatory woof.

"I'm reading," said Breck.

"H-how c-c-come?" asked Cyrus.

"Because I like to."

The two of them circled behind Breck, peering over his shoulder. "You can understand that?" asked Footy.

Breck shrugged. "Most of it. I'm working on the rest."

"What does it says?"

Breck read a sentence, then smiled at them.

"Th-that's real n-nice," said Cyrus.

"That's Shakespeare."

"Sh-Sh-Shakespeare."

"Mr. Gilbert says Shakespeare lived a long time ago."

Now they sat on the log next to Breck, one on each side like bookends. "Read to us some more," said Footy.

"'How now, my love! Why is your cheek so pale? How chance the roses there do fade so fast?'"

Chewing on his lip, Footy asked, "What's that mean?"

"I think it means they're in love."

"Oh."

"See?" Breck pointed to the page. "It says 'my love.' L-O-V-E. Say 'love.'"

"Love," Footy said.

"Now spell it. L-O-V-E. Love."

"L-O-V-E. Love."

"Very good. Now you do it, Cyrus." After Cyrus spelled "love," Breck read some more, pausing occasionally to spell a word and have them repeat it. By the time daylight began to wane, Breck felt better than he had in days. "Can we meet here again tomorrow?" he asked.

They both nodded while Footy said, "Miss Sarah, she's too busy with all them sick folk for her to work in her garden anyhow. We gots all the time in the world."

"Tomorrow it is, then."

So, while down in New Orleans, tens, maybe hundreds, died, while Fox Creek groaned under the weight of so many sick, and while William languished in his bed, ears roaring with quinine, Cyrus, Footy, and Breck met on the forested knoll. And though bristling with heat and limp with humidity, the days passed pleasantly enough under the shade of Shakespeare, Sir Walter Scott, and James Fenimore Cooper.

On their sixth lesson, Breck watched as Footy labored to write his letters on a slate, the tip of his tongue protruding from between his lips.

"A-L-A-S," he wrote, "W-H-I-T-H-E-R W-A-N-D-E-R Y-O-U?"

"Very good." Breck consulted his book. "Now write, 'bawdy house.'"

"But I don't know how."

"I'll spell it, and then it will be Cyrus' turn. B-A-W—No, no, Footy. That's a U, not a W. Try it again. B-A-W-D-Y H-O-"

Suddenly Rascal woofed, awakened from sleep. At the same time, there was a rustling behind Breck.

He turned.

Out of the underbrush stepped Kate and Monette. Both looked hot and tired, as if they'd been crawling through bushes. Breck watched as Kate surveyed the scene. Her gaze moved from Breck to Footy to Cyrus, to the dog, the pine torch, the books, the slate, and the chalk covering their fingers. She put her hands on her hips. "And just what do you think you're doing?"

It was an awkward question for Breck. Not once while he'd instructed Cyrus and Footy had he questioned his actions—whether what he was doing was wrong or right.

But now that his sister confronted him with narrowed eyes and a scowl on her face that reminded him not of his mother, but of his father, he suddenly remembered what he had until then forgotten: it was against the law in Louisiana—in the entire South, for that matter—to teach a slave to read. He knew that if they were caught, all of them would be punished. Cyrus and Footy would be whipped. Or sold.

Much as he liked his sister, at times she was an annoying pest, a tattletale if she did not get her way. The only way to keep this a secret would be to include Kate, knowing that if he told her to leave, everyone would soon know what he had been doing in the forest on the knoll. "Come join us," he said at last.

The invitation seemed to unbalance her, as if she'd expected secrecy and was now a little disappointed. She blinked with uncertainty, then said, "All right," and seated herself on the log.

"You too, Monette," said Breck, feeling an unexpected warmth when Monette smiled at him in return.

# Chapter 5

EVEN BEFORE THE LANDAU rumbled to a stop in front of the big house, Sarah was running. Out the door, across the brick gallery, and onto the drive, knowing it was most unladylike, heedless that her dress cap, trimmed with Mechlin lace and pink rosebuds, flew off her head. "Mother!"

"My Sarah," replied Emma from atop her seat in the landau. "How good it is to see you." Sarah's mother, even at sixty-two, was a beautiful woman. Crowned with hair of a most lustrous silver, she sat erect, regal almost, belying her diminutive stature. Eyes green like Sarah's, to the casual observer, they appeared shining, like jewels, her most arresting feature. But to an astute observer, shadows of sadness painted the lids, the brows, and underneath the eyes. The sadness went deep, only adding to her beauty. She smiled now at Sarah and extended a hand to John, saying, "Help me down."

Emma's feet had barely touched the ground before Sarah embraced her. "Oh, Mother, I've missed you so." Tears surged to Sarah's eyes, and she suddenly wished she were a child again, with no responsibilities, no concerns for the future, no fears.

Her mother seemed to sense Sarah's need, for she did not push Sarah away after an appropriate amount of time, but held her, murmuring, "There, there, my dear. I'm here now, I'm here."

After a while, Sarah asked, "How did you know I needed you?"

Now Emma did pull away, searching Sarah's eyes. "But didn't you send your coachman with the message for us to come today?"

Sarah shook her head, no.

Then John spoke. "Likely William did." John was, many believed, a most unremarkable man. Deliberate of speech, quiet, he exuded nothing extraordinary. Many found him plain, homely almost, with a broad forehead, thinning hair, and hazel eyes set too far apart. But Sarah saw none of the imperfections, seeing only her brother—an intelligent, kind-hearted, generous individual, who would do anything for anyone at any time of the day or night.

"But you know William's in bed with swamp fever," said Sarah.

Her mother said, "I'm sure William has his ways."

Sarah nodded, remembering just yesterday when William had dressed and gone to the fields during a downpour, despite her protests that he remain in bed. He'd lasted only an hour, returning to the big house almost delirious with fever, moaning over and over, "The cotton's rotting, Sarah. The cotton's rotting."

Poor man, she thought. Likely when he was out, he'd sent someone to fetch John and Emma. Realizing this now, her heart swelled with gratitude for such exertions on her behalf.

"At least it's not Yellow Jack." John pulled his black bag from the landau. "It has made its appearance in Bayou Clare despite all our precautions. Let's hope it stays there and doesn't migrate." He gave orders to his coachman, and the three of them moved into the parlor, where Sarah instructed Uncle Henry as to their refreshment.

"Well," John said, draining his glass of sherry, not wishing to waste time, "tell me where everyone's located, and I'll get started."

Sarah rose from her seat. "I'll go with you."

But John sensed her reluctance to leave their mother, her need to rest, thinking, The poor girl looks exhausted. Weariness stamped every aspect of Sarah's features. Dark circles surrounded her eyes, her mouth hung almost slack, her auburn hair—normally so neat and coifed—was in disarray, stray curls sweat-plastered to her forehead and neck. "Stay here with Mother. Just tell me where everyone is, and I'll take care of everything."

His first stop was the master bedroom. It was shuttered, unbearably hot, the only light coming from a candle atop a bedside table. John shooed away the servant boy and lifted the mosquito net. William was sleeping. Although, as a physician, John was long accustomed to witnessing the ravages of disease, it was still a shock to see close friends and family succumb. One day vivacious, the next day prostrate, helpless, waiting for death even. With eyes sunken, beard overgrown like stubble in a cornfield, William appeared corpse-like, emaciated. His skin was the color of old paste, his breathing quick and shallow. John touched his brother-in-law's forehead. Damn fever, he thought, taking from his black bag medicines to purge the bowels and induce vomiting. Powdered calomel and rhubarb. Jalap. Ipecac. Castor oil. With such a fever, it was necessary to drive it from the body with the force of a sledgehammer, followed up by vigorous doses of quinine, and bleeding should inflammation occur.

When John was finally ready—bottles, spoons, and pills organized on the bedside table—he realized William was watching him. "How do you feel?"

"Like shit." His voice was cracked, weak.

John made William say "ah," then examined his tongue, and then asked him how often his fevers were coming.

"Every two days. Just when I think I'm well, it's back again. God, I hate this."

"I'll have you up and around in no time, my friend."

"Yes," said William, casting a bleary glance at the medicines. "I can see that."

"I'm sorry, but it's quite necessary."

"So, you tell me." William put a hand to his head, wincing.

"Headache?"

"Splitting. John, do me a favor."

"Anything."

"There's negroes of mine that are shirking their work. They know I'm sick and Sarah's too kind-hearted. They're taking advantage of the situation, pretending to be sick when they're not."

"Don't worry yourself. I know what to do."

"There's more."

"Isn't there always?"

"Three of my boys ran off like partridges. Word has it they're living the high life in the woods."

"Leave it to me. I've got one missing as well."

"My cotton's rotting, John."

"So's mine."

"It's been a godawful year."

"I know, William, I know. Open wide now."

It pained Emma almost more than she could bear to see her daughter's exhaustion. She determined then and there to send over two of her most trusted women to tend to Sarah's tasks so she could rest.

For now, they sat in the schoolroom, away from Mehitable's prying eyes, where they could speak in private. The schoolroom was square and good-sized. Bookcases lined the plain white walls. Emma recognized some of the books that Sarah had taken as her due when she'd left home to marry William. A rectangular table dominated the center of the room, and it was at this table that the two women now sat, each nursing a cold glass of lemonade.

"How is William?" Emma asked.

"Well, he seemed to feel better yesterday, but instead of resting like I told him to, he insisted on going to the fields." Sarah sighed. "So, of course, the fever's back. Sometimes I swear he's hardheaded as an axe."

"Why, Sarah, your father was exactly the same way. It would have taken an earthquake, a fire, and a plague to keep him down. So very headstrong and bullheaded. But, even so, I loved him, that I did."

"You know I love William, Mama. More than anything."

"Of course, of course, dear. I know that. I've known that since the first time I laid eyes on the two of you together. You know, dear, you're very fortunate in that regard. Many ladies go through their entire marriage with only a shred of love to hold it together, if that. Kind of like trying to hold together a bale of cotton with a cobweb," said Emma with a laugh, satisfied when she saw a glimmer of a smile from Sarah. "Now don't you worry about William. He's a fighter. Being hardheaded does have its advantages, mind you. I'm sure he'll pull through like he always does."

Her daughter looked away and said nothing, twisting a lace handkerchief in her hands, biting her lip, reminding Emma so much of when Sarah was a little girl. She longed to take this beautiful creature into her arms and hold her. Instead, she asked, "And the children?" Emma was anxious to see her grandchildren, but at present, they were nowhere to be found—playing, no doubt, as children do.

"No sign of sickness yet, God be praised. I pray every day for their health."

"As do I, Sarah dear, as do I."

They reached across the table and held hands. It was more than just a bond between mother and daughter; it was the bond of women everywhere. The bond of motherhood. Emma knew the fear of losing a child preyed on all mothers' minds, haunting them. That fear had become a reality for Emma, not once, but six times. At her family cemetery back at Woodleigh, six infant tombstones rose above the sweet grass, above the fragrant blooms that Emma tended so lovingly.

*Another little lamb has gone*
*to dwell with Him who gave,*
*Another little darling babe*
*is sheltered in the grave.*

Now Emma squeezed Sarah's hand, praying her daughter would never be forced to endure the anguish of losing a child.

Emma remembered Sarah's birth, a strange combination of dread, hope, and love. Don't love her, Emma had told herself, even as she expelled the child from her womb. She won't survive. She'll die like the others, and I shall tend seven tombstones, not six. But Emma could no more stem the flow of love than a levee of sticks could hold back the Mississippi. To Emma's delight, the child thrived. Now, in what Emma considered to be her venerable old age, Sarah and John were the joys of her life—her reason for living.

What pleasure it was to watch a child grow. It almost took the pain from her, the aching pain for her other losses. Now Emma knew that such pain never went away entirely; it merely dulled, and the dulling took years. Sarah had always been a beautiful child. From the time she first toddled around, her "big brother John" took her everywhere he went, seemingly as pleased as Emma that he finally had a sibling to play with, though seven years her senior. Even when John returned from Philadelphia at the age of twenty, a new medical doctor, young Sarah followed him on his rounds to the neighboring plantations.

It was on one of those visits that Sarah became reacquainted with William Jensey. She was young, fifteen; William was hardly older than that. Emma remembered the fear when John informed her of the burgeoning relationship. No! She wasn't ready to let her baby go! (Especially to a man whose own mother did not know the meaning of the word "gentility," and despite the fact that his father was descended from an established, respectable South Carolina planter family.) Emma adamantly prohibited Sarah from making the medical rounds with John, but of course, the young lovers found a way. They always do, thought Emma with a smile.

She pulled a half-finished blouse from her sewing bag. She'd brought plenty of sewing in case she had to stay several days. While Woodleigh was not far away, their lands adjoining, the drive was bumpy, inconvenient, sometimes wet and muddy, mostly hot and bug-filled. Besides, she longed to spend time with Sarah. As she began to stitch the collar, she said, "John has told me the most wonderful news."

"What news?"

"You mean to tell me you don't know? The news regards you, my dear, and William."

Sarah flushed. "I was waiting to tell you."

"You should know by now never to wait with such news if your servants already know. By then, it's too late."

"I'm sorry I didn't tell you first."

"Nonsense. I never expect to be the first to know. I'm just delighted that I shall soon have a third grandchild. And seeing as John appears to be a confirmed old bachelor, I guess that means I'll have to rely solely on you for my grandchildren. So, my dear, it comes as welcome news indeed."

Sarah looked up from her own sewing and smiled.

"When is the child due?" asked Emma.

"Christmas."

"Well, then, I shall have to get busy making baby clothes. Perhaps a Christmas outfit for a newborn?"

"You and John must come spend Christmas with us."

"I wouldn't miss it for the world. In fact—" Emma paused.

"What?"

"Perhaps I should come earlier, around the beginning of November or so. I can take care of household business while you rest. Mustn't take any chances, you know."

"Oh, Mama, that would be wonderful."

But even as her daughter uttered these most welcoming words, Emma detected a heaviness to her voice that was more than just fatigue. "What is it, Sarah? Is something bothering you?"

This time Sarah did not look up as she sewed a pair of pantalettes, attaching the lace with meticulous stitches. Emma could not see her eyes, seeing only her cap, and the beautiful auburn hair that escaped in neglected tendrils. "No," her daughter replied. "Nothing's bothering me at all, other than William being sick, of course."

But for some vague, unsettling reason, Emma didn't believe her. She couldn't figure why she didn't believe her daughter. After all, it had been a long time since Sarah had been untruthful. There was something, something in the bend of her daughter's neck, in the way she stabbed the fabric, something that Sarah was not telling her.

In spite of the heat, Emma shivered.

The smells wafting from the kitchen that evening were at once familiar and enticing. Monette and Kate were passing by the pond on their way to the stables to visit Tiptop when the smell assailed them with the deliciousness of a whispered secret.

"Praline candies!" declared Monette, immediately recognizing the creamy, sugary, nutty smell that conjured up visions of Ma'amzelle Rosalie's shop, of her plump white arms, and how she always reached out to tweak Monette's cheek while praline candy melted on Monette's tongue, and everyone around her chuckled and said what a sweet child she was.

But even as the two girls detoured around the big house toward the kitchen, Mammy Hester was hollering out a window at Kate, saying, "Lord a'mercy, there you is! I just about wore myself out looking for you. Your Grandma Emma's here, and she been wanting to see you something fierce! Where you been, anyhow?"

"Grandma Emma!" shrieked Kate, immediately bounding toward the house, telling Monette over her shoulder to hurry and pretty please fetch some praline candy for her!

Monette had not met Grandma Emma yet, but Kate had told her all about her—how wise and gentle she was, kind too, and how she gave Kate gifts and always told Kate how much she loved her. Monette was anxious to meet Grandma Emma too, to be loved by her as well, but first things first.

Pralines!

Smiling with anticipation, mouth watering already, Monette stepped into the kitchen. There were the pie cupboards, piled high with crockery. Cast-iron pots, pans, skillets, and lids hung from pegs hammered into the wood-planked walls. Bundles of dried herbs dangled overhead. Seated around the table, where two candles burned atop the red, checkered tablecloth, a bevy of dark faces peered at her, and the murmur of voices fell away. She was instantly shy, wishing they would stop looking at her, wishing Kate was with her.

For the first few days after arriving at Fox Creek, she, too, had taken her meals in the kitchen, sitting small and quiet while everyone chatted about who was pregnant, or that new girl, Minty, or did you hear about Hannibal over on the Cobb plantation who choked to death on a chicken bone? Monette was content to sit there, small and quiet, until one day one of them turned to her and asked where she'd come from, and who her mama and daddy were. Immediately, the inside of her head began to roar—like a tree full of cicadas had grown inside. She could feel everyone around the table staring at the top of her head, waiting for an answer while she examined the bracelet on her wrist that Kate had given her, wondering through the whirring confusion in her head if those were real jewels. She stood then, quietly folded her chicken, peas, and corn muffin into her napkin, and left.

Anymore, she only went into the kitchen long enough to fetch her meal before taking it elsewhere, pretending she didn't see the cook scowling at her. Instead, she found it far more satisfying to share her meals with Kate in the playhouse, or to picnic at their secret spot, or to eat in Kate's room while they pretended they were at a royal banquet and Monette taught Kate how to say "Please," "Thank you," "Excuse me," "I couldn't possibly eat another bite," and "That was simply delightful!" *En français,* of course.

Monette turned away from their staring eyes and found what she was looking for—hot praline candies, cooling on a greased flour cloth atop a table next to the window, smelling simply divine! Her mouth watered. *Miam, miam!*

"Them's for later," Aunt Delia said to her. "Made 'em special 'cause of company. You come back later, I can give you one."

Monette's gaze dropped to her own shoes. *"S'il vous plaît,* Aunt Delia, but—"

"Don't you talk none of your French to me, you knows I can't understand it. You wants to talk to me, you speak English like the rest of us do."

Monette was tempted to flee the kitchen empty-handed, to tell Kate sorry, but her mouth remembered the taste of praline candy, the soft crunch of nuts. "If you please, Miss Kate told me to fetch her some pralines. And to hurry."

"Did she now?" Out of the corner of Monette's eye, she could see Aunt Delia putting her hands on her plump hips. "Well, then, why didn't you say so? What you standing there for? Fetch her some pralines."

Monette stacked six, seven, eight pralines into a napkin. She gathered up her bundle, not looking at Aunt Delia or at anyone as she whispered, *"Merci,"* and scurried out the door, the pralines still warm in her hands.

While passing through the spare bedroom that led from the rear loggia to her own room, Kate found Grandma Emma kneeling beside the bed, hands folded. Kate knew she was praying, because she'd seen her own mother pray like that, and she herself had tried it once or twice, only to discover that it hurt her knees.

Even so, Kate knelt beside her grandmother, folded her hands, and closed her eyes. Dear God, dear God . . .

Her forehead creased with effort, trying to think of what to say. Dear God, today I went to secret school, but don't tell anyone because it's secret and then we'll have to stab your eye with a needle. She waited for a few seconds, trying to think of more to say, but when nothing came to her, she proclaimed a resounding, "Amen."

She opened her eyes to find her grandmother smiling at her. Emma took one of Kate's hands in her own. Kate loved the silky feeling of her grandmother's hands.

"God loves you, Katherine, dear."

A warmth filled Kate—not because God loved her; she really didn't stop long enough to ponder that—but because Grandma Emma loved her. Of all the people in the world, it seemed Grandma Emma loved her best. To have her grandmother all to herself like this was like having an enormous piece of taffy and not having to share it with anyone.

"Come with me." Out on the gallery, the setting sun painted the sky with brushstrokes of purple and orange. Grandma Emma sat in a rocking chair and pulled Kate onto her lap.

As the sun settled behind the trees, Grandma Emma began to hum. Kate felt the vibrations through the woman's chest and melted back into her grandmother's arms. When the humming stopped, Kate asked, "Was that a song?"

"One of my favorites. It's a hymn called, 'How Sweet the Name of Jesus Sounds.'" She then sang the hymn for Kate as they rocked.

"That was pretty," Kate said when she finished.

"It was, wasn't it? There are many beautiful things on God's sweet earth, dear Katherine, and song is one of them."

"Are palmetto bugs beautiful?"

"Well, I suppose they're beautiful, so long as they're not buzzing in your hair or swimming in your soup."

Kate giggled. "Are alligators beautiful?"

"In their scaly, ugly way, I suppose they're beautiful too."

"Is Grandma Mehitable beautiful?"

Emma chuckled. "Let me put it this way: if it weren't for Mehitable, you wouldn't be here in my arms. For that, Mehitable is beautiful, and I shall always appreciate her."

Kate turned and looked up at Emma. "Am I beautiful?"

"You, Katherine dear," said her grandmother, hugging her at the same time, "are a bright star in God's universe."

"Are you a star too?"

Emma nodded.

"Which one?" asked Kate.

"What do you mean, which one?"

"Which star?"

Emma looked past Kate into the darkening sky. "I think I would be a star in a constellation. A big constellation with all my children and my dear, dear George, God rest his bullheaded soul. Each one of us a brilliant star. That one, maybe. Or that one."

Kate kissed her grandmother's cheek then, inhaling the smell of talcum. "Don't go yet," she whispered.

"Don't go where?"

"Don't go to God's universe yet. Stay here with me."

Emma smiled at her and tweaked her nose. "Why, here I am, dear Katherine. Here I am."

Just then, Monette stepped onto the gallery, smiling shyly as she approached.

Kate sat up straight, returning Monette's smile. "This is my best friend, Grandma. Her name's Monette," she said, pleased when Monette curtsied, saying, *"Bonjour, Madame, comment allez-vous?"*

"Never been better," Grandma Emma answered, laughing when Monette opened up a napkin filled with pralines, which they all three happily devoured.

# *Chapter 6*

For two days, they could not hold their secret school because of the rain. When, finally, the five of them met again, the forest steamed around them—hot, lush—a living, breathing entity clothed in a damp, rich verdure.

It was Cyrus' favorite part of his day because he got to be with Monette. Each morning, when he arose to the clang of the bell, he slipped Monette's bonnet out from under his cornshuck pallet, brushing it against his face before returning it to its hiding place. He'd found it down by the creek a few months ago, and it still smelled like her. But coming to secret school was even better than sniffing her bonnet because she was there. He got to see her again. To be near her. To sometimes hold her hand.

Today he thought she looked especially fine, with her pretty green dress and a crisp, new bonnet to match. She cradled her doll, and it reminded him suddenly of their time together in the slave pen, on the day when Finney had returned her dress and given her a handful of ribbons. "Y-you looks aw-awful pretty t-t-today, Mon-Monette," he said with a smile, wishing the others weren't listening too.

"*Merci, mon ami.* You are very kind."

"Is you gonna yap at Monette all day like you done before," asked Footy, "or is we gonna learn ourselves how to read and write?"

"I-I-I ain't yappin'."

The children sat facing each other across two logs. They'd found another log on their first day, not too far distant, and dragged it with much groaning and straining (and barking from Rascal) until it lay parallel to the other log, three feet apart.

Now they took turns with the slate, wiping it off and passing it to the next person, while Breck kept his finger in the book, glancing at the page occasionally to spell a new word. "No, Cyrus," Breck was saying. "Mop starts with an M. Spell mop. M-O-P. Mop."

Cyrus frowned, aware that Monette watched him. He wiped off what he had written and began again. "M-m-m—"

"Wrong," said Kate, who sat across from Cyrus. "It doesn't have three M's, silly. It only has one M. Anyone can spell mop. Mop is easy. M-O-P. There. See? Now try it."

It sounded so simple when she did it like that. Mop, he said in his mind. Mop. Like what to scrub floors with. Mop. M-O-P. "M-m-m—"

Kate sighed with exasperation. "There he goes again."

"How comes you always stutters?" asked Footy.

Cyrus looked at the ground and shrugged, wishing it wasn't his turn any longer. How could he explain that he didn't know why he stuttered, he just did? That he only stuttered in front of white folk? That they scared him? That he knew they looked at him and thought him stupid? If he tried to explain all that, they would laugh at him. Kate might even pinch him; she'd already done that twice when no one was looking.

Instead, a blankness entered his mind, a welcome blankness in which he felt nothing, thinking only, it don't matter none. Don't matter at all. A grin spread across his face.

"Sometimes you don't stutter," Footy continued, unabated. "How comes you can't talk straight like that all the time?"

Again, Cyrus shrugged, smiling, saying nothing, aware that all of them were waiting for an answer.

"It doesn't matter," Breck said at last. "Just spell it on the slate, Cyrus. Don't spell it out loud."

When Cyrus finished, knowing it was wrong, knowing it was sloppy and backward, he handed the slate to Breck.

"Very good, very, very good," said Breck.

"*Bravo*, Cyrus!" Monette clapped her hands. "*Très bien!* I see improvement!"

"Now it's Monette's turn," said Breck. He handed Monette the slate. Cyrus watched as Breck briefly consulted his book. "Spell lady. L-A-D-Y. Lady. It's from *Antony and Cleopatra.* Cleopatra was a lady."

"That's a hard one." Footy rolled his eyes. "'Cause it only her fourth day."

"She can do it." Breck gave her the chalk and placed his hand over hers. "I'll help you. Do you remember how to write an L?"

"I am afraid I have forgotten. There are many letters to learn."

"Then I'll show you." Their hands began to move. "That's good." Breck nodded as together they scrawled out an L. "Very, very good."

Kate frowned. "That's not what you say when my letters are crooked. You say to do it over."

"That's because you should know better. Monette's just learning."

"*Oui.* I have never made letters before, *jamais!*" Monette said, smiling at Breck. "I think making letters is fun. I like it. I like learning to read too."

"But remember to never tell," said Breck. "It's our secret. Or else we'll have to poke a needle in your eye."

"*Oui.* I do not want a needle in my eye."

When, later, Breck finally slapped the book closed and said, "That's enough for today," Cyrus left the forested knoll without a word, ignoring Footy's pleas to wait up.

That night, long after the final bell, the comforting blankness ebbed away. Confused, Cyrus tossed upon his pallet, knowing only that things were not as they used to be, and he longed for the blankness to return. It don't matter none, he told himself again and again.

Don't matter at all.

Now he was afraid to talk, afraid to open his mouth, speaking only when necessary. Gradually, as one day melted into the next, Cyrus became acutely aware of something else that caused him exquisite pain. Already, Monette's letters were better than his, and he'd had more schooling. No matter how hard he tried, many of the letters looked the same, sounded the same. Whenever he passed the slate, a streaky smudge of chalk and sweat, nothing was right. Everything was wrong. A knot formed in his stomach each time it was his turn. He repeated to himself, don't matter at all, while he pretended not to hear when Kate would say, "Wrong." Or when Footy would say, "That ain't how you spell a E. Ain't you figured that out yet?"

But the biggest agony of all started when Breck first laid his hand over Monette's. Cyrus hadn't been able to sit next to Monette that day, or on any of the following days. Instead, Kate sat on one side of her, Breck on the other, while Cyrus and Footy shared their own damp log that sometimes erupted with bugs. On the day Breck laid his hand over Monette's, something poured out of Cyrus' heart, seeping like blood, lost forever, as if he were being placed on the scales all over again and sold like a hog.

On the following Sunday, in the heat and dampness of mid-August, secret school ended abruptly for Cyrus.

It had rained during the night, and steam rolled from the soft ground beneath his feet in a stifling, stinking wave. A peacock perched on the branch of a nearby live oak, his cry shattering the stillness.

Cyrus stood for inspection in the first row, grinning, waiting to be called forward to receive his rations. He'd eaten the last of his bacon and cornmeal yesterday morning.

"You gots to learn to stretch it over a week's time," one of his cabin mates told him. "Even if you goes a little hungry, you gots to control yourself."

He did not have to wait long. His cabin was called, and he went forward with his four cabin mates. Today, William was performing the inspections, while Breck stood beside him. Breck had told Cyrus that his father was sick, real sick, and Cyrus believed it. He look like a stick, thought Cyrus. A tall, sick stick.

To his surprise, William spoke directly to him, something he'd only done once before. "Cyrus, listen up. Tomorrow, when the bell rings, report to Quincy, my driver. You're going to the fields to pick cotton. You understand?"

At first, Cyrus didn't say anything, trying to comprehend what William had said. *You're going to the fields to pick cotton. You understand?* Then he swallowed and said through his grin, "Y-y-yes, M-M-Mars W-William."

"Quincy, get this boy some pants, stockings, a straw hat, and a pair of shoes. Work him as a half hand for two weeks, and then switch him to a three-quarter hand. I think he can handle it."

Pants? Stockings? Shoes? Cyrus gathered his rations and rejoined the line, still grinning. *This am a good day. Lordy, this am a good day. I gets some new clothes, and I don't got to go to secret school no more.*

Cyrus had been absent from secret school for one month when Monette heard a distinct rustle come from the bushes behind them, not far away.

Rascal jerked from sleep and woofed, just as Breck grabbed the dog's collar. "Stay, boy."

Kate looked up. She'd been reading aloud. "What is it?"

"I heard something." Breck put his finger over his lips. "Back there in the bushes."

"I heard it too," said Monette.

"Oh lordy," Footy croaked, his eyes wide. "It am a bear."

Horrified at the thought, Monette gasped. She had never seen a bear, only heard of them. Kate told her how they peeled the skin off children layer by layer, and then licked their insides. "I am frightened. Let us leave, please. *Tout de suite.*"

"Shh." Breck motioned her to be quiet. "I'm going to have a look. Footy, come with me."

"No sir, Breck sir, I don't think so."

"I'll come with you," offered Kate.

Monette was astonished, for she saw no fear in Kate's face, only an excitement. Did Kate want to get peeled and licked? "Don't go," Monette pleaded. "It is too dangerous. What if it catches you?"

Breck nodded. "You stay here, Kate, and look after Monette. I'll be right back. Footy, come with me."

"Oh lordy." Footy got up slowly from the log. With a final, despairing look at Kate and Monette, he followed Breck and Rascal through the brush and disappeared.

"Don't worry," Kate said, patting Monette's hand, "I'll protect you."

Monette half expected a bear to charge through the bushes, even though she could only imagine what a bear might look like—a huge, roaring monster, tall as a tree. But instead of a bear, Breck and Footy eventually emerged from the brush, hot and sweaty, with burrs stuck all over them. Rascal was nowhere to be seen.

"Well," said Kate, "what was it?"

"Bad news," replied Breck. "Someone's seen us."

"What do you mean?" asked Monette.

"We found footprints all over a muddy spot back there. Whoever was there could see and hear what we were doing. From the looks of it, he was there for quite some time."

"So what does that mean?" asked Kate.

Breck began to gather up the books. "It means school is closed. At least for now."

"School is closed?" Monette searched both boys' faces to see if they were in jest, but knew from the heavy way Breck sighed and from the way Footy moped around, disappointment scrawled all over his face like misspelled words, that it was all too true. Just like that, secret school was closed. She hadn't realized until that moment how much she'd enjoyed it.

"We can't take the chance of getting caught." Breck looked first at Monette, then at Footy. "I'm sorry—sorry I got you into this. I should never have done it. It was wrong. Let's hope whoever he was keeps his mouth shut."

"But—" asked Monette, "how will we learn to read?"

"Yeah. How we gonna learn ourselves enough to read Shakespeare like you can do?"

Breck shook his head. "Sorry. Really, I am."

While Monette did not understand what was happening, why secret school had to be secret at all, why it was wrong, it hurt her to see Breck so sad. "*Ça va, mon ami.* Let me help you with the books."

"No, it's better that we all split up like usual, so no one will suspect anything." Breck stood holding the torch, the books and slate tucked under his other arm, seemingly reluctant to leave. "Well, I guess that's it."

"I will miss secret school," said Monette. "I had learned all my letters."

"Leastways, I didn't get gobbled by no bear," said Footy.

Kate tugged on Monette's hand, saying, "Let's go." Together, the girls took the forest path and left the knoll behind, Monette talking in French about the demise of secret school and how sad it all was, and whether bears *really* peeled off the layers of your skin and licked your insides, while Kate nodded as if understanding every last verb and nuance.

Again, the day was humid and heavy, the distant clouds pregnant with rain. After they visited their secret spot, just to be sure it was still there, still secret, they stopped by the playhouse and rearranged the various rugs and chairs, dishes, and dolls before strolling up the pine- and oak-alley toward the big house. The lower gallery of the big house was floored with brick and flush with the ground. Shaded by the upper gallery, it provided a cool place to sit in hot weather. Sitting on the gallery were Sarah and Emma. Each of them sewed a garment and, as Monette approached, she heard them talking about the yellow fever,—that it had killed hundreds in New Orleans, that poor Sophia Taggart's little boy had died of it just a few miles away, and when would it ever go away and leave everyone alone?

Sarah looked up and spied Kate. "Oh, there you are. Come see what I'm making for your new brother." As Monette drew near, she could see the tiny garment Sarah held up, all tucks and gathers and lace. A new brother for Kate, thought Monette, surprised when a deep emptiness cracked open inside her, like a fissure in a rock suddenly rent apart, an earthquake of the soul. In the instant she peered into the fissure, she was terrified by the darkness, the raw pain that bled from the opening as if something had crawled inside and died. Monette quickly looked away, forcing the fissure closed. But in that instant, she was left breathless, knees weak, heart galloping like Tiptop gone mad.

It took all Monette's willpower to keep standing on her feet, to smile at Miss Sarah, pretending she had not glimpsed anything more than the hem of delicate lace, that the new brother was her brother too, and that Miss Sarah was her own dear mother. A pretending that now seemed substantial and happy and infinitely preferred.

Kate said, "That's pretty, Mama."

"*Oui. Très jolie.*"

"Katherine dear, are you all right?"

"Just tired."

Monette frowned, thinking that was impossible. Kate was never tired. But when she thought about it, she realized that ever since they'd left the secret hideaway, Kate had been uncommonly quiet, and in their walk down the alley, a walk which they usually ran, Kate had lagged behind.

"Come sit with us a while," said Emma, patting an empty chair beside her. "I'm sure it's just the heat."

"Monette," said Sarah, once Kate had wilted into the chair, "fetch Katherine a glass of lemonade. Aunt Delia put a fresh pitcher in the butler's pantry."

"*Oui, Madame.*"

"Monette, please respond with, 'Yes, Miss Sarah,' as do the others in my household."

"Yes, Miss Sarah."

The butler's pantry was located at the back of the house. All food from the kitchen building was first taken through the rear loggia and into the butler's pantry to be transferred onto serving dishes and chinaware before being served to those in the dining room. The pantry had a central table surrounded by shelves and cupboards on all four walls.

Monette ran from the lower gallery, through the dining room, and into the pantry. She was thirsty too, and so took two glasses from a shelf and poured them full, thinking that she'd have to remember to take some lemonade with her the next time they went to the playhouse. Monette took a sip from her glass just as she spied a sponge cake on the table behind the pitcher, and beside the cake, a small crock filled with fresh cream.

Sponge cake! She remembered sponge cake from . . . from . . . it did not matter. Only that cake, like lemonade, was a treat. Hurrying now, she fetched two plates from the counter, thinking how nice it was that the plates were just sitting right there, and cut two pieces of cake, wondering if she was using the correct utensil, as there always seemed to be a utensil particular for each food, dish, or culinary task. As she transferred the slices of cake to the plates, wondering if Miss Sarah and Miss Emma might like some as well, a chunk of cake fell into the crock of cream, which she then proceeded to carefully fish out with the tip of her little finger, thinking nobody liked lumpy cream. Certainly not!

She never saw the blow coming.

All she knew was that she had been standing licking cream off her finger, trying to figure out how she would carry two glasses of lemonade plus two plates of cake and whether she would need to make more than one trip, when her head exploded with stars, and she tumbled into the table and into the cake. The pitcher of lemonade crashed to the floor, the glasses and plates shattered, the crock of cream hit the wall with a splatter of white, and Monette began to shriek.

She collapsed to the floor and curled into a ball, screaming as someone beat her, as someone yelled, "I knew you were nothing but a thief! Sneaking around and taking things that don't belong to you! Now the cream is ruined! Dirty yellow nigger!"

Monette shrieked louder, hurting so bad, oh so bad, screaming for Miss Sarah, for Kate, for Miss Emma, anyone, to save her, please save her from this nightmare. It was like the bear peeling her skin and licking her insides. Then there were voices swirling above her like fog, fading, fading, until she slipped into a world of gray where there was no more beating, and all was silence and peace.

# Chapter 7

TWO POUNDS OF PORK. A plug of tobacco. A gourd filled with molasses . . . The cost of slipping away.

"You gots 'til the end of the row at most," the driver had told Retta earlier. "You gots to be back 'fore Mars William comes to the fields."

No need to say why she needed to be back before Mars William. They both knew. Retta then lagged behind the others, picking slowly, waiting until all were ahead of her, until all had their backs to her before she slipped back into the brush and through the trees that lined the cotton field. It was good to be careful. No telling who might snitch. After hiding her bag of cotton, she hurried through the underbrush. *'Til the end of the row . . .* Barely enough time to do what had to be done.

It took her a spell to find them. Mars Breck, Missie Kate, that uppity mulatto, and her own Footy. She watched her son for a long while, her heart racing.

She knew she was late when she returned to fetch her bag of cotton, but felt no sense of relief that she'd landed a lucky kick on the dog's chops and sent him cowering, no sense of relief that Mars William had not ridden by yet. By the time she took her place in her row, picking furiously, her hands trembled with rage—a consuming, white-hot rage that made her want to throw her head back, scream, and shake her fists to the heavens.

It was late in the evening when Footy walked into their cabin, as if nothing was wrong, as if Retta had not noticed the change in him over the last few weeks, nor seen the letters drawn in the dirt behind the cabin before she wiped them out with her foot.

The baby pulled on Retta's nipple, playing, patting, satiated with milk. Retta had no patience for playing and gave the baby to her eldest daughter before buttoning herself up. "Put him to bed. Footy, come here. I needs to talk with you."

Footy looked suddenly wary, as if he sensed trouble in her tone of voice. Trouble is right, she thought. You's in heaps of trouble, boy. "Now you girls go on," she said to her daughters. "Mind your own business. Me and Footy needs to talk." No sense in everyone knowing what was happening, she believed. In fact, no one else was ever going to know, not if she could help it.

Footy stood beside her. Even through her anger, she sensed his nervousness. She spoke quietly, aware that his breathing immediately quickened. "I knows what you been doing, Footy. That's right. I done seen you today. Now I's telling you, and telling you good, you stop what you's doing. Stop it right now. Don't you go there again, you hear? Ain't no one in this family gonna bring grief on me."

When Footy furrowed his brow, not seeming to understand, she said, "What you been doing in the woods ain't right by the law, and white folks is what makes the law. White folks *is* the law. Mars William find out you been breaking the law, and he gonna break you. He gonna break me. He gonna break your daddy. He gonna sell you far 'way from here, 'cause black boys what reads and writes ain't nothing but trouble for white folks. You understand me, boy? You hear what I's saying?" Angry tears coursed down her face, and her voice hardened. "Mars Breck don't think of stuff like that. He just act like it don't matter none. Well, chile, it does matter. It matters a heap. I ain't having my family ruined just 'cause Mars Breck thinks it fun, or wants to experiment, or some such foolishment like that. You hear what I's saying, boy?"

Now Footy was crying, nodding. His eyes were closed, and her heart ached for him. Angry. Aching.

She wagged her finger. "Don't you tell your daddy. Don't you tell no one what you done. Don't you never write nor read 'nother word so longs as you live. Swear to me, Footy, swear to me now."

Footy opened his eyes, and the tears rushed down. "I promises, Momma. I's sorry. I's so sorry. I promises."

Just then, Obediah came in the door. He was late most nights, trying to finish the dance hall.

Retta said nothing more, rising from her chair to prepare for bed. She was tired, more tired than she'd ever been before. It seemed she carried a weight about, a weight that pressed down upon her shoulders, heavier, more wearisome by the day. Lord, sweet Lord, when will this ever end?

Her husband took her hand, and together with the children, they bowed their heads in their nightly prayer. Retta moaned, low and gentle, as Obediah prayed, "Someday, Lord, someday. Someday you's gonna lift this yoke from us. Someday, Lord, someday—"

Knees popping in protest, Mammy Hester took the steps to the attic as quickly as her old woman's body would allow. Light from her candle variously illuminated the stairwells, the hallways, the cobwebbed corners, which no amount of swiping with a broom seemed to keep in order for long. She reached the top, and after steadying herself against the doorframe, lifted the latch and entered.

Her bedroom was as comfortable as she could make it. The occasional mud dauber's nest glued to the rafters didn't bother her. She swatted them and tossed them out the double windows opposite the fireplace. On wintry days she was allowed to keep a small fire going, and so, in the evenings, when her tasks were completed, she often sat in the rocker with her feet just inches from the closest ember. In the corner nearest the windows stood a dresser with a pitcher and bowl (albeit, chipped) with a mirror above. The fact that the mirror was foggy in places and had cracked long ago ceased to concern Mammy. She could see just enough to be certain she had nothing stuck between her teeth, that her turban was good and tight, and that nothing untoward lurked out the end of her nose. Against the far wall lay a four-postered bed, a hand-me-down from William and Sarah on the day they purchased a new bed from London. Getting on in years, as was Mammy, it protested now whenever she rolled over, loud and squawking as a hen ousted from a warm nest. Despite the discordant symphony of wood joints and planks, it was comfortable enough, cradling her bones into a pleasant sleep each night, a pleasantness Mammy attributed not only to the firmness of the moss mattress, but to the crucifix which she'd hammered into the wall above the bed, a guarantee against ghosts, witches, and malicious spirits of the general variety.

On this night, the shutters were closed. The room was stifling, the damp air seeming to distill on the inside of her lungs, smelling of dust and mice. Beneath the mosquito net and the fading colors of the thin, summery quilt atop her bed, lay the child. Mammy set the candle on the bedside table, a little taken aback to see Monette's large amber eyes peering at her. They were startling eyes. Odd-colored, certainly. Haunting. The pain, the confusion of the afternoon were easily seen in their depths, even without the telltale swelling, the darkening bruise around her left eye and cheekbone.

As if that weren't bad enough. Lord a'mercy. "I's so glad you's finally awake," Mammy whispered. "You done had such a fright."

Of course, Monette began to cry, as the old woman had known she would. Mammy Hester drew up the net, sat on the bed to the crunch of moss, and wrapped her arms about the child. Ain't nothing but a sparrow, she thought. "There, there, honey chile. Go 'head and pour out your sorrows. The sweet Lord above sees and counts every tear." She stroked the girl's hair, tracing her braids.

Eventually, the girl managed to say through her tearful hiccups, *"S'il vous plaît,* Mammy Hester. Do you know where my doll is?"

Mammy pulled away and gazed into the face that seemed golden in the candlelight, even at the shimmering strand of saliva that stretched like a gossamer thread from Mammy's *fichu* to the child's damp mouth. "That doll sure am special to you. Was that doll a gift, honey? From your Momma?"

The child seemed bewildered by the question, her breath smelling of an empty belly. "I don't know. *Je ne sais pas.*"

"Well, surely someone special made it for you. It didn't just drop out the sky into your arms now, did it?"

When again Monette said she didn't know, Mammy Hester sighed, promised to return with her doll in a wink, and left the room. After fetching the doll from the clothesline outside, Mammy scrounged up some food from the kitchen—a bowl of strawberries which would spoil if not eaten soon, bread and cheese, plus a glass of milk. When Mammy returned to her bedroom, the child was sitting up, holding her arms out for the doll even before Mammy set the tray down on the bedside table. "I done washed it for you this morning and she's all clean and smelling like a rose. I must a knowed you was gonna need her."

As Monette hugged the doll, Mammy pulled the rocking chair to the side of the bed, telling the child to go ahead and eat, no sense being shy, that she was no doubt hungry as a gator.

Mammy watched Monette, her delicate fingers sifting through the berries to find just the right one, her fingertips and mouth stained with pink, the way she pretended to feed the doll. No doubt Monette was a strange child, strange as the color of her eyes. As the child sipped the milk and nibbled the cheese and bread like a tiny mouse, Mammy wondered about Monette. After all, she was a favorite subject around the servants' table in the kitchen whenever she was absent, a subject they engaged in often, for, excepting the first week or so since she'd come to live at Fox Creek, Monette had rarely, if ever, taken her meals with the domestic servants. Instead, she went on picnics with Kate. Or simply folded the food into a cloth before exiting the kitchen, saying only, *Merci*. Leaving behind not only her absence, but the whisper of speculation.

"Likely the chile of some colored concubine. White mens, they likes a little chocolate stirred in their milk now and then."

"Ain't that the truth. But after they gets their fill, well then, they cast them off like they's a dirty old smelly shirt or something."

"Maybe she the daughter of one of them fancy French quadroons what goes to them balls and everything. Maybe she ain't got no daddy."

"Naw, she too dark-colored to be a daughter of no quadroon. She half and half."

"'Sides, every chile got a daddy."

"Maybe her daddy's black as night, and her momma's a quadroon. Ever think of that?"

"Naw, quadroons hates us black folk. Thinks they's too good for us."

"The way I sees it, it don't matter none who her momma or daddy is, 'cause she done been sold. She one of us now. And that's that. There ain't no going back for her, like there ain't no going back for any of us. When you's sold, you's sold. And that's that. It's plain as cotton that she ain't never been no slave before, neither."

"Yep, that's for true. Yep. You got that right."

"I can count on two fingers how many times she done eat her meals with us."

"Why, just the other day, I seen her eating in that playhouse of Missie Kate's. She and Missie Kate, they was giggling something awful."

"Why, fact of the matter is, she act just like she got white skin like Missie Kate. She act like she done had tea parties ever' day since she was borned."

"It gonna be a hard day when she finds out she ain't white."

"Yes'm. You said that right. A hard day, yes'm, a terrible hard day."

Mammy Hester was startled to realize Monette was looking at her. That she'd pushed away the tray and now sat with her back against the headboard, holding her doll. Mammy stirred, wondering if she'd dozed off, realizing she was stiff from sitting. It never took long anymore for her bones to stiffen. "What you say, chile?"

"What happened to me?"

"What does you mean?"

"Why does my head hurt? Who was kicking me? *S'il vous plaît*, why am I here in this room? Where's Kate?" As the girl spoke, her lower lip began to tremble and two great tears gathered, one in each eye like dewdrops.

The old woman sighed, remembering. She'd been tidying Mr. Gilbert's room when all hell broke loose. Down she'd run into a melee of screams, white faces, and porcelain shards. On the floor lay Monette, senseless.

Of course, it was Ole Miss Mehitable, a bad-tempered biddy whom all the servants despised. A woman who did nothing but whine about her ailments while spying through the house with the agility and silence of a cat, using her cane only when it suited her. Mammy Hester pursed her mouth, remembering how it was. When Miss Sarah bent to care for Monette, Ole Miss Mehitable put her handkerchief to her forehead and cried, "Land sakes! I believe I'm about to faint!" Immediately, all rushed to hold the woman up, and Miss Sarah ordered that she be whisked off to bed. Three servants were set to fanning her while another massaged her feet and another rubbed her temples. When finally, finally! Mammy Hester finished tending Ole Miss, she returned to the pantry. There lay the child.

Mammy Hester scarcely noticed Missie Kate, huddled in the corner of the pantry, ashen-faced and crying. She should have noticed, but didn't. Not then. With all the strength she could muster, Mammy picked Monette up and carried her up two flights of stairs to her attic room. She could not have done it had Monette weighed anything more than a sparrow's wing.

"Why, it was Ole Miss what done hit you, Ole Miss Mehitable. She clobbered you with her cane. That woman, she sure do like to use that cane. I been clobbered with it once or twice myself. She said you was eating and drinking like you owned the place or something."

Monette said nothing, looking puzzled.

So, thought Mammy Hester, the terrible, hard day had finally come. The day when the child realized that her skin was as brown as the rest of theirs. A lighter shade, to be true, but still, in a world of whites, black was black and white was white. Perhaps it was just as well the child was beaten. Perhaps some good could come of it after all—an understanding of her place in the world before it came to trouble. Oh, lordy yes, to not know your place in the world was like thinking you were a dog with wings. Sooner or later, you'd jump off the cliff thinking you could fly. "Listen, chile. This don't got to happen no more if you follows the rules. Know what I mean? I tells you the truth now, you gots to learn your place."

Still, she said nothing, so Mammy Hester continued. "See now, Monette, we all gots to learn our place sooner or later. The sooner you learn your place, the sooner you's a lot happier. You see, I's happy 'cause I knows my place and besides, I—I puts my trust in the good Lord. He knows all what I'm thinking and everything. If I gets sorrowful thinking maybe life is unfair or some such, I knows that the sweet Lord above understands. You see what I'm saying, chile?"

Still Monette looked puzzled.

Mammy scooted her rocking chair closer and leaned forward. The chair creaked, legs touching the bed's frame. The candle flame flickered, and part of the wick dropped, sizzling into the molten wax. "Now gimme your arm. I's gonna show you." She took the child's proffered arm and inched up the sleeve, doing the same to her own. She then held her bare forearm next to Monette's. "See what I mean? We's both the same. We's both brown as maple syrup. I may be a tad darker, in fact a lot darker, but that don't—"

Here Monette surprised Mammy by pulling away, almost roughly, as if Mammy had just told her there was no such thing as Christmas or the baby Jesus or stars in the sky. Without taking her eyes from Mammy, Monette tugged her sleeve down until it once again covered her arm.

Mammy cleared her throat, ready to try again, thinking maybe it was because the candlelight was a little dim, or maybe she just hadn't explained it well enough.

But then Monette whispered in a voice so quiet Mammy had to strain to hear, "Where's my sister?"

"Who? What you mean to tell me you gots a sister?"

"Kate. Where's Kate?"

For a spell, Mammy Hester said nothing, too tired for this. Then she got up, knees complaining, and went to the washstand. She poured some water into the bowl, knowing the child was simply too young to understand, knowing that her terrible hard day was yet to come. Well, Mammy had done what she could. There were other things more important by far. Especially tonight.

Mammy washed her face and dried it with a towel, then dampened the towel and returned to wash Monette.

"Please, Mammy Hester, please tell me. Where's Kate? I want her."

The old woman sighed, dabbing the bruised face and easing up when Monette winced. "Well," she said slowly, wishing she could have kept it from her, at least until the morning, "it were a good thing Dr. John was done fetched. He and Miss Sarah, they's with Missie Kate now. They ain't left her side yet."

"But—but I want her. I—I miss her." Again, Monette's eyes welled with tears, as if she knew what Mammy was about to say. "I want to sleep next to her. *Please.*"

"I'm telling you now, you can't. She gots the yellow fever, and you's gonna stay away from her. Fact is, I need to check in on them again. Should have done that a while back. They's gonna be wondering where I run off to." Mammy stood, trying not to think of the long night ahead and the dread possibilities. After returning the towel to the dresser and pausing to straighten her turban in the mirror, she kissed Monette on the cheek, told her to be a good girl now, replaced the mosquito net, took the candle, and left.

# Chapter 8

STAY AWAY. DON'T GO in there. Miss Kate is very sick, they always said.

For days Monette fled whenever Miss Mehitable lumbered up the stairs, her cane pounding each step like cracks of thunder. Cloaked in a darkened corner of the guestroom, hugging her rag doll, Monette watched as the door to Kate's room opened and closed. Opened and closed.

One time, she darted out from her hiding place and grabbed the skirts of Miss Sarah as she passed by. "*Pardon, Madame* Sarah, may I see Kate?"

Miss Sarah looked down, her eyes focused elsewhere, as she said, "Not now. Be a good girl and leave us to do our work." Monette glimpsed a curtain of yellowed gauze flickering in the dull candlelight before the door pulled closed on Kate's room, leaving a sour smell in her nostrils that lingered even after she climbed into bed that night with Mammy Hester.

On the morning of Baby Betsy and Cousin Cordelia's funerals, Monette took her doll and left the big house, forgetting her bonnet, forgetting even to watch for Ole Miss Mehitable. She ran through the ornamental gardens and under the canopy of trees that dotted the vast lawn. She paralleled the creek for a spell before finding the tunnel of bushes. As she crawled through, she was aware of the panting of her breath, the skittering of her heart. Parting the curtain of Spanish moss, she stepped into the glade, their secret spot. They had not been there since the morning she'd been beaten by Ole Miss, since Kate had fallen ill. It seemed impossible that it had remained untouched, ruffled in their absence only by the breeze and birds and insects as they caressed the flowers and sighed from branch to branch. Monette longed to lie beneath the magnolia, to recapture the memories when all was secure and secret, when the pink blossoms overhead were filled with fairies and princesses and treasures, but there was not much time.

She set aside her doll, and after picking a sufficient number of flowers, settled herself and began to weave the blossoms together, working quickly, soon enveloped in a sweet, bruised fragrance. She knew it was messy, that some of the flowers didn't fare well against such handling, but it would have to do. When she was finished, she gathered the chains together, fetched her doll like an afterthought, and sped back toward the big house.

She hid behind a tree, watching as they climbed into the carriage, stiffly attired in black, silent except for the clothing that crackled and swished. She waited until the reins snapped, until the glossy black carriage lurched forward to the clip-clop of hooves, rumbling down the drive, until it disappeared under the dappled shadows of the trees.

In the big house, all was silent. Listening almost. To the slightest creak, to the glide of Monette's slippers as she pressed each stair, to the shiver of her breath. She grasped the knob to Kate's bedroom, opened the door, and entered.

No longer the bright, pink room she remembered—gay light streaming through the windows, the orange glow of a fire banked in the fireplace—it was now as if the room itself was spent, dying. Gray shadows hovered like ghosts, seeping around the four-poster bed and under the shuttered, curtained windows. In a chair beside the bed sat Miss Sarah, dressed in black, hands clasped over the swell of her belly. Her head lay back, her lips slightly parted, and Monette heard the slow, deep breathing of sleep. Although her auburn hair was pinned in place, her clothes neatly pressed, Monette sensed the dishevelment. The despair.

*My mother. Ma chère maman . . .*

Monette had heard all the arguments—everyone trying to persuade Miss Sarah not to enter Kate's room, saying who knew what deleterious effects Kate's illness might have upon Miss Sarah's unborn child, upon Miss Sarah herself. But she'd brushed everyone's arguments aside as if she were swiping crumbs off a table. "If it is Kate's time to go," she'd told them, "and I pray to God that it is not, then what kind of mother would I be if I let her pass from this world to the next without me by her side? My daughter needs me, and so I will go."

Monette tiptoed toward the bed, trying not to wake Miss Sarah, not wishing to be chased from the room in what might be her only chance to see Kate.

*My sister needs me, and so I will go.*

An image came unbidden. A body laid out. A halo of candles. The stench of greenhouse roses. A cold, hard hand. Gold coins instead of eyes. Monette gasped for breath, panicking, almost fleeing the room as a wave of sickness washed over her. She swallowed hard, her throat dry, and then focused her eyes on Kate, forcing the memory, the dream—whatever it was—away, away. . . .

Kate lay on her side beneath the *moustiquaire;* and it was only as Monette lifted the gauze and slipped beneath it that she heard Kate's shallow breathing and saw her eyelids flutter. Monette was frightened. The yellow skin. The heat that radiated from Kate. The sour stench. The faint odor of onion. The tiny flecks of black that spattered the pillowcase. Her beautiful hair, once so long and lustrous, now cropped just beneath her ears. "Kate," she whispered.

She called her name again, louder.

With a moan, Kate flung her arms about and rolled onto her back, still sleeping. Monette glanced at Miss Sarah, relieved to see she had not moved.

"Kate."

When again Kate did not rouse, Monette began to drape her with flowers—blossom chains of lemon yellow, royal purple, and sunset pink. The necklaces were especially difficult to place because she had to lift Kate's head without further damaging the delicate blooms. Petals blossomed around Kate's wrists, atop her forehead like a crown. Then Monette took the red flannel *gris-gris* from around her neck, where it had lain for as long as she could remember, as familiar to her as her heart, and placed it around Kate's neck, kissing the small pouch goodbye. She kissed Kate's cheek too—a cheek iron-fevered and dry as cinder. Finally, she placed her doll under Kate's arm before sitting back on the bed, gazing at her handiwork.

I have brought you bits of treasure—treasure from our secret spot. *Gris-gris* to keep you safe, to make you well. A doll so you will not be lonely. When you awaken, you will know I have been here.

Then, glancing toward where Miss Sarah yet slumbered in her chair, unmoving save for the rise and fall of her breath, Monette lay next to Kate, resting her head on the pillow. For a long time, Monette stroked Kate's hair, brushing sodden strands from her face. As she did so, a love filled Monette, swelling inside her with the sweetness of a lullaby. It was a simple love, a child's love, asking for nothing save to continue loving.

*"Je t'adore,"* she whispered. "Please do not die."

—— *ell* ——

Sarah had not meant to fall asleep, but her exhaustion pressed her head to the back of the chair, and before she knew it, she was awakening—lethargic, her head filled with cobwebs.

In the deepening gloom, she saw them. Hands clasped, face-to-face, both of them slept beneath the mosquito net. Sarah glimpsed the faded bruising on the tiny servant's cheek, the flowers clustered over and around Kate as if she were a princess on a funeral pyre, their vibrant colors belying the dullness of the room, the yellow pallor of her daughter's skin. She frowned, seeing what looked to be a *gris-gris* containing God-knows-what, and a rag doll that Sarah had more than once thrown in the trash.

Sarah fetched the pan of vinegar water and the bottle of niter. Sighing, careful not to awaken either of them, she moved aside the netting, the sheet, the nightclothes, the doll, the flowers, cutting away the *gris-gris*—intending to burn it later, as was prudent—and sponged the sick child.

As she did, tears began to fall unbidden. Into the pan of water. Onto Kate's bare skin. Onto her own hands, frail with worry. For in that moment, Sarah knew: Kate would live. Her fever had broken, and she was sweating.

—— *ell* ——

A sliver of moonlight filtered through the window glass. At first, Monette was confused, wondering where she was, while fragments of her day pieced themselves together like the remnants of a quilt. Kate dying . . . the chains of flowers . . . the *gris-gris* . . .

Monette rolled over. Beside her, Kate lay on her back, sleeping. Monette knew, as surely as she knew whether it was light or dark or sunny or raining, that the spirit of sickness had left Kate.

Monette lay there for a while, not yet fully awake, watching her friend sleep, hearing her breath slide in and out of her mending body, a quiet sound like the swish of silk. Though she should have been ecstatic that Kate was not going to die, she still felt uneasy, as if only part of a story had been told and the ending remained obscure—an ending she did not want to hear. Her unease did not come from Miss Sarah, for the chair was empty, swathed in the silver of moon dust.

*Look...*

The word seeped into the night air as if whispered by a ghost. The air felt suddenly alive, aware, filled with not only the heat of the night but also with a vibrational pulse that caused Monette to sit up, wide awake and listening, blood quickening.

*Mwana na mono, my daughter...*

*Tala!... Look!...*

Again, she peered at Kate's sleeping form. Now she understood her unease. The flowers she had so carefully arrayed around Kate were gone. And the *gris-gris*—where was her *gris-gris?* Her doll? Monette knew, even before she searched the bed, that they too were gone.

It was then that Monette both smelled and saw the fire—or rather, what was left of it. The tang of smoke. The faint glow of a few pebble-sized embers. She slipped out from beneath the *moustiquaire* and crossed the room, dropping to her knees before the fireplace. The hearth bricks pressed into her knees, rough, faintly warm. She heard her own breath, frantic, heard herself whimpering. She stabbed the ashes with the poker, holding it with both hands, for it was heavy. Then she found something. Dangling on the end of the poker like the flag of a ragtag army, was a shred of fabric. Even before holding it up to the moonlight, Monette knew what it was—the surviving remnant from her doll's apron.

Upon realizing that her doll had perished in the fire, consumed by flames while Monette had slept peacefully just feet away, the emptiness inside her split open again, unbidden. Pain clawed out of the chasm like a demon released, piercing her heart with its talons and paralyzing her lungs so that she choked, a sob catching in her throat.

*Look...*

Again, that whisper. This time, it seemed not a ghostly whisper reverberating through the air, but one emanating from the chasm within—from the emptiness that both spoke and seared.

*Look . . .*

She took the poker and spread the ashes. There, against the back bricks of the fireplace, a cord peeped out from under the ashes. She leaned over the old fire—sooty now from head to toe—and pulled it out. It was her *gris-gris* bag, surprisingly intact and unharmed. She dusted it off, untied it, and withdrew the contents, placing them one by one onto the hearth bricks—knowing what was inside, but needing to check anyway. There was her red agate. The braid of sweetgrass, smelling not of ashes or smoke but of vanilla. The bone, half as long as a chicken drumstick, bleached a silvery-white, smooth and oddly comforting. A green Y-shaped stick. A plait of black hair, stiff and wiry—as familiar to her as her own hair. And, in the bottom of the bag, the salt and pepper, which she kneaded through the fabric to assure herself the lucky grains were still there.

She dropped the items back into the flannel and cinched it shut. Draping it about her neck, she felt a profound relief as the bag settled against her chest—a piece of her returned, retrieved as if from the bottom of a well of darkness.

The twin boys were born on the third day of December, a clear, frosty day that put an end to yellow fever. Delivered by old Dr. Smith from St. Marysville (who, in Dr. John's opinion, could hardly see the end of his nose, much less a pair of forceps) and arriving nearly three weeks premature, the twins were nevertheless good-sized babies, robust and pink, each with the requisite ten fingers and ten toes.

The parish of West Feliciana, finally relieved of constant illness, erupted into a flurry of visiting. Fox Creek Plantation was a favorite destination on Saturday nights, where fox hunts were rewarded afterward with a hushed glimpse into the big house and the sight of two identical sleeping babes, and where the negro dances—a fiddling flurry of calico and hobnailed shoes—lasted far into the night.

Sarah had never been happier. They had lost only four negroes during the season of sickness, a paltry number compared to some plantations, which had lost upwards of twenty or thirty hands. Her husband had fully recovered from swamp fever. The children's lessons had resumed with both Mr. Gilbert and Monsieur Déclouet. Kate had regained her health. And the twins were a delight.

As for herself, Sarah was finally relieved of the nagging dread of childbirth. The births had been fairly straightforward, and she laughed now, knowing she had worried needlessly. Of course, everything would be fine. Sarah felt her strength returning sooner than it had with either Breck or Kate, so she surprised everyone by creeping down the stairs and into the parlor on Christmas morning.

"Mama!" shrieked Kate.

Breck smiled and said, "We have presents for you."

Mammy Hester, Sarah's co-conspirator, beamed and fussed, ordering her directly into one of the cushioned chairs and propping up her feet.

The tree looked so festive, with candles, ribbons, strings of popped corn, and—beneath the tree—there were gifts for everyone. A silver brush, comb, and mirror for Kate. A fancy writing box for Breck, with pens, paper, and ink. A cut-glass bottle of perfume for Mehitable and a powder compact for Emma. A pair of pantaloons for William, and a new beaver hat and scarf for John. Sarah received new kid gloves from William, plus two new chemises, nicely trimmed by Emma. So many gifts!

They gathered around the piano and sang carols while Emma stumbled through the chords, and everyone pretended not to hear the mistakes. Afterward, Sarah played her mandolin and then read the story of Christmas from the Gospel of Luke. While she read, the household servants gathered, listening, reminding her of her neglected duties with regard to their religious education. Then and there, she promised to do better. Come the New Year.

A week before Christmas, William had asked every negro on the plantation what they wanted, jotting down their requests. Later that week, he drove the wagon to St. Marysville and filled the order. So, just before Sarah's strength gave out on Christmas Day, she hobbled to the gallery. All the negroes were gathered on the front drive, dressed in their finest. Together with William, she handed out their gifts: pipes, chewing tobacco, colorful turbans, handkerchiefs, hats, slippers. One by one, they came forward—curtsying, or removing their caps—saying, "Thank you, Mars William. Thank you, Miss Sarah. Merry Christmas to you."

It gratified Sarah to hear their exclamations as they unwrapped their gifts. As a final gift to them, the twins were presented.

"This is George William Jensey, named after Miss Sarah's father and myself." William held up the eldest infant, who was older by twenty minutes. "You may call him Master George." Then, holding the youngest, he said, "And this is Thomas Jefferson Jensey. You may call him Master Thomas."

Sarah couldn't help the pride that filled her heart. She looked out over the negroes and saw the same pride reflected on their faces.

"Merry Christmas, Mars George. Merry Christmas, Mars Thomas," they said, smiling.

By the time Sarah returned to bed, her legs trembled and her heart pounded with weakness. But it was worth it, she thought. Such a happy day. In spite of all our difficulties this year, God has truly blessed us. Outside, she could hear the final preparations for the Christmas feast they gave every year to the negroes. She knew that once they'd eaten their fill of puddings, hams, chickens, jellies, and breads, they would meander to their newly completed dance hall and dance until the New Year dawned. She slept to the scent of sandalwood, left burning in the brazier.

When her one-month convalescence was finally at an end, Sarah was ready. It was hog-killing time, and, together with Emma and Mehitable, she supervised the butchering and rendering of one hundred fifty-seven hogs. In early October, she'd sent ten boys to the swamps to run out the hogs. After two rainy, muggy days of running and squealing, the hogs were finally corralled into pens, where they were fattened on corn. Now, she ordered the carcasses cut into hams, shoulders, and jowls, separating the prime sections. She supervised the making of sausages. Salt and lard caked her hands. Smoke poured from the smokehouse, permeating her clothes and hair.

"You're working too hard too soon," warned Emma.

But Sarah shrugged her off. For the first time in months, she felt exhilarated. Alive. She was blessed, and she knew it. She poured herself into her work. Making brushes from hog bristles. Soap from lard and lye. She ordered barrels of lard stored beneath the earth to prevent the lard from turning rancid. Once the hog-killing season ended, Emma, perhaps sensing that her daughter had mended both body and spirit, returned to her own plantation at Woodleigh amid showers of thanks and farewells.

During this time in early January 1844, Sarah finally threw her daughter a party—a long-overdue celebration of Kate's eighth birthday, a day that had come and gone with scarcely a kiss or hug during the height of fever season the previous September. With Kate's illness, the pregnancy, and the arrival of the twins, time had simply gotten away from Sarah. In preparation, Sarah drew Kate aside and told her to write a list of all the girls in the parish whom she wished to invite to her party. There would be a giant, frosted pink cake, games to play, and ponies to ride.

Later, Kate handed her the list. Looking at it, Sarah sighed. Dear, dear Katherine.

Eighteen names straggled across the paper in a blotchy, crooked line. Kate didn't seem to realize anything was amiss and smiled up at her, ink smudged on her lower lip.

"There's only one thing wrong, dear Katherine," Sarah said gently.

"What?"

"I'm afraid Monette cannot be a guest at your party."

Kate chewed her lower lip, regarding her with those beautiful green eyes that so often turned impish. "Why not?"

They had been standing in the parlor, but now Sarah sat on the sofa and patted the cushion beside her. Kate sat, a perfect picture, Sarah thought, of loveliness. Though she no longer had flowing hair past her waist, her short curls framed her face, adding a rounded softness to her features. Her summer freckles had faded, and now her skin was as porcelain-fine as Sarah wished it to be.

"You see, Katherine, Monette is not like your other friends. It wouldn't be appropriate to have them all together."

"But why?"

"Monette is of African descent. While it's fine for you to be friends if no one else is around, when your other friends come to visit, Monette must know her position in the household. She must act like a servant. She *is* a servant."

Kate's forehead creased, and Sarah knew she was thinking hard.

"But she is my friend. My best friend."

Sarah smiled and patted Kate's knee. "Of course, she is your friend. Your very dear friend, one who helped you recover from Yellow Jack, and for that I will always be grateful." Sarah paused. How could she explain this? "Mammy Hester is my friend, too. She's been with me for as long as I can remember, and I love her dearly. I can't imagine life without her. But even so, you must never allow the servants to forget their place. They are negroid and you are white. While they can be your friends, they can never be your equal. Do you understand?"

"But why?"

"Why? Because it has been ordained by God, that's why. Oh, dear Katherine, how can I explain to you the wisdom of the Lord? Only that He is wise and wonderful, and so good to me. You must trust me in this, Katherine. I have given it much thought and prayer. You see, the African race is weaker than the white race. They cannot help being weaker—it is simply the way God made them. God has placed them in our hands to—to guide them through life. It is our responsibility to care for them: to clothe them, feed them, and—and house them. We must do our duty as sons and daughters of God to provide for all their needs, both physical and spiritual. That way, we may all stand blameless before God on Judgment Day."

The child said nothing, and for a while, Sarah was content to let it be—to enjoy a spell during which her daughter was thoughtful and quiet, instead of thoughtless and boisterous. Sarah hoped it was a portent of life to come—joyful years of training her daughter in plantation management: shared threads of needlework while they discussed the food stores, the servants, the supply of candles . . . It was the domestic realm of womanhood, and Sarah longed to share it with Kate.

"Can Monette still have a piece of birthday cake?"

Sarah laughed. "Of course. As long as you understand that Monette is a servant. She is there to serve you and your friends. Do you understand what I'm trying to tell you?"

When Kate nodded and said, "Yes, Mama, I think so," Sarah held her daughter close. It was not an easy lesson, she knew. For some children, it came more naturally than others. But it was an important lesson—one in which Sarah would be remiss not to instruct her children. Ever since they'd purchased Monette, Sarah knew she'd been entirely too lax in her duties as mistress. It had been too easy to allow the girls an intimate, unsupervised friendship. Now, it was time. Then and there, Sarah resolved to attend to Monette's training as a household servant—for Kate's benefit as much as for Monette's. Yes, it was time.

# Chapter 9

THE JUNE DAY WAS unpleasant, the moist heat rising in sultry waves. Sweat trickled down Breck's chest. Beneath him, his saddle cooked his backside, and his pants were damp. He pulled the brim of his hat lower, cutting the glare of the sun.

He knew he looked like his father: both tall, both steady in the saddle, both wearing identical broad-brimmed leather hats. Ever since Breck could remember, whenever his father went to the fields or went hunting, he always wore his leather hat, a hat stained with tobacco, tree sap, and gun grease. Last winter, at Coleporter's Mercantile in St. Marysville, William had purchased a smaller version for Breck, new and stiff and smelling of cowhide. He'd slapped it on Breck's head, peered under the brim, and said, "How's that fit?" Now, Breck sensed the glances cast in their direction. He could almost hear the talk: There goes Mars William and Mars Breck again. Ain't they a sight.

As soon as William had regained his health last autumn, Breck had begun accompanying his father into the fields. Once a week, Breck's afternoon lessons were cut short, and he walked out the rear loggia to meet his father, standing with two horses saddled. Breck no longer rode a pony. "In another year, you'll be as tall as your mother," his father had told him last Christmas. "It's time you rode a horse." So, Breck's pony had been replaced.

His new hat, his new horse, his height—he donned them all, wore them like a badge, a badge of identity that said:

You are William's son.

Then there was talk of buying Breck a rifle. A rifle he could take with him to the fields, and use to shoot small game. "Next Christmas," William promised. "When you're big enough so you don't shoot off your toes."

Already this afternoon, they'd stopped at the jail, still under construction. While William talked with the carpenter, Obediah, in low tones, while motes of sawdust floated lazily in the thick air, Breck inspected the jail like his father had told him to. Not really knowing what he was looking for, he nonetheless rapped the walls with his knuckles and peered under the building to check the supports. After the jail, they rode to the blacksmith's shop and checked the progress on the leg irons. The shop was swelteringly hot, the glowing forge seeming to utilize all breathable air, leaving nothing but a choking mass of wood smoke, hot iron, and sweat. Breck was relieved when they finally rode out to the cotton fields.

Feeling his horse move beneath him in sure, easy strides, Breck felt ill. Again. It seemed to come more often now, a vague tightness that lodged in the base of Breck's stomach every time he accompanied his father to the fields. Breck rode beside him, wondering. Was it the heat?

Far ahead, the mule team and plow scraped the row, throwing the dirt away from the cotton plants and into the furrow. Following the plow, a line of hoes flashed with sunlight, chopping in tandem to the pulse of their song: *Green Sally up, Green Sally down, Lift and squat, gotta tear the ground . . ."*

His father gestured toward the workers. "Tell me why the cotton isn't harmed when the plow scrapes the dirt away from the sides of the ridge."

"Because the roots of the cotton grow down, not sideways."

"Why do we scrape the dirt from the sides?"

"To expose the roots of the grasses, to make it easier to chop."

"What do we do when we're finished chopping?"

"Push the dirt back where it was, leaving a furrow."

"And then?"

"Start again."

"Why?"

"Because by the time we're done, the grasses have grown back."

Breck didn't understand why his father looked amused. He only knew they were the same questions, again and again. It had been this way for months now, and Breck was weary of it. He disliked having to leave his lessons to roam the fields, where it was hot, where the rows of cotton and work to be done never ended, where he grew thirsty, hungry, catching only an occasional glimpse of Cyrus. He'd rather be reading, studying with Mr. Gilbert, dancing with Monette, or rafting the creek with Footy. But he knew better than to voice such an opinion to his father, and so stayed silent.

Soon, one of the men from the hoe gang approached them. It was Quincy, the head driver. Breck was accustomed to listening as William and Quincy discussed which field needed hoeing, which field needed clearing, and which worker was acting up. Today, Breck could tell by the rigid walk of Quincy that it was the latter. His stomach tightened.

"Problem, Quincy?" asked William, reining his horse to a halt.

"Yessir, Mars William." Quincy removed his hat and stood at the shoulder of William's horse. He stared at the ground, crushing his hat in his hands as he spoke. He was a tall, spare man, with a broad forehead and a long nose.

Breck liked Quincy. From what he had seen, the man seemed to be honest and hardworking.

"It that new darky, Sawney," Quincy was saying. "That one you bought a few weeks ago at that Blackstone auction over in Jacksonville."

"I know who he is, Quincy. Tell me what he did." William leaned an arm on his saddle horn. Curled around the saddle horn was the whip William always carried. It was a part of his saddle. A part of his horse.

There were odd moments, moments of mingled clarity and confusion, in which Breck was shocked to realize that he really didn't know his father. That this man who leaned forward in his saddle, who squinted under the shadow of his hat brim, who had, in times past, proclaimed beauty in the colors of a butterfly's wings or in a sunset, was, in fact, a stranger, as if Breck was seeing him, once again, for the first time. Breck looked away.

"He refused to hoe 'longside the rest of us, saying he knowed how to do his job and everything, and to just leave him be and he gonna show me what he means. But I can't allow that 'cause then everyone will want to just get left alone, and then what do I got?"

William said nothing.

"You see, Mars William, it like this. Sawney, he do that on purpose. He know I can't allow no such thing like a field hand working by theyselves when they's supposed to be on a hoe gang, and so I told him to go to the post for a whipping, that as soon as you comes to the field, you's gonna show him who's boss. But he just keep on chopping like he don't hear me none, and so I says it again, only louder. Then he says for me to go to hell. And—"

"Where is he now?" William interrupted.

Quincy pointed. "Over there yonder."

Away in the distance, Breck saw a solitary figure, hoeing.

"Son, follow me." In a second, William was galloping his horse across the field, clods of dirt flying behind him.

Twenty seconds later, Breck reined to a halt beside his father. The field hand faced them, leaning on his hoe. He was in his mid-twenties, by Breck's guess, lighter-colored than most of the field hands, of average height and medium build. An old scar, shaped like a half moon, cut through one of his eyebrows. He wore the usual clothing of a male field hand: linen pantaloons, a straw hat, and a coarse linen shirt. The shirt was dark with sweat and open to the waist.

"What's the problem, Sawney?"

"Ain't no problem, Mars William. Ain't no problem at all. 'Cepting that driver of yours gots some ill will towards me."

"That so?" William turned in his saddle, whistled, and motioned Quincy from across the field to come over. "How about we just wait until Quincy says his piece? Then you can say yours."

Even though Sawney's head was lowered, his eyes cast downward, Breck sensed the tension in the man's body. The rippling jaw. The quickened breath. The hands gripping the hoe with a force sure to snap the handle in two. He wondered if Sawney had that same queasy tightness—as if someone had hold of his middles.

It seemed forever before Quincy stood before them, repeating what he'd said before: ". . . and then I told him to get hisself to the whipping post, and he told me to go to hell."

"Sawney, did you refuse to go to the post?"

"No sir, I mean, yessir, but there's a reason for that. You see, Mars Blackstone, he allowed me to work on my own, see, and he don't bother me none—"

"This isn't the Blackstone Plantation," said William.

"Yessir, I know that, Mars William, but I—"

"Hoe gangs have to follow the scraper. Makes the work go faster. Working by yourself doesn't accomplish as much."

"Yessir, you's right about that, Mars William, but I—"

"Every hand follows the orders of the driver, or else there's a whipping. Every hand knows the rules."

At that, Sawney raised his head and looked William full in the eye. "Mars William, you said I could say my piece."

Breck saw his father's jaw tighten, and his plain brown eyes narrowed.

For a long while, no one spoke, and Breck became aware that the mule team no longer pulled the plow, that everyone in the field had stopped hoeing, and that the rhythmic pulse of their work song had petered into silence.

"Don't really matter none, does it," said Sawney finally, still staring at William, "'cause you's gonna whip me no matter what I says. Ain't that right?"

It was then that Breck saw the hatred. It roiled from Sawney like the effluvia from the swamps. Stifling, poisonous. Breck's heart began to beat wildly. From his side vision, he saw Quincy move away slowly, one foot behind the other.

William grabbed his whip and urged his horse closer to Sawney.

Sawney backed up, holding his hoe like a weapon.

William bellowed, "Sawney, get down on the ground and receive your whipping!"

"No sir, I will not!"

Before Breck knew what was happening, the hoe flashed through the air like an axe, missing William's head by an inch.

In an instant, the tail of the whip snapped through the air, and Sawney was running—down the furrow, darting between cotton plants and down the next furrow, William on his horse thundering after him.

Breck saw the gleam of his father's rifle. He heard the crack of its discharge as Sawney stumbled and fell in a cloud of dust. Even from where he sat, Breck saw the stain on Sawney's thigh.

Then his father was back beside him, breathing hard. "Quincy," he ordered, "have some of the boys carry him to the hospital. Fetch Miss Sarah and have her meet you there."

"Yessir, Mars William." Quincy left, and Breck heard the driver giving orders, telling the boys to move Sawney to the hospital. To go easy now—they didn't want to hurt him no more than he already was.

William removed his hat and mopped his brow with his sleeve. "You all right, Son?"

Breck tried to answer. To say, Yessir. But his mouth wouldn't work. No sound issued. Then, as if he watched from a distance, as if it were not really happening to himself but to someone else, Breck burst into tears.

With his boots and stockings scattered across the master bedroom where he had thrown them, William sank back into his chair. He closed his eyes, allowing himself to feel a brief comfort in the touch of his wife. Sarah knelt at his feet, rubbing first one foot, then the other. Her touch was tender, yet strong—enough to make him almost forget the events of the day. Almost.

"Damn that Sawney. If he hadn't of run, I wouldn't have shot him."

"Hush, William. It's over. No sense getting upset again."

"I hate it when they run, Sarah. I'd rather they do anything but run."

"I know, I know."

William brooded, wincing when she rubbed a sore spot on his heel. "Will he live?" he asked for the third time, knowing he'd asked before, knowing the answer.

"Yes, he'll live."

"Should have aimed higher."

"Stop it, William."

"Next time, I'll kill him."

"Next time, you'll do nothing of the sort."

"Hell if I won't."

Sarah frowned, and William noticed an escaped wisp of hair curling against the side of her neck beneath her ear, an auburn tendril against creamy porcelain. "We can't afford to waste a thousand dollars every time someone turns tail and runs," she was saying. "Besides, he's a human being—"

"Human being be damned. He's a damned black rascal, is what he is."

A smile played on her lips. "You sound like your mother."

William scowled. He was nothing like his mother. He was everything like his father. Everything.

"Well, supposing you did shoot to kill, that would make you worse than Capt. Cobb, because at least you know better."

Everyone agreed Captain Morton Cobb was the meanest man in the vicinity, certainly the meanest man William had ever known. Cruel, heartless, Capt. Cobb didn't half feed his negroes, and then worked them almost to death besides. Last month, he'd castrated three of his males and flayed the skin off the backs of several of the women, one of whom died the following day. Even though the jury acquitted, the whole parish knew Cobb was guilty. "Capt. Cobb is a scamp. Next time he shows his face around here, I'm going to make him see stars, and I'll be damned if I'm worse than he is. He has no justice about him. He's cruel because he likes to be."

She said nothing, bending her head over his feet, the tendril of hair tickling the top of his foot.

He watched her a while before saying, "Breck disappointed me today."

"So you've told me."

His fingers drummed on the arm of the chair. The sight of Breck sitting on his horse, bawling his eyes out, was enough to infuriate any father. Good God! As if he didn't have enough to worry about without his son turning into some mewling woman. "I'm taking him on my next hunt for runaways."

Sarah looked up, surprised. "Don't you think he's a little young?"

"He's ten. He's old enough. Or he'll be old enough by the time I'm through with him. I started when I was ten, and I was more than ready."

"William, please—"

"Hush, woman," he said, more sharply than he intended. A bruised look passed over her face, but he ignored it, sinking farther into the chair. It irritated him when Sarah argued about things she knew nothing about. What did she know of hunting for runaways? What did she know about a boy growing to manhood? Of keeping one hundred and fifty-odd people housed, fed, clothed, and productive? "I'm taking Breck to town tomorrow. It's time he had a rifle of his own."

"Why do you push him so hard? He's just a boy."

Wrenching his foot away from her grasp, he sat up, exasperated. "Good God, woman! How old was I when my father took ill and could no longer run the plantation? I'll tell you how old I was. I was eighteen. Eighteen years old, by God! If my father hadn't taken the time to teach me everything he knew, we'd have lost the place. By the time I was eighteen, I knew more about running the plantation than most men twice my age. That kind of knowledge doesn't happen by accident."

He continued when she said nothing. "Every afternoon, from the time I was Breck's age, I was beside him in the fields. Why do you think we do so well compared to some of our neighbors? It's because I know what I'm doing. It's because I refuse to hire a damned overseer. It's because when there's trouble in the fields, I handle it myself. It's because the negroes know where they stand with me. They know exactly what's expected." He softened his voice when he saw her face. Downcast eyes. Thick, dark lashes against her cheeks. Trembling mouth. She always did that to him. "I want the same for our son, Sarah. I want Breck to be able to take care of you so that if I—"

In a whisper of petticoats, she was beside him, wrapping her arms about his neck. He breathed the lilac on her skin. She was his tonic. His elixir. His cure for every hurt imaginable.

"I'm sorry, William. I didn't mean to upset you. I just don't want to see him hurt."

William pressed her against him. "I'll make sure he doesn't get hurt. I love him too, dear wife. I love him too."

In the adjacent room, Breck lay atop his bed, staring woodenly at the canopy. He heard no more of their argument. All was silent, except for downstairs where the servants prepared the dining room for supper. There was the clank of dishes, the clink of silver. He knew he would not eat tonight. Could not eat. Could not sit at the same table as his father and endure his scrutiny.

He was ashamed, so ashamed.

Remembering what he did in the field. His father's horrified look that quickly melted into disgust. He'd handed Breck his handkerchief. Clean yourself up, he'd said, looking away. The tone of his voice said it all.

*Breck disappointed me today....*

## *Chapter 10*

Finally, the twins were asleep. Monette had fussed with them for hours, it seemed. No sooner would one fall asleep than the other would cry, and soon both would be squalling, their faces contorted with outrage. Desperate, ready to burst into tears of frustration and weariness, she'd fed them bits of sugar through the bars of the crib, then stuck a sugared finger in each of their mouths until they settled, suckled, and slept.

From the time the twins were six months of age, they had been moved from Sarah and William's bedroom into the only spare bedroom remaining in the big house. For the two months since, Monette had cared for them day and night. Sleeping in Kate's trundle bed, with the door separating the twins' room from Kate's wide open, she crept sleepily out of bed whenever they fussed.

"You's their little nurse," Mammy Hester had told her. "I's just your age when I starts to take care of little chilluns. Soon you's gonna be a mammy just like me. Chile, I tells you true, it am a privilege and a honor when white folks wants you to take care of their chilluns. Ain't nothing better. Lord a'mercy, mm-mm-mm, ain't nothing better than that."

But Monette didn't want to be a little nurse—especially to two squalling babies. Instead, she longed to slip out of the house with Kate and run to their secret place, to spend hours in their playhouse dressing each other's hair or gossiping about the neighborhood, to wrap her arms around Kate as they rode Tiptop through the fields and forest. But little Georgie and Thomas seemed to know when Monette stepped foot outside the big house, and the ruckus would begin. Always, Monette dashed back to the twins' room, her feet noiseless upon the steps, hurrying before Miss

Mehitable could rap her across the backside with her cane for neglecting the babes.

Now, Monette slowly withdrew her fingers from their mouths. She ignored the stink that hovered over their crib and left without glancing back. She crossed Kate's room, cast in the shadow of the August evening, and crept out onto the gallery, from where the murmur of voices and the tinkle of laughter had beckoned her all evening.

Fingers of light penetrated the woods as the sun sank into the arms of the distant pine forest like a weary lover, spent, ready for sleep. A breeze meandered through the chorus of crickets and the whirring of palmetto bugs, chasing the mosquitoes away, cooling the moisture on Monette's face, and whispering through the dampness of her dress.

Below the gallery, set in the ground about fifteen feet away from the big house, two torches snapped and burned, as smoke vanished upward into the gloaming. The torches drew the insects away, while lending a faint flickering light to the gallery.

The people on the gallery took no notice as Monette moved behind them, a shadow among shadows. The man named Marshall barked in laughter and blew a cloud of cigar smoke. Miss Mehitable's chin sagged on her chest, and Monette thought she heard a faint snore, which she knew, given time, would explode into a full-phlegmed gargle. Miss Sarah smiled at one of Marshall's jokes, while Mars William drew on his cigar before saying something in return that provoked another round of laughter. Breck sat beside his father, quiet as usual, his face cast in shadow, hands folded on his lap.

Monette slipped into the chair where Kate already sat, the chair amply sized for the two of them. She laid her head on Kate's shoulder.

"Oh, there you are," whispered Kate.

*"Oui. C'est moi."*

"Adults are so boring. Nothing they say is ever funny."

"I know. I am glad I am not an adult. Then I would have to be boring, too."

"Thirsty? You can have my lemonade."

Monette took the glass Kate offered her, cleaning the rim with her pinafore before drinking.

"Papa says I'm going to get a real horse someday, like Breck's. Maybe next year. But I don't want a real horse. I like my pony. I'm going to ride Tiptop until I'm as old as Grandma Mehitable. I love Tiptop."

"Me too. We will ride Tiptop forever."

"Papa says I'm a good horsewoman. He says I'm a natural, like him. My mother's not a natural. Papa says she sits on a horse like she's sitting on a cactus."

There was a burst of laughter again from the adults, and this time Monette heard the fleshy laughter of Miss Mehitable. "Land sakes," the woman was saying, her voice dull with sleep, "If that don't beat all!"

Kate sighed. "See what I mean? That wasn't funny at all. I never want to be an adult. Anyway, Mama says Frances Parsons is having a birthday party next week, and I'm invited. I'm sewing a sampler for her gift. Mama says Obediah will frame it for me if I ask him. It says, 'The Lord is my Shepherd.' That's a psalm. Mama says I'm getting skillful with the needle."

As the last trace of sun vanished in the forest, Monette remembered a day last winter—a day of pink cake and pink frosting. A day when, instead of sitting next to Kate and sharing it with her, she'd watched as a dining room filled with fresh-faced girls sang to Kate and gave her gifts, afterward devouring the cake that Monette had helped to frost. She recalled watching them as emptiness gnawed her from within—an emptiness having nothing to do with hunger, the chasm opening only barely before she slammed it shut. Instead, she endured their haughty glances, their mouths filled with pinkness, pretending she did not care, that she was one of them, giggling and chatting, too, despite the fact she'd had to clean up after them, eating her slice of cake long after the party was over.

"I wish I could have some *gâteau d'anniversaire* right now," she said with a sigh to Kate.

"Some what?"

"Birthday cake. You have forgotten your French!"

"Oh. Well, if Frances has any—any *gaddo de anniversary* left over, I'll wrap it up and bring it to you. If she asks me what I'm doing, I'll tell her it's a secret—hey, I know a secret. A *real* secret. Want to know what it is?"

Monette nodded. Like Kate, she loved secrets.

Kate cupped her hand around Monette's ear and whispered, "Grandma Mehitable doesn't wear any drawers."

In spite of her weariness, Monette giggled.

"And she has whiskers down there. I've seen them myself. All gray and ugly."

A wave of hilarity washed over Monette, and she clamped her hand over her mouth. Whiskers! Old woman whiskers! *Down there!*

"And guess what? When she goes to the privy, she passes gas. And not just a little gas, either. Loud, long, bubbly gas."

"*Pouah!* That is very nasty."

"It's true, I swear. I've heard her. Next time I'll take you with me and we'll hear her together."

While the girls stifled their giggles, Sarah listened as the men talked of Mexico—talked about the rumors they'd heard in St. Marysville today. "They say that England's loaned Mexico forty thousand dollars," Marshall was saying.

"Why would England do that?" asked Sarah, trying to be polite, glad Marshall couldn't see her face in the dim torchlight. Just the mere sound of his voice irritated her. Set her teeth on edge. For the hundredth time tonight, she wished she hadn't accepted the men's invitation to join them on the gallery. She had mending to do. Hems to let out. Sleeves to lengthen. The twins were growing so fast. They promised to be big children.

"It's just your typical politics," said Marshall. "Nothing that would interest you ladies."

"But to satisfy your burning curiosity, my dear," said William, with a note of sarcasm, "England wants Mexico to invade Texas. That's why they loaned them the money. Anyone with a lick of sense knows it's all aimed at slavery."

"Slavery?" asked Breck.

"You see, Son, if Mexico can win Texas, which I highly doubt, the Texas territory will be declared slave-free, at least that's the rumor. As usual, England's sticking her nose in our business where it doesn't belong, taking away our inalienable right to decide our own destiny. England's nose casts a considerable shadow."

Marshall laughed. "I, for one, will be the first in line to whack it off. With pleasure, I might add."

Then, from inside the house, Sarah heard the unmistakable sound of a baby's cry. Soon, there was not just one cry, but two, a boisterous infant duet. Realizing that no one was tending the twins, Sarah rose. "Excuse me, I must see to the children."

The men stood and bowed as she left. Truthfully, she was thankful for the interruption, thankful to escape Marshall's presence, wondering what her husband ever saw in that man.

She smelled the twins halfway across Kate's room. It was an old smell. Sour, almost. I am too weary for this, she thought, as she entered the twins' room. She fumbled with the match holder and finally succeeded in lighting the candelabra, the odors of sulfur, tallow, and beeswax a welcome relief. The twins clung to the bars of the crib, screaming, their faces red and furious. Tears trembled in their eyes, glistening in the candlelight.

"My babies. My sweet babies." She kissed them on the top of their heads and ruffled their hair, ignoring their cries of indignation when she did not lift them out. Where was the little nurse? Why didn't she change them into fresh diapers? How many times must she be told to keep the children clean? Sarah sighed, knowing Mammy Hester was away visiting her family at Woodleigh. Sarah was alone with the two infants.

"Monette?" She searched the room. Sometimes the child hid from people, peering at them from darkened corners. Her impatience rising, Sarah checked the attic, the parlor, the dining room, the pantry. . . . The girl was nowhere to be found.

Back she went to the gallery. "Katherine, have you seen Monette? I can't find her anywhere."

"Why, yes, Mama. She's right here. She's sleeping."

In the dimness, Sarah discerned the outline of a child, thumb in mouth, head propped against Kate. "Monette, wake up." Sarah shook the girl's shoulder, and the child stirred. The twins continued to scream in the background. "Monette, the babies are filthy. You must clean them up."

The child blinked at her, uncomprehending, with eyes that looked liquid in the semi-darkness. *"Je ne peux pas supporter de faire quelque chose, Madame,"* she said finally. "I'm too tired."

Sarah struggled to keep her voice calm. Her own tears threatened to overwhelm her. "We are all tired, Monette. Now do what you are told and obey me like a good girl."

*"Oui, Madame."*

"Say, 'Yes, Miss Sarah.'"

"Yes, Miss Sarah," she said sullenly.

Sarah followed the child into the twins' bedroom. Her ears hammered. Such a racket! "You take one, and I'll take the other."

"Yes, Miss Sarah." The child reached through the bars and began to undress Thomas, slowly and clumsily, as if she were yet half-asleep.

"Your duties to the twins come first, before anything else." Sarah was leaning over the railing, stripping a wet gown and diaper from a sobbing, scrunch-faced Georgie. "I have too much to do to be minding them every time they fuss."

"Yes, Miss Sarah."

"Monette!" Sarah straightened, gasping. "How long has it been since you changed their diapers? They're absolutely drenched! Just look at them! Both their bottoms are bright red and crusty! No wonder they're crying!"

"I—I changed them right before I went to the gallery, Miss Sarah. Honest I did. *Je le jure.*"

Tears of exasperation burned the backs of Sarah's eyes. "Telling a falsehood is a sin before God, child. Now hurry and fetch a pan of warm, soapy water and two fresh washrags. Hurry before my ears split."

"Yes, Miss Sarah."

All traces of lilac had long vanished by the time both boys were cleaned and changed, and the crib remade with fresh linens. Sarah settled the twins in their crib, realizing that her ears rang, her back ached, and a headache pulsed behind her eyes. As she stood, rubbing her temples, wishing she could slip out of her corsets and into bed, tiny arms wrapped about her waist and squeezed. She'd forgotten the child was there.

"Thank you, Mama."

Sarah said nothing, not knowing if she was too angry to speak, too weary to correct her, or if it was because she was strangely moved by the child's words and action. After a minute or so, during which she heard Marshall's barking, throaty laughter, she disengaged the girl's arms. "It's late, Monette. Go to bed."

⸺ ✐ ⸺

It was that ridiculous dancing man again. That Monsieur what's-his-name. Along with his infernal racket and that damned clapping mulatto. Good Lord! As if she didn't have enough troubles. Now her afternoon nap was ruined, and her head positively throbbed.

Disgusted, angry, wishing William would hurry and build the new additions to the big house like he'd promised, Mehitable rose from her bed, crossed the room, and cracked open the door to the parlor, peering through. Accompanied by Kate as she pounded on the piano, Breck and Monette danced and twirled, hands clasped. Mehitable pursed her lips. The girl's dress was flying up and down in a most indecorous manner, petticoats flashing for all to see. Gracious! The only time in her life she'd seen such behavior was when Miss Vera Botswa shook her ripe melons in front of everyone at last summer's cotillion. Now here it was happening under her own roof, sanctioned by Sarah, ignored by William. Granted, Breck was still a child. How old was he? Ten? Eleven? It was difficult to remember. But still, everyone knew that when men were encouraged early, they started early. It was a simple fact. They could not help themselves. Now the mulatto was ruining not just one, but two of William's children.

Intolerable. Absolutely intolerable.

Mehitable was determined to speak with Sarah again. Not likely it would do any good—her daughter-in-law was as stubborn as a goat—but still, it was the least she could do for her grandchildren. But while Mehitable smoothed her hair and pinned on her day cap, a sudden dizziness overwhelmed her. She clutched the armoire, waves of blackness rolling through her, thinking, It's the heat. The blasted heat and that confounded noise. It's too much for any woman.

Once the dizziness passed, Mehitable felt weakened, drained. Perhaps, she thought, she should move to South Carolina after all. Not only did her youngest daughter know how to heed the advice of her elders, but surely the heat wasn't nearly so crippling. Mercy sakes, how on earth could it be? As it was, Mehitable's legs now trembled, and she feared she would fall. She called for Sarah, for Mammy Hester, for Henry, for *anyone* to help her, knowing no one could hear her over the ruckus. Determined to get help, she fetched her cane and lumbered through the office and into the rear loggia, where she saw the houseboy.

"Nat, boy, fetch Miss Sarah. I'm having an attack."

The boy looked at her blankly, as if he didn't understand that she might be dying. "But Miss Sarah, she out in the orchard."

Mehitable felt the blood rise in her face, and her headache surged. "Mercy sakes! I don't care if she's in China! Do like I say, boy!"

Nat shuffled toward the back door, head hanging, showing no indication of the urgency she felt.

She gave him a sharp poke in the back with her cane, propelling him out the door. "Molasses moves faster than you! Hurry now, or I'll be dead by the time you come back, and it'll be your fault. And fetch me some ice."

"Yes'm."

Mehitable mopped her brow with her handkerchief. Knowing Nat and his dawdling ways, it would likely be Christmas before Sarah arrived. Goodness. Such heat. Such dampness. And the flies. Almost as bad as that racket.

*Heavens to Betsy, the racket.*

It sounded to her like the mulatto was singing. Was that possible? It was a girl's voice, and it certainly wasn't Kate's, whose voice was pure and sweet. No, this voice was vulgar and chesty. Singing in French, of all things. Lord have mercy. What next?

Mehitable was searching through the cupboards of the butler's pantry when Sarah entered.

"Mother, what's wrong? Nat said you were sick."

"I can't find the sugar for my lemon water, and I think I'm having an attack."

"Sit, Mother."

Grateful her daughter-in-law was finally here, finally able to care for her, Mehitable sat. Sweat streamed down her face, between her breasts, and under her arms. She'd meant to fix a tall glass of lemonade to revive herself, but the sugar was nowhere to be found. "It's gone."

"What's gone? Mother, what are you talking about? What's wrong?"

"Yesterday you fetched a new cone of sugar because the one from last week was already gone, and now that one's gone too. I tell you someone's stealing the sugar, Sarah."

"I'm sure it's here somewhere. You just rest, and I'll take care of everything," said Sarah, who proceeded to look in each cupboard.

Mehitable could have saved her the trouble, told her she'd already looked everywhere, three times over, but knew that Sarah, stubborn as she was, would look anyway. Crossing her arms, Mehitable watched as Sarah scoured every inch of the pantry, saying, "I told you so," when Sarah turned up empty-handed.

"I'm sure there's a likely explanation."

"Of course, there's an explanation. There's a thief in the house. Call the servants together."

"I don't really wish to make a—"

"In my day, we didn't tolerate the servants having the run of the house."

"Of course not, only—"

"If you don't do it, I'll make certain William does. You can be sure he'll get to the bottom of it. He can't abide a thief any more than I can." Observing Sarah's face, Mehitable knew she'd delivered Sarah a blow just as surely as if she'd slapped her. Well, it couldn't be helped. Sarah deluded herself into thinking she was capable of handling the household without interference from William. But she was entirely too soft for such management. The house negroes were as spoiled as any, and it was getting worse. It took a much firmer hand than Sarah's to keep a heap of adults and children gainfully employed day in and day out, from laundresses to gardeners, from coachmen to cooks, from mammies to maids.

"Very well, Mother. Have Nat call the servants."

When the servants finally assembled in the rear loggia, Mehitable thought she'd never seen a more worthless, shiftless passel of darkies. Reeking like animals, circles of sweat under their arms, most of them were too old or too young to work in the fields. Instead, they spent their time pilfering from the pantry and snoozing whenever one's back was turned. It was a wonder anything got done. It was a wonder she didn't have to do everything herself.

Mehitable curbed her impatience while Sarah asked each of them if they knew anything about the missing sugar. Of course, they all said no. It was the way she asked it. As if she encouraged them to say no, so there would be no punishment. In Mehitable's day, if no one confessed, they *all* received punishment. No supper. No passes for a month. No Sundays off. Thrashings all around if necessary. It was a known fact that darkies couldn't keep their hands to themselves unless the threat of punishment loomed large. Heavens to Betsy, even a babe would have sense enough to realize that. Mehitable clucked her tongue and shook her head. For all her beauty, Sarah was the stupidest woman.

As Sarah made her way down the line a second time, asking, "Did you steal the sugar?" and each one in turn widened their eyes, shook their head, and exclaimed, "Why no, Miss Sarah, I ain't never stole nothing in my life," Mehitable watched them. Scrutinized them.

When Sarah reached the end of the line where the little mulatto stood, dressed to the teeth in Kate's hand-me-downs like a mule in gold harness, Mehitable knew.

It's the mulatto.

She's lying.

The crack in the ceiling meandered down the wall like a bolt of lightning, dividing, then dividing again. A line of ants marched down the crack, and where one disappeared, the rest followed—in, out, over the moisture-swollen plaster, trickling down the wall and to the cone of sugar. Earlier, the cone of sugar had been hidden in the corner of the sill, hidden even when the curtain was drawn and the window open. But now the sugar lay exposed, and ants swarmed over it, black on white.

Monette watched the ants, knowing that what she'd done was wrong.

But the twins had screamed so loudly. Sugar softened their cries, and lulled them to sleep.

Sarah stood beside the window, outlined in a haze of light. Wisps of auburn hair trailed against her neck and across her shoulders. Her green eyes looked troubled, angry almost, and her forehead creased with lines.

Mehitable sat in a rocking chair beside the empty crib. The rocker groaned as the large woman shifted her weight and scowled at Monette, her face hard despite the soft folds of flesh. Just minutes ago, Mehitable had found the sugar. Shrieked in triumph. Summoned both Sarah and Monette to the twins' room. Now both women confronted Monette, the cone of sugar plain to see.

"Did you steal the sugar?" asked Sarah.

"No, Miss Sarah," whispered Monette, her heart pounding in her ears.

"What did you say? I can't hear you."

"I said no, Miss Sarah, I did not steal the sugar."

"She's lying," said Mehitable.

For a while, no one said anything. Through the window came the high-pitched squeal of the cotton press, followed by the caw of the peacock. Monette's knees trembled and her stomach twisted sour. Tears built, stinging and painful, begging for release, until Monette could no longer stem the salty stream that began to course down her cheeks and trickle into her mouth.

Then, in a swish of petticoats, Sarah left the window and knelt next to Monette. She touched her on the hand, a gentle touch, cool on such a hot day. "Child, remember, it is a sin to tell a falsehood. Now tell me the truth. Did you steal the sugar?"

Monette hesitated, sensing Mehitable watching her, watching the tears as they slid down her face. Thinking, *Liar.*

"I promise you won't be hurt. Just tell me the truth."

"Oui, Madame."

"Please speak English, Monette."

"Yes, Miss Sarah."

"Yes, what?"

"I took the sugar."

Mehitable grunted. "I told you so."

"Why did you steal the sugar?"

"I didn't steal it, I took it."

"It is the same thing, Monette. You took something without permission, and that is called stealing. Now tell me, why did you steal the sugar?"

"To—to keep the babies from crying."

"I see. So you fed it to them?"

"Yes, Miss Sarah. But I brushed off the ants first."

Sarah sighed and rose to her feet, the scent of lilac fading as she moved back toward the window. Once again framed in a square of light, Sarah stared outside, saying nothing for so long that Monette wondered if Sarah had forgotten about her. Forgotten about the sugar. Maybe she should leave. She wished she *could* leave, for Mehitable continued to watch her, forcing Monette to look away, down at the carpet, at her own pink slippers.

"It's my fault, Monette. I'm afraid I've misled you."

"Oh, Lord have mercy," said Mehitable. "Here we go again."

"I'm afraid I've given you the wrong impression. You are a servant, Monette. Do you know what it means to be a servant?"

"Yes, Miss Sarah." But as Monette spoke, it was as if the ground beneath her rocked, as if she stood on a castle of sand, which now crumbled away, and she was, suddenly, falling into the abyss, an abyss filled with nothingness and all terror. She wanted to cover her ears with her hands, to not listen, to scream instead, hearing Miss Sarah's voice now as if it came from far above, somewhere where there was light and love and family.

"You are not my daughter, Monette. And you are not Katherine's sister. You are a servant. Servants do what their masters tell them. Servants are obedient and honest. They do not lie or steal. Do you understand what I am telling you?"

"Yes, Miss Sarah."

"You are not to participate in music and dance lessons any more from Monsieur Déclouet. It gives you the wrong impression. Do you understand me?"

"Thank heavens! It's about time! I've been telling you that for ages!"

"Yes, Miss Sarah."

"You are no longer to share Katherine's bed. I will have a pallet put into this room. You will stay here and look after the twins. You are their servant, their little maid. Do you understand?"

"Yes, Miss Sarah."

"That is all for now. You may go."

Monette fled the room, away from Mehitable, away from Sarah. She stumbled down the stairs, out the back door, and into the bug-filled heat.

Down the walkway, she ran, dimly aware that people watched her from all sides, whispers buzzing like wasps.

The privy was empty. She closed the door, the air thick with heat and the stench of waste. Her knees buckled, and, with a choked sob, she collapsed. Then, oddly, she was no longer there. Like a bird escaped, she now floated far above, in the stars perhaps, watching with detachment as a little girl began to savagely claw her arms. She saw the child's skin erupt with blood, beading like dew, mixing with tears, smearing now. And she knew why. High in the stars, with a simple clarity, she knew and understood. The girl clawed to erase herself, to erase the voice whispering out from the emptiness within her, howling like a bitter wind, dry as bone dust, whispering, shrieking,

*Mwana na mono . . .*

*You are lost . . .*

*lost. . . .*

# Book Three

*"Knowledge makes a man unfit to be a slave."*

Frederick Douglass

# *Chapter 1*

*November 1849*

KATE KNEW MONETTE WAS right. She wouldn't be in such an awful fix to get ready if she'd gotten up when Monette had told her to. But when the morning sun had peeped into the guest room where she was staying, she'd snuggled deeper. Sleeping felt so good. Downright marvelous, in fact. Only when Monette announced the breakfast tray, with hot biscuits and a slab of honeyed ham, had Kate finally crawled out of bed.

"It's much too early," she said as she stood, shivering, her mouth filled with biscuit.

"Well, you don't want them to leave without you, do you? Now up with your arms."

Kate obediently lifted her arms so Monette could slip a chemise over her head. As soon as the undergarment dropped into place, Kate snatched another bite of buttered biscuit from her breakfast tray. Soon layers of petticoats hung from her waist, a couple of them conspicuously spotted with ham grease. Or was it butter? Thank goodness she wasn't old enough to wear corsets yet; they seemed like an awful fuss. Petticoats were bad enough. Kate thought, likely now that I'm fourteen, Mama will make me wear corsets. I'm certainly tall enough. Taller than Mama.

"Stop eating, wash your face, and sit. I need to do your hair. You can't go riding looking like you've just rolled out of bed."

"But I *have* just rolled out of bed."

"Stop being so difficult and do what I say."

Kate scrubbed her face at the washstand, accepted a towel from Monette, and sat with a loud sigh at the vanity. "If I'd have known you were going to be so bossy, I would have brought Mammy Hester with me instead."

Their eyes met in the mirror. Monette tried to look stern, but Kate wasn't fooled, merely amused. Monette didn't look or sound in the least bit stern, certainly not like Mammy Hester, who could look downright formidable with her bony arms placed on her hips, and her forehead creased into a thousand lines, saying, "Now you mind what I says, Missy Kate, or there's gonna be heaps of trouble."

No, Monette was about as stern and commanding as a mouse sipping a cup of afternoon tea. Stern or not, Kate envied Monette's natural grace. Whereas Kate was tall, Monette came up to Kate's nose, certainly a height much more becoming in a female of the species! Whereas Kate was big-boned (no matter how much she tried to be slender), Monette was willowy, fragile almost, as if she might break in half in a stiff wind. But stiff wind or not, Monette, in Kate's estimation, was beautiful, with slender hands, delicate features, and gorgeous amber eyes that elicited more than a few comments wherever they went. Now, as Kate gazed at her in the mirror, she saw the tug of a smile at the corners of Monette's mouth. Kate suppressed a giggle.

Monette placed both her hands on her hips in a perfect imitation of Mammy Hester and declared, "Lord a'mercy, chile! What you gone and done now?" while Kate burst into choking laughter, spattering biscuit crumbs onto the vanity mirror.

As Monette brushed Kate's hair, Kate savored the taste of freedom. Freedom! It was so wonderful to get away from the constant supervision of Mama and Mammy Hester and, of course, Grandma Mehitable. (Not to mention the pestering of the twins!) Even if it was for just a few days.

Yesterday, she had arrived with her father and Breck at Tanglewood Plantation, guests of Mr. Marshall McCain. Initially, Mammy Hester was supposed to go with Kate, to chaperone, to attend to her toilette and all that other nonsense. But Mammy Hester had come down with a nasty cold. "You can't go without Mammy Hester," Sarah told Kate sadly, shaking her head, seeming to sense her daughter's distress. "It isn't seemly."

Stricken, Kate pleaded with her. "Let Monette go instead! Monette knows everything Mammy Hester does. She can take real good care of me. . . . Pleeease!"

Sarah only relented when Mammy Hester concurred, saying that Monette was as good a maid as any God had ever created, and that she'd be more than happy to mind little Georgie and Thomas in the meantime.

Thank heavens, thought Kate. Freedom! Sweet, delicious, wonderful, wicked, freedom!

Suddenly impatient to be outside, to breathe the fresh air of the sugar fields, to feel a horse beneath her, she pushed Monette away and strode to the closet, where she pulled out her riding habit. "Hurry. Help me dress." She tossed the skirt over her head and struggled to pull it down.

With a sound of exasperation, Monette said, "Let me help. You'll end up in knots if you don't stop trying so hard. Plus, you're messing your hair."

Finally, after a measure of tussling, pulling, tucking, primping, and smoothing, Kate stood fully dressed before the mirror. It was her favorite riding habit, one her mother had sewn for her as a gift on her fourteenth birthday. Made of pale green cashmere, it had a tight bodice and a full skirt (although the hem had been let out once already), from under which peeped her lace-trimmed petticoats and pantalettes. Atop her head perched a dashing felt hat, forest green, pert, with a band of white satin, plus a pale green downy feather that was quite becoming, especially in a breeze. Her forest green gloves were of the softest calfskin, with boots to match.

"My cloak," she said, knowing even before Monette placed the fur-trimmed cloak around her shoulders that she looked fetching. A lady. Well, almost. Anyway, it was fun to pretend. So long as she didn't have to wear those stupid corsets that pinched and made ladies gasp at the slightest effort. How ridiculous!

Set along the banks of Bayou Bend, Tanglewood Plantation lay a mere two miles from the Mississippi River coast, and within a three-hour carriage ride from Baton Rouge, including the time it took to harness the horses. The big house was one-storied, sprawling, with a wide gallery meant for whiling the evenings away. Behind the big house lay a sea of haphazard outbuildings, each constructed as if the result of a sudden thought, an impromptu change of plans, a moving from here to there like debris on an ocean wave. To the left and right, the cane fields stretched as far back and as wide as the eye could see, the leafy stalks swaying in the breeze, each higher than twice a man's height. In the distance, the blackened chimneys of the sugarhouse spewed smoke into the November sky, soiling the air with soot and sugar.

Kate rode one of Marshall's little mares, thinking how wonderful it was to be here—to be visiting, away from pursuing her studies, away from watchful eyes, from reprimands. No matter that Marshall's plantation was ugly. No matter that it lacked the influence of a woman to lend it color and beauty. It was a man's plantation. And somehow, Kate felt right at home.

Beside her, Breck sat easily atop a bay gelding. She envied him, that he could sit with one leg on each side of the saddle, whereas she had to ride sidesaddle. She just *knew* that if she could ride the other way, the man's way, that she could ride even faster, jump even higher, and perhaps be the first, finally, to corner a fox. She also envied him the advantages of his height, that Breck's height was admired, looked up to, whereas her height, as Aunt Virginia always put it, was most unbecoming in a lady. But here in the sugar fields, none of that mattered. Kate could be as tall as she wanted. Who was here to see? Just Papa and Marshall, who rode together twenty feet ahead, and they didn't count. And, of course, Breck.

Breck was handsome, she supposed. It was difficult to look at her brother—someone she had known all her life—and think, yes, he's definitely handsome or no, he's not, although some of her acquaintances had assured her that yes, he was most assuredly, dreamily handsome! To Kate, Breck was just her brother, handsome or otherwise. His soft brown hair curled under the brim of his leather hat, and his face was beginning to turn into a man's face, lengthening, creating masculine angles and lines, the brown eyes radiating intelligence. Was that possible? wondered Kate. Could people radiate intelligence? She didn't know, only knowing that Breck had forever loved his studies, seeming to devour them, while she still limped along, bored and distracted.

Spying a wagon track, Kate said to Breck, "Race you to the end!" Before he could answer, she urged her horse into a gallop and took off. She heard the drumbeat of hooves, felt the wind upon her skin, making her eyes water and her hair fly out behind. Like a bird dashing against the bars of a cage, a wild feeling of exhilaration fluttered inside her chest, and it was all she could do not to burst into an insane laughter. Soon he was abreast, as she'd known he would be. She urged her horse to go even faster, but knew the little mare was giving all she could. Breck pulled ahead, and by the time they reached the end of the wagon track, she lagged by three lengths.

As she wheeled to a stop beside him, a flock of birds took off, their wings thrumming through the air. Now she let her laughter loose, a bubbling laugh of pure joy. "What fun!"

Breck smiled, panting a little. "I always have to be on my guard with you around. I never know what devious scheme you have in mind."

"I'm plotting all the time, Brother. Horrible plots, and deciding who's my next victim!"

"Why am I not surprised?"

"Well, I suppose because nothing ever surprises you."

They turned their horses around and began trotting back to where Marshall and William waited for them at the beginning of the track.

Breck said, "So who is it?"

"Who is what?"

"Your next victim. You said you were plotting. I sure hope it isn't me."

"Well, you can be certain that whoever it is will never know until afterward. Otherwise, it spoils all the fun!"

By the time they joined the others, Kate could tell her father was irritated. She hurried her horse along, remembering the last time that her father was irritated with her, he'd given her a taste of "switch pie." Fortunately, he didn't say anything, merely drawing his heavy brows together and giving her a hard look, before continuing beside Marshall down the rows of sugar cane. But in that instant of his hard look, her giddy happiness vanished, flown away like the flock of birds.

They approached an area where the negro hands were working, sweating despite the chill of the November day. The workers moved among the stalks, singing cheerily amidst the *whack, whack* of their machetes and the dry rustle of leaves. Cut cane was stacked like hay; the soil darkened with cane juice. To Kate, even the air seemed thicker, stickier, as if she was breathing in the sugar itself.

Just then, a white man rode up. Marshall introduced him as Tad, his overseer. Tad shook hands with William and Breck, and tipped his hat to Kate, saying, "My pleasure." As her father didn't employ an overseer, Kate had only seen a few others when she visited other plantations. She'd heard terrible stories, though, about how overseers, as a rule, were lazy, abusive, and stupid as stumps. Kate was a little disappointed when Tad didn't drool, or look monstrous, or greasy, or any of the other characteristics one might expect from one who was lazy, abusive, and stupid. He sat in his saddle looking ordinary enough.

"Status?" asked Marshall.

Tad spat and said, "Finished cutting the east border field. Soon as we're done hauling to the sugarhouse, we can start hauling here."

"How many cart loads of cane so far?"

"Somewheres between fourteen and fifteen hundred. Don't have the exact numbers right off the top of my head, but I can get them for you."

"What's the tally on the sugar?"

"Right around two hundred thousand pounds."

William whistled.

"That's right, big boy," said Marshall with a grin. "What have I been telling you? Sugar's the way to go; the world's clamoring for it."

The blackened smokestacks of sugarhouses were becoming more and more familiar to Kate. Even on the three-hour carriage ride to Marshall's, she'd counted five sugarhouses, the air smelling like taffy and making her stomach grumble and her mouth water.

"How many pounds you figure to harvest in all?" asked William.

"We'll likely quadruple it, maybe more."

William pushed up the brim of his hat, excitement dancing in his eyes. "How many pounds last year?"

Marshall eyed him, clearly enjoying himself. "Over a million, big boy."

After the overseer left, William turned to Breck. "Hear that, Son? During a year when we lost half our cotton to worms, Marshall here raked in over a million pounds of sugar."

"That's what I've been trying to tell you all these years." Marshall paused to light a cigar, offering cigars to both William and Breck, who accepted and followed suit. Marshall blew a cloud of smoke, seemingly refreshed by the ritual, a ritual which left Kate wishing, not for the first time, that she was a man and could puff a cigar like it was her God-given right.

"The way I figure it," Marshall declared, "if you've got two cash crops, even if one goes belly up, you've still got money. You're too attached to your cotton, William. Too set on doing things just like your daddy did. But the world's changing. Gotta keep up with the times." Marshall turned in his saddle and whistled to one of the cane cutters. "Cut these kids some cane, would you?"

Before Kate could hardly wonder what was happening, there was a flash of machete, and one of the workers walked over to her and Breck, handing each of them a piece of cane about a foot long. She took hers and brushed it off. She looked at Marshall, unsure of what to do.

"Go ahead, chew on it," urged Marshall. "It ain't ladylike, I know, but what the hell. We won't tell your mama."

Kate happily complied, devouring the raw sweetness and spitting out the fibers like she was born to it. But it wasn't long before her beautiful calfskin gloves were stained with sugar juice. She knew Mammy Hester would have a bonafide fit when she saw the gloves, saying, When was she ever going to grow up? or some such. Oh well. It was too difficult to please everyone. It seemed that no matter what she did, someone was bound to be unhappy about it.

After Kate left, Monette tried to keep herself occupied, bathing, dressing herself in a fresh calico skirt, blouse, and starched white apron, stoking the fire, cleaning up the morning's hurried toilette, and setting out Kate's change of clothing before finally creeping out to the kitchen to ask if there was any more food. She was hungry and had yet to eat.

There were three of them, including the cook. One stirred the contents of a pot suspended above the fire, another kneaded dough, her hands dusted with flour, while the last sat at the table chopping vegetables. At least, they *had been* stirring, kneading, and chopping. For upon her entrance, they stared, their actions suspended, as if she were some haunt from the grave.

Finally, one of them spoke. "What you need, girl?"

When they offered her a chair at the kitchen table to eat, she refused, knowing they did not mean the invitation—that they instead wanted her gone. She left the kitchen carrying a tray of cold ham, peas, and two molasses-smothered biscuits, her face growing warm as she walked the path toward the big house, voices carrying easily in the chill air:

"What you doing inviting that uppity yellow nigger to sit here with us?"

"She ain't no yellow nigger; she's a white nigger, that's what she is. Thinks she's white, and we's nothing but a heap of trash. I sees it in her eyes."

Back in Kate's room, she chewed mechanically, washing down the food with water that tasted of silt. Afterward, she set the tray aside and moved to the window. Perhaps Kate was returning. She peered out at the green expanse, seeing nothing but cane.

Actually, she was glad to be away from Fox Creek. Here, at least, there was nothing to do but tend to Kate. At Fox Creek, there were always more tasks to be done—tiresome, irksome tasks that caused her to fall into an exhausted sleep each night and awaken each morning bleary-eyed and stiff. Of course, besides the usual sweeping, dusting, scrubbing, and polishing, there was also mending, fetching firewood, tending the twins, and training to be a lady's maid.

One year ago, when the twins were almost five years of age, she'd moved from sleeping in their room to sharing Mammy Hester's bed in the attic. She'd thought it was a blessing—until that first night when Mammy Hester shook the rafters with her snoring. Over the past year, Monette had grown somewhat accustomed to the nighttime ruckus, but many mornings she awoke feeling like she'd scarcely slept.

Then there was Fatima . . . but at the thought, she shoved Fatima from her mind like she was spitting out something rotten.

Oh, when would Kate return?

It was a dream of a sugar field. Instead of individual stalks of cane, it seemed like one organic being, a field of green, swaying to the same rhythmic thought. She, a child, on his horse, galloping through the fields on a summer's day, his arms like a father's arms, tight about her, cradling her, wild joy in her heart as she heard him say, *Ah, ma chérie, do you not love the wind in your hair?*

Then, in the distance, the sky darkened and thunder rumbled. Soon, rain pelted down in sheets, turning the green fields into gray, the soil into mud. Suddenly, a river rushed in front of them, a raging torrent, blocking the way home.

He set her into the low branches of a tree. *Wait here, ma chérie,* he said. *I shall return.* She gazed at him, at the rain streaming in rivulets down the brim of his hat, thinking, *He shall save me.*

Drenched and shivering, she watched as he urged his horse into the river. Halfway across, the horse began to flounder, rider and mount suddenly separated, sweeping past her, down the river. Then, far away, slowly, slowly, they sank without a sound. Where they had been was nothing. She opened her mouth to scream, but no sound came. She clung to the branch, screaming her silent scream, knowing he would never return.

Then she was in a clearing, surrounded by a crowd. She lay on her back in the clearing, in the mud, naked, crying tears that would not shed. The people said nothing, just circled around her, staring at her nakedness. She wanted to run for the shelter of one of the nearby buildings, but couldn't move. Her arms. Her legs. Exposed and frozen into place.

Then out of the crowd he came, his face veiled in the fog of her dream. His body hardened with fieldwork. Black as coffee beans. An enormous man.

He covered her with his shirt, then gathered her up in his arms and kissed her forehead. She felt the heat of his calloused hand against her thigh.

*You's safe with me,* he whispered. *Ain't nothin' never gonna hurt you. Not while I gots breath in my body.*

As he carried her away from the staring eyes, she nestled into his arms, pressing her cheek against his chest, cradled in the smells of field, sweat, and soil. . . .

✐

"Monette?" Someone was shaking her. "Monette? Wake up, sleepyhead."

Sleep rolled from her in waves before Monette remembered where she was—at Marshall's, in the room where she and Kate stayed.

Kate was talking at her. "You've let the fire burn out. Hurry and build it up again, because I need you to heat my irons and dress me for dinner. My hair goes limp as a rag in this weather. After dinner, Papa and Mr. McCain are going to race their horses, and I certainly don't want to miss that, so hurry up. Besides, I'm starved, and it's almost two o'clock, you lazybones."

After a bit, the fire was burning and the irons were heating. While Monette dressed Kate, Kate chattered on—about the sugarhouse. The vats of molasses. The fine, sweet smell. How Papa was going to build them a sugarhouse too. Oh, wasn't it going to be grand? She'd heard of sugarhouse parties that lasted until dawn!

Monette scarcely listened, still numb with sleep. She'd only meant to lie down for a short spell, to catch a quick nap, but the nap had turned into a deep slumber of restlessness. And the dream—*Mon Dieu, l'rêve!* It was a recurring dream, one that had disturbed her sleep for months now, visiting her with increasing frequency. Each time she dreamed it, she awakened with a *mélange* of feelings, as if both pain and love intertwined like lovers refusing to separate. What it all meant, she did not know. She only knew that she both hated and loved the dream. She feared the pain it aroused, ached with it, yet at the same time yearned for the dream with such passion that she felt certain that were the dreaming to stop, she would simply cease to be.

She glimpsed her own puffy eyes in the vanity mirror as she brushed Kate's hair. She tried to match Kate's happy mood, to recapture their fun of the morning's toilette, but it was like catching butterflies with a string.

So she brushed Kate's hair until it crackled. Kate had refused to cut her hair since her near-death from yellow fever, save for a smidgeon off the ends every few months. Auburn, shining, and wavy, it now curled to her waist, voluminous and soft. "Kate's glory," Miss Mehitable declared, and Monette agreed (much as she disliked agreeing with anything Ole Miss said). Set against her green eyes and her pale, sometimes-freckled face, Kate's hair gave an illusion of beauty where, perhaps, without it, she might have been considered ordinary or, at most, pretty. It *was* her beauty.

". . . then we raced to the end of a wagon track. A quarter mile, maybe more. It was neck and neck. I almost beat him, but Breck won by a whisker. You should have seen it."

"Uh-huh."

"Then Marshall had them cut me some cane. When we raise cane ourselves, I shall order them to cut you a piece, and you shall see for yourself. I'm afraid my new gloves are perfectly spoiled. Of course, maybe the juice washes out. I hadn't thought of that. Then Mammy Hester would never know. Why don't you wash out my gloves after dinner, and then we'll see? It can't hurt . . ."

Monette wrapped a tendril of Kate's hair around one of the irons and held it a second or two before releasing it. A part of her listened to Kate, understanding Kate's excitement—her race with Breck and the wonders of a sugarhouse—while another part of her wandered away, as images and voices variously flitted across the canvas of her mind, as though painted by the hurried brush of a distraught artist. . . . The horse and rider vanishing beneath the water's swirling rage, swallowed without a sound—not even a farewell . . . Her nakedness in the clearing . . . Everyone gawking at her . . . The man's black hand upon her thigh, the comfort of his warmth . . . His face, lost no matter how hard she strained to see him . . . Then the voices, nasty and crawling as worms:

*What you doing inviting that uppity yellow nigger to sit here with us?*

*Thinks she's white, and we's nothing but a heap of trash.*

*I sees it in her eyes.*

"Ouch! Monette! You're pulling my hair!"

"Oh, *désolé pour ça.* Sorry."

Kate glared at her in the mirror, rubbing a spot on the back of her head. "What's gotten into you anyhow? You've been acting like a sour grape."

When Kate continued to glare at her, clearly expecting an answer, Monette said, "There's not much to do when you're gone, I—I missed you, *ma chérie.*" Anymore her accent was discernible only to the discriminating ear. Unless emotion got the better of her, or when she was especially fearful, or, as was the case now, she was not being entirely truthful. Then the words migrated to the back of her throat of their own accord, and her voice thickened, and the language of her childhood slipped off her tongue.

"Well, you certainly don't act like you missed me." Kate picked up the hand mirror and held it up behind her so she could see the back of her head, as if evaluating the damage done. "I mean, here I am, and you've hardly said two words to me. I might as well be invisible. I might as well talk to the wall. It might actually be more stimulating."

"Sorry."

Kate set down the hand mirror as Monette fetched another iron from the fire. "Walls do have ears, you know. Grandma Mehitable always says so anyhow." Suddenly, Kate's face brightened. "Oh, Monette, I almost forgot to tell you! I heard the most delicious bit of news. Apparently, Mr. Vanderkloot, a weak, silly man if there ever was one, asked Miss May Rockwell for her hand in marriage, and she said yes—stupid girl, I guess she deserves him—but then she changed her mind and said she'd prefer to marry a mule, so I guess she's not as stupid as she looks. But Kloot—that's what they call him—he actually had a mule he said he could give her, if that was her preference. Well, you can imagine May's father didn't take kindly to that! Not to mention May herself. She said if he ever showed his face again, she'd fix it with a horseshoe. Can you imagine?" When Monette said nothing, Kate frowned at her in the mirror. *"Monette!"*

"What?"

"Oh, honestly. Sometimes, I swear you don't hear a thing I say. And can you *please,* pretty please, hurry up? They're probably ready to start the horse race without me, and I think I'm going to faint with hunger besides."

Monette released the last curl. "Just a while longer."

"Anyway, when I marry, I certainly don't want some dolt like Kloot. I'm going to marry someone exquisitely handsome and smart."

Taking the ribbon Kate handed her from the ribbon pot, Monette tied it prettily in Kate's hair, smiling at her in the mirror. "There. Finished."

In a flash, Kate was out of her chair, kissing her on the cheek, and saying, "You're an absolute dear. Whatever would I do without you?" before running out the door, leaving Monette behind in a room that smelled suspiciously like scorched hair.

# Chapter 2

"Miss Sarah, I's terrible sick. My head aches something awful."

Sitting at her desk, Sarah ignored the complaint and continued writing in her medical log. The previous patient had just left her office, and she found that if she didn't record a complaint before the next one assailed her, she later became confused as to who had what, and what she'd given to whom. Once she finished jotting her entry, complete with diagnosis and remedy, she turned to the new complainant. Does it never end?

Fatima stood in the doorway, one hand pressed against her forehead. There was nothing about the girl that indicated she was one of the laziest, most deceitful servants Sarah had ever had the misfortune to own. Thirteen years of age or so, Fatima was almost Sarah's height, seeming cheerful, a little pudgy, with a wide nose and a scar across her chin. But whenever Sarah caught a glimpse into the girl's eyes, a contrived innocence peered out.

This morning's complaint was, no doubt, contrived. It was not the first time.

"Plus, my throat's on fire, Miss Sarah. I's dying, maybe."

"Come a little closer and let me look." Suppressing a sigh, Sarah felt the girl's forehead and peered down her throat. Temperature: normal. Throat: healthy and pink.

If it weren't for the girl's mother, Lizzy, Sarah would long ago have sent Fatima to the fields. The girl vexed her—as if she didn't have enough on her mind. But Lizzy was such a good worker—obedient, strong, and capable—everything Sarah wanted in a housekeeper. Sarah knew that

Lizzy went to extraordinary lengths to hide Fatima's laziness, to do the girl's work whenever possible, and so Sarah didn't have the heart to send Fatima to the fields. For Lizzy's sake.

I'm too soft, thought Sarah. Mehitable always declared her softness a failing, but Sarah wasn't so sure. Every plantation needs a softness, she believed. A softness from above that counteracts the firmness. A gentleness of stewardship over these people whom God had ordained her to care for. That she was a steward, she knew. She would not desecrate that stewardship by causing undue sorrow. Although sometimes, especially in the presence of Fatima, she was sorely tempted. Her softness was in evidence the day she'd purchased Lizzy and Fatima. She'd been visiting a friend in Woodville when Lizzy approached her, all mumbly and wide-eyed. "Missus gonna sell us," she whispered through the sizeable gap between her front teeth, "me and my daughter both. You gots to buy us, Miss Sarah. I done heard you's a good woman, fair and all. I promises to do everything you says afores you even opens your mouth. I promises to keep your house sparkling clean. Please, Miss Sarah, please."

After conferring with her friend and discovering that, indeed, Lizzy and Fatima were scheduled to be sold the following week at auction, Sarah purchased both of them on the spot.

"Thank you, Miss Sarah, thank you," was all she heard for two months every time she passed Lizzy in the house. "Thank you, Miss Sarah, thank you."

"Fatima, there is absolutely nothing wrong with you."

The girl's eyes grew large and insulted. "Oh, but there is, Miss Sarah, there is! I's suffering something terrible. If you don't give me some medicine, I's sure gonna die. I just knows it." To prove her point, Fatima's eyes suddenly rolled back in her head, and she flopped onto the floor.

Sarah went back to writing in her log. She would make certain that Fatima received a remedy she wouldn't soon forget, a remedy certain to make Fatima avoid playing sick the next time she grew too lazy to work. These faked illnesses were becoming far too common. Already, there were nine reported sick today, and at least four of them were undoubtedly faking. Let's see, thought Sarah. An emetic? Perhaps syrup made from the dried root of ipecac. She jotted in her log before finding the labeled bottle in the supply cabinet. Measuring out the proper dosage, she knelt next to Fatima.

"Drink this."

The girl groaned but managed to raise herself enough to drink the medicine. She made a face. "That ain't poison, is it?"

"It's a cure for what ails you. Now go drink a big glass of water, then return to your cabin, lie down, and rest. I'm sure you'll feel a change come over you shortly. Let me know if you need any more medicine."

"Yes, Miss Sarah. Thank you, Miss Sarah. You sure is good to me, Miss Sarah." The girl left, head bobbing, eyes cast downward, hands clasped demurely—the perfect picture of innocence and obedience.

Sarah sighed, jotted what she hoped to be her final entry of the day into her medical log, and then quickly brought out her manuscript on etiquette and health for young ladies. As if, should she delay, she would lose courage, drowning instead in pills, plasters, and prescriptions.

She dipped her pen in the inkwell, thought for a few minutes, then wrote, *Nothing indicates the good breeding of a young lady so much as her manners at table. . . .*

Several days later, Sarah instructed the household servants in their catechism. A few years ago, with the help of Father Whitmer Scarborough, she had begun instructing her servants in the ways of the Lord, a duty in which she was remiss no longer. Now she resolutely performed catechism three times per week, despite Mehitable's stern disapproval and William's feeling that all that godliness would lead to nothing but trouble—how it led to a mistaken sense of equality in the eyes of God. On Tuesdays, Thursdays, and Saturdays, Sarah gathered the servants together for their lessons. Of course, all the servants now attended Holy Trinity Episcopal Church every Sunday for their weekly instruction from Reverend Scarborough. Such a difference it had made in all of them, especially Monette, who was now obedient in all things—a trusted and valued servant. However, Sarah still waited for such a profound effect upon Fatima.

Sarah sat in the parlor, her dress arranged comfortably around her, a shawl over her shoulders, for the December air was chill despite the roaring fire. At her feet sat the younger of the household servants: Fatima, Monette, and Nat. Scattered in various chairs behind the children were Sarah's grown servants, nine in all: the coachman, the gardener, the butler, the head seamstress, the head laundress, the head cook, the hospital attendant, and, of course, Mammy Hester and Lizzy. Sarah opened her

*Catechism for Colored Persons* to a carefully selected page—a lesson not only directed at Fatima, but a lesson that begged repeating again and again for the good of all.

"What command has God given to servants concerning obedience to their own masters?" Although her voice was soft, Sarah prayed it carried the necessary weight and conviction of a proper mistress.

They replied in spurts—first one, then another—stumbling through the words like lame oxen plowing a rocky field. "Servants be obedient be obedient be obedient to them to them that are your masters masters masters according according according to the flesh to the flesh flesh flesh."

A shaky start.

"What does He mean by 'masters according to the flesh'?"

"Our masters in this world world—our earthly masters masters."

Better.

"How ought servants to try to please their masters?"

"Please them well in all things."

Sarah was delighted. Now they sounded as one—a chorus. It always took a few tries.

"Is it right in a servant, when he is commanded to do any one thing, to be sulky, and move slow, and be impudent, and answer his master again?"

"No."

"If the servant professes to be a Christian, ought he not to set an example to all the other servants of love and obedience to his master?"

"Yes."

"And if his master is a Christian, ought he not especially to love and obey him?"

"Yes."

"But suppose the master is cross and hard to please, and threatens and punishes more than he ought, what is the servant to do?"

"Stay at home and do his best to please him."

"Is it right for the servant to run away, or is it right to harbor a runaway?"

"No."

"What did the Apostle Paul do to Onesimus, who was run away? Did he harbor him, or send him back to his master?"

"He sent him back to his master with a letter."

"What is God's will to servants about stealing?"

"They must not steal."

"Ought servants to tell lies and deceive their masters?"

Sarah watched Fatima's face as the girl replied sweetly along with the others, "No."

All innocence. No guile. Such a liar.

"Is it any praise to a servant to be punished for his faults, or ought he to think hard of it?"

"No."

"Will God love and bless all good servants?"

"Yes."

"What will become of all bad servants?"

"They will be punished."

Some prompting required, but overall, Sarah was pleased. She closed her book. After giving a brief lecture on the duties of servants toward their masters, and after offering what she believed was a most fervent prayer, she led them in the singing of a hymn, and then dismissed them.

She sat before the fire, alone now, the book in her lap. She drew her shawl closer around her, shivering, for some reason unable to stay warm. Always, it seemed, the weight of responsibility pressed upon her. She felt weakened under its weight. Breathless, almost. She gazed into the bright fire, which had been stoked upon the servants' dismissal. "Oh, Lord," she whispered, "help me." Yellow flames snapped and curled. She pressed the book to her chest and bowed her head.

"Lord, O Lord, You have given me this flock, and I, as their chosen shepherd, must lead them. Guide my hand, O Lord, guide my wisdom, that I might be found blameless before the Judgment Day, holy in Your sight. Guide my hand, Lord, so that each of these, thy children, shall follow You all the days of their lives, in obedience and servitude, in the calling that You have ordained for them. Guide my hand, O my blessed Father, and give me strength to fulfill my duties. In the name of Your beloved Son, our Redeemer. Amen."

The day following Christmas, Sarah left her office through the rear loggia and stepped outside. The air was brisk, smelling of wood smoke. Four years ago, they'd finally finished the additions to the big house. Now, two separate but matching buildings faced one another across a rectangular clearing that stretched out behind the big house, with the kitchen forming the final side. Each addition was one-story, raised off the ground a foot or two on brick pilings, with two generous rooms and a gallery. Sarah wrapped her shawl tightly around her, crossed the space that divided the big house from the south addition, and knocked on the door of William's office.

"What's wrong?" he asked, frowning as he opened the door and drew her inside, out of the cold.

She rarely bothered him while he was in his office. Not that he didn't welcome her visits—he seemed to, anyway—but she didn't want to become a nuisance. So now, whenever she did happen to visit his office, he always assumed something was awry.

"Nothing's wrong," she said as he closed the door behind them.

A slow fire burned in the fireplace. William led her to one of the two chairs facing the fire. After she settled herself, he asked, "Sherry?" handing her a petite, stemmed, crystal glass filled with the rich, sweet liquid, when she said, Yes, please, that would be lovely.

He dragged his chair across the rug until it was beside hers, the upholstered arms touching. Then he sat, holding his glass of sherry, staring into the fire. He was dressed in his work clothes, intending, she was certain, to check the quarters once he was finished here with whatever needed doing. Going over the year-end figures, likely. His hair hung well past his ears, and she thought, he needs a haircut. Even so, with his untrimmed appearance, she thought him handsome. Yet when she considered each of his features alone—his plain eyes, his heavy, uneven brow, his crooked teeth—they were none of them handsome by any stretch. Though, as a whole—well, she'd long ago ceased trying to figure it out. She just loved him, she guessed. That was the sum of it. As she sat studying him, he withdrew a cigar from his jacket pocket and lit it, inhaling in little puffs.

She knew he was curious why she'd come, but for a while she was content to merely enjoy the closeness of his presence. It was difficult to explain. During the day, every day, both of them were surrounded by seemingly endless hordes of folks wanting, needing, shirking, wheedling, faking, pleading. So often, the only time they were truly alone together was at night, when they finally fell into bed, bone-weary. Sometimes, she thought, I just want William to myself. No demands. No interruptions.

*Just us.*

She reached out and squeezed his hand.

He turned from the fire and gazed into her eyes. "What is it, Sarah? What's wrong?"

"I—I've missed you."

As she watched, he seemed to soften—to lose all his hard edges, to just become—her husband. He smiled then, the smile crinkling the corners of his eyes. "How did you know I was thinking about you?"

"Were you?"

"Always." He kissed her hand.

"Did you like my gift?" She'd given him a hand-carved cigar box made of mahogany. Expensive and tasteful.

He pointed to his desk. "Already put it to use."

"The twins loved their little ponies," she said, smiling. William had given them a pair of gray, dappled ponies, complete with saddles and gigantic red bows. The twins had ridden until they'd nearly fallen off from exhaustion. "They're good boys."

"Yes, they are. They have a good mother."

"And a brilliant father."

"Stupid and homely."

"Intelligent and handsome."

"Sarah."

"What?"

"I adore you."

She said nothing, basking in the glow of the fire, the warmth of the sherry, and the love of her husband.

He said, "Do you remember the Christmas when all we could afford was a handkerchief for each other?"

She laughed. "Do you remember the Christmas when all the fire would do was smoke because of the winds, and so our turkey was black on the outside and raw in the middle?"

"What made it worse," added William, "was that it was Breck's first hunting trophy. He was proud as could be, but then the bird ended up as dog chow."

"Poor boy. Yes, I do remember that one."

He smiled, his expression wistful. "How about when the Christmas tree fell over and caught the drapes on fire?"

"That's a memory I'd prefer to forget. Almost caught my dress on fire, as well."

"I'll always treasure my memories with you, Sarah. Good or bad."

"Hmm. Is that a compliment?"

"It is."

"Then, dear William, I shall accept it as such."

He paused to puff on his cigar, then asked, "Why are you so kind to me, Sarah?"

"Why shouldn't I be? You've always been good to me."

He looked at her, his face open and honest. "I try to be good. I do. In fact, I don't believe I've ever done anyone wrong. Not to my knowledge, anyway."

"No, I don't believe you have."

"*Am* I a good man, Sarah?"

"Of course you are. Are you concerned that you're not?"

"Just wondering what you think."

"If you're worried, why don't you come to church with me?" She knew she was broaching a touchy subject, knew instinctively she should back away, but wanted so desperately for him to attend church, to become a Christian, to know God as she did. But as the words came out of her mouth, she couldn't help but glance above the fireplace. Displayed on the mantel beneath his rifle was the neck bone of an ass, a curious item by anyone's standards. The one time she'd asked him about it, she was mortified to hear him reply that it was the natural representation of a priest praying, followed by a resounding, "Bah!"

Instead of getting angry like usual, stomping off in a huff, he merely smiled, seeming amused, leaning forward to flick his cigar ash into the fire. "Couldn't stand to be surrounded by all those hypocrites, yourself excepted, of course."

"Of course." With a sigh, she let the matter drop. Another time.

He reached out and touched her hair. "You know I like it better when you wear your hair down."

"You know I can't. It isn't proper. I'm a married woman."

"Proper be damned." All at once, he set aside his cigar and glass of sherry and rose to his feet. He moved behind her and began removing the pins, telling her to hush when she protested.

Soon her hair fell down around her shoulders, over her bosom, and down the back of the chair. She closed her eyes and breathed deeply as he ran his hands through her hair.

"As the God-fearing woman that you are, Sarah Margaret Breck Jensey, you should know that this is the way your hair was created to be. Not pinned up and shackled under a goddamn lacy cap. Any fool should know that pinning up such lovely hair, a miracle of creation itself, is a goddamn sin, and someone somewhere's going to Hell for it. Isn't that the way Christianity works? Isn't there always a price to pay?"

She laughed and rose to her feet, setting down her glass of sherry. Its warmth had traveled to her head, and she felt a little giddy. "You do know swearing is a sin."

"So, punish me." He pulled her into his arms, laughing, and she let herself go to him.

A few minutes later, there was a knock at the door. Someone saying, "Come quickly, Mars William."

She saw the hard lines return to his face as he strode to the door and flung it open. A blast of cold air swirled about the room. "What is it, Quincy?"

"You gots to come quickly, Mars William."

William shoved his hat on his head and was gone, leaving her alone before the fire, their time together over.

Another memory, only.

## *Chapter 3*

IT WAS A BEAUTIFUL book, bound in blue leather as soft as Kate's calfskin gloves, its title embossed in curling letters of gilt. Although she knew she was alone, Monette glanced around Breck's bedroom anyway before picking up the book from his desk. Its pages were thin and filmy, edged with gold, and marked with a scarlet ribbon. She traced the letters with her finger, wondering what they said.

Breck had received the book for Christmas. She knew this, because she'd peeked around the doorway yesterday, observing him as he opened his gifts in the parlor, surrounded by his family and the glowing candles of the Christmas tree. Now she understood why his face had lit up as he'd unwrapped it. It was a treasure.

A sudden, intense yearning filled her, a yearning so powerful, that it startled her: *I want to read.*

Taking a breath, she set her duster aside and sat at his desk, knowing she mustn't be long, for Lizzy expected the room to be cleaned within the hour. Gray light filtered through a window, its hazy rectangle settling on the book and illuminating the pages.

"F," she said aloud, again startled. How had she known what letter it was?

Then a distant memory formed in her mind.

*Secret school.*

That was what they'd called it. She had almost forgotten. No, she *had* forgotten. How long ago was that? Six years? Seven? Since before her memories began.

Secret school . . . and who had been at secret school? Several of them. Kate, Breck, and . . . Monette creased her forehead, trying to remember. It was so difficult, like trying to see a faraway building on a foggy day. No matter how she strained, her mind could not focus the image.

Yet she knew her letters.

The plantation bell rang, shattering Monette's concentration like glass. She slammed the book shut and rose from the desk so quickly that the chair flew back with a clatter. Heart thundering, she stood staring at the book, her duster, the chair lying on its side, the rectangle of light long since faded into the drabness of day.

Panicked, Monette set the chair aright, grabbed her duster, and straightened her clothes as if reading a book had caused them to fly into disarray. She would have to hurry back later and clean like fury.

In the new north addition, apart from the big house, Breck's room opened directly onto a gallery. As she flew out of Breck's room and clattered down the gallery steps onto the grass, Monette felt guilt stamped upon her face—as if anyone who looked at her would know she had been in Breck's room, opening his books, reading his treasures, sounding her letters.

As she hurried into the yard to take her place in line, she thought: *I have sinned.*

The yard behind the big house teemed with field hands and servants. They seemed to mill about at random, unorganized, until gradually forming into lines, crushing the grass underfoot with clumsy homemade shoes. Normally, the bell rang twice per day: once to arise, and once at bedtime (except on Sundays, when they gathered for inspection and to receive their weekly rations). So, whenever the bell rang in the middle of a non-Sunday, it meant only one thing:

*Trouble.*

Monette hurried to her usual spot beside Mammy Hester. The household servants always gathered together. Within that grouping, husbands stood with wives, and children with parents. In Monette and Mammy Hester's case, they shared a room, and that was enough. Face hot with guilt, Monette mumbled a quick hello to Mammy Hester, not daring to look at her. Instead, she took her place in line, facing the big house like a soldier in a regiment.

"Huh," grunted Mammy Hester. "Don't Mammy Hester even rate a kiss, or is I just getting too ugly for such nonsense?"

"Sorry, Mammy Hester." Monette quickly brushed the woman's bony cheek with her lips, embarrassed to have forgotten their customary greeting. She added, "I don't think you're ugly. I think you're beautiful as a flower."

"Huh," Mammy grunted again, but Monette could tell she was pleased. "Lord bless me, if I didn't know better, I'd think you was buttering me up so you can borrow my new Sunday hat I gots for Christmas from Miss Sarah."

Monette smiled. "How did you guess?"

Shaking her head in mock exasperation, Mammy Hester patted Monette's shoulder and then faced the big house, perhaps wondering along with Monette what the trouble was now. Stolen pig? Runaway? Epidemic on its way?

Mars William sat astride his horse, leaning over the saddle as he conferred with Quincy, the head driver, who stood beside him. On the other side of Mars William sat Breck on a black gelding. He gazed over everyone's heads, seemingly focused on nothing at all. In his hands, he held a ledger.

Still, they waited.

Then, from the other side of Monette, startling her with foul breath and a tickling in her ear, a voice whispered, "Don't I get a kiss?"

Monette recoiled.

Fatima.

"Please leave me alone."

Like the underside of a rock, teeming with moistness and creepy things, the whisper continued, "I seen you racing out of Breck's bedroom like your hair was on fire. Whatsomeever you done, I's gonna tell."

Fear flashed through Monette, but even so, she knew Fatima was lying. Like boys tossing lines in a creek, she was merely fishing for a bite.

"Please go away."

"Make me."

Fortunately, just then, Fatima's mother hissed, "Get on over here, girl, 'fore Mars William sees you outta line."

Before Fatima left, she pried a scab off her arm and popped it into her mouth. "That's what I does to yellow niggers." Then she was gone, standing by Lizzy, chewing slowly, her face a mask of innocence.

Monette hated her.

Fatima, who pressed her against walls, giggling when she felt Monette tremble. Fatima, who scattered smoldering ashes across the floor, saying she hoped the whole place burned down. Fatima, who spat in the gravy. Fatima, who pinched bruises onto Monette's arms, whispering, "Yellow nigger," as she squeezed her fingers together. "Dandified, frenchified, yellow nigger."

Monette knew it was wrong to hate; Miss Sarah told her again and again—told all of them—that hatred seeped into your heart like poison and made you think and do bad things. Miss Sarah said to love your enemies and to ask for forgiveness. Just last week, Miss Sarah said that those who hate would go to the everlasting lake of fire and brimstone—that only those who love their fellow man could go to heaven. Monette shivered, trying not to hate, trying to love like Miss Sarah wanted her to, but her thoughts darkened whenever she looked at Fatima. Whenever she thought of Fatima.

*Fatima.*

Oh, yes, Monette hated her.

So Monette did the only thing she knew how, the one thing that protected her when her thoughts loomed like monsters, all darkness and fear. It was automatic, an unconscious act of the mind. She pushed the thought of Fatima far from her. Pushed it away, away . . . until Fatima no longer existed. Gone. Vanished.

Monette unclenched her fists, unaware she had squeezed her hands so tightly. She sighed as the muscles of her jaw released, and her breathing calmed.

Mars William was calling roll.

Breck was writing in the ledger.

A hush pressed down from the sky, enveloping them in silence, leaden and gray. It took a long time, this counting. Each family shuffling forward. Monette taking her own turn, along with Mammy Hester.

Finally, after all the families had been called forward, Mars William took the ledger from Breck. He studied it, then handed it back to his son.

"According to the ledger," he said, loud enough for everyone to hear, "there should be one hundred and seventy-five of you. But this morning, there are only one hundred and seventy-two. Now, how do you explain that?" He pushed his hat back and peered out at them, as if one of them were going to explain it.

Monette looked down. She did not want Mars William looking at her.

"Well, now. Since none of you seem to know, and since all of you are standing there like angels with harps and halos, I'll explain it so you can understand the situation along with me. Sawney, Primus, and Sam have absconded. They have taken what lawfully belongs to me and disappeared. Now I'm sure you're standing there right now deep in puzzlement asking yourselves what they took that belongs to me. Well, I'll tell you. Themselves. That's right. Three healthy males, ages thirty, twenty-four, and twenty-three. Worth almost four thousand dollars. That's right, four thousand dollars. Now I ask which one of you would stand by and do nothing, do *nothing,* if someone stole something of yours worth four thousand dollars?"

He paused again.

Monette stayed as still as she could, although her nose itched and she thought she might sneeze. She'd learned long ago to become still and small if Mars William was looking for answers.

"What I should do is tack their hides to the side of the barn, but I'll tell you what. Since it's the Christmas holidays, and I'm feeling a little of the holiday spirit myself, I promise to go easy on them if you'll just tell me where they are. Not only that, but whoever comes forward with information leading to their capture will receive five dollars. Now, considering how my generosity's been taken advantage of, absconding during the holidays and all, that's a pretty kind offer. I'll even give you a pass to town to spend your money. And no one has to know except you and me."

Out of the corner of her eye, Monette saw Mars William lean forward on his saddle horn as if pressing his point home. His voice became hard and steely. "Of course, there's always the possibility that one of you's harboring the fugitives, or stealing food for them, or some such rascality. If I catch any of you going behind my back when such a kind offer's been put on the table, there will be hell to pay. Any questions?"

They were dismissed.

Monette murmured a quick goodbye to Mammy Hester and hurried back to clean Breck's room, her duster still in hand. As she exited the yard, someone called to her. "Monette! Wait up!"

Still hurrying, she glanced back, anxious to finish her task, wondering who was shouting her name. She frowned when she saw that it was that big boy from the fields. Cyrus, if she remembered right. Why did he always pester her? Pretending she neither heard nor saw him, she slipped inside Breck's room, closing the door behind her. There.

Time to dust and polish.

# Chapter 4

KATE STOOD BEFORE THE crackling fire in the parlor, her dress arrayed about her in shimmering folds of crimson. The child's voice lifted higher, higher, seeming not to strain at all as she hit what Sarah knew to be a high A. Sarah strummed her mandolin, thinking, dear God, my daughter has the voice of an angel.

Kate finished and everyone clapped, smiling at one another.

"Just the way it should be sung," said Sarah.

"Bravo!" said Emma. "Katherine dear, you are truly a nightingale."

"A fine performance," said John.

"Couldn't have done it better myself," said Mehitable.

"It's called an aria." Kate tossed her hair over her shoulder. "At least, that's what Monsieur Déclouet calls it."

"Well done," said Breck, smiling. "You've impressed me."

"Bravo! Bravo!" echoed the twins, still clapping joyfully.

Only William remained silent, sunk in the shadows of the parlor, farthest away from the fire, farthest away from the twinkling candles and the fresh pine scent of the Christmas tree. Sarah knew he was brooding about the runaways. Whenever anyone absconded, William always fell into what Sarah believed was a cross between helpless despair and blind rage. The matter was made worse by the fact that Sawney was one of the runaways, a field hand who was a constant thorn in William's side. William had wanted to hunt for the runaways this very evening, but Sarah had forestalled him, saying, "There will be plenty of time to search tomorrow. For tonight, let's enjoy each other and our family as we'd planned." He'd argued, but had finally given in. Now, looking at him, Sarah rather wished she had let him search for the runaways as he'd wanted. He certainly looked sour and in no mood for arias. In fact, Sarah was positive he hadn't heard a single note Kate had sung.

She closed her eyes briefly, thinking, I'll worry about William later.

For now, family.

As Kate basked in the afterglow of the family's approval, Sarah glanced about the parlor, as if to assure herself that her family was still there.

Ever since their births six years ago, the twins had attached themselves to Uncle John. It seemed whenever they were with him (which wasn't as often as Sarah liked, seeing as John was kept constantly busy between his doctoring and plantation duties at Woodleigh), the twins stopped their fidgeting and ceased their questions, content to merely be in John's presence. Both towheads, little Georgie and Thomas nestled now in John's lap following their boisterous approval of Kate's aria. They leaned their heads together in comfortable camaraderie. Sarah could tell by their leaden blinks that it would not be long before they fell fast asleep.

Emma and Mehitable sat side by side on the settee. Two more different ladies, Sarah was sure, could never be found on God's green earth. Opposite in stature, in bearing, in voice, in temperament, in every characteristic that could possibly be opposite, yet Sarah loved them both. How strange life was. What a testament to the power of love.

And Breck. Sitting so gentlemanly beside Emma. Nothing in his features belied his troubled thoughts. Yet, Sarah knew he was troubled. About what, she wasn't sure. Many things, she supposed, only knowing that he had been troubled almost from the day of his birth. For years she'd sensed his turmoil, but try as she might, she could no more unlock the door to his mind than she could tear down a brick wall with her bare hands. Breck seemed to keep her at a distance, to respect and love her as a good son should, but to never truly let her in. The older he became, and the more he withdrew from her, the more Sarah released him to God. She had no choice. For the older *she* became, now thirty-four years of age, the more she realized that Breck did not belong to her. That he never had, and never would.

She turned her attention back to Kate. Never, Sarah believed, had her daughter looked more lovely than on this evening. Dressed in a new gown, trimmed with creamy lace and crimson brocade, Kate stood with her shoulders back and her head held high, seeming elegant with the statuesque sweep of her long neck. For the first time, Sarah suddenly realized that no longer was Kate the tall, gangly child. Tonight, especially, the child's face captured the glimpse and glow of womanhood. *Is it possible?* thought Sarah. *Is my little girl becoming a lady?* "Katherine dear, how about, 'Flow Gently, Sweet Afton'?"

"Certainly, Mama."

Sarah played an introduction, and once again, Kate's voice filled the parlor with sweet, pure notes.

*"Flow gently sweet Afton among thy green braes,*
*Flow gently, I'll sing a song in thy praise.*
*My Mary's asleep by thy murmuring stream;*
*Flow gently, sweet Afton, disturb not her dream, . . ."*

As the music wove its magical strands around Sarah, a sweetness, a deliciousness of life overwhelmed her. *My life is full,* she realized, *and regardless of what has come before and what comes after, I am at peace.*

⁓ℓℓ⁓

Like a feather caught in an updraft, floating ever higher, the sweet strains of mandolin and melody drifted up the staircase and into the attic bedroom where Monette lay awake on her bed, the candle on the bedside table casting a jaundiced glow about the attic room.

Just minutes ago, she'd helped Mammy Hester and Uncle Henry serve hot, mulled cider and holiday bread with nuts and dried fruit to everyone gathered in the parlor, feeling more and more alone even as they became increasingly festive. Standing in the doorway, seeing the candles glowing on the tree, John affectionately ruffling the twins' hair, Miss Sarah embracing Kate, telling her how beautiful she was, Monette had left and gone silently to her room, knowing her absence would go unnoticed—at least until they needed something, or until Mammy Hester came grumbling, wondering where she'd run off to.

Monette absently picked at the yarn tacking, noticing the quilt's musty odor. It had been a while since it had been laundered. But laundering at Christmastime was not easy. The family's garments were paramount, followed by their bedding, and, of course, the kitchen laundry and linens from the dining table. Monette breathed the musty smell, imagining it smelled of lilac, like the one time she'd dared to lie in Miss Sarah's sheets and nestle her face into the pillow and breathe in the scent of Kate's mother.

From downstairs, Kate began singing another song.

*"There was a place in childhood,*
*That I remember well,*
*And there a voice of sweetest tone*
*Bright fairy tales did tell;*
*And gentle words and fond embrace*
*Were given with joy to me,*
*When I was in that happy state,*
*Upon my mother's knee*
*My mother dear, my mother dear!*
*My gentle, gentle mother! . . ."*

Rolling onto her back and closing her eyes, Monette let the music enfold her like a tender caress, wondering simply, as she had wondered a hundred, a thousand times before, whether her own mother had ever set her upon her knee. Whether her mother had ever wrapped her arms about her, ever whispered into her ear, *Monette, my dear, how beautiful you are.*

## Chapter 5

A GRAY AND RAINY February day. Another horrid school morning. Kate sighed, irritated, hardly able to believe it was already half past seven, and that Monette was here with the breakfast tray, telling her to get her lazy bones out of bed. And what a horrid night. Tossing and turning, unable to get comfortable, feeling cross that she was tossing and turning, and so tossing and turning even more because she was cross.

Not only that, but she didn't feel well. Not *real* well, anyway. Perhaps not even well enough for school. But pondering this possibility, she rejected it. She knew she'd have to be really sick to get out of lessons. (The last time she'd gotten out of lessons, she'd had yellow fever, not counting the time she'd tested Grandma Mehitable's new bottle of sherry just to see what all the fuss was about.)

She threw back the covers and got up, knowing there was nothing for it but to get ready.

That's when Monette started to scream.

Where Kate had lain was a puddle of blood the size of a pancake. Bewildered, Kate peered down at herself, wondering where the blood could be coming from. Even as she lifted her nightgown, she knew. She felt it, trickling from between her legs and down her thighs. Suddenly, her knees felt weak. "Get Mama," was all she could say.

The screaming disappeared into the back bedroom, then the hallway. A trail of screams. The rapid tramp of feet up the stairs as the screaming moved above her head. Then, down the stairs the screaming came, and suddenly Mammy Hester was there, eyes wide, her mouth hanging open, while Kate stared back weakly, battling a wave of dizziness, leaning against the bedpost. I'm dying, she thought.

"Lord have mercy!"

Monette stood behind Mammy Hester, still screaming.

Mammy Hester turned. "Land sakes, chile! Hush that awful racket! Now fetch Miss Sarah. Hurry—"

Just then, William rushed into the room, breathing hard, his face chalk-white. "Christ almighty," was all he said.

Then Sarah entered.

"Mama!" cried Kate.

After one look, her mother turned and pushed William and Monette out the door, latching it behind them. Then she found Kate a wooden chair and made her sit, shoving her head between her knees. "Mammy dear," she said calmly, "set a basin on the rug before the fire and fill it with warm water."

"Yes'm, Miss Sarah."

"I'll need fresh towels and, of course, the necessary accouterments."

"Yes'm, Miss Sarah."

"Inform Mr. Gilbert there will be no school today for Miss Katherine."

"'Course, Miss Sarah. No school today." After bustling about a bit, Mammy Hester left the room.

"What's happening, Mama?"

"Hush now. You're going to be perfectly fine."

"What's happening?"

"Patience, dear Katherine. First things first."

Kate shivered as her mother stripped her of clothing, stood her in the basin, and began washing her with a soft cloth. Water slipped down her skin and into the basin, billowing into a watery pink. Some of the blood had dried, and Sarah scrubbed until Kate's skin smarted.

Now that the fuss was over, Kate asked her mother again and again what had happened. But it wasn't until she was dried and dressed, with her "accouterments" in place, that Sarah finally told her.

———ele———

If this was what it meant to be a woman, Kate didn't want any part of it.

The belt was horrid.

A gigantic wad of cotton toweling ran between her legs like a diaper, pinned to a belt at the front and back. She hated it. It itched. It got caught in between. It made her waddle. She wanted to rip it off and toss it out the window. Then, if *that* wasn't bad enough, to be told what these—these—*womanly flows* were for!

"They're for babies," Mama said. "When you're married, your husband, well, you see, he—he comes to you and loves you and, well, makes a baby inside of you. It's all very—well, um—very natural, Katherine dear. Once you have a baby growing inside, then the flows stop. Until after you have the baby, that is. Then it happens once per month. It's all part of the womanly process. It's the way God made us. It's nothing to be frightened of. Oh dear—I mean, it's just not polite to talk about it, is all."

It was late now, the moon a shimmer of yellow behind the clouds. Kate sat under the magnolia tree in her and Monette's secret glade, her back against the trunk. A lantern burned weakly beside her, the candle in need of trimming, for it was smoking and blacking the glass. The dampness of the grass was already seeping through her cloak, her gown, her petticoats, and her accouterments, but she decided she didn't care. Let herself be damp.

One would think she could find privacy within the closed doors of her bedroom, but it was not so. Always there was someone bustling in or out, throwing wood on the fire, changing the linens, informing her it was time for supper, telling her to get her lazy bones out of bed, that it was time for lessons, or time to practice her music, or to help Mama with the sewing, or the butchering of the hogs, or the canning of preserves. Always, always there was someone. But here in the secret place, where none knew but Monette, there was privacy in abundance.

Tonight, her hair fell in waves down her shoulders and back. She hugged her knees to her chest.

So that's what they were for.

The womanly flows.

For making babies.

She'd seen it in the fields. Stallions with mares. Bulls with heifers. The hound dogs, even. It was hilarious. But when she tried to imagine it with people instead of horses . . .

Appalled, Kate suddenly realized that *Mama and Papa . . .*

*. . . he comes to you and loves you and, well, makes a baby inside of you.*

No, this being a woman thing was not at all what she wanted.

Kate stared out into the darkness, listening to an owl hoot.

What a day.

Every time she turned around, it seemed, the pad needed changing. Unable to do it herself with all her skirts and petticoats and whatnot—it was downright impossible—she'd been forced to holler for help. And while Mama was showing Monette how to change the pads, she mentioned something about corsets.

Oh, Lord.

What a day.

That evening, well, it was simply horrid, too. Entering the dining room for supper, trying not to waddle, it was as if everyone stared at her, knowing. As if they'd had a big plantation announcement. Papa even stood as she seated herself. "Evening, Kate," he mumbled. "You're looking well."

She could feel his embarrassment, and she blushed, remembering what he'd seen. While the twins gawked, Breck gaped back and forth between her and Papa, as if knowing *something* was going on, even if he didn't know exactly what it was.

Oh, Lord.

Then the belt began acting up. Itching her. Climbing. She wanted to squirm. Adjust. Scratch. She could actually feel herself *flow*. Such an odd feeling. But instead of squirming, adjusting, or scratching, she sat there saying stupid things like, please and thank you, or yes Mama, or no Papa.

What a day.

Suddenly, Kate snapped her head up, listening. She heard a shuffle. The sound of rustling, branches being parted. Someone was entering through the tunnel of bushes. "Who's there?" she hissed.

Out of the darkness came a whisper, "Oh, *mon amie,* thank goodness I've found you. I don't like being alone in the woods at night."

"Monette! Don't sneak up on me like that! Criminy—you scared the daylights out of me!"

Monette materialized out of the darkness, moving toward her into the shadowy circle of lantern light. "Everyone is wondering where you ran off to," she said. "Your mother is pacing the gallery."

"Well, everyone can just keep wondering," Kate replied, hearing the grumpiness in her voice. "I need to be alone for a spell."

Monette stopped in front of Kate. Twigs and bits of leaves stuck to her skirt. Two sodden patches of mud dampened her skirt front, where Monette must have knelt down. "Then I should leave?"

"Of course not," said Kate, looking up at her. "You're my best friend, so you don't count."

"What do you mean, I don't count?" Monette looked both perplexed and hurt.

Kate took Monette's hand, rushing to add, "What I mean is, silly girl, I like being with you, and you've never bothered me a day in my life. So, when I'm with you, it's the same as being alone." Kate giggled then, her mood suddenly lighter. "Oh, never mind. I can't explain it. I'm just glad you're here."

Monette smiled. She bent and kissed Kate's forehead. "Me too." She then gathered some moss into a pile, and settling next to Kate, said, "This morning, I thought you were dying."

"I thought I *was* dying with all your screaming. You about gave me a heart attack. I've never heard anyone shriek so loudly."

Monette looked at her, and Kate was surprised to see the concern on her face, reflected in her amber eyes. "Then you aren't dying?"

"Of course not, silly. It's a bother, certainly. But Mama says it's perfectly natural. That it's just a womanly transition."

"A what?"

Kate wasn't sure exactly what "transition" meant either, so she rephrased it. "It's for making babies."

"Babies?"

Kate lay down, pillowing her head in Monette's lap. Monette played with her hair while Kate told her about making babies, about husbands and wives, and stallions and mares. She was surprised when she felt a smugness at being the one to tell her. That she *knew* something about life itself. Womanhood. Uncomfortable and irritating as it was. After Kate finished her explanation, Monette was silent, as if the thought of procreation was too dreadful to believe.

"To think that a man and a woman do this," Monette finally said.

"It's true."

"But why?"

"To make a baby, I suppose. Otherwise, what would be the point?"

"I'll never do this."

"Me neither," replied Kate, peering up at Monette. "Pinky promise?"

"Pinky promise."

But even as they linked their pinkies, again Kate was surprised by a gentle flutter against her breastbone. Despite the irritation of the day, the wad of toweling, the stares, there was something about all this—this woman stuff that was mysterious. As if a secret doorway beckoned. That one day, *one day,* she would know what lay beyond.

Once the February rains finally stopped, the yard behind the big house erupted with activity. Overnight, it seemed, spring had arrived.

The yard was the hub of the plantation. Enclosed by a split-rail fence, it measured 240 by 300 feet, and contained some of the most important structures in Fox Creek: the smokehouse, the dairy, the jail, the hospital. . . . Fifteen buildings in all, each surrounded by its own flurry of activity during one particular time or another.

The laundry was one of those flurried hubs. For weeks, laundered items had been unable to dry completely, often taken down still damp from the lines before mildew set in (for everyone knew mildew stains ruined a garment), and then washed and hung again, hopefully for the last time. During the first few sunny days, the head laundress and her crew had already laundered more garments and linens than in the three weeks prior. Heads wrapped in turbans, they squatted beside and stooped over the huge cast-iron kettles, blinking in the steam, sometimes singing, sometimes yakking up a storm, stirring the mounds of clothes with paddles until the water cooled enough for their hands. Clotheslines stretched from the laundry house to the hospital, the lines so heavy there was scarcely room for a rooster to walk underneath without getting its tail feathers wet.

While the laundry continued its hectic pace, Sarah ordered the drives swept. During the rains, the winds had blown Spanish moss from the trees, burying the drives until the carriages could no longer pass. It took two old men and a gang of children three days to clear the drives. Again and again, they filled the wagon with moss and drove it to the yard, where the moss was picked through, then hung over the split-rail fence to dry, later to be made into mattresses.

The supply of candles was almost gone, scarcely enough for three weeks more. In another pocket of activity, Sarah began the task of replenishing the supply. Mutton tallow mixed with beeswax (with a little camphor and alum) made the most perfect, clear-burning candles, and it seemed no one else could dip them to the perfection she demanded. In one day, Sarah dipped eighteen dozen candles—a good day's work, even for a chandler.

"Them's mighty fine candles," said Mammy Hester, nodding with approval. "Nobody makes them like Miss Sarah do."

Sarah beamed under such praise and locked the candles away in the storehouse, patting the keys at her waist after the final lock was turned. Another task completed.

Busy as it was, it was Sarah's favorite time of year. It was the time of year when things that had been put off for another day, another week, or another month, could now be accomplished. It was the time of year when the promise of new life was fulfilled. She could already see tiny green shoots pushing through the soil of her spring garden, planted in January. Soon, the entire plantation would burst with new plant and animal life—from roses and plums and strawberries to chicks and lambs and piglets. It was a new beginning. A new year.

God be praised.

Sarah made her rounds to the various buildings, consulting with those in charge, giving instructions, and overseeing all the activities. This year, Kate accompanied her on her rounds. As Kate was fast becoming a young lady and an accomplished seamstress, Sarah believed it was time to delve even further into the responsibilities of the plantation mistress. Sarah knew many ladies—ladies like herself, mistresses of plantations—who ignored the training of their daughters in such matters, finding it easier to direct the operations themselves without having to be a teacher and mentor besides. But Sarah believed that such an attitude was shortsighted, perhaps even bordering on lazy. After all, the day Kate married might be the day she began her duties as mistress. Sarah didn't want her daughter unprepared. She'd known young ladies who'd become plantation mistresses as young as fifteen. While Sarah had no intention of allowing Kate to marry so young, still, it did happen, and that was just a few months away. Besides that, there was still finishing school, which would take Kate away from home, further removing her from the sphere of Sarah's influence. But that was another matter entirely, and one Sarah did not have time to think about. Not now, anyway.

Her tasks at the loom house completed, and satisfied with her chat with the head seamstress, Sarah donned her sun hat and headed to the gardens with Kate. Trailing after them was a trash gang, composed of young children, pregnant women, and the elderly—those who were too young, or who could no longer work the fields for health reasons.

"Let's see now, I need the walkways brushed and scrubbed down to the brick. They've grown over with moss in places. And make sure the debris gets hauled away in the wagons. I don't want to see it scattered about the beds willy-nilly, like last time. See these beds? I want them spaded so they're nice and soft. I'm going to plant japonicas here, and some azaleas. Now, won't that look lovely? And see this hedge? It's a mess and needs a trim. Tamar, bring me my gloves. And see here, I need all these pots gone through. There must be a thousand of them. Toss the ones that are broken and clean out the others. I'll be potting my cuttings starting today, and I'll likely use them all. Basil, be a dear and fetch Miss Katherine and me some lemonade. I declare, it almost feels like summer!"

Kate knew her mother was in heaven. She could hear it in her voice, see it in the shining of her green eyes as she looked from task to task, her face softly lit by a delicate smile. Kate knew that the darling of her mother's life was her ornamental garden, and that if she could spend every moment of every day gardening, she would be completely content. But try as she might, Kate could find no joy in the garden, no thrill in running her hands through dirt, feeling it cake beneath her fingernails. As she followed her mother into the potting shed, hearing her mother breathe deeply, happily, Kate sneezed, her nose itching with the musty odor of soil, mildew, and mice.

She'd rather be riding her horse.

She'd rather be doing a whole lot of things than following Mama around. Such tasks as laundry, weaving, carding, candle-making, and smoking meat really didn't interest her. She knew, however, that such tasks were necessary because she was a woman now. And women, as a rule, were experts at all the boring things in life: reading, sewing, soapmaking, preserves, healing the sick, birthing babies, on and on and on. It was the realm of womanhood that she would be happy to do without.

Kate resolved then and there that, as a plantation mistress, she would be the one elegantly dressed, inviting heaps of company every day for fox hunts, horse races, and parties until dawn. There would be music and dancing and fine food and plenty of funny jokes, and if someone wasn't funny, or if they were stupid, or couldn't dance, well, they just wouldn't be invited again.

Besides, with almost two hundred people working *for* you, the work should be finished without you having to do it yourself. Otherwise, Kate thought, what's the blasted point?

"Well now, Katherine dear, let's get started. We've got a lot to do."

Pot the rose cuttings. Transplant geraniums. Outside to plant dahlia tubers. To the hot house. Set out the annuals. Check on the progress of the trash gang. It was sweaty work, and Kate told Basil to hurry and fetch her another glass of lemonade, which he did.

She guzzled it down. "Mama," she said, wiping her mouth on her sleeve, watching as her mother knelt in one of the beds and forked the soil around a sweet olive.

"Mm-hmm."

"How did you and Papa meet?"

"What, dear?"

"How did you and Papa meet?"

Sarah gazed up at her from beneath the brim of her straw hat, her eyes shaded from the sun. Today her mother wore her "gardening clothes," a brown cotton blouse with sleeves extending to the wrists, and a brown skirt—the color of dirt. "Why, it was not long after your grandfather passed away. My brother and I came here to Fox Creek Plantation to see your grandmother, Mehitable. She was ailing, and your uncle John was the new medical doctor in these parts. I was just keeping him company."

"So that's when you met Papa for the first time?"

"Why, no, honey, like anyone who lives here in West Feliciana, we all know everybody. No one's a stranger. You know how it is. I'd known your father around town and at the various functions just like I know anyone. But I was just a child when he left for university, and, well, when he came home, I guess I was all grown-up. Or mostly grown-up anyhow."

Kate chewed on her lip, thinking. Then she asked, "So, was it love at first sight? As grown-ups, I mean?"

"Well, I don't know." Her mother stopped working the soil and tilted her head, looking thoughtful. Tendrils of auburn hair escaped from her hat, curling to her shoulders. "I guess it was love at first sight. I mean, I thought he was handsome—"

"You thought Papa was handsome?" Kate asked incredulously.

"Well, of course, dear. Maybe it was the way he looked at me. He made me feel—I don't know, beautiful, I suppose. Special. Every woman wants to feel beautiful and special."

"Did you love him?"

"Not right off. Oh, Katherine, I don't know if I should be telling you this. It doesn't seem right."

"Oh, Mama, please. I've wondered for such a long time now, and all Mammy Hester will tell me is that you two were love birds and no one could keep you apart. Please, Mama."

Sarah sat back on her heels and removed her gloves. "Well, it was a love that grew over time. It wasn't there all at once, although I did admire him from the start, taking over the plantation like he did after his father's death. Oh, I don't know how to explain it; it's not something I talk about very often."

"Mammy Hester says you were only fifteen."

Then Kate saw it. Her mother blushed. She'd hit the nail on the head! Mama had only been fifteen!

Sarah bent back to her task, facing away from Kate, stabbing the soil with her trowel. "When your father and I married, I was eighteen. A respectable age for marriage."

"But you were fifteen when you fell in love, weren't you? Did you—did you—"

"Really, Katherine, I don't see what this has to do with anything. Hand me my rake, would you?"

Even though the conversation was clearly over—from her mother's side, anyway—Kate was satisfied. Wildly happy, almost. Fifteen—just a breath away.

## Chapter 6

All was silent. Kate lay in bed, suffering from cramps. Breck was in the schoolroom with Mr. Gilbert. Miss Sarah tended to the sick at the hospital. The twins played outside somewhere. Fatima was sweeping her way through the butler's pantry.

Monette was alone.

She opened the book, always delighted at the sound of the pages as they turned, like dry leaves rubbing together, like the rustle of crinoline. As if the sound was made just for her. A secret sound.

She knew some of her words now. It had been a laborious, yet wondrous, process of sounding her letters, stringing them together to create a word, like beads on a necklace. Again, secret. She sounded each word, rolling it across her tongue as if to savor each nuance, each syllable—a banquet of consonants and vowels, a forbidden feast, an altar upon which she sacrificed her sinlessness.

That she sinned, she knew.

She had tried to stop herself, to dust around the book, to ignore it, but simply could not help herself. The words were a sweet elixir, a bottle filled with sin.

Each time she came to Breck's room, she pulled the drapes closed, casting the room into shadow. With trembling hands, she lit the three-armed candelabra, sat at his desk, and opened his book, believing no one could see her—not even God—pretending she had not heard the sermon about the slave Hagar, who hid herself away. And who, when confronted by an angel of the Lord, cowered and said, *Thou God seest me.*

Today, like so many days, she was enveloped in language. Wrapped in its blanket like an enraptured lover, whispering endearments. Her voice cradled in the stillness of the room, candlelight casting subtle shadows across the page. Just a little longer, she thought. Then I shall clean. Just a little longer. No one shall know.

"R-A-S-P. Raassp. Rasp of the S-W-O-R-D. Sss-word. S-word? What is an s-word? *Je n'en ai aucune idée!*"

"It's a sword," said a voice from behind her.

Monette stood and whirled, the chair crashing to the floor.

It was Breck.

Her breath caught in her throat. "How long have you been watching me?"

"Long enough."

"I—I thought you were in the schoolroom with—"

"I was. But I needed to fetch some supplies. Mr. Gilbert is taking me on a morning excursion."

For an instant, she considered running, bolting like a rabbit from the meadow into the shelter of trees, but even in thinking it, she knew it was ridiculous. Where would she go? Where could she hide that they would not find her? Breck's eyes revealed nothing of what he was thinking. Was he disappointed in her? Angry? Panic coursed through her veins, sharp and biting. She had been caught doing something she'd been told again and again was forbidden. She suddenly remembered Reverend Scarborough sweeping a stiffened finger over the congregation and thundering, "He that knoweth his master's will and doeth it not, shall be beaten with many stripes!"

She hung her head and whispered, "Please do not tell. *Je vous implore.*"

Wisteria drooped from the oaks, pregnant with purple. Vines snaked up tree trunks before exploding into a plethora of wild honeysuckle and jasmine. Camellias, pines, china trees, magnolias, chestnuts, poplars, Spanish moss—a savage garden. An intoxicating temple built for birds. It had rained during the night. Little by little, the late-March sun banished the morning chill until the steam rose in sultry waves.

On this particular morning of wisteria, with Miss Kate unable to join them, Mr. James Gilbert had taken the opportunity to trek with Breck into the dense woods opposite Fox Creek for a dual lesson in biology and art. Now they sat amid the jumble of forest, breathing the earthy dampness while birds chorused and fluttered. Seated on a log, each with his own sketchpad, they drew in the manner of John James Audubon, whom Gilbert admired, owning the complete volumes of *Birds of America*. Many of the birds, he knew, Audubon had drawn in West Feliciana, a source of great pride for the parish. Before them, removed from a trap set yesterday, a juvenile wild turkey lay on its back, the skin of its torso pinned back, its innards exposed. They had already drawn the turkey intact, in what they hoped was a natural pose. Now they attempted to draw its insides, with attention to proportion, coloration, and proper labels. Not an easy task, even for Gilbert.

It was too steamy for Gilbert's taste and, besides that, his allergies, like the wisteria, were in full bloom. The pollen from the oak trees coated everything: his clothing, his hair (what was left of it), his eyes, his nostrils, the lenses of his spectacles, even his paints and his sketchpad. Everywhere, a golden dust. It was enough to drive any Northerner insane.

He missed the seasons. He missed the tangible cutoff from autumn to winter—a November snowfall, bulbs pushing their tender shoots through the snow to herald the tempest of spring, the hot days of summer, although not *crushingly* hot. Not like the drugged, torpid days of a never-ending Louisiana summer that made him wish he were dead.

Ah, well. They had warned him.

But, unlike his fellow graduates at the University of Philadelphia, who scattered to various teaching institutes to live out their days in dismal classrooms at pitiful wages, Gilbert had heard of the lucrative possibilities as a plantation tutor. Up to five hundred dollars per annum, room and board provided. He had naively dismissed the Southern weather as a mere inconvenience, ignored his friends' admonitions regarding the strangeness of Southern ways and their peculiar institution, kissed his sister goodbye, and boarded a vessel heading south.

During the first year, his resolve was sorely tried. If it weren't for Breck, he would have left long ago. Bugs, alligators, heat, and humidity (sweet Jesus, wasn't that enough?), followed by a scorching case of swamp fever. Gilbert didn't think he would survive, thinking he would become one of the grass-covered mounds in the plantation cemetery, and that his sister and her husband would someday receive a letter from Miss Sarah saying how sorry they all were.

During the more lucid periods of his illness, Gilbert's intention, once he recovered, *if* he recovered, was to head back North. Experiment a disaster. Colleagues correct. But while still breathless with weakness, unable to even pack his trunks for the carriage ride to Bayou Clare, much less board a steamship for the long voyage North, his pupil surprised him by coming every evening, reading to him during his convalescence, discussing the classics, and doing his figures, until Gilbert finally concluded that he was here for a reason. That, critters and sickness aside, this was where he belonged. For now. With a scholarly-minded boy destined to become a planter, an occupation esteemed by Southerners as the pinnacle of manhood. (Besides, they said you built an immunity to swamp fever after a while.)

That was seven years ago.

Gilbert slapped a mosquito on his neck and set his sketch aside, his eyes itching and watering. He removed his spectacles, cleaned them with his handkerchief, mopped his face and neck, and blew the pollen out of his nose. After tucking his handkerchief into his pocket and replacing his spectacles, he observed Breck, something Gilbert liked to do just as he liked to observe a bird, or a river, or a field dotted with cotton pickers. He was an easy boy to teach. Boy, man, whatever he was. Gilbert wasn't sure, knowing only that boys were rarely six feet two inches tall, and men were rarely fifteen years old. Gilbert figured time would sort things out. Meanwhile, during these years of Gilbert's influence, he was doing everything in his power to feed the boy's insatiable appetite for learning. Not for the first time, Gilbert felt a deep sadness that this young man would waste his life in the fields raising cotton. A boy like this, with a mind such as he had, should be housed in the best institutions this country had to offer.

But it was not his decision.

Breck looked up from his work, seeming to sense that his instructor watched him. "How does it look?" He held out his sketch for Gilbert to see.

It was stiff, rudimentary. The boy certainly was not an artist. It would have to be enough that his pupil learned attention to detail. Observation.

The traits of a good scientist. "It has promise. Your labels and proportions are correct, but your colors are off."

Breck studied the drawing, his cheek smudged with paint. "It's hard to see the colors sometimes with all the flies. Gives it an illusion of darkness."

"Agreed." Gilbert knocked the bird with the toe of his boot and the flies scattered, only to land again. "We're close to being done anyway."

"My father says painting's a woman's occupation."

Unable to keep the snap from his voice, Gilbert said, "It's biology, not art," disliking any reminder of William Jensey. They'd had more than a few run-ins. He remembered the time when William began taking his son out into the fields during the afternoons—first once per week, later increasing to three times per week—instead of allowing him to remain for his full six hours of instruction.

Gilbert had confronted William, and the heat of the conversation had risen by degrees until William finally said to Gilbert in that voice that could turn steely in a second, "Breck is my son. Someday he will be a planter. While he will indeed go to university when he is of age, and while math, science, and the classics are vital to his cultivation as a gentleman, I am sure, book learning must be balanced with his education in the field. Of what use is geometry when he is faced with fields of rotting cotton, or a labor force that rises against him because they sense weakness or ignorance on his part? Whether you like it or not, Mr. Gilbert, planting is his future. Seeing as your salary has not been decreased, I cannot see where it is your concern."

Breck looked away. "Biology doesn't require an exact replication of color. That is a skill of an artist."

Gilbert smiled, thinking, nothing escapes this boy's attention. "I must admit I think it a shame that a man cannot draw what he sees, put the miracle of nature on paper without someone demeaning his effort by calling it woman's work. Well, let it suffice that we have done enough creativity for one morning. Call it what you want."

Gilbert made to rise, but stopped when Breck did not move. He knew his student well enough to know the boy wanted to remain. Perhaps to talk. Very well. Gilbert allowed himself to lean back against the trunk of a tree. He folded his arms and closed his eyes, enjoying a spell outside the schoolroom. The chattering of the birds soothed him. The flitting from branch to branch. He would have to remember to save some of the turkey's feathers for the classroom.

"Why aren't negroes allowed to read?"

The question surprised Gilbert, prickling him with such shock that he realized he must have dozed off. "Excuse me?"

"I said, why aren't slaves allowed to read?"

"Well, uh, to be perfectly honest, I'm not certain." Gilbert ran a hand through his thinning hair. "It's the law, I know. But other than that, I—I guess it's because they're not well adapted to intellectual pursuits."

"Do you really believe that?"

The boy looked at him with such intensity, that Gilbert felt uncomfortable. Darkies? Learn to read? For what purpose? "I've never really thought about it before. Why?"

"No reason. Just wondering." At that, Breck gathered his supplies and put them in his satchel. "Sorry. Papa's expecting me." After tightening the straps of his satchel, he turned and smiled. "Thanks for the art lesson."

Gilbert watched as Breck ducked his head under a curtain of Spanish moss and disappeared up the deer path toward Fox Creek. As Breck slung his satchel over his shoulder, walking tall like his father, Gilbert suddenly realized that, though daily surrounded by almost two hundred people, the boy was, perhaps, the loneliest person Gilbert had ever known.

By the time his horse was saddled and ready to go, it was well past one o'clock, the hour appointed for Breck to meet his father in the fields. William was in the northeastern section, at least a mile distant. Breck mounted his horse, called his spotted hound, Rascal, and set off, loosening his shirt along the way, for it was as sultry as the kitchen on bread-baking day.

From the middle of the long northern border of the Jensey property, Fox Creek meandered south for a half mile before splitting into two tributaries. The western tributary, continuing as Fox Creek, wound its way south past the big house, slicing the entire property almost in half, leaving the smaller western property across the creek from the big house wild and wooded. The eastern tributary, Jensey Creek, exited the property in the middle of the eastern border, formerly isolating the northeastern corner of the property, an island to itself. But now, a new bridge spanned Jensey Creek, connecting the cultivated portion of the property with the, as till now, untamed northeastern section.

Breck urged his horse over the bridge. There was a hollow clatter of hooves on wood, and then they were on the other side. Rascal trotted ahead, nose to the ground, occasionally pausing to investigate the crawfish that scurried about the drainage ditches.

A few months ago, the northeastern section of the Jensey property had been a tangle of woods suitable for hunting and hideaways, but that had changed radically. It had become sugar land.

It was not a decision that had come to them lightly. For months, Breck and William had discussed the past few years' performance in terms of cotton. The truth was downright dismal, what with the loss of a major portion of their crop due to cotton worm, and then the rest of it being worth next to nothing, due to the bottoming out of cotton prices. Breck's father had been forced to borrow over eight thousand dollars from his factor for the third year in a row, just to continue operations.

"At this rate," William finally admitted, "we can't survive but a couple more years."

Breck agreed. How many more years could they take a loss before they called it quits? Sold the plantation and headed to Texas, where, in the aftermath of the war, land was for the taking? Where they could start again? It was a thought that was foremost in their minds. How much longer can we struggle? How much more money do we lose?

"What we need is a second crop," Breck had suggested one night, pleased when his father seemed to listen intently. "That way, if the cotton prices are low, or if the cotton worm comes again, a second crop will carry us through."

William replied, "Old Man Parsons swears that ribbon cane can be grown this far north. Says it has a tough rind. Protects the sugar juice from the cold. Not that he knows a damned thing."

That evening they'd hunched over William's desk late into the night, scribbling figures back and forth, both knowing that their future—everyone's future—depended upon what they decided. Finally, they determined to investigate sugar for themselves, starting with the visit to Marshall's Tanglewood Plantation last November.

While at Tanglewood, Breck had watched his father grow increasingly excited as the week advanced. "We can do this," he kept saying to Breck. "We can make this work."

Breck had no doubt his father was right.

Sugar was the future.

So, despite the cholera epidemic raging at the time in New Orleans, they immediately boarded a steamboat and visited their factor. After explaining their plans, they mortgaged some of their field hands as collateral, and then spent the remainder of the time discussing the prices of sugar-processing equipment, including a mill and a steam engine, while William continued to say, "We can do this."

Now, four months later, thirty acres of the northeastern property were already planted with seed cane. Breck rode along the cart track that paralleled Jensey Creek, crossing each of the small bridges that spanned the drainage ditches leading away from the creek.

Unlike cotton, sugar demanded both plenty of water and plenty of drainage. To do this, the land had to be entirely flat and crisscrossed with drainage ditches, like a patchwork quilt.

"Take my advice," the factor had told them in New Orleans. "Don't risk the lives of your prime hands to level the land and dig the ditches. Hire a crew of Irish."

"I hate the Irish," William had said.

"I know, I know, but look at it this way. You lose even one prime negro to an accident or illness, and you've lost yourself, what, twelve hundred dollars? But you lose an Irishman, and you've only opened a vacancy that twenty more Irishmen will be begging to fill. Besides, how are you going to spare thirty field hands for months on end? You've got other crops to worry about, and now you've got a sugarhouse to build."

"I know, I know. But God, I hate the Irish. Bunch of no-account white trash."

Now, Breck approached the hubbub of activity. Smoke from giant piles of burning brush cast everything in a hazy brown. In the distance, Irishmen leveled the land, moving soil from higher elevations to lower, some waist-deep in the earth, their shovels flinging soil, digging the now-ubiquitous ditches. Another team of Irishmen, shirts off in the heat, felled trees, while another team sawed and split the wood, loading it into wagons to be hauled away as firewood. Elsewhere, men harnessed teams of oxen to stumps. To a chorus of commands, the oxen dug in their hooves and strained against the stumps—a slow strain like the initial break in a levee, followed in due time by a flood of dirt and snapping roots.

Breck spied his father resting his arms on his saddle horn, surveying the work. William straightened and pushed his hat back as Breck reined to a stop beside him. "Afternoon. How was your lesson with Mr. Gilbert?"

"Good."

"What did you study?"

"Biology." Having a hunch his father wouldn't understand a trip to the woods to draw birds, Breck quickly added, "Earlier this morning, we studied Latin."

A wry smile played at his father's lips. "Hated the subject. Had a professor who drilled it into me as if the world wouldn't spin unless I could pass his damned exams, pardon my French. He seemed to delight in torturing me. Damned ass. Hope he's roasting in Hell." William lifted his hat and smoothed his unruly hair before snugging the hat back on. "You know what, Son? Having wasted many a youthful afternoon stumbling like a fool over a language deader than Caesar, in all my years here on the plantation, not once have I had use for Latin. I've found straightforward English works best. The more straightforward, the better. You get my drift?"

"Yessir."

"You see, Son, understanding is key." He gestured toward the Irishmen. "Whether they're Irish or whether they're your driver or one of your field hands, it's imperative that folks know where you stand. They need to know what they can expect from you. If your negroes work badly in the fields, every last one of them knows they'll be working late, until the day's work is done. If one of our boys is found off the plantation without a pass, or if he steals from us, or sells produce off the plantation, he knows he'll get twenty lashes per offense. And if someone's impudent—"

"—he gets to cool his heels in jail," Breck finished. As did every hand who worked the fields, Breck well knew his father's rules. For as long as Breck could remember, the rules had remained unchanged, like the everyday rising of the sun. He recognized the validity of what his father was saying. Working late in the fields, for instance, did wonders for the next day's productivity. No one wanted to work late, and slackers were not well received by the rest of the workforce.

"Any planter worth his salt knows that the punishment should only be severe enough to encourage good behavior," his father was saying, shooing away a pestering fly. "Of course," he added with a smile, "it's essential that the negroes see their good behavior rewarded."

Breck realized his father was in a sunny mood. A mood attributed, no doubt, to the fine weather, the progress with the sugar fields, and having an attentive ear. "As I always say, keep your negroes contented, don't give them occasion to complain—"

"Yes, I know," Breck interrupted, "give them frequent holidays, especially for work well done. A fine dinner, a dance, et cetera, et cetera, feed them well—"

Here William leaned over in the saddle and poked Breck conspiratorially with his elbow. "Plus, a little whiskey every now and then to wet the pipes doesn't hurt either, so long as they don't abuse it."

Breck smiled, the sunny mood infectious. He allowed himself to bask in the warmth of the sun pressing against his back, the feel of a smile playing on his lips, the sight of the Irishmen's tents, set helter-skelter amid clothes hanging out to dry, and coffee pots nestled in the ashes of cold cook fires.

After discussing the day's work with the Irish foreman, William and Breck urged their horses into a walk down one of the cart tracks, William taking up the conversation where they'd left off. Rascal circled ahead once again, nose to the ground. "It is my humble opinion that planters who are at times lenient and at other times strict leave their negroes in a state of confusion."

Breck nodded.

"Communication is the key."

"Yessir."

"Communication and consistency. If you show any sign of weakness, people will take advantage of that. They can smell weakness like a dog can smell blood. They'll go for the jugular every time."

Immediately, Breck was reminded of Sawney, a field hand whose sole occupation appeared to be clamping onto William's jugular and never letting go. He was still at large after running away almost three months ago (though Primus and Sam had been quickly apprehended). But Breck would no more mention Sawney to his father than he would mention that he had decided to become a priest or a traveling minstrel. Just the sound of Sawney's name set the storm clouds brewing on William's brow, turning his skin into an unhealthy, mottled red. So instead, Breck said, *"Homo homini lupus est."* Upon seeing his father's look of incomprehension, he translated, "Man is wolf to man."

William laughed and clapped Breck on the back. *"Touché!* Now let's go see how the seed cane is coming along." He dug his heels into his horse's flank and cantered away, with Breck soon beside him.

"You see," his father was saying, "a plantation might be considered a piece of machinery. To operate successfully, all of its parts should be uniform and exact. As the head of the plantation, you and I, we're the compelling force. Unless we're invested, unless we're *interested* in the proceedings hereabouts, we can expect nothing but indifference from our negroes."

Soon, they were in the fields of seed cane, the leafy green shoots standing from six inches to over a foot in height. Breck dismounted, knelt, and examined one of the cane shoots, rubbing its leaves and feeling its fibrous texture while assessing the shoot's overall health. Unlike cotton, unlike corn or peas or potatoes or any of their other crops, Breck felt an affinity with the cane. It surprised him, this affinity. As if the cane were his, truly his, born of the night when he'd suggested they try a second cash crop in an effort to save the plantation. Throughout the process, his father had trusted him, relied on him, and Breck didn't want to disappoint. For the first time in his life, he felt a connection to his father, and even to his father's father, Octavian, who had first settled the land in the Jensey name. As if, finally, they were bound together by the soil, by their desire to see the plantation succeed.

William knelt alongside Breck, scooped up a fistful of soil, and let it trickle through his hand. Mixed in with the rich smell of soil, Breck caught the scent of gun grease, leather, and tobacco.

"Don't think I've ever seen a finer day," his father said with a satisfied sigh. "Caught a bird in my hands this morning. He was trapped in a sticker bush, poor fellow. Had a red tuft on the top of his head, was colored olive gray, and had feathers so soft that it was almost like fur. Pretty little thing, tiny as can be. Wish your mother could have seen it."

Breck smiled, imagining his father cradling a bird, feeling the fragile heart beating in his hands. "Sounds like a ruby-crowned wren to me. Pretty late for them to be this far south. You should draw a picture of it while you still remember what it looks like. I've got some paints you can use."

His father nodded, as if taking his suggestion under consideration.

Breck yanked a weed from the soil, then another. After pulling a fistful, he tossed them aside, stood, and brushed his hands on his pants. "Need to send the hoe gang here tomorrow."

William stood too. Behind him, his horse whinnied gently and blew into William's ear. He put a hand on the horse's muzzle, patting him absently. "Think we can make this work, Son?"

Breck gazed at his father—at the face that was beginning to show signs of age, shadowed now by the brim of his hat, revealing years of field and weather; at the sincerity shining from his eyes. The time was long past when Breck had to crane his neck to look his father in the eye. *"Amat victoria curam."* Smiling at his father's quizzical look, he translated: "Victory favors care. Those who take pains."

William laughed as he climbed back into the saddle. "Well said. Now let's go take a look at our stables. Got a new horse yesterday I've been wanting to show you."

***

It was late afternoon by the time Breck left the stables and headed toward his room. Breck's room was now in the north addition, on the west side. He liked it because it was private, without all the bustle of the main house; although Georgie and Thomas occupied the bedroom adjacent to his, they were rarely to be seen.

He climbed the gallery steps and entered his room, closing the door behind him. It was uncomfortably warm, the drapes pulled shut, the room cast in shadow. He tossed his hat onto the bed.

"Monette?" he whispered. "You here?"

It was only a heartbeat, a breath of thought, before she stepped out of the armoire, straightening her dress and apron. *"Oui."*

# Chapter 7

THEY WERE THE SORRIEST set of human beings William had ever seen. They lay sprawled beneath the shade on the edge of Piney Lake, basking like alligators in varying degrees of filth and contentment. Jackets had been tossed aside when it started turning warm. Suspenders loosened. Hats forgotten. Shirts half-unbuttoned and smudged with mud. Empty bottles of sherry and champagne scattered.

By God, it didn't get any better than this.

Last night, there had been a party. William had brought the fiddler up from the pine quarter, determined to dance the evening away with family and friends. Not only did the evening dance away, filled with general merriment and frolicking, but the night danced away as well. And no sooner had William fallen dead asleep on the settee, lost in a deep snore, than Marshall was shaking him awake, saying, "Get your lazy ass up. Time to go fishing, ol' buddy. I'm hankering for a fish fry."

They stumbled through the house, whispering loudly, bumping into furniture, shaking anyone awake who looked a likely candidate. Then, five men set off into the dawn with three servants, six horses, three baskets of food and drink, and enough tackle to reel in a wagonload of fish.

"See, the thing of it is," Marshall was saying now, his drawl thick and lazy as the heat, "I can't for the life of me figure the advantage of marriage. Correct me if I'm wrong, but a lady's got to have the best of everything. The finest house, the latest fashions, all them whatnots from Paris—"

"Furniture," said William, his eyes closed, hardly listening as he lay on his back.

"That's right. French furniture with all that curlicue shit."

"You see, Marshall," said a voice from the vicinity of the food baskets, "the way I see it is, you're a coarse, base creature with the cultural taste of a wharf rat. Of course, you wouldn't want to be married because then you'd have to be responsible for someone besides yourself. It'd interfere with your general love of disorder and your propensity for rakishness."

There was a round of chuckling, and, without opening his eyes, William knew the speaker to be Alexander Saffin, a senator and fellow planter, and his neighbor to the southwest. William's age, Saffin was taller than average, solidly built, thickening around the middle like they all were, his classic profile reminding William of a Greek statue. In his fourth year as senator of Louisiana, Saffin was known throughout the parish as an outspoken, intelligent man of high morals and dedication to civic duty, aspiring someday to become governor. But, as William often told Saffin jokingly, he didn't hold it against him.

Marshall replied, "Trying to drum up the votes by bringing out my finer points, eh, Saffin? Well, it won't work. I'd never vote for a high-minded man like yourself. Hell, your head's so high in the clouds, all I can see is your ass."

After more chuckling, William's brother-in-law sat up. John had been lying next to William, and now he stretched, scratched, and yawned widely. "Well, as the only other bachelor in the party, I feel obliged to say that I get awfully lonely at nights and would be happy to find a wife. I mean, I'm not getting any younger, and growing old alone—well, it scares me. And I'll buy her all the French furniture she wants."

William sat up too, a little woozy, surprised by John's speech. First of all, in all the years William had known Sarah's brother, the man had scarcely strung more than two sentences together at once. This speech was outright verbosity. Secondly, John had never before expressed his loneliness. John? Lonely? Perhaps it was the sherry. Hell, all their tongues were flapping just a little more than usual.

"You've got to come over more," suggested William. "Stop keeping to yourself so much. Makes a man crazy."

John nodded.

"Know what your problem is, John?" asked Marshall.

"No, but I've a feeling you're going to tell me."

"You see, the ladies don't find you particularly attractive. In fact, if I may be so blunt—"

"Just this once."

"—you're a downright ugly son of a bitch. Now, if you want my advice, you gotta open your mouth more so the ladies know there's more to you than just plain ugliness."

"Thanks, Marshall."

"Don't mention it. Before you know it, the ladies will be crawling all over you like maggots on spoiled meat."

"Sounds delightful."

For a while, no one said anything, seemingly content to nibble on food, wash it down with warm champagne (the sherry being depleted by noon), and check their lines for a bite. Already, William had caught eight fish, but things were slowing down. Heat of the day, he supposed, when everything went suddenly still, stuporous, needing a nap. Affected the fish as well as the humans. Off a ways, the servants lay sleeping. His own eyelids felt leaden as he lay down again beside John. Everything seemed to sleep except the insects—a constant drone of wings, a tickle on the face, or a crawling up the arm—and, of course, Marshall.

"I mean, take William here, for example. He's about as pretty as a stump, but most ladies find him attractive anyway. It's tough to figure. And doggone it if the man didn't marry the most beautiful belle in West Feliciana."

William rolled over and scowled at Marshall. "Look who's talking. You're such a plug-ugly piss pot, my hound bitches run and hide at the sight of you." Seeing the answering gleam in Marshall's eyes, William knew the man was full of himself today. He wondered what Marshall would say if he knew that Sarah couldn't stand him. Likely, Marshall already knew, but probably didn't care any more than he cared about a lot of things.

"See, John?" continued Marshall, pausing long enough to light a cigar. "If it could happen to William, it could well happen to you. But, enough of the encouraging banter. My point is, why make it happen at all? Sure, you're lonely, but is that a good enough reason to shackle yourself to the same woman year after year? What happens when you find out you don't really like her? That she only married you for your fat wallet, and now you're stuck buying her chandeliers and doodads?"

William exchanged glances with John. John rolled his eyes and lay back down.

"Don't listen to him, John," said Saffin, his speech a little slurred. "Marriage has its rewards. Marshall's just too thick in the head to appreciate any of them."

William looked at Saffin, who lay sprawled a few feet away, having finally crawled out of the food baskets. He was curious as to what rewards Saffin might be referring to, seeing as William believed Saffin to have married a shrew of a wife. Well, maybe not a shrew exactly, but a woman who didn't hesitate to speak her mind, dabbling in matters she had no business dabbling in, often grinding a man's pride beneath her pretty slippered heel while smiling sweetly and drinking a cordial. William did his best to steer clear of Mary Grey Saffin, as he didn't want to say something to her that would injure his relations with Saffin. Something like, Shut the hell up.

But Saffin didn't elaborate, choosing to stay quiet concerning the rewards of marriage. William shrugged. Who knew? Maybe their marriage was happy. The Saffins did seem to enjoy one another's company. It was difficult to guess regarding other people's private lives, and William had given up trying long ago. Besides, he'd learned it was far safer to keep his nose out of other people's business. Among other things, it kept the nose clean.

"My philosophy is," drawled Marshall, tilting his head back for a swig of champagne, "why buy the cow when you can have the milk for free?"

"You're a sick man, Marshall McCain," concluded John, closing his eyes.

Marshall belched. "Sick, rich, and happy."

Now Judge Walter Rockwell spoke, a man William had known since boyhood. He was a man of integrity, a political pillar of the community, portly and balding, as many pillars tended to be. Today, he was more than a little soused. Drunk as a skunk, thought William. Can't hold his liquor. But, by God, a man shouldn't have to hold his liquor all the time. Especially on a day like today. Entirely too much effort. "Found out last night my youngest son's getting married this June."

"Congratulations, ol' buddy," roared Marshall. "A toast! A toast! To Judge Rockwell and his son, Stephen!" He tipped back his bottle, while everyone followed suit.

"Who's the bride?" asked William, wiping his mouth with the back of his hand.

"A wisp of an Irish girl named Mary. Hey, same name as your wife, Saffin."

"Doubtful she's like my wife if she's Irish. My Mary's pure Brit, through and through. Born with a teacup and a high brow."

"Well," replied Judge Rockwell, downing a gulp of champagne, "our little Mary may not be pure Brit, but she's old Irish. Family's been here for decades, practically. Plenty of money. No immigrant bogtrotter for my son. Wouldn't allow it."

William felt the color rise in his face. God, he hated the Irish. He hated anyone who wasn't full-blooded American, everyone else be damned. He would only be too glad to see the Irish leave his land. *Bon voyage,* hail and farewell, and all of that. But even as he thought it, he knew he'd have to have them back again and again to clear more land, at least if he wanted to expand his sugar production. This year, he'd planted thirty acres of seed cane, which would in turn provide enough cane to plant the newly cleared ninety acres. While they wouldn't have a sugar crop this coming winter or the next, the winter of '51-'52 would see the first sugar crop at Fox Creek Plantation. William planned to have at least four hundred acres of sugar under production within five years. It was an enormous undertaking, and one in which he was learning to rely on Breck more and more.

"My daughter Lucy seemed rather sweet on Breck last night," Saffin was saying. "Now I'll probably have to listen to her lovesick babble for weeks. Breck was the perfect gentleman, dancing the quadrille with her. An amazing thing to watch your children grow up, isn't it, William?"

"Word of advice," said Marshall. "Don't let your children grow up. Whole new kettle of fish."

"What would you know?" asked Saffin. "Seeing as you have none."

"Who says I have none?"

Actually, William hadn't really noticed Lucy's attraction to Breck. It was something that didn't occur to him. Yes, he'd watched his children dance, laugh, and enjoy the company of others, but it had never occurred to William that Lucy's attention to Breck was anything more than childish play. William shrugged. Lucy was a good girl, from a fine family. Even if there was an attraction there, what could it hurt? So long as Breck went to university first and finished his education, as every gentleman should, before settling down. "To answer your question, Saffin, yes, it's amazing to watch my children grow up."

"Family," said Judge Rockwell with a loud hiccough, "is what it all boils down to. Family. And that, Marshall, is why you get married. Wouldn't trade it for anything." With that, the judge's elbow slipped out from beneath him, and he was out cold, sprawled like a washed-up river rat under the Louisiana sun.

Later that evening, after the fish fry, Sarah found herself alone with William in their room. She'd gone up to freshen herself and change into her evening gown when he entered. She dismissed Mammy Hester and sat still, dressed in her undergarments, watching in the vanity mirror as he approached her from behind and wrapped his arms about her.

She breathed in his smell of cigar, leather, and—thank goodness—soap, and leaned back into him, his breath tickling her ear. "You're drunk."

"I know."

"Having fun?"

"I needed this."

"I know," she replied, smiling.

He turned her head gently toward him and kissed her. "I can't live without you," he murmured, kissing her lips, her cheeks, her hair. "My true love. My only love."

She felt her heart flutter, thinking, when do I get too old for this? When does the time come when he no longer makes my heart race? Never, I hope. Never. . . .

He picked her up and carried her to the bed as if she weighed nothing. She knew she should protest. She knew she should say something like, This is inappropriate. We have guests. But she could not. For once he loosened her corset, and put his hands on her, all propriety ended. She was a woman in love. Forever. It was her weakness.

Afterward, she lay on the bed surrounded by heaps of undergarments, watching as he dressed himself. "I'll fetch Mammy Hester," he was saying, "to put you back together."

"Yes. And please give everyone my apologies. Tell them—"

"I know." He leaned over the bed and kissed her again. "Tell them you had a small headache, but you're better now and will be down shortly."

"Mmm."

He smiled. "I love it when you have headaches."

After he left, the memory of their love lingered like his scent, and she wondered. Lately, he was so passionate. Desperate, almost. Frantically making love to her, saying over and over again that he loved her.

As if she couldn't hear him.

As if one day he might awaken only to discover that it was all a dream.

It was one of those hellish spring nights when the thunder rolled across the sky in a continuous, ominous rumble, when lightning seared the backs of a man's eyeballs, and when, no matter how hard one tried to keep the rain at bay, it seeped under one's hat and coat, cold fingers trickling underneath one's clothes, until a man shook in his boots and longed for the warmth of the home fires and a bowl of steaming stew to heat his middles.

Jake Oswald was no exception. While he considered himself a hardy soul, accustomed to the rigors of farm and field, after nearly an hour of slogging through the gullied roads on horseback, he'd resigned himself to a perpetual state of clenched teeth—thoughts of returning home, his only comfort.

His companion, Amos Wood, a big bear of a man, looked no less miserable. Head low between his shoulders, face averted from the worst of it, rain waterfalled off the brim of his hat, drenching his chest-length beard. (Normally, Chubb Wilton also rode patrol, but after the first few bends in the road, he'd called it quits, and soon horse and rider had disappeared into the rain.) Even the hounds slunk along, showing none of their usual gusto, instead cowering near the horses, glancing up occasionally at Jake and Amos as if to say, Whose idea was this?

Indeed, if it were any other night, Jake too would have called it quits. But he couldn't afford to—not when, for the past three nights, someone had raided his chicken coop; not when, just this morning, he'd awakened to find his best hog missing and a trail of booted footprints leading from the pigpen to the swamp out back. Standing there in his long johns and boots, unshaven and shivering, he'd thought, *runaway,* while both fury and expectation coursed through him—fury for the theft of his chickens, eggs, and hog; expectation because a runaway caught was money in his family's pocket, opportunity for advancement. But when he rushed into the house, intending to grab his pistol and britches, he found his wife,

Alice, bent double over a tub of dirty dishes. She clutched her swollen belly and stared at Jake with full-moon eyes, gasping between pants, "Fetch Mildred, my time is come."

Fourteen hours and one daughter later, Jake was finally on patrol, britches on, pistol ready, despite being soaked to the bone.

It was just around one of the bends in the road, where the branches of the black willows on each side met overhead in a leafy canopy, that Jake saw him, illuminated in a series of lightning flashes: a black man crouched near a tree trunk, half-in, half-out of the brambles, hurriedly plucking up various items from the muddy grass—a comb, what looked to be a shaving strop, a silver spoon—and bundling them in a cloth, as if in his haste to cross the road, the bundle had slipped from his grasp, or had perhaps been torn from his hands by the brambles.

Then there was darkness.

A heartbeat.

Another flash of lightning and Jake cried, "You there!"

Upon Jake's cry, the black man's head jerked up and the dogs leapt forward, as surprised as any, while Amos Wood hollered, "No kill! No kill!" to keep the dogs from mauling the man to death.

In the next flash, the man was standing straight, arms in the air, surrounded by a snarling, seething mass of fur and teeth, glancing up warily at the two men as they approached on horseback.

Jake reined to a stop under the black willow. Already his pulse had quickened, and he yelled over the driving rain, over the rolling thunder and the yap of the dogs, "Let's see your pass, boy!"

"Beg—begging your pardon, Mister, but I—I done dropped my pass down here in the grass. You—your dogs is trampling it."

Jake threw a glance at Amos. They'd heard it all before. The blustering. The bellyaching. The bullshit. It would have been pathetically funny had Jake not been so miserable, so wishing he could return to his wife, to his newborn Ginny, pink and soft.

When Jake nodded, Amos whistled once, twice, and finally had to get off his horse and haul the dogs off, laying into one of the bitches with his boot. He stood to the side, holding the dogs by their collars, two in one hand, three in the other. The dogs whined and lunged against him, tongues hanging.

"Go ahead then, find your pass," said Jake, watching as the man got down on all fours and searched the earth like a varmint searching for grubs. A minute passed. Another. Jake shivered, the early morning's upset taking root once more, any patience he'd had wearing thin as a blade. Damned thief. Where's my hog? "That's enough, boy, you're coming with us!"

Just then the man snatched something from the mud. "The pass, I done found it!" Grinning widely, he limped over and handed it to Jake.

The next flash of lightning told Jake what he needed to know. Cupped in his hand was a gloppy muddy mess, paper hardly in evidence, any writing long gone. "You call this a pass?"

From beneath a palmetto hat, wide, innocent eyes blinked briefly up at Jake. The man appeared to be older than Jake, in his late twenties or early thirties, skin colored like tobacco, expression dull as a hitching post. "But, but, Mister, it *was* a pass. I swears it. My massa, he—"

"Whatcha got there, Jake?" Amos asked.

Jake allowed the rain to wash the muddy mess off his hand while the black man's eyes further widened under the brim of his hat, while he stammered that he was telling the truth, please, please, for God's sake, they gots to believe him. Then Jake smiled. "Well, lookee here. I think we got ourselves a runaway. Amos, I think it's time you let them dogs go, don't you?"

In the next heartbeat, the next flash of lightning so powerful that it seemed to rattle his teeth loose and stand his hair on end, Jake saw two things: first, the runaway's full-on gaze changed from wide, dull, and innocent, to narrowed, scheming, and hate-filled; second, where the man had previously appeared to be unarmed, now he grasped a razor in his hand, a six-inch blade that he swept through the neck of the lead hound, deep and swift.

Then, like a heavy curtain falling over Jake's eyes, darkness fell.

He heard himself cursing, heard the man running away. Heard the gurgle of blood and breath from the dying hound. Heard Amos struggling to mount his horse, shouting, "Christ almighty! Get him! Get him!"

For a moment all was wheeling horses, frightened whinnying, yapping dogs, thunder, and darkness. Then the lightning lit up the sky and Jake spied the man plunging into the dense undergrowth at the side of the road, hounds at his heels. In the time it took to draw breath, Jake straightened his horse, slammed his boots into the mare's flanks, and was off, Amos beside him, horses' hooves slapping through the mire.

Upon entering the woods, branches ripped Jake's hat from his head, scratching his face. He plunged on, heart galloping with anger and disbelief, chasing the trail of baying hounds, praying his horse wouldn't turn an ankle.

"Sweet Jesus!" Amos was hollering. "Sweet Jesus! Did you see that? He killed her! The bastard killed her!"

Jake scarcely noticed when they barreled through a swollen bayou and out the other side. He urged his horse on, on, over rotted logs, past another dead hound, weaving between tree trunks, between brambles, closer, closer, searing light alternating with blinding darkness.

Three hundred feet inside the wooded swamp, Jake saw him. Bareheaded now, the runaway stood with his back to a giant cypress tree, breathing hard, razor in his hand, the three remaining dogs snapping and barking just out of the razor's reach.

Before his horse had even stopped, Amos was grabbing his pistol and swinging himself from the saddle. "Bastard!" he was screaming. "Bastard!"

Jake didn't even remember getting off his horse. But suddenly he was blocking Amos' way, arm planted stiffly against the big man's chest, surprised to hear his own voice saying calmly, "Can't let you kill him, buddy." Even as he uttered the words, he wondered why he was saying this, yet he knew he meant it, meant it more than anything he'd meant in his life.

Amos stared wild-eyed at Jake, as if he didn't remember who Jake was, as if the past two years' friendship had suddenly been forgotten.

"Can't let you kill him, buddy."

The big man blinked. Though Jake knew Amos could have easily shoved him aside and fired his pistol anyway, knew their friendship would survive such a conflict, and though the law allowed a white man to kill an armed black man, no questions asked, Amos lowered his pistol and nodded, releasing a breath that smelled of onions, beans, and grease.

The rest was fairly simple. They'd done it plenty of times before. With a well-aimed snap of his bullwhip, Jake disarmed the man before Amos moved in with the hounds, pistol-whipping and trussing up the runaway like a turkey for Christmas. As Jake stood back and watched Amos deliver twenty-five well-deserved licks with the bullwhip, old scars gnarled like tree roots across the runaway's naked back, Jake suddenly knew why he'd stopped Amos from killing the man.

It was because when the midwife had handed him his daughter, his firstborn, wrapped in one of his old flannel shirts, when he brushed her soft cheek with his calloused, soil-gullied hand, he'd had to turn around, embarrassed by the emotion that swelled in him like a blossom opening to the sun. With his back to Alice and the midwife, he'd gazed at his daughter, at her tiny fingers, her delicate eyelashes. And as tears welled in his eyes he'd thought, I'm your daddy, Ginny baby, I'm your daddy. No matter what happens, I'll take care of you. No matter what.

Standing in the ooze of the swamp, remembering how it was, he wiped his cheek with the back of his hand. Half watching as Amos delivered the punishment, grunting with the effort. Half watching as the runaway flinched with each lick.

*Thieving nigger. You owe me.*

# Chapter 8

RELIGION DID NOT SUIT Kate. Neither did God, for that matter. But it was not her choice. When one was fourteen years old, one didn't have a choice about such things. Go to school. Study. Go to church. Pray. Eat. Go to bed. Wake up. It was a world of absolutes—choiceless facts of life that could not be avoided.

When she was an adult though, Kate told herself, things would change. When she was an adult, she would stay home from church just as Papa and Grandma Mehitable did, scarcely saying goodbye when everybody else—Mama, Breck, the twins, and all the household servants—filed solemnly out of the house and climbed into the church-going carriages. One day, when Kate had casually suggested that she would stay home too, you'd have thought she'd declared allegiance with the devil. The look of silent pain on her mother's face—not to mention the profusion of Lord a'mercies from Mammy Hester, delivered hands-on-hips—was enough to make her repent and allow herself to be steered into the carriage for the long, bumpy ride to church. (Not that she'd repented of not wanting to go to church, only that she'd voiced her desire aloud.)

Sitting and standing and kneeling, up down up down, while Reverend Scarborough (whose spectacled, rawboned countenance could change from benevolence to aggrieved severity in the time it took a soul to sin) droned through a litany of creeds, of prayers, of beseechings to God Almighty, amid much solemn lifting and blessing of wafers, Bibles, crosses, silver goblets, and who knows what else.

Good God Almighty. It was enough to drive any fourteen-year-old insane.

Who was God, anyway? It was not as if Kate had not done her part in trying to reach Him. She'd prayed to Him before, begging Him for things she never received, asking Him questions after which He remained stubbornly silent. Of what use was a God like that? Where was the God of the Bible who rained manna from Heaven whenever someone was hungry, or who thundered His commandments so they could be written on tablets of stone? Kate knew now that no such thunderous God existed in St. Marysville. Instead, the God of Holy Trinity Episcopal Church was a God who kept to Himself and didn't deign to give answers to questions even when one's knees began to throb from kneeling so long.

Just when she thought it couldn't get any worse, Mama had surprised her one day with a new set of whalebone corsets. "For you," she said, smiling. Without realizing the abjection of Kate's spirits, Mama had proceeded (with Mammy Hester and Monette's help) to strap Kate up, not just that morning, but every morning after, pulling the laces tighter with each passing day. Now, when Kate sat in church, ramrod straight out of necessity, everything pinched and ached. Her hips, her ribs, under her arms, her belly, her shoulders. Good God Almighty, she prayed, where are You when I need You? I can't breathe! This, during a spring heat wave, no less, when no matter how many times she fanned herself, it could never wipe away the unladylike moisture that seeped from beneath her bonnet, trickling down her temples, her neck, her back—and down just about every crease God had created as a good place for sweating.

But all that changed on the morning of April 13, 1850. It changed through the form of a young man named Edward Scarborough, nephew to Reverend Scarborough. Even the air didn't seem so hot anymore. There he sat in his family's rented pew, gaze fixed on the Reverend, seeming to absorb every word that fell from his uncle's mouth as if uttered from the Great Mouth of God. His straight back, the blond wisps of hair just above his starched collar, his broadening shoulders. (How old was he? Fifteen? Sixteen?) A great sigh escaped Kate.

*Edward . . .*

The next Sunday, Kate determined to make Edward notice her. "Tighter," she said, when Mama made to tie off the corset. Kate held onto her bedpost, her fingers white with the strain as Mama yanked and yanked. "Tighter," she gasped.

Mammy Hester clucked her tongue. "Why Missie Kate, if Miss Sarah goes any tighter, your plumb foolish head's gonna pop off. What's got into you, anyhow?"

As Monette threw petticoat after petticoat over her head, Kate said, "My new dress. The yellow one Grandma Emma sewed with the little daisies embroidered on the sleeves. And my white bonnet with the pale-yellow sash and parasol to match. Oh, I can hardly wait! Hurry, Monette, hurry!"

Then, finally, there she was in Holy Trinity Episcopal Church, engrossed in Edward's every move—the way he brushed his hair back from his face with a tender toss of his fingers, the way he pressed his forehead against the pew in front of him whenever he knelt, the way he stood during prayers with his head reverently bowed, the way he scarcely glanced at his prayer book but knew what to say anyway—when suddenly, the service was over. Never had religion been so wonderful. Afterward, when they were invited to the Scarboroughs' for tea, Kate thought she would die with giddiness. "It must be God's grand design," she whispered in French to Monette, her sole confidante in the Edward Matter.

*"Oui."*

But the afternoon disappointed Kate in every regard when Edward only talked with the adults (as if he were an adult himself!), discussing such things as religion and politics and weather and crops and whether or not there was going to be an epidemic this season, seeing as it was getting to be that time of year. There she sat on the gallery with Breck, balancing a delicate teacup on her lap, careful not to spill, nor to stain her lace gloves, and not once did Edward so much as speak to her. Or look at her. In fact, Edward seemed to look everywhere *except* at her. Well! There were clearly some faults in God's Grand Design!

Then the miracle happened. The parting of the Red Sea. Manna from Heaven. Lazarus raised from the dead. . . .

For as Kate prepared to climb into the carriage for the return trip home, a ball of anger crouched in her bosom, ready to burst forth with either wild weeping or an agonized pounding of fists (she didn't know which), Edward reached out and took her gloved hand in his.

"Oh!" she said, startled, acutely aware of the moistness of his hands through the thin lace of her gloves, the intense blue of his eyes as he gazed at her for at least a second, maybe more. Lingering, almost. Her heart skipped. Her breath caught in her throat.

"Mind your step, Miss Jensey," he said, as he helped her into the carriage.

*Edward . . .*

His voice, so manly, so deep.

*Oh, Edward . . .*

To the crunch of wheels and the jangle of harness, they parted.

⸻ ℓℓ ⸻

Reverend Scarborough was pleased.

Moments ago, Miss Katherine Jensey had delivered her catechism for confirmation, replying promptly to each question. She'd rehearsed the Articles of Belief, the Ten Commandments, the Lord's Prayer, duty toward neighbors, etc., etc., with astonishing accuracy and conviction. Truly, she was a remarkable and motivated novitiate! But the clergyman knew it was premature to voice his pleasure aloud. First things first. No one was allowed confirmation or baptism into the Episcopal Church until they could prove their readiness—readiness of a spiritual quality rather than one of rote. Such discernment was not a simple task. Enjoyable, yes. Ordained by God, yes. Simple, no.

Today, he and Edward sat facing Miss Katherine and her little handmaiden across the dining table at Fox Creek Plantation, on this their seventh meeting together, while outside, a light rain began to fall. Now it was the little maid's turn for her baptismal catechism, a catechism especially written for souls ignorant in scholarly matters, souls of a more simple, childlike nature.

Thumbing to the correct chapter in his *Catechism for Colored Persons,* adjusting his spectacles, and clearing his throat, Reverend Scarborough said, "Now then. On we go, little—Monette, is it? Well then, Monette, my child, when is a person fit to be received into the church?"

"When he has a new heart," the servant replied. Seated beside her, Miss Katherine beamed at the servant's response, appearing likewise delighted that her young charge had decided to commit her soul to Christ.

"Oh my. Yes, yes. You're absolutely correct about that," said Reverend Scarborough. "But how can you tell that *you* have a new heart?"

"By my feelings and actions."

"Indeed, indeed. Now then, how do you feel toward Jesus, the Savior of Sinners?"

"I love him and trust in him."

"Good, good. Very well then, how do you feel toward your sins?"

Here the servant girl paused. She lowered her gaze to her lap and replied softly, "I am sorry for them, and hate them."

"Excellent," replied Reverend Scarborough, smiling inwardly with pleasure. The maid's demeanor was one of humility, shame, and repentance for her sins—a posture befitting every baptismal candidate, regardless of the ignorant nature of their soul.

"May I, Uncle?" asked Edward. Upon Reverend Scarborough's nod, Edward pulled the book toward him. Several months ago, Edward had announced his intention to follow in his uncle's footsteps by becoming a clergyman. While he was yet too young to begin such training, Reverend Scarborough thought it would be good for the young man to accompany him to Fox Creek, where there resided two souls longing to deepen their relationship with the Lord.

Reverend Scarborough sipped his tea as Edward continued the catechism, his voice and bearing astonishingly mature and direct for one so young. "What do you feel you would like to do all your life?"

Again, the servant girl paused.

Miss Katherine was smiling at Edward as if she knew the answer too, but would not breathe a word of it, rightfully allowing the little servant to answer of her own accord. Even now, as her maid recited the catechism, Miss Katherine's eyes plainly sparkled with her love for Jesus Christ. It brought warmth to an old clergyman's soul to see that his efforts among his flock were still bearing fruit, even after all these years.

"Love and serve God," whispered the maid.

"Do you feel that you love God more than all?"

"Yes."

"Do you now love to pray and to go to church? Do you love the Bible and all God's people?"

"Yes."

"You say you have these good feelings, but what makes you sure that you have them? What proof can you give me that you have them? Do you act up to these feelings?"

As Edward's voice rose in volume and passion, Reverend Scarborough had a brief but poignant vision of Edward addressing a congregation of devout souls, with the power of God illuminating him. Yes, Edward would do well. He was a chosen instrument of God. A lump of clay in the Master's hand, ready and willing to be formed into the perfect vessel. Reverend Scarborough felt a sudden, intense joy in his heart, as if all the years of training and yearning and praying had culminated in this day. This day of sitting in a dining room surrounded by silver and crystal, listening to the patter of rain, enjoying the breeze of the shoo-fly, while three precious souls committed their lives to Christ.

The maid replied, "I do my best to act up to them."

Again, that sparkling in Miss Katherine's eyes. That purity of divine love. And the little servant girl—an appropriate measure of fear and trembling.

"When you fail to act up to them, do you feel sorrow and shame before God?" Again, that passion. Almost thunderous in this enclosed space.

"Yes."

"In what manner is a tree known to be a good tree?"

"By its fruits."

Reverend Scarborough was pleased. So pleased.

Yes, they were ready.

On a blustery day in late spring, when clouds blew from the north and a hint of rain pinched the air, Kate hurried toward the stables, hoping her mother wouldn't spot her.

Kate could tell that this was one of those days when her mother was intent on gardening. Not only was Sarah dressed in her drab gardening clothes, but she had that blissful, blank gardening look about her face that Kate was beginning to recognize as a foretelling of drudgery. Seeing her mother's intention, Kate made a quick resolve to go riding. After all, Mama hadn't actually *asked* her to do anything, had she? Besides, Kate thought, I can go riding if I damn well please.

When Kate entered the stables, she was surprised to see her father there with the twins. She'd forgotten that William had said at breakfast that he was taking the twins fishing at the lake. Of course, they would ride there. "Oh, hello, Papa," she said, feeling caught and foolish.

William was helping little Georgie onto his pony. "Kate. What are you doing here? I thought you were with your mother."

Thinking quickly, she decided fishing was better than gardening. "Thought I'd go fishing with you."

He helped Thomas onto another pony and checked the saddle to make certain it was cinched tight. "You're dressed rather fine for fishing, don't you think?"

She laughed. "I swear, Papa, you don't know anything about clothes at all. This is just some old rag Mammy Hester found in the back of my closet." (In fact, it was her finest riding outfit.) "Besides, I promise to keep out of your way. If I do that, then it doesn't matter what I wear, does it?"

"Get your horse saddled," was all he said.

The whole way there, the twins chattered. Did they think they'd catch a fish? Maybe not just one fish, but a whole passel of fish. Big fish. Maybe a wagonload of big fish. Maybe Georgie would catch them all, but Thomas wouldn't catch any. Maybe it would be the other way around, suggested Thomas. But, of course, Georgie decided, if that happened, they'd share.

"Heck," said Thomas thoughtfully, "if we have that many big fish, we'll share with everyone. We'll invite the world to a fish fry."

"And," added Georgie, "we'll have fiddle music."

Kate followed William's horse down the wooded path, only half listening to the twins' banter. It was hard to listen to anyone completely when one's mind was forever on Edward Scarborough. His handsome image, the sound of his voice, and her feelings toward him, never fully left her mind at any point of the day or night. If Monette was doing her hair, chatting in French, Kate was thinking about Edward. If Kate was answering her mother's questions, she was thinking about Edward. If Kate was sleeping, she was dreaming about Edward. Last night, she'd awakened in the dead of night with heated thoughts of Edward tumbling through her. She'd touched herself below, shivering with the cool press of her fingers, wondering, wishing. She even slipped a fingertip into the forbidden passage, only to withdraw it quickly, knowing that to do so was a dreadful, mortal sin. Surely, Edward would never love a sinner. She'd sighed, rolled over, then hugged and kissed her pillow until she slept again. *Oh, Edward . . .*

"Papa," she asked, once they'd settled at the lake and the twins had cast their lines, "do you think I'm beautiful?"

William looked surprised and a little uncomfortable at her question. Casting his line into the water, he sat on the bank between her and the twins. "Well, you take after your mother, so I suppose that makes you beautiful. Why do you ask?"

"No reason, just wondering." She played with a stick, poking it into the soft ground. Just then, the wind gusted, rippling across the lake and rustling through the trees overhead, the sky threatening a storm. Tendrils of hair slipped out from beneath Kate's bonnet and snapped across her face.

William clamped a hand over his hat. "Probably should have waited for a better day, what with the rain we've been having, but they've been pestering me for weeks now."

Tucking her hair back under her bonnet, Kate asked, "Papa, how tall do you think I'm going to be? Aunt Virginia says height is unseemly in a woman."

Georgie interrupted, "When do the fish get hungry, Papa?"

"Well, Son, sometimes they bite right off, and other times it takes a spell. But you've got to be quiet and still, otherwise you scare them off, because then they know you're planning to yank them out of the water and fry them for supper. No one wants to be fried. Fish are smart that way."

"Wonder how they know," said Georgie.

"I wouldn't want to be fried," said Thomas.

William reached out and rumpled Thomas' hair. "Take my advice. If you see a fat worm dangling from a hook, don't bite it."

The twins giggled.

"Quiet now," whispered William. "It's fish-biting time."

Kate tried again. "Papa, how tall—"

"Virginia is a babbling windbag with a brain the size of a turnip. Pay her no attention."

"But how tall do you think I'm going to be? Mammy Hester says I grow taller by the day."

"I suppose you'll be just tall enough so your feet touch the ground."

"Papa! I'm dead serious!"

"I know."

"Well?"

William sighed. "How should I know how tall you'll grow? You'll be as tall as you're meant to be, I suppose."

"Oh! You're no help at all."

She stabbed the ground with her stick, frowning when he said, "You're going to be five feet, ten and a half inches tall. Satisfied?"

Of course, she wasn't satisfied. She knew her father was just making it up. Sometimes he evaded her questions with the skill of negroes shirking work. But, she thought, with a prickle of anxiety, what if Papa was right? What if she *did* grow that tall? She would positively loom over Edward. Like Aunt Virginia said (turnip-brain as she was), it just wouldn't be seemly. A misery enveloped Kate. She closed her eyes, hating that familiar feeling. Oh, why did true love have to be so painful?

Then a memory came. Blessed relief. Holy water poured on unholy wounds. On the last day of her catechism, Edward had smiled at her while saying to Reverend Scarborough, "Uncle, I agree with your assessment. She's ready for confirmation." He took her hand and bowed his head over it, as if unaware that she was already two fingers taller than he was. "May God bless you, Miss Jensey."

Oh! Surely Heaven must be near to such feelings! A week from tomorrow, those feelings would culminate with the sacrament of confirmation. Kate knew that on that day, that stupendous, miraculous day, everything would change. (For one thing, God would never allow one of His chosen to grow to unseemly heights!)

A wild feeling of contentment, of pure, unadulterated bliss, swept over Kate. Everything would be all right. She just knew it. She sighed and opened her eyes. Her father was adjusting his line. He drew it in and cast it out again, and then checked the boys' lines in turn. Dear Papa, thought Kate. You are so, so good. In a flash of insight almost stripped naked with its intensity, she knew she loved her father. Even for all his gruffness, his shortness with her, she loved him. "Papa," she said, giddy with the rush of emotion, "will you come to my confirmation next week? I declare it's going to be special. Bishop Polk will be there and everything."

Her father looked away. "Made a promise years ago to never step foot in a church, and I don't intend to break that promise."

"But it will only be for a little while. Then you can carry on with your promise like it never happened."

"Another time."

"But Papa, there won't be another—"

Just then, one of the twins shrieked. A glance at his fishing pole told Kate that Thomas had a bite.

"Lookie, Thomas," cried Georgie, his eyes wide with excitement. "You got a fish!"

"Now bring him in slow," cautioned William. "Don't want to lose him."

It wasn't long before Thomas pulled a fish from the water and, with a little help, withdrew the hook from its mouth and then set the fish in the basket. "It's still alive," he breathed, watching as the fish flopped. "Maybe we should let it go."

"Well, that's certainly a fine, plump fish," said William. "One of the finest I've ever laid eyes on. If you put it back, no one will believe you caught it."

"Oh," said Thomas sadly. "Sorry, fish."

Kate waited until Thomas' line was baited and cast. "Papa," she said, "what I was saying was that—"

"Dammit, Kate," he said shortly, "I thought you said you were going to stay out of my way and not be a bother."

Again, the wind gusted. Again, her hair flew from beneath her bonnet, snapping across her face, stinging her cheeks. She drew her arms around her knees. She hadn't realized until that moment, just how cold it was.

# Chapter 9

"HIDING FROM SOMEONE?" STARTLED, Breck turned, unsure how to respond, believing the speaker to be in earnest until he saw the smile playing at the corner of Captain Stephen Decatur Rockwell's lips.

They stood beneath one of the great live oaks at Jericho Plantation, the longtime residence of Judge Rockwell and his family. Just two hours earlier, on an island draped with weeping willows in the middle of a pond, Judge Rockwell's third and youngest son, Stephen, resplendent in his military uniform and medals of valor earned in the recent conflict with Mexico, had wed Irish Mary, a petite, red-haired girl near drowning in yards of creamy silk, veiled in lace and orange blossoms. While the couple had exchanged vows, while swans and geese drifted lazily by and the air chorused with birdsong, Breck stood mechanically, wishing he were home. Around him, the half-dozen unmarried ladies fanned themselves vigorously and looked as if they might swoon, whether from the humidity or from love lost now that handsome Stephen Decatur Rockwell was no longer available, Breck wasn't sure, and really didn't care. That more than a few had cast their glance in Breck's direction had not escaped his notice. But he'd kept his face a mask of polite propriety, a mask, he was learning, as essential to the Southern gentleman as his cravat.

Now dusk was fast approaching, and an army of servants, Monette among them (for everyone had brought a handful of house servants), bustled about, carrying lanterns, setting torches ablaze, and whisking dirty platters off to the kitchen. A few musicians tuned their instruments in preparation for the promised dance and festivities.

"Actually," answered Breck with a bow, "yes."

"Ah, my lips are sealed!" Stephen said, laughing. "Your secret is safe with me. I nevertheless feel it my duty to warn you that all the young ladies are wondering where you've run off to. But I trust they'll mend their broken hearts in due course."

Breck smiled, accepting the glass of champagne Stephen offered, feeling the suffocating tightness that had plagued him since the morning begin to release its grip. He liked Stephen. He always had, even when Breck was a mere lad of four, and Stephen a young man of fifteen, black-haired, with eyes the pale blue of a winter's sky. As far as Breck could remember, though, this was the first time Stephen had sought him out for conversation. Man to man, so to speak. As surprised as he was flattered, Breck straightened his posture, placed a hand on the lapel of his embroidered waistcoat, and raised his glass, saying, "A toast to the bridegroom. May you and your wife enjoy a lifetime of happiness."

Now it was Stephen's turn to bow. "I am honored."

"Mary's a beautiful woman. She seems quite devoted to you."

"Indeed. I'm a lucky man."

"I hear you're traveling to Europe for your honeymoon?"

"For eight months. England, France, Spain, Italy, and, of course, to Mary's ancestral home in Ireland. Been in her family for over four hundred years now."

Breck was painfully aware of his own sheltered existence. The farthest he'd ever been from home was New Orleans. He hadn't even been to the State of Mississippi, only thirty-odd miles to the north. Breck sipped his champagne, envying Stephen. Envying him his knowledge of the world. The valorous medals pinned to the breast of his uniform. His seeming ease with any situation. "And after Europe?"

"Do what every gentleman does, I suppose. Build a fine home, work the land, raise a family, care for my wife, do my civic duty, and hope by the time I die I've done some portion of good in the world." Stephen sipped his champagne, his eyes smiling. "Forgive my asking, but how old are you now?"

"Sixteen."

"Ah, sixteen. A memorable age, though, admittedly, most of my memories of that time are acutely painful. But, memorable nonetheless." Stephen smiled. "So, Breck Jensey, I'm afraid I have a confession to make.

I did not wander under this tree by happenstance. I was sent to you as a man on a mission."

"A mission?"

"Indeed. A mission of utmost importance." He lowered his voice to a conspiratorial whisper. "Of utmost urgency."

"Let me guess. Lucy Saffin sent you?"

"Ah," said Stephen in mock exasperation, "your intuition has rendered my mission dead in the water. It is a good thing I did not have to face you across the battle lines, else I'd have been required to alter my strategies—"

As Stephen talked, Breck spied Lucy at the edge of the pond surrounded by a gaggle of young ladies. There seemed enough flounces and parasols and flower-laden headgear between them to clothe all of Paris. Lucy herself was the picture of the Southern belle—all silk, lace, and curls, her tinkling laughter floating up to where Breck stood under the live oak.

Though Breck had known Lucy since they were children—hardly a rare occurrence as all the children of the plantations in these parts knew one another—her address toward him had changed of late. It was an uncomfortable change, in his opinion, as if the air now thickened whenever he was around her, as if she expected something from him that he did not wish to give. Seeming to sense his gaze on her, Lucy cast her glance ever so casually in his direction. Too late, Breck looked away, taking a quick swallow of champagne, pretending his face was not flushing. He realized Stephen was watching him.

"Alas," Stephen said, "I'm afraid there's no remedy. At least none I've found."

Breck nodded, sighing. "I fear you're right."

"They will not rest until you, like me, are happily joined in matrimony."

"Tell me, Captain Rockwell, now that I know who sent you, what exactly *is* the nature of your mission?"

"You mean, besides befriending a guest whose countenance could not have been more deceptively benign? Let us just say that the dance is about to begin, and your presence has been requested by more than a few."

"But shouldn't you have the first dance? As—as the bridegroom, I mean?"

"Seeing as you are correct in your assessment, and seeing as I will not leave the shelter of this tree without you, the consequence of which would throw all subsequent festivities into an uproar, perhaps it is best that you offer your surrender and come with me."

Knowing the battle was lost, without another protest, Breck capitulated. Together he and Stephen strolled out from under the tree. Hardly had they taken ten steps when they were surrounded by the young ladies, all of them acting as if the intersection were mere coincidence. Stephen whispered, "So it begins." With a wink, he released Breck, rendered his apologies to the ladies, and hurried away.

Breck smiled and bowed. He took Lucy's gloved hand as she tucked it under his arm and led the way across the lawn toward the dance arena, murmuring appropriate responses to the excited chatter, meanwhile ticking the seconds off in his mind, pretending he did not watch Monette as she worked under the eave of the big house.

*　　　*　　　*

William heard Alexander Saffin's breath whistling through his nostrils even before he felt the man's elbow jab his ribs.

"See? What did I tell you?" Senator Saffin pointed his brandy at their children as they strolled across the lawn, looking, for all intents and purposes, like adults. "She's sweet on him. We're going to be in-laws, Jensey, mark my words. I'm sure the advantages of my uniting with such a heathen family will become apparent in due time, although I'm at a loss momentarily."

William allowed himself a smile, knowing Saffin was joking, half-drunk probably. William's own head felt pleasantly off-kilter. They sat in the shade of a live oak, reclining in chairs meant especially for the comfort of the gentlemen: his brother-in-law John, Marshall McCain, Judge Walter Rockwell, and others—longtime neighbors and friends, plus a few more recent acquaintances. Servants fanned the air, stirring a breeze that smelled of cigar smoke, snuff, and magnolia. A male servant moved among them, silent as a shadow, filling glasses with port, brandy, Scotch, or Madeira, as each gentleman desired.

"I'll have you know," said William, his tongue a little thick and clumsy, "my Sarah attends church regularly and holds catechism for our house coloreds. A more god-fearing woman does not exist."

Marshall butted in. "Ah, but has she changed *your* heathen heart?"

"She's changed my heart, yes, but I'm afraid I remain an unrepentant heathen. Religion is against my principles."

"And what, pray tell, are your principles, exactly?" asked Frederick Taggart, his large bulk partially shaded by the trunk of the tree.

The wealthiest landowner in West Feliciana, with over 6,000 acres and 450 slaves, Taggart was, in William's estimation, a pompous ass. Maybe it was Taggart's high opinion of himself, his enviable success in nearly every avenue of agriculture, his mustache, so bushy it obscured his bottom lip, or the fact that he held a financial note on nearly every planter in the parish, including William, payable whenever Taggart demanded. William didn't know. None of these things were the reason, he supposed. Maybe it was because Taggart made William feel less than a man, as if he were nothing but a cracker with a patch of weeds and a hog to his name.

As it was, William forced a smile, watching water droplets slide from Taggart's glass and dot his pants. "I make no secret of my principles. I mean to enjoy life and provide for my family, and perhaps have a good laugh at the end of it all."

"Spoken like a true heathen." Saffin smiled and nudged William's ribs again. "However, seeing as you're still walking and talking among us, the Almighty must still hold some shred of hope for your redemption. The smallest shred, I must emphasize."

"God hasn't smitten me yet."

"I wouldn't let my guard down, if I were you, William, my boy," drawled Marshall. "That God's a sneaky rascal. Always smiting folks when they least suspect it. What's particularly infuriating, he refuses to smite the ones that really deserve smiting."

"Referring to yourself again, Marshall?" asked John, who sat reading the paper, squinting through his spectacles in the deepening twilight.

Marshall's voice hardened. "Referring to those damned Yankees, to that damned Congress, and to anyone else who deserves damnation."

More than a few nods of agreement and expletives followed Marshall's pronouncement.

It was a subject foremost on everyone's mind: Northern aggression. The winds of secession were blowing more and more furiously, until William worried that North and South might, indeed, come to blows. This year, 1850, more so than any previous year, loomed like an ominous cloud. Would the new territories acquired from the war against Mexico be slave or free? Would the slave trade be abolished in the District of Columbia? Was the nation a confederation of states come together, each entitled to govern itself as its populace desired? Or were the states mere divisions of a federal government that could make sweeping mandates affecting every man, woman, and child within its borders—a government that was becoming increasingly Northern in its outlook and action, disregarding Southern interests? For months, Congress had alternately acted like statesmen and schoolboys, on occasion delivering brilliant speeches and exhibiting uncommon wisdom, on other occasions devolving into name-calling, bullying, and even fisticuffs. Would good sense ever prevail? And who, pray tell, was the determiner of good sense?

"You'd damn your own mother, Marshall, if you thought it would further your interests," mumbled John.

Saffin set his own newspaper aside and stood. William caught a whiff of brandy and sweat. The would-be governor of Louisiana leaned against the trunk of the tree, holding his glass out for a refill as the servant passed by. "Should we become embroiled in war," the senator was saying, "and I pray to God that it will not come to that, your son, Judge Rockwell—your fine son who has bound his future with a fair maiden this day—will be on the front lines leading the charge." The judge looked away while Saffin aimed his finger at various men. "Your sons too, Taggart, and yours, Gustine. For all we know, we're already at war. Perhaps tomorrow or next week we will receive word, and in the next breath, we'll be packing their saddlebags and watching them ride off."

Though Saffin sounded like so much drama, as politicians often did, William knew that Saffin could be right. News took a long time to wend its way down the Mississippi. It was a tragic fact that in 1815 the Battle of New Orleans had been fought weeks after the war had officially ended. Thousands had fought needlessly under a banner of peace. To William's surprise, he became aware of a small fear quivering deep inside him, a fear that had always been there, he supposed, but only now realized: fear for the future of their nation, for the future of his holdings, and especially for his son, Breck, who would soon be old enough to enlist. William gnawed on the end of his cigar, thinking, is it possible? Will the nation really divide against itself? Through the years, William had dismissed such an eventuality, but now that it was truly a possibility, the thought scared him more than he'd thought it could.

"No sir," Saffin drew on his cigar, the end glowing orange. In the distance, the musicians began to play. Strains of violins floated across the lawn like a gentle breeze. "This will be no war on foreign soil, fought in some distant land against nameless faces. It will be brother pitted against brother, fought on our very land."

Taggart grunted and threw back his Scotch.

"Saffin, you always were full of humbug," said Marshall. "It's no wonder you were elected to office. People always love humbug mixed with bluster and sentimentality. No, it's my belief that all we have to do is show a bit of backbone, a bit of Southern fire, and our Northern brethren will sign the secession papers so fast we'll scarcely have time to cock a pistol."

"My thoughts exactly," remarked Mr. Hugh Vanderkloot, a pale, skinny man—all fop and gawk, in William's opinion. "I promise to drink every drop of blood shed in this so-called conflict. Hardly a mouthful, I'll warrant."

Marshall barked with laughter and thumped Mr. Vanderkloot between the shoulders. "That's the spirit!" he cried, while Vanderkloot choked on his port, and Saffin rolled his eyes at William.

"As always, Senator," drawled Taggart, his bushy mustache wagging, "you're full of bleeding-heart nonsense. These United States were not formed because we cowered behind locked doors, afraid of our own shadows, God forbid. Instead, our country was built on the courage and conviction of good men, brave men who would not be governed from afar, but who would govern themselves. It was for that ideal of self-government and self-determination that our forefathers bled on the battlefields." Taggart spat. "They did not tuck tail and run, nor did they give in to the threats of bullies."

Saffin faced Taggart, suddenly looking older than his thirty-eight years. "If the time comes to fight, Taggart, I will fight, and I will not prevent our sons from going to war. But before that day comes, I will do everything in my power to prevent it. Our forefathers, as you say, bled on the battlefields to form this republic. I will not stand idly by while it is torn asunder by a few hotheads."

Taggart leaned forward in his chair. The air itself seemed suddenly alert, wary, as if it were seconds before a lightning strike. "The ideal country that they fought to form has turned into the very tyranny that they bled on the battlefield to escape. Every day, gentlemen, that tyranny is shoved down our throats. Southern interests are denied. The North will tell us what to do, and we will like it." Taggart's voice rose. "If the South must choose secession to abide by the principles of self-governance, then I am at her service. And if that makes me a traitor, then by God, so be it!" He sank back into his chair, jowls quivering.

William gulped his brandy, feeling as uncomfortable as the rest of the men looked. He loosened his cravat, wondering who was right and who was wrong, knowing they were both right and both wrong, that it was all a mess. Wondering how the hell it got so bad, angry at the North for sticking its nose where it didn't belong, angry at himself for not knowing the answer, knowing only that he would kill anyone who tried to take what was rightfully his by law.

Saffin turned away, saying nothing, gazing over the lawn toward the festivities. One of the torches snapped, spitting embers.

Here Judge Rockwell heaved himself up from his chair, stubbing out his cigar in a dish so provided. "Damnations be damned. This is a wedding celebration, gentlemen. And I, for one, am off to witness my son whirl his bride around the dance floor. And after he's finished whirling his bride around, I'm going to whirl my own bride around." Whereupon the judge fetched his walking cane and proceeded across the lawn toward the merriment, leaving the men behind.

Marshall mumbled under his breath, "As if the fat bastard can whirl anyone anymore."

"The judge is right, my friends," said Saffin. "There's a time and place for everything, and the time for such sobering predictions must be postponed. Gentlemen, come. It is now the hour to frolic. Despite your advanced ages, surely you remember how it is done." And off he marched in the wake of the judge.

But when William rose and made to follow, relieved to frolic his worries away, John caught his arm and shoved the newspaper under William's nose, pointing at one of the advertisements. "Read this." William took the paper and held it up to the light of one of the torches.

*COMMITTED to the jail on the fourth day of April, one negro man, appears about 30 years old, medium-colored, 5'9" tall, about one hundred and seventy pounds, crescent scar through right eyebrow, old gunshot wound on right thigh, walks with a limp, bears many scars on back. Refuses to give name, or where from, very recalcitrant, claims to be free. A dangerous fellow, armed with knife when captured. The owner is desired to prove his property, pay charges, and take him away. S. J. GOODMAN, Jailor.*

John said, "Sounds like your boy, Sawney."

William handed the paper back to John. He sighed and rubbed the bridge of his nose, feeling a headache coming on. "At least one thing is resolved this evening."

# *Chapter 10*

IT WAS A NEW dress, white, with gathers on the bodice, tiny satin bows at the throat and sleeves, and a row of lace stitched around the bottom hem. Mammy Hester presented Monette with the dress on the morning of her baptism. Up in the room they shared, with a dry kiss and a bony hug, Mammy whispered, "You looks like an angel, chile. A real angel."

Monette nodded, rubbing the stiff fabric between her fingers, unable to speak because of the tears bunched in her throat and gathered behind her eyes, remembering. So many evenings when she'd come to the door of their attic room, it was barricaded. She'd heard, "Just a second, I's plumb naked," and a quick rustling from within. Then, after a spell, Mammy Hester would open the door, clad in her nightgown. All that time, Monette realized now, she'd been sewing a baptismal dress for her.

"Well, ain't you gonna say nothing?"

Monette wrapped her arms around the woman. "Thank you, Mammy Hester. You're too good to me," she said, her accent thickening before she lapsed into her native tongue altogether, a familiar, comfortable retreat, like the fitting of an old shoe. *"Je ne mérite pas une si belle robe."*

"There there now, chile. Ain't no reason to cry. This be a happy day. This be the Lord's Day. This be the day Jesus gonna gather you to his bosom like a hen what gathers her chicks. Lordy sakes, I's so proud of you, I's just fit to bust inside."

Touched as she was by the old woman's gesture, the new dress did not ease Monette's rising dread.

All the way to church, she held Kate's hand through a drizzling rain. The carriage splashed through muddy holes, each bounce jarring her spine, her teeth, her panic. I am a sinner, she thought, looking away from Miss Sarah's tender gaze, from Mammy Hester's broad, wrinkle-faced smile. Not only that, but I have not renounced my sin. *I will not.*

At least two nights a week now, whenever she could, she hid in Breck's room, trembling with the fear of discovery, waiting for his return, waiting for the time when they would sit together, the two of them alone, the bedroom shuttered, a single candle burning, breathing air that smelled of books and fire and secrecy. They kept white soap and vinegar close by for scrubbing the ink stains from her hands, as if by removing the stains, she could blot out her sin. She could not explain her fascination, her determination to read and write. She only knew that the sounds, sentences, and stories pierced the sameness of her days like a brilliant light shining through the holes of a ragged blanket.

Into the church she filed with Kate, taking her seat alongside the other candidates, aware of the smiles and nods of the parishioners. Monette's dress lay in stiff folds around her, dotted with rain, her petticoats tinged with mud.

She had not wanted to be baptized. "No," she'd said, turning away when Kate had first asked her. But Kate begged pitifully, crying, clutching Monette's sleeve, saying Edward's manservant had just been baptized, that it was a sin to not have one's servant baptized. Besides, Kate herself was going to be confirmed, that she'd committed her soul to the Lord, and she certainly didn't want to commit her soul alone. That if Monette really loved her, she'd be baptized. Upon Monette's further refusal, Kate flung herself onto her bed, burst into tears, and prayed, "Oh God, please soften the hard heart of your naughty servant girl!"

Monette relented. She would be baptized. But guilt pulsed through every fiber of her body when, the next morning, Miss Sarah gathered Monette into her arms, kissed her with a kiss of lilac, and whispered, "It has brought me such joy that you have decided to turn your life to Christ. I hope you will be an example to others of your kind."

Now Monette watched with detachment as Kate knelt in turn before the bishop, a pork chop-faced man as formidable as he was immense. He smothered Kate's head with his oversized hands, voice booming through the sanctuary.

"Defend, O Lord, this thy servant . . ."

Outside, the thunder rumbled low. There was a roar of wind. Candles guttered, smoked. The bishop raised his voice as rain spattered the stained-glass windows, pocking Jesus' crown of thorns, running rivulets down his gaunt cheeks. Monette squeezed her eyes closed. The hardness of the pew ground into her spine, the bones of her pelvis. She clenched her jaw, willing herself to breathe. Just *breathe.*

"Go on, Monette. You're supposed to go up front. The bishop and everyone's waiting." Kate was seated beside her now, her knuckles digging into Monette's ribs.

Beneath the gold brocade of his tall, pointed miter, the bishop was frowning, his eyebrows drawn together in disapproval.

"*Go on!* What on earth is *wrong* with you?"

Monette forced her body up, out of the pew. Forced her knees to bend, her hips to move, her feet to climb the stairs. She joined the other baptismal candidate, who already stood before Bishop Polk at the baptismal font. As godparents, Miss Sarah and Miss Emma moved to stand behind Monette.

The bishop addressed the candidates, prayed, exhorted, and finally addressed them again, his colorful vestments glistening in the candlelight.

Monette watched his mouth move, a meaningless flapping, while a clanging, swirling tempest roared in her head.

"Dost thou renounce the devil and all his works, the vain pomp and glory of the world, with all covetous desires of the same, and the sinful desires of the flesh, so that thou wilt not follow, nor be led by them?"

Monette heard herself answer, "I renounce them all; and, by God's help, will endeavor not to follow, nor be led by them."

"Dost thou believe all the Articles of the Christian Faith, as contained in the Apostles' Creed?"

"I do."

"Wilt thou be baptized in this Faith?"

"That is my desire."

"Wilt thou then obediently keep God's holy will and commandments and walk in the same all the days of thy life?" The other baptismal candidate had already answered, but the bishop cleared his throat, waiting for Monette. Again, thunder rumbled, and the sanctuary paled, bereft of light as though it was the end-times at last, the sun turned to darkness, the moon to blood. Words lodged in Monette's throat like hot coals, refusing to come out her mouth.

*And what of lying lips?*

*Lying lips are an abomination to the Lord.*

The bishop cleared his throat again, louder. "Wilt thou then obediently keep God's holy will and commandments and walk in the same all the days of thy life?"

Monette blinked, spitting the words out. "I will, by God's help."

After exhorting and expounding some more, and after baptizing the other and marking his forehead with a wet-fingered cross, the bishop led Monette to the font. She almost resisted. Almost pulled away from the arm that steered her toward the Holy Water.

*Where shall all liars have their part?*

*In the lake which burneth with fire and brimstone.*

Now it was too late. He scooped a handful of water and poured it on her head as lightning flashed through the sanctuary. "I baptize thee in the name of the Father and of the Son and of the Holy Ghost. Amen."

*Can we ever tell a lie and the Lord not know it?*

*We cannot, for He knows all things.*

"We receive this person into the congregation of Christ's flock; and do sign her with the sign of the cross . . . " Words continued to spill from the bishop's mouth as he took his wet finger and marked a cross on her forehead.

Monette let out a muffled cry, drowned in a crack of thunder.

*God hates the liar.*

All Monette wanted to do was undress and lie upon her bed. She felt drained, as if it had been her body crucified upon the cross, her blood that everyone sipped as they knelt at the chancel rail.

But there was Fatima. Like a dark stain upon the attic step. Waiting for her as the storm raged outside.

"Go away," said Monette, her heart lurching.

But already Fatima was grabbing her arm, her fingers squeezing together. She lowered her face into Monette's. "I see'd you up there at church today."

Monette tried to pull away, but Fatima squeezed harder, pressing her against the railing. The hard wood bit into Monette's back, hurting her, but the older girl was bigger, stronger, and Monette knew better than to struggle. Struggling always made it worse.

"So pretty up front in your shiny new dress. All them white folks be smiling at you like you was something special, while all us stupid niggers be sitting in the back."

Monette turned her face away as best she could, despising the sight of Fatima. Outside, the wind gusted. Somewhere, a shutter banged. "What do you want?" she asked flatly.

Fatima said nothing, her breath moist and warm on Monette's face, smelling of lard. Then, slowly, the girl raised a pudgy hand and plucked one of the tiny bows from Monette's dress.

Monette felt the tug, heard the snap of threads over the rumble of thunder, and, without looking down, knew her dress was torn, that bits of thread stuck out like tiny hairs.

"A bow. That's what I want. A white bow from a yellow nigger."

Another tug, another snap.

Tears smarted in Monette's eyes, tears for her dress and all of Mammy's hard work, followed by tears of humiliation, crying like a child in front of Fatima. "Please stop."

"You see, it like this." Tug, snap. "I done see'd you crying up there when that priest done poured water atop your head." Tug, snap. "I knowed why you's crying, see, 'cause I just know things like that. I knows everything 'bout you. There ain't nothing you can hide from me." Tug, snap.

"Please let me go."

"You see, everybody else thinking you's crying 'cause you gots religion. But I says to myself, no, that girl ain't got no religion. That girl, she going to Hell. That's why she be crying. 'Cause she can feel the flames a'scorching her toes." Fatima put her lips next to Monette's ear, her voice licking the insides, a wet whisper. "'Cause she can hear the devil hisself calling her name, 'Monette, Monette!'"

Hatred coursed through Monette, hot and biting, and now she pushed against Fatima, fists pressing into the girl's soft flesh, saying through clenched teeth, "I hate you!" Tears coursed down her cheeks as she struggled, her breathing ragged, the taste of salt in her mouth. Again, the wind gusted, the shutter banging like gunfire.

Fatima smiled, hardly blinking as Monette's fists flailed against her chest like a fragile moth beating against window glass. "See, bitch," she hissed, "that's exactly what I's talking 'bout. Hatred."

Then, to Monette's relief, the girl released her. Monette tumbled to the step above, gasping, bruising her hip, angry at herself when fresh tears burned her eyes.

She watched Fatima through the veil of tears, watched her uncurl her fist and gaze at the bows on her palm as if she'd forgotten they were there. "Hmm. Don't need these for nothing. They just a bunch a white trash." With a flick of her wrist, she tossed them over the railing, turned, and sauntered down the steps without looking back, while the bows of satin ribbon fluttered to the floor beneath.

Of course, Monette wouldn't be in his room, waiting. After all, Breck had been gone for five days now, and besides, it was late, past eleven. Breck knew she wasn't there, but he called her name anyway, feeling a childish disappointment when only silence answered. Silence, and the thrum of the rain outside, sounding like a thousand birds' wings.

It took a minute or so of fumbling with the match holder, but Breck finally managed to light the candelabra, the shadows in his room—the armoire, the bed canopy, the massive candlesticks on the mantel—growing monstrous. Half of him was irritated with Uncle Henry for not having a fire burning in the grate to chase off the stink of dampness; at the same time, it was just as well. The darkness and chill fit his mood.

After hanging his coat on a peg, not caring that he was still soaked through, he sat at his desk, shivering. He ran his hand through his hair and moved a few books around, knowing that she'd been there in his absence. At the thought, weariness stirred in his bones, deep as marrow, a weariness that had been there all along, but which he had consciously suppressed, relegating it to a time when he could allow it to manifest in a bone-bending stupor.

He buried his head in his hands.

Why was it that just when it seemed the plantation and all its parts were functioning smoothly, something always happened to twist things awry? Why? When, five days ago, his father had said that they needed to go fetch

Sawney from jail, it had sounded easy enough. Saddle up the horses, a day there, a day back. But no sooner had they packed and left, taking the road to the landing at Bayou Clare, than the skies opened and dumped an ocean of rain.

By the time they arrived at the jail, and after proving their ownership to the magistrate, both William and Breck were cross as badgers, in no mood for anything but a warm fire and dry clothes. But then there was the jailer, a smug, corpulent man smelling of sausages, who seemed to take a smirking pleasure in both William's and Breck's sodden discomfiture.

Standing next to William, Breck could feel his father's anger rise, palpable as heat, while the jailer rattled off a list of charges, cheek distended with chaw, his voice moist and gargling: "Six dollars for apprehension in the woods, ten cents a mile to jail, let's see—fifty-four days of incarceration at twenty-five cents a day, of course there's the advertisement costs, the turnkey . . ." The man could scarcely conceal his pleasure as he pushed the paper across the counter. Total: $30.70.

William exploded. "By God! That's enough to buy a—a—"

Here the jailer shrugged and crossed his arms, looking contented as a toad.

For a second, Breck thought William might hurdle the counter and cane the man. The vessels bulged on his father's forehead; Breck saw the pulse throb. But then his father was rubbing his temples with his hand (no doubt thinking better of horsewhipping a jailer), saying through clenched teeth, "Fine. Fetch our boy and we'll be on our way."

The nightmare continued.

Rain, driving sideways.

Breaks in the levee, crevasses like lakes.

Water up to the horses' knees.

Sawney, roped up, stumbling ahead of them amid floating debris, alligators.

Meanwhile, William growing sicker by the hour.

Earlier this evening, five days and four nights after first setting off, they'd finally arrived home. Breck had handed Sawney over to Quincy, telling him to lock him in jail, that he'd deal with him later. Then, with the help of Uncle Henry, Breck had hauled his shivering father off to bed, grateful when his mother took over his father's care, getting him out of his wet clothes, spooning quinine down his throat as if he were a babe, saying how much she'd worried about them, that she'd prayed and prayed for their safety. But before Breck could leave, before he could shed his own wet clothes, his father clamped a fevered hand on Breck's wrist and pulled him close. At first, Breck was surprised, thinking his father meant to embrace him, but then his father was saying in his ear, his voice hard despite the tremor, "Whip the bastard. Duck him, then whip him to within an inch of his goddamn life. I'll not have him get the better of me. I won't have it."

"I promise, Papa. I'll take care of him, I promise."

Now, with a creak of the chair, Breck rose from his desk and slowly peeled off his clothing, dropping his shirt, pants, stockings, and undergarments in a heap by the cold fireplace, knowing Uncle Henry would take care of them in the morning. He crossed the room, naked. Pouring water from the pitcher into the bowl, he splashed the liquid against his face, shivering again, startled by the reflection peering at him from the washstand mirror. A boy older than his years. Hardened with shadows. Eyes guarded. In need of a shave.

He quickly grabbed a towel and pressed it against his face.

## *Chapter 11*

OH, EDWARD SCARBOROUGH WAS so infuriating! How could a boy—a man, any man, for that matter—be so insensitive to womanly charms? How could any man have his eye so single to the glory of God that he ceased to have peripheral vision? Didn't God have enough men praying to Him and obeying His every command without Him having to snatch one away from Kate? Was God really so desperate? Didn't God know she *loved* Edward?

It seemed that ever since her confirmation months earlier, Edward hadn't so much as glanced in her direction. Oh yes, he looked at her, but only like he looked at anybody. The fact was, he didn't *look* at her. And there certainly was a difference. It didn't matter what Kate did, what she wore, how she acted, or what she said. Nothing mattered. It was as if she wasn't there. Kate cried into her pillow at night, beating it occasionally while feathers puffed about the room, and sometimes suffered Monette to hold her in her arms while Kate reviled Edward's name in every manner she could think of. Now that she was a woman, it just wasn't fair. Was it really supposed to be this hard? Did it always hurt this much?

One night, when her mother was in her room, Kate asked, "Did it hurt when you fell in love with Papa? Did you—did you—?" Kate couldn't finish her sentence because she fell back on her pillow and burst into tears.

Sarah gathered her into her arms, whispering such things as, Hush now. Don't cry. After Kate calmed down, rocked in her mother's arms like a baby, Sarah said, "Your Papa and I loved each other very much. What hurt was when we couldn't be together because we were so young. And you, my dear," she said with a kiss, "are only fifteen. There's plenty of time for you to fall in love and start a family. I wouldn't worry about it just yet. Enjoy your childhood for just a while longer. Now be a good girl, say your prayers, and go to sleep." Then Mama brushed the damp hair from Kate's face, blew out the candle, and left her alone. Kate sighed, feeling unsatisfied and angry. It was what everyone said: You're young. You have plenty of time to fall in love.

Grandma Mehitable was much more blunt: "Don't be ridiculous."

Kate clenched her fists and pounded the pillow. Nobody understood. Nobody. Youth had absolutely nothing to do with the pain in her heart. Pain was pain.

But, Kate was learning that blessings, like miracles, come in many disguises. On a crisp December day, when smoke spewed from the sugar mills, Kate attended a birthday party for Cousin Juliana. She sat around a table with girls much older, knowing she'd only been invited because she was a relation. The older girls scarcely gave Kate a glance, only suffering to address her occasionally out of politeness. Cake? More tea? Sugar? She'd previously told her mother she'd rather not go, but Sarah had tsked and said, "Nonsense. It's what ladies do. You want to be a lady, don't you?" So, there she was, gritting her teeth through the insipid conversation, to the occasional giggle behind gloved hands, to the air of aloofness cast in her direction every so often.

Then came the blessing.

*Oh, Edward!*

It started with a whisper: "They say she's from darkest Africa."

"Well, she must be, otherwise how could she know her charms and spells? Believe me when I say, she *knows* her charms and spells."

"Reverend Scarborough says such charms and spells are the work of the devil. He says New Orleans is the devil's own cauldron of iniquity, and that this bubbling iniquity has spilled out, scalding us here even in English Louisiana with witches and sorcerers and goodness knows what else."

"Oh, Priscilla, that's such utter nonsense! Tell me, do devil's instruments work in ways of love? Can a witch really divine your future? Only God could know such things."

"She tells your future?"

"Of course, silly. What good is a witch who can't tell the future?"

"Has she told you yours?"

"Why, yes, she has."

"And?"

"Why, she says I'm to marry the most charming man from out-of-town."

"Who? Who?!"

"Well, of course she didn't *tell* me. It has to be mysterious, or else it won't work. As I was saying, she said I'm to marry the most charming man from out-of-town, and that he would enter my life starting in the new year—"

"Why, Juliana, that's just a few weeks away!"

"—and that he would ride a white horse and ask me for a drink."

"What else did she say?"

"That we would marry come summer, and that we would be very happy and have eight healthy children between us."

"Eight! Why, if that's my future, I'd rather not know."

"Not me. I want to know everything. Even the day I die."

"Did she tell you when you were going to die?"

"Not exactly."

"What did she tell you then?"

"That I would live to be an old lady and die in my bed, surrounded by my family."

"Oh, that's the way I want to die, too. Real peaceful-like."

"Not me. I want to die in a tragic accident, so everyone can be sorry that they ever said anything to me cross-eyed."

"But really, Juliana, tell us. What else did she say?"

"Well, there *is* one other thing."

"What."

"That there would be something in my life that would cause me great sadness."

"What."

"She didn't say what. Only that it would be terrible."

"Well, you could have saved your money, Juliana, because I could have told you that much. After all, who lives to be an old lady without some tragic event happening in your life, whether it's—it's your parents dying or your children or even your favorite dog? I mean, we all have to die, don't we?"

"Hush, don't say that. You'll bring bad luck to Juliana."

"Well, witch or no witch, I want my fortune told like Juliana's. I want to know whether the next man I hand a drink of water to is going to be my future husband or not. I mean, what if he's your future husband and instead of giving him a drink you ignore him, or you're with some other lout that you only *think* is your future husband? Your whole life would be ruined just because you didn't know."

"So tell us, Juliana. How do we find this hoodoo woman?"

"They call her Crone Juju. She lives on Emma Breck's plantation."

"Woodleigh."

"That's right. You're only to come at midnight because that's when her power is at its fullest. That's her witching hour. And don't forget to bring five dollars."

"Five dollars! Why, that's highway robbery!"

"Wouldn't *you* pay five dollars for your future husband? Anyway, as you're heading north up Fox Creek Road, just past the southern border of Woodleigh, there's a path leading through the woods. Follow the path to the swamp. Take a lantern."

*       *       *

Just as Kate was about to give up, tears of frustration rising until it became physically painful to hold them back, she found the trail. She understood why she could have missed it, especially in the dark. It was a mere footpath, inches wide, an earthen thread disappearing through the tangle of brush. "This way," she whispered to Monette. Holding the lantern high, she stepped onto the path.

Strands of spider silk snapped as she moved forward. Wisps of Spanish moss brushed her forehead like ghost-fingers, and she parted them, aware of the creak of the lantern hinge, the stink of melting tallow, and Monette's breathing behind her, too close. Shapes and shadows loomed, seeming to move, slither, watch, whisper. For all of Kate's life, she had wandered these woods on horseback, with her father, with Breck, or Monette. She had always thought of these woods as *hers.* But on this night, knowledge stabbed her between the shoulder blades like a knife. Not only were these not her woods, but she was an intruder. As if, when night fell, they belonged to someone else. Some*thing* else.

For the second time in her life, Katherine Emma Jensey felt fear. Real fear.

The first time, she'd been ten years old. It was her first ride atop her big new horse, Mamie. No sooner had she sat in the saddle than Mamie began to buck, and before Kate could draw her next breath, she was flying through the air. It was strange flying, as if it took an eternity, although it really only took a second or two. She thought of how much it would hurt when she landed; she determined which part of her body would land first; she figured she would have a hole or two in her new riding suit; she heard people around her screaming and wondered how silly she looked, and, in a sudden afterthought of terror, she thought she might actually die. When she did land, her arm was at a crazy angle, and she heard herself screaming along with everybody else. She realized she hated fear, even more than she hated the pain of a broken arm, and determined never to feel fear again, even if Mamie threw her into the next parish. "I'll get rid of the horse," William had said, his face tight. "They told me she was gentle."

"No," replied Kate. "Keep her. I like her. She's got pluck."

Now Kate felt fear again. But it was a different kind of fear. Not the flash of terror she'd experienced as she'd flown through the air, but an insidious kind of fear that seeped into her blood and chilled her from the inside out. Good God Almighty, she thought, we could get lost. And no one knows we're here. She swallowed hard and forced her feet to continue, wondering if Edward was worth all the fuss.

Of course he was.

Then the ground softened beneath her boots. A crunching. As if she'd stepped on something alive and had crushed it into the mud. She turned to Monette, seeing the whites of her widened eyes, knowing her eyes looked the same. "Let's hurry," she whispered. "I don't like this place."

Monette nodded, grasping Kate's cloak as she turned and quickened her step.

The forest opened into a murky blackness, and the lantern light reflected off mirrored pools of ink-black. Cypress knees jutted from the watery depths like the undulating spine of a sea serpent.

"*Mon Dieu.* This place is evil."

Kate shivered. "Nonsense," she said, anxious to dispel the fear, ignoring the stink of decay. "It's only the dark that makes it seem so bad." Determined to match the bravado of her words, she marched as quickly as she could, and, after a while, thankfully, the ground grew firmer, and the forest closed in. After a few hundred feet, the woods parted to reveal a clearing framed by trees and palmettos and the dark curve of a bayou.

Perched like a stork on the bank of the bayou, was a cabin. It stood on pilings a few feet above the ground, a tumbledown affair that looked slapped together with scraps from every rotten building that had ever collapsed into the swamp. Weak light emanated from between the boards.

Monette tugged her arm. "Do not do this. *S'il vous plaît, mon amie,* this is a terrible idea. It will come to no good. Witches are *malfaisant,* evil."

But Kate shook her off and headed toward the cabin. "Are you coming or not?" she asked, hiding her relief when Monette shut her hanging mouth and followed.

It was as if someone had been waiting for them. For when they climbed the steps and onto the half-collapsing, sloped surface of the gallery, the door opened, moaning on its hinges. Of course, Kate told herself, why should she be so surprised, seeing as the old woman—Crone Juju, was it?—was a witch and could tell the future and all. Naturally, she would know who was coming and when, otherwise she wouldn't be worth two cents, let alone five dollars.

Beside her, Kate felt Monette stiffen. Darkies. Sometimes they could be such superstitious chickens. Kate tossed back her hair, straightened her shoulders, and marched into the cabin. Upon entering, the light in her lantern expired. Kate squelched a startled shriek, her heart pounding. It was a sudden breath of wind, she told herself. Nothing more.

The cabin was a mere twelve feet square. In the center of the room, several pine knots burned in a half-gourd set on a large floor cloth, casting looming shadows against the walls. The cabin was, in Kate's opinion, ugly and barbaric. There were animal skeletons, herbs, roots, toads—human hair and fingers and toes maybe—hanging everywhere from the rafters and walls. Kate frowned, thinking, Papa would never allow such a cabin to exist at Fox Creek. He would torch it to the ground and then sprinkle the smoldering pile with lime to stop the spread of disease.

"Hello! Anybody home?" Except for the guttering pine knots and the shadows creeping upon the walls, there was no movement. No sound. She peeked behind the open door. Nothing. How odd.

"Monette, do you—" The question died in Kate's throat, for Monette looked the very picture of terror—eyes widening, mouth hanging as she tried to form words—pointing at something behind Kate.

Kate whirled. There. Against the far wall. What she'd thought was merely a chair, a pile of clothing, a fireplace—now she didn't know what she'd thought it was—materialized into a woman sitting hunched upon the floor. Crone Juju was small—no bigger than Monette—and withered, black as the night swamp, her head wrapped in a turban. Well. Kate didn't know what she'd expected to see, but this so-called witch was certainly disappointing. Now she found it hard to believe she'd been terrified. Terrified of what? A raggedy old woman, all bones and whiskers?

"Sit," was what she said.

Seeing no chairs provided for guests, Kate grunted with disgust and sat upon the floor with Monette. Who knew what creepy critters were just waiting to skitter up her drawers? Juliana should have warned her. Feeling Monette's hand slide into her own, Kate shook her off, fumbled in her skirt pocket, and withdrew five dollars. "I've come for my fortune." As she laid the gold coin on the floor cloth, she felt an unexpected leap of excitement. Here it was. Her fortune. Her life revealed, charted from point to point like a map she would follow to a faraway destination.

*Oh, Edward . . .*

Crone Juju spoke from the shadows, and Kate didn't know if the witch was looking at her or away, or whether she had her eyes closed, or whether she was blind even, perhaps with gaping eye sockets. "Gimme something what belongs to you."

"Why, I just gave you five dollars, and now you want more?"

"Your essence be through all things close to you, whatsomeever touches you." Crone Juju's voice, though seeming withered and feeble as the witch herself, filled the cabin. "See, child, if I sees your essence, I sees the spirits of your future. Without it, can't see nothing. Might as well be blind."

"Oh." Hesitating, Kate untied her bonnet and tossed it to her. Crone Juju caught the bonnet and held it to her face. Kate grimaced. She'd have to burn it now. The witch was sniffing her essence.

Lowering the bonnet to her lap, Crone Juju began to stroke it, as if it were a cat. "Now I sees the spirits. They's everywhere. They's moving in this room all about."

"What do they say?"

"They say he of no-account."

"Who?"

"The one you's pining for."

"Edward?"

"Yes'm, that be the one."

Kate frowned into the semidarkness. "Edward's not of no-account. He's going to be a clergyman, and he's kind and good and very pious."

"I's just saying what the spirits tell me. Ain't no use setting there arguing. You see, chile, the spirits know. They got sensibilities, and it be our task to hear what they says."

"Well then, the spirits are wrong. I'm going to marry Edward. Someday."

Crone Juju chuckled. "Oh, chile, you ain't never gonna marry nobody."

Her words took Kate's breath away. Like a slap. She felt an outrage, a deep hurt, like someone had just snatched her most prized possession and torn it to shreds. Marry no one? Pine away in spinsterhood like the Miss Wigfalls, Lecida and Matilda, with sour faces and dour dispositions? The thought was ridiculous. Of course, she would marry. Everybody married. Everybody except those who were worthless and ugly, whom nobody could possibly love.

Monette slipped her hand into Kate's, but again, Kate brushed her away. She was in no mood for coddling. "What else?" she demanded, holding back tears of frustration for the second time that night.

"Hush, chile. What you in such a hurry for? You gots to be quiet and let the spirits do the talking." The old woman swayed back and forth. Then, with a flick of her wrist and a sound like rattling dice, she tossed the contents of her hand onto the floor cloth. She stopped swaying, leaned forward, and studied a scatter of bones. Her breath wheezed in and out.

Kate considered scooping up her five dollars and leaving, but again, despite her frustration, curiosity beckoned. After all, just because the old woman was an obvious charlatan didn't mean it couldn't be interesting. Kate would just have to remember that it was all a lie, something Crone Juju dreamt up to lure unsuspecting girls into her cabin so she could steal their money and get them in trouble for consulting devil's instruments. Kate sniffed and wiped her nose and waited as the woman stroked the bonnet, pondered the bones, and said nothing. Close by the cabin, Kate heard a heavy splash.

Finally, Crone Juju spoke. "Spirits say you's going away soon."

"Going away? Where?"

"They don't rightly say. Just that you's going away for a long time and you better start packing your belongings."

Kate frowned. "But—but that's ridiculous. Fox Creek is my home. I have no intention of going away unless I'm going to visit Grandma Emma or to New Orleans to attend the theater. Of course, I'll be going to finishing school, but that's not for a long while yet. I mean, really, I don't think I need to pack quite yet. I think you must have stupid spirits, or you don't listen very well."

Now Kate did see the woman's eyes. Liquid black, seeming to float in the dim light, coming closer, disembodied almost, staring at her. *Good God Almighty.* Kate's scalp prickled. "What—what I mean is, surely spirits of the future should be able to know where I'm—I'm going, don't you think?" Kate groped for Monette's hand, squeezing it tightly.

Crone Juju said nothing.

Kate lowered her head and closed her eyes. Now that she'd made the witch mad, she would cast a spell on her. A dying spell. Or a snake spell, where she put snakes into your body. Kate had heard of it before—snakes, spiders, anything creepy—crawling inside you while your skin rippled right before your eyes, driving you insane.

"You's different from your mama."

Kate gasped, raising her head and opening her eyes. "You know Mama?"

"'Course, chile. This done be her plantation 'til she up and got herself hitched. 'Course I knows her. She be a fine woman. I helped born her into this world. I was the one what cotched her when she come out of the womb, the first one what held her as she done weep her first cry." Kate watched, horrified, as Crone Juju crushed the bonnet, imagining her mother as a tiny white babe, similarly crushed and mauled with those horrid black hands. "Spirits say you gots lots of misery a'coming your way, chile. They say to brace yourself, for it gonna be terrible."

"What kind of terrible misery?"

"Terrible, terrible misery. It be 'bout your mama. 'Bout your papa too. 'Bout many folks."

Kate stared at the wall now, hating the sight of the old woman, telling herself this was not real. This was not happening. That the old woman was a fake. Her scalp crawling anyway. "I don't want to hear anymore," she whispered. "Keep the money."

## Chapter 12

T HE HOUND TROTTED ALONGSIDE, glancing at Breck occasionally as he rode his horse. Breck noted that Rascal had that look of sheer contentment that only dogs seemed capable of achieving, as if the two of them were setting out on some grand adventure. "No great adventure today, my friend. Just inspecting the quarters like Papa asked."

Upon hearing Breck's voice, Rascal seemed to smile all the more. Ah well, thought Breck, he'd likely be content if they just trotted around like this all day doing nothing. In fact, doing nothing was exactly what Breck had planned for himself. As it was a holiday, the last day before the new year, he'd intended to retire to his room and read at least one of the three new books he'd received as Christmas gifts. Then, if there was time, perhaps he'd work on his model of a ship, fashioned after the *HMS Bounty*, the same *Bounty* of Captain Bligh and the mutineers. Mr. Gilbert had assigned him the project over two months ago, and Breck enjoyed crafting and assembling the little pieces: the masts and spars, canvas sails, planks for decking, miniature barrels for storing food and water. . . . Ah well. Tomorrow, maybe.

At breakfast, William had announced that he and Sarah would spend the day visiting neighbors, and who wanted to come along? Of course, Kate and the twins exclaimed a resounding, "We do!" while Breck felt relieved that he would have the day to himself. His relief was short-lived.

"As long as you're staying here," William said, "do a thorough inspection of the quarters. Sometimes the holidays give the negroes an uppity air. Makes them impudent and lazy. If anyone gives you trouble, lock them in jail for the holidays. That'll cool their heels." Breck knew better than to argue, merely nodding, seeing the chance of a day to himself slip away. Why was it he never had a holiday?

Then Breck had an idea. He needed a miniature cookstove constructed for his ship. Of course, there were many other items made of iron that he needed as well, such as anchors and cannon, but first things first. Going to the quarters would present the perfect opportunity to ask the blacksmith about constructing the cookstove. Perhaps it could even be ready by the end of the week. So, with his horse saddled, a diagram of the cookstove in his pocket, and Rascal by his side, he left for the quarters.

The quarters had recently been whitewashed with lime. Cholera was plaguing New Orleans, and St. Marysville even had a few folks who'd succumbed. Although cholera had yet to hit Fox Creek in all the years of operation, they took no chances, having the negroes empty their cabins of belongings, air their bedding, and scrub the structures top to bottom, finishing with a whitewash inside and out. It was a tiresome process, and one in which the negroes complained incessantly. But as far as Breck was concerned, a few disgruntled hands were far better than a cholera epidemic. So it was that when Breck entered the pine quarter, all was tidy. Breck was pleased. Today's inspection would be easy. He could hurry through, give instructions to the blacksmith concerning the cookstove, and return to his room. He'd almost have the full day ahead of him. Perhaps he could get to his model after all.

The inspection of the pine quarter went well. As he'd predicted, all was in order, and the hands seemed in an especially good mood, thanking him repeatedly for their Christmas gifts.

On his way to the cypress quarter, Breck stopped at the blacksmith's shop. Seeing as it was a holiday, Breck really didn't expect to find Jermain working at the forge. As expected, the shop was empty, the fire out. No cookstove today.

The cypress quarter was in even better condition than the pine quarter. Maybe word had already reached them that Mars Breck was performing inspections. Breck knew that such a lightning-fast grapevine was not just conjecture, but reality. It was something planters had to deal with, like it or not. In this instance, it paid dividends. Breck complimented each head of household on a job well done.

"Thank you, Mars Breck," each of them replied. "Thank you for the kerchief," or "Thank you for the pipe," or "My missus thanks you for her new comb. She say it don't tear her hair like the other one done."

As Breck prepared to leave, he realized he had yet to see Jermain. He asked one of the drivers where Jermain was, and was told, "Jermain, he at the shop."

"No, I've just come from the shop. The fire's out and he's not there."

Breck noticed the driver scuffing the dirt with his shoes, showing undue interest in the marks he made. "Well now, if he ain't at the shop, Mars Breck, it be my guess he over at the pine quarter. He's sweet on one of them gals over there. You know Jermain. He burning on fire just like his forge. Gotta put it out."

Breck blushed, wondering if the driver had meant to embarrass him. "But I—I've just come from the pine quarter and didn't see him."

"Well now, Mars Breck, you don't expect a fellow to reveal hisself while he doing his private business, now do you? I 'spect that if you tries to find him tomorrow, you have better luck."

It was obvious to Breck that the driver had no clue where Jermain was, and that he was wasting Breck's time. After asking several more people as to the whereabouts of Jermain, he whistled to Rascal and headed back to the pine quarter. Perhaps he *had* missed him. Perhaps Jermain was one of those lumps under the covers, lumps Breck didn't bother to inspect.

But at the pine quarter, Jermain was nowhere to be found, lumps and all. By this time, Breck knew from the sudden way everyone disappeared, scattering like mice to their holes, that Jermain had run away. Not only was Jermain gone, but Breck realized what he should have recognized earlier: Sawney was also missing.

During the six months following Sawney's capture, Breck had clung to the false hope that somehow the ducking and whipping he'd administered to Sawney had fixed him. "Taken the starch out of him," as his father was fond of saying. But even as Breck had applied the lash, guts trembling, teeth clenched, his father's voice in his head telling him over and over that it was a just punishment, that Sawney had known the consequences, that it was a necessary component of a well-ordered plantation, Breck had known the man would run away again. That he'd run until his dying breath. William agreed. Once he recovered from swamp fever, they'd fitted Sawney with an iron collar—a thick ring encircling the neck with three prongs projecting around the head and face, a bell hanging from each prong—making him impossible to miss.

Yet miss him he had.

Breck squared his shoulders and straightened himself in his saddle, trying to look bigger and older than he felt. The situation required immediate action. He hollered for Quincy, the head driver. "Ring the bell. Gather the hands in the yard for a head count."

Once the workforce had assembled, Breck faced them from atop his horse. A sea of faces. Downcast eyes. Blank expressions. Yellow, red, green, and blue checked turbans. Calico skirts motionless. Hats in hands. New kerchiefs.

One hundred eighty-one of them, or so there should be, counting two new babes in arms, born last month. He told Quincy, "Call them, starting with the household servants," irritated when his voice cracked with the sound of adolescence.

A breeze kicked up, stirring the dry December dirt into a fine dust as if it were mid-July, causing the calico skirts to sway like curtains at an open sash. It took a long time, this counting. Families summoned forward. Shuffling. Quincy calling out cabin groups as Breck ticked the names off Papa's ledger. Each group or family silently melting back into the wall of black.

When the count was finished, Breck studied the ledger. It wasn't possible. He didn't want to believe it. Yet, there it was.

"There are five missing," he finally said. Into a silence broken only by a baby's cry and the rustling of the wind through the trees, Breck read the names. Again, silence.

An aura of guilt hung in the air, and Breck was surprised that he had not noticed it before. It hung there like a vast cobweb, tangible almost, a cold brushing against his skin, unmistakable now. *They knew. They allowed me to inspect the quarters, grinned at me, thanked me for their gifts, and all the while they knew.*

Without a word, he passed the ledger to Quincy and took a moment to collect his thoughts, to calm himself, surprised by the anger and humiliation rising within him. He clenched the reins in his hands. Finally, knowing what must be done, he urged his horse forward and began to move among the rows. He looked into each face. "What do you know about the missing men?" he asked, knowing they would not answer, knowing such a question was fruitless, unable to stop himself, to admit that none of them, not even Footy, would confide in him.

Over the next week, they searched for the runaways. The neighbors—John, Saffin, Judge Rockwell and his sons—joined the search with rifles, hounds, and horses. It seemed everyone had someone missing. After three days, they caught two of Saffin's, one of John's, and one of William's. At the end of the week, the men gave up and, except for an occasional outing, did what they normally did—promised to look out for one another's negroes and keep an ear to the grapevine. Runaways rarely got far in the Louisiana swamps. They were bound to turn up when they got hungry, and someone, somewhere, always knew something. But now it was the new year, and life pulsed on, runaways or otherwise. There was work to be done. It was time to plant the cane, to plow the ground for corn, for oats, for potatoes, and to finish ginning those last hundred bales of cotton. . . .

Breck and Monette had been reading together for ten months now. Since last March, they'd met in his room, secretly, whenever they had a chance. Breck knew he should end the sessions. After all, Monette could now read and write as well as he. She was sharp, quick to learn, absorbing everything he said, watching him with those eyes that shone with bronze, gold, and amber all at once.

But he could no more end the sessions than he could stop breathing. For him, they were his deliverance. With Monette, he could speak freely. He told her things he could not tell others, talking with her like he once used to talk to Footy, afterward lying alone in his bed at night, wondering why.

He told her about how, when his father had returned home from his round of Christmas visiting, he'd stormed through the house, slamming doors, bellowing, "Damned negroes, I'd sell the whole lot of them if I could find anyone fool enough to buy them. See if I'll give them another holiday. See, Son, they do this on purpose. The second you let down your guard. Favorite trick of theirs, running away on a holiday, thinking you won't check on them. Gives them a few days' head start before anyone even knows they're gone. They'll do anything just to do nothing. I should just shoot the whole lot of them. Ease my pain. Christ! What's a man to do?"

Of course, Monette already knew what Breck was telling her. She'd been there. She'd heard. No one could escape the sound of his father's voice, cracking like gunfire. But Breck told her anyway. He needed to talk. He needed someone to listen.

He also told her about his humiliation. About everyone knowing, yet saying nothing. Footy, Cyrus, Uncle Obediah, Quincy. Everyone. He told her even though she'd been there. She'd heard and seen it all.

Then he turned to her, asking, "You would tell me if you knew something, wouldn't you, Monette? About the runaways, I mean?"

"Of course, I'd tell you. If I knew."

He felt comforted, knowing she spoke the truth, feeling the tension somewhat ease out of him as she laid her book aside, came to him, and rubbed his shoulders as she often did, her fingers surprisingly strong, her touch warm and gentle.

One evening, it was getting late and still Monette lingered. The two of them sat at his desk, a book propped open before them. In her hand, she held a reed pen. She was supposed to be copying a sentence. But for the last minute or so that Breck had observed her, her hand had remained poised above the paper, her mind obviously far away, unaware that a drop of ink had just dripped from the tip of the pen. Her face looked golden in the candlelight, her complexion soft and smooth. He knew she should return to her room, that after being gone so long, someone was bound to start asking questions, that the danger for both of them was mounting, but he could not bring himself to make her leave. Just a little longer. *Please.*

Outside, he heard the ringing of the plantation bell and the answering howl of the hounds.

She started at the sound, bending her head to her task once again, humming now. The pen scratched across the paper. She finished her sentence and glanced into the book, the vibrations of her song soothing the air like the hush of a lullaby.

"What are you humming?"

She stopped, a puzzled expression on her face, as if unaware she'd been humming at all. "I don't know." She smiled. "Strange, isn't it?"

He shrugged. "Not so strange. Perhaps you made it up. Maybe you're a musical genius," he suggested with a smile.

"I've heard it before, I think."

"In your dreams?"

He'd expected her to laugh, but instead she looked at him with such seriousness, whispering, *"Oui, mon ami,* I think so."

Then Breck found himself listening as she told him about her dreams, about acres of sugar fields, of a man with white hair, of a horse, a storm, and a river. Her accent became increasingly pronounced and peppered with French, a habit of emotion that Breck found particularly endearing. "That is not all. I dream they drown, the man and the horse. *Miséricorde,* it is *horrifiant!* They are swept away and there is nothing I can do. I'm left *seule*—standing on the riverbank alone. I am screaming, but no matter how hard I scream, I cannot hear myself." She tapped her chest and her voice lowered, trembling. "It is like my scream is stuck, wedged tight, and can't get out. It is *coincé*—how do you say? It is *trapped.*"

Breck resisted the urge to draw her into his arms. He watched her as she spoke, as she wetted her lips with her tongue, wondering briefly what she would taste like. Immediately, he was ashamed for thinking such things while Monette shared what was, he knew, something very private and painful, at least as painful as his own humiliation.

"That's only one dream," she was saying. "There are others."

"They are just dreams, Monette." For a while, she didn't answer, instead gazing at him, her eyes large and trusting and yet, he now saw, troubled as well. Then, as if granting herself permission to speak, she said, "Please, Breck, tell me about my past. What do you know?"

The question startled him. Breck shook his head, not knowing what to say. "What do you mean?"

"Where do I come from? *S'il vous plaît, mon ami,* if you know, please tell me." Her face looked stripped bare, naked in its intensity.

"You mean, you can't remember?"

"Nothing. I remember *rien.* The past few years, only."

"I—I'm sorry, Monette," he said gently, "but I don't know what to tell you. We purchased you in New Orleans when you were about six. I don't know anything about your past or where you came from. How could I?"

"You know nothing of my father? Or my mother?"

Breck shook his head, and a silence grew.

After a while, she laughed. But it was a sad laugh, the kind of laugh people do when they realize they've lost their fortune. "Would you believe I used to pretend that Miss Sarah was *ma mère*—my mother?"

"That's not so hard to believe," Breck said, smiling.

"Kate was my sister, you were my brother, and—" she motioned around her, "all this was mine too, Fox Creek Plantation. I used to run around thinking that I'd always lived here, and that nothing had ever been different, and that nothing would ever change. It was *bébête*, I know. Childish."

"But you believed it, didn't you?"

She looked surprised by his comment. He wondered if he had hurt her feelings, wondered if maybe, on some level, she still believed it. "I don't expect you to understand, Breck. It hurts not knowing who your mother is. Or your father. Not knowing if they are alive or dead, or whether they are wondering this very instant about you and where you are and whether they will ever see you again." Her voice faded and she looked away.

He watched her, wishing he could say something, anything, to comfort her. He knew she was right. He really didn't understand how it must feel and wondered what it must be like to know nothing of your past. To not know who you were or where you'd come from. She looked so fragile sitting there, staring at the fire as if the flames held answers in the heat of their embrace. Again, he yearned to take her into his arms, to comfort her at the very least.

*She's beautiful,* he thought, his breath catching. Of course, he'd known this for years, since the day he'd seen her on the auction block in New Orleans, but on this night, her beauty took his breath away. He found himself gazing at her thick, dark lashes. Her high cheekbones, her mouth, her profile (so perfect), the curve of her neck. His gaze dropped and he felt himself flush, seeing the slight swell of her chest. He suddenly became aware that his breathing had quickened. He looked away, his heart racing.

"Breck, what's wrong?" She was watching him. "I've upset you, haven't I? I shouldn't have asked."

He could say nothing.

She rose from her chair and moved behind him. With the touch of her hands upon his shoulders, a fire spread through him. A molten fire, more powerful than anything he'd ever felt before. *Oh God!* "Monette," he whispered hoarsely, rising from his chair, deeply embarrassed. He turned, removing her hands from his shoulders.

Her eyes searched his. "What's the matter?"

"You must leave, Monette. The bell has rung." He heard the trembling in his voice. He glanced away, then back again.

"But why? Some nights I have stayed much—"

"Please. Don't ask. Just leave."

"But I—"

He pushed her gently toward the door. "Go to your room, Monette. I can't explain. Just go."

"But what do you mean?" Tears shimmered in her eyes. "What about tomorrow night?"

"You know that company's coming for a fox hunt."

She just looked at him, saying nothing. Then she fetched her shawl from where it lay draped over her chair and wrapped it about her. When he saw her lips quivering, he almost lost his resolve, almost took her in his arms, his restraint causing physical pain. "I've never told anyone about our meetings," she was saying. "I've kept our secret. I swear to you."

"It's nothing you've done, Monette. Believe me. You're still my friend. But you must go now."

He turned away from her, waiting, his heart clenched and hammering, closing his eyes when she whispered, "Then good night, Breck Jensey. I hope you catch many foxes," shutting the door softly behind her.

On the other side of the door, Monette stood in the darkness, bewildered. What had just happened? What had she done wrong? She wrapped her arms about herself, shivering.

She recalled the way he looked at her just now, or rather, away from her. As if she were ugly, as if he could no longer tolerate the sight of her. Were they not friends? Did he not like her anymore? The thought of losing his friendship, losing the affection that had steadily grown between them, was, suddenly, painful. It caught her by surprise, this pain.

Then she heard a low moan from inside Breck's room. She caught her breath, listening. He moaned again, and when he did, she felt her face flush with heat. She should not be listening, this she knew! Horrified, embarrassed, she fled through the darkness, fumbled stupidly with the back door of the big house, and ran up the stairs. Inside the darkness of the attic room, she stood with her back to the door, panting, face warm with remembering, for the first time thankful for Mammy Hester's raspy snore. Down below, between her legs, Monette felt a stirring—not as a flower blooming into the ripeness of womanhood, but instead a dull heaviness, a seeping away, as if the weight of her soul could no longer be borne.

# *Chapter 13*

So far, the hunt had been, in Kate's opinion, absolutely exhilarating. The hounds had started the fox in the crispness of the early morning, and to the sound of the fox horn and the chorus of baying hounds, they were off. The Rockwells, the Saffins, the Taggarts, the Scarboroughs, Uncle John, Marshall, and anyone else who felt like pounding the turf and feeling his heart run wild.

Kate had followed at a distance, not too awfully concerned about the fox or the hounds, instead following Edward. He was dressed in a short black coat, and breeches. A white neckerchief, stout with starch, swayed in broad folds across his chest. His blond hair peeped from beneath his black hat. How handsome he is, thought Kate, unable to take her gaze from him. Edward preferred not to jump the fences or ditches, instead going around them or through the gate, if one was to be found. Although Kate would rather have soared over just about any fence, ditch, or hedge in West Feliciana, she meekly followed Edward through each gate, saying, "Why, thank you, Mr. Scarborough. How kind of you."

And whenever his blue eyes gazed into hers, her heart tumbled in her chest.

*Oh, Edward . . .*

She knew she looked fetching. Grandma Emma had made her a new riding outfit, as she'd outgrown her other one already. A grand black coat, cut to within an inch of her life, designed to enhance her figure, which, Grandma Emma said, could use a bit of enhancing. (Oh, to have a waist like Lucy Saffin, idiot that she was!) Plus, her tan riding skirt, draped in glorious folds down the side of her horse, Mamie, and her hat, black, with crimson ribbons caressing her hair. She knew her cheeks were rosy with cold, for she felt the chill in her teeth, and in the delicious ache of her ears. A man would have to be blind and stupid not to notice her.

Then Edward took a wrong turn. She knew it was a wrong turn, had heard the hounds a while back coming from a different direction, but happily followed Edward, turning Mamie onto a rutted road that disappeared into a wood. Perhaps it was part of God's plan. Now she would have Edward all to herself. She urged Mamie onward, wanting to close the gap. (Kate had fallen behind when she'd stopped at a thicket to relieve herself, first allowing Edward to ride ahead a great distance. He'd ridden at a furious pace, seeming in a hurry to catch something. Certainly, it wasn't a fox!)

The trees touched overhead in places, the winter's sunlight dappled. A rabbit skittered across the road, fleeing Mamie's flying hooves. Kate couldn't see Edward anymore—she'd lost him around a bend. "Mr. Scarborough, oh, Mr. Scarborough! I believe you've taken a wrong turn!" She rounded the bend, and still he was nowhere to be seen. Why didn't he wait for her? Didn't he know she was trying to catch up?

Four bends later, Mamie beginning to quiver from exertion, she found him, along with Lucy Saffin and Breck. Kate reined to a stop, smothering a flash of disappointment. She smiled. "Why, Lucy! Breck! Here I thought only Edward and I had made a wrong turn. How silly of all of us."

Her brother gave her a knowing glance, as if he could see through her charade. But he said nothing, merely nodding his head in greeting.

Edward looked away.

"Why, hello, Kate," said Lucy, smiling her dimpled smile. "Breck and I were just enjoying a spell in the woods. Chasing a fox is awfully tiring, you know, wears a body out. Besides, they always circle back around, don't they? I believe they do, anyway. So, we'll just join in again when it comes back. Maybe we'll even be first to the fox!" She laughed and tossed her curls, as if she'd said something terribly clever.

Kate resisted rolling her eyes, a tempting occupation in Lucy Saffin's presence. The girl annoyed her. A year older than Kate, Lucy was as daft and airy as a pillow. Her banter was enough to make Kate want to rattle some sense into her. And the way she looked at Breck: soppy with love, drooling almost. It was enough to—well, it was just ridiculous, is all.

Didn't she know Breck wasn't interested in her? That he was too much of a gentleman to tell her otherwise?

"Come," said Lucy, "let's all ride together. How fun it shall be."

"I must say, Miss Saffin," remarked Edward, "you look particularly radiant today."

In point of fact, Kate thought Lucy looked anything but radiant. Small waist aside, she was a rather plain girl, pasty-faced at that, with dullish dark-brown curls and a chin just a tad too prominent. Kate knew Edward was just being polite. Clergy were always polite. It was part of feeding God's flock.

"Why, thank you, Mr. Scarborough," Lucy replied.

"Please, call me Edward."

"Why, then, thank you—Edward."

The four of them rode their horses abreast.

Lucy was going on and on, saying, Oh, hadn't they heard? The St. Charles Hotel in New Orleans burned to a crisp last Saturday, and now was nothing but a pile of smoldering rubble, and wasn't that a terrible shame (such a splendid hotel!) and that next month she was leaving to attend finishing school in New Orleans, and what a fine school it was, who had attended in years past, and all about her new wardrobe. Finally, practically breathless, she asked, "Are you going to finishing school, Kate? After all, every girl who wants a proper education simply *must* go."

Kate chewed her bottom lip. Attend school in New Orleans? But—but that would mean she'd have to leave Edward! While she knew Lucy was right—no education, no *proper* education, would be complete without finishing school—the thought of leaving home for months on end left Kate feeling panicked, as if her future, *life itself,* would no longer be under her control, as if, should she leave, nothing would ever be the same again. "Mama says she needs me at home right now. I'm much too valuable." She felt Breck's sideways glance and ignored him. "I mean, what's the rush? Besides, our tutor has taught me so much, I just don't think some finishing school could provide anything that I haven't already learned."

"Yes," Breck added. "Kate has learned so much from our Mr. Gilbert. She just can't get enough."

"Has Mr. Gilbert taught you Greek, Kate?" asked Lucy. "They teach Greek at the finishing school."

Kate laughed lightly, wanting to choke her. "Why, Lucy Saffin, you sound like an erudite! For me, I prefer living life in full measure rather than living with my nose in a book. Besides that, I *do* know French. *Je suis actuellement une vraie experte à la langue,*" she finished, knowing she'd mangled her assertion of expertise horribly, hoping Lucy wouldn't know any better.

"I know Greek," said Edward. "And Latin."

"Oh, bless you," said Lucy, glancing briefly at Edward. "Breck, what about you? I'm sure a smart, young gentleman like yourself should know a few languages."

Beside her, Kate heard Breck sigh. "I admire those who have an aptitude for languages, especially those who seek to learn the classical languages. For myself, while I know French and Latin, I'm afraid our tutor scarcely knows Greek. But I'm sure when I go to university—"

"Why, Breck Jensey," Lucy exclaimed, "I could teach you Greek! What better way than to learn from a friend?"

"Thank you, Miss Saffin, I'll be sure to remember your kind offer."

Lucy giggled. "Please, call me Lucy. There is no need for such formalities among friends, is there? I mean, we're next-door neighbors and have been our whole lives. Oh, I suppose I *will* miss the plantation when I leave home for school. You will write me, won't you, Breck? Otherwise, I might get awful lonesome."

"Of course, Lucy."

"I'd be happy to write as well," offered Edward.

"Why, thank you, Mr. Scarborough. How very thoughtful."

Wanting to steer the conversation away from Lucy, Kate said, "There's a witch on Grandma Emma's plantation. She can tell your fortune for five dollars."

Edward frowned, his eyebrows drawing together. "A witch?"

"Has she told you your fortune, Kate?" asked Lucy. "It had better be some fortune for that kind of money."

Kate had been about to launch into a wild description of her visit to the witch, but seeing the look on Edward's face, thought better of it. "Don't be silly. Who believes in such hoodoo nonsense anyway?"

"My uncle says that conjurers and witches are the devil's instruments," said Edward.

Remembering the horrid little witch, Kate rather agreed with him. After all, the witch had told her she wouldn't be marrying Edward or anyone. Likely, that was just the sort of deception the devil would wish her to believe. Nothing but lies. "She certainly looks like the devil's instrument."

"Why, Kate Jensey," said Lucy, gasping, "you sound as if you've seen the witch! Have you?"

"Why, uh, no, I just know what she looks like from what others have told me." Kate glanced quickly at Breck, aghast when she realized that he knew she was lying. The corner of his mouth curled up, as if he were amused. *Well, you just stay amused, dear brother. So long as you keep your trap shut.*

Lucy tossed her curls. "Well, I think anyone stupid enough to go see a witch deserves whatever fortune they get. Don't you agree, Breck?"

"What if it's a fabulous fortune?" asked Kate. "Lots of money, fame, and true love? Would they still deserve it?"

"How does money, fame, and true love compare to being cast into the lake of fire and brimstone?" asked Edward.

Kate blinked. Truly, Edward had a certain single-mindedness about religion. "Well, I don't suppose it compares very well—"

"Jesus himself was poor. It is no shame to be poor."

No one said anything for a while. Kate fiddled with her horse's mane, thinking that the conversation hadn't gone well at all. Certainly not like she'd imagined the hundreds of times late at night while hugging her pillow. Now she'd made Edward upset at her. Now he would think she was sinful, consulting devil's instruments. Lusting after fortune and fame. *But Edward, dear Edward, if you only knew that I went there—endured that horrid little witch—for you, for us.*

Just then, Lucy cried, "Oh dear! I believe I've hurt myself! A branch has poked my eye."

"Why, Miss Saffin!" declared Edward. "Are you all right?"

"I've just said that a branch has injured my eye. I don't know of too many people who think that's all right." Lucy bent over in her saddle and pressed her gloved hand over her eye. "Breck, would you be a darling and take a look at it?"

Breck leaned over in his saddle while Lucy removed her hand. She gazed at Breck, tears shimmering, while he peered at her eye, lifting her eyelid with a finger. Finally, he sat back. "It doesn't appear to be cut, which is good."

"I need to return to Fox Creek to rest my eye. Else, who can say but I might be blind by morning?" Her lip quivered. "I'll need someone to escort me, Breck."

"Of course," replied Breck.

"I'd be happy to escort you," Edward offered.

"Oh, that won't be necessary. No sense everyone ruining their day. You and Kate have a marvelous time together now." Then she and Breck turned their horses around, and, like that, they left, coaxing their horses into a canter.

Kate was stunned, half admiring. Why, that little minx! She planned the whole thing! Lucy no more had a branch in her eye than an elephant! Suddenly she wanted to hug Lucy. Now Edward was hers!

"Do you think she'll be all right?" Edward asked, gazing after Breck and Lucy.

"I think Lucy's perfectly fine."

"Perhaps I should go after them."

"Why, Edward, there's nothing you can possibly do to help. Besides," added Kate, glancing at him sidelong, "Lucy said for us to have a marvelous time together, and we can't disappoint her now, can we?"

"I—I suppose not."

"Come," said Kate, prodding Mamie forward, "let's enjoy what's left of the morning. As Lucy said, maybe we'll even see the hounds corner the fox."

Around the next few bends, Kate wondered what she should talk about. Now that she had Edward alone, all to herself, finally, what was there to say? Should she declare her love? Talk about religion? "The weather has certainly turned chilly, don't you think, Edward?" Kate dropped the reins and rubbed her arms vigorously, hoping he'd take the hint and wrap her in his coat. She sighed when he merely nodded and kept riding. She tried again. "My father says he thinks it's going to be a short winter. That means, he'll be able to clear more fields for sugar. By next fall the sugarhouse will be finished. Won't that be fun? I'll invite you to my parties. We can make candy together."

"Thank you, but I don't like candy."

"Oh." Kate sniffed and wiped her nose on the back of her glove. "Well, I don't suppose you have to *eat* the candy. After all, half the fun is making it. I hear some taffy pulls can last all night. You have to rest your arms for weeks. Then, of course, there's the dancing."

Edward gave her a stern look. "My uncle says that dancing is of the devil. It provokes unhealthy urges in the unmarried."

Kate blinked. Unhealthy urges in the unmarried? She flushed and turned away from Edward's disapproval, wondering if he'd guessed the kinds of unhealthy urges she'd had at night. Oh, what a sinner he would think she was! If only he knew it was true love! Can true love be a sin? Kate swallowed hard. Perhaps it was time to tell him. To confess her love. Her true love. "Edward, I—"

"Miss Jensey, I've been meaning to ask you something."

Kate's heart leapt. Could it be that he was going to propose courtship? She gazed at him, searching his eyes for a glimmer of love. She leaned toward him, hoping she wouldn't slip from her saddle when he embraced her, or kissed her even.

"Perhaps it isn't appropriate to ask you such a thing, but—"

"Oh, Edward!"

He looked at her oddly, cleared his throat, and then said, "Do you—do you think that Miss Saffin—I mean, Lucy—has a fondness for me?"

Kate sat back, saying nothing, gazing upward through the trees at the sky, at the clouds that seemed to have come from nowhere, darkening overhead. She smelled rain in the chilling breeze that suddenly gusted through the forest road, sweeping the tree branches to and fro. Her crimson ribbons flapped behind her, one whipping around to slap her cheek. She looked back at Edward. At the stiff, starched folds of his neckerchief. At the way he sat on his horse, as if he were sitting on corncobs. At his blue eyes, which but moments ago held the depths of the universe, but which now seemed small and dull, rather like fish eyes.

Kate cleared her throat and spoke with a calmness that surprised her. "Lucy Saffin told me that you're a cold-hearted bore, and that she hated you. She said she wishes to never see you again and hopes you gallop off a cliff with your god and your devil both." Satisfied with Edward's wounded look of dismay, Kate slapped Mamie with her reins, dug in her heels, and left Edward behind in a swirl of winter's dust.

She had a fox to hunt.

## *Chapter 14*

Ham. Venison. Catfish. Cornmeal and pecan stuffing. Gravy. Potatoes. Peaches preserved in syrup. Hotbreads. Dewberry jam. Cake. Sweet potato pies with fresh cream. On the sideboard, brandy for the gentlemen. Sherry or mint juleps for the ladies. Then there was dripped absinthe *frappé,* a drink common among the Creoles and quite the rage in New Orleans.

Preparations for dinner had started early in the morning, following the hurried breakfast, after the hunters had left to gather their hounds and their horses and to rustle up a fox to chase. Monette brushed the hair from her face, damp with perspiration. It had been and would continue to be a long day.

As soon as the hunting party was gone, the housekeeper, Lizzy, wagged her finger at the troop of servants. Nat, hurry them dirty dishes out to the kitchen and scrub them clean. Monette, clean the crumbs off that old crumb cloth and get it ready for the next go-round. Then set out the fine china. Mm-hmm, yes. That's right. Polish the silver, Henry. Fatima, dust and polish every square inch of the dining room and that rear loggia. What you say? Again? 'Course, I mean again, girl. You know how Miss Mary Grey Saffin swipes her gloved fingers in places where ain't nobody got a right to swipe. Wouldn't want to embarrass Miss Sarah with no dirty dirt.

It was just after two in the afternoon when the hunters returned, the fox cornered, the hounds fed and retired, the horses returned to the stables. Coats were hung, scarves unwound, hats pulled off, amid exclamations of:

"Did you see the way it backtracked through Fox Creek?"

"Clever devils, those foxes."

"Took the hounds near twenty minutes to figure that one out."

"Patience is a virtue when fox hunting."

"Oh, but the end! How thrilling!"

"I swear my hands are frozen solid. Kindly let me near the fire before my fingers fall off."

"Oh, if the food doesn't just smell delightful! If I don't eat right this minute, I swear I'll have to go and eat my horse!"

"Let's hope it doesn't come to that, dear. Fox hunting would hold a different appeal if we all had to walk."

"Run, you mean. Neither the fox nor the hounds would care to wait."

"Judge Rockwell wouldn't last more than two steps."

"Well, he'd just make it illegal, if it came to that. More than one way to skin a fox, you know."

After the ladies returned from adjusting their hairpins, with coils and caps neatly in place, cheeks flushed, Mammy Hester beaming from behind them like a proud mother hen, all were seated around the dining table. Reverend Scarborough offered a blessing, and the meal began.

Monette smoothed her pinafore, ignoring the growl in her stomach, pretending she did not see Breck sitting at the table next to Lucy Saffin. Pretending her face did not flush remembering the sounds that had issued from his room the night before last.

The servants all knew their duties. Uncle Henry mixed and poured the drinks. Nat and Fatima fetched the steaming pots from the kitchen and set them in the butler's pantry, where Monette quickly transferred the foods to silver platters, or fine porcelain, or chafing dishes. Then Monette and Mammy Hester and Uncle Henry served the food to the guests, while Lizzy kept a supervisory eye over the proceedings, filling in where necessary.

Whenever they had company, work was doubled, tripled even. Today Monette was hungry and tired. Yesterday, just as the company arrived, she'd begun bleeding. Down there. For the first time. Mammy Hester had helped her with a cloth, ragged and holey. The cloth bothered her. Worming up into places it didn't belong. Now she knew why Kate hated it so much. Constantly now, Monette glanced at the back of her calico skirt, wondering if she was soaking through.

"Stop all that peeking," whispered Mammy Hester, pulling her into a corner of the dining room. "You's gonna twist yourself into a knot. Don't you worry none now. I's gonna keep an eye out for you. You starts to leak, I'll holler."

"Oh, thank you, Mammy Hester. But don't holler too loudly." She caught a glimmer of laughter in Mammy Hester's eyes and resisted the urge to giggle herself. It wouldn't do for the servants to be giggling in the corner.

Finished serving the breaded catfish, Monette entered the butler's pantry, the swinging door closing behind her. What she saw caused her heart to tumble. Fatima stood, bending over the counter, smiling at her. A glob of spit dangled from her bottom lip, over the gravy pot.

Not again. "Don't do it," begged Monette. "Please."

"Try and stop me." The spit waggled.

"I'll tell."

"No, you won't, 'cause I'll kill you if you do. I'll stab you with this here knife." As Fatima said "knife," the spit plopped into the gravy, trailing a string of saliva. Fatima stared, then wiped her mouth, stirred the pot with the knife, and handed the pot to Monette. "Serve it up to them white folks. They won't know the difference."

The pot was hot. Gasping, her hands suddenly afire, Monette set it back on the counter. She took a deep breath, angry at herself when tears stung her eyes. "Maybe I won't tell Miss Sarah, but I will tell your mother."

"My oh my. Is you crying? Oh, poor baby Monette, the yellow nigger what thinks she better than everybody else, she be crying. Come here, baby honey, and let me—"

Just then, arms laden with a tray of dirty dishes, Lizzy bustled into the pantry. Under her white turban, her face shone with perspiration. Stains darkened the underarms of her indigo blouse. "Where's the gravy? All them folks be needing gravy for their taters and stuffing. Can't have taters and stuffing if you don't got no gravy."

"But Fatima," began Monette, pointing at Fatima.

"Why, there it is. For heaven's sake, Monette, what you doing standing over the gravy pot for, letting it get cold as January?"

"But I saw Fatima—" The words caught in Monette's throat, for Lizzy's face suddenly hardened and her eyes narrowed.

"I don't want no complaint or I'll have your hide, Miss Monette Too-Good. And I don't care what you seen."

There was a burst of laughter from the dining room. A man's voice. Another burst of laughter.

"But Fatima spit—"

Lizzy shoved Monette roughly aside and poured the gravy from the pot into the gravy boat. "They expects it to be hot, and that's what they's gonna get." She bustled out of the butler's pantry as quickly as she'd swept in, carrying the gravy boat, the door swinging shut behind her.

Fatima doubled over with laughter. "Your face. Oh lordy, you should see your face! You looks like you just swallowed a turd."

Monette busied herself with slicing more ham. Darkness pulsed behind her eyes. Her chest constricted and she found it hard to breathe. Fatima continued to laugh. I hate you, Monette thought.

Meanwhile, Nat dropped off a pan of hot biscuits and left again. Mammy Hester bustled in and told Fatima to stop that laughing and for heaven's sake, what was she standing around for, acting like a plumb fool? To hurry and fetch more food from the kitchen as the white folks was waiting. Fatima strolled over to the platter of ham and, while Monette watched, powerless, teeth clenched, Fatima shoved a hunk of ham into her mouth and grinned before sauntering across the room and out to the back loggia.

Mammy Hester sighed. "I swear, that girl do make me want to do some wickedness."

Monette transferred the biscuits to a cloth-lined basket and handed it to Mammy Hester. "I wish she didn't exist."

"Why, honey chile, we all does. But I learned long ago that wishing don't change nothing. Wishing ain't nothing but a waste of time. Best thing you can do is go 'bout your business and don't pay her no never mind." Mammy leaned over and pecked Monette's cheek. "Don't you let that girl upset your sweet self for another second. She ain't worth it. Now fetch that plate of ham and let's go. Them folks in there done worked theirselves up an appetite."

Monette did as she was told, following Mammy Hester into the dining room. She looked blankly at her hands as she held the platter, going from person to person. "Sir, would you like some ham?" "Ham, Mars William?" She looked at the fine swirls of gilt on the edges of the plates, at the silver serving fork, the lace tablecloth, at the flash of an emerald on a lady's hand—anywhere except at them, at Miss Sarah, Kate, and Breck, as they sat and chatted with friends and neighbors, all the while eating a part of Fatima.

Monette stared into the darkness, her ear vibrating with Mammy's snore. She was tempted to poke her as she sometimes did, hoping the old woman would mumble and roll over so Monette could fall into a quick sleep. But on this night, Monette knew that even if she poked Mammy Hester, she would still be unable to sleep. Not only was it the cramps, crouched in her belly and bowels, but it was the tightness of her jaw. The clench of her fists. The remembering of Fatima, despite her efforts to forget her.

Ever since that afternoon, after the dinner party, she'd felt sick. Nauseated. Her bowels had certainly loosened, and Monette had made frequent trips to the privy, sometimes barely making it in time. At this evening's toilette, just as Kate was tearfully describing that horrible Edward and what a terrible, frightful bore he was and how could she have possibly thought she was in love with him, Monette had rushed from the room with a gasp, leaving behind such a nasty odor that, when she returned, she found Kate fanning herself on the gallery, the windows flung open to the January air. "Mercy sakes," Kate declared. "That was worse than Papa's!"

Even though it really was funny, Monette had not laughed, any more than she could laugh now. Knowing that Fatima would be waiting for her tomorrow. The next day. And the next.

A lifetime of Fatima.

Monette sat up. Her bowels heaved and sloshed.

*Sacredié!* Here I go again.

She flung back the covers, hurriedly put on her shoes, and flew out the door, throwing her shawl over her shoulders at the same time. She clattered down the stairs, the pressure from her bowels increasing. Not here! *Mon Dieu!* Then she was outside, running. A large bird took flight from off the laundry house roof. Powerful wings pulsed through the sharp air, momentarily blotting out the three-quarter moon that hung bright over the distant treetops.

Inside the darkness of the privy, Monette fumbled with her nightgown, her drawers, her belt, and cotton padding, before finally sitting down and releasing her bowels. Relief and weariness overwhelmed her. She rested her face in her hands, deciding to crawl into bed with Kate instead of returning to the attic room and Mammy Hester's never-ending snore. Miss Sarah would never know. She never did. Besides, thought Monette, I have a secret to tell Kate. I'm a woman now. She'll definitely want to know that.

It was a comforting thought, and so by the time Monette finally stepped out of the privy and headed toward the big house, she felt a relief that was more than physical. She was wondering just how she would tell Kate, when she saw a movement out of the corner of her eye, wondering if it was the bird come back.

It took Monette a second to realize what she was seeing.

There, in the vicinity of the pond, someone darted from tree trunk to tree trunk. Monette's breath caught. There was something familiar about the way the person moved. Furtive as a thief. Casting a glance toward the big house every now and then as they hurried over the tree-studded lawn.

It was Fatima. A basket over her arm. Headed in the opposite direction of where she dwelled in a cabin in the yard. What was Fatima doing? Monette wondered. Where was she going in the dead of night with a basket full of—full of what? Miss Sarah's silver? One of the gold and crystal *girandoles* that were Miss Sarah's favorite? Monette realized her heart was hammering, that a part of her screamed for her to return to the big house. To slip into bed with Kate. To forget Fatima. Instead, Monette began to follow, knowing only that whatever the reason Fatima was sneaking around, and whatever was in the basket, it was a secret.

And Monette intended to find out what it was.

She kept Fatima in sight as the girl neared the creek. Reaching the road that led to St. Marysville, Fatima turned south, paralleling the creek. Monette followed her a long time, so long she began to doubt the wisdom of her actions, wondering whether she could outrun Fatima, should it become necessary. Finally, Fatima left the road, disappearing under the shadows of pine and poplar.

Quickening her pace, Monette reached the place at the edge of the forest where Fatima had disappeared. Monette paused, then entered. Soon the trees enclosed her. The forest smelled of dampness, the moon peeping between the branches high overhead. A leaf trailed its dew across her face. She heard her breath, shaky and rapid. The crack of a stick underfoot. Her eyes adjusted quickly, and she saw a movement straight ahead. Fatima. She was easy to follow, for not only could Monette see her clearly in the darkness, but the girl was also clumsy and loud. Fatima followed a rough trail, as though she'd been this way not just once, but many times.

On occasion, Fatima stopped and looked behind her. Whenever she did, Monette would stop too, becoming as still as one of Miss Sarah's garden statues. Fear splashed through her veins, and she almost bolted back to the big house when once Fatima peered straight at her. But after staring a while, squinting, Fatima continued through the forest. She can't see me, Monette realized. Her vision's bad.

Finally, Monette saw a light. Like tentacles, the light seeped between the hanging moss and brushed the surface of the black swamp, casting the cypress knees into deep shadow.

She had to hurry to keep up when Fatima began to run toward the light. As Monette entered a small clearing, she suddenly understood. What Fatima was doing. Where she was going in the dead of night and why.

It was a runaway camp.

There were a dozen men or so. Monette recognized some of them as men from Fox Creek, from the fields. She didn't know their names, but knew they'd been missing since Christmas, knew there was a five-dollar reward for information leading to their capture. "What you bring us this time?" one of them asked, as he held up a lantern and rooted through the basket. There were two bottles of champagne, venison, a leg of ham, biscuits, breaded catfish, cake, candles.

"Whooee!" one of them whooped, sinking his teeth into a biscuit while popping the cork off a bottle. "Don't get no better than this!"

"Damn, girl! You done good!"

Rough bark beneath her fingertips, Monette hid behind a tree, observing while they feasted, licking their lips and fingers, passing the bottle, talking with their mouths full, while they told joke after joke, growing increasingly louder. They ripped the meat from the ham bone, chewing. Grease glistened on their faces.

Monette had never actually heard a field hand speak freely. Now, listening, her face heated. Some words she'd never heard before, but from the resulting cackles and backslapping, she knew they were terrible, sin-filled words. Only one of the men kept apart, rarely speaking, never smiling, an iron collar around his neck that tinkled with bells whenever he moved. It didn't matter. They were all horrible. All of them. Worse than Fatima. Coarse, disgusting, disrespectful, with manners like beasts. Miss Sarah would be mortified, especially if she heard what they said about her. What they said about Mars William, Kate, and Breck.

Monette knew what she had to do. Immediately.

But as she turned to leave, Fatima and one of the men crept to the edge of the clearing and locked in an embrace, kissing, their tongues not only touching but intertwining, licking, smacking. Monette stared. There was a pull of clothing, grunts, moans, unbuttoning, and before she scarcely realized what was happening, they were doing it. *It.* The humpity-bumpity. Right in front of her. The man's hips moved fast. Faster. Fatima threw her head back and groaned, her fists filled with the flesh of the man's backside.

Monette's heart roared in her ears. *Mon Dieu!* Nauseated, her bowels racing once again, despising the pleasure on Fatima's face, Monette turned and slipped back through the woods.

By the time she knocked on Breck's door, gasping for breath, shoes covered in mud, she was hot as July.

"Who is it?"

"It's me," she whispered loudly.

The door cracked open. She saw the outline of his tousled hair. The shine of his eyes. "Monette, what is it? What's the matter?"

She slipped inside, closing the door behind her. "I have found them."

# *Chapter 15*

D ESPITE SARAH'S AVERSION TO the girl, she nonetheless felt the stirrings of pity. She couldn't help it. Fatima lay on her stomach on the hospital bed, whip marks scoring her back in a crisscross of swollen, blood-crusted streaks. Sarah wrung out a rag and continued to wash the girl's back. "Hush now, hush. You'll only make it worse with your carrying on."

Yes, Sarah knew it hurt. But much as it hurt, and much as she pitied the poor girl, Sarah knew that Fatima had been asking for it. Aiming for a whipping as if she'd been an arrow aimed at a bull's eye. It was only a matter of time before such rebelliousness of character would cross paths with the workings of the plantation, with William. There were rules to follow. Consequences. The Bible was filled with rules and consequences. It was, Sarah knew, part and parcel of a well-ordered, God-fearing society, even if one didn't much like it. Sarah rarely allowed herself to think of it, though, for the knowledge of life's harsh commandments, of life's seeming inequities, caused her pain. She'd learned long ago to stop questioning and leave it in God's hands.

"Hush, child," she whispered, rubbing a liniment made from lard and mullein leaves over Fatima's wounds.

Later, finally finished, having given Fatima a sip of laudanum, just a sip, Sarah exited the hospital. She saw Lizzy sitting on the gallery, wringing her apron, her eyes reddened and swollen with crying. Sarah stepped off the gallery, sighing when Lizzy threw herself on the ground in front of Sarah, blocking her way.

"Oh, Miss Sarah. Pray, Miss Sarah. Have mercy."

"Lizzy, get off the ground."

Instead of rising, Lizzy flung her arms around Sarah's ankles, weeping onto the work dress Sarah had finished sewing only last week. "Pray, Miss Sarah. I done heard you's gonna sell my baby. Oh, pray, Miss Sarah. They'll put her to work in the fields, and you know the fields is terrible hard. Please, please. My baby needs me."

Sarah looked at the turbaned figure bent before her. The woman's body, as she shuddered with sobs. Again, pity flooded her. Why, dear God? Why must it be so hard? Why must it be this way? Especially with such a strong, competent housekeeper, one who, in every other way, had never disappointed her? "Lizzy, your daughter is with child."

Lizzy looked up, her face wet with tears and stunned with shock.

"She says that one of the field hands from the Saffin plantation is the father. Saffin has generously agreed to purchase Fatima, so as soon as your daughter's well enough, she'll be married. Fatima's going to be a wife and mother, Lizzy. She's chosen her lot, and there's nothing I can do about it."

Lizzy clutched handfuls of Sarah's dress. She blinked tears from her eyes and sniffed. "Miss Sarah, you knows womens what works on one plantation sometimes has husbands what works on another. They gets together every week or thereabouts. I knowed two womens what does that. Why, Mammy Hester does that. They's happy as—happy as pie. Please, Miss Sarah."

Sarah hated this. Despised the position this put her in. Despised the look of hope on Lizzy's face, for Sarah knew what she had to do. Closing her eyes for a second, she prayed for strength. Then, trying to keep her voice steady, her breathing calm, she said, "Lizzy, you're a good housekeeper. You know how much I depend on you. But you also know that your daughter's a lazy, dishonest worker. I've told the Saffins as much, and they're willing—"

"She'll change, Miss Sarah. God's honest truth! She'll change. I swears it!"

"Fatima broke the rules, Lizzy. I can't be letting her back in the big house when I can't trust her to not steal the food, and when I know she's sneaking around behind my back and doing—well, doing goodness knows what. She's had her chance, and I don't want her back."

Lizzy wailed and clutched tighter. She was a big woman, and Sarah struggled to keep her balance. "I'll watch her night and day, Miss Sarah.

You knows I keep my promises. I'll never sleep for watching her. I'll make her work like what you wants her to. Please, Miss Sarah!"

"It's too late for that. Fatima aided and abetted runaways. That's against the law, Lizzy." Hardness crept into Sarah's voice. "Of all the workers I've ever had, over all the years of my life, Fatima is the one who deserves to be sold. Maybe at the Saffins', she'll learn to work."

"She'll be good now, I promises. Don't send her there. You's the kindest, most peaceable mistress in these here parts. Everyone knows that. I'll do anything you wants. Pray, Miss Sarah. Pray forgive her!"

Realizing this conversation was going nowhere, Sarah began to extricate herself from Lizzy's grip. It wasn't easy, and Sarah found herself prying Lizzy's fingers from off her dress, her ears ringing with Lizzy's screams, until Sarah thought she might start screaming herself. Instead, she clenched her jaw and wrenched herself away from the woman. As she did, she felt a tug at her waist, heard a rip of threads, knowing now her dress would need repair. Surprise, anger, and humiliation coursed through her. "This conversation is ended, Lizzy. You will not bring it up again, or I swear to God, I will have you punished!" She turned from Lizzy's gap-toothed face and headed to the big house, shaking, angry at herself for her outburst, yet relieved she would no longer have to bear that deceitful girl, Fatima.

William sat at his desk in his shuttered office, face pressed into his hands, willing the pain to go away. Just this morning, even as Breck shook him awake in the darkness, telling him about the runaway camp, William's tooth had begun to throb. A maddening, piercing throb that only grew worse as all the men—Saffin, Judge Rockwell, Marshall, Taggart, Scarborough, Breck, and John—rustled up rifles, horses, and hounds, and headed out into the forest. It was an easy thing to bust up the camp, what with the extra men and the added hounds. Normally, he would have jumped for joy at the capture of the last of his runaways, especially Sawney, but the pain in his mouth was too great.

Upon returning to Fox Creek and with the rise of the sun, the company had ordered their belongings packed, the horses harnessed to the carriages, and off they'd gone with wives and children, waving goodbye, each with a runaway or two in tow. A profitable fox hunt, all in all.

If it weren't for this damned tooth.

William rubbed his fingers over his day-old beard, hearing the scrape of whiskers, wincing, knowing he needed the tooth pulled. He'd examined himself in the mirror, seen the swollen gums, the blackened enamel. But lordy, having a tooth pulled was a painful ordeal.

Someone knocked at the door.

A timid knock.

William rose, strode to the door, and flung it open. It was the little mulatto, Monette. The girl shrank back, looking as if she wanted to flee. William would have smiled, but knew it would hurt too much. Instead, he motioned for her to enter before returning to his desk.

Rarely had William paid the mulatto servant much mind, any more than he'd paid much mind to Mammy Hester or Lizzy. After all, he was more than happy to leave the workings of the big house to Sarah. It was a load off his mind, and he wasn't displeased with the way she handled things, despite what his mother thought. Overall, the household seemed to run smoothly with little upset.

"Monette, is it?" asked William, trying to ignore the pain that shot through his jaw.

"Yes, sir." Her voice was so quiet that, had it not already been deathly still in his office, he never could have heard her. Color crept into the girl's cheeks, and William saw the signs of emerging womanhood despite the girlish, pigtailed hair.

"Miss Sarah speaks very highly of you. You're a valued, trusted servant."

The girl made no reply, staring at the floor in front of his desk.

William cleared his throat. Winced. Damn tooth! "Monette, I want to personally thank you for what you did last night. You did the proper thing by showing us the whereabouts of those runaways. I always reward servants who do what's proper." William waited for some reply, but, receiving none, opened a drawer and pulled out a five-dollar gold piece. "This is yours. Next time you're in town, you can spend it as you wish."

This time the girl looked up. William noticed the delicateness of her hand as she held it out. He dropped the coin into her palm.

"Thank you, Mars William," she whispered, and before he hardly realized what was happening, she was gone, the door closing behind her. William grunted, shook his head, and pulled out his journal. Long ago, he'd made it a habit to jot down the goings-on of the plantation, from crops planted, rows hoed, to births, deaths, punishments received, visits made, family outings, and even his love for Sarah when he was feeling especially wistful. He dipped his pen in the ink well and wrote:

*Jan. 23, 1851 – Thin clouds-   East wind verry disagreeable-   Found runaways living the high life in the woods- Quite a camp-   All my stuff- Wondered where my cigars went-   Took runaways back to quarters & commenced giving each a hundred stripes in front of everyone-   Let the dogs overhaul Sawney a bit- Hope it takes the snuff out of him- Most disobedient defiant hand I've ever had the misfortune to own-   I'd sell him if any one was fool enough to buy him-   D— rascal-   Takes pleasure in thwarrting me-   Pressed yesterday- men & boys trashing cotten-   getting ready to start plowing tomorrow if rain holds off-   Set women spinning-   Sold Fatima to Saffin for two hundred dollars-   Need to find a husband for Monette- She's near breeding age if not already-       Paid her five dollars for finding runaways-   Have toothache*

Monette awakened with a gasp in the pale morning light, sitting upright in bed, dreams swirling like torrents of rain.

The horse. The river. Sinking with despair into the mud.

Silently screaming, screaming.

Her nakedness in the clearing. The man, deep-voiced, muscled. The huge man who covered her with his shirt, who gathered her into his arms, who smelled of soil, his face elusive as a ghost's.

She fell back onto the bed, thankful she was alone, that Mammy Hester was away visiting her husband and family at Woodleigh. She listened to the rhythm of her heart as it slowed, wishing she could slow her heart to nothing. Place her hands atop the hollow of her chest like a saint praying, and simply say, *Stop. No more.* Maybe then the ache inside her would release its grip, freeing her from the pain of forever longing, of never knowing.

"Monette!"

Kate's voice bellowed up the staircase. Monette wiped her tears on the back of her sleeve. *Mon Dieu!* It is Sunday morning, and I am to dress Kate for church, and then there are inspections! She whipped back the covers, the floor cold beneath her feet, banishing her previous thoughts of death as being no more than the maudlin drip of a sentimental fool.

She was rummaging for her Sunday dress when Kate banged on the door. "Get up, you lazybones!"

"Coming, Kate. I overslept!"

"Hurry. I'm frightfully hungry and I can't get my hair to work right. Looks like I ran it through the cotton gin."

"I'll be down as soon as I get dressed."

"Geez. And you call *me* lazybones!"

Later, after Monette had finished with Kate's toilette, after breakfast had been served and eaten, Monette hurried to the yard for the weekly inspections. She slipped into line alongside the other household servants, head lowered, wishing it was over, missing Mammy Hester's presence beside her.

She was relieved to discover Mars William was allowing Breck to perform inspections today. While Breck often found something out of place or dirty with the other servants, she knew he'd never say anything against her, even if she went to inspections with a mud pie on her face and under both arms. As it was, she hadn't re-braided her hair from yesterday, nor had she scrubbed her face and ears like she was supposed to have done.

Family by family, or household by household if they had no family, Breck began roll call, beginning with the household servants, each stepping forward in turn. When it was Monette's turn, she could feel his gaze on her. She wanted to look up into his face, but knew better. Instead, she stood motionless, her expression as blank as she could make it, watching as the wind caught her skirt and flattened it against her legs.

After, she threaded her way back through the lines to her usual place. But with each step, she became increasingly aware. Something was wrong. Terribly wrong. They were watching her. *All of them.* Out of the corners of their eyes. And the feeling in the air—blowing in the wind, cutting between her legs with the flapping of her skirt—it was anger. *Rage.* Monette spotted one of the men she'd seen at the runaway camp, the one with the iron collar. His face was stony, chiseled with hatred. *Mon Dieu!* He'd like to kill me, I think!

She found her place, her heart skittering, thinking, but I did nothing wrong! I followed the rules, only!

While the hands from the pine and cypress quarters underwent inspection, she recalled little incidents in the household that had occurred over the past few days, ever since they'd caught the runaways. Mammy

Hester not speaking to her much, instead clucking her tongue and shaking her head and saying Lord a'mercy over and over. Uncle Henry suddenly deaf whenever Monette asked a question. The laundress glaring at her, snatching the dirty clothing from Monette's hands. The cook not telling Monette that the pot was hot and so letting her scorch her fingers. Lizzy ordering her to scrub out every last fireplace in the house, not once, but three times over, a job Lizzy knew she hated. Nat running away when Monette told him to help her. Suddenly, it was all too clear.

*They know.*

How they knew, she couldn't guess, for after pointing out the runaway camp that night, while yet shrouded in the denseness of darkness and forest, Mars William had ordered Breck to take her back to the big house. She'd sat behind Breck on his horse, her arms wrapped around his waist, bursting with joy that Fatima was finally caught, relieved that the unspoken tension that had existed between her and Breck for the last week was, at last, over. She'd nestled against Breck's back, holding him close, wondering at the feel of him, his hardness, so different from Kate. As Breck had set her down, pulling on the reins to head back into the woods, she'd beamed with happiness when he'd smiled at her, saying, "I knew I could trust you, Monette."

When, finally, inspections ended, Monette fled the yard and ran up to the attic room, where she closed the door. She flung herself atop her bed, tears bursting from her with the violence of a spring freshet. It's not fair! They don't understand! Fatima spit in the gravy! She is a wicked, wicked girl. A liar, a thief, and a fornicator who will burn in the Lake of Fire and Brimstone! Don't they know we're all better off without her?

After allowing herself a good cry, Monette rose from the bed and peered in the mirror above the dresser. A crack zigzagged diagonally across the mirror like a lightning bolt, slicing her reflection in half. In between the patches of fogged silver, she saw the reddened whites of her eyes, the puffy skin beneath like half-risen dough, her skin blotchy and unlovely.

Sighing, sniffing, she unbraided her hair and brushed it with the hairbrush Kate had given her for Christmas. After the requisite one hundred strokes, she plaited her hair, half smiling at herself for being so dramatic earlier. Really, what did it matter what they thought of her anyway? When did she ever care what a field hand thought of her? As for the rest of them, she knew she could make it up to them. Maybe not Lizzy, but Lizzy had been concealing Fatima's lazy deceitfulness for a long time, and it had finally caught up with her. It was nothing more than what Lizzy deserved—what they both deserved.

By the time Kate rapped on her door, telling her it was time to go to church, that everyone was waiting in the carriage, Monette was ready. Her face and ears were scrubbed clean, she smelled of soap, and her bonnet was tied snugly. She opened the door and smiled at Kate, planting a soft kiss on Kate's cheek. "Let's go, shall we? We're going to have a *splendid* day, *mon amie!*" She linked her arm in Kate's and down the stairs they went, Kate laughing, saying, yes indeed, they'd have a splendid day, even if they did have to suffer momentarily by going to church. Even if she did have to set eyes on that horrible, boring Edward Scarborough, a man, no, a boy, who no one could prevent from going to church no matter what, save perhaps a Holy Miracle from above: thunder, lightning, floods, or maybe swarms of locusts if she was lucky.

# *Chapter 16*

DUE TO THE NIGHT'S pounding thunderstorm, the early May afternoon was hot and muggy. Sarah's ornamental gardens appeared none the worse for wear, bursting in a profusion of buds, blossoms, and greenery, interlaced with the soft drapings of moss that caressed her shoulders or her cheek like a lover. She'd just been to the greenhouse and told Wash, the gardener, and Robert, the coachman, to set all the greenhouse plants outside, and to clean out the greenhouse from top to bottom. One of the shelves needed fixing, too. Plus, the windows were sprouting green gardens of their own.

Sarah snipped a rose off a bush and placed it in her basket, along with the others she had gathered. Tonight, there would be a fresh bouquet on the supper table.

Thank goodness for her ornamental garden. A living, growing sanctuary—cool, if anything could be called cool in such weather—inviting, and a balm for whatever ailed her. She paused to sit on one of the stone benches she'd purchased last year. After all, if one couldn't take the time to enjoy one's handiwork, then what was the fuss all about? Besides, she was tired. Her ankles and feet were swollen and beginning to throb. Plus, it was a day without her usual morning sickness, a miracle of blessedness, and she meant to take full advantage. She pulled off her garden gloves and set them in the basket atop her bouquet, the air thick and sweet with the fragrance of roses, Cape Jessamine, and honeysuckle.

"Dear Lord," she whispered.

Her head was tilted back, and she was listening to the hum of dragonflies, and the chorus of birds, when a voice said, "Mammy Hester told me to bring you this."

It was Kate. She held out a glass of water. Droplets condensed on the outside of the glass, trickling off to spot the blossom-strewn, brick pathway beneath.

"Why, thank you, Katherine dear." Sarah drank deeply, and then patted the bench beside her. "Come sit a while. Keep your mother company."

Kate sat, peering at her from beneath a broad-brimmed hat. "Mammy Hester says you have no business being out here in such weather, and in your condition, and that you should come inside and rest."

Sarah ignored her exhaustion, smiled, and patted her belly, at the same time pushing away that familiar, nagging fear, and telling herself that, like last time, everything would be fine.

Even though she was only in her fourth month, Sarah was quite large, and her feet were already giving her fits, what with the swelling. Resting always helped, and she was the first to admit that she adored Mammy's foot rubs—foot rubs that melted away both the swelling and her apprehension. "Yes, well, Mammy Hester always knows how to take care of me better than I know myself. But if I don't look after my garden, who will?"

Kate looked away. "I told her you wouldn't listen."

A cardinal landed on a nearby statuette, a brilliant red against the gray stone. "How is the mending coming along?"

A deep sigh escaped her daughter. "Fine."

"But?"

Kate fiddled with her dress, rolling the fabric between her fingers. "Even if I keep at it forever, I won't finish until Christmas."

"Mending is just one of those jobs, Katherine. We do what we can. I certainly could never keep up with it if I didn't have you to help me."

"I know, but—"

Sarah waited, knowing that it was far more than mending and a glass of water that had brought Kate out to find her in the garden.

"Papa and Breck are leaving tomorrow for New Orleans. I thought—I thought, maybe—"

Not again, thought Sarah. Does this child never give up? "Katherine, we've been through this before. I told you that I can't do without you, even for a few days, until after the baby's born. I simply must have your help."

"But that's not until October!"

"Besides, you know full well that your father and Breck aren't going to New Orleans for pleasure. They're meeting with their factor. They plan to buy the equipment for the sugarhouse, plus they need to purchase some extra help, hire an engineer to set everything up, and you—"

"I know, I know, Mama. But Lucy Saffin's invited me to visit her family there in New Orleans. They bought a second home in the city, you know, for social events, and—"

"Since when have you and Lucy been friends? You never played with her even when you were little. I thought you said she was a numskull."

Kate shrugged. "Since she invited me to the theater, I guess."

"But I thought she was attending the academy at—"

"She is, Mama, but sometimes she gets permission to attend theater with her family. It promotes the social graces and an appreciation for the arts. She said we could go to the theater together. Oh, Mama, you know I haven't had any fun around here for *ages*. Plus, the theater season will be over soon, and then it will be too late." Twisting her dress into knots, Kate looked wistfully at her as if attending the theater was the most important thing on God's green earth. The dear child. Always in such a hurry to grow up. "I'd be back by next week, and then I promise to help you every day until the baby's born, without a word of complaint."

A squirrel skittered up the shadowy tresses of a crepe myrtle tree and began to call loudly. Sarah sighed. "Your father wouldn't want to chaperone you. You know how he is when he has nothing but business on his mind."

"Breck would escort us if I asked him. I know he would. Please, Mama. *David Copperfield* is playing at the Varieties on Friday. I hear it's simply *divine*."

"Oh, really, Katherine, I don't know." Sarah drew a rose out of her basket and held it to her nose, breathing deeply. If only she could find answers to life's perplexities as easily as she found pleasure in her gardens. It was difficult having a daughter who wanted to grow up in an instant. It was hard to know when and where to stand firm. Sarah knew that if she applied no control over Kate's adolescent development, soon Kate would do nothing but visit, dance, party, and have no concerns other than her hair, her dresses, and boys. While such things were of importance in high society, ultimately aiming toward a marriage union, they were small comfort when faced with a plantation to run. The way Kate was headed, Sarah wouldn't be surprised if her daughter became a plantation mistress within two or three years. Just last week, Kate had received four gentlemen callers, three of them from neighboring plantations, one of them without a scrap of land or a negro servant to his name. (William, bless his heart, had wasted no time in showing the scamp the door!) More and more, they seemed to be lining up, hats in hand, distracting Kate from her duties.

Sarah handed the rose to Kate, but instead of smelling it, she just held it on her lap, waiting. "Katherine, while you're here, there's something I've been meaning to talk to you about."

Curiosity sparkled in her daughter's eyes, like sunlight off the bayou.

"By the time the baby's born, you'll be sixteen years old. At that time, I think it would be appropriate for you to attend Mme. Dupré's Finishing School for Young Ladies in New Orleans."

Kate's eyes widened. "Really, Mama?"

"I've been inquiring. Two of Judge Rockwell's daughters attend, and, of course, that's the school Lucy—"

Kate flung her arms around Sarah. "Yes, Mama! Thank you, Mama!"

Closing her eyes, Sarah basked in the feel of her daughter's arms around her, a feeling she was often denied. Kate smelled of soap. Of sandalwood. Then they were laughing, softly. Both their hats had slipped off their heads and down their backs with Kate's impetuous gesture, and now they snugged them back onto their heads. In doing so, Sarah made a sudden decision. "If your father says you can go to New Orleans with him, then I shall give my approval as well."

Kate shrieked and jumped to her feet. "Where's Papa?"

"Why, I expect he's in the fields this time of day. You could wait and ask him at supper tonight—" Sarah found herself talking to empty air, for Kate had gathered up her skirts and darted down the path toward the stables, her hat flopping against her back. "Katherine, dear, you're not dressed for riding! And put your hat on your head! Remember your skin and how it freckles!" Sarah realized Kate hadn't heard her, or, if she had, knew none of those things made any difference to her daughter. Not when she had her mind made up.

Sarah dabbed her forehead with her handkerchief.

Mercy, how *hot* it was. She had to put the roses in water before they wilted. Rising from the bench with a grunt, she limped toward the big house, trying to ignore the throb in her feet, thinking, yes, a foot rub sounds mighty fine right about now.

_ele_

She was waiting for him in his room, as he'd known she would be. Breck had slipped Monette a note at supper, which merely said, *Tonight.* The note had discreetly disappeared, and she'd continued serving small dishes filled with strawberries and cream as if nothing had happened.

As he lit a match, striking the sulfur head against the rough crisscross of the cast-iron match holder, the armoire door swung open, and there she was, smoothing her dress and her hair. She smiled at him, something that always made him catch his breath, as if there wasn't enough air between the two of them to breathe properly, as if she'd cast a spell over him. He looked back at what he was doing; the match was already half consumed, and he quickly touched it to the wick before it burned away entirely.

"What are we reading tonight?"

Breck glanced at the stack of books on his desk: *A Midsummer Night's Dream, Le Comte de Monte Cristo,* the *Iliad* . . . "Whatever you want."

She withdrew *The Scarlet Letter* from the stack, seated herself at the desk, and opened the book to where they'd left off. "Chapter Six. 'We have as yet hardly spoken of the infant; that little creature, whose innocent life had sprung, by the inscrutable decree of Providence, a lovely and immortal flower . . .'" Monette looked up. "Are you going to sit, or must I crane my neck?"

In answer, Breck pulled up another chair to the desk and settled himself to listen as Monette resumed the chapter, each word a caress. "'. . . a lovely and immortal flower, out of the rank luxuriance of a guilty passion. How strange it seemed to the sad woman, as she watched the growth, and the beauty that became every day more brilliant, and the intelligence that threw its quivering sunshine over the tiny features of this child!'"

*Yes,* thought Breck, looking away, *a guilty passion . . . every day becoming more brilliant . . .* He forced himself to stare at the wall, to listen to the story, to ignore the heat gathering in his body. Again he asked himself, when am I going to end this? For over a year now, they had been meeting secretly, reading, discussing things afterward—not necessarily the books, or the stories, just *things*. Breck knew he should end it, lock his door, tell her that it was wrong, but he could not.

He could not, because he was in love. The first time he'd admitted his feelings, a night no different from all the others, Monette was again reading while Breck listened and watched. As he watched, he knew. It was a clear, quiet thought, yet forceful enough to leave him nearly breathless.

*Monette, I love you, I love you.*

Pondering his love, he realized that he'd loved her from the start, from the very first day he'd seen her standing atop the auction block in the rotunda of the St. Charles, trembling with fear. Since that day, he'd tried to ignore his feeling of love, to purge it, diminish it, telling himself that it was not right, but the more he tried to stop it the more he realized that love had stolen him, kidnapped him, and he was, simply, captivated. Now, with each breath of every day, his thoughts were consumed with her, wondering where she was, what she was doing, when he would see her next, imagining the feel of her skin and the taste of her lips.

Much later, finished with the chapter, Monette yawned and pushed the book away. "I'm tired tonight."

Breck restrained himself from brushing a wisp of hair from her face. "It's the heat."

"I spent the whole afternoon ironing and packing Kate's things for her trip to New Orleans." Monette absently coiled her braid around her finger. "She has many pretty things. She'll be the most beautiful, well-dressed young lady at the theater, I think."

Breck sighed. How his sister had corralled him into escorting both her and Lucy to the theater, he didn't know. He was still reeling from the speed with which it had happened. Even his father was a little stunned by it all. One minute they were planning a business trip to New Orleans, the next minute they were worrying about what to wear to the theater and whether their shoes were blacked. "She'll either be the most beautiful," Breck replied, "or she'll die trying. I'm glad you'll be coming, too, Monette."

She shrugged. "Miss Sarah said I was to provide a calming influence on Kate. To keep her out of trouble."

"Good luck."

"You'll visit with Lucy Saffin?"

"Who, me?"

Monette giggled. "Of course, you."

"Unless I want to be thought an inconsiderate bore, then yes, I'll visit with Miss Saffin." Breck watched as the girl looked away. Did it bother her that he would visit with Lucy? "But even then," he whispered, "I'll be thinking of you." Before Breck realized what he was doing, he reached out and caressed her cheek with a fingertip.

She gazed back at him, her eyes pools of amber in the low lamplight. "Do you like Lucy?"

Breck withdrew his hand. "Lucy is a fine girl from a fine family. I've known her all my life."

"Kate says Lucy's a numskull."

"Why am I not surprised?"

"Well, is she?"

"Is she what?"

"A numskull."

"Why are you asking me this, Monette?"

She shrugged, saying nothing.

"If I had to choose between you and Lucy," said Breck, "I would choose you."

"If she's a numskull, then that's not necessarily flattering."

Breck frowned. "Monette, what's wrong?"

Instead of answering, Monette pushed her chair back and stood. "Good night, Breck." Out she went, closing the door behind her, leaving Breck clueless as to what he'd done wrong.

That she was upset, he knew.

But why?

Again, scarcely realizing what he was doing, Breck hurried out the door after her. A crescent moon hung suspended in the cloudless night sky. The air chirruped with crickets. "Monette!" he whispered loudly. She was a few steps ahead of him. When she did not turn around, he took her hand and pulled her toward him, gathering her into his arms. The top of her head came just below his chin. He felt her heart pounding against him, her breath against his neck, her warmth, the press of her breasts, so close. He'd never held her like this before. *Dear God.* Again, he felt the stir in his loins, that familiar tightening in his chest, as if he couldn't breathe.

*Dear God.*

From the seat beside her bedroom window, Mehitable held the curtain aside and leaned forward. Yes, there were the two of them, all right. Pressing together shamefully, where anyone could see. One was her grandson, the other that wanton mulattress, what's-her-name.

Mehitable was not surprised, no, not surprised at all. How many times had she told William that there was trouble brewing in that little servant girl? It was no wonder. For years, Sarah had spoiled her rotten, allowing the servant unbridled freedom with Kate, teaching the servant that religious nonsense, which inevitably put wild notions into darkies' heads—notions of equality before the Lord, salvation, and other such rubbish. Led to nothing but trouble, and such nighttime seductions were proof.

Mehitable watched as the two continued to embrace. She watched for signs of groping, of kissing, of rearrangement of clothing. Instead, she breathed a sigh of disappointment as the two separated, Breck returning to his room, the girl to the big house.

No matter, she thought, setting her jaw.

*I'll be watching you.*

# Book Four

*"Then I will speak upon the ashes."*

Sojourner Truth

# Chapter 1

*May 1851*

MONETTE TIPTOED AMONG THE dozens of candles, some of the candlesticks so tall they loomed over her head, casting shadows that shifted like specters as she crept around the coffin. She didn't want to look, yet could not avert her eyes.

A rosary peeped out from his hands, the crucified Jesus touching his thumbnail. They were pale hands, bone-thin, spotted with age, hands that had once caressed her cheeks, her hair, hands that had reached for her while laughter danced in his eyes. Her gaze shifted to his face. But instead of seeing the expected tenderness, the strong, straight nose, she saw a haze. As if someone had whitewashed his face away, stroke by stroke.

Her inability to see his face frightened her. Like the striking of a match, her spark of fear illuminated the chamber, and it was then she realized she was surrounded by hundreds of red roses—greenhouse roses, grown in the heart of winter. The cloying stink of roses began to fill her nostrils and throat, as if the sickly sweetness were poured from a vessel, viscous and heavy, smothering her so she could not breathe.

But when she turned to flee, a hand clamped around her wrist.

*His* hand.

Dead, rigid, pulling her toward the coffin in a vise of icy fingers, bruising her flesh, the rosary cast upon the floor. He was sitting up now, joints popping, his face no longer whitewashed but twisted with hate and fury, a young man, opening his mouth, saying, "It is in your blood and cannot be helped," while worms dropped from his mouth.

She tried to pull her arm back, to scream, but could not. Her bones turned to jelly, her voice to silence, while every cell in her body shrieked *No! No!* as he drew her toward him. Her shoes scraped the floor. *No! No!*

*Mon ami! Me sauver!*

Arms wrapped around her from behind. Strong arms. Hardened with muscle. When his arms wrapped about her, alive and warm and black as the shadows, her fear vanished, and the hand that gripped her wrist released her. Without a sound, the body fell back into the coffin, and the lid slammed shut.

She was weeping.

The man behind her pressed her against his body, folded her into himself, his breath warm, whiskers brushing her cheek, his arms cradling her. *I's here. I's here. Ain't no cause to cry now. Hush, baby. Hush. It be just a dream. It can't hurt you no more.*

Then he was kissing the back of her neck with a tenderness that caused her knees to weaken. The warmth of his kisses spread through her body, stirring secret places long ago forgotten, corners of her soul that she thought were dead.

*Mon amour . . .*

In the morning, all was astir as those catching the steamer for New Orleans hurried through their toilette, their breakfast, and last-minute preparations. All was astir except for Monette, who lay in bed, complaining of a terrible pain in her stomach, coupled with a throbbing headache.

Mammy Hester clucked her tongue and shook her head. "Heavens to Betsy, chile, what you mean, you's sick?"

Kate's face crumpled with dismay. "But you *can't* be sick! We're going to New Orleans together! I need you!"

Miss Sarah sent a wailing Kate to her room, then placed a hand on Monette's forehead. She checked her throat and probed her abdomen, studying Monette's face as if she knew Monette was lying. Monette looked away. Finally, like an answer to prayer, Miss Sarah tucked in the mosquito net, told her to get some rest, that Mammy Hester would accompany Kate to New Orleans instead. She assured Mammy, amid a flurry of protests, that yes, she'd manage just fine without her for a time, thank you very much, at least until Monette was well enough to attend Miss Sarah's toilette herself. To hurry now and pack. Miss Sarah left then, saying she would check on Monette later in the day, while Mammy Hester stomped about the room, mumbling under her breath and no doubt boring holes through Monette's back as she lay on her side, staring at the wall.

At mid-morning, the carriage pulled away, wheels rumbling, leaving Monette with nothing but the hum of mud daubers flitting about and knocking into the rafters, and her feverish thoughts tumbling one over the other in a cascade of confusion. She tossed in bed, plumping her pillow, flinging off her thin blanket, and finally throwing open the shutters as the day warmed.

She recalled last night, the heat and tremor of Breck's body as he held her, the shaking of his breath, the press of his lips against her hair, the answering response of her own body, the fluttering, down low, heated, surprised. What did Breck mean by it? By the embrace? Was he simply hugging her goodnight, as friends often do, or had their relationship suddenly shifted? Was it now more than books and letters? She liked Breck, loved him even. How could she not? He was so good to her. She sat up in bed and embraced her pillow, breathing in its musty smell, telling herself that what happened last night was a simple hug. Nothing more. Yet, like a fox that hears the distant sound of a trumpet, she knew that there was danger there. Like her dream, it frightened her.

Then, her dream—*miséricorde! mon rêve!*—still so vivid, the stench of roses seemed more substantial than the daylight streaming through the windows. The man in the coffin, somehow familiar, at first the giver of tenderness, then turning into a stranger, a younger version of himself, grasping at her, dragging her toward him. More than once, Monette examined her wrist, half expecting to see bruises. She wept into her pillow, her head now truly beginning to throb, eyes swollen, praying for the images to go away. *Va-t'en!*

Each time she prayed for the nightmare to go away, it was as if his arms wrapped about her again. *Him,* the man who cradled her, who saved her from harm, from terror itself. Though the man was a dream, insubstantial and illusory, she felt his warmth still, his lips touching the skin of her neck. A shiver swept through her, gentle as a whisper, passionate as flame. *Mon amour.* She fell back on the bed, legs spread, arching her back, sighing and crying. Sighing with the thrill of desire, crying because he was not real.

Miss Sarah visited her twice, at noon and in the evening, each time bringing a tray of food: jellied pork, stewed collards and potatoes, bread, cheese, and lemonade. Monette drank the lemonade, answered Miss Sarah's questions, Yes, No, Yes, until Miss Sarah left. Monette picked at her food, not hungry, ashamed that Miss Sarah had gone to all that trouble for nothing.

When night finally fell, after the house had been silent for some time, Monette arose. She lit a candle and dressed quickly. Part of her screamed for her to return to bed, to *not do this,* but she set her jaw against her protests, against the fear that caused her to startle with every creak and groan of the settling house.

She knelt by one of the bedposts next to the wall and set the candle on the floor beside her. Using a fork, she pried up one of the floorboards, exposing the gaping rectangular hole beneath. She'd known of the hiding place for a long time, several years at least. She'd first hidden her *gris-gris* in its dark recesses after she'd been told that it was sinful, an abomination in the eyes of a Christian God. Something ignorant people dabbled with, invoking impotent powers that had nothing to do with God and everything to do with evil. Still, she could not bring herself to toss it away. So, it remained buried in the hole in the floor. Bone, stone, stick, grass, hair. Someday she would get rid of it. But not yet.

Now she hesitated, wondering whether there were spiders in the hole, big spiders. She reached a hand inside, stifling a shriek as her hand passed through cobwebby strands. She felt about, *Mon Dieu! Mon Dieu!* her fingers briefly touching the flannel bag, then nothing but the building itself, her eyes once again stinging with tears that seemed to fall anymore without provocation, until her fingers passed over it, a slight elevation. She picked it up.

*I always reward servants who do what's proper.*

*Spend it as you wish.*

After brushing off the cobwebs, she wrapped the coin in a rag and stuffed it down her bodice.

———℮ℓℓ———

A noise awakened Sarah. She opened her eyes, blinked, saw the faint outline of the moonlit window, her thoughts still peopled with dreams. At first, she lay there uncomprehending, drifting back to sleep, but when she heard the sound again—a creaking, a shuffling—she sat bolt upright, shock spilling through her veins.

*Someone is out there.*

She reached for William, remembering he was not there, even as her fingers grazed his pillowcase. Nor was Breck, nor Kate, nor even Mammy Hester. Not for the first time since they'd left, she wished she'd taken Georgie and Thomas and gone with them to New Orleans, pregnancy and all, despite the legions of tasks and people that required her attention.

After the initial shock, Sarah told herself that, of course, it was Monette needing to use the privy. Mr. Gilbert fetching a glass of water, rambling about, unable to sleep. Yet, despite her sensible explanations, her terror remained. It was a familiar terror, shared, she knew, by white women everywhere. Born of insurrection, of poisoned mistresses, of houses torched to cinders. During the day, such terrors were easily dismissed. Why, Fox Creek Plantation was her home! She'd grown up just a few miles yonder at Woodleigh! And, so far as Sarah knew, her labor force respected her. Some, Sarah would have sworn on the Bible, loved her even, as she in turn loved them. But at night, such terrors assumed hideous proportions, not so lightly dismissed.

Sarah squeezed her eyes closed and pulled the bed linen over her head, telling herself she was being silly, to stop acting like a child, all the while half expecting to smell smoke, or to hear the swish of a machete the instant before it chopped her skull in half like a melon.

❧

"You's back," Crone Juju said when Monette deposited the coin on the floor cloth next to the burning pine knots. "I been waiting a powerful long time."

Monette tried to swallow, but couldn't. Here she stood in the dwelling place of a witch, an individual who had made a pact with the devil, who rode brooms at night, brewed evil potions, whose very association could damn Monette to Hell forever. If someone had told Monette six months before that she'd return here again at night, this time alone, with nothing but a lantern borrowed from the kitchen, she'd have thought they were insane, likely spouting nonsense while under the delusion of sherry, whiskey, or port, as she'd seen many of the gentlemen and even some of the ladies do while visiting Fox Creek. Visit the old witch alone? At night? Not "Fraidy-cat Monette," as Kate called her. Monette, who jumped at shadows, who shrieked and did the crazy dance whenever a mouse dashed across the floor, or a spider loomed overhead.

Tonight, Monette didn't feel brave, only desperate, like a person who finds herself on a sinking ship, suddenly faced with the choice to either swim gallantly toward the faraway shore or perish. Her voice came out scratchy and small. "I—I've come for my—I'd like my—please, please, may I—I need help—"

"I knows what you needs, chile. I wouldn't be much good to nobody if I didn't know what folks be needing. Ain't that for true?"

"Oh, *je suis désolé*. I'm so sorry."

For a while, Crone Juju said nothing more. Still standing by the door, Monette waited, every nerve afire, trying not to gawk at the skunk pelt tacked to the walls, the bundles of dried herbs, the half-gourds filled with objects: small bones, liquids, fingernails, hair. . . .

Crone Juju had been sitting against the far wall, knees pulled to her chest like a beggar, but now she rose, grunting. "I tells you, chile, these knees ain't what they used to be. Sometimes it just don't pay to get old. Now, do whats I tell you. Put down your lantern and come here and take my hand." The old woman held out a hand, a hand square and surprisingly large for the woman's size. When Monette didn't budge, other than to set her lantern on the floor, Crone Juju motioned with her fingers. "Come now. The night be waiting."

The thought of crossing the room and taking the witch's hand horrified Monette, as if, should she do so, there would be no going back. No possibility of flight. As if, by taking the witch's hand, she too would be making a pact with the devil and burn in Hell forever. But the thought of returning home without answers, still not knowing, *never* knowing who she was, where she'd come from, who the people were in her dreams, *if* they were real at all, was more than she could bear. Clenching her fists, Monette straightened her spine like she'd seen Kate do a thousand times when faced with a difficult situation, and forced her feet forward until she stood before Crone Juju, the top of the old woman's head coming no higher than Monette's mouth. She heard the woman wheeze, the rattle of wind in her chest, and smelled her breath, like damp soil, an odd, earthy smell as if something might sprout from her at any moment.

The woman took one of Monette's hands, pulling her even closer. Her touch, like her breath, was warm, damp. "Heavens, chile, you acts like I's gonna gobble you up or something. Now uncurl that fist 'lessen you wants to punch me with it."

Crone Juju studied Monette's palm, face so close to it Monette could feel the tickle of the witch's breath, wondering how the woman could see her palm at all in the near darkness, wishing she could yank herself away and run. Crone Juju poked Monette's hand, grunted, wheezed, and grunted again. Then the witch was looking up, peering into her face. Monette tried to draw back, but the woman now held her upper arm in a firm grip. Her face was close. Too close. Monette saw the crinkles around each eye, the bags sagging beneath, the eyes themselves, which seemed to not be normal eyes at all, hardly human, belonging instead to another creature altogether. Those eyes now studied Monette, lids narrowing as the witch drew in her breath sharply. Without releasing Monette, she fetched the gourd of burning pine knots and held it up to Monette's face. Monette shrank away from the heat, from the smell of hot pitch, sharp in her nostrils.

"Lordy sakes, your eyes, they be—chile, what you know of your mother?"

The question shocked Monette. Her *mother*? "I—I—"

Such a simple question, and yet how could she possibly explain to this witch the countless times she'd wondered about her mother? Who she was. Where she came from. Why she let Monette go. *If* she let her go at all. Maybe Monette was taken from her. Maybe her mother was still alive somewhere, likewise wondering where Monette was. All these questions and hundreds more she'd asked countless times on countless nights, while listening to Mammy Hester snore, while polishing the silver, while snuffing the candles, while sweeping, dusting, mending. . . . Such a simple question, and yet the answering of it held more sorrow than she could express. Monette could no longer meet the witch's stare. She looked away, still trembling. "I—I know nothing about her."

"Yes," said the witch slowly. "I sees that now." With this, she lowered the light and let go of Monette's arm. "I can help you. But now you gots to lie down."

"Lie down? What do you mean, here?"

"I says I can help you, but I can't if you ain't willing. It be up to you. It be your five dollars."

Soon Monette was lying on the floor cloth, shivering despite the damp heat of the night. Coming here now seemed a folly greater than anything she'd ever done, for the woman's hands were on her now, firm, probing, kneading her forehead, her temples, her neck, her chest, her abdomen, her groin, while Monette squeezed her eyes closed, begging God to have mercy, to forgive her, to let her live to see the sunrise.

"Hush now. I ain't gonna hurt you none. You gots to relax. Hush now. Hush. Stop that fool whimpering."

A weight pressed on Monette from above, blanket-like, covering her from head to foot, almost paralyzing, her limbs growing thick and heavy. Then there came the smells of roses and smoke, the smells enveloping her, soon drifting inside her body with the stupor of a dream. And from somewhere there was a laugh, someone chanting, hands on her again, a voice saying, "Sleep, chile, sleep. . . ."

# *Chapter 2*

A LTHOUGH NOT ONE SOUL in all of Louisiana had formally declared Lucy Odetta Saffin a beauty, on the evening she stepped into her family's private box at the *Placide's Varieties Theatre,* more than one male head turned an appreciative glance in her direction.

They saw a girl of fifteen, sixteen years of age, with dark brown hair swept up. Had the gentlemen been familiar with the styles of antiquity, they would have rightly determined the hairstyle—complete with golden circlets and braids—to be of Roman origin. Were they not so familiar, they would simply have agreed that it was, indeed, a flattering style, showing off the young lady's sloped, white shoulders, the youthful ripeness of her bosom, and the plump roundness of her arms.

"Isn't that the senator's daughter?" some of the more curious inquired of their neighbors over the tunings of the orchestra in the pit, casting an even more appreciative glance when informed that, "Why yes, that's their box. Can't remember her name, offhand. In fact, that's Senator Saffin and his wife behind her now."

Lucy was not unaware of the attention she garnered, though she gave no sign. Instead, she accepted her father's arm while moving gracefully to her chair at the rail (the art of grace being practiced at great lengths at school). She arranged her gown, sat with shoulders back, chin down, hands clasped (oh, Mme. Dupré would be so proud if she could see her now!), submitted to her father's peck on the cheek, and said, "Thank you, Papa," before he joined Lucy's mother behind her. Aware of the warmth in her face, hopeful it provided a becoming flush of pink to her sometimes too-pale complexion, Lucy cautioned a quick glance below to the dress circle, wondering who was in attendance this evening, and whether anyone still gazed in her direction or noticed the elegance of her gown, its arabesque design on ivory brocade, beribboned with deep navy, a color quite in vogue this theater season.

Thrilled that yes, indeed, she was the object of admiration, Lucy casually turned her gaze toward the stage and the bustle of the orchestra in the pit, as if velvet curtains and the tuning of violas were of enormous interest. She felt her pulse thrum in the hollow of her neck and wondered when Breck Jensey was to arrive and whether he would find her beautiful.

Lucy had scarcely slept the previous night. She'd flung herself about, complaining of the damp heat, sighing with every thought of Breck, until finally her bedfellow (sweet Susie Caldwell, whom Lucy had decided upon first meeting was the dearest, loveliest girlfriend in all the world) complained. "Lucy Saffin! If you don't stop floundering about like a fish in a frying pan and let me get some sleep, I declare I'll do some wickedness for which we'll both be sorry!" The voicing of the complaint had quite the opposite effect, however, for then both of them were wide awake. For the remainder of the night, side by side, they'd surmised about the upcoming evening at the theater, congratulating Lucy upon her maneuvering in getting Breck to attend ("Pure genius," declared Susie, "inviting Kate Jensey like you did!"), and giggling about what Breck might say to her and the wonderful things she would no doubt say in return. "Oh, how I wish I were going," Susie had pined.

"Next season," replied Lucy. "I promise. For now, I don't want Breck distracted by anyone but, of course, yours truly! Besides, you're much too pretty to be allowed in his vicinity!"

Lucy was smiling with the memory, wishing Susie could see her now, when the curtain behind the box parted, and the Jenseys—Breck, Kate, and William—all stepped into the Saffins' private sanctum to a chorus of good evenings and how are yous.

Lucy's heart tumbled. Would she ever grow accustomed to the sight of Breck? Tonight, he looked divinely handsome, a classic male beauty that made her breath catch and her corset seem all the more confining. Like an ornate frame surrounding a masterpiece of art, Breck's evening attire of black pantaloons, white waistcoat, and black dress coat complemented and accentuated his strong, square jaw, made his smile seem all the more brilliant, his height and posture, godlike. All previous attentions from the young males of the theater forgotten, Lucy extended her gloved hand to Breck, stifled the joyful giggle that so wanted to burst from her lips, and said, "Oh, it's you!" as if she'd completely forgotten that he was to share their family's box this evening.

For the first eleven years of her life, Lucy had paid little attention to Breck, or at least no more attention than she paid to, say, Percy Taggart from Hickory Grove, who could bend backwards and touch the ground and then stand back up again, or Victor Cobb, who usually had a black eye or two at any given time and who was always dueling with sticks.

But one sweltering Fourth of July at the St. Marysville town square, where the community had gathered for a barbeque and speeches, everything changed for Lucy. A sudden thunderstorm had overtaken the celebration with a fury that took everyone by surprise. One minute they'd been wiping the chicken grease off their faces and talking about their crops and who was having a baby, the next minute everyone was scattering for cover like hens escaping the stew pot. Eleven-year-old Lucy fell behind, scurrying to gather her new paper dolls (which she'd brought so she and Frances Parsons could play during the speeches), when suddenly Breck was there alongside her, helping her pick up the little dresses and bonnets, which the pounding rain quickly turned to a pulpy mush. Lucy wailed, "Oh, they're ruined!" But instead of dismissing her anguish as childish, or explaining that they were just paper dolls, Breck looked as if he understood, even as if he were equally distressed on her behalf. He then took her hand and together they raced to the shelter of the people-stuffed gazebo, where they were covered with blankets, and each given a few sips of sherry to revive their spirits.

A week later, a package arrived at Belrose Plantation. It was a new set of paper dolls with a note saying, *For Miss Lucy.* Although the dolls were poorly drawn and cut, and certainly not styled according to the latest fashions, Lucy was smitten, knowing Cupid's arrow had truly pierced her heart. From then on, Lucy Saffin loved Breck Jensey, and vowed to someday become his wife, *knew* she would become his wife, a vow that strengthened in determination and resilience with each passing year.

The gaslights reflected off Breck's wavy brown hair as he took her hand, bent his head, and brushed her glove with his lips. "Good evening, Miss Lucy. You're looking radiant. I trust you've been well and have been making good progress at school."

Lucy would have said something in reply, but suddenly Kate was there, pressing her cheek to Lucy's own, the circumference of Kate's evening dress forcibly ending all social introductions with Breck, who retreated to the second row of chairs to sit with his father and Lucy's parents. "Thanks for inviting me," Kate was saying. "It seems ages since I've been to the theater!"

Lucy smothered a flash of irritation and smiled at Kate. Never had the two of them been close, always seeming interested in other things. But Lucy was determined to change that. After all, Kate *was* Breck's sister, a tie of kinship that had certainly come in quite useful tonight! "Why, Kate Jensey, you look lovely. Is that a Paris gown?"

Kate laughed. "No, silly, we have a dressmaker right here on Canal Street."

"Those stripes and those roses, why, they're simply *divine!* That pink, it brings out the color of your skin and the red highlights of your hair." Lucy drew Kate close and whispered conspiratorially, "It's a shame your gown doesn't match your headdress, though. I think a spray of tiny roses might have been the perfect thing. But here, come, sit on my left. We'll gossip together."

After Kate settled herself and Lucy received her hellos from Breck's father, Lucy swiveled in her chair. "Why, Breck, surely you don't mean to be a bore and sit back there and talk politics all night, do you? Sit here with Kate and me. Not only can you see better, but I dare say the conversation will be better as well." She giggled and stole a glance at Kate before gasping and pressing a gloved hand to her mouth, as if she hadn't meant to say what she did. "Oh, Papa! No offense intended."

"Nonsense, Lucy." Her father smiled and winked as he motioned Breck toward the chair Lucy offered. "You young people enjoy yourselves."

Lucy turned back around, but not before she saw her mother's eyebrow rise in that familiar caution, meaning, Mind your manners, young lady.

As the gaslights dimmed, the curtain rose, and the audience quieted to the tune of coughs, clearings of throats, and a whimsical number by the orchestra, Lucy fetched her opera glasses from her reticule. "Oh, just look at the scenery," she whispered as Breck sat beside her. "Isn't it lovely?"

"Not nearly so lovely as the company," he whispered in reply.

Warmed as she was by his compliment, Lucy nevertheless remembered to stick out her bottom lip, as Susie had instructed ("Not too much, else he'll think you're not genuine!"). When Breck inquired as to what was the matter, Lucy said, "You didn't write me, like I'd asked. Why, Breck Jensey, if I didn't know you better, I'd swear you didn't care a whit about me. Three months at school, and not one letter from you!"

Breck appeared taken aback by her remonstrance, but recovered gallantly, smiling in a way that made Lucy's heart tumble again. "I promise I shall write you upon my return home. I shall be remiss no longer."

On the other side of Lucy, Kate watched the opening of the play through her opera glasses as the formidable Aunt Betsey entered the domicile of David Copperfield's young, widowed, pregnant mother. "Mrs. David Copperfield, I think," said Aunt Betsey. "Yes," the widow replied. . . .

Kate clenched her opera glasses, while the sound of Breck and Lucy's whispered exchange murmured on. *Why, that little vixen! Lucy only invited me to the theater so she could be with Breck! How* dare *she! And Good God! Do you hear her babble on and on? As if anyone* cares *what she has to say? As if her blather is even worthy of an idiot!*

Anger seared Kate's chest. Anger toward herself for falling for such a ruse, and also a hurt-filled anger knowing that Lucy had so easily dispatched her. *My gown doesn't match my headdress? Well, Miss Saffin, you smug little viperous senator's daughter, I'll have you know I picked out this very outfit, headdress and all, from* Godey's Lady's Book. *And if you weren't such a cretin, you'd know that! To think I was actually looking* forward *to visiting with you and seeing the play!* Kate wanted to say all those things and more to Lucy, but instead sat with spine erect, immobile, watching intently through her glasses as if she cared anymore whether the actors delivered their lines properly or perhaps dropped dead through a hole in the stage floor.

When the curtain fell at the end of Act One and while the theater yet resounded with applause, Kate excused herself and hurried out to the hall, presumably to powder her nose. The hall was semi-dark, lit only by two gas lamps turned low, the carpet red, the wood paneling stained chestnut. She fled down the hall, making it no farther than the top of the stairs before hot tears gathered in her eyes, stirring her pot of anger all the more. Oh! She was furious with herself for shedding even one tear over someone as vapid and contemptible as Lucy Saffin! She paused at the top of the staircase, vision blurring, afraid she might start boohooing before she could make it down the steps to the ladies' closet. As she dug in her reticule for her handkerchief, trying to feel where it might be (a difficult task with gloves), a man's voice startled her from behind. "Why, Miss Jensey, is that you?"

Kate spun.

Midnight-black hair and winter-blue eyes shimmered through her veil of tears. It was Stephen Decatur Rockwell, a man she'd known all her life. She'd never known him well, never had reason to seek anything beyond his acquaintance; he was, after all, near twice her age. She'd last seen Stephen at his wedding one year prior when he'd wed Irish Mary. Kate hadn't even known they'd returned from their honeymoon abroad.

"Mr. Rockwell!" She hastily brushed her tears with her gloves, praying he didn't notice, wishing he would go away.

There followed the briefest heartbeat of silence, as if in that measured beat Stephen took in her distressed appearance, her tear-filled eyes, her (no doubt) blotched and reddened face, understanding in an instant that she'd been about to bolt down the stairs, fleeing some upset. Stephen withdrew a handkerchief from his pocket and held it out. "You look as if you could use this."

"No, thank you," she replied, sniffing, feeling silly and caught.

"I insist. What kind of gentleman would I be if I left a young lady in distress without coming to her aid?" He continued holding out the handkerchief. "Take it, please. I will stand here until you do. Please, I beg of you. For my sake at least. I shall look ridiculous come ten o'clock this evening when all the people stream past me down the stairs."

Envisioning such a possibility—the dashing Stephen Decatur Rockwell standing in his military dress uniform decorated with ribbons, medals, and badges, with his arm outstretched, proffering a handkerchief to the empty air—Kate suppressed a smile, took the handkerchief, and turned away from Stephen. She wiped her eyes and blew her nose, remembering too late how unladylike it was to blow her nose in front of a man. She turned back around, unsure whether to return or keep his handkerchief. "Sorry."

"It's yours," he said.

"Thanks. You're—you're very kind." She glanced over his shoulder, embarrassed to be the object of his scrutiny, shyly returning her gaze to his bearded face, at a loss for words. "You—you have returned from your honeymoon?"

"Indeed, I have, as you can see," he said, smiling. "To answer your next question, yes, it was pure heaven. We saw Paris, London, Rome, Prague, Istanbul—all the big cities and even the insignificant hamlets. Our horizons were broadened, and our palates challenged. I would highly recommend such cultural expansion to anyone."

Stephen talked on about his honeymoon in such an affable, self-assured manner that Kate felt herself relaxing. The anger that had smoldered like a fire inside her bosom began to dissipate. She was thinking of how different he was from Edward Scarborough, who couldn't string two nice words together and who scarcely acknowledged her presence, when suddenly, Stephen's smile fell, and he stopped talking.

"I am boring you with my twaddle."

Kate laughed. "No, no you're not. Believe me. You've lifted my spirits."

He dramatically clasped his hand over his chest. "Ah, mission accomplished. Now, Miss Jensey, forgive my asking, but before I lift your spirits entirely to the heavens, I must know, or again, I am not a gentleman. Was there some rogue responsible for your state of distress?"

"Why, no." Kate found herself giggling, thinking of Lucy as a rogue.

"Come now. Where is he?" Stephen looked about him as if he might find a rogue lurking in the shadows of the gaslights.

"There is no man."

"Fie! I must challenge him to a duel!" Stephen placed his hand on the hilt of his sword. "No one besmirches the good name of my friend, Miss Jensey, without me to answer to!"

"You are being silly."

His face fell, but his eyes still danced with laughter. "Alas, I find silliness becomes me. Especially in times of great despair. So. You are certain there is no rogue who must feel the cold of my steel pass through his fiendish heart?"

"Quite certain, but I thank you for your gallantry."

Stephen bowed just as Breck approached. The two shook hands and exchanged a few pleasantries before Breck rolled his eyes at Kate and said simply, "Save me."

"Now," said Stephen, bowing again, "I must beg your leave and hurry back to my wife, who is doubtless wondering what mishap has befallen me. Miss Jensey, I leave you in better hands and bid you *adieu*. And please," he paused, "give my best to Miss Saffin." With that, Stephen winked at Kate as if he'd known all along the subject of her distress, hurried down the stairs, and was gone.

Back inside the box, Kate felt none of her anger. She sat next to Lucy, even smiled at her when Lucy exclaimed too loudly, "Why, Kate, you were gone forever. The second act is half over!"

Kate murmured a reply, having no recollection of what she said to Lucy, either then or later that night as she lay in bed at the St. Louis Hotel gazing out the window at the gaslights of the French Quarter, as a breeze whispered through the filmy curtains, brushing Kate's skin with coolness. All she remembered was the winter-blue of Stephen's eyes, his laughter and teasing, the boldness of his presence, and how, when she spied him returning to a box opposite the theater, he had glanced across at the Saffins' box and met Kate's eye, smiling one last time before sitting between Irish Mary and Judge Rockwell, while, on stage, David Copperfield declared his love for Little Em'ly and they shared an innocent kiss.

## *Chapter 3*

W HEN CRONE JUJU LAID her hands upon Monette and told her to sleep, Monette dreamed again. Initially, her dreaming was fragmented, like reflections seen in a shattered mirror, moving, shifting, never fully beheld—the green of sugar fields, the white of his hair, the red of roses—a kaleidoscope of images, at once blended, then distilled into shards, edges both blurred and sharply jagged. But then, with a gentle touch on her shoulder, like a bird alighting, he was there, standing beside her. She felt the warmth of his hand and gazed up at him, for she was very small. A child only. Music was playing from somewhere in the *grande maison*. A woman was singing. The air smelled of recent rain, fresh and earthy and warm.

Together they walked to the stables, his hand holding hers, gently, as if he held a flower in his grasp and knew that, should he so much as fold his hand, he would crush the fragile petals. His horse was already saddled—a gray, dappled like sunshine through the leaves.

They were off. Cantering along the cart tracks, across the bridge that stretched over the swollen bayou, and into the forest, beneath the drapings of moss, through the meadows, she in front of him on his saddle, his arm wrapped about her. She felt the rumble of his chest when he laughed, felt the vibrations of his voice as he told her a story about a princess who fell asleep for one hundred years. Sometimes she even thought she felt his heart beat against her back, as if, should she press herself into him even more, their hearts would soon beat in tandem, like lovers who match the stride of their walk.

They were singing a song of fair maids when the sky grew dark, and thunder rumbled.

*Ah, ma chérie,* he said, stroking her hair, *Our sweet afternoon is over. We must hurry home, or we will get wet.*

She laughed then, imagining the cup of *chocolat chaud* that would be waiting for her, the rubbing of her skin with dry towels, the tsks of her nurse, the exchange of glances over the bent head of the nurse, as if they shared a delicious secret.

*Hold on, my little one!* He urged the horse into a gallop. His arm tightened around her, she holding fistfuls of the horse's mane. The rain began to fall, softly at first, then driving and cold until they were surrounded by a soupy gray. Thunder boomed overhead.

She was no longer laughing. She was cold instead, and wet through. She shivered against him, unable to stop the whimper that escaped her lips.

He reined the horse to a halt. The beast stamped in the mud, snorted, and tossed his mane. She felt him quiver beneath her, as if he, too, were frightened. In the distance, through the soupy gray, a wall of water approached. A white crest at the fore. There was a roar, like the ocean tide.

With a command from the man, the horse was springing upward, onto a small patch of risen ground, a tree at its center. The wall of water washed past them, surrounding them, rising, rising, until their island disappeared as well. The horse whinnied and shied. Water swirled about his fetlocks.

Before she could ask what was happening, she was being taken from the horse, set upon the lowest branch of the tree, told to climb upward, to not let go no matter what happened. This she did, not understanding. The branches were slick and wet in her grasp. Moss trailed in her hair, wet tendrils against her cheek as if the tree itself was weeping. She looked down at the man, at the rain streaming off the brim of his hat, at his mouth, no longer smiling, his face pale and lined with fear. She wanted to cry then, to tell him she was cold, that she was frightened, and that she'd torn her dress, but said nothing, clenching her jaw to keep her teeth from chattering.

*Wait here, ma chérie,* he said. *I shall return.* He turned to go. She blinked back the rain and watched him, thinking, *He shall save me.*

Horse and rider waded into the deeper water. Soon the torrent reached his stirrups, his thighs, his hips, fast and roaring. At first, the horse swam. Then the beast was sideways, shrieking grotesquely, flailing like an insect on its back. The rider was now cast adrift. The reins tore from his hands. She watched, horrified, as both rider and horse swept past her and disappeared into the gray nothingness, sinking beneath the water's surface.

Lightning jolted the sky. Thunder hammered as if with a fist.

Her mouth was open. She knew she was screaming by the hoarse feeling in her chest, as if it had suddenly ripped open, rawness exposed to the fury of the storm, as if her very self erupted out of her chest, vomited out her mouth.

She awakened from her dream not knowing where she was or who was screaming so shrilly or why there were hands upon her body. For an instant her dreaming merged with the reality of the night, fragments of both swirling together like two birds caught in a whirlwind. Then she remembered.

*The witch.*

*Candle flame.*

*The stench of roses.*

*The heaviness of sleep.*

*The man. . . .*

Monette lay on a rough cloth on the floor of Crone Juju's hut, the floorboards uneven against her back, a knothole jamming her hip. Once she realized that it was she who screamed, she ceased. A silence followed, filled only with the soft patter of rain on the roof and the breathing of the woman who crouched beside her. Monette made no effort to stem the salty tears that spilled down her temples. Her throat ached. Her head throbbed, a drum of pain.

Then, finally, Monette looked at the woman, at her shriveled face, her dark eyes sunken in her head, and knew she was no longer afraid of her. Crone Juju returned her gaze.

"The man in my dream—"

"Yes."

"He is real."

"Yes, chile."

"And the dream—"

"Yes, chile?"

"It's not a dream at all. It's a memory. *Un souvenir.*"

"That it is."

Monette turned her gaze to the shadowed cobwebs of the ceiling, the dream still so vivid she could yet feel the rain upon her face, the horse quivering beneath her, his arm around her. She could hear the roar of the water, the clap of thunder, see the gathering fear upon his face. It was a memory, this she knew. A memory from *before.*

"Who is he?" she whispered, and when the old woman gave no answer, tears once again slipped down Monette's temples, trickling into her ears, pain pressing upon her chest so that her breath shortened.

*Who are you?*

*You who called me ma chérie, who are you?*

It wasn't until Monette prepared to leave, standing at the door of the hut, her legs feeling so wobbly she wasn't certain she had the strength to return to the big house, that Crone Juju placed some rose petals in Monette's hand and told her, "Put these in a bowl of water and set it under your bed. Spirits like that. Smells good, and they's attracted to pleasing aromas. You do that, maybe he visit your dreaming. Tell you who he is." The old woman pecked Monette on the cheek and said, "Go on now, chile."

Monette, fearing dawn would soon be upon her, departed.

If Sarah had thought she'd find time to plant her strawberry runners, or put out the remainder of her greenhouse plants, or write a bit in her manuscript while the others were gone to New Orleans, she was sorely mistaken. First, there was Mehitable, sicker than the dickens, yet refusing to stay confined in her bedroom, instead growing roots right in Sarah's office, snorting and coughing and advising and tut-tutting until Sarah thought she'd go crazy. Then there was the man on horseback at the back door, asking if Sarah had any niggers for sale, bad or good, young or old, they were all the same to him. No sooner had she sent him on his way (declaring to Lizzy she'd rather sell her negroes to the devil and that his impudence was downright astonishing), than the Miss Wigfalls arrived for a visit, chatting about the weather, the neighbors, and asking when, oh when, was William going to finish plowing their corn field like he'd promised?

In the few days since her family had left for the city, Sarah had done nothing but scurry from one body to the next like a gossipmonger at a community fish fry. Her back hurt. Her morning sickness was in full bloom. Her feet were swollen, throbbing, and as she winced her way down the stairs and into her office, she swore she'd never let Mammy Hester and her fine foot rubs wander out of reach again. As if all that weren't enough, she hadn't been sleeping well, either.

Despite the fact that Sarah would have preferred to stay in bed or perhaps whisk over to Woodleigh for a long overdue visit, the air in the office smelled fresh and welcoming. A bouquet of lavender lay in a basket on her desk, tied with a ribbon, adding a fruity sweetness to the air. Sunshine streamed through the east window accompanied by the usual din from the yard: a baby crying, the chop of an axe or two, a burst of laughter from the kitchen, the shouts and squeals of children at play. Sarah was relieved to see that Mehitable was not there. Perhaps she'd taken that sleeping draught like Sarah had suggested and would order a breakfast tray sent to her room as well. Maybe, Sarah hoped, if sick call went well, and if Mehitable stayed out of her way, there might even be time to write a little in her manuscript, to finish that chapter on caring for the teeth and gums, how to keep the breath sweet, and how regular brisk walks kept the lungs clear and invigorated the mind.

Sarah's hope was short-lived. She was in the middle of counting her supply of blue mass pills when she heard the unmistakable sounds of Mehitable's entrance into the rear loggia: the rap of the cane, the groans, the rustle of yards of crinoline, the clearing of the throat before the woman declared, "Lord have mercy. Where is everybody? Sarah? Sarah!"

"In here, Mother," Sarah responded, thinking, please William, hurry home. I need you more than ever.

Mehitable's bulk soon blocked the doorway. "Gracious. I guess it's considered old-fashioned anymore to help an ailing lady to her chair?"

Suppressing a sigh, Sarah left off her counting, took Mehitable's arm, and steered her to the wingback chair by the window, saying, "You're certainly looking better than yesterday, Mother. Did you sleep well? Have you had breakfast?" while the baby fluttered inside her like a butterfly and the number she was keeping in her head slipped away like sand in a sieve.

"Of course, I didn't sleep well." Mehitable sat in the chair with a grunt. "It's a wonder I sleep a wink with all the things troubling me, and yes, I've had breakfast, if you could call it that. I've told Delia time and again I like my bacon done crispy, not chewy. My teeth aren't what they used to be. I felt like a dog gnawing on a bone. Mark my words, Sarah, when you get to be my age, you'll pine for the days when you could take things like chewing for granted. Land sakes! It nearly makes a body want to stop eating altogether! And I can't abide dentists!"

Sarah sat at her desk, gathered the blue mass pills into a pile again, and opened her journal of inventory. *Blue Mass Pills – 1200 quantity rolled October 2.* She said without much hope, "Mother, how would it be if you visited Mrs. Parsons today? The two of you have always enjoyed—"

"What, that old biddy? She's a fool if God ever made one. I never did abide her ways with those negroes of hers. Passel of lazy rascals is what they are. Takes two of them to help one do nothing."

*Twelve, fourteen, sixteen . . .*

Then there was someone in the doorway. "Excuse me, Miss Sarah, but my son's feeling poorly today—"

"Mercy sakes, can't you see Miss Sarah's busy counting?"

The interruptions mounted. Sarah lost count of her pills four, five times. Tamar, needing medicine for Basil, whose bowels were acting up. Aunt Juda, swelling with the dropsy. Sam, one of the field hands, shifting from foot to foot, complaining of fever and pain in the joints. Mehitable, saying William would know how to fix him. The baby inside, fluttering. Her nausea, growing more insistent.

Sarah was dipping her pen into the inkpot, preparing to record the total (finally, the total!) when someone else burst into the office.

"Miss Sarah, come quickly!"

"Merciful heavens!" exclaimed Mehitable. "If it's not one thing, it's another. My word, Sarah, I don't know how you get anything done."

It was Tabb, Tamar's husband. He was breathing hard, his shirt damp with sweat. Sarah set down her pen and stood. There was something about the tone of Tabb's voice that caused her heart to falter, as if counting blue mass pills were suddenly as insignificant as counting flies. "What is it, Tabb?" Was that blood on his sleeve?

"You gots to come quickly."

"What is it?" Already Sarah was pulling off her apron, striding across the rear loggia, out the door and into the heat. "Is it—is it Basil?" she asked, hoping it was not, for she had a soft place for the child, due, she supposed, to helping bring him into the world and because he was a favorite playmate of the twins.

"It's Quincy." Tabb was pulling her by the arm. Up ahead, in the vicinity of the hospital, a crowd gathered.

"What's the matter with Quincy?"

"Hurry, Miss Sarah, 'fore it be too late."

The crowd stood clustered, no doubt, around Quincy. When they saw her approaching some of them ran toward her. "Oh, Miss Sarah, Quincy, he got hit with a hoe." "Hurry!" "It am bad, Miss Sarah, real bad."

The crowd parted as she walked through. Except for someone crying, the others grew silent, watching her, as if they believed she could raise folks from the dead, provide manna, or fetch water from a rock. She wondered if they could see her tremble. If they knew she dreaded what she was about to see. If they knew her thoughts, childlike and quivering: William, please, I can't do this anymore. . . .

When Sarah saw Quincy, she gasped. Nausea and dizziness washed through her, and she clamped a hand to her mouth. "Oh, dear God." Quincy lay on his back. His hands were clenched in front of him like claws, shaking as if with the palsy. Instead of a scalp, an abundance of fine hair, his head was a gooey mass pulsating with blood. It was difficult for Sarah to imagine a human body carrying so much blood, but there it was, soaking every inch of his clothing, pooling darkly in the grass beside him, dripping into the eyes that stared at her, pleading. Even his voice seeped from his mouth like blood from a wound. "S—Sawney." Then his eyes rolled up into his head, and his body sagged with a sigh.

Sarah knelt beside him, checked his pulse, heard herself say, "Aunt Page, lay out some clean linens in the hospital and start some water boiling. Robert, hitch up the wagon and go tell my brother John to hurry on over. You, you, and you, take Quincy inside to the first bed. Careful now."

At the start of the ruckus outside, Monette slipped upstairs. Ever since she'd awakened, Lizzy had dogged her with this task and that. Sweep out that parlor. Dust them shelves. Polish that mirror. Take them linens out to the wash. Churn that milk. Take up them ashes. Fetch more wood. Anymore, it seemed Lizzy took a fierce pleasure in working Monette from sunrise to long past sundown. Monette knew it was because she had gotten Fatima into trouble and now Fatima was living on another plantation. But

Monette would rather work all day than to have Fatima spilling her wet whispers into her ears, pushing her up against walls, saying nasty things, and spitting into food. Yet the backlash from Lizzy was more than just keeping Monette so busy she could hardly scratch—it was the way Lizzy watched her. With eyes narrowed. With an intensity that said, *Someday you gonna be sorry, girl.*

With the commotion, Lizzy, Nat, Uncle Henry—everyone who had ears—had rushed outside, leaving Monette in the dining room setting out the silver for the midday meal. She hesitated, hand hovering with fork and spoon over the place setting. Then, setting the silver aside, she ran out of the dining room, through the butler's pantry, and flew up the stairs in the rear loggia.

Because of the slope of the roofline, the attic was a narrow affair, divided into three rooms. At opposite ends of the middle room were two bedrooms: Mr. Gilbert's and the room Monette shared with Mammy Hester. The doorway to Monette's room was open, casting an ambient light upon the windowless, middle room. Like a catchment basin holding the overflow, the middle room had always been used for storage. Old, rolled-up carpets stinking of peppercorns and tobacco, champagne baskets filled with lamps, tablecloths needing mending, chipped but usable plate, trunks filled with coverlets, dresses for babes, for mourning, for special occasions, bonnets and fans long gone out of fashion, books musty and brittle with age—a flotsam of household goods washed up from the ebb and flow of eating, sleeping, dressing, working, playing, loving, birthing, and dying.

Now that she had a respite from Lizzy, Monette scarcely knew where to begin, hardly even knew what she was looking *for*, only that, when she saw it, she would know. Whatever *it* was. After struggling with a rusty clasp, she opened the nearest trunk to a creak of hinges and a billow of dust, the stink of camphor strong and pinching.

Miss Sarah's evening dress.

A mantel clock with a cracked glass.

A crocheted shoulder cape, the fringe crushed and tired-looking.

Early this morning, with a bowl of rosewater beneath her bed like Crone Juju had instructed, Monette had dreamed of him again. They meandered through a garden. She, like before, a child. Her hand, warm in his. Under an archway they strolled, a lizard darting along the hot flagstones before them. Then there was a house. A big house. A *grande maison,* with stairs mounting to the *galérie* that wrapped around the second floor. Above, two dormered attic windows peered out from the hipped roof like the bulging eyes of an alligator, watchful and waiting. While Monette gazed upward, the house shifted, blurred. It was evening, and she now was gazing up at the front of the Fox Creek big house, the sun setting at her back. Pulling her by the hand, the man stepped through the entrance like a visitor who'd forgotten to knock. Miss Sarah was sitting in her favorite chair by the fireplace, sewing. Kate played Bach on the pianoforte, striking a sour note. Mars William reclined opposite Miss Sarah, chewing the end of an unlit cigar. Breck read by one of the crystal-laden *girandoles,* glancing at the dining room door as if expecting someone. When the man entered with Monette in tow, no one paid them the slightest attention. Ghostlike, they walked through the various rooms to the back of the house and began climbing the steps, not stopping until they stood in the attic, surrounded by trunks, baskets, rugs, and dust.

From this dream Monette had awakened with a start, the plantation bell pealing with the thrum of her heart. She'd awakened, but not before the man had knelt before her, his blue eyes penetrating and calm. He cupped her face in his hands and whispered, *Find it, ma chérie.*

Now she rummaged through the contents of a second trunk, a third. *Find it.*

She was sorting through a basket, shoving aside yellowed linens that stank of mildew, when the hairs rose on the back of her neck. Someone was creeping up the stairs, this she knew. For a second, she froze. Then, like a mouse realizing it has just moments before the cat awakes, Monette crawled into the crevice between a stack of trunks and the wall, into the angle created by the sloped roof joining the floor, peeping around the edge of the bottom trunk, praying the windowless room would be dark enough to hide her.

It was Miss Mehitable. Her head, shoulders, and ample figure rose by degrees as she climbed out of the stairwell. Then the woman was standing in the center of the room, silent, cane in hand, swiveling her head to peer into the shadows.

Monette shrank back into the crevice. A splintery floorboard pressed into her knee. She shut her eyes. Heard her pulse in her head, thready and fast. There was dust in her throat, and she wanted to cough.

*Sacredié.*

The floor creaked, a series of creaks that crept toward Mr. Gilbert's room, then back toward Monette's before returning to the center of the room. Then there was a brush of fabric against a trunk. Closer now. The sound of breath drawn through nostrils. Monette felt the woman standing over her even before she opened her eyes and saw the toe of a shoe, not twelve inches away from her nose. Monette considered bolting, yet knew she would never get away fast enough. Besides, the woman was blocking her exit. So, Monette did nothing, her neck crawling with the expectation of a hand clamping itself upon her back collar as if she were an animal caught.

Then there were shouts from downstairs. The sounds of people running. The door slammed shut.

Monette heard Ole Miss grunt as the shoe moved away. The woman crossed the floor heavily, dress swiping against trunks and baskets with the sound of a broom sweeping the floor, before marking her descent upon the stairs with a thwack of her cane against the spindles.

When Monette was certain Ole Miss was gone, she wiggled out from her hiding place and bolted down the stairs. She paused on the second-floor landing, verified through the window that yes indeed, both Ole Miss and Lizzy were outside, then descended the last flight of steps and rushed into the dining room.

When Lizzy entered not thirty seconds later, it was with all the innocence Monette could contrive to look her dead in the eye, smile sweetly, and say, "Why, yes'm, of course. I did as you asked me to."

# Chapter 4

WHEN THE STEAMBOAT ARRIVED at the town of Bayou Clare, William Jensey was in high spirits. Never had a trip to New Orleans been more enjoyable. Initially reluctant to bring his daughter upon what was supposed to be a business trip, he was the first to admit that it did a body good to jest with friends, to attend the theater, to wager on the ponies (even if none of his were racing)—to allow satisfaction in the finer things of life. It was, after all, these finer things that reminded a man once again of what was truly important: love, joy, friends, family, and, of course, hounds, horses, and Cuban cigars. His only regret was that he hadn't insisted that Sarah come along.

"Don't worry, big boy," Marshall drawled from where he stood beside William at the rail, as the two of them watched the roustabouts moor the vessel to the landing. "She's kept your bed nice and warm for you." Marshall said something else too, but booming as his voice was, it couldn't compete with the ear-splitting blast of the *Barbara Allen's* whistle.

William grinned down at the smaller man—at the pock-scarred skin, the crooked nose, the eyes squinting back at him through the smoke that curled upward from his teeth-clenched cigar—glad Marshall had agreed to accompany him home. Not only would they spend a day or so hunting and fishing, but William could take advantage of Marshall's expertise now that the construction of the sugarhouse was scheduled to begin. "Mind yourself, Marshall," he replied, once the sound of the whistle died away. "I have a daughter with big ears nearby."

"A fine daughter she is, too. Grew from a weed to a flower in hardly the time it took to blink my eye."

William glanced over to where Kate stood a few feet away, chatting with Breck, and Senator and Mrs. Saffin. A flower? While William admitted to a certain pride when it came to Kate, a father's pride born the day of her birth and as natural as breathing, more often than not that pride was overshadowed by her behavior—boisterous, loud, stubborn, often thoughtless.

Sometimes it was everything he could do to restrain his temper, although he did have to admit that she'd acted respectably during this most recent jaunt to the city. As much as could be expected, anyway, without her mother along to offer the proper guidance. Someone must have said something funny, for now they all laughed—Kate in the manner of a man: head back, mouth wide open, teeth exposed, garnering more than one disapproving glance from other passengers. "She should be at boarding school, but Sarah wants to keep her home until after the baby's born. I think a few years away will do wonders for her disposition. Teach her refinement—a foreign notion to her at present."

"Nothing wrong with a wild filly, my friend."

"Fine talk in terms of horse flesh, but when it's your daughter, trust me, it becomes wearying."

The smaller man thumped him on the back. "You worry too much," was all he said, as if that summed it up.

Again, William glanced at Kate. When his daughter caught him looking and shot him a smile designed to melt a father's heart, William smiled in return, thinking, Marshall's right. Maybe I do worry too much.

Out on the landing, amid porters, trunks, carts, horses, and farewells, while the muddy waters of the Mississippi swirled and eddied around the brush and tree trunks of the shoreline, the Saffins parted company, saying they should all do this again soon, and the Jenseys and Marshall settled into the family's carriage for the journey home to Fox Creek, leaving the servants' mule-drawn cart to lumber along at its own pace.

William sank back into the seat, knees jutting high as his chest. Content to watch the timbered hills roll by, thick with beeches, magnolias, and yellow poplars, the succession of split-rail fences, the horses out to pasture, he only half listened to Marshall's banter with Kate and Breck, the sweet warm breeze reminding him of the time he gave Sarah a bouquet of lavender and white roses. . . .

Long before the big house came into view, William had fallen asleep. Now, with a "Whoa," from Robert, and a setting of the brake, William awakened and rubbed his eyes, his neck stiff, wondering what was for supper and whether Sarah had missed him.

It was after William had alighted and as he was helping Kate navigate the step down that his coachman, Robert, said quietly from beside him, "Mars William, there be something I gots to tell you."

"Oh, I swear," Kate was saying loudly, "I'm famished!"

"Let's hope the home fires are roaring, and they've got a pig on the spit." Marshall clambered out after Kate. "And I could do to wet my whistle."

"Mars William, please, there be something I gots to tell you."

"Breck," said William, pointing into the carriage, "fetch that package. Hide it from your mother. I'll give it to her this evening."

"Please Mars William—"

William snapped, "Can't it wait 'til later, Robert?"

"Yessir, yessir, why it sure can. Yessir. But, but it be about Quincy, you see."

"Quincy?" There was something about Robert's voice that caused William to turn his full attention to him. The coachman stood with his head lowered. Gray flecked his hair and beard. He crushed his felt hat, turning it round and round as if it were a wheel rolling.

The carriage springs squeaked as Breck alighted. "What about Quincy?"

"Problems already, big boy?" asked Marshall, turning back around while Kate stepped inside the front entrance, hollering, "We're home, Mama!"

Robert glanced up briefly at the three of them. Swallowed so hard William watched his Adam's apple bob up, then down. Robert stared at the ground again. Shifted his feet.

"Spit it out, Robert," said William, fighting the urge to rattle the teeth out of the man's head.

"You see, it happened the other day—"

"*What* happened?"

"You see, the way folks tells it, it started out as an argument. Quincy, he was just doing his job, you know, telling folks what to do 'cause that's his job and you was gone to the city, and Sawney, well, he don't like no one to tell him what to do, as you probably already know."

"Get on with it."

"Well, see, no one saw what happened exactly 'cause no one was there 'cepting Quincy and Sawney, and well, Sawney, he up and scalped the hair right off of Quincy's head."

"He *what?*" asked William.

"Scalped the hair off?" asked Marshall. "What do you mean, scalped the hair off?"

"That's—that's what I mean. I mean, Sawney took that hoe and done sliced the hair right off Quincy's head, skin and all."

"Good God," breathed William, feeling the blood drain from his head. His best driver. *Scalped.*

"Where is Quincy now?" asked Breck.

"He at the hospital. Been there going on four days now. Dr. John says—"

"And Sawney?" From the first mention of Sawney's name, a familiar rage had risen inside William. Anymore it seemed as if the rage was always there, like a pot of smoldering embers, ready to burst into flame at the first wisp of air.

"Well, he run off, neck collar and all."

"Goddammit!" William threw his straw hat to the ground. Kicked the carriage wheel. Kicked his hat. Slammed his cane against the carriage, further enraged when a piece of enamel chipped away. "See what happens when I leave town? Everything, goddammit, *everything* goes to hell!" He swore some more, stomped his hat, restraining himself with an effort when he realized that Kate and Sarah stood in the doorway, looking no less shocked than if he'd just plunged a dagger deep into his own breast.

"If there were no witnesses," Breck was saying, "and Sawney ran off, how can you be certain who scalped Quincy?"

"Well, see, that's the thing. Quincy crawled hisself to where the hoe gang was working. Then they carried him to the hospital where he told who done it 'fore he lost consciousment. I heard him say so myself. He said, 'Sawney.' That's what he said. And since Sawney's gone, well, it's a sensibility that he be guilty."

William ran a hand through his hair, feeling drained, wishing, not for the first time and probably not for the last, that he could just forget all this planting business and live in a hovel next to a lake with nothing but a rifle and a horse and a fishing pole.

"Well, big boy?" said Marshall.

Heaving a sigh, William retrieved his straw hat from where it lay against the carriage wheel. The upper part was crushed, half separated from the wide brim, his boot print stamped upon its surface in several places. He tried to brush the dirt off, to push the hat back into shape, knowing it was futile, knowing he looked half the fool, wishing he'd worn a different hat as this one had been his favorite, perfect for those daytime excursions in pleasant, mixed company. "We'll head out after supper. He's been gone four days. A few more hours won't make much difference." So saying, he put the hat on his head, cockeyed as it was, and strode to his wife, crushing a surprised Sarah to his chest. He breathed in her familiar scent of lilac, kissed her hair, saying, "God, I missed you," not caring that everyone was gaping, wishing to hell that he could live a life of peace.

⸺ℓℓ⸺

Night fell quickly in the swamp.

Weak, ragged threads of light died away as twilight succumbed to a liquid darkness. It seeped between the branches of the cottonwood, giant sycamore, and cypress trees, and dripped down the blackened moss to settle in the soft mud.

Beneath the vast canopy of trees, the swamp's heartbeat slowly pulsed—alive, throbbing—a rhythmic silence broken by a startled splash, a slithering. The heartbeat quickened as a man stumbled over twisted roots and through the mire. His clothes hung in tatters, his pants shredded up to his knees, his shirt and coat torn from clawing his way through briars and brambles. An iron collar surrounded his neck, three prongs jutting outward and up, the bell at the end of each prong hammered closed, their clappered-tongues silenced. The upper part of one shoe flapped about his ankle, the sole gone, sucked away, the foot scraped and bleeding. Despite the inky blackness of the night, he ran.

Into the heartbeat of silence.

Just minutes ago, Sawney had been asleep, perched atop a crook of branches, back against the trunk, trying not to startle awake at every splash, every soft plop of muck, trying to sleep at least an hour or two to chase away the exhaustion that plagued his limbs, to forget the pain of his hunger, to subdue the hatred raging in his heart. But then a low keening penetrated his dreams. It continued, mournful, until he jerked awake, heart hammering.

*Nigger hounds.*

In one bound he was out of the tree, off and running.

His lungs burned. His foot screamed as the wounds reopened.

Then, slowly, the howling of the hounds faded away and Sawney heard only his pulse thrumming in his ears, his gasping for breath, his frantic splashing as he crashed through the murk. He even dared to hope that he'd imagined the hounds. That they'd been a nightmare. Nothing more.

Then he heard them again, closer, much closer. He realized that now they came not from behind him, but from his right. Had he circled upon himself? Had they changed direction?

Branches swatted his face and chest. Became tangled in the prongs of his collar. Spider webs caught him across his neck, his open mouth, snapping in protest as he ran blindly through them. Curtains of moss parted and trailed down his shoulders and back as the ground beneath his feet grew firmer.

Still the hounds came, closer.

Untying a bag of pepper from around his neck, he sprinkled the grains behind him as he ran. But then, with a cry of surprise, he stumbled over a log, whacking his shin, and sprawled headlong into muddy water, the air in his lungs expelling with a bubbling whoosh, the bag of pepper flying from his grasp.

He scrambled up, covered in mud and slime, wanting to scream, wanting to kill.

The hounds were almost upon him. He drew a knife from his waistband. For such a crude knife, it was well-balanced, long, sharp, and deadly. Praying he did not get sucked down forever, praying he did not step on an alligator, or a snake, to get at least one chance at those hounds before they ripped him to pieces, he waded deeper into the watery muck, away from the firmer ground, mud oozing up around his ankles, shins, and knees. When the water reached to just below his waist, he squatted, the surface of the water up to his nose.

Hardly had the water settled around Sawney, than they were there. He stiffened and held his breath, listening. The pat of their feet. Their excited whining. The pant of their breath. The snuffling of their noses on the ground. He tried to see them but saw nothing except a vague shape of trees above his head, cast in a faraway moonlight. Then one of them howled, and suddenly, like waking from a nightmare, they were gone. Crashing through the underbrush until all was silent again.

Shivering, he waited, the familiar hatred rising so strong he could taste it. It was the same hatred that had impelled him to hurt Quincy. Quincy, bending his backbone to another man's will, spewing his master's words like vomit, ordering him to go to the whipping post.

That *they* would come, he knew. High on their horses, removed from the slime, they would follow their dogs through the swamps, firearms at the ready, searching for evidence of his passing. If he crawled out of the mire now, he might make new prints, or he might run in circles unawares and stumble right into them. But if he stayed hidden, they might not look deeply, might follow the tracks of the dog pack without so much as a quick glance around. So he waited.

After what seemed an eternity, they came. First a distant yellow light. It grew like a sickness, seeping around tree trunks, through the choking moss and strangling vines, through the torrent of underbrush, growing stronger, stronger, until he could hear voices and the movement of horses.

Beside him, a soft swish. A plop. A brush against his arm.

Then, like their hounds, they were there. Sitting atop their horses on higher, firmer ground, holding up their torches and looking out over the vast, inky pool of murk where he hid among the cypress knees. There were four of them. William Jensey, his brother-in-law John, son Breck, and another man, short and ugly, whom Sawney didn't recognize. He tightened his grip around the haft of the knife, unaware that he was clenching his teeth, his thighs screaming from the effort of squatting.

"The dogs went that way."

"Not so fast, Son." William dismounted, knelt, and picked something up out of the mud. "He's been here. See? Here's his bag of pepper. Probably dropped it by accident."

"Likely threw the hounds off the trail," said John. "They might be off on a wild goose chase."

"Old trick," said the ugly man.

"They'll be back," said John. "They're never fooled for long."

"Meanwhile," said William, "let's take a look around. See if we can find where he went. Maybe we can put the dogs back on the trail."

"If we can't find him this time, William," said John, "I'm done for the night. Got a long day ahead of me tomorrow and I'm beat."

"Won't take long and then we'll go home, I promise."

Sawney watched as the others dismounted and spread out. He watched Breck find some footprints, heard them speculate he'd lost a shoe. Then John found the place where he'd tripped over the log, where he'd scraped some moss off in a slimy streak. But what they couldn't find, what he knew they couldn't see, were his prints in the soft mud beneath the shallow water leading toward the depths where he hid. He hoped he looked like a cypress knee, jutting darkly from the water, shadowy, iron prongs like sticks, not even worth a passing glance. But even as he hoped it, something slithered into his shirt, something cold, long, and sinuous.

*Son of a bitch!*

He closed his eyes. Heart beating wildly. Willing himself to stay silent. To not move. And in the midst of his willing, he knew.

He was being watched.

Without moving his head, Sawney snapped his eyes open. Breck Jensey stood but ten feet away. Torch held high. Staring right at him. Knowing. Looking just like his father, a man Sawney despised even more than he despised Quincy.

Sawney's first impulse was to leap from the water, to stab the boy, to kill the snake that brushed against his ribs, to scream loudly, insanely, before they shot him to death. But there was something in the boy's eyes that arrested him. He could not move.

*I's a dead man.*

"See anything, Son?" his father asked from the other side of the pool.

The boy held Sawney's gaze for a little longer before turning back to his father and saying, "No, nothing."

Sawney released his breath, not realizing he'd been holding it.

"Anything, John? Marshall?"

"Nothing."

"Not a thing, big boy. And I'm with you, John. I'm beat."

A long sigh. "The hounds are coming back. Let's call it a night."

Within minutes, just as Sawney's thighs began to spasm, they were gone. The snake, the hounds, the humans, the horses, taking with them the torchlight. It faded away and disappeared, slithering around the tree trunks, leaving nothing but blackness, nothing but the pulse beat of silence.

## Chapter 5

IT TOOK THREE WEEKS for Quincy to die. Perhaps the sting of death would have been lessened had his murderer been apprehended, but Sawney was still at large. They'd tried to find him on numerous occasions, and had finally resorted to hiring negro hunters from Mississippi whose advertisement read that the undersigned had an excellent pack of hounds and that persons desiring a negro caught would do well to contact.

Reports of the runaway surfaced here and there: a dead cow over at Rockwells', a missing hog at Saffins', the Cobbs' barn burned, along with two calves and a dog. (Although the last accusation infuriated William. "Where's the proof?" he demanded. "Where are the witnesses? I'll be humbugged if I'll pay that lying rascal Cobb a brass nickel! His barn was nothing but a pile of sticks and scraps anyhow.")

John tried everything to save Quincy's life. From warm poppy fomentations to leeches to hot flannels and fly-blisters. From laudanum to decoctions of wormwood, to cinchona, to salves of beeswax and sweet oil. A cornucopia of cures that would surely have revived a scalped elephant, much less a man. But despite all of John's efforts, despite Sarah's prayers and attention to Quincy's comfort, despite William's reassurances to Quincy that *of course* he would get well, Quincy slipped from this life to the next during the first week of June, on a shirt-soaking, humid day when all hands were setting the sweet potato slips, the cane was two to three feet high, and the cotton crop promised to be as good as any, not counting the stand taken over by grasshoppers, worms, and by bugs of the general variety, a day when everything stank of growth and manure and sweat.

Breck sat in a chair on the hospital's gallery, looking out over the yard. Voices murmured from inside the hospital. Someone walked toward the door, boots on a floor, and then William was on the gallery with him, hat in hand, his face weary and lined and pinched, looking older than Breck had ever seen him. His father gazed out to where the women stirred the laundry in cauldrons, surrounded by steam and chickens and clothes hanging out to dry. Normally the sound of their chatter was an ever-present reality, as assured as spices in Aunt Delia's pumpkin bread, but today they wrung out the clothes in a silence dreary as gray water. Things were strangely silent even at the nursery, a building usually bursting with boisterous children, its gallery home to rocking chairs and toddlers and old aunts cradling infants. Now, other than the occasional face peeping out the window, there was nothing.

"He's gone," his father said. "Quincy's gone."

Breck nodded. From the time he'd stepped into the hospital room at noon and seen Quincy lying stiffly—cheeks hollow, eyes sunken and glassy, struggling to draw each wheezy breath—he'd known the man was dying. Breck had murmured his goodbyes. A lump forming in his throat. Feeling uncomfortable. Like an interloper, an intruder in one of the most intimate experiences of a man's life. Then he'd left to wait on the gallery. Now, upon his father's announcement, the lump in his throat swelled as if he'd swallowed a cocklebur.

"Quincy was the best driver I ever owned," his father was saying, "and a good man. Been with us since he was eleven or twelve or thereabouts. Used to run around with me getting into all kinds of mischief." His father peered at him, and Breck was astonished to see moisture in William's eyes. It was the first time he'd seen his father near weeping. "Used to pole the creek together. Like you and Footy." Several crows took flight from the split-rail fence. William brushed his eyes with the back of his hand and sighed deeply, his gaze following the birds. "I fear his wife will take it hard."

Breck picked at a spot on his pants, wishing it were over. "We going to bury him today?"

"Much as I hate to. Too blamed hot to let him sit around. Well, time to inform the masses, I guess."

His father stepped onto the grass, paused, then turned back to Breck. And where the softness had been in his eyes, a fire now burned. "I'll kill him, that Sawney. I swear to you, Son, I'll kill him if it's the last thing I do." With that, he replaced his hat and set off stiffly in the direction of the plantation bell.

Breck watched him, wondering what his father would say, what he'd do, if he knew that Breck had let Sawney go. He'd never intended to let the man go. Wanted him caught just as much as the next fellow, he supposed. Sawney was destructive. A thief, and now a murderer, certainly more trouble than they could handle, or *wanted* to handle. But that night in the swamp when their gazes locked, Breck was struck dumb, his voice incapable of forming the simple words: I've found him. Or, there he is. Instead, Breck had stared at the man, at his eyes reflecting the glare of the firebrand, at the man's head, mud-slicked, half submerged, at the debris dangling from the iron prongs encircling him as if he were part of the landscape, and said nothing. Even now, sitting on the porch, watching his father's tall figure stride away, he wasn't certain why he'd let Sawney go. He supposed it was because of what it brought out in his father. A darker, more menacing side that Breck both feared and loathed. Maybe it was simple mercy. Or maybe it was a grudging respect for someone who refused to be obedient no matter the cost, perceiving in some vague way that in Sawney's struggle for freedom lay his own.

The sound of the bell rippled through the air. The shudder and sigh of an entire plantation. Breck stood, aware that with the bell's ringing, everyone had stopped what they were doing and that all eyes had turned toward the hospital. The laundry workers, paddles in hand. The children, filed now out onto the gallery of the nursery, two old aunts in the doorway. The kitchen crew, crowding out the back kitchen door, hands white with flour.

Breck stepped off the gallery and put on his hat.

Overhead, two vultures circled.

And from the vicinity of the dairy house, someone began to wail.

The cemetery for the Jensey slaves was a motley affair. Located adjacent to a cotton field and nearer the cypress quarter than the pine quarter, it was a grassy series of elongated mounds and valleys oriented at haphazard angles to one another, as if a gigantic mole had burrowed beneath for the last half-century. For the most part, the graves were unmarked, save for the occasional willow tree that sprang from a grave, roots long ago passed through the body of the deceased, bone to root, dust to dust.

The funeral procession had begun at the hospital, led by the Jensey family, all astride their horses. More than a few gaped at Miss Sarah astride a petite chestnut mare, for only those born before 1838 could recall seeing her ride, an occupation she appeared to happily leave to her husband and children. Indeed, she looked ill at ease in the saddle, knuckles strained white around the reins, as if the gentle mare who liked nothing more than to munch her oats might suddenly take off, flying over hedges and dashing through streams and swamps in her race to Kingdom Come.

Behind the Jensey family shuffled Quincy's wife and children in varying degrees of sorrow, followed by the rumbling ox cart which conveyed the pine coffin. The remainder of the Jensey slaves brought up the rear, dodging the steaming piles of ox dung. The procession streamed out of the yard and down the road, through kitchen gardens ripe with turnips, collards, peas, strawberries, beans, squash, and an abundance of watermelon (the Jensey's favorite during the dog days of summer), through the cypress quarter, and into the cemetery, where they gathered beneath a giant willow.

Years of manning the plow had both built and hardened Cyrus' body. Earlier predictions as to his eventual size now rendered unnecessary, Cyrus was, at almost nineteen years old, the largest man in the plantation workforce, both in height and girth. A stranger to Cyrus would have thought him intimidating, perhaps capable of snapping a man's neck the way one might snap a chicken's. Those who knew him could have told the stranger that Cyrus wouldn't swat a fly, much less snap anyone's neck. That his massive hands, armored with calluses, had done nothing more violent in all his years at Fox Creek than furrow the dirt or accidentally kill some weeds or grubs or worms during the course of guiding his plow.

He stood next to Footy under the shade of the willow in a valley between two mounds, hat clutched to his chest, the trailing end of a willow branch resting on his head like a laurel. Sweat stained his shirt under both arms, trickled a path down his spine and chest. He wished he'd had time to bathe, to scrub his hair, to change into his one clean shirt that he'd laundered the night before, but following the announcement of Quincy's death, he was set to work unhitching his team of oxen from the plow and harnessing them to the cart, helping to place Quincy in his casket, nailing it shut, and sliding the casket onto the cart's rough planks. And even though he'd then wanted to hurry back to his cabin to change, people were already arriving for the funeral procession with scarcely a breath between.

Where Monette was, he did not know.

He'd waited for her by the hospital as more and more people arrived, cooks, house servants, babes in arms—everyone. He'd waited long after the Jenseys led the procession out of the yard, the clot of people unwinding along the road to the cemetery like a ball of string. Finally, unable to wait any longer, he'd joined the tail end of the procession, glancing back at the big house again and again, wondering, *Monette, where is you?*

Someone was saying a prayer. A bee, heavy with pollen, brushed Cyrus' shirtfront. Everyone had their head bowed, and though Cyrus also lowered his head, and though he was sorry, real sorry for Quincy, had shed tears for him while hammering the casket closed, he cast his glance about. Had he missed her?

"She ain't here," Footy whispered from beside him. "You can stop all that fool lookin'."

"But where is she?" Cyrus asked, waving a mosquito away.

"How should I know? Maybe she sick."

*Sick!* Just the thought of his little Monette lying prostrate on a bed somewhere, sick, needing him, perhaps even dying like Quincy, sent a shiver of fear through Cyrus, as if the muggy heat had suddenly turned icy. Could he do so, he would gladly run to the big house and carry her to safety, to the hospital, hold her in his arms and never let her go. Could he do so. But the chasm between the fields and the big house loomed so large, the Mississippi River might as well run between. The big house stood like a fortress, impregnable except for a chosen few. Cyrus had only dared to enter the big house once, two summers ago. He hadn't been feeling well, not *real* well anyway, had a niggle in the back of his throat and coughed at Miss Sarah to show her what he meant, all the while looking around him at the lamps, the chairs, the desk with cubbyholes and slots and crannies, the books and papers, the well of ink, the paintings on the walls. And when Miss Sarah gave him a pill and told him to go rest for the remainder of the day, Cyrus had shuffled his feet as slowly as he could, hoping Monette would see him and they could talk together like old times. But in the minute it took him to shuffle out the back door, he'd seen nothing more alive than a cat slumbering in a corner of the loggia.

Even on Sundays, when all the workforce gathered in the yard for inspections and to receive their weekly food rations, Cyrus was relegated to the back row, seeming miles away from where the house servants stood near the front. He'd have to holler to get her attention, which he did on occasion after inspections were over, not understanding why, oh why, she always hurried away so quickly, why she never heard him. Had she gone deaf? Perhaps that was why she was sick.

"I hope she don't die," whispered Cyrus, wondering if people could actually die from going deaf.

Footy rolled his eyes. "Course, she ain't gonna die, fool. She probably got the sniffles, or a bad toe, or something like that. Now hush 'fore you gets us in trouble."

Then, with an "in the name of Jesus Christ we pray" and an "Amen," the prayer ended. People coughed and moved about. A baby started to fuss. Mars William spoke, asking if there was anything anyone wanted to say about Quincy, because he was a good man, and good men were hard to find.

Cyrus looked away from Mars William, hoping he wouldn't call on him to say anything. Cyrus couldn't speak in crowds. Could hardly speak, period.

The one time he'd met Monette face-to-face since he'd moved to the fields, he'd acted like the fool Footy always said he was. The one time in eight years. It had happened three summers ago, when he was fifteen or so. He'd been fishing at the creek with Footy on a lazy Sunday afternoon. After catching a few fish, they headed back to cook them up for supper. Just over the creek bank, on the path headed straight toward him, strolled Monette arm-in-arm with Missie Kate, not five feet away, looking just as startled as he felt. He snatched his hat off his head, nodded politely, tried to form the words, "How do, Missie Kate? How do, Monette?" but his mind clouded, he found himself unable to breathe properly, and all that came out of his mouth was an agonized, "How d-d-d-d—" that seemed to last a lifetime. Cyrus knew disgust when he saw it, for Missie Kate had it written all over her face. She pushed past him with an *Ugh!*

But that wasn't what stuck in his memory like a bone in his craw. It was when Monette looked at him as if he were a stranger, as if she feared him even, saying nothing more than, "Excuse me," hurrying after Kate, leaving him alone on the path with Footy and three fish and a heart flailing around his insides like a wounded bird.

*Monette, where is you?*

—ell—

Over the past few weeks, Monette had searched the attic whenever she had a chance, which wasn't often. Once, on a Sunday afternoon following dinner, when it was so crushingly hot that everyone drooped onto their beds, languid as convalescents. Once, when Lizzy was off visiting Fatima at the same time Mr. Gilbert was gone to town. And now, while everyone was at Quincy's funeral.

The first time, Monette had rummaged at random, deciding afterward that she had to be more methodical: begin at one end, work her way from this side to that side, moving toward the center of the room, and finish at the other end. During all her methodical searching, she wondered what it was she was looking for, how she'd know when and if she found it, and, worst of all, whether she'd already passed it by but hadn't recognized it as anything more than what it was: a rug, a dish, a lace collar, a book, a pair of winter boots. . . .

Today, as on the other two days, the heat of the attic was unbearable. At least in her attic bedroom, there were two windows she could open. But the center attic room was windowless, and though she'd opened the door to her bedroom and the shutters were wide open, not a breath of air stirred.

She would not be here were it not for the dreams, the memories. The man from her past, a man whom she loved—she knew she loved him, although she didn't know why—taking her by her child's hand up the attic stairs and telling her night after night, *find it, find it.*

Hurrying, ears tuned to the creak of stairs, sweat soaking her clothes, eyes stinging with salt, Monette rifled through six trunks, eight, nine, moving between trunks and baskets after a quick going over of their contents. She shuddered more than once when spiders scurried out of her way, some ambling fatly, looking as if pickings in the attic were the best around.

There was the bonnet Kate had given her, the one she'd torn while trying to follow Kate into the top branches of the magnolia. There was Kate's old sheet music—yellowed, crumpled, smudged, and scribbled with pencil. The ivory and silver comb and mirror set Kate had received as a gift, her favorite before Monette dropped the mirror and it cracked. A sheaf of compositions, homework assigned years ago to Breck by Mr. Gilbert. She blew the dust away, wanting to read the compositions, to laugh with him later about his mistakes—if even he made any—but she was drenched in her own stink, this was taking too long, and she wasn't even halfway through searching the attic.

*"Zut!"* she said aloud, sneezing.

For a silly, terrified moment, she wondered if Miss Mehitable had heard her, but immediately dismissed the thought. Ole Miss was sleeping in her room. Monette had made sure of that before coming to the attic. The woman's snores had vibrated through her bedroom door like the squawk of an out-of-tune fiddle. No, she was safe. For now. Besides, Monette assured herself, even if Ole Miss awakened soon, she would no doubt assume everyone was at the funeral.

Crawling to the back, clearing a path as she went, Monette crouched under the sloped roof. Flies droned, circling. She heard the scrabbling of a bird on the roof overhead. In the distance, the screech of a peacock. She checked the contents of a basket—nothing to speak of, a set of bowls, a bent pair of shears, a lady's fan, broken—then moved it aside. Beneath was a chest encased with two leather straps, one of which dangled loosely, nibbled by mice. She unbuckled the remaining leather strap, then fumbled with the clasp of the chest. It was rusted, stuck.

*Ça alors!* I'm too hot for this!

Monette fetched the bent pair of shears from the basket and whacked the clasp smartly with the handle, horrified by the loud clank, telling herself that after this, she was finished for the day.

She pushed up the lid, rusty hinges creaking, dust filling the air.

At first, she saw nothing out of the ordinary. Baby clothes of white linen, embroidered, stinking of camphor. A mourning dress of black bombazine. Digging deeper, underneath, was another garment. And as her fingers grazed the soft velvet, she knew.

She had found it.

*It.*

Hardly daring to breathe, Monette withdrew it from the chest and spread it out atop the other clothes. Even crushed as it was, worn, neglected, stained, she knew it had once been a fine dress, costly, the color of mint julep, with rows of flounces, tiny buttons, ribbons, and bows. Touching it, seeing it, a vibration started deep inside her and flowed outward, like a long-forgotten song whose melody grows more discernible by degrees.

This is *my* dress. Not a hand-me-down from Kate, but mine. *La mienne.*

She rubbed her cheek against the fabric, melody of memory singing down her limbs, surging to the tips of her fingers, the ends of her toes, through her breath, her heart, as if his hand, once again, caressed her cheek.

She smiled, remembering his kindly face, his hair of snow, his eyes crinkled at the corners as he returned her smile.

*Ah, ma chérie, my daughter.*

*Papa Léon. It is you.*

# *Chapter 6*

M ONETTE WAS HUDDLED ON the floor, dress pressed against her cheek, when there came a sound from downstairs. At first, she took no heed, but when the sound came again, a clink like glassware, she snapped her head up, a cry wedged in her throat.

*Mehitable!*

Pausing no more than a blink, Monette stuffed the remaining garments back into the chest and shut the lid. With her dress in hand, she scrambled back between the trunks and dashed into her bedroom, cursing her own heaving breath, the sound of her shoes on the floorboards. She shoved her dress under her bed, then whirled, half expecting to see Miss Mehitable glaring at her through the open doorway, knowing what she'd been up to. But there was no one.

Outside, through the open window, Monette heard a door open, then shut. She sighed with relief when she saw it was Ole Miss leaving her bedroom in the south addition, looking cross as a preacher in Hell. She ambled toward the privy, a task which, Monette knew, took Ole Miss no less time than it would take her to run a mile.

Now thirsty, feeling as wrung out as the rag she used to scrub the floors, Monette smoothed her calico dress and hurried downstairs, the relative coolness a welcome relief. She was in the butler's pantry, guzzling a glass of water, when she heard it again. A clink of glassware. Coming from the dining room.

Monette cracked open the door and peered through.

It was Marshall McCain. Hat off, shirt sleeves rolled up, he stood at the sideboard, having just poured a glass of brandy. He downed the brandy in two gulps, wiped his mouth with his forearm, then looked directly at her, his eyes small and frightening. "Fetch me something to eat, girl."

"'Scuse me, M-m-mars B-Breck," Cyrus stuttered after the funeral ended, the final hymn still humming through the willow branches. He hovered at Breck's elbow, where he stood before the grave, hat off. "D-d-does you know wh-wh-wh-where Monette is?"

Breck looked at him. He said nothing, put on his hat, and strode over to where the rest of his family was unhitching their horses and climbing into saddles. Cyrus followed. In one fluid movement, Breck mounted his horse. Cyrus shielded his eyes, gazing up, the sun bright behind Breck's head.

"D-d-does you—"

"I heard you, Cyrus. To answer your question, I don't know." He turned his horse to leave, but Cyrus put a hand on the horse's halter, stopping him, surprising himself as much as it appeared to surprise Breck.

"S-s-s-sorry," he said, quickly removing his hand.

Straightening in the saddle, Breck eyed him, his face closed like the door of the big house.

Cyrus dropped his gaze to Breck's boot, to the glistening hide of the horse's flank, the rifle in the gun holster.

When Breck spoke again, his voice was softer, and Cyrus wondered if he was remembering the times when they used to pole the stream together, catch frogs, and hunt for arrowheads. "Maybe she'll be at the dance tonight. Sorry, Cyrus."

"What you go and do that for?" asked Footy, after Breck had ridden away. "You's lucky Mars Breck didn't just up and slap your fool black hide."

Cyrus was only half listening, still watching Breck ride away. "You think she'll come, Footy?"

"What you talking 'bout?"

"You think Monette will come tonight? To the dance? Mars Breck said she might." Cyrus looked at Footy, hopeful.

Footy stared back, his eyes seeming to bug out even more than they usually did. Then he nodded his head slowly, saying, "Yeah, Cyrus, I does.

I think she'll be there all right. Just like I think I can lower my bucket into the well and it come up full of whiskey every time."

Cyrus was still trying to figure out exactly what Footy meant by this—whether he thought Monette was or wasn't coming to the dance—when Footy laid a hand on his arm, and his voice came out low and solemn, like it did sometimes when he talked about how his sister up and died from convulsive fever, and how the convulsions shook the cabin timbers before she finally lay still. "Look, Cyrus, forget her. I mean it, you gots to forget her. She a house servant, and house servants don't pay no nevermind to us field hands. And that's the truth of it. 'Sides, since when has she ever come to one of our dances? She probably forgot all 'bout you anyways."

Footy said more, but Cyrus was no longer listening, his gaze turned instead in the direction of the big house, wondering where she was now, whether she was thinking of him, knowing she would look real pretty at the dance this evening, whatever she wore.

Monette set the tray on the table beside Marshall: a thick slice of ham, bread, butter, apricot jam, a bowl of fresh strawberries, cream, and half a pickled cucumber. She arranged his plate, his silverware atop a napkin, the smell of brandy and tobacco strong. Then she curtsied, waiting for him to dismiss her.

But he did not. Instead, he placed his napkin on his lap, took a bite of ham, and began to butter his bread, asking in that loud, stinging voice of his, "Where is everybody?"

Monette cleared her throat, wishing she could go to her room and be alone, wishing he would stop looking at her. Rarely did a guest of the Jenseys pay the house servants any more attention than one might spare a stool. "The—the driver, Quincy, he died and—"

"Speak up, girl."

"Quincy, the driver. He died today, and they've all gone to bury him."

Marshall shoved a hunk of bread into his mouth and chewed noisily. "And you didn't go?"

"No sir."

"Why not?"

She shrugged. "I don't know."

He ate for a while, saying nothing, instead slurping, chewing, licking his fingers, and swishing his brandy around in his mouth before gulping it all down. She watched him out of the corner of her eye, agreeing with Kate that Marshall McCain looked rather like a scuttling crab when he ate. But then he turned his small eyes on her, eyes the color of river mud, and she looked away, her face stony, pretending he did not scare her.

"Monette, is it?"

"Yessir."

"Dish me some strawberries. No cream."

"Yessir."

She spooned some strawberries onto his plate.

"Are you ill, Monette?"

"No sir."

"Your hands are trembling, and you're soaked in sweat like you just ran around the horse track with a horde of devils nipping at your heels."

Monette said nothing.

"Maybe," he said, laughing, holding out his empty glass, shaking it from side to side for a refill, "I interrupted you in the middle of something."

She took the glass, flinching away from the casual brush of his fingers, glad to escape his closeness, if only for a few seconds. At the sideboard, she poured more brandy from the decanter, the fumes making her temples throb, willing her hands not to shake. For the first time in her life, she prayed Miss Mehitable would lumber into the big house, causing a racket loud enough to wake the dead. She set the glass on the table and stepped back, glancing at him just as he popped a strawberry into his mouth.

He caught her looking and smiled. "Or maybe you're just frightened." Juice bubbled in the corner of his mouth. "Do I frighten you?"

Again, she looked away. At the crumbs on the tablecloth, still left from breakfast. At the etched glass fly catcher filled with sugar water and poison. "No sir."

Here, Marshall barked with laughter. He slapped his knee, wiped his mouth with his napkin, and tossed it on the table. "You're a terrible liar. Do you know how I know you're a terrible liar? Huh, Monette?"

"No sir."

"Because I can smell it." He tapped the side of his nose. "I've got a good nose for smelling, and can smell all kinds of things. For instance, not only can I smell a liar, but I can also smell fear. Ever smelled fear, Monette?" He popped another strawberry into his mouth.

She heard the squelch of his chewing. His breath in and out of his nostrils.

"I asked you a question."

"No sir."

"And, I can smell a woman." His voice lowered. "Are you a woman, Monette?"

Monette closed her eyes, feeling her pulse pound in her neck, roar in her head, imagining Marshall lying on the floor, a pair of bent shears sticking out of his chest.

"Look at me and answer my question. I'm not going to hurt you."

She opened her eyes. Clenched her jaw. Stared at his hands.

"Here. Smell this." He scooted his chair back, stood, took a strawberry from his plate, and held it under her nose. "Go ahead. Inhale its perfume. That's it. See what I mean? The nose is a powerful tool. Tells you all kinds of things." He stood close, too close. His sourness exhaling all over her face. "Now bite it."

He pressed the strawberry to her closed lips, its flesh cool and firm, the tiny hairs softly prickling.

"I said, bite it."

As he said this, from the rear loggia came the unmistakable sounds of Miss Mehitable: the rap of the cane on the floor, the grunts, the Lord a'mercies, the slam of the door.

With a snort, Marshall stepped back, took Monette's hand from where it hung limply at her side, and placed the strawberry into her palm. Then he sat back down and stabbed the cucumber with his fork, saying, "You can go."

# Chapter 7

IT WAS SARAH'S MOST uncomfortable pregnancy yet. Maybe it was because of the heat—capable of melting bone and sinew by mid-morning. Maybe it was her size, her belly so enlarged she could scarcely believe she was only in her fifth month. Could it be she had miscalculated? Her feet swelled without mercy, pinching and throbbing inside her largest pair of shoes. Or perhaps she had merely forgotten the more uncomfortable aspects of her previous pregnancies. After all, everyone knew that the memory of pain dulled with time, like a ship sailing ever farther toward the horizon.

On this evening following Quincy's funeral, Sarah sat at the mistress' station opposite William at the head of the table, smiling, making small talk, laughing politely when appropriate, pretending not to pick at her food, willing herself not to vomit.

Marshall was telling a joke, talking around the ham he'd just put in his mouth, after first assuring William that, yes, yes, it was a clean joke, appropriate for the ears of the gentler sex. "What's the difference between the Prince of Wales, an orphan, a bald-headed man, and a gorilla?" He grinned, clearly enjoying himself in that way that Sarah detested so much.

Everyone thought. Alexander Saffin and John (both of whom, along with Marshall, Breck, and William, planned to go on an early-morning deer hunt), Kate, Mehitable, Emma, and the twins.

George—who, at seven and a half years old, had informed everyone that he was George now, *not* Georgie—said, "Intelligence?"

Saffin, touching his own thinning scalp, said, "Quantity of hair, perhaps?" They all laughed.

After a few more failed attempts to solve the riddle (amid requests of "Tell us! Tell us!") Marshall answered, "The Prince of Wales is an heir apparent. The orphan has ne'er a parent. The bald-headed man, sorry Saffin, has no hair apparent. And the gorilla has a hairy parent!"

While everyone laughed again, Sarah excused herself and hurried into the butler's pantry where Monette was slicing bread and Mammy Hester was wiping her hands on her apron. One look at her, and they knew. It was a familiar routine. There was a flurry of brown hands, and a basin appeared from nowhere just as her stomach turned inside out. Mammy Hester wrapped her arm around Sarah's shoulders, saying, "Oh, my poor honey chile. When this ever gonna stop?" and eased her into one of the chairs. Monette dampened a cloth, and when the heaving subsided, washed Sarah's face as if she were a babe herself, afterward handing her a glass of water to rinse out her mouth.

"Let them go ahead and laugh away in there, Miss Sarah," said Mammy Hester. "You just rest here a spell. Lord a'mercy, you looks like something what the cat dragged in."

Sarah nodded, weakened, her belly muscles sore. Her fatigue was more than nausea, more than the pregnancy itself. It was the restless nights, brought on by the dread of giving birth, coupled with an occasional, fleeting terror that was gradually worsening. Beginning about a month ago, it seemed she slept with one eye open, every sense alert and strained.

There had been a fire last night. Javier Gustine's carriage house. Arson suspected. Saffin had given them the news when they'd returned this afternoon from Quincy's funeral, Sarah weary from riding and glad to be on the ground again. Saffin and Marshall were sitting on the gallery, brandies and cigars in hand. Sarah had expected William to erupt into a white-hot fury upon receiving the news, but he surprised her, surprised everyone, by nodding calmly and saying, "Let's hope those negro hunters from Mississippi are worth their salt." He then poured himself a brandy, lit a cigar, and whiled away the rest of the afternoon with his friends, their jokes and laughter carrying through the window of Sarah's bedroom as she lay panting in the heat.

The door to the butler's pantry swung open, and Emma came in, the door swinging shut behind her. She hurried to Sarah's side. "Sarah, dear, are you feeling all right?"

With Emma's entrance, Mammy Hester and Monette returned to their tasks and were soon bustling about the butler's pantry, while Nat and Zoe (the cook's eleven-year-old daughter and Fatima's replacement) brought food from the kitchen. They were laughing and chatting, but fell to silence and hurried out when they saw Sarah and Emma, leaving the heavy smells of fried chicken and eggplant in their wake.

"I'm fine, Mother. My stomach just turned, is all."

"Why don't you go upstairs and rest? Let me play the hostess." Her mother's green eyes looked so tenderly into her own. "It's not like I haven't done it before."

Sarah shook her head and forced a smile. "No, thank you, that's all right. I have to admit I'm weary of my room. I've been staring at those same four walls a lot lately. I've got every crack and stain memorized."

Emma sat and took Sarah's hands in hers. Her hands were surprisingly cool. "All the more reason why you should come to Woodleigh for a visit. It's been so long."

Her mother had asked her this many times before, and Sarah always replied that she'd love to, but that she was much too busy. Maybe later. But this time, when her mother asked, Sarah felt like a child again. Like a four-year-old needing to curl into her mother's lap and allow her to stroke her hair and whisper sweet things and rock her until she fell into a deep slumber. "Yes, Mama. That sounds fine."

"When?"

Sarah laid her hand atop her belly. "Soon, Mama, I promise. Really." To Sarah's surprise, tears stung her eyes. She looked away, hoping her mother hadn't seen, knowing she had.

With a swish of fabric, her mother's arms enveloped her. Sarah dropped her head to her mother's shoulder, her body wilting like a flower, as if all the tension, the misery of every time she'd leaned her head over a basin, melted away and disappeared. She heard the door to the butler's pantry open and close, open and close, the clink of dishes, more laughter from the dining room, but at that moment, she cared about nothing, nothing except the feel of her mother's arms around her, loving her.

Monette's hand brushed against Breck's as she leaned over the dining table to refill his water glass. Breck was in the middle of nodding at Saffin. But whether the senator was talking about how the secession crisis of last year had been averted by a series of compromises, or how the new Fugitive Slave Law now made it more difficult for slaves to escape, or the location of the best fishing holes at Piney Lake (all topics he bandied about with equal ease), Breck could no longer say. Because with Monette's touch, an electrifying shock wave surged up his arm, restarted his heart, stopped up his lungs, his ears, and clogged his brain.

To him, it seemed impossible that everyone in the dining room didn't observe the shock wave. That they didn't turn to one another and remark in astonishment, did you see that? His father to his mother: This must be your doing. All that equality before God nonsense. Saffin to Marshall: You see, it's the institution that corrupts them. It's like dangling a beefsteak in front of a dog and expecting him not to eat it. Kate staring at him, open-mouthed: You *love* her?

But the conversation carried on as usual under the breezy *creak-creak* of the shoo-fly. Monette moved around the table, refilling water glasses. Breck pretended to focus on Saffin, nodding. Thomas dropped his fork on the floor. Then everyone laughed at something Saffin said. Breck laughed too, but late.

He hadn't met with Monette secretly since his return from New Orleans a few weeks ago, since they'd discovered Sawney missing and all hell had broken loose. There were many reasons why he hadn't, he supposed. Not enough time, exhaustion from so many manhunts, too many days spent supervising in the fields because of Quincy being near death, on and on. And at first perhaps, these were reasons enough. But Breck knew the real reason was none of these. It was a decision he had made, a decision born of a heightened sense of danger. With Sawney's disappearance, it seemed everyone was on edge. As if, around each corner of every outbuilding, Sawney crouched with hoe in hand, ready to scalp any unsuspecting soul who had been foolish enough, oblivious enough, to not smell the danger, a smell acrid as the forest air the second before one pulls the trigger, firing a bullet between the eyes of a doe.

Breck didn't know if he was being paranoid or not. Maybe the general sense of danger had everything to do with Sawney and nothing to do with him and Monette. Maybe. But one night about a week ago, lying naked on his bed, Breck forced himself to look frankly at the situation.

If they were ever caught . . .

*If Monette was caught . . .*

His father had never made a secret of the fact that he abhorred relations between white men and their servant women. Not only were such relations illegal, but he also thought them a disgusting aberration of nature. That such amalgamation was the surest way for the great United States to fall into ruin. For well-oiled plantations to crumble into chaos. Breck had seen him chase mulattos—grown children of a neighboring planter, well-dressed with hats and canes and bonnets and silks—from the quarters at Fox Creek where they were passing through. Yelling at them to not come back. Ever. And to tell that father of theirs to keep his spawn where they belonged. So Breck could well-imagine his father's outrage should he learn of Breck and Monette's secret liaison. Never mind learning that Breck *loved her.* Over and over, he heard his father's voice thundering in his head, Good God! Have you learned *nothing?*

Not only was Breck in love, but he was simultaneously thumbing his nose at every law written in the books by teaching Monette to read and write. Was he a fool to have allowed it? Surely, he did not think that they could spend the rest of their days comfortably reading Shakespeare and Sophocles without a care in the world? Slaves had been imprisoned. Strung up and flogged. *Sold,* for less. He could not bear it if Monette were to suffer for *any* reason, much less because of his recklessness. He could not bear to never see her again, to know that she was owned by someone else, enduring God knows what. Yes, he was a fool. *A fool!* That night, lying there in the darkness alone, breathing in the memory of her scent, he had pleasured himself, moaning, imagining she lay beneath him, and that the world remained ignorant of their bliss, that the danger was only his imagination. Afterward he lay in a pool of his sweat, feeling raw, dirty, unsatisfied, and angry.

Today at the funeral when Cyrus, voice husky as the mating cry of an alligator, kept pestering him about Monette, it was all Breck could do not to punch Cyrus in the face, an animal reaction that both shocked and repulsed him. If Breck would not, *could not,* further his relationship with Monette, why then this reluctance, more than reluctance, this *refusal* to allow someone else to court her? Someone who had, obviously, loved her for a very long time, for Cyrus wore his love like a garment, hanging all over him and plain to see. But when Cyrus had asked him if he knew where Monette was, Breck no longer saw the long-ago boy who used to pole the creek with him. Instead, all Breck saw was a brute of a man, stupid as oatmeal, smothering Monette beneath his dirty, smelly embrace.

"Breck will wait another term, isn't that right, Son?"

They were all looking at him. Wait another term for what? Breck nodded and said, "Yes, that's right," then lifted his glass of brandy and took a larger gulp than he intended.

His father cocked an eyebrow as if he knew Breck hadn't been listening. "I need him here to help me with this year's sugar harvest. Got to make certain everything's in good running order before he heads off to college next year. Can't do it without him."

Saffin smiled at Breck. "You're what, seventeen now?"

Breck nodded.

"Have you chosen your course of study yet?"

"Law." Breck cleared his throat and said it again when his voice came out as a croak.

"A worthy profession," said Saffin. "Who knows? If you have an interest, perhaps when you graduate I can find a place for you on my staff. There's always room for bright young men who have a mind for the intricacies of politics and who appreciate the subtle shades of democracy." Here Saffin winked at William, as if they shared a private joke, as if Saffin's invitation was based less on shades of democracy than upon his daughter, Lucy, a girl whom Breck found about as alluring as he did little Amy Parsons, five years old and still making mud pies.

"Once again, Saffin, spoken like a true politician," said Marshall, talking around the potatoes in his mouth. "All flowery nonsense and ambiguity."

Breck raised his glass to Saffin. "Thank you, Senator. I'll be sure to remember your generous invitation through the long months of study."

"Do you know yet which university?" asked Breck's uncle, John.

Breck glanced at William. They'd had long discussions about this very topic. Breck had wanted to go up North at Mr. Gilbert's urging, where the quality of education was arguably unrivaled. But William had put his foot down, deciding to keep him close to home. Not only so he could be close to Fox Creek should his father need him, but because the Northern institutions, in his father's opinion, now crawled with raving fanatics who polluted the impressionable minds of Southern boys with abolitionist propaganda. "I'll be attending the Centenary College at Jacksonville. They've already accepted me."

"Jacksonville!" exclaimed Saffin, beaming. Breck had the sudden, uncomfortable impression that Jacksonville wasn't nearly far enough away from Lucy. "Why, that's wonderful! Hardly a stone's throw away. It must be a great comfort, Miss Sarah, to know your son will be close by."

At the end of the table nearest the butler's pantry, Breck's mother nodded. Despite her ready smile, Breck thought she looked tired. Dark half-moons under her eyes. Her complexion wan, like aged linen. "Yes," she replied, "it is a great comfort."

"Sarah," said John. "Why don't you go rest?"

"Please, Sarah," said Emma, "just for a little while."

Sarah hesitated, then nodded. After she excused herself with a brief apology, Breck and the rest of the men sat back down.

"William studied law," said Mehitable, belching, telling Kate to pass her the snap peas. "Isn't that right, William?"

"Yes, Mother," William said before returning his attention to Saffin. "And while Breck may attain a law degree, as have many Southern gentlemen, his priority is to Fox Creek. He is a planter, first and foremost."

"Naturally." Saffin leaned back in his chair. "As your eldest son, it is only fitting." He turned to George and Thomas, smiling and winking. "Not that the two of you won't make fine planters some day. But you've got a little growing to do yet."

George looked at Saffin, his expression serious. "We went to the fields yesterday. Cotton's looking good. We should get a good price for it this year."

Everyone chuckled, and George looked pleased with himself. Thomas, not to be outdone, said, "We need to send the hoe gang to the willow bottoms tomorrow. The weeds have taken over."

"Well," said Saffin, laughing, "I guess I was mistaken."

"Finally, he admits it," quipped Marshall.

Saffin raised his glass. "To Georgie—"

"*George.*"

"My apologies, young man," said Saffin, inclining his head. "To Masters George and Thomas Jensey, planters *extraordinaire*. Destined to raise the world's finest cotton and to grow the best sugar that ever found its way into a teacup. Here's to you!"

"Hear! Hear!" they all cried, Breck included, clinking glasses and smiling.

"And to Breck Jensey," continued Saffin, "one of the finest young men in all of Louisiana. I'll eat my buttons if he doesn't someday become one of the leaders of our great nation."

Breck felt the blood rush to his face, saw Monette glance at him quickly from where she stood against the wall, as if she perceived more than anyone present that he was both embarrassed and pleased in equal measure.

"Hear! Hear!" everyone cried. Clinking their glasses and smiling once again, they drank jovially, some holding out their glasses for more as Monette and Uncle Henry alternately poured brandy, sherry, and water, depending upon both preference and age, while Mammy Hester bustled in from the butler's pantry with a tray, announcing bread pudding for dessert.

Breck drank, noticing the graceful angles of Monette's arms, the way she leaned in between each person. The tiny beads of sweat on her forehead and neck. But when Monette leaned in to fill Mehitable's sherry, Breck realized with a jolt, like a hot brand to his brain, that his grandmother was watching him.

And in that split second before he looked away, he saw. Eyes like pinpricks. Mouth rigid. A coldness to her features he'd never seen before, her face chiseled from marble rather than flesh, as if one of his mother's garden statues had grown furious after so many years of culinary abstinence, and so wrested itself off its pedestal and stomped indoors to dine.

Breck bent his head over his plate, pretending undue interest in bread pudding. Even so, he felt her eyes on him, watching, as if she were not fooled.

⸻ ℓℓℓ ⸻

It was late, well past ten o'clock. A candle burned atop Breck's bedside table, the flame motionless, suffocated into submission by the heat's damp embrace. Ten-foot-tall drapes stood sentinel, observing the gradation of shadow, from a grainy yellow to the deepest black. Outside, two dogs barked, riled over something.

Monette leaned toward the mirror in the armoire, studying herself, her breath making little puffs of moisture on the glass. She peered into her eyes—swirls of amber around pupils made large in the semi-darkness—so different from the pale blue of Papa Léon's.

*I am the child of a white man.*

She touched her cheek, recognizing the shape of his cheek within her own. The shape of his nose, his brow, her chin. She wondered how she could not have seen him before, encased as he was beneath her skin, her very bones molded from his.

Stepping back, she looked at her body beneath its calico dress, a print of blue and yellow during the daylight, now a vague wash of black and gray. She was thin. Too thin. Her neck was long, her collarbones sharply defined. Her breasts remained small, as did her waist. She pulled up her skirts, her petticoat, and peered at her legs. Thin too, and long. But there was a shapeliness to them that she'd not noticed before. She turned around, glancing at herself from over her shoulder, lifting her skirts higher. Not wearing any drawers due to the heat (oh, how Kate would laugh!), her buttocks appeared like half-moons. There was a fullness that spoke of womanhood, and she wondered what it would feel like to have a man touch her.

Immediately she dropped her skirts, remembering Marshall, the way he'd looked at her, his hand brushing against hers in a casual lie, the revulsion. Her every impulse had cautioned her to flee. To stab him. An impulse that now seemed ridiculous and would certainly cost her her life, even if she dared to commit such an act. No doubt he was a dangerous man. She'd heard as much from the other servants, that she should stay away from him because he had an appetite for chocolate. And she would stay away. She was good at that.

She faced the mirror again and began to unbraid her pigtails, wondering what was keeping Breck. She could afford to stay a little past eleven, as there was a dance tonight for the negroes, something they liked to do whenever someone died, especially someone as influential as Quincy. Monette hadn't known Quincy at all, but he'd seemed pretty decent. Still, she'd never gone to one of their dances and never planned to. She couldn't imagine being among masses of field hands, men like those whom she'd observed at the runaway camp, whose filthiness of body and coarseness of manners were only exceeded by their ignorance and foulness of mouth. The thought of dancing alongside one of them was not only frightening, but absurd. Who were they to her? Even as she dismissed them, she wondered about the man in her dreams, a man black as a full-blooded African, a man who, inexplicably, she felt drawn to, despite the color of his skin.

It is only a dream, she told herself, smiling a bit at her own mawkishness. Besides, how can it be a memory? I have known no man. I have never even been kissed.

Released from its bonds, her hair fell in a mass of curls and waves about her shoulders, ending midway between her shoulder blades. She combed it with her fingers, hating its kinkiness, wishing it could be silky like Kate's. She watched herself in the mirror, fingers sliding in and out of the black tresses, wondering whom she would marry. Like a fog dissolving and the barren landscape made clear, she realized that there was no one. Even if she had but one drop of African blood in her, she could never marry white, not even Breck. It was forbidden. And the thought of someday marrying a house servant, or worse, a field hand, seemed as ill-fitting and horrifyingly laughable as a match between a thoroughbred and a burro. In that moment, her hands now stilled with the realization, she felt alone. A mulatto island. Isolated in a sea of black and white.

She heard a step outside, the scrape of a shoe. Before the door handle turned, she hurried into the armoire, shutting the door quietly, hearing her own breathing along with the sound of the bedroom door opening and closing.

There followed such a long silence that Monette began to fear that perhaps it wasn't Breck after all. But then she heard his whisper. "You can come out now."

She stepped out of the armoire, straightening her hair and clothing, hoping she did not look too silly and rumpled. She smiled. "I've missed you."

"It's late, Monette. I'm very tired." He said this as he crossed the room, loosening his shirt before sinking into one of the cushioned chairs and yanking off his shoes.

Monette could see only the shadow of his face. "I didn't come here to read, Breck. Not tonight. I'm tired too," she said, unable to keep from yawning at the thought. "Lizzy keeps me busy. I think she hates me because of Fatima."

"Then why are you here?"

Monette blinked. Was she imagining the curtness in his voice? And was that brandy she smelled? "I found something today." When he said nothing, she sat on the bed facing him. The mattress of moss crunched with her weight, and she smelled the lavender she had placed in his linens. "I found a dress. It used to be mine when I was a little girl. When I was—*sold.*" The word didn't want to come out. It seemed wedged in the back of her throat, and she had to pry it away. Spit it out. The actual event of being sold was not in her memory, but she knew she must have worn the little green dress by the simple fact that it was here at Fox Creek, and it was hers from *before.* She gazed at Breck, wishing she could see his eyes, see what he was thinking, how he was responding. "Please, I want to know—I *have* to know—tell me what you remember of that day. What you know of—of *me.*"

"Monette, I—I don't know what to tell you. We've been through this before. I really know nothing of you."

"You were there, weren't you?"

"You were put on the auction block and we bought you, yes. But I know nothing of your past. And yes, you were wearing a pretty dress. Green, I think it was. You were very small, I remember. We all were. You, me, and Kate. It was a long time ago."

With his words, Monette realized she'd been hoping Breck could fill in the missing pieces of her life, even though, like he said, she had asked him before. But now she realized how unlikely that was, a dream again, like peeling back an ear of corn hoping for gold nuggets. "My father—he was white."

Even with his face cast in shadow, Monette knew Breck was studying her. "Yes, I know."

"But how do you know such a thing?" she asked, surprised. "I—I thought you said you knew nothing about me."

"Monette, you are a mulatto. Mulattos are conceived through relationships with white men and black women. It's always this way. A white woman would never consort with a black man."

"Why not?"

Breck turned toward the candle. Now she did see his face. It looked tight, brittle, as if it might shatter should he smile or grimace. "Because white women are attracted to power, while white men are attracted to helplessness. I'm sorry to put it so bluntly, Monette."

She drew silent, wondering. Had Papa Léon loved her mother? Had he been attracted, as Breck said, to helplessness? "My father, Papa Léon, he was the master of a plantation."

Breck turned toward her. Now it was his turn to be surprised. "Master of a plantation? How do you know?"

"I remember. That much at least, I remember. It was a sugar plantation with vast fields of cane, plus forests and meadows. I have images of it in my mind."

"And your mother?"

Monette shook her head and a silence grew between them. She wanted to tell him that she didn't know anything about her mother. Not even in the realm of her dreams. That it was as if her mother had never existed. That somehow, against all laws of the universe, Monette had arrived into her father's arms without a mother to bear her, to kiss the downy softness of her newborn head.

Breck finally spoke. "What happened that you were sold?"

Now Monette looked away, remembering, seeing . . . *The afternoon ride on horseback, the storm, the wall of water approaching, horse and rider, gone.* "That dream I used to have? Remember I told you? It wasn't a dream at all. It was a memory. My father died that day. He—he drowned in a crevasse." Her voice fell to a whisper. "I saw it happen. I was there."

"I'm so sorry, Monette."

Upon hearing the tenderness in Breck's voice, tears sprang to Monette's eyes. It was tenderness she longed for, someone to say they were sorry. Someone to wrap their arms about her and rock her, saying, Hush baby, don't cry, it's all right now, it's all right. She sat on the bed, weeping, aching for Breck to come to her, to hold her. But he did not. Instead, when she looked at him through her shimmer of tears, he sat with his head in his hands, fingers laced through his hair. "Breck—"

He said nothing. Did not move.

"Breck, what's the matter? Don't you like me anymore?"

Still, he said nothing.

Her heart twisted, as if with a knife. She tasted anger and heard herself saying, "Am I not helpless enough for you, Breck Jensey?"

"Monette, stop it."

"Do you love Lucy Saffin?" she asked, thinking it all made sense now. Lucy, a white girl from a white family for a white boy. "Is that it?"

"Enough, Monette."

"Then, what? *What's wrong?*"

Breck stood then, towering over her. She hoped that he might pull her to her feet now, take her in his arms, tell her that Lucy meant nothing to him, maybe even tell her that he loved *her*, Monette, but instead he crossed to the washstand, poured water into the bowl, and splashed his face. Drying himself with a towel, she heard the scrape of whiskers, and him saying, "You can't come here anymore, Monette."

His words stung as if he'd slapped her. As if the floor had opened and swallowed her whole. "*Can't come?* What do you mean?"

He put the towel down and turned toward her. She finally saw his eyes. They were distant, cold. The eyes of a stranger. "What I mean is, I'm in love with Lucy Saffin."

"You lie!" she whispered fiercely. *Was* he lying? Perhaps she was the one so foolishly deceived. Perhaps when Breck was alone with Lucy they talked about Monette, laughed about her—the poor little mulatto who believed she was receiving the key to knowledge when she was, in reality, receiving nothing but the bitterness of her own servitude. A great hurt welled up inside Monette. Choked her. Blackened her vision. As if he had his hands about her neck and squeezed.

"Think what you want, Monette, but the fact remains that you may not come here anymore. Never. I'll tell Lizzy that I want someone else to clean my room."

"Has none of this meant anything?" She spat her words at him. "Or was it just a game to you?"

When he said nothing, showing no more emotion than the wall behind him, she could stand it no longer. The sight of him, his betrayal of her, made her sick. She looked around to gather her things, to leave, realizing stupidly that there was nothing to gather. It was all his. The books, the pens, everything. Her days of reading and writing were over. And her friend, lost to her. A friend she'd cared for deeply, trusted implicitly, loved even. She forced herself across the room to the door. But before she could make herself leave, she turned and faced him, saying, "I hate you, Breck Jensey," feeling no satisfaction when he flinched as if she'd slapped him.

Outside, she scarcely noticed the crescent moon, the cooing of the pigeons perched on the eaves, the wink of the fireflies. Instead, she was running. Into the big house, up the stairs, slowing when she reached the bedrooms on the second floor, thankful that the guest room was open and empty. She slipped through it into Kate's room.

Kate was sitting up in bed, braiding her hair over her shoulder, candle on the bedside table. With Monette's unannounced entrance, Kate looked up, startled, having just been pondering whether orange was a becoming color for her or whether it really accentuated her freckles like Lucy had asserted. "Monette! What's wrong? Are you crying?"

"I—I had a bad dream," Monette said, before bursting into a rash of wild weeping. She then ran across the room, and flung herself, tears and all, at a surprised Kate, who'd lifted the mosquito net at the first sign of tears.

Wondering what on earth kind of dream would warrant such a response and thinking that Monette was sometimes just too tender for her own good, Kate nevertheless drew Monette into her arms and held her tightly, feeling a sudden, nostalgic sense of yesterday, of a time when they'd shared every moment together, both waking and sleeping. It was a sweet memory, so when Monette's sobs began to subside into a soft hiccoughing, Kate simply pulled the covers back and said, "Get in."

She then blew out the candle and nestled into Monette's arms, while the darkness stole over them like a blanket.

## *Chapter 8*

I T WAS ALL POSITIVELY mortifying. How she'd let her mother talk her into this, Kate didn't know. A weakness for the plight of widows and fatherless children, she supposed, a weakness shared by any person who claimed even half a heart. A weakness certainly possessed by the Ladies Charitable Society of St. Marysville, the organizers of the benefit, of which her mother was a long-standing member and of which Sophia Taggart was president.

Undoubtedly, the Taggarts' plantation, Hickory Grove, was the ideal location for just such a benefit, the benefit including not only a picnic basket auction hosted by the young ladies, but a barbeque and barn dance later in the evening. Hickory Grove was, simply, the delight (and envy) of West Feliciana Parish.

Of course, everyone knew it was because Frederick Taggart was so immensely wealthy that the construction of a new wing or a private racecourse, complete with a miniature grandstand, was no more painful to his pocketbook than was the purchase of a tea caddy or perhaps one of the new fountains that sprayed its mist into a summer's eve, providing a coolness Sophia found refreshing. The architecture of the big house, white and double-storied, was inspired by the Greeks. The gardens—meticulously hedged and perfumed with flowering shrubs, trees, and perennials of every variety—were inspired by the gardens at Versailles, exceeding even, most agreed, the vibrancy and cultivation of Sarah Jensey's gardens at Fox Creek (although some would argue the point). It was a plantation of galleries, gazebos, statues, and archways, where white-coated servants awaited to fulfill every guest's whim and amusement.

On this early summer morning, under the shade of sycamore and live oak, Kate stood primly on the makeshift stage, head up and shoulders back. She faced a crowd that seemed to number in the quadrillions, though it really was no more than one hundred seventy-nine persons, including Old Man Parsons, whose feeble frame looked as if he had but a few days left to wander the earth (if wandering could be defined as planting oneself in a chair never to arise and dozing through most everything of interest).

Displayed on a table at Kate's elbow was her picnic basket. It was decorated quite handsomely, in her opinion, with a checkered white and blue bow and a spray of orange blossoms and sweet bay that didn't wilt in the heat like so many of the more delicate sprays on the other baskets. Not only was the basket attractive in appearance, but the day before she'd labored in the kitchen, sweating and miserable, preparing its contents. Under the tutelage of her mother and Aunt Delia, Kate had rolled pastry, peeled, pared, kneaded, shucked, chopped, and fried, until she seriously began to wonder if widows and orphans were really as bad off as everyone let on. Laborious as the task had proved, Kate was nevertheless proud of the dinner she'd prepared. Today the aromas of fried chicken, fresh bread, cinnamon, and apples, wafted from the picnic basket and her stomach rumbled.

"Three dollars!" cried Victor Cobb.

"Three fifty!" countered Hugh Vanderkloot, raising a pale, bony finger.

Kate felt herself redden. She exchanged a glance with her mother who stood off to the side, looking appropriately chagrined. Mortified, no doubt, on behalf of her daughter. *Victor Cobb? Hugh Vanderkloot?* Mother! How could you do this to me? Your own daughter! Thrown to the—to the—*dogs!*

Having never participated in a basket auction before, Kate didn't realize until too late the disadvantages of being last up. Simply put, all the good, eligible men had already bid upon a basket. And who in their right mind needed two dinners? Uncle John had bid for Priscilla's, Stephen Decatur Rockwell for five-year-old Amy Parsons', Percy Taggart for Juliana's, Breck for Lucy's. . . . (Breck had had to bid vigorously to beat out Edward Scarborough, who bid as though his life depended on it. And what was Breck thinking anyway, bidding for Lucy Saffin? Did he *want* to spend any more time with her than he had to? Had he lost his marbles?)

Twenty-some ladies ranging in age from five to thirty-five, all taken. Except for her. Who, now, was the object of pity, bid upon by two of the most unappealing male figures who ever respired in West Feliciana Parish, perhaps in all of Louisiana. Victor Cobb, eighteen years of age, a truculent smash-faced fellow who overly liked to punch, kick, whip, crush, smack, slap, and otherwise violate just about everything and everyone, be it a butterfly or his bondservants, a young man who increasingly took after his father, Morton, in every regrettable respect. Then there was Hugh Vanderkloot, who clad his knobby knees and buttermilk skin in silks and velvets and frills, whose clamminess of hand seeped through the fabric of any glove gracing the hand of a lady, no matter how stout the glove. The thought of sitting on her blanket with either one of them, chatting sweetly while sharing the meal that she'd worked so hard to prepare, was, well, positively mortifying.

*Mother! Save me!*

"I have a bid of three fifty, that's three fifty from Vanderkloot," boomed Reverend Scarborough in his best Thou-Shalt-Not voice, normally reserved for the pulpit. "Do I hear four dollars, four dollars for this beautiful young lady, a-devout-Christian-and-model-of-piety?"

Victor Cobb raised his hand.

"Excellent! Mr. Cobb's bid is four dollars, that's four dollars, do I hear five? Five? That's not too much to ask for this fine young lady from a respectable family. And if those delicious aromas coming from her basket are any indication of what's inside, you're in for a treat. No doubt she's worked her delicate fingers to the bone to satisfy even the most discriminating and voracious appetite. Now-who'll-give-me-five-dollars?"

"Four fifty," said Mr. Vanderkloot, smiling wanly at Kate, who resisted the temptation to roll her eyes and stomp off the stage in a huff. Instead, she filled her lungs and straightened her spine, determined to give no one the satisfaction of sensing her humiliation. Even so, she could not stop the burn of tears at the backs of her eyes, the tremble in her middle. All that work, all that *sweating,* for *this?* And, good God, is that Lucy Saffin standing over there under her parasol looking smug as a fat hen, as if all of this were terribly *funny?*

"Four seventy-five!" called Victor Cobb, the plug of tobacco in his lower lip bulging like a canker.

"Do I hear five dollars? Five dollars to feed-the-poor-starving-orphans and to shelter-and-clothe-the-widows? Our Lord who died to save us commands us to do no less. Four seventy-five going once—"

"Five!" cried Vanderkloot.

*Lord Who Died to Save Us, save me!*

"That's five dollars, yessir, the bid's five dollars. Five dollars going once, going twice . . ."

Then, just as tears truly threatened to overwhelm Kate, someone from the back of the crowd called, "Twenty-five dollars!"

The crowd gasped and craned their necks, trying to see who it was, no doubt delighted at this unexpected turn of events.

But even before the crowd parted and he stepped forward, and even were it not for the telltale thrill that raced up her spine, starting low and tingling upward, Kate knew who the bidder was. As if she could ever forget the tenor of his voice, his easy, gentle drawl. It was Stephen Decatur Rockwell, smiling at her, touching the brim of his hat in greeting, looking as handsome as he had while standing at the top of the stairs at the *Placide's Varieties Theatre.*

She'd replayed the scene in her mind for weeks. The two of them. His dashing figure, uniformed and resplendent with medals of valor. His willingness to make a fool of himself on her behalf. His treatment of her, not as a child, but as a lady, a lady in distress. The remarkable blue of his eyes, wintry yet warm. Of course, she knew he was married. Happily, by all accounts. His Irish wife pregnant with their first child. She recited these facts to herself again and again, as if she couldn't quite keep it all straight. And of course, she knew he was twice her age or thereabouts. Goodness knows she'd tried in the past weeks to interest herself in eligible males who were closer to her own age, but invariably found herself comparing them to Stephen, mentally ticking off their faults, yawning discreetly behind her gloved hand, relieved when they finally rode away.

Now, standing on the stage, she smiled down at Stephen.

Images of plump orphans and happily domesticated widows must have paraded across Reverend Scarborough's mind, for after only a brief, startled hesitation, he pounded the table with his gavel, grinned broadly, and cried, "*Sold* to Mr. Rockwell for twenty-five dollars! And-in-the-name-of-the-Father-Son-and-Holy-Ghost-*Amen!*"

Kate sat next to Stephen atop a checkered quilt, slippered feet tucked beneath her skirts, slowly twirling her parasol as she listened to little Amy Parsons prattle happily about this and that while eating the last of the gingerbread. Kate thought she was a pretty child, rosy-cheeked and fresh-faced, her blonde pigtails long and thick. A red cardinal flew from a sycamore overhead, alighting on the lawn next to Amy, where it began pecking the crumbs from the grass. The air smelled heavy, languid with the leftover scents of bread, pies, cakes, oranges, and cinnamon.

Beneath the canopy of shade trees, a sea of other picnickers surrounded them, spaced such as to provide a modicum of privacy, all in various stages of ingesting the contents of the picnic baskets. Empty bowls, cups, gloves, forks, and bottles littered the blankets. The murmur of conversation and the occasional laughter swelled and receded like a gentle tide. Both Kate's mother and Grandma Emma sat in a group of ladies some distance away beneath an orange tree, Sarah's enlarged belly tastefully hidden beneath folds of creamy muslin. Kate thought she looked somewhat peaked as she fanned herself, listening to Aunt Virginia, whose mouth was moving and whose hands were gesturing.

Amy lay back on the blanket. "I'm full," she declared with a satisfied sigh.

Stephen smiled, glancing briefly at Kate. "As well you should be, Miss Amy. I believe you ate more than a regiment of soldiers. If I didn't know better, I'd think one of those little legs was hollow." He reached over and tweaked Amy's big toe. "Aha! Just as I suspected."

The child giggled and sat up. She pulled her pantalettes above her knee and rapped on her leg as if upon a door. "That's sweet potato pie in there, I think. Oh, heavens to Betsy, that was so yummy!" Then she looked at Kate quite seriously. "Sorry I couldn't eat the whole thing."

Kate grinned. "Why, silly, no one expects you to eat a whole pie. Only a pig eats a whole pie. But I can give you some to take home, if you like."

Amy nodded, while Stephen winked, saying, "I'll bet I can eat a whole pie," at which point, he belched.

"Stephen!" Kate gave him a playful punch, pretending to be aghast, while at the same time doubling over in a fit of giggles along with Amy. She saw Stephen watching her, an amused, playful glint in his eye.

After the laughter subsided, Amy's expression grew wistful. She sighed, absently plucking grass blades and tossing them to nowhere in particular. Now a cluster of birds hopped about just out of arm's reach, watching her every move, dashing in occasionally to peck at the ground before flitting away. "I wish I were an orphan."

"An orphan?" Stephen matched her tone of seriousness. "What on earth for?"

"So I can have people raise money for me and feel sorry for me and—and such like."

"Well, if that's what you want, Miss Amy, I'll feel sorry for you right now." And so saying, Stephen assumed a sad expression, the back of his hand pressed to his forehead dramatically. "Oh, woe!"

Kate followed suit, placing a gloved hand over her heart. "Why, poor, poor Amy Parsons. She's homeless and nobody loves her or wants her."

After they all laughed again amid a few more expressions of woe and mirth, Amy stood abruptly and announced, "I think I'll go play now." With a thank you and a goodbye and a kiss on the hand from Stephen, she ran, zigzagging across the shaded grass between the other picnickers, her pigtails flopping behind her, until she disappeared behind the hedges from whence came the happy sounds of other children at play.

Now that Amy was gone, a shyness and awkwardness stole over Kate like a shadow. Stephen, too, was quiet, reclining on one elbow, a blade of grass poking out one side of his mouth. He appeared to be gazing at a half-clad statue of a woman, gray robes draped casually about her hips, stone breasts exposed to the elements. Kate flushed and turned away, giving her parasol an extra twirl. Should she thank Stephen and take her leave? Retire indoors to rest as some of the other picnickers were already doing? For, though it was only noon, the heat and humidity were steadily increasing. She could feel the beads of perspiration on her forehead. Moisture trickled between her breasts and down the small of her back.

"Stephen, I—I want to thank you."

"For what?"

She gave a faltering smile, overcome with self-consciousness, especially now that he was looking at her. She wondered for a fleeting, guilt-filled second if he was thinking of her breasts, imagining them. "For—for coming to my rescue, of course."

"Somehow," he said, smiling sideways, "I just couldn't imagine the headstrong Miss Kate Jensey enjoying a picnic with either Victor Cobb or Vanderkloot. Just a guess. Though maybe I was mistaken," he added with a wink, laughing. "Maybe they would have swept you off your feet and left you moonstruck, lovesick, and calf-eyed all at the same time."

"Not hardly!" shrieked Kate, laughing too, until she realized they garnered more than one raised eyebrow from nearby picnickers, including a glower from her mother. Kate lowered her voice. "Although I must admit, you're right in one respect. My mama always says I'm too headstrong. She says I'm like a colt barreling toward a fence, too spindly to jump over, yet too stubborn to stop."

"Well, are you?"

His blue eyes gazed at her intently, melting her insides like butter on a hot day. And she wondered briefly if Irish Mary felt this way whenever he looked at her. "Am I—am I what?"

"Headstrong?"

Kate nodded, unsure whether such an admission pleased him or not. Then and there she determined, not for the first time, to become less headstrong, more demure, the very picture of femininity, though the thought of such remolding of her own character frightened her.

"Sorry, Kate, I shouldn't have asked. It was forward of me. *My* mother says I need to mind my own business and stop trying to fix everybody's problems."

"And *my* mother talked me into doing the auction in the first place. She wouldn't take no for an answer."

"Yes, mothers are wonderful for that sort of thing. Wherever would we be without them?"

"Nowhere, I suppose." Kate bit her lip, thinking it would be rude not to ask: "I—I hear your wife, Mary, is about to be a mother?"

Stephen was silent for a bit, seeming to contemplate the significance of her question, the years of responsibility it prefigured. Then he nodded. "Yes, Kate, I'm going to be a father. Next month, according to Dr. John." When he looked away, profiled, gazing at the statue again, Kate read his expression perfectly. *He loves her. He loves his Irish Mary.* And though the understanding should have come as no surprise to Kate—husbands were supposed to love their wives, after all—nevertheless the knowledge pierced her. A bayonet to the breast. Wielded by the most honorable of

military men. She wished, suddenly, that she was instead sitting next to
Hugh Vanderkloot, all fop and gawk as her father described him, where
the height of her pain was nothing more than a little humiliation, sheer
boredom, and the clammy press of his hand through her glove.

# *Chapter 9*

S ARAH WISHED SHE HADN'T come. There were many excuses she could have used—her pregnancy, the multifarious tasks that required her attention, and the heat. But when Sophia Taggart was on a mission—and mission it was—she was not a lady to be refused. Two weeks ago, she'd sailed into the Fox Creek big house like a ship in full regalia, soft-spoken yet commanding, her posture straight as a fence post, telling Sarah exactly what would be expected of her at the fundraising event, as if Sarah's involvement was a foregone conclusion. And Sarah had acquiesced, later shaking her head no when William told her that he could send a man over to the Taggarts with her apologies, and that Sophia Taggart, along with her bully of a husband, could go fry an egg.

But now, sitting in the shade with her mother, her sister-in-law Virginia, Sophia Taggart, Mary Grey Saffin, and several other ladies (ostensibly to chaperone the picnickers), Sarah wished she'd listened to William's better judgment.

Virginia was leaning toward them, her voice continuing low. "They say her labor lasted three days. Three days! Can you imagine? Poor Jane! And even though the doctor bled her, he waited far too long to do it, the fool, everyone said so. When she died, they say her husband was so beside himself that he was going to shoot the doctor for his negligence. Thank goodness cooler heads prevailed, or else he would have been hanged for murder, and then both the young lovers plus the baby would have been dead. A tragedy if there ever was one. As it is, he's remarried, and word has it his new wife is already pregnant. A honeymoon baby, by my calculations."

"My labor with Campbell lasted over fifty hours," said Sophia to a symphony of gasps from the other ladies. Sarah recalled a time when Sophia Taggart had been a beautiful woman, but fifty-four years of living, plus the bearing of seven children (not counting the two who had died in infancy or the miscarriages), had taken their toll. Her once glossy black hair was lined with gray, and her face had long ago succumbed to the forces of gravity. As commanding as Sophia could be, there was also a gentleness to her, a compassion that had, at numerous times, benefitted more than just orphans and widows. Once, when Sarah was ill, Sophia had come bearing tonics and a potted geranium; the tonics she'd poured down Sarah's throat, the geranium she'd set near the window, the bright pink flowers cheering Sarah long after Sophia had taken her leave.

Today Sophia sat straight, no doubt whaleboned to the extreme, her forehead furrowed as though the memory of childbirth was, in itself, excruciating. "It took me a full six months to recover, and I'm still not perfectly well. Don't believe I ever will be." Sophia sighed. "Campbell would be seventeen years old now, if he'd lived. God bless his sweet soul."

"Bless his soul," they all said, Sarah recalling that little Campbell had died during the yellow fever epidemic of '43, the same epidemic that had nearly claimed the life of her own dear Katherine.

"My first labor lasted even longer than that," said a young lady, a friend of one of the others. Sarah couldn't recall her name, thinking she didn't look any older than twenty. The young lady's voice fell to a whisper, and her lips trembled. "No one thought I would live. Not even the doctor. I was so weak afterward I couldn't even nurse my own baby."

There were murmurs of sympathy all around before several other ladies launched into whispered stories of giving birth, of the pain, the suffering, the screaming, the friends who hadn't been so lucky, the babes who'd only breathed a few breaths, the babes who'd not breathed at all, their faces blue as indigo.

*Dear Lord! I can't do this again!*

Just when Sarah thought she'd start screaming herself, the familiar fear and nausea rising, Emma reached over and took her hand with a reassuring squeeze. She then turned to the ladies, exclaiming, "Why, Sophia, if that isn't the most beautiful dress your daughter is wearing. Surely that came straight from Paris?"

Now the ladies turned their attention to the picnickers, to where one of the Taggarts' daughters, Ulyssa, sat beneath a china tree with her fiancé, indeed looking quite fetching in her hooped dress of blue lawn, a leghorn hat with white ribbon, and a white lace parasol to match.

"Would you believe," answered Sophia, "my woman Nancy made it for her as a gift for her twenty-first birthday?"

"Your Nancy is quite skilled," said Sarah, smiling, feeling a tiny kick under her rib and wondering if it, too, was grateful for the change in subject.

"Trained her myself," said Sophia. "She was perfectly useless before that. Came to me without a skill in the world."

Mary Grey Saffin, who had remained silent during the talk of birthing and babies (word had it that after giving birth to Lucy, she'd ousted her husband from their marriage bed because she couldn't bear to have her figure ruined), said, "Yes, they do have a tendency toward uselessness, don't they?"

"I've always believed," said Virginia, "that if it wasn't for us putting industry into their hands, they would spend their days sleeping and shirking. They've proved as much, time and again."

"And yet," said Mary, plucking what looked to be a hair off her lap and letting it fall to the grass, "that Harriet Beecher Stowe would have us believe that negroes are all hardworking saints while we are cruel, heartless beasts."

Sarah groaned inwardly and caught a glance from Emma, who seemed equally wary of such a discussion. *Uncle Tom's Cabin.* Harriet Beecher Stowe. North versus South. It seemed, other than babies and birthing, as if no one could talk of anything else, at least not since the first few installments of *Uncle Tom's Cabin* had appeared in *The National Era* earlier this month. Sarah had herself picked up a copy from atop William's desk, curious, unable to stop herself from reading, although she knew it would do nothing but cause her anguish. And it had. After finishing, she'd laid it down, aghast, trembling.

*So that is what they think of us?*

"Please, Mary," said Sophia, frowning. "Must we bring up such topics? This was to be a pleasant day."

"And pleasant it is, and shall remain. I am only saying that we Southrons are not the cruel, heartless beasts Stowe would have everyone believe. I, for one, feel my heart beating in my chest, so I know I am not heartless.

I, for one, have upon occasion accidentally cut myself, or pricked a finger while sewing, so I know my blood runs red, and it is the same red that runs through Mrs. Stowe's holy veins." Mary's eyes glittered, and her chest heaved with the passion of her words.

Like her daughter Lucy, Mary was an average beauty. Her features were sharp—somewhat pretty, fox-like. Her cheeks were a bit too rosy, resembling those of a drunkard, though, admittedly, Sarah had never seen her imbibe more than was proper. And although she'd known Mary for most of her life, Sarah admitted that Mary was not someone with whom she felt much kinship, although, Lord knows, she'd tried to foster a relationship many times. Perhaps it was because, at times like these, Mary's thoughts seeped from her like an unpleasant odor, as if they'd been moldering inside her. And, in Sarah's opinion, more often than not, they were unladylike thoughts, frightening thoughts, better left to the gentlemen. Unladylike thoughts that were likely the result of being married to a senator, daily being surrounded by coarse topics, political rhetoric, and outspokenness. Sarah believed that the senator's wife was particularly susceptible to such unladylike leanings due to her minimum of motherly responsibilities, responsibilities that never failed to soften a lady's edges and place her within her proper sphere. More to the point, Sarah believed the woman lacked maternal instinct altogether, reminding her of the mother cat who ate her kittens and afterward licked herself clean.

"You sound like your husband," said Sophia.

"Thank you, Sophia, I shall take that as a compliment. As I was saying, this Mrs. Stowe sits ensconced quite comfortably in her study up North, sipping her tea and penning books with her lily-white hands in an attempt to ease the bitterness she feels in her heart toward us Southrons."

Sarah looked away from Mary, crushing her handkerchief in her hands, feeling her face flush. Beside her, Emma shifted in her seat.

"While," continued Mary, "if truth be known, neither Stowe, nor any Northerner for that matter, cares so much as a whit for those poor hapless souls that they pretend to love. Let *them* spend year after year caring for the physical and spiritual needs of the African race, a race that is by nature lazy, dirty, stupid, ill-smelling, and in need of governance. Let *them* spend year after year surrounded by such woolly heads, having not one day of peace in the face of their childish demands, and then, and only then, will people like Stowe have the authority to speak out against the institution. And yet she, and others like her, bid the savages to rise up and slit our throats. All in the name of Christianity. All in the name of a higher good. They are hypocrites—"

"Mary, please," begged Sophia. "Let us not speak of—of such atrocities."

"What, you do not want to hear about our houses going up in flames while the Jenseys' slave Sawney runs around free as the wind? Imagine all of them free, running around and slitting our throats while we sleep—"

There was a collective gasp. Sarah stood abruptly, the blood draining from her head. Beside her, Emma, too, was standing, taking Sarah's hand, telling Mary that such talk was inappropriate, especially in light of Miss Sarah's delicate condition, and that she should be ashamed of herself. Sarah couldn't look at Mary, nor at any of the ladies. Instead, trembling, she turned from them and gazed out at the picnickers, at the birds that swooped low, wings thrumming. "If you will excuse me," she heard herself saying, "I—I need to retire indoors to rest. I'm not feeling well."

"Certainly, Miss Sarah," said Sophia, standing. "I shall accompany you."

And with Sophia on one side and Emma on the other, Sarah made her way to the big house of the Taggart plantation.

Normally, the barn at Hickory Grove was the stuff of barns everywhere, filled with the usual cows, pigs, straw, scythes, plows, carts, and all the accompanying but oddly satisfying aromas of manure, grease, dust, and hay. But on the evening of the benefit, nary an animal was in sight; the barn had been swept clean, the floor spread with a layer of fresh sawdust. Bales of straw lined the perimeter, meant for young and old and everyone in-between to rest a spell if either the heat or the festivities overwhelmed them. Streamers of blue, red, and canary yellow festooned the rafters. And instead of the usual smells, it smelled of freshness, fun, and frivolity.

At the center of the back wall, atop a dais built just for the occasion, a band played. Jaunty strains of fiddles, mandolin, and piano (the instrument hauled in for just the occasion and soliciting more than a few comments!) floated in amongst the posts and beams, causing shoes to tap, even the shoes of those who weren't twirling their partners around the dance floor.

"Why, Breck," exclaimed Lucy with a laugh once the dance ended, "I swear if I had any more fun, they'd declare it illegal!" She'd already danced quite a few numbers with several of the other young bachelors, and the Highland *Schottishe* was a particularly lively number. Lucy was out of breath, perspiring more than was ladylike, hoping he didn't notice.

"Illegal or not, Miss Lucy, I'm certain all the young men present today would risk imprisonment for the pleasure." He looked down at her in the way that made her heart do a *Schottische* of its own.

The next dance was announced, and as the dancers rearranged themselves, Lucy begged Breck for some rest and refreshment. He escorted her to the perimeter, tucking her arm under his. "Water? Punch? Champagne?" he asked, as she seated herself on a straw bale.

She giggled, feeling giddy already. "Champagne."

"I shall return."

Lucy watched him weave his way through the crowd to where the food and drinks were being served outside, his tall figure, so erect and manly. She leaned back against one of the giant posts, sighing. Truly, it had been, and continued to be, the single happiest day of Lucy's life. Just wait until she told Susie Caldwell!

Was it only yesterday that Lucy had bid Susie goodbye? That they'd clung to one another, sobbing like the schoolgirls they were, knowing they would not see one another again until late July, when the new school session began? How long ago it seemed now. "Breck's in love with me!" she would whisper to Susie the next time she saw her. "Yes, he's in love! With *me!*" And she imagined she and Susie clasping one another by the wrists and jumping up and down as if they were five years old again and testing the fortitude of a mattress. "You should have seen the way he bid for me and my basket! Even though that horrid little clergyman—what's his name—kept upping the bid, Breck refused to be beaten! Such a gentleman! And such a picnic we had. I swear his eyes were only for me! He said my cooking was simply divine, not to be rivaled even by his own Aunt Delia's!"

"Miss Saffin?"

Lucy looked up, smothering a frown when she saw it was Hugh Vanderkloot, a man who couldn't buy a wife even for a million dollars. That morning, it had required all her self-restraint not to laugh aloud at his vain attempts to win Kate's basket and company. And Kate, striking the very picture of outraged femininity! Then, horrors, to be purchased by a married man who was, no doubt, moved to do so only out of pity, or perhaps out of a concern for the welfare of orphans. Lucy had resolved to tell Susie every juicy tidbit. Oh, how they'd howl!

Now Lucy smiled, making certain the smile did not reach her eyes. "Why, Mr. Vanderkloot. I trust you are enjoying the evening?"

"Yes, I am, Miss Saffin. Except my—my—" he faltered.

"Except what, Mr. Vanderkloot?"

"Except my evening shall not be complete unless you agree to be my partner for the next dance." Here he bowed with a frilly flourish. Nearby, a tight circle of girls erupted into giggles, as if they'd overheard, which Lucy thought impossible, as Vanderkloot had spoken in a whisper as vapid as dishwater, and the music played boisterously.

Lucy flushed and fumbled in her reticule. She extricated her fan, flipped it open with a flick of her wrist, and began to fan herself with vigor. Again, she smiled. "How kind of you to offer, Mr. Vanderkloot, but I simply must rest. I hope you understand. My constitution is fragile and easily disturbed."

"Of course, Miss Saffin, of course I understand completely. I—I just thought that—"

Rescue came in the form of Breck, carrying two glasses of champagne.

"Why, Breck, how gentlemanly of you." He seated himself beside her, and she took her glass, sipping the golden liquid, saying, "Mmm, thank you kindly." Then, looking at Mr. Vanderkloot as if startled, having forgotten, perhaps, that he was still standing there with a moist, bovine expression upon his face, she said, "Oh! You may go now."

"Poor wretch," murmured Breck as Mr. Vanderkloot wandered away.

"Poor? Why on earth do you call him that?"

Breck looked at her. She couldn't read his eyes. "Because every man, no matter who he is, deserves to be loved. To find love and have it returned in full measure."

"That's easy for you to say. After all, he was not asking *you* to dance." Lucy laughed, then realized Breck was serious. "Well, surely you can't mean that. Why, I believe that love must be earned. One must display honorable characteristics. Characteristics like chivalry, boldness, courage, and devotion. Surely you don't believe that someone who is, perhaps, cowardly or dishonest or mean-spirited, is worthy of the same love?" Disliking the look on Breck's face, Lucy's voice trailed away. She felt suddenly uncomfortable, as if the ground was slightly off-kilter. She gulped her champagne.

"So, Miss Lucy, I take it you've never done anything mean-spirited?" He said this lightly, smiling, and the sudden, uncomfortable mood that had descended upon Lucy lifted, leaving her wondering if it had been her imagination.

Lucy shrugged, relaxing. How overly sensitive she was! She'd have to remember to tell Susie that they'd maybe had their first lover's quarrel. Maybe. About what, she wasn't sure. "Why, I've never acted mean-spirited," she declared with a laugh. "It's not in my repertoire as a lady." She lowered her voice to a conspiratorial whisper. "Unless you count the time I was four and I pulled your sister's hair for snitching my doll."

"I'm certain she deserved it."

"What about you? Have you ever done anything mean-spirited?"

Breck sipped his champagne, looking lost in thought, absently watching the dancers, his sister Kate kicking up the sawdust with her father, William Jensey. Breck finally admitted, "Don't tell anyone, but when I was six, I set the corncrib on fire."

"You didn't!"

"I did. I was the proverbial naughty child playing with fire. Never did own up to it until last year, when I told my father."

"What did he say?"

"'Don't do it again.'"

They both laughed, Lucy wondering if her giddy feeling was due to love, joy, or the champagne. All of them, she supposed, mixed together in a heady cocktail that she swore to savor for the rest of her days. She loved Breck Jensey, pure and simple. "And dishonest?" she asked, his candor warming her. "Surely you have never been dishonest, have you?"

Breck knew the question was coming. He merely smiled at her, noticing the drab hazel of her eyes, wondering what she would think of him if she understood the depths of his dishonesty. Loathe him forever, he supposed. And dishonesty not just toward Lucy, but toward just about everyone—his father, Cyrus, Monette. . . .

Hardly a minute went by when he was not thinking of Monette. Aching for her. Reliving the agony of when she'd turned and said, *I hate you, Breck Jensey.* Remembering the incredible hurt in her eyes, hurt that he had inflicted, that he would never forgive himself for.

Breck looked into Lucy's hopeful eyes and willed himself to love her, for her to mend his shattered heart, knowing he never would, and that she never could, wondering if life was simply a series of compromises. Dishonest compromises that presented to the world a face of honesty and integrity. As if, should one ever boldly live the truth of his life, he would be reviled and destroyed. And, as a measure of his dishonesty, he planned to write her a letter the moment he arrived at college, informing her that he was interested in someone else, that they could remain friends, but only friends. "And if I have been dishonest?" he asked.

"Why, of course, as a gentleman, you would have to make reparation to the injured party."

"What if they had wronged me first?"

"Well, then, that's an entirely different matter." Lucy leaned toward him, and he smelled the rosewater on her skin, saw the face powder dusted on the tiny hairs of her cheeks.

His gaze lowered, and he saw the swell of her breasts pushing against the tight bodice, rising and falling with each breath she took. Her upper breasts were exposed, not vulgarly, but providing more than a hint of the plump white lilies beneath. He felt his breath quicken.

"If someone has wronged you first," she was saying, looking pleased, "unless he gives you satisfaction, then you must challenge him to a duel."

"A duel?"

Her voice lowered. "Would you fight a duel to protect my honor, Breck?"

Breck drew back, realizing they were being watched. Lucy's mother, for one, her eye as piercing as an eagle's. Perhaps she had seen him ogling her daughter's bosom, a mistake he would not make twice. "You know there are laws against duels."

Lucy stuck out her bottom lip in a pout worthy of any schoolgirl. "You mean you wouldn't fight, not even for me?"

Thankfully, the dance ended, and a Virginia Reel was announced. Breck masked his annoyance and stood, proffering his hand. He forced himself to smile. "You are always an exception, Lucy Saffin. Dance?"

As she giggled and he pulled her to her feet, he noticed Monette standing in the corner, half hidden behind a beam, observing him. How long had she been there? he wondered, feeling a sharp jab in his heart as their eyes met. Then he looked away, making a show of looping Lucy's arm in his own. He led Lucy out onto the dance floor, smiling at her, not listening as she chattered about something. Then they lined up facing one another, gentlemen on one side, ladies on the other. The reel started, and he began to dance.

~ ✺ ~

Monette had seen enough. She dodged a few people here and there: an old man dozing on a bale of hay, a group of white-coated servants, a few of whom eyed her as she left the barn. Outside, a breeze stirred the palmetto fronds and blew against the moisture on her skin. Stars sprinkled the night sky like spilled salt. The music was quieter out here, mingling with the chorus of katydids and frogs. There were people outside too, gathered in clusters, some talking in low voices, some smoking cigars, some heading out on the track back to the big house, servants in tow, for it was approaching midnight.

It had been a long day, beginning with the preparations at Fox Creek, followed by the carriage ride to Hickory Grove. Of course, she'd had to remain close to Kate all day. Not too close, as that was considered impertinent, but close enough so that when Kate needed to rest or to freshen up, Monette would be there, assisting her charge in every regard.

From a distance, she'd watched Kate picnic with Stephen Rockwell and the little girl. She'd watched Breck and Lucy too, although Monette was unable to decipher anything other than two people eating and conversing. Then, after the picnic, Kate retired indoors, along with many of the other young ladies. In one of the ladies' chambers, Monette undressed Kate, loosened her corsets, thankful that Kate was somewhat subdued and quiet. And when Kate lay down on a bed alongside Miss Sarah, arm flung atop her mother's pregnant belly, Monette left and curled up in the hall, too uncomfortably hot to sleep, trying to ignore the other servants who wanted to whisper among themselves.

Afterward, had followed the barbeque and the barn dance.

She'd known it was a mistake to come inside the barn, but she'd been unable to resist. She had to see for herself. Was it true? Did Breck really have feelings for Lucy, as he'd asserted? She'd watched their dialogue, the way Lucy leaned in close, Breck glancing at Lucy's bosom, a bosom that invited gawking. She'd seen the whispers between them, the laughter, and the more she watched, the more she felt deeply betrayed.

Now Monette began to walk toward the big house, not intending to go far (Kate would need her again when it came time to retire), yet wanting to stretch her limbs, to experience nothing except the beat of her heart, the bend of her feet inside her shoes, and the swing of her arms. The trees grew tall on both sides of the cart track, boughs interlocking overhead so that Monette saw only an occasional glimpse of the stars peeping through, and the half-moon directly overhead.

*I'm in love with Lucy Saffin,* he'd told her, hardening to stone before her eyes, forbidding her to enter his room again. Monette hadn't needed to be told twice. Even if Lizzy, the housekeeper, hadn't smugly informed her that her new assignment was William's office instead, Monette would never have entered Breck's room again, come dust, cobwebs, an unmade bed, or Lizzy's fury. The simple fact that Breck didn't *want* her in his room was enough.

For the past three weeks, she'd raged over his betrayal of her, his casting her aside as if she were nothing, praying he would change his mind, knowing he wouldn't. Grieving over the loss of their friendship, plus the loss of her reading and writing, as if mourning a beloved child.

Along with her rage-filled grief, she'd been forced to admit something that frightened her: once both Kate and Breck left for school, her life would radically change. Without their companionship, what would her life entail? Would she become like Lizzy, obsessed with dust and "dirty dirt," as she called it, and soiled linens? Become like Mammy Hester, looking after Miss Sarah's newborn until it no longer needed her? Of course, she knew that someday she would be the mammy of Kate's children, she and Kate still sharing secrets, stories, and rides through the forest. But that was a long, long time away. And meanwhile . . .

When Monette reached the end of the cart track, the tree-enclosed tunnel opening into a torch-lit expanse of gardens and buildings, she turned around and began to head back to the barn. She walked fast now, longing for bed, for sleep, for this day to end, hoping Kate was ready now to retire.

She both heard and saw them before they saw her. Three men walked toward her. One of them carried a lantern that swung on its hinges with a rusty scrape, a mosaic of shadow and light shifting overhead in the canopy of leaves and hanging moss. She recognized them as servants of Morton Cobb. They were laughing. One of them told a joke, and they laughed again, staggering, slapping each other on the back.

*They're drunk.*

Seeing them, hearing them, she recalled the time she'd hid outside the runaway camp, horrified as the runaways violated everything and everyone—grease glistening on their faces, cussing, the man rutting like an animal on top of Fatima.

Monette stiffened as the men approached. She thought about turning back, moving quickly, taking refuge in the big house, but before she could act, they saw her.

They stopped walking, and their laughter fell away. In the gap of silence, Monette heard the faint sounds of mandolin, fiddle, and piano.

"Why, looky here, boys," one of them said. "It be that, that, what's-her-name, Jensey."

"Ain't she a purty sight."

"Kind of like ice cream on a hot day."

They laughed again, slapping one another as if they'd said something hilarious.

Monette put her head down and forced her feet forward, her ears suddenly roaring with the scream of her heart.

"Why, come here, baby, you looks awful lonesome. Let me give you some company."

"Oh, he's some bad company, girl. You don't want him. 'Sides, he ugly. You come here to me, I'll show you a fine, good time. I know how to give you what you want. C'mere, girl."

One of the men smacked his lips. "Look at the way she move. Mmm. Mmm. For sure I'd like me a taste of that." He made chewing noises, and they all laughed.

Abreast of them now, Monette could smell the liquor, the sweat, the beef tallow burning in the smoking lantern. She could feel their eyes on her, crawling like insects, and she wished she'd escaped to the big house while she'd had the chance. Now, she quickened her step.

*Kate, mon amie, tout de suite! J'ai besoin de toi!*

There was a moment, a tense moment, in which every fiber in her body shrieked, that Monette thought they would grab her as she passed by, push her into the thicket, hurt her, but then she was past them, running toward the barn, panting, their laughter filling her ears like slime, their voices nasty as vermin, saying that they'd heard all about her, yessir, every juicy mouthful, calling her names,

*cunt,*
*yellow nigger,*
*whore.*

# *Chapter 10*

THE SUMMER OF 1851 was one of the hottest ever. Were it not for the thunderstorms that punctuated the July days like childish outbursts, West Feliciana's crops would have withered in the fields, the lush gardens of her finest plantations shriveling until they were nothing but crisp, faded memories of spring's fecundity.

July saw the labor force at Fox Creek laying by the crops and performing the multitude of tasks required in anticipation of the harvest, not only of the cotton, the corn, peas, potatoes, peaches, fodder, and all the variety of crops, but also of the first sugar crop ever to be produced on Jensey land. The drainage ditches were dredged. Roads were mended, and the encroaching brush cut back. The strongest were set at the plows. Depending on the weather, the women hoed or spun or planted potato slips or pulled fodder. In preparation for the constant running of the sugarhouse furnace, a crew chopped the wood previously harvested from the clearing of the sugar fields. This last was an especially laborious task, for, according to William's calculations, the furnace would require approximately 600 cords of wood to produce the anticipated 200 hogsheads of sugar.

"Don't think for one second your cooper can handle it," Marshall had advised him. "You better buy or hire a good cooper, otherwise your sugar and molasses will leak into the bottom of every ship from here to New York and piss off just about everyone."

William took his advice. Not only did he hire an experienced cooper, but he had a second cooperage constructed near the sugarhouse. Soon, the cooper and his gang were churning out hogsheads and barrels—hogsheads large enough to contain a whopping 1000 pounds of sugar, and barrels sized for the standard 45 gallons of molasses—all made with staves shipped from the upper Mississippi valley, as the woods of Louisiana were simply too tender. (Tender as the backside of a woman, according to Marshall, an assessment agreed upon by those knowledgeable about staves and who'd likewise had the agreeable opportunity to gauge the backside of the gentler sex.)

By the beginning of August, the sugar crop at Fox Creek had reached maturity, thankfully tall enough that the tedious chore of hoeing the weeds could cease, as the weeds could no longer compete. Come the middle of the month, the corn harvest began, along with the cotton picking, William offering a one-dollar reward to each day's fastest cotton picker.

The area surrounding the cotton gin and press became a hive of activity. Workers hauled bags and baskets stuffed with cotton to the scaffolds, to the mule-powered gin, to the screw press, where teams of oxen plodded a circular rut into the hard-packed soil, turning the screw tighter and tighter, wisps of cotton floating in the air like snow. And, as was true at this time every year, the high-pitched squeal of the cotton press became as familiar a sound as the wail of the peacocks, audible even to the Jenseys when they sat down to supper under the breeze of the shoo-fly, discussing the events of the day, who was marrying whom, and whether the watermelons had ever tasted sweeter.

But William's crowning achievement was not the cotton, satisfying as it was, nor the corn, nor any of the other rooted, living plants that came and went with the seasons. It was the sugarhouse, completed at last. Had it been a Greek edifice with columns aspiring to the heavens, William could not have been prouder. It was, in essence, a testament to his life. Not something handed to him from his father, perpetuated, improved perhaps, but *his*. Begun with his own hands and finished. Something he could pass on to his sons, to Breck. Something that would, he believed, bring prosperity to the Jensey family. Perhaps, finally, the years of barely scraping by were ended.

Standing at the eastern juncture where Jensey's Bayou joined Fox Creek, the sugarhouse was an imposing L-shaped building constructed of brick, measuring 120 feet at its longest, the shorter arm two-storied, dominated by two massive chimneys. Although William would have preferred to build the sugarhouse closer to the plantation complex, as it stood almost a mile away from the quarters, he and Breck had figured it was best to build it near the sugar fields, adjacent to the waterway, hopefully lessening the overall traveling back and forth when all was said and done. Time would tell if they'd made the right decision.

William could hardly wait. Come October or thereabouts, the workers would move into the sugar fields, the cane carts would rattle down the cart tracks, the steam mill would fire to life, the rollers would rumble, the furnace would be stoked for days on end (maintained at just the right temperature), and the gleaming, empty copper kettles would soon bubble and froth, and, by God, thought William, life would be sweet, life *was* sweet.

On his last trip to New Orleans, William had hired an engineer, a sugarmaker named Ogden Birchett, whose duty it would be to train and oversee William's workforce, to advise William, and, of course, to produce the finest sugar to ever dissolve on a tongue. Birchett had already visited twice for advisement purposes, and, come the end of September, he would occupy the new two-room cottage they'd built not far from the sugarhouse. The cottage, plus an office, the cooperage, the woodshed, and the landing fronting Fox Creek, completed the sugarhouse complex.

Even the Sawney issue was resolved, thank the stars. Not long after the benefit at Hickory Grove, while the memory of dancing the night away still lingered like sawdust in the air, the Taggarts' barn had burned to the ground. Hardly a cinder left standing. Cause unknown, arson suspected. The next night, the negro hunters from Mississippi chased a runaway matching Sawney's description into the river, though, admittedly, he hadn't been wearing a neck collar. Torches blazing, horses' fetlocks in the shallows, they'd watched as the man sank once, twice, three times. It was two weeks before they found the body. And while it was discolored and swollen, much of the flesh chewed away, William thought he recognized Sawney's teeth, saying to Breck, "We got our boy." He felt sure of it when the mysterious burnings ended. Save for the usual runaways from just about every plantation around, life returned to normal. The hunters were paid, the cotton harvested, the sugarhouse finished, and finally, Sawney dead.

Yes, life was sweet.

It wasn't until September peeped its head around the corner of August that Sarah finally visited her mother at Woodleigh. Due to deliver in a little over a month, Sarah was ungainly, as big around as a barrel of molasses, by William's estimation.

"Twins again?" Emma asked when Sarah alighted from the carriage, holding onto John's arm for dear life.

Sarah tried to smile, unsure how to respond. Much as Sarah dearly loved George and Thomas, she secretly hoped she carried only a single babe, as the reality of raising two more infants overwhelmed her. (Though this hope inevitably left Sarah feeling guilty and faithless, for she knew such a thought was a reproach against God—the God of Creation who planned all things for her good.) And always, beneath the surface of her calm, simmered the memory of childbirth itself, like a wound that would never fully heal despite the abundance of bandages. "Hello, Mama," was all she said, thankful when her mother did not press the issue. Instead, Emma ushered her inside for a glass of iced lemonade and to rest her feet awhile, saying how wonderful it was to have her home at last.

Sarah and Emma spent the next few days relaxing on the upper gallery, relieved from the heat in part by the jalousies, which kept out the sun but encouraged the breezes. Together, they sewed baby clothes, mended, and chatted, Sarah feeling fifteen again, wondering where the years went. Sarah even brought out her easel and paints, something she hadn't dabbled in since she was Kate's age. She painted a sunset, her mother sitting on a rocker, the orange tabby snoozing in the corner—all crudely rendered, she knew, but she found a sense of girlish freedom in the dabbing of paint on canvas.

"Oh, how lovely," Emma would say, peering over Sarah's shoulder, her hands cool on Sarah's neck as she pinned back a stray wisp of hair.

"Mm-hmm."

In the evenings, they strolled arm in arm through Emma's gardens, drifting apart occasionally to pick a flower or two. Most evenings, their walk led them to the family cemetery, more by happenstance than by design. Surrounded by a low iron fence and a hedge, they laid flowers atop the tiny graves of Sarah's infant siblings, as well as atop the graves of Sarah's father and grandparents, who had immigrated to Louisiana from the West Indies in 1793. Her grandparents had passed away at the turn of the century, her father from an infection in the lungs just three months before Sarah was born.

One evening, as Sarah laid a bouquet of pansies on her grandmother's grave, Emma said, "I've been thinking. . . ."

Sarah stood and said nothing, waiting, breathing in the perfume of honeysuckle. Nearby, perched on the lower branch of a live oak, a squirrel scolded them, brazen with indignation. A breeze rustled the leaves overhead, stirring the Spanish moss like the beards of old men caught in a wind, and Sarah prayed the breeze was a forecast of cooler days to come. Or maybe it was another thundershower on its way.

"John and I have discussed this at length."

"What is it, Mama?"

"We'd—we'd like to give you and William some land."

"Land? But why?"

"Oh, it was an easy decision, really. Once it occurred to me, I couldn't let it go, and the more I thought about it, the more it made sense. Anyway, John's in complete agreement. We've decided to give you five hundred acres off our southeastern border—"

Sarah gasped. "Five hundred acres? My goodness, Mother!"

"Don't look so surprised, or that baby might come sooner than we expect!" Emma laughed. "Of course, I'm jesting, dear, but you can't be too careful."

"But Mother—"

"Come. Let's walk back to the big house. I asked my cook to make us some ice cream. It'll be just the thing to wrap up a beautiful day.

"You see, Sarah, I'm not getting any younger," Emma said as they strolled over the lawn, arm in arm once again. "As for John, well, I think it's pretty clear he's not going to be married anytime soon. Never, if his past is any indication. But you and William, well, your family is growing, and soon your three sons will be vying for their own slice of the pie." She glanced at Sarah's belly. "Who knows? Maybe more than three."

"But Mother, we can't possibly—"

"Nonsense. Utter nonsense. I knew you'd argue, but in this matter, I'll brook no argument." This she said with a smile, patting Sarah's hand, and Sarah knew her mother well enough to know she meant it. "William's invested so much into his sugar venture, and we want to see it succeed as much as he does. These lands we want to give you adjoin your sugar fields.

So, you see, it's perfect. You can turn them into even more sugar land. Besides, I think John prefers his doctoring to anything sprouting from the soil—"

"But Mother—"

Emma halted, gazing at Sarah with those emerald eyes that Sarah had always loved, even as a little girl. She cupped Sarah's face in her hands. Sarah felt the whisper of Emma's breath, smelled the peaches she'd had for supper. "Listen to me. You are my daughter. This is my gift to you. My gift to you and your children. Please honor me by accepting it."

Then, for reasons Sarah could not explain, perhaps it was the touch of her mother's hands on her cheeks, the gift of land, her mother's love, tears welled in Sarah's eyes, and she began to weep, laying her head on Emma's shoulder even as her mother slipped her arms around her. "Oh, Mama."

"Go ahead and cry, child. It's all right."

So, they stood together, mother and daughter, arms around one another, saying nothing more. When the sun dipped low and the mosquitoes started to get pesky, Sarah dabbed her tears, and, together, laughing now, they headed indoors to where the ice cream was simply delectable.

⸺ elle ⸺

Sarah opened her eyes, unsure what had awakened her, but knowing something had. She sat up, heart in her throat. A swath of moonlight cut a rectangle across the foot of her bed.

Though it had been eighteen years since Sarah had left home, her bedroom at Woodleigh remained unchanged. The same dolls she'd played with as a girl still peopled the room—sleeping in wicker carriages, riding the wooden rocking horse, taking tea at the knee-high table—all frozen in time, dressed in silks, laces, bonnets, the fabrics frayed and faded. Gilt-framed portraits hung on the walls, her favorite, that of herself sitting on her mother's lap, four years old, with a preadolescent John standing at Emma's elbow, hand tucked in his jacket like Napoleon.

The room was as it should be.

Had she been dreaming? Was it the baby? Was it time? But even as she thought it, Sarah dismissed the possibility. She was not in labor. That she knew. Whatever the reason, she was wide awake now, every sense keen.

As was true each night, the glass-paneled doors leading to the gallery stood open, filmy curtains billowing gently in a honeysuckle breeze. Sarah threw back her thin bedcover and the mosquito net, heaved herself out of bed, and lumbered across the room, suddenly anxious to close the doors, as if her life, somehow, depended on it. *You're being silly*, she told herself, even as she hurriedly pulled the doors shut, turned the key in the lock, and bolted both doors to the floor.

*Silly.*

She stood and leaned her forehead against the doorframe, waiting until her breathing calmed, until her heart resumed its normal pace in her chest, then drew aside the curtain and peered through the glass.

Save for the cane-bottomed chairs, a broom propped in the corner, and what looked to be a forgotten cup, the gallery was empty. The staircase leading to the lower gallery, also empty.

*You see? Pure silliness.*

She let the curtain fall. Her hand slipped to her belly, feeling the roundness, the firmness beneath the cotton nightgown. "Little baby," she whispered, wondering as she often did whether it was a boy or girl, "can you hear me? Mama was just being silly. That squirrel in the cemetery has more pluck. Hopefully, little James, you'll be far braver than your silly mama, and handsome like your papa. Or, baby Caroline, if it's you in there, my little angel, I pray you're infinitely brave and beautiful and, of course, wise and wonderful." Her hands caressed her swollen abdomen and she smiled, hoping it was a girl, her little Caroline, yet knowing she would be content either way, wondering how on earth she'd ever get back to sleep now.

She rearranged the dishes at the play table—porcelain cups, saucers, gold-rimmed with hand-painted birds amid profusions of flowers, in browns and burgundies and blues. Had she really been so diminutive that she could sit at this table with her dolls? She remembered playing tea by herself, or with a friend if one happened to visit. There was Mary Grey Saffin (of course, she wasn't Mary Grey Saffin then, only little Mary Grey, three years Sarah's senior), sipping from her teacup, saying her father was going to Washington, D.C., next month, and didn't Sarah wish she had a father too? (After more than thirty years of Mary, Sarah was quite used to her peculiar ways and strong opinions. She'd long ago forgiven Mary for her heartless remark at the benefit last June, determined that such pettiness would not injure a relationship destined to span a lifetime, but still wishing that Mary would learn to cultivate more heart than brain.) Then there was little Floride Simons, Sarah's best friend at one time, dead now for thirty years, a victim of the yellow fever.

Sarah was standing, straightening the ribbon under the chin of her favorite doll, Mottie, when she heard something.

A scrape, like a boot on a rough surface.

Muffled. Coming through the open window nearest her bed.

Floorboards creaked as Sarah crossed to the window. She parted the curtain and peered out, again aware of her breathing, faster now, seeming loud, her pulse in her neck.

She saw nothing, nothing but what she expected to see from her vantage on the third floor—the dense foliage of trees, shrubbery, hedges, walkways and steps, the expanse of lawn beyond, the gardener's shed—everything hazy and indistinct, shrouded in a silvery veil of moonlight.

Then she saw a movement.

It was a glimpse so brief that she immediately doubted herself, but in that instant, she saw him. A black man crouched by the well. An iron collar about his neck, and what looked to be prongs jutting outward.

Sarah gasped, blinked, and he was gone.

Vanished.

Where he'd stood was a shrub, man-sized, its trunk split like legs. Above the shrub, the iron lid to the well, handle protruding. Sarah laughed at herself. She clutched Mottie to her chest and kissed the cool porcelain cheek, breathing in the dust of her hair. "You see, Mottie? I haven't grown up entirely. I can still be silly." And with one last glance outside, seeing nothing, Sarah climbed back into bed. She set Mottie on the pillow next to her, holding the doll's hand, whispering silly things until she finally fell into an uneasy sleep.

# Chapter 11

IT SEEMED IMPOSSIBLE THAT Miss Sarah could get any larger without producing a child, but she did. When the second week of October rolled around and no labor pains were forthcoming, even William began to look worried, joking to the family that maybe if they set her on a fast horse, they might succeed in jarring the baby out of her.

At Sarah's invitation, Emma came to Fox Creek to stay until after the baby was delivered. John might as well have come to stay, for he dropped by nearly every day, placing his stethoscope on Sarah's ever-expanding middle and listening attentively before returning the stethoscope to his black bag. Then, predictable as a clock, he'd say, "Send for me as soon as you feel the first contraction. And, of course, send a boy to fetch old Dr. Smith. He's got farther to travel." And off John would go in his buggy. As the days crawled by, Sarah sent for both doctors twice, but both times, even before they arrived (old Dr. Smith to attend to the birth, Dr. John to attend to old Dr. Smith), she knew it was false labor.

The entire plantation, the entire parish, for that matter, seemed to hold its breath, waiting for Mrs. Sarah Jensey to finally come down in size, relieved of a baby that threatened to break both records and scales. There were bets as to the sex and size of the baby. A male child was the hands-down favorite. James the Giant, it was joked. As for size, at first, any bets larger than eight pounds were ridiculed, but soon, bets exceeding nine pounds were not uncommon. (It was whispered that Javier Gustine placed a hefty wager for an equally hefty 10 pounds, 4 ounces, though Sarah could not be persuaded to believe it.)

There was one big baby at Fox Creek that was already creating a pleasant stir. Chancet, his racing years over, had sired a foal that had every indication of taking after his father and tearing up the racetracks in every parish from here to yonder. Hardly a day went by that William didn't visit the stables, watching Arrochar as he frolicked in the pastures, his near-black coat glistening. The colt seemed to delight in kicking up his hooves and dashing around, hardly having time to gulp his mother's milk before he was off again, finally flopping down in the shade to sleep.

William conferred periodically with Uncle Abram as to the colt's health, weaning, and training, pleased that Uncle Abram agreed that this was a horse worth reckoning. Only one thing worried William: Cato, the jockey, was no longer the spring chicken he used to be, and lately, he'd been unable to sink as low in the saddle, saying his back was paining him. "We need a new jockey," William told Uncle Abram on a morning when the sunrise splashed the sky with oranges, pinks, and purples, as if someone had tripped with the paint bucket.

"Well now, it's a good thing you mentioned that, Mars William, a good thing, 'cause I been thinking. If you don't mind me offering my opinion on such matters, I been thinking that the boy Footy, he be the one. Don't hardly figure he weighs more'n a stalk of wheat, nohow."

Actually, William had been planning on purchasing an experienced jockey the next time he was at the Metairie track, but Uncle Abram's suggestion gave him pause. Footy? Was it possible?

So, while the sun worked its way to finally rise above the treetops, they discussed the jockey question at length, finally deciding that yes, training Footy was at least worth a try. So long as he wasn't afraid of horses and didn't mind flying at speeds that sucked the tears right out of your eyes. "I'll send Footy here today," said William in conclusion. "Start him as a stableboy. Get him familiar with horses, and we'll take it from there."

"Yessir."

With all matters pertaining to horses and jockeys settled to his satisfaction, on the twentieth day of October, with over two hundred bales of cotton already shipped and the cotton storehouse bursting at the seams, William sent eighty-odd workers to the sugar fields, where the harvesting of sugar began. That first resounding *thwack!* made by the first machete was an exciting sound, a sound born from years of preparation and industry. William thought he'd never heard or seen anything finer than the crackle of cane and the slow disappearance of row after row as the stalks fell to the machetes. Throughout the next few days, work proceeded feverishly. Breck's school lessons were temporarily suspended while he and William supervised the work in the fields, cane towering above their heads even as they rode their horses down the rows. And to think this was only the beginning. There were now an additional five hundred acres just waiting to be tamed into sugar land, thanks to Emma and John's generosity.

William was equally pleased with the progress at the sugarhouse. The sugarmaker, Ogden Birchett, was proving to be worth his weight in gold, which was a substantial, though well-deserved, compliment. Sporting ill-fitting dentures and a cleft chin, Birchett appeared capable of directing a novice workforce, handling the steam engine, the rollers, the kettles, and the furnace with equal expertise and calmness. And the sugar, by God, the sugar! Maybe it was because it was a first-year crop. Or because it was grown on virgin soil. Or maybe Birchett was, as everyone said, simply the best. Whatever the reason, William thought it the finest sugar he'd ever tasted, bar none, and Breck agreed.

Jensey sugar. By God, it was finally real.

Now all that remained was for his wife to have that baby.

For the first time in Kate's life, she envied Lucy Saffin. Attending Mme. Dupré's Finishing School for Young Ladies in New Orleans, Lucy was likely practicing the harp, painting watercolors, or preparing to attend the theater as the fashionable crowd did on Saturday evenings. Whereas Kate was stuck in the Fox Creek schoolroom with a particularly dreadful Mr. Gilbert, who, at that very moment, was in a particularly dreadful, mean, nasty, and cantankerous mood, seeming to delight in torturing her.

"Do it again," he said, setting her paper before her on the table.

"But I—"

"*Again.* This time, *think.*"

Kate sighed irritably, picked up her pen, and started over, wishing Mr. Gilbert would tie a millstone around his neck and jump into the Mississippi. Who cared about the Pythagorean theorem anyway? Who cared about hypotenuses, or right triangles, or laws of cosines?

"Stupid equation," she muttered.

"What?"

"Nothing."

Mr. Gilbert wasn't the only one she was miffed at. Frankly, it seemed the entire world was positioned against her, as if all humanity had discovered that the true meaning of life was to make Katherine Emma Jensey totally miserable. Breck, getting to go out to the sugar fields while she was stuck here with Mr. Mean. Monette, all peevish and pouty anymore, saying she was too tired for this and too tired for that. Mama, insisting Kate stay at home to help with the baby, saying Kate could begin school later, in the first week of February, when the new term began. February—why, that was *ages* away! And what did "help with the baby" really mean, anyway? What with Mammy Hester, Monette, Grandma Emma, and everyone else on the plantation around to help, why on earth did Mama need her around too? She'd tried to explain it to her mother a million times, but her mother always assumed an expression—lips tight, eyelids half closed. An expression of martyrdom that said, You Are Causing Me Pain.

But that wasn't the real reason Kate was out of sorts. For months, Kate had planned a sugarhouse party. Well, more imagined it than actually *planned* it, because, as the harvest season approached, Mama had, once again, put her foot down. No sugarhouse party. At first, Kate had refused to believe her mother was serious, thinking surely she didn't mean to interfere with *tradition* (or what would certainly *become* a Fox Creek tradition), an annual event destined to be talked about by everyone, far and wide. But the more Kate had argued, not only that day, but the next and the next and the next, the more her mother resisted, finally dealing the death blow by assuming her You Are Causing Me Pain expression.

"But I've already invited everybody!" Kate had wailed, and though it was not entirely true, it *felt* true.

"I'm sorry, Katherine dear, but you'll just have to uninvite them. I simply can't have a house full of guests when I'm due to deliver."

"Surely by then you'll already have had the baby, or watermelon, or whatever it is you're having. We can have the party after the baby's born, can't we? *Pleeease,* Mama!"

"Katherine Emma Jensey, this discussion is over. You know that I—"

But her mother never finished what she was going to say, for Kate ran howling up the stairs and flung herself on her bed, weeping off and on for the next few days from a combination of disappointment and the fact that her corset didn't really allow for such carrying on.

"It's not fair," Kate muttered now, her pen scratching across the paper.

"What?"

"Nothing."

Kate sensed Mr. Gilbert peering at her over his spectacles. She hunched over her paper, pretending to concentrate.

"Well, Miss Kate, since fairness appears to be an issue for you today, how about I give you a couple more problems so you can be satisfied you've learned your lesson fairly?"

"No, thank you, Mr. Gilbert, Sir."

"Why, it's no hardship for me, I assure you."

It was another ink-blotched hour of academic drudgery before Kate was finally released from the schoolroom. Monette was in Kate's bedroom, snapping a bed linen in the air. The linen billowed like a ship's sail before settling neatly onto the bed, scenting the room with lavender.

"Be glad you don't have to go to school," Kate grouched, collapsing into the wingback chair next to the bed. "Mr. Gilbert is such a horrible, cruel, purposeless man. Who cares about theorems? I certainly don't care about theorems. Do you care about theorems, Monette?"

Monette was smoothing the linens, tucking in the edges. She bustled around to the foot of the bed, not looking at Kate, her skirt of blue gingham swaying, her apron crisp and fresh. "I don't know what theorems are, Kate."

Saints alive. Was that snippiness in her voice? Was the entire world on a mission? Was there something they all knew that she didn't? "Oh, for Pete's sake, please don't tell me you're crabby, too. I can't abide any more crabbiness. I swear, if I hear one more crabby, snippety word, I'll start screaming. Or maybe I'll start yanking out someone's hair. Maybe yours. Then at least you'll have a reason to be a Little Miss Crabby Sourpuss."

Monette gaped at Kate. "What on earth's eating you?"

"What's eating me? Why, tons of things. My—my corset's pinching me in half, for one, and I've ink stains all over my hands. Mama's been cross lately and she won't let me have a sugarhouse party for all the goodness in the world, Breck has all the fun and gets to do everything that's interesting because he's a *man* and I'm *not*, and, besides all that, lately you've been nothing but a bitter, nasty, hard-to-swallow *pill*."

Seeing Monette's shocked face, her mouth hanging open, her honey-colored eyes all huge, Kate felt a giggle tickle its way up her throat. Now that she'd said it aloud, it all sounded rather ridiculous. And when Monette said, "A—a pill? I've been a pill?" Kate could hold it in no longer and burst into laughter.

"Oh, Monette, you should see your face!"

"I'm a pill? You think I'm a pill?"

Still giggling, feeling now light and happy, Kate stood and clasped both Monette's hands in hers, first removing the pillow from her grasp and tossing it onto the bed. A half smile now softened Monette's face, and Kate thought she'd never looked prettier, with her hair a mass of black curls and skin creamy as caramel. Saints alive. Whatever would I do without Monette? she thought, leaning forward and kissing her cheek resoundingly. "What do you say we go riding? It's been ages."

Monette's smile faded. She looked down. "I can't. Lizzy's got a pile of chores for me and—"

"Oh, pish posh. Lizzy may be your Miss Bossy Boss, but she's not mine. If I say we go riding, we go riding."

An hour later, after sailing out the back door shouting, "Monette's going riding with me!" to an open-mouthed Lizzy, Kate was galloping Mamie across the pastures, down lanes and cart tracks, with Monette's arms wrapped around her from behind. Though there was scarcely a cloud in the sky, the air was cool, refreshing after the stuffy schoolroom. Kate rode Mamie hard, the wind making her eyes water. Down past the racetrack, the borders of the cotton fields, the swamp bottoms, and through the woods. And just when Kate feared Monette might peel off, unable to hang on any longer, and certainly long after the mare was laboring hard, Kate wheeled Mamie to a stop near the entrance to their secret spot. "Let's go in," she said.

In Kate's opinion, the glade was still a magical place. Secluded, bejeweled with blossoms, pulsing with animal life, it had been their sanctuary for years now, still secret, unknown by anyone else, so far as Kate knew. Entering the clearing (though Kate had to admit that scrambling through the tunnel on all fours was more strenuous than she remembered), she was captivated once again. "It's been waiting for us," Kate whispered, something she always did while here, as if the sanctuary was a cathedral, and she, a nun, bound in vows of silence and obeisance.

Hand in hand, they strolled through the clearing. They stopped to pick the autumn flowers, to watch a rabbit who observed them in equal measure, clover poking out the side of its mouth, whiskers quivering. Kate tucked a flower behind Monette's ear, adjusting her black curls. "Remember when we used to make flower chains? You taught me how."

Touching the flower behind her ear, Monette smiled, her fingers tracing the petals. "Did I?"

"We were quite the beautiful princesses, you and I. All the handsome princes from the surrounding kingdoms begged for our hands in marriage—"

"Rescuing us from dragons, I suppose?"

"Mean, nasty dragons, almost as evil as Mr. Gilbert. All the princes promised us everything if only we would marry them. But of course, we always refused, remember?" Kate stretched out her arms, laughing, and began to twirl. "Our kingdoms were vast, and our palaces made of gold and sprinkled with fairy dust. And of course, no matter what, we always lived happily ever after, you and I!"

Kate stopped spinning when Monette didn't laugh. When instead she sighed and looked up, as if expecting storm clouds to gather and there to come a chilling downpour. "It is a shame that fairy tales do not come true."

"Why, Monette! *Tu n'as pas honte?* I thought we left all that gloomy-doominess back at the house!" She gestured around her. "Here, there are no such things as gloomy-doominess, or bossy housekeepers, or idiot schoolmasters, or—or Pythagorean theorems, thank heavens. And certainly, no sourpuss faces. And if I see or hear anything that's remotely cross-eyed," Kate said, wagging her finger in Monette's face as if she were a naughty child, "well, then, I shall have to toss you in the dungeon!"

They both glared at one another, mock tension between them. Feeling once again giddy, wild, relieved to be out of the house, Kate lunged for Monette, grabbing her wrists, giggling when they started to tussle. Monette struggled to free herself, beginning to laugh, too.

"I'm sorry," Kate said between fits of giggles, "but you definitely were pouty just now—ouch! You broke the rules and you've got to—hold still, there now!—got to go to the dungeon—hey!"

Monette freed herself and bolted away through the flowers and grasses, stumbling a bit on the hem of her skirt before she hiked it up, running fast. Kate chased her, wondering what her mother would say if she could see them now. Running like savages. Laughing so hard it was difficult to breathe. Kate sometimes catching Monette, grasping a handful of gingham before Monette twisted away, running again. Around the trunk of the huge magnolia. Monette on one side, Kate on the other. Monette always dodging her no matter which way Kate ran around the tree.

Finally, happily, Kate gave up. Still laughing, she collapsed to the ground, too out of breath, her corset too tight, the world beginning to spin, her vision pulsing with the beat of her heart. "Oh, save me, save me, save me."

Monette tumbled over her before flopping onto the grass beside her, panting.

"It's not fair," Kate said, once her breathing calmed somewhat. "You don't have to wear a corset."

"Your legs are longer, so we're even."

"Since when did you get to be so fast?"

Monette propped herself up on her elbow. "Since I've had to chase you around to get you to behave, I suppose." She ripped up some grass blades and tossed them at Kate.

Kate grinned. "I'm beginning to think I'll *never* behave."

"So I've learned."

"Well, little Miss Sourpuss, don't tell me you've never misbehaved. Never done anything bad or wrong?" Though said in jest, Kate was taken aback when a shadow flitted across Monette's face. Just as suddenly as it had come, it was gone. Had she imagined it? Was it possible that there were secrets Monette was keeping from her? When Monette only shrugged in response, saying nothing, Kate determined that, whatever the secret, she would find it out. What delicious fun! She whispered, "I'll tell you a secret if you tell me one."

Monette hesitated, then nodded.

Sitting up, Kate arranged her skirts so she could sit cross-legged, pleased when Monette did the same. They faced one another, knees touching. Overhead, a Blue Jay called loudly, launching himself from a tree branch. A leaf spiraled down.

"You must promise to never tell a soul," Kate said.

"I promise."

"Pinky promise?"

"Pinky promise," replied Monette, and they linked their pinkies.

"I—I'm in love with—" Kate faltered, the words catching in her throat like a plug of cotton. Now that it was time to reveal her secret, it felt a little like ripping off her nightgown and running around naked at midnight. She felt exposed, vulnerable, yet still, somehow, pleasantly wicked. Kate cleared her throat and whispered, "I—I'm in love with—Stephen Decatur Rockwell."

For a second Monette just looked at her blankly, as if she'd just said they were having cornmeal mush for dinner and wasn't that grand? Then a look of comprehension spread over Monette's face, and she gasped. "But he's married!"

"You think I don't know that?"

"But—but you *can't* love him!"

"Love didn't ask me. It just happened."

"Does he love you?"

"No more than he loves any other young lady. I mean, he's nice to me and certainly chivalrous, but, well, he's in love with his—his Irish wife. And now they've got a new baby boy and they're happy as larks by all accounts."

While Kate talked, Monette had picked a few flowers and now began weaving a chain of blossoms. "So, what are you going to do?"

"What can I do?" Kate shrugged, taking a daisy from Monette and pulling off its petals one by one. *He loves me, he loves me not . . .* "Fall out of love, I suppose. Although how one does that, I haven't a clue. Gouge out my heart, I guess."

"Maybe just the right man needs to come along."

"And who would that be? Hugh Vanderkloot, maybe? Or Victor Cobb? Or how about that horrid Edward Scarborough?" As Kate spoke, she recalled the words of Crone Juju, words that, until now, she'd made herself forget: *Chile, you ain't never gonna marry nobody.* Maybe, thought Kate with alarm, the old witch was right.

"But there are others—" Monette was saying.

"No one I'm interested in. You see, it's hopeless." Now that it was all out in the open, Kate rather wished she'd not brought up the subject of secrets. Instead of it being the exciting fun she'd imagined, she was beginning to feel as mournful as Monette. Before the afternoon disappeared completely into an abyss of pity, Kate said, "Your turn," plucking the final petal from her daisy.

*He loves me not.*

While waiting for Monette to reveal her secret, whatever it was, Kate began weaving her own chain of blossoms. "I promise I won't tell," she prompted, fingers already sticky.

Finally, Monette's voice came low and soft, "I have these dreams."

Kate frowned. Monette's deep, dark secret was about *dreams?*

"For years now, I've dreamed of a man. He's strong. And powerful."

"Powerful like a king?"

"Powerful as in—" Monette flexed her arms, "physical strength. It's difficult to explain, but he comes to me in my dreams—"

Kate gasped, shocked, hands frozen in the middle of twining daisies. "Don't tell me you and he do the *hump*—"

"*Mon Dieu!* Of course not!"

"Well, all right, what then?"

"Always in my dream I'm in some faraway place, some clearing or courtyard, I don't know where. And even though there are people everywhere, I'm alone and afraid."

"But what about the man? Your prince?"

Here Monette paused, glancing quickly at Kate as if wondering how much to reveal, while a cool dappled sunlight played across her features like a lover's caress. "At first, he is not there. Instead, I'm lying naked in this clearing. I can't move and—and everyone is staring at me."

"Naked!" Kate cried, gasping. "What a nightmare! I would rather die than have everyone see me naked!"

"It *is* a nightmare. Lying there, I feel so helpless. But then the man, the powerful man—"

"Your prince."

"*Oui,* my prince, as you say, he comes from nowhere and wraps his arms around me, protecting me."

"While you're *naked?*"

Monette looked away. Kate saw the color rise in her cheeks and wondered if she was sorry now that she'd revealed her secret.

"And yet, I don't know. It's as if I've known him before, and yet how could I have? I mean, he's a man, *après tout,* a grown man. He—he loves me. I know he does."

Kate concentrated on her daisy chain, thinking, so that's it? Monette's big, fat, delicious, juicy secret? It was all just a little anticlimactic. She remembered the time a few months back when Monette had burst into her room, all teary-eyed and upset because of a silly nightmare. Perhaps Monette just needed to learn a little perspective. To understand that dreams were, well, just dreams. "It *is* just a dream," Kate said, when Monette offered nothing more. "At least the person I'm in love with is actually real and can walk and talk and truly break your heart." Disappointing as it was, why then, Kate wondered, did she feel as if there was something more, something that Monette still was not telling her? Could it be? Was there more to the secret? Or maybe Monette had not just one, but two secrets? Maybe many secrets? "So, that's it? That's your big secret?"

"*Oui.*"

"There's nothing else?"

"*Rien.*"

A silence descended, along with a growing darkness. The sun had fallen behind the trees and an evening breeze rustled the leaves in the branches overhead, a cool breeze bordering on cold, swirling down like falling leaves, making Kate shiver. But just as she prepared to stand and suggest a visit to their long-ago playhouse, that maybe there were candles and matches there and wouldn't that be fun, Monette leaned across and placed her crown of flowers on Kate's head. "You're still a princess, *mon amie.* Your prince will come."

Inexplicably, as the flowers resting on her head sweetened the air with a bruised fragrance, Kate felt touched, gifted with a friendship that suddenly seemed profound and precious. A friendship that nothing could injure, come hell or high water or secrets or anything. Kate took the circlet of flowers she'd assembled and set it on Monette's head. After arranging her curls just so, Kate sat back and smiled, gazing into Monette's amber eyes, feeling somehow spacious, grand, as if a larger part of her had expanded to fill the universe. "Sisters forever," she whispered.

# *Chapter 12*

WHEN MONETTE SAW THE stables and adjacent carriage house, she knew something was afoot. No less than seven carriages of different sizes and hauling capacities stood outside the carriage house. The respective coachmen were in various stages of unharnessing the horses, leading teams to the stables, or cleaning the enamel of accumulated dust, polishing the conveyances to a shine once again.

"Footy, what's happening?" Kate asked as Monette slid off Mamie.

Footy stood just outside the stable door. All around, torches blazed in the deepening twilight, smoke mixing with the smells of straw and manure. "You better hurry on up, Missie Kate," he was saying, holding the halter as Kate dismounted. "They been looking for you."

"Who's they?"

"Why, everyone. Your mama and papa, and a course, all them guests."

"What guests?" Monette heard the impatience in Kate's voice and knew that if Footy didn't answer her in two shakes, Kate would boil over like hot taffy.

"Why, there be the Saffins, and a course, Marshall McCain. And then there be the Rockwells with their baby—"

Kate's eyes grew huge in the torchlight. "Oh my God! The Rockwells!" No sooner was this said to Monette, Kate whirled, and with a shout at Footy to take care of Mamie, she was off, hurrying toward the big house so fast Monette had to run to keep up with her long strides. "Oh my God, oh my God. I've grass stains all over my dress. I've sweated like an ape. Do apes sweat? Oh my God. The Rockwells. Did you hear, Monette? Hurry!"

At the big house, they slipped through the back door and up the stairs, unnoticed save for Nat, who told Monette that Lizzy was looking for her, and boy was she mad.

"Never mind that," Kate said, breathless. "Just go tell Mama I'm here and not to worry. I'll be down as soon as I freshen up!"

While Monette stoked the fire and heated the irons, helping Kate out of her dirty clothes and into clothing more appropriate for company, a myriad of voices, laughter, and even singing, drifted into Kate's bedroom from the parlor below. Then someone was playing the pianoforte, Mozart by the sound of it.

"What should I do when I see his wife?" Kate sat at the vanity, fussing with the face powder, the ribbon pot, the pomade, the hairpins, examining her face in the mirror, frowning over every blemish and freckle.

Monette released a tendril of hair from the iron. "Tell her she looks lovely."

"And his baby? What about his baby?"

"What do you mean, what about his baby?"

"Well, what should I say?"

"Tell him his baby looks like him. Men like to hear that."

Kate cocked an eyebrow, gazing quizzically at Monette in the mirror. "Since when did you become such an expert on men? Is there something you haven't told me?"

"I know nothing about men," Monette admitted with a laugh, thinking it was true, remembering Breck, and how his betrayal of her had completely surprised her, unnerved her, *hurt* her, a bolt of lightning from a sky of summer blue. Remembering Marshall McCain and how he'd paid her undue attention, wondering now if she'd overblown it all, as he hadn't spared her so much as a disinterested glance since then. And then there was that night at Hickory Grove Plantation, when those men had called her names so vile, she blushed to think of it. Men? She knew nothing of men. In fact, they were beginning to frighten her. . . .

Hairpin clasped at the corner of her mouth, Monette said, "There, *mon amie,* you are beautiful once again," giving a final tweak to the tortoiseshell comb and *bandeau* in Kate's hair.

Like a child released from the dinner table, Kate sprang to her feet with a squeal of delight. And, after rendering an appraisal of herself in the armoire mirror, twirling once in her peaches-and-cream tarlatan dress,

Kate brushed Monette's cheek with her lips and hurried out the door, leaving behind nothing but a whiff of the magnolia fragrance she'd dabbed behind her ears and the sound of her footsteps gliding down the stairs.

⸻ ℓℓ ⸻

"Puss . . . puss wants a corner!" cried fourteen-year-old Frances Parsons, all blonde curls and prettiness.

There followed a second's pause before all became pandemonium, everyone rushing from this corner to that corner before "puss" could beat them to it. Breck hurled himself out of his corner and dashed across the second staging of the sugarhouse, bumping into Stephen Rockwell, into Kate, amid various giggles and shouts and scuffles, before finally catapulting himself into another corner a chin's whisker before Vanderkloot, leaving the latter without a corner, and everyone laughing and panting for breath.

"Ha!" shrieked Frances. "Kloot's the puss now!"

The evening came as a surprise to Breck. Not because he hadn't known there would be a sugarhouse party. He had. After all, he'd helped his father plan it. "What's a sugarhouse without a party?" his father had asked him two days ago, his eyes glinting with that mischievousness that often heralded a break in routine, whether it be an afternoon fishing at Piney Lake, a jaunt to New Orleans, or a fire hunt at midnight. And so commenced last-minute arrangements—all very hush-hush, of course, so Breck's mother couldn't object. They'd invited the neighbors. Rustled up some musicians. Informed the kitchen staff. The household staff. Ogden Birchett, the sugarmaker. All was in readiness for a night of frivolity. No, the evening came as a surprise to Breck because, though he'd dreaded the party the way young men abhorred the staid conversations of old men, he was finding the evening enjoyable. As if, for the first time in months, he could breathe again. As if his future held a glimmer of something beyond abject misery and longing for someone he could not have.

Earlier, following the late supper, they'd crammed together in two cane carts, singing *Corn Cobs Twist Your Hair* as lustily as barmaids while the carts rumbled down the lanes and milk spilled across the moonless night sky. Then they'd sung *Rothsay-O!* and *Turkey in the Straw*, the verses growing increasingly boisterous, so that by the time they reached the sugarhouse—the air smoky-sweet—even Breck's mother was laughing with the rest of them.

"Puss . . . puss wants a corner!" said Vanderkloot.

Breck darted out of his corner, colliding into Frances Parsons. There was a brief "Oh!" from Frances. A shy smile of white, straight teeth framed in slender lips. Eyes of cornflower blue. And while Breck was momentarily nonplussed, wondering when Frances had left behind her braids of girlhood and started putting up her hair and wearing lace gloves, she maneuvered around him and ran, giggling, into the one remaining corner, leaving Breck alone as "puss" in the center of the room.

Breck grinned, glancing around at the dozen or so people hugging the corners of the various hidey-holes assigned such a function. "Puss . . . puss wants a corner!" he cried, diving once again into the ruckus and stumbling across the wooden boarding as he raced around people, colliding pleasantly, laughing until it hurt. Until William hollered from below that it was time for a taffy pull and would all the youngsters and the young-at-heart come on down to aid in the new business at hand.

— ele —

Monette's face still stung from where Lizzy had slapped her.

"Bitch," Lizzy had said, her hand connecting like a sack of rocks, so hard it threw Monette onto the brick of the rear loggia and started her nose bleeding. "What you doing leaving me with all the work? What you mean riding off into the blue yonder when there be company coming? Bitch, that's what you is. Good for nothin' yellow bitch."

Walking now along the track to the sugarhouse, Monette wiped the dribble of blood away, wishing there was a moon, wishing she'd brought a lantern. But she hadn't thought of it. The second the door to the butler's pantry swung closed on Lizzy, Monette ignored the housekeeper's last command to clean off the supper table, a command cast over Lizzy's departing shoulder like hog slop. Instead, Monette stood, brushed herself off, and left for the sugarhouse, thinking, I will tell Kate. We will see who gets the beating.

She'd never been to the sugar complex. Kate had told her all about it, though—especially the sugarhouse—how grand everything was: brick, smelling firewood-fresh and sugar-sweet, with a detached office, a cottage for the sugarmaker, and everything else required to produce the cones of sugar both ants and humans liked so well.

Now Monette paused, unsure which direction to go. So far, she'd kept on the track because of the corn, or cane, or cotton—or whatever it was—that grew along the edges. A prick of a branch or a brush of a leaf let her know when she strayed too far left or right. But now, the track appeared to open on both sides. Directly ahead, she heard the murmur of the creek, hardly perceptible unless she held her breath. Dense shadows of trees and brush loomed directly ahead too, both creek and trees blocking the way.

It was a fork in the road.

And as she paused there, nose dribbling, face smarting, a voice swelled inside her, like floodwaters rising:

*Mwana na mono—my daughter, go back.*

*Forget the sugarhouse.*

*Clean the dining room like Lizzy ordered.*

*Accept the slap as your due.*

*Mwana na mono, go back.*

She hesitated. Nearly turned around. Then she touched her cheek. And in the touching, she recalled Lizzy's eyes of granite, as her hand swiped the air, her voice tight with hatred:

*Bitch! Good for nothin' yellow bitch!*

Monette sniffed the air, turned in the direction of the sugary smoke, and moved forward through the darkness.

"It's my turn," Vanderkloot announced. They were variously seated or standing in a clumsy circle on the main floor of the sugarhouse—all thirty of them or so—cloaked under the light of the pine torches, warmed by the fire blazing in the furnace. There were the Saffins (minus Lucy), the Gustines, a smattering of the Parsons clan, Vanderkloot, the Rockwells, William, Sarah, Emma, John, Mehitable, Breck, Kate, George, Thomas, and, of course, the ubiquitous Marshall, whom no one could dissuade from a fine party where hot punch—boiled cane juice mixed liberally with French brandy—was served.

Hot punch or not, the party was turning out to be simply hideous, in Kate's opinion. Oh, there was nothing about the party *itself* that presented a problem. Besides the hot punch, the sugarhouse itself was simply divine, what with all the dusky aunties and uncles stirring the giant copper kettles while steam wisped about their grinning, glistening faces, and the sugarmaker strolled here and there, chatting with them and keeping an eye on it all. And of course, there were the games, the ride in the cane cart, the songs, the taffy pull. . . .

No, it was simply hideous because no one should be expected to suffer as she was suffering. (Was there no end to suffering? No mercy whatsoever?) Her misery had returned in the parlor, upon kissing Irish Mary hello and telling her she looked lovely tonight. Honestly, Kate hadn't *really* expected Irish Mary to look so pretty. She'd instead expected to be the giver of undeserved compliments, rather like a benefactor showering gifts upon the indigent. But in fact, Irish Mary looked positively radiant. She was petite, and her skin, without a freckle to be found, was the epitome of perfection, making Kate suddenly feel cloddish, all arms and legs and gangly horsiness and youth. Irish Mary's flaming red hair was lush and thick, a wealth of lushness only new mothers possessed. Her eyes glowed with happiness. And if all that weren't bad enough, Stephen hovered over her shoulder—so obviously bursting with pride!—while his wife cradled their baby.

Kate had swallowed the despair and guilt wedged in her throat, smiled at the red-haired, pink-skinned baby, eyes just like his mother's, and heard herself say (stupidly, horrifyingly, my God, what was she thinking!), "Why, Stephen, I declare he looks just like you!"

Both Irish Mary and Stephen had gaped at her. Irish Mary, flummoxed, as if she were a newly informed cripple, presented with the task of learning to walk without any legs. Stephen, as if he perceived Kate's thoughts, every stupid or mean thing she'd ever thought or said. Kate could feel the blood rush to her face, setting the roots of her hair on fire. But then Stephen was smiling. They both were, he and Irish Mary. At each other, at her, and he was saying, "Why, thank you, Miss Kate. I shall take that as the sincerest of compliments." Then his hand fell to his wife's shoulder, and he'd gazed upon his child and his Irish Mary in such a way that Kate felt, for a sickening, dizzy moment, that she might vomit down Irish Mary's bodice, splatter chunks of food all over those milk-engorged breasts.

"I love my love with an L," Vanderkloot was saying, casting Kate what was no doubt meant to be a meaningful glance, which she returned with a stony stare, "because she is *lovely,* because her name is *Liberty,* and because she lives in—in *Lafayette.* I will give her a *lock.*"

When Vanderkloot began twisting a lock of his hair, as if he would gladly hack off all his limp, lackluster strands and pile them onto Kate's lap forevermore, Kate sighed and focused on the rafters.

*Idiot fop.*

"—I will feed her on *licorice* and make her a bouquet of—of—" Vanderkloot paused, started, paused again.

"Forfeit!" cried Judge Rockwell. "You must pay a for—"

"Wait, wait! Here is my answer—I'll make her a bouquet of *lavender!*"

After a few more people went, it was Kate's turn. While she was yet wondering whether she should pass, and whether such passing would be considered rude and unbecoming of a hostess, her words rushed out in a torrent: "I love my love with an R, because he is *ridiculous,* because his name is *Rogue,* and because he lives in a *rat hole.* I will give him a *rake.* I will feed him on *rotten rump roast* and make him a bouquet of—of *raspberry thorns!*"

There followed a silence during which everyone was no doubt wondering whether she was in earnest, perhaps piqued about something? But when she flashed what she knew to be a brilliant smile, every bit a lie, every bit as miserable as drowning herself in a bucket, everyone laughed and clapped, while Thomas pointed out that neither "hole" nor "thorns" began with the letter R, and George frowned, saying that he doubted "rat hole" could be found on a map.

"Bravo!" cried Senator Saffin. "Three cheers to Miss Kate for her wit!"

"Now that's my idea of a terrific relationship," quipped Marshall.

Surprisingly, with their response, Kate's spirits lifted. A triumphant repartee. Victory over misery. But her triumph was short-lived. Looking about the circle, she caught Stephen's gaze. It was a brief glance, no more, but it was enough. His winter-blue eyes, bewildered, his face stricken, as if he'd just awakened from a happy dream to find the sands shifting beneath him.

⸻ ❧ ⸻

Light blazed through the windows of the sugarhouse—golden teeth in the maw of darkness. The twin chimneys belched smoke, invisible against the night sky save for the sparks and the inking out of stars. In the clearing surrounding the sugarhouse, teams of mules rested, heads down, hitched to the cane carts, oblivious to the laughter that seeped from the sugarhouse like honey from a honeycomb.

Monette paused at the edge of the clearing. Now that she was here, faced with the task of entering the sugarhouse, finding Kate, explaining what Lizzy had done, Monette wondered if she was making a mistake—waltzing into a party in front of Mars William, in front of Breck, everyone—wondered whether she should wait and tell Kate in the morning instead. But then there was Lizzy, back at the big house, waiting.

She shivered, rubbing her arms, undecided. Behind her, where the road ran next to the creek, an owl hooted. From somewhere nearby, a wet sound, like water poured from a jug held high.

No doubt Lizzy was furious by now and itching to slap her silly the instant she presented her naked face. Her cheek stung anew with the thought of Lizzy. Pressure dilated her chest until Monette's breath shortened.

*She should not have hit me.*

*She had no right.*

Before Monette could change her mind, she marched into the clearing, startled when a man's voice said, "Well, look who's here."

She whirled.

It was Marshall, buttoning up the front of his pants.

She realized that the wet sound she'd heard was him urinating. That he'd been standing all along at the perimeter of the clearing, just ten feet away. Peeing into the countryside like Monette and Kate used to do when they'd wandered too far away to use the privy or were just too absorbed in their play to be bothered.

Seeing him, her pulse quickened, jumping into her throat. Even in the gloom, illuminated only by what emanated through the sugarhouse windows, she could see him looking at her with eyes made black in the night. Alligator eyes. Hungry. He was smiling, the pockmarks on his face shadowed like cratered cheese.

"You're hurt."

She wiped the blood dribbling out of her nose. "It's—it's nothing."

The owl hooted again—a call that now sounded like a warning: *Go! Go! Go!*

"Pardon me, *Monsieur* McCain, but I need to find—" She stepped sideways now, edging toward the sugarhouse, but with her every step, he moved toward her, closer. "I—I need to find Miss Kate."

"Well, the least you can do is let me look at it. Maybe I can help."

"It's nothing. *Rien.*"

"I said, let me look at it, girl."

Though quiet, his voice sliced like a machete. Monette froze as he drew close, thinking, *Kate! Toute de suite! I am alone!*

The heel of his boot scuffed the dirt. A moth landed on his pants before flying off again, wings fluttering crazily, the sound suddenly thrumming inside her head, a thousand wings beating, weak and fragile. Then his hand was on her face, turning her toward the light, and she smelled him. His sweat. The brandy. The stink of cigar smoke. And from some distant place inside her, she realized his hand was soft. That it shouldn't be soft. That being soft was somehow wrong.

"There's water at Birchett's place. We can clean you up."

He gripped her upper arm and began to pull her in the direction of a small house that she only now noticed. She thought of resisting, and for a moment, she did. Her feet planted, growing roots, refusing to move. But then he was pulling her, harder, and she was following, her feet obedient, her legs alternately bending, straightening, left, right, a part of her screaming, *Pull away! Run!* another part of her shutting down, mechanical, blank, as if with Lizzy's slap, both her brains and her will had oozed out of her nose along with her blood.

The door was unlocked. Hinges creaked. It was cave-dark, stinking of beans. He shut the door, then stumbled into something. A chair, maybe. The sound of spindles hitting the floor.

"Shit!"

His fingers stabbed into the flesh of her arm, and she gasped. He was pulling her through the darkness. She stubbed her foot against something, stumbling. She heard someone keep asking, Where is the light? Where is the light? realizing that it was her voice, her mouth, tongue, lips.

Then he was pushing her up against a wall, hard. The corner of a picture frame jabbed her behind her ear as Marshall's mouth crushed hers, as he pried her mouth open with his tongue, and she began to cry, to choke, squeezing her eyes closed, tears burning, his hot breath smothering, tongue tasting like ashes. *No! No!* She didn't know when he hiked up her skirt, but suddenly she felt the bruise of his knuckles against her inner thigh. She felt a tug, heard the rip of fabric, felt him briefly fondle her before he began fumbling with the front of his trousers. He was panting now in her ear, a wet breathing, grunting, whispering *whore*. She was struggling, trying to push him away. To say No, to beg him to stop, *arrêtez!* but his hand was mashing her mouth, smearing spit and blood and salt tears. Her head roared, beating. Her heart slammed against her ribs. He continued to fumble with the front of his pants, now jerking his hand back and forth quickly, saying, Fuck, goddammit, fuck, fucking whore—a jerking that went on and on until the picture fell off the wall, frame crashing to the floor, wood splintering. With the falling of the picture, Marshall cursed again, took his hand from her mouth, and slammed the wall with his fist before slapping her across the face. It was a vicious slap, harder than Lizzy's, catching her by surprise, stealing her breath. Her head snapped against the wall. Her knees buckled. He pulled away, and she crumpled to the floor, her bones suddenly turned to water, a piece of wood jabbing her hip.

Then he was kneeling beside her, fingers squeezing her cheeks together, hard against her teeth so that it hurt, and she gasped and tried to pull away, blood seeping into her mouth. His voice was in her ear. "You tell a soul, and I promise I'll gut you. Slice you like a hog from your ass to your nose and feed your guts to whoever's hungry."

So saying, he released her and stood. She heard his boots clomp across the floor. The door opening, closing, then nothing.

## Chapter 13

"WELL, YOU SURE SEEM to be having a good time tonight," Kate said, her tone implying that she was not. "I guess being allowed to drink more than one glass of hot punch does wonders for one's disposition."

Breck laughed. "Please don't tell me that having a good time is a crime."

They waltzed around the sugarhouse to some Scottish-sounding tune, rendered quite proficiently on the fiddle by one of Saffin's men. Breck had waltzed with Kate a hundred times before under the tutelage of Monsieur Déclouet, and now they moved amongst the other dancers almost without thinking, the skirt of her dress swaying and shimmering in the torchlight.

They'd partnered by playing "forfeits." Little Amy Parsons had obtained some item from each lady present, placing them on a tray from which the gentlemen chose an article, being subsequently paired with its owner. When Breck's mother had refused to put something on the tray, saying she couldn't possibly, William marched over and removed her brooch, setting it on the tray amid her protests, saying that if ladies in her condition could not abide waltzes, all the more reason to waltz, as her condition must find a cure. Whereupon his father promptly chose the brooch for himself. When the tray came to Breck, he chose Kate's handkerchief, embroidered with bluebonnets, feeling a surge of brotherly protection as Vanderkloot was next in line, eyeing the handkerchief like a frog eyeing a fly. Even Grandmother Mehitable was dancing with one of Gustine's younger sons, a man of nineteen, recently graduated from university, who, judging by his expression and the distance he kept between them, looked as if he would have preferred dancing with a porcupine.

"Well?" Kate asked.

"Well, what?"

"Why *are* you so happy?"

"Tell me, sweet sister of mine, is there anything in your book that isn't a crime? Saying my prayers or doing penance, perhaps?"

"Just answer the question."

Breck glanced over to where Frances Parsons danced with Marshall. "I'll tell you why I'm happy if you tell me why you're mad."

She sniffed and looked away, and he knew she wasn't going to answer.

He leaned toward her, whispering. "Let me guess. Does it have anything to do with feeding Mr. Rogue rotten rump roast in the rat hole?"

"Breck!"

"If you weren't so thick in the head, I'd swear I could see right through you," he said, laughing again when she punched his shoulder and told him to mind his own business, though he could see a smile tugging at the corners of her mouth. "Besides, Kate, I thought you wanted a sugarhouse party. You've been begging for weeks and now that you have one, well, let's just say you've turned into an ice princess."

He felt her droop a little, a frozen layer chiseled away. "Oh, I don't know, Breck. I think—I think I've just hurt somebody terribly. Somebody that I care a lot about."

Breck pretended shock. "Since when have you been sorry for anything you've ever said? According to the apology ledger, you're in my debt a thousandfold."

"Am not."

"Are so."

"Am not."

"If you started apologizing now for every mean thing you've ever said to me, you wouldn't balance the ledger until, I calculate, Christmas at the earliest. Just in time to give me a present."

"You are full of yourself tonight, aren't you?"

Again, Breck laughed, knowing she was right. He was full of himself. For the first time in years, it seemed his life was finally headed in the right direction. The sugar venture was exceeding his wildest expectations. He and his father were getting along, developing a relationship built on mutual respect, seeing eye to eye in most every matter. Come next year, Breck would head to college. Someday, obtain a law degree. And tonight, for the first time, he could take a breath without thinking of Monette (was that even possible?), take a breath without feeling like he was withering, his lungs collapsing inward to squeeze the blood from his heart. Tonight, he could look at someone like Frances Parsons and think that maybe, someday, removed by years and geography, he could give his heart to someone else.

The waltz ended. While others clapped, Breck kissed Kate on her forehead. "No matter how bad it gets, you've still got me. Now do me a favor and at least pretend you're having the time of your life."

She smiled at him, appearing grateful for his brief attempts to bring her out of her doldrums. "So long as I don't have to dance with you-know-who."

Breck clapped his hand over his chest. "I solemnly swear I shall protect you against the villainous dragon, come fire, flood, or famine."

"I'm counting on it," she said, laughing now.

Breck danced a couple more times. The polka with Irish Mary. A Scottish reel with Grandma Emma (who got tangled up a few times and couldn't remember all the steps, but laughed anyway).

He was still humming the tune to the reel when, not long after, he left the outdoor privy and began to cross the darkened clearing, heading back toward the sugarhouse, feeling pleasantly tired now, wondering how long the party would last and whether they would dance through the night. He didn't notice a figure detaching itself from the shadows, running toward him across the clearing, until he heard someone approaching from behind. Footsteps on the ground. A panting mixed with weeping. The sound of his name, called once, twice.

He turned.

It was Monette.

He caught a glimpse of her in the flicker of light from the sugarhouse windows before she flung herself at him. Instinctively, he wrapped his arms around her, holding her, startled, confused. Was that blood on her face? "My God, Monette! What are you doing here? What on earth's the matter?" He tried to pull away, to look at her, to see if it *was* blood, whether she was injured, but she clung to him fiercely, weeping, her body quaking. Moisture seeped through his shirtfront, and his heart began to race.

With hardly a thought, he picked her up in his arms. She wrapped her arms around his neck, cradling her head against his shoulder as he headed toward Birchett's house. He would get to the bottom of this—whatever it was.

But when he put his hand on the door, a difficult maneuver with Monette cradled like a babe in his arms, she stiffened. "No," she whispered, her breath hot and slick against his neck. "Not there. *Please, Breck, not in there.*"

He was breathing hard now, angry, feeling somehow, in some way, that whatever was wrong, whatever had happened, it was his fault. His fault for forcing Monette away. He never should have done it. He should have found a way to be with her, to protect her. Skirting the edge of the clearing, he entered the sugarhouse office, a place where he spent most of his time anymore. It was shuttered, blindingly dark, as he'd known it would be. "I'm going to set you in a chair. I need to light the—"

"*No!*"

There was a desperation in her voice he'd never heard before. Her arms tightened around his neck, and he felt the wild flailing of her heart against his.

"Don't let me go. Don't—please, Breck. Oh, please don't. I need you. I need you to hold me."

"Hush, hush," he breathed, wanting to calm her, to help her, bending his head, kissing her cheek, amazed by its silkiness, moisture like dew beneath his lips. "Hush. I won't let you go, I promise." As he spoke, as he held her trembling in his arms as though she were a delicate flower, every thought he'd ever entertained of letting her go, of perhaps someday loving someone else, pledging his troth to another, vanished. Love for her returned like the heated blast from a furnace, and he found himself just standing there, crushing her to his chest, breathing, breathing . . . feeling his own tears as well—tears released from an imprisonment so deeply guarded that the pain of freedom took his breath away.

*Monette! My Love!*

Taking four steps—five—he lurched to the edge of his desk and set her atop it, still clasping her to him. Papers crackled and swished to the floor. An inkpot slid off, bounced, and rolled along the floorboards. He scarcely knew when his lips found hers, only knowing that suddenly he was kissing her, tasting her, wanting her, whispering that he loved her: *Oh God! You're everything to me! Everything!*

He slid his hand up her legs, wondering at her softness—how did women become so soft?—sliding farther, all the way up, now wondering at the tender folds of flesh, groaning when she wrapped her legs around him, her breath full on his face, heated. He released his pants, aching to take her, to have her. The culmination of all his fantasies—all the nights lying awake, dreaming of her, pleasuring himself. *Oh God! Oh God!* He positioned himself, pushed against her cleft. She gasped as he entered her, arching her back, squeezing her legs tighter. There was a slight resistance inside, but then he pushed harder, broke through. He was deep inside her now, gasping at her softness, her wetness, her heat, his body trembling, afire.

*Oh God! Monette!*

*Take me, take me . . .*

## Chapter 14

THERE WAS TROUBLE BREWING tonight—of that, Mehitable was certain. She smelled it the same way she smelled rain coming on: a current in the air, expectant . . .

It hovered among the torches of the sugarhouse, over the steaming kettles, sliding among the workers and the dancers with a stealth that no one seemed to notice—except her. That was the way with trouble, she thought. Most people remained stupidly oblivious until the clouds parted and the deluge began. Then, like idiots, they scurried for cover, wondering where the sunshine had gone and why trouble had to rain on their picnic.

She sat on a chair next to Sarah, both hands gripping the head of her cane, grinding the point into the floor as she watched the dancers glide about, thinking, I'm no idiot. And I'll not stand for it.

There was Mary Grey Saffin, drinking more than her share of hot punch. Anyone could tell just by looking at her that the woman was drunk. And she, a senator's wife! There was one of Gustine's sons (God only knows the man's name, as the Gustines churned out sons the way hounds produced puppies), dancing entirely too closely with Frances Parsons, a girl with the brains of a partridge. And there was Irish Mary, looking decidedly unhappy as she danced with her husband. Goodness! Was their marriage in trouble already? The consequences didn't bear thinking about! Well, as they say, they've made their bed.

Then there was Breck. He'd left the sugarhouse ten or fifteen minutes ago and hadn't returned. She watched the door, anxious, the cloud of trouble swirling about her until it achieved hurricane force, so powerful she wondered why everyone in the sugarhouse didn't stop their ridiculous waltzing, grab one another, and dash for cover.

Unable to stand it another second, she rose to her feet, gasping from the stiffness in her hips. She brushed off Sarah when her daughter-in-law asked her if there was anything she needed—anything she *needed?* How about an end to *blindness,* to *stupidity?*—and lumbered toward the door. She hadn't really intended to go outside, but upon peering out, seeing no light anywhere, no sign of her grandson, a sense of stillness that screamed deception, Mehitable knew just what she had to do.

There was a groan from Breck. Then he shuddered, gasping, his arms tightening around her, squeezing. With a final groan, a final thrust, he collapsed on top of her, releasing his breath with one long sigh into her hair. As he did so, a hot dampness spread between her legs, trickling down her buttocks. Monette could feel his heart galloping, its frenetic pace matched by the racing of her own heart, her own breath, blown into the crook of his neck. She was suddenly aware of the dampness of her clothes, the sweat that glued their bodies together despite the night chill.

Her mind reeled, stunned with the speed with which it had happened. One moment he was carrying her, comforting her—she, so relieved to be in his arms at last, needing him to hold her. The next moment, she was on a desk and they were kissing, and then he was pushing his way inside her, hands on her hips, and they were doing it. *It.* No longer an abstraction. No longer an act exclusive to the imagination, to be wondered about, spied upon, scorned, yearned for, dreaded. An act that, though painful at first, was both thrilling and horrifying in equal measure. Thrilling, because of the way her body had responded, a flame within, ignited, engulfing her when Breck said he loved her. Knowing he would protect her now. Horrifying, because she didn't know if she'd wanted to do it at all, her body acting of its own accord. As if conscious decision had played no part—like tumbling off a cliff, having no choice but to fall.

And then there was Marshall.

*No! Do not think of him! It is over! He cannot hurt you again!*

*Breck will protect me.*

*He loves me—Il m'aime.*

With the thought, Monette tightened her arms around Breck, kissing the hollow of his neck—the nightmare, the banishment of the last few months finally, finally ended.

Upon her kiss, Breck raised himself onto his elbows. She felt the brush of his lips across her forehead, his still-quickened breath in her hair. "You all right?" he whispered.

*"Oui."*

In the ensuing silence, she waited, wanting him to again say he loved her. That he would never let anything hurt her again.

"I—I don't know what came over me. I—I'm sorry if I hurt you, if I—" His voice trailed off, and an awkwardness wedged between them, palpable; she could taste its uncertainty.

Monette suddenly wished he was off her, out of her, so that she could clean up, pull her skirt and her blouse back down. He must have been thinking similarly, for he began to pull away, straightening. But then came the sound of a metallic scrape, a door handle turning. A sound lasting a second, no longer. They both froze, mid-breath, and Monette's heart stuttered with fright. The door flung open. A figure stood framed in the doorway, thrusting a lantern into the room.

Breck knew from the look on his grandmother's face that she could see everything. See him between Monette, pants pooled around his ankles, her bare legs still encircling his waist. He knew he had that look on his face, that look hunters often joked about when they startled a deer with their torches—blank, numb, horrified.

He'd never seen his grandmother shocked before, but he saw it now. Her widened eyes. Her jaw, falling. She inhaled, an odd-sounding shriek, animal-like. The lantern slipped from her hand, crashing on the doorstep with a shatter of glass, a clank of metal. And with its falling, the light mercifully extinguished. He heard steps running away, toward the sugarhouse, as the smell of melted tallow seeped into the room.

A pile of books dropped from his desk to the floor, scattering, pages crumpling as he tore himself away from Monette. He yanked up his pants, his blood racing, his mouth dry. My God! What had they done? What had *he* done? How could he have been so foolish? He heard Monette too, sitting up, the rustle of her clothing as she put herself back together, her panicky breath, close to weeping.

"Hurry and go back to the big house and wait for me there."

"But—"

"There's no time to argue! My God! Don't you realize? Don't you know my grandmother can't keep secrets? *Won't* keep them?" He forced himself to not panic, though he wanted to run, to flee, to find a quiet place away from everyone and scream and rage. He fumbled in one of his desk drawers for the matches, then found the lantern that he kept on a table next to the door. The match scraped. He smelled the sulfur, saw the sudden flare, his hands trembling as he lit the wick and blew out the match. Taking the lantern, he turned. She was standing by the desk, clothing rumpled, her blouse spotted with blood. He saw now that her lip was swollen, cut. One of her nostrils was caked with dried blood. Her left eye also appeared to be blackened, swelling too. Earlier, had he known, he would have been appalled by her appearance, but now he was beyond shocked. He saw his own horror reflected in her eyes.

He handed her the lantern, wrapping her fingers around the handle when she did not take it of her own accord. "Please, Monette. *Please!*" He shoved her toward the door, knowing her terror, for the same terror screamed in his own chest, threatening to come clawing out of his throat. "Now run! Go to your room and wait for me!" Then he shoved her out the door. Glass crunched under her shoes. She looked back once, but then turned and began to run, lifting her skirt with one hand, one of her shoes flopping. The lantern light swayed across the clearing, then trailed along the cart path in a sickly glow before it finally disappeared, swallowed by the darkness.

# Chapter 15

S ARAH DREAMED SHE WAS drowning. They were in a paddleboat. All of them—William, Breck, Kate, the twins, her mother, Emma, her brother, John—and she fell overboard. Without a cry, without warning, with only a whisper, like brushed silk, she sank beneath the waves, the darkness closing over her head, her lungs already burning. She surfaced once, saw them looking at her. Squeezed shoulder to shoulder along the rail, mute with horror, paralyzed with helplessness.

She tried to call to them, to say, Save me, or Help me, or simply, *Please,* but water rushed into her mouth. It poured down her throat and into her stomach, so that she sank again, saying nothing, her pregnant belly a boulder, dragging her down, down. As her vision blackened, as the air in her lungs frothed into liquid, she awakened. Opened her eyes. Gasped for breath. Her heart, wild. Her lower back, aching dully.

It was morning—likely eight o'clock, no later. Diffuse gray light peeped from behind the heavy drapes. Outside, she heard a carriage departing—the clop of hooves, and Frances Parsons' young voice bidding farewell.

The party last night had ended abruptly. Apparently, William had received word of something gone wrong, a not infrequent occurrence. He declared an end to their festivities and left to attend to business, while the remaining group concluded the evening with a cart ride back to the big house.

Sarah rolled over, gripping her belly in her hands. William's pillow was undisturbed. Whatever the business, it was important enough to have kept him out all night. For herself, she'd been so exhausted—still half angry at

William for planning the party despite her wishes—that she'd felt justified in excusing herself from the guests. She left all to her mother and her mother-in-law, and fell into bed the second Mammy Hester slipped her nightgown over her head, Mammy telling her to have sweet dreams.

Sweet dreams? Did one have sweet dreams this late into a pregnancy? Two weeks overdue? No, it was an ugly dream. A hateful dream, and one best forgotten.

She closed her eyes, not wanting to get up, not feeling well. She could hear the commotion below. Guests still departing. The distant clink of dishes from the dining room. Marshall's barking laugh. The house crawled with people. And she, just wanting everyone to go away. To leave her to have her baby. She waited until the company of voices migrated outside, finally disappearing in the jingle and clatter of departing carriages. When she'd rung the silver bell a third time, and still Mammy had not come, Sarah swung her legs over the edge of the bed and heaved herself to her feet, everything aching—her knees, her ankles, her hips, her back.

*Please, God.*

Out in the rear loggia, wrapped in an oversized shawl, she stopped the houseboy, grateful he was running an errand in her vicinity so that she wouldn't have to shout down the staircase, or, heaven forbid, waddle downstairs. "Nat, fetch Mammy, and tell her I'm awake. And where is Master William, do you know?"

Nat shrugged, staring at the floor, looking so blank and useless that she was tempted to grab his shoulders and rattle his teeth together, wondering if all those years of catechism had been wasted on this particular soul, wondering, as she often did, if Nat wasn't more suited for the fields. "Just go fetch Mammy," was all she said, sighing when he proceeded down the steps at his usual plodding pace.

From the window in the rear loggia, she could see the kitchen, the yard, and the vegetable gardens spreading out beyond. Smoke from the kitchen fires, from a dozen other fires, and from the sugarhouse over a mile to the northeast hung languidly, trapped under an invisible ceiling, unable to rise into the sky above. Even from inside the big house, she could smell the smoky denseness—a grayness that seemed to penetrate every pore, seep into her blood, weigh her down, and lace fingers with the familiar fear crouched in her womb.

The baby kicked, and she grimaced. It kicked again, harder. The ache in her low back intensified, and she kneaded the muscles, dreading what was to come. She wondered if she should just go back to bed and stay there, hoping today was the day—terrified that it was. She stared out the window, wishing Mammy Hester would hurry. As if getting dressed would solve everything.

Old Pompey wasn't so old that he couldn't still set a rattrap. Once a day, he entered the cotton storehouse and navigated his way between the bales of cotton, down makeshift corridors so narrow, his stooped shoulders brushed against the creamy down.

Today was a good day. Lately, his back had been paining him—aching during the night so much that he could never get comfortable, almost relieved to hear the ringing of the plantation bell, telling him it was time to rise and shine. But today, by golly, he felt good, yessir. His back was feeling dandy. Fit as a fiddle. Even his wife commented that, if she didn't know better, she'd think he had a spring in his step.

He knelt between the bales and the wood-planked wall, grunting, placing the trap on the floor, noting the telltale rat droppings. The air was thick here, unable to circulate, as if, should he take too deep a breath, he'd clog his lungs with cotton. But the claustrophobic atmosphere didn't stop him from chuckling. From thinking, *Brace yourself, Hettie. Come tonight, I's gonna surprise you with how much spring I still got! Yessir. We's gonna make some music clacking our old bones together!*

With an experience born of setting hundreds of traps, Pompey carefully pried open the jaws, the jagged iron teeth itching to rip into the flesh of anything fool enough to whet its appetite on the molasses-coated trigger pan. He held his breath, set the trigger, and backed away, pleased when the trap remained open—its gaping mouth looking as famished as a gator in a drought.

"Soup's on," he whispered, chuckling again, just as pleased with his good mood as he was with the trap. "Come one, come all, by golly, yessir. See what old Pompey's got for you."

Next, he checked the traps against the south wall, which he'd set yesterday. One was empty, and he let it be. The other held a rat as big as his foot and deader than a squashed bug.

Pompey was squatting, releasing the trap, when he smelled smoke. To begin with, he didn't pay it any mind, as it was a generally smoky day anyway, one of those days when it seemed nothing wanted to leave the earth and instead clung to the ground like a wet blanket. But when the smoke came again, stronger, and he heard what he swore to be a crackle of flame followed by a whoosh of fire, he stood, trap in hand, heart flopping like a fish out of water. The rat slid off the iron teeth and plopped onto his shoe.

"Ralph? That you?"

A younger man might have made it out in time. A younger man might have dropped the trap, sprinted down the narrow aisles, around the corner, sliding against the splintered wall before flinging himself through the circle of flames, out the wagon-sized door, onto the grass outside. But old Pompey's thinking was sometimes as slow as his reflexes, and by the time he figured out it was not his imagination—that it *was* fire, big fire, and that he needed to move, to forget the rattraps, to drop everything, to get out—it was already too late. With a roar, fire engulfed the cotton tinder, igniting even the fluff floating in the air. Pompey's last thought, back pressed against the wall, hair beginning to singe, unable to hold his breath any longer against the thick, black smoke that stung his eyes and made them stream with water, was,

*This ain't the way I wanted to die. No sir. This ain't the way . . .*

William drew on his cigar and exhaled slowly, observing his son, who sat with folded arms. Breck ignored him as if he were nothing more than an indoor shrub, instead gazing alternately at the fire in the grate, at the neck bone of the ass on the mantel, at the rifle mounted above, wearing a stony expression that William did not want to admit frightened him. He flicked the cigar ash into the tray, ignoring his own weariness.

Though it was early morning, though he could hear the bustle of various folks outside, William's office behind the big house was still shuttered. He'd chased off the servant who'd come to open the room, telling her to first stir the fire, add more wood, bring them some food and water, and, for Chrisssake, some brandy, and then to leave posthaste. She'd rushed through her tasks, as if she sensed a pot soon to boil over, scathing everything and everyone.

It had been a hellacious night, beginning at the sugarhouse, when his mother approached him. William knew from the pallor in her cheeks, and the odd glaze in her eyes, that something was amiss. He'd only seen her look that way twice before in his life: the first time, some thirty years ago, when one of his sisters was discovered dead—drowned in Jensey's Bayou; the second time, when the kitchen cook chopped off all four fingers of her left hand with a cleaver while his mother was smack-dab in the middle of instructing her as to the supper menu—an act his mother swore to this very day had been purposeful. "See to your son," she said. "He's in the sugarhouse office. See to him." When William questioned her about it, knowing deep in his gut that something was horribly wrong, she would only shake her head, saying hoarsely, "Hurry."

He finished his hot punch in one swallow, handed her the empty glass, took a torch, and strode out to the sugarhouse office. He was surprised to see Breck there in the dark. His son was crouched down, picking up papers and books strewn about the floor. There was a wet smear on the desk, and the room smelled suspiciously like—like *sex*.

"What happened in here?" William asked, infuriated when Breck said nothing, and avoided meeting William's eye, merely continuing to gather papers, tapping them into neat piles, as if that were the most important task at midnight. William yanked the boy to his feet, almost startled to discover the boy was near as tall as he was. "Who was she?" William demanded, his suspicions confirmed by Breck's lack of denial. William felt the blood drain from his face, the floor seeming to rock beneath him. Good God. Just what had his mother seen? Had it been Frances Parsons, all of fourteen years and a minute old? Breck had been calf-eyed around her all evening. Her father, and her brothers, would *demand* satisfaction. Breck's reputation would be ruined. *Ruined!* William racked his brain, trying to remember if Frances had been missing at any point in the evening, but, for the life of him, could not recall.

Rather than get into it at the sugarhouse office, not the most comfortable of places even in the best of times, William had returned with Breck to his office in the south addition behind the big house (after first making his excuses to his guests, saying he and Breck had urgent business to attend). He motioned his son into a chair and said neither one of them was leaving until Breck spilled his guts. So saying, William sat on the edge of his desk, lighting a cigar with what he believed to be the patience of a saint, trying to banish the image of his son rutting like a bull on top of Frances.

He'd always had trouble with the boy, ever since the first day he'd taken him to the fields—something made especially apparent on the day his son bawled his eyes out after witnessing the unpleasant encounter with Sawney. Their relationship had been an uphill battle ever since, fought in silence, for the most part. Only in the last couple of years—since taking on the sugar venture—had there been a feeling of father-son *camaraderie,* of working in tandem toward a common goal. He'd finally been proud to call Breck his son, a planter like himself, worthy to carry on the Jensey name, expand the Jensey lands, and create a fortune worthy of their South Carolina ancestry.

Now, hours after leaving the sugarhouse, William had finally migrated from the edge of his desk to the more comfortable chair by the fireplace and was in the process of smoking his fourth cigar. His eyes felt bleary, stinging, like two red-hot coals burning a hole through his brain. Breck had yet to say a word. Neither of them had dozed so much as a wink. And the tension between them grew by degrees, until William wanted to leap across the rug that separated them and whip some sense into him, or throttle the confession out of him. Good God! Instead, William concentrated on making what he judged to be a respectable smoke ring.

Though he'd been waiting since early morning for his son to speak, when the sound of Breck's voice broke the silence, it caught William by surprise. "I will tell you everything, and I mean everything, but you must, in turn, make several concessions."

William stared at him before his pent-up fury boiled over, and he exploded out of his chair. "I'll be goddamned if I'm the one making concessions here! You seem to forget who did something wrong, and it wasn't me! I'll be the one making demands. Not you."

Breck shrugged. "Suit yourself."

"Goddammit!" William felt the veins bulge in his neck, grabbed the nearest object—a pencil box given to him by Saffin—and threw it across the room, where it splintered against the door. He stood panting, staring at the pieces, thinking that he'd really liked that pencil box, before turning to Breck. "Just tell me this. Was it Frances?"

For a second, his son looked blank, as if William had spoken in Chinese. Then, a look of horror spread across his face. "Good God, Father, what do you take me for?"

"Then it was not Frances?"

"No!"

Relief flooded through William like a balm. Thank God! There were small mercies, after all! But no sooner had relief soothed his battered spirit, it flitted away again like a bird undecided where to roost. "If it wasn't Frances, who was it?"

"I've told you my terms."

This time, William did fly across the rug, blood rushing, eyes pulsing. He scarcely knew what he was doing until he saw his own fist raised, Breck still sitting in the wingback chair, regarding him with a coolness that infuriated him all the more.

"Are you really going to hit me?" Breck asked. "Do you really know me so little that you think it would serve any purpose? Other than maybe to satisfy your own rage?"

Part of William wanted to smash Breck's face beneath his fist, but part of him wanted to crush him in an embrace, to wind back the clock and have things be as they were, nothing changed, Breck as his companion, a savvy business partner, becoming more and more his friend. William's arm fell limply to his side. Was it possible he was losing his son? His firstborn?

He turned away, retrieving his cigar, taking a gulp of brandy, wishing someone would remove the knife from his heart, and wondering if all his children would turn out to be this difficult. He wandered to the fireplace, setting his glass on the mantel next to the neck bone of the ass, a ridiculous-looking bone shaped like an equally ridiculous-looking preacher kneeling in a ridiculous posture of prayer (prayer being a ridiculous notion, ironically practiced by the spineless, those who could not handle life on its own terms, his own Sarah excepted). "I'm not saying that I will grant any of your concessions."

"What are you saying then?"

"That I will at least listen to them."

"Listening is not enough. I require—"

"Breck, dammit, can't we at least start there?" William looked at his son, the knife twisting. "How can you expect me to grant concessions when I know nothing of their nature? I don't even know *who* I'm granting concessions to. You're not playing fair. Will you at least grant *me* that concession?"

"You don't understand. You—"

"Do you really think me so heartless?"

Now it was Breck's turn to stare at him. To look ashamed. William waited, knowing the time had come, dreading what the boy was going to say.

"I—I want a guarantee of the girl's safety," Breck began, leaning forward in his chair. "That she will not be punished—"

William frowned, not certain what Breck meant. "Punished?"

"Also, under no circumstances is she to be sold. I want her to have her own—"

"You—you're telling me she's a *slave?*" Blood roared into William's head. His vision pulsed, eyes burning. A slave? My son fucked a goddamn *slave?*

From somewhere, there came a banging—loud, insistent.

"I don't think—"

"Good God, have I taught you *nothing?* Was it too much to ask of you to keep your pants buttoned? To keep your hands off the servant girls? You know what kind of trouble that causes."

Now Breck was standing, his voice rising. "It wasn't like that—"

"It was the mulatto girl, wasn't it? Christ! I knew she was trouble! My mother always said so!"

Again, that banging, that hammering. Someone at the door. Someone yelling, "Mars William! Mars William!"

"Not now!" he barked in reply. Christ! Could no one leave him in peace? Was his life destined to be nothing but chaos? Nothing but heartache? Knives in the back?

"You said you would listen!"

"To ridiculous idiocy? To the ravings and fantasies of—of a pubescent *boy?*"

Just then, the door burst open.

"I said, not now!" William roared, at the same time registering the fact that the man was grimy with soot, and out of breath—a man who worked at the cotton gin, only coming to the area around the big house when it was time for inspections. What the hell was he doing here?

"But—but, Mars William, the cotton storehouse—it on fire!"

William blinked, each word falling from the man's lips like a brick, hard, unyielding, unable to be absorbed, at the same time realizing that the plantation bell was ringing, and had been ringing.

Breck, too, stared. "What?"

"The cotton storehouse be on fire! It be up in flames right now."

"Oh God," breathed William. And he rushed out the door, Breck on his heels, off to fight a battle that he knew was lost before it began.

From the first spark, it took hardly a blink for the cotton storehouse to collapse into a fiery heap. Even from where Breck stood over eighty feet away, squinting in the smoke, the heat was more blistering than a forge on a summer's day. He knew it would take days for the fire to burn out completely, as each bale was so tightly compressed. A crazy part of him wanted to leap into the ruins with buckets of water, crying out that it was not too late to save them. But his brain knew what his heart could not bear: seventy-odd bales of cotton, destroyed.

Beside him, his father stood stiffly—a sun-bleached board, ready to ignite come the tiniest spark. They were listening as Uncle Ralph told them how he'd seen it all. Said he was toting a basket of cotton from the ginhouse to the press when he noticed a thick, black smoke billowing from the mouth of the storehouse. And, hardly before he could sound the alarm, bright orange flames shot up. Two fellows burned themselves trying to put out the blaze. But old Pompey, well, it was a pitiful shame, because Ralph sure liked the fellow, always had, but figured Pompey was playing his harp now, God bless him.

"Did you see anyone?" William asked, his bloodshot eyes smoldering beneath the brim of his hat in that way that Breck both feared and despised. His father's once-white shirt was now rumpled and fingerprinted with soot. Breck returned his gaze to the burning cotton, suddenly disliking the sight of his father. "Anyone suspicious?"

"Did I see anyone? Why, I don't rightly recollect, 'cause folks be—you know, folks be screaming and hollering and running every which way like it be Judgment Day or something similar."

Once William dismissed Ralph, Breck ventured to ask, "You don't think it had anything to do with Sawney, do you?"

His father gazed upward into the smoke-filled sky, and Breck wondered if he was remembering the day of Quincy's funeral, when he'd vowed to kill Sawney if it was the last thing he ever did. "Maybe those Mississippi hunters were mistaken. Or maybe they just wanted their money. Were sick of the chase." William's jaw tightened. "Maybe they just took me for a goddamn fool." Here, he looked at Breck with such intensity that Breck took a step backward. It was a look that said, no one makes a fool of William Jensey. *No one.* He jabbed his stiffened finger into Breck's chest. "Our little conversation? We'll continue it after I've checked on our boys at the hospital. I'll see you back at the office."

So saying, his father marched away, leaving Breck standing alone with a sudden dread that the worst was yet to come.

# Chapter 16

Sarah watched from the second-floor loggia window, gripping the sash with white-hard knuckles, while the smoky blanket hovering over the plantation turned increasingly black, like a doomsday prophecy come true.

"Mama, what on earth is all that fuss?" It was Kate, emerging from her bedroom with the bewildered, puffy look of someone awakened from too little sleep. Her feet were bare beneath her nightgown. Auburn hair dangled in a thick braid over one shoulder. Sarah held out her arm, drawing Kate close, as her daughter stood next to her and peered out the window. Kate's eyes widened, and she gasped. "A fire?"

"It appears so."

"Where?"

"One of the cotton buildings, I believe. At least, that's what I'm hearing from outside. It certainly looks like that's where it's coming from."

For a while, they said nothing, only watching as the air grew more dense, the sun now a vague ball of grimy yellow. The laundresses scurried about, yanking the linens off the lines, no doubt seeking to save them from the rain of soot. Everywhere else, people had stopped their tasks and gazed in the direction of the fire, as if, by sheer willpower, they could penetrate the haze and witness the conflagration.

"Will Papa be able to put it out?"

Sarah let out a breath, wishing she could say, Yes, dear, Papa can put it out. Instead, she said, "You know how cotton is."

"But—what if we lose it all? The cotton?"

"I don't know, Katherine dear. All we can do is pray." As Sarah spoke, her back tightened, hardening. She caught her breath. *Any day but today.*

Once the contraction passed, lasting a minute, perhaps, she found Kate looking at her, her jade-green eyes searching Sarah's. "Is it the baby?"

Sarah kissed her daughter's cheek. "Fetch Monette and get dressed. I'll be needing you today."

"But Mama, is it—"

"Go on now. I'll be fine. Just hurry."

Kate's eyes widened. "Good God," she breathed. "First a fire, now a baby."

"Watch your language, young lady. Now go do what I've asked."

Not far from where Monette lay on her side in her bedroom, breathing in the musty smell of the patchwork quilt, a mud dauber climbed the wall. Pausing first before hauling itself over every bump and crack in the plaster, it reached the ceiling, only to fall to the floor. It gained its feet clumsily, heavily, and started up the wall again. Monette watched, one eye swollen shut, wondering why it didn't fly up to join the other mud daubers flitting around in the nest above, wondering how many times it would attempt the feat, as it had been climbing and falling, climbing and falling, since dawn. Wondering whether it would keep at it until it died from exhaustion, from hunger, or even from loneliness.

As she watched, the events of last night pulsed through her mind like the throbbing of her wounds: unceasing and painful. Lizzy's slap. Marshall's attack. Her running to Breck, and the way everything happened *so quickly,* how she suddenly found herself underneath him on the desk.

She knew now that Breck loved her. Yes, he loved her deeply. But even as she tried to comfort herself with this thought, tried to love Breck the way he loved her, her dreams broke through like an ocean through a levee. The huge man coming out of the fog to rescue her. Black as coffee beans, face a mystery.

*This man* she loved—deeply loved . . . She felt as drawn to him as if an unbreakable, golden strand connected her heart to his. Forever. Her heart ached, scraped raw with longing.

But, she told herself, this man is only a dream, while Breck is *real.*

Would he, could he, help her now? Would he protect her? Or would he look away while she was punished? Whipped? *Did Breck have any real power at all?* The spidery fingers crawling up her backbone screamed the answer, and she pretended she could not remember what had happened to Fatima—the fornicator who deserved what she got. Twenty lashes. Wages for her sin.

She watched the mud dauber fall again, imagining the pain of the first lash. Would she scream? How many lashes? Would she die? Would everyone watch?

From behind her, she heard Kate bounding up the stairs—knew it was her even before she shouted, "Monette! Wake up!" and flung the door open, stirring the smoky haze that had slowly filled the room all morning despite the shuttered windows. Monette closed her one good eye and curled into herself, hugging her knees to her chest as Kate's words came out in a rush. "The cotton's on fire, and not only that, but Mama's in labor. So, I need you to get me dressed *pronto*. My gray wool dress will be perfect because it won't matter if it gets dirty. I was planning on giving it to you anyway—"

"I can't."

There was a pause, during which Monette prayed Kate wouldn't attempt to roll her over. Because once Kate saw her face—the cut and swollen lip, the black eye, the bruise on her cheek—she'd demand explanations, explanations Monette didn't want to give. Kate let out an exasperated breath. "What on earth's eating you?"

"I said I can't."

"What do you mean, you can't? Of course you can. You've got to dress me so I can help. Mama's going to have her baby any second, and Papa's out fighting a fire, and everyone's gone home except for Grandma Emma and Uncle John, and—and, well, you've just got to help me!"

Monette pulled her pillow over her head, sorry the cotton was burning, worried for Miss Sarah, but wishing Kate would just go away. Leave her be. Relieved at least that Kate appeared to know nothing of what had transpired last night. "Get Mammy Hester to help you. I'm sick."

Finally, after Kate further begged, cajoled, commanded, and shouted, she mercifully left, slamming the attic door. Monette heard footsteps descending, a voice crying, "Fine! Be that way! I guess you don't care about me after all! And I don't care what you say, you're *not sick!*"

With Kate gone, Monette sighed and got up. She fetched the chamber pot from under the bed, ceramic scraping over the rough planking. Squatting, she relieved her bladder, wincing at the soreness between her legs. She shoved the chamber pot back. Then, that done, she tended her face at the washstand. The water was cold, soothing against her bruised face. Even so, she found herself drawing in her breath sharply as she dabbed the washrag over her eye, her cheek, her nose, her lip, which had split open again and now drizzled blood. Next, she removed her garments—her white blouse, stiff and soiled; the calico pattern of her skirt concealing stains like a secret—and slid them under the bed, where they would stay until she could launder them herself. Naked, shivering now—for it was chilly—she took the chunk of soap, worked up a lather, and scrubbed hard between her legs, at the bloody crusts on her inner thighs, as if by scrubbing hard, by digging through the layers of skin, she could rewrite yesterday, blot out her sin, erase herself so that maybe God could not see her. Erase what was to come.

She dressed in a fresh blouse and skirt, then combed her hair, pretending she couldn't see the dirty water tinged with pink—water that shrieked, *Fornicator!* Pretending her stomach did not crawl with dread, sending out tentacles that slithered down her legs, her arms, worming into her heart, her lungs, her skull.

Dressed now, every hair in place, smelling of soap, Monette knelt near the wall, next to one of the bedposts. She struggled to lift the floorboard, tearing back a fingernail, but finally succeeded in prying it up. Trying not to think of the spiders lurking in the hole, she reached in, cobwebby strands brushing against her fingers, as she found the flannel bag and pulled it out. Her *gris-gris.* An abomination in the eyes of God. Evil. Even to touch it, she knew, was a sin.

Back on her bed, she untied the leather thong. She emptied the contents, digging out with her fingernail some of the grains of salt and pepper that had slipped into the seams of the patchwork quilt.

Despite the fact that she had not looked at them in years, the objects were at once as familiar to her as her skin. The red agate, smooth, cool to the touch, the size of a pigeon's egg and the color of blood. The stick, shaped like the letter Y, still green, strong, as if cut only yesterday. The braid of black hair, frayed now, wiry strands poking out here and there. The sweetgrass, also braided, smelling faintly of vanilla. And the bone, bleached smooth and finger-like.

Seeing them again, touching them, letting the scent drift into her, they seemed a part of her—bone of her bone, hair of her hair—as if they spoke, not of evil, but of love. As if someone were embracing her from far beyond, whispering in her ear,

*Mwana na mono, my daughter, you must be strong now.*

Back in his office, William poured himself a glass of brandy, the lack of sleep catching up with him. What was supposed to have been a night of fun among friends had turned into a nightmare. First, the fiasco with Breck, then the fire, the loss of all that cotton, not to mention the loss of Pompey, plus two men burned and out of work for who knew how long? A couple of weeks, according to John. Just at a time when he could least afford the loss of manpower, when harvesting the sugar was top priority before a killing frost came to ruin it all, freezing the cane juice in the stalk. And, judging by the nip in the air, the first frost could come at any time.

He gulped his brandy, feeling it burn, wishing he could just forget the events of the past twelve hours and go to bed. And where the hell was his son? He topped off his glass, put his hat back on, and headed out to the gallery to wait.

The smell of fresh-baked bread wafted from the kitchen, mixing with the haze of sooty smoke that William knew would take days to dissipate. Behind the kitchen, William could see most of the yard. A woman carried a pail of milk out of the dairy house, bent sideways with the weight of it, white froth sloshing over the top, startling a rooster in mid-crow, who scurried out of her way. Elsewhere, everyone bustled about—not talking, heads down, striding about their work with a purpose born, no doubt, of William's injunction: a command bellowed minutes ago from the hospital gallery, for everyone to get the hell back to work, to stop standing around with their mouths agape, or there would be sore hides tomorrow.

Part of him didn't want to admit that Sawney could be responsible for the fire. To admit such would mean that the man wasn't dead after all, that he'd defied William again, that the negro hunters from Mississippi had been mistaken. Or, worse, that the hunters had lied to William's face.

And life, once again, would become a series of manhunts, of fetching Sawney from jail, of headache and heartache and rage punctuated with fragments of simulated peace. Standing on the gallery, gazing out over the yard, William downed the rest of his brandy. *Oh God, let it not be true. Let the fire have been an accident. Let Sawney be dead.*

He saw Breck now in the yard, passing between the cabins of the domestics, walking toward him. He's too soft, William realized. All this time, he'd believed Breck's zealous participation in the sugar venture to be a sign of his manhood, a coming-of-age. Instead, William believed now, it was a cover for his weakness—his inability to confront issues head-on and mete out appropriate punishments and rewards when necessary. And, for the first time, William seriously doubted Breck's ability to take over the plantation, to govern it with the mastery it required.

He watched Breck until the boy stood on the ground next to the gallery, returning William's gaze over the rail. Beneath the brim of his hat, Breck's chestnut-brown eyes were steady, though underlined with shadows. And, for a second, William thought he detected fear, coupled with dislike.

With all the drama over the fire, William had yet to consider what to do about Breck's situation. The thought of continuing their discussion now seemed more than William could bear. He could feel the brandy slogging through his veins, urging him to finish their discussion tomorrow, after they'd slept. But Breck put an end to that as a possibility when he said, "She is not to be punished."

Upon Breck's words, the brandy in William's blood boiled, his vision darkened, and, before he knew what he was doing, he slammed his glass against the rail. Glass shattered. A shard sliced William's thumb, and he dimly realized he was cut. *Goddamn!* He could feel the pounding behind his eyes, and he spoke through clenched teeth. "You are in no position to be making demands."

"You said you would listen to my conditions. You said—"

"That was before I knew she was a goddamn *slave.*"

William watched as Breck's face shut, like a curtain drawn. "This discussion is going nowhere," his son said, voice tight and low, and William wondered, with incredulity, whether his son was about to cry. "If you lay one hand on her, I swear I'll—"

"You'll *what!*" challenged William, too loudly, noticing a few heads turning in their direction. With an effort, his head pounding now with a sudden headache, he lowered his voice. "Come inside."

"Not until you promise me she will not be harmed."

William was tempted to jump the rail, to grab his son by the collar, and drag him into the office. But, even as he restrained himself, there was a shout from nearby. More shouts. A commotion coming from the yard. A man on horseback was approaching. It was the sugarmaker, Ogden Birchett. In front of him, with his chin held high, leashed to the horse by a rope tied to his iron collar, limped Sawney.

# Chapter 17

"Pardon the intrusion, Mr. Jensey, but I found him inside the sugarhouse office." Birchett reined his horse to a stop just feet from where Breck stood in front of the gallery. "Would've gotten away too, except he cut his foot on some glass. Gave me a chance to nab him." Birchett patted the pistol holstered at his side.

It had been months since Breck had seen Sawney in the swamp, his head poking above the inky water like just another cypress knee. From the looks of it, time had not been good to Sawney. His shirt hung in tatters, grayed with dirt; his pants were torn at the knees, shredded at the ankles, muddied. One shoe clung stubbornly to one foot, held by a shoelace choked with knots, the toe open. The other foot was bare, responsible for the trail of bloody footprints. And beneath the shreds—the holes, the frayed edges of clothing—Breck glimpsed the scars and scrapes, bites and bruises, of a life lived on the run.

"Had this on him." Birchett threw a dagger into the ground, where it stuck fast.

Breck filled his lungs with the smoky air, his heart clenching, wishing he could be somewhere else, anywhere else, yet knowing, as surely as he knew the earth spun on its axis, that this day was bound to arrive. A collision of destinies charted from the time his father had first shot Sawney in the fields—from the time Sawney had first stared into William's face and defied him.

Sawney drowned in the Mississippi? No. It was too easy, too tidy, too *wrong.*

From behind Breck, he heard his father crossing the gallery—boots on wooden planks—down the steps, one at a time, slowly, like a clock ticking. A crow cawed, the cry drifting from the eave—flat, cold. Birchett's horse shifted its feet, blew air out of its nostrils, and folded its ears back, as if it sensed something amiss. Elsewhere, Breck felt people watching—buckets set down, bread burning in the oven, curtains parted in the big house. The watching enveloped everyone in a silence thick as the soot that rained like dirty snow.

Sawney had been staring at the ground, but with William's approach, he raised his eyes, looking full into William's face. It was a look of such defiance that Breck wondered which of them was the one pursued, the one beleaguered beyond the limits of endurance. Breck considered fetching the loaded rifle from over the mantel in the office behind him, then hurrying back outside—

Stopping a foot away from Sawney, William towered over the runaway. Voice low, face shuttered, he asked, "You set fire to my cotton storehouse?"

"Yes."

Breck saw his father taken aback. The word like a slap. Unexpected. Stinging. A second passed, no more, before the face shuttered again. "Taggarts' barn? Gustines' carriage house?"

"Yes, and yes."

"You scalped my driver? Quincy?"

This time Sawney made no response. Instead, he continued to stare at William, chin high, eyes like coals of hatred, fists clenched at his side. Watching them, Breck feared Sawney would attack William. Choke him. Gut him, maybe, with a hidden knife. Breck tensed, ready to leap between them if necessary, not realizing he'd been holding his breath until his lungs began to burn, heart jittering.

William's face darkened. Without a word, he strode to Birchett, whipped the pistol out of its holster, and returned to stand before Sawney. He cocked the gun, pointed the barrel at Sawney's forehead, and pulled the trigger. Breck didn't realize he'd cried out until his voice hung in the air, along with the click of an empty pistol.

Sawney looked shocked. As if, of all things, he hadn't expected this.

From inside the big house, a woman screamed. William cocked the hammer and pulled the trigger again. And again. Producing nothing but a metallic click with each snap of the hammer. Someone was running out of the house now, toward them, auburn hair billowing behind, belly clutched in both hands.

"Father, stop," Breck was saying, holding his hand out for the gun. His father turned his gaze to Breck. His eyes were bloodshot. Distant. As if he couldn't remember he had a son. "Don't do this. Please."

In answer, William handed the pistol to Breck, then bounded up the gallery steps and into the office. When he appeared again seconds later, Breck's mouth went dry, and he felt the blood drain from his head.

Whether it was words—coherent, meaningful—or simply the shrieking of animal terror, Sarah didn't know; only that she was screaming, for she could feel the scraping in her chest, the rawness in her throat. She was running—feet bare, still in her nightgown—dumbly surprised that her legs could carry her so quickly in her condition, seeing William enter his office, his shadow disappearing from the gallery. Seeing Breck standing there, dumbfounded, horrified, holding a pistol as if he couldn't quite figure how he had come into possession of it. Seeing Sawney, the figure from her dreams, her nightmares, reeking of hatred, watching her approach.

*William!*

*My son!*

*No!*

In the next instant, William was back on the gallery, rifle in hand. He hesitated, glanced over at her, then—surprise in his eyes. Breck cried, "Mama!" as she passed. She stumbled up the gallery stairs just as William began to descend, no longer looking at her, his gaze locked on Sawney. She caught his arm, his muscles rigid and unyielding beneath her hands.

*No!*

Her legs wilted, spent, as a contraction tightened. William was dragging her now, and she clung to him, screaming, feeling the tears drain down her cheeks, a stick jabbing the tenderness of her foot, the contraction growing stronger, *stronger.*

"Mama, please!"

"Goddammit, get off me, Sarah!"

William flung her to the ground, and she fell on her side—hard, pain flaming through her midsection, searing up her spine. She gasped, groaned.

Breck's arms cradled her from behind—her son, weeping, "Oh God, Mama! Mama!"

There was the retort of a rifle. An acrid sting of gunpowder. Then Sawney was falling beside her, his breath expiring into her face, his chest blossoming into a savage red. His look of triumph was the last she saw as her vision dimmed, and day turned into night.

## *Chapter 18*

That evening, a storm blew in. Wind howled around the big house, repeatedly slamming a shutter that refused to stay battened. Rain pelted sideways, leaking through every chink in the roof and seeping between the window frames like tears. The fire in the master bedroom fireplace fluttered and smoked, hissed and flared, doing little to dispel the October chill. Candles guttered in the draft. The room stank of tallow, smoke, and childbirth.

An hour ago, the bedside table had been strewn with various medical supplies: forceps, laudanum, scissors, a needle, waxed thread, castile soap, a lance, a bloodletting bowl, and various linens stained with blood, birth waters, or smeared with hog's lard. Now, save for a Bible and a wax-spattered candelabra, the table was barren.

Sarah lay neatly on the bed, covered with her favorite *courtepointe*—the edges tucked in, a nosegay of lilac beside her cheek. Her hair was brushed, gleaming auburn in the firelight. Her eyes were closed, hands clasped on her chest, breath thin as the thread of fraying silk.

At the foot of the bed stood Reverend Scarborough, spectacles perched on the end of his nose, reading, "We humbly commend the soul of this thy servant, our dear sister, into thy hands, as into the hands of a faithful Creator, and most merciful Savior; most humbly beseeching thee, . . ."

The cold of the wall pressed into Kate's back. She closed her eyes against the sight of her father kneeling at her mother's side, face stricken. She wanted to embrace her father, tell him she loved him. That she would take care of him now. Likewise, she wanted to be the one next to her mother as she lay dying, to be the one holding her hand, pressing it to her cheek, telling her how much she loved her. To beg her, please, please, don't die. Instead, Kate squeezed her eyes shut, tasting the bitterness of her helplessness.

It seemed unreal. A nightmarish slumber from which she could not awaken. Everything had gone wrong. Everything. And so quickly. Mid-morning, she'd been in her room as Mammy Hester dressed her, still stewing about Monette and her pill-ishness, already anxious about the events of the day. Then she'd heard shouts. The sound of gunfire. *Her mother screaming.* Scalp erupting with prickles, wearing hardly a stitch of clothing, Kate panicked, crying, "Oh my God, hurry! Hurry!" By the time Mammy finally pulled the dress down and buttoned Kate up sufficiently, everyone was saying that her father had killed Sawney, and that her mother was in her confinement.

Kate had grabbed her grandmother's arm as Emma made to enter the master bedroom with a towel-laden Lizzy in tow. "Grandma, what's happening? Is Mother—?"

Kate's voice trailed off as her grandmother's emerald eyes turned toward her. She looked vague, distant, saying in a tone that pierced Kate's heart with icicles, "Pray for your mother, Katherine dear. That's the best thing you can do right now. Pray for her."

Kate asked more questions but soon found herself talking to the door. Yet in the instant before Emma closed it, Kate glimpsed inside: she saw the profile of Uncle John, her father in the corner with his head buried in his hands, several servant women bustling about, and her mother thrashing amid twisted sheets, weeping and moaning in pain.

*Mama ...*

Oh yes, she'd prayed. For the rest of the morning and all afternoon, sitting outside the master bedroom, the wood of the cane chair creasing her back. Praying, praying, praying, while her mother's agonized screams grew in intensity, echoing throughout the house. While the wind began to blow, the first rain spattered the windows, and the day darkened. Praying, praying, praying, her prayers seeming to go no farther than her lips, a mockery, as if the conclusion were foregone, written in the heavens, unchangeable even by the hand of God. Praying, praying, praying, as if by doing so she could smother the sense of foreboding that crawled up her throat and threatened to come roaring out her mouth like a demon.

*Mama ...*

When she'd opened her eyes, ashamed of her weariness, Breck stood before her, face pinched and eyes shadowed, his approach masked by the sound of the full-throated storm. And as he looked at her, saying nothing, from inside the bedroom came the mewling of an infant. A sputtering cry that sounded at once weak and pitiful. Soon Mammy Hester was bustling out of the room, eyes swollen, face wet, infant in arms. "Hush, hush, baby, dry them little tears."

Kate leaped from her chair, ignoring the stiffness in her legs, asking, "How's Mama?" while Breck said, at the same time, "How is she?"

But Mammy Hester refused to look at either of them, instead hurrying down the stairs, saying, "Lord a'mercy, chilluns, why don't you light a candle rather than sit there in the dark like you's haints?" By the time Mammy's figure faded down the stairs, Kate realized she hadn't asked whether the baby was a boy or a girl. A brother or a sister.

When Grandma Emma appeared some time later, Kate knew what she was going to say before she opened her mouth. A script. Written in the lines on Emma's face. "It's time, children. Time to say goodbye."

*Mama . . .*

It wasn't really a goodbye—just a bending over, a kiss upon her cheek, a whisper in her mother's ear that she loved her, yes, so very much. Smelling the lilac. Kissing the auburn hair. Aching because her mother didn't respond. Kate stepped back, finally, to let a tearful George take his turn, then pressed herself against the wall, the house trembling behind her.

"Wash it, we pray thee, in the blood of that immaculate Lamb, that was slain to take away the sins of the world; that whatsoever defilements it may have contracted in the midst of this miserable and naughty world . . ." Kate tried to deafen herself to Father Scarborough's voice, to hear nothing but the wind, the rain, the house groaning, quivering, the window shutter banging, banging, banging, the occasional, distant cry of the infant from wherever Mammy had taken it, but the priest's voice rose. ". . . apply our hearts to that holy and heavenly wisdom, whilst we live here, which may in the end bring us to life everlasting, through the merits of Jesus Christ thine only Son our Lord. Amen."

Kate didn't know quite when the atmosphere in the room shifted—whether it was with the priest's amen or a gust of wind or perhaps an unheard sigh from someone present—only that she was aware

of something different. A shift. Something that used to be, now gone. The
air thicker, heavier. Her heart suddenly decades older.

She opened her eyes, knowing.

Kate watched—they all did: Breck, the twins, both her grandmothers,
Uncle John—all silent, hangdog, and dumb as beasts—as her father lifted
his head, searching Sarah's face. He moved her hands to her sides, quickly,
as if the speed with which he did things now could make a difference, and
pressed his ear against her chest. Rain pummeled the side of the house in a
sudden gust. The fire choked. A burst of embers spat up the chimney with
a snap.

Suddenly, William threw his head back and a cry ripped from his throat.
He cast himself upon Sarah, pressing his cheek against hers, his shoulders
heaving. Kate watched her father while a deadness seeped into her veins
like mortar. She watched until her father raised his head, face contorted,
and screamed at everyone to leave him be. For Chrissake! Please. Everyone.
Just leave him be!

Out in the rear loggia, the unlit air was cold and drafty. Kate felt
the banister under her fingers—the smooth, worn wood. A banister her
mother's hands had caressed countless times as she'd gone up and down
the staircase through the years.

Kate padded down the steps in her slippers and entered the parlor,
ignoring Mammy Hester's startled questions, scarcely hearing the baby's
cries. She lifted the latch on the front doors, not knowing where she was
going, not caring.

With a roar, the wind blasted the doors open. Cold rain slapped her
face. The wind ripped the hairpins from her hair, casting it out behind her.
Curtains billowed like ship's sails. Doilies and table linens flew to the walls.
A newspaper flapped across the room, and Mammy Hester was hollering
something.

Drawing in her breath, wondering vaguely if she'd ever be able to draw
breath again, Kate crossed the gallery, struggling now, for her dress was
caught between her legs, sodden already. She clambered down the gallery
stairs, and then was running, running. . . .

*Mama . . .*

*Oct 27, 1851 – Cloudy cold morning- Wet wind from the Southwest- Hard storm last night- Damage severe though not as Bad as it could have been- trees fell on dovecote and on jail- Thank goodness no one inside except pigeons- Hands harvesting cane- Hired ten of Marshall's men to help —Sugarhouse in full blast and proceeding- Birchett a godsend- will highly recommend- Yesterday cotten storehouse burned to the ground- Old Pompey lost- Can't remember a time in my life when he wasn't around- A good man if there ever was one- Boys say 73 bales of Cotten gone- great losses- Hope Insurance proves adequate- Last Night at seven o'clock, a Sunday, my beloved Sarah died – the love of my life – if I was the cause of it will never forgive myself- Old Dr Smith too ill to come- damn him- John says Sarah had a large tumor that killed her —bled out- know he did everything he could- Children distraut- Kate inconsollable- Baby Caroline hangs on though my guess is she will not live long- I look out and see nothing but a cruel World and a cruel God- Sawney is dead*

The pen slipped from William's hand, splattering ink into the journal. He knew he should blot out the blunder, but instead watched the droplets black out the name Sawney, dot through the 73 bales, and Old Pompey.

William sighed, stretched his stiffened limbs, and then got up to warm his ink-spotted hands by the waning fire. He was frowning at the neck bone of the ass, wondering where his Sarah was now, whether there really was a God, life eternal, wishing for her sake that there was—please, let it be true!—when there came a knock at the door.

Without waiting for a reply, Breck entered the office, hatless, hair tousled with wind. His face was unshaven, his shirt rumpled, eyes bleary, and he smelled of rain and of the ubiquitous smoke which left the inside of William's nose feeling raw and irritated. Watching his son seat himself in a chair next to the fire, William realized that the rage he'd felt toward Breck yesterday was gone. Maybe not gone, but coagulated into the huge mass that now hung heavy in William's heart. He loved Breck, yes, this he knew, all his failings aside. He wanted to tell him, started to, but the words refused to form. He turned back to the neck bone, fingering it, saying instead, "I've decided to send you to a military institute. Think it's the best thing for you at this point. You'll leave in a few days, after—after your mother's decently buried. John's agreed to accompany you."

William had expected outrage, objection at the very least, and found his stomach and shoulders tensing. He released his breath when Breck merely said, "Where?"

William turned. His son was leaning over, elbows propped on his knees, staring vacantly at his mud-caked boots. "Kentucky."

At first Breck made no response, seeming frozen in position. Outside, William heard Mehitable's cane on the gallery and knew she was making her way to breakfast. William's own stomach growled, but the thought of eating, of sitting at the dining room table with Sarah's empty chair opposite, made him ill.

Oh God, he wondered, Am I to blame for her death? John says she would have died anyway.

*Oh God. Sarah, my love. Forgive me.*

As the heaviness in William's heart threatened to burst, to his surprise, Breck's face sagged into his hands and he began to weep with great shuddering sobs, the sight of which caused tears to prickle the backs of William's eyes.

He let Breck cry for a good while before finally going over and placing a tentative hand on his shoulder. "Son—" was all he could manage to say, wishing suddenly that Breck could stay on at the plantation, continue to help with the sugar, help rebuild the cotton storehouse, knowing that it was not possible. Not after—after what he'd done. Knowing also that Breck needed the discipline at a military institute to toughen him for the demands of running a plantation.

It was as William was fetching his hat by the door, preparing to leave, that Breck finally looked up, his face splotchy and swollen. "I love her, Papa. I love her."

William said nothing. Simply snugged the hat on his head and stepped outdoors, the wind snatching his breath away, making his eyes water.

Monette was standing at the window of her attic room when the door opened.

It was Lizzy, white-turbaned, calico-skirted, chest heaving under her blouse and starched *fichu*. Monette wondered if the housekeeper intended to slap her again. Shake her until her teeth rattled. Ask where she'd been for the last day while the world went to hell, while Miss Sarah died and a babe was born and a storm blew through. Instead, after regarding her for a while—no doubt congratulating herself on the outcome of her slap—Lizzy said, "Mars William, he be asking for you. He outside now."

Refusing to give Lizzy the satisfaction of seeing her fear, of detecting the sudden pounding of her heart, her sweaty palms (though she'd been expecting this summons), Monette walked calmly past Lizzy and descended the two flights of stairs with Lizzy close on her heels, risers creaking beneath them.

Outside, behind the big house, a cold wind caught Monette's skirt, billowing it out in front of her like a bell. The air smelled rain-fresh, vaguely of smoke. A rooster crowed, strutting near Mars William, who sat tall on his horse, his figure framed by gray, rolling clouds, whip coiled around his saddle horn. Monette looked down quickly, ears roaring with the pound of her heart. The horse pawed the ground, mashing tender shoots of grass under its hooves.

*Breck! Mon ami! Save me!*

Mars William said, "Come with me." He wheeled his horse around and urged it into a walk.

From behind Monette, Lizzy pushed her, a knuckle in her spine, propelling her forward. *"Yellow bitch,"* she whispered.

Monette followed Mars William and his horse. Between the kitchen and the north addition, past the yard, past the orchards now swirling with leaves, navigating rotted fruit and limbs strewn across the road, skirting uprooted trees, past the family cemetery, and up another road.

*Breck! Where are you? Save me!*

When they reached the cart track leading to the sugarhouse, Monette began to founder. Mud oozed over her shoes. Squelched between her toes. Cold and icky. She was breathing fast now, wanting to cry, wanting to ask Mars William where he was taking her, what he planned to do, why he had that whip with him . . . dreading the answers. Instead she concentrated on pulling one foot at a time out of the wallow while not losing her shoes.

Finally, Mars William turned his horse around and waited for her to catch up. When she did—unwittingly reaching out a hand to steady herself on the horse's flank—he said, "Get on." He reached down and pulled her out of the mud, setting her behind him on his saddle as if she weighed no more than a child. At first, she was too frightened to touch him, but when the horse began to walk again, lumbering with some difficulty through the mud, rump shifting from side to side, she had to clutch Mars William's coat to keep from sliding off. She could smell him now—the leather, the cigars. She wondered what he was thinking, knowing he knew what she and Breck had done. How could he not? A gust of wind blew her hair sideways, into her eyes, pinched her cheeks with cold, now carrying the smoky smell of cooked sugar. A splotch of rain pocked the top of her head and she shivered.

Upon reaching the sugarhouse, Mars William set her down in the mud. There were a dozen or so people in the clearing, field hands she recognized from inspections and some she did not know, men and women both. As she stood there, unsure what to do, mouth so dry she could not swallow, more people appeared. They emerged from the fields, from the sugarhouse. They set the brakes before climbing off wagons and hitching the mules. Everyone was looking at her, saying nothing, gathering. Faces closed and tight. Clothing flapping like flags. Monette didn't realize she'd touched her *gris-gris* until she felt the press of the blood agate against her heart, the jab of the stick against her palm.

From behind her, still on his horse, Mars William's voice cut through the wind. "Monette will be working in the fields now. Darby, I'll leave it to you as the driver to secure her a place in the quarters and keep her occupied. I'll be back later today to check on progress at the mill. That's all."

So saying, Mars William began to leave, muck squishing under the horse's hooves.

Monette knew it was foolhardy, dangerous even, but could not stop herself. She ran after Mars William, leaving both her shoes stuck in the mud as if she'd flown straight up out of them. Under her bare feet, the mud was slick and cold. She waddled, crab-like, wind in her teeth, but finally grabbed his boot. Pulled on the leg of his pants. Tears were falling now, her vision blurring. She heard herself begging, weeping, "Please, Mars William, please, I implore you, don't leave me here. I'll do whatever you want, I'll mind everything you say, please, please, have mercy! Don't leave me!"

He shook her off somehow, rattled his foot around as if ridding himself of a rat, saying nothing, simply urging his horse onward while she slipped and fell to her hands and knees with a wet sound like spilled oatmeal. Mud splattered up her clothing, onto her blouse, slapping a cold smear across her chin and lips. She could hear herself begging still, a shrill sound, bleating upon her own ears with a hysteria that seemed to be coming from another. Someone else who watched as Mars William urged the horse onward, watched as the beast plodded away, head bobbing slowly, up down, up down, as the rain began in earnest. A few fat drops to start with, quickly followed by a deluge that turned her hair into soggy ringlets and plastered her shirt to her back, swallowing both horse and rider into the grayness beyond.

---

Cyrus watched through one of the sugarhouse windows. He'd seen them ride into the clearing. He'd heard the instructions, that Monette would work in the fields now. He'd watched as Monette cried and fell in the mud. As the crowd closed in and the rain began to fall, beating on the sugarhouse roof like drums.

His heart quickened.

*Monette, oh Monette. You is come back to me. You is come back.*

Cyrus ran into the rain, mud slopping up his calves. He pushed his way through the crowd—past Retta, Tamar, past Sam, Primus, Tabb—until they all stepped back, watching him. Until the growing noise that had begun to sound like kennel dogs fighting, drowned into silence.

Monette lay on her back, the front of her blouse torn away, her rain-wet breasts exposed. The half print of a muddy boot branded her hip, another her ribs, her thigh. Her face was battered and bruised, one of her eyes swollen shut. Blood seeped from a gash on her forehead.

Cyrus could hear his own breathing as he removed his shirt. She was watching him. Like a wounded animal, wary, watching, as he covered her nakedness, gathered her in his arms and stood. He felt her press against him, her body clinging, cold, trembling.

"You came," she whispered.

They moved out of the way, the crowd. They moved out of the way as if Cyrus were behind the plow, driving a team of oxen, coming through. And once they fell away, dissolving into the downpour, Cyrus began to run, pants chafing his thighs, feeling as if he could run forever. All the way to Heaven, maybe.

# *Author's Note*

This book came about by accident. Decades ago, my husband asked if I wanted to accompany him on his business trip to New Orleans. I jumped at the opportunity, as I'd never been. I also thought, what a great opportunity for me, a fledgling writer, to base a story there!

Initially, I planned to write a ghost story for a middle-grade to young adult (YA) audience, set in the spookier corners of the city. How fun would that be? Aware of my own ignorance (a Northerner), I dove into research and was thus armed with at least a nascent knowledge by the time I stepped out of the airport and into the sultry air.

As part of my own excursion during my husband's seminar, I rented a car and ventured north to visit several plantations. Although my YA novel (still unplotted) was to be set in New Orleans, I nonetheless felt drawn to the plantations—more specifically, to the history and legacy of slavery.

I wasn't sure why I felt such a pull. Maybe it was because I'd read too many novels about plantations, each time hoping that maybe *this* was the novel to include the "other side" of the story. But each time I finished, I was left dissatisfied. Why were there only White characters and storylines? Didn't those characters—or their authors—recognize that their very lifestyle was dependent upon enslaved people toiling day after day?

Looking back, I know how naïve I was. I'd started reading adult-level novels in sixth grade, so I had no context for critiquing them—no understanding that these types of novels often amounted to a White glorification of a bygone era. Instead, I just felt a deep unease—nameless and simmering.

So, when the chance came to see the plantations for myself, I knew I had to go. I don't know what I was expecting—perhaps a more balanced history? A recognition of the enslavement of *millions* of individuals? But the plantation tours were much like the books: centered on a White perspective, with drawling hostesses hooped to the nines in crinoline, each plantation steeped in a pleasant, curated version of Southern hospitality.

After each tour, I was left to wander the grounds on my own—and that's when I would visit the slave cabins: silent witnesses to the disparity between a glorified White history and the suffering and blood of an enslaved people.

My ghost story plans evaporated like mist. Instead, I became consumed by the slave narrative, particularly how it intersected with the dominant White-centered narratives of the time. This intersection came into sharp focus one sunny morning, when I stepped out of my guest cabin at Tezcuco Plantation.

I was feeling buoyed by a sense of purpose, a calling. I walked across the dirt path to an abandoned well, overgrown with honeysuckle, the air heady and sweet.

A Black woman was sweeping the ground near the well.

"Good morning!" I chirped.

What happened next rocked me to my core. I will never forget the long look she gave me. I may as well have run into a brick wall.

Her look seemed to say: *You, a White woman, having just spent the night as a guest at a plantation, are not my friend. Do you not know that the ground you stand on is soaked in the blood of my ancestors? I refuse to be a part of your fantasy.*

Without a word, she went back to sweeping.

Each time interactions like this occurred, a few more scales fell from my eyes. I saw a shantytown crammed with Black families, huddled in the literal shadow of the stately townhomes where wealthy White families lived. People walking down the street—White with White, or Black with Black—rarely together. The Confederate statues and flags. The museums explaining the "War of Northern Aggression." (This was the '90s and early 2000s, remember.)

Over the course of my research, I returned to Louisiana multiple times—each time a little wiser, each time the weight of my understanding growing heavier. I read dozens of slave narratives written by those few who had escaped and could tell their stories. I read narratives from the Louisiana Writers' Project (1934–1943)—oral accounts told by Black people who *could still remember being enslaved.* I also read dozens of diaries, letters, and logs written by elite Southern Whites and plantation owners—both men and women—to help me understand their view of the world.

In particular, I ran across three diaries of slave owners that influenced me greatly in the writing of *Fox Creek*. The first account is the diary of Louisiana Creole sugar planter, Valcour Aime. Known affectionately as *Le Petit Versailles,* his plantation was the stuff of fairytales—fountains, botanical gardens, a zoo, and even a miniature railroad built to transport guests around the estate. Believed to be the wealthiest man in Louisiana, upon Aime's death, it was discovered that he was deeply in debt. His plantation was subsequently sold piecemeal, and nothing of it remains today. Papa Léon is loosely based on Aime.

The second account was the diaries written by James Henry Hammond, governor of South Carolina from 1842-'44. One day in 1852, he was "dreadful ill" and saddened to find himself "abandoned" by all, as he believed himself a good man: "I, who never willfully harmed or desired to harm a human being, who never wronged one that I know of." This statement, taken against the backdrop of his horrifying treatment of his slaves, including the habitual rape of young teens—both White relatives and Black slaves—is stunning. Hammond's belief in his goodness, his inability to see beyond his own needs and desires, and his placement of himself as the central figure in his worldview of domination, was critical to my understanding of how a patriarchal, slave-owning culture could prosper.

The third account, and one I relied on heavily in forming William Jensey's character, was *Plantation Life in the Florida Parishes of Louisiana, 1836-1846: as Reflected in the Diary of Bennet Hilliard Barrow.*

Most entries were mundane:

*February 23   Cloudy     cold    too wet to plow*
*March 25     Clear     gave the women a dress*
*June 12   Cloudy    warm — 6 hands in swamp getting out cypress fence*
*July 31  Cloudy sultry morning — 9 women spinning — Finished a shop & dance room for my negros*[1] *... one child verry ill Sunday  croup & worms light shower at noon — never saw better crop ...*

But every so often, punctuating the humdrum of everyday life like lightning bolts, we see the undercurrent of the plantation:

*Nov 2  Cloudy   cool — Dennis came in sick on Tuesday — ran off again yesterday… will carry my Gun & small shot for him — I think it will break him of his rascality…*
*Nov 28  Cloudy   damp & warm — Whiped all my grown cotten pickers to day, Dennis did not come up When called, ran off I expect…*
*Nov 29   Dark Foggy morning, warm   caught Dennis Last night at the scaffold yard… gave him the worst Whipping he ever had — & ducking — Finished picking cotten*

It's easy to conclude that Barrow—like Hammond, and even like Aime—was a terrible person. But humans are complex beings, and Barrow was no exception. He loved his wife and children. He took care of his neighbor's fields when they couldn't. He did his civic duty in the community. He cradled a small bird, noting its characteristics. He enjoyed life to the full: horse racing, fox hunting, or a fish fry with friends. Like Hammond, he stated: "I acted for the Best and so far have never injured any human being to my knowledge …"

In forming my characters, I felt it vital to present the slave owners as everyday people—not as the Simon Legrees of movies and literature, although, like Morton Cobb in my novel, those psychopaths certainly existed, and, even flourished under such moral license. Instead, I wanted to present slave owners as relatable. Why? Because, in my opinion, people like Barrow weren't outliers in the human spectrum. They were ordinary people, helping friends and defending family, believing themselves "good" even as they perpetuated and were blind to the suffering and cruelty surrounding them.

Finally, after three years of full-time study, when the voices of my characters would no longer stay still, I began to write.

I would like to say that my writing was linear: that I started one day and added to the manuscript on each subsequent day until the day came when I wrote "The End." But life intervened.

During that time, I was contracted by both Knopf Books for Young Readers (Random House) and Dutton (Penguin) to write eight books for middle-grade and young adult audiences. Somewhere in there, I also attended seminary and earned a Master's in Religion, with an emphasis on global eco-justice—justice for both the environment and the marginalized peoples who often bear the brunt of climate change, pollution, and habitat destruction.

And then I climbed Mt. Kilimanjaro in Tanzania, and, at the same time, co-founded an organization, Orphans Africa, which builds boarding schools for orphans in various locations throughout Tanzania. We're still building schools. We're still working hard.

So, for my novel *Fox Creek,* it's been a long haul—nearly thirty years in the making.

Taking so long to finish the book has had a consequence I never saw coming: the cultural milieu has changed. I am a privileged White woman writing about Black characters. In the 1990s, conversations about cultural appropriation were rare—either that, or I was not listening for them. Now it's front and center. Who am I to speak through a character who is Black? After all, White people have whitewashed Black history to the point where, even today, many still believe the fallacies—such as the idea that Black people were better off as slaves, or that they were all happy.

Cultural appropriation has been used to erase the voices of marginalized peoples. After all, who writes the history books? People of privilege and power—the victors, the oppressors. People like Hammond. And who *doesn't* write the history books? Those who are vanquished, those living on the edges—the invisible, the powerless.

I see this dynamic in my work in Tanzania. We work with orphans—some of the most economically disadvantaged children—in a country where nearly one out of every eleven people is an orphan, and the median age is just eighteen. It's not hard to imagine how an orphan in that situation might become just another burden in an overextended community. In the remote regions where we work, there are no social services. Orphaned children are simply too young, too poor, too hungry, too invisible, too sick (fill in the blank) to survive. And when an orphan dies, there is no ripple effect. No one outside their village knows that anything has happened. Certainly, no history is being written by a people struggling just to stay alive.

So, with regard to cultural appropriation, all I can say is this: from the time I first set foot in New Orleans, I felt compelled from deep within to write this book, as if the Universe were saying, *Look . . . listen . . . write.*

At the same time, I would remind my readers that I am, at heart, an artist—an artist of words, who paints the world through the prism of her eyes and the voice of her heart, as all artists must. I paint the people in many shades of color. I paint the men, the women, the children. I paint the background. I paint the culture. I paint those who suffer, and those who cause harm. Please, hang my portraits—my paintings—beside those of others, and let them stand the test of time.

And finally, I believe that what ultimately connects us, in Truth, isn't our gender, our culture, our skin color, or even our shared traumas—although these can be powerful unifiers. What connects us, in Truth, is the beating heart of who we are as human beings.

For all readers, especially White Americans, when we name former slave owners as "other" than ourselves, *un*-relatable, we create a distance between us and them, thereby escaping the burden of our history. It's an easy out. But in order for us to grow as a nation, we must see ourselves reflected in their lives—not in the sense of condoning their actions, but in the sense of understanding how the perpetration of such atrocities could have occurred in the first place by seemingly normal human beings. We must ask ourselves, in what ways are we blind today to the degradation or oppression of others? For, I believe, that only in asking this question, framed alongside our shared history, can we truly start the task of healing the chasms that divide our great nation.

I pray that, together, we have the courage to stand in the muck and ugliness of one another's pain, as well as in the beauty, freedom, and creative expression of our diversity and our differences. I pray that we connect with one another so deeply that we forge a bond that extends beyond any lived experience or action. For it is in this collective understanding that we are enlightened by a love for one another that transcends all.

---

1.  *I have preserved the original language of the diary entries, which contain outdated and offensive terms like "negros" [sic]. As throughout my novel, I have chosen to keep this language as a historical artifact, consistent with the understanding and social milieu of the characters. However, I do not endorse the use of, or the normalization of, such terminology.*

# *Acknowledgements*

Thank you to my fellow writers through the years, who heard and read my manuscript in all its evolving forms. Without your encouragement and your honest feedback, I couldn't have stayed the course. Thank you to authors Heather and Judy L. for our Wednesday coffees, and for your willingness to dive deeply into the manuscript. Thank you to Colleen, Susan, Lisa, Judy N., Dace, Lorian, Marge, and Anita—all accomplished authors—for our monthly literary read-aloud critiques, and for our occasional weekends spent together walking on the beach and brainstorming all things literary.

I would also like to thank the kind and generous folks in Louisiana, who helped this Northern girl begin to understand the more languid rhythm of the South. Thank you to Shirley at the Barrow House Inn, to Mary Donovan at the Episcopal Historical Center, and to Ann and Helen at the West Feliciana Historical Society Museum. Thank you also to the staff at LSU's Hill Memorial Library.

Closer to home, I give my thanks to Christine at the King County Library, who tirelessly fetched me books from hither and yon. Thank you to Audrey at Episcotalk online and to Judy N. for helping me understand the sacred rites and rituals of the Episcopal faith.

A million thanks to Judy L., Judy N., Kaisa Swenddal-White, and Leroy M. Nill, for their help with the French translations. *Merci beaucoup!*

A huge debt of gratitude goes to my husband Carl for his generous support. His was the shoulder I leaned on, and the ear I filled regarding the characters, the storylines, my frustrations, and triumphs. In addition to his emotional support, Carl financially held down the fort during the years it took to research and write this book. Thank you also to the rest of my family— my mother Norma, my father Don, my sister Andrea (also an author), and my sons Ian, Aaron, and Ethan, for their love and support during this process. I have been truly blessed.

Finally, while I leaned upon many people during this writing process, I claim sole responsibility for any mistakes, exaggerations, or misrepresentations in the book.

# *About the Author*

*Fox Creek* is M. E. Torrey's first novel for adults.

Torrey holds a B.S. in Microbiology and Immunology and an M.A. in Religion. She currently resides in Washington State and has lived and traveled extensively throughout the world.

In addition to her writing and traveling, she is a co-founder of the charity, Orphans Africa. The charity works in Tanzania, building boarding schools for children orphaned by disease and poverty. Her organization has educated thousands of children, empowering them to step into their giftedness. Over the years, the students have become doctors, bankers and financiers, nurses, teachers, business entrepreneurs, secretaries, drivers, mechanics, tailors, electricians (including solar & automotive), and more. The schools are now owned and operated by Tanzanians and continue to aim toward complete self-sustainability. (www.orphansafrica.org)

M. E. Torrey, also known as Michele Torrey, is the author of twelve books for children (Knopf; Union Square & Co). Those books are available at www.micheletorrey.com.

Visit Torrey at www.metorrey.com.

www.ingramcontent.com/pod-product-compliance
Lightning Source LLC
Chambersburg PA
CBHW030331010826
48973CB00004B/965